Rosa Nouchette Carey

Heriot's Choice

A Tale. Third Edition

Rosa Nouchette Carey

Heriot's Choice
A Tale. Third Edition

ISBN/EAN: 9783744790314

Printed in Europe, USA, Canada, Australia, Japan

Cover: Foto ©Andreas Hilbeck / pixelio.de

More available books at **www.hansebooks.com**

HERIOT'S CHOICE

HERIOT'S

A Tale

BY

ROSA NOUCHETTE CAREY

AUTHOR OF 'NELLIE'S MEMORIES,' 'NOT LIKE OTHER GIRLS,'
'WOOED AND MARRIED,' ETC.

THIRD EDITION

LONDON

RICHARD BENTLEY & SON, NEW BURLINGTON STREET

Publishers in Ordinary to Her Majesty the Queen

1891

TO

The Rev. Canon Simpson, LL.D.

THIS STORY

IS AFFECTIONATELY INSCRIBED BY

THE AUTHOR

CONTENTS

CHAPTER I

PAGE

'SAY YES, MILLY' 1

CHAPTER II

'IF YOU PLEASE, MAY I BRING RAG AND TATTERS?' . 12

CHAPTER III

VIÂ TEBAY 25

CHAPTER IV

MILDRED'S NEW HOME . . . 37

CHAPTER V

OLIVE 49

CHAPTER VI

CAIN AND ABEL 62

CHAPTER VII

A MOTHER IN ISRAEL . . 75

CHAPTER VIII

'ETHEL THE MAGNIFICENT' 88

PAGE

CHAPTER IX
KIRKLEATHAM . . 101

CHAPTER X
THE RUSH-BEARING 114

CHAPTER XI
AN AFTERNOON IN CASTLESTEADS . . 126

CHAPTER XII
THE WELL-MEANING MISCHIEF-MAKER 137

CHAPTER XIII
A YOUTHFUL DRACO AND SOLON . . 150

CHAPTER XIV
RICHARD CŒUR-DE-LION 161

CHAPTER XV
THE GATE AJAR . 175

CHAPTER XVI
COMING BACK . 185

CHAPTER XVII
THREE YEARS AFTERWARDS—A RETROSPECT . . 199

CHAPTER XVIII
OLIVE'S WORK . 211

PAGE

CHAPTER XIX
THE HEART OF CŒUR-DE-LION . 223

CHAPTER XX
WHARTON HALL FARM . . . 236

CHAPTER XXI
UNDER STENKRITH BRIDGE 249

CHAPTER XXII
DR. HERIOT'S WARD 259

CHAPTER XXIII
'AND MAIDENS CALL IT LOVE-IN-IDLENESS' . . . 273

CHAPTER XXIV
THE DESERTED COTTON-MILL IN HILBECK GLEN 286

CHAPTER XXV
ROYAL 299

CHAPTER XXVI
'IS THAT LETTER FOR ME, AUNT MILLY?' . 311

CHAPTER XXVII
COOP KERNAN HOLE 325

CHAPTER XXVIII
DR. HERIOT'S MISTAKE 338

CHAPTER XXIX
THE COTTAGE AT FROGNAL 351

PAGE

CHAPTER XXX
'I cannot Sing the Old Songs' . . . 364

CHAPTER XXXI
'Which shall it be?' 376

CHAPTER XXXII
A Talk in Fairlight Glen 388

CHAPTER XXXIII
'Yes' 402

CHAPTER XXXIV
John Heriot's Wife 414

CHAPTER XXXV
Olive's Decision . . . 428

CHAPTER XXXVI
Berengaria 441

HERIOT'S CHOICE

CHAPTER I

'SAY YES, MILLY'

'Man's importunity is God's opportunity.'

'O fair, O fine, O lot to be desired !
Early and late my heart appeals to me,
And says, "O work, O will—Thou man, be fired,
To earn this lot—" she says—"I would not be
A worker for mine own bread, or one hired
For mine own profit. O, I would be free
To work for others ; love so earned of them
Should be my wages and my diadem." '—JEAN INGELOW.

'SAY yes, Milly.'

Three short words, and yet they went straight to Milly's heart. It was only the postscript of a long, sorrowful letter—the finale brief but eloquent—of a quiet, dispassionate appeal ; but it sounded to Mildred Lambert much as the Macedonian cry must have sounded of old : 'Come over and help us.'

Mildred's soft, womanly nature was capable of only one response to such a demand. Assent was more than probable, and bordered on certainty, even before the letter was laid aside, and while her cheek was yet paling at the thought of new responsibilities and the vast unknown, wherein duty must tread on the heel of inclination, and life must press out thought and the worn-out furrows of intro- and retro-spection.

And so it was that the page of a negative existence was turned ; and Mildred agreed to become the inmate of her brother's home.

'Aunt Milly !' How pleasant it would be to hear that again, and to be in the centre of warm young life and breathless

1

activity, after the torpor of long waiting and watching, and the hush and the blank and the drawn-out pain, intense yet scarcely felt, of the last seven years.

To begin life in its fulness at eight-and-twenty; to taste of its real sweets and bitters, after it had offered to her nothing but the pale brackish flavour of regret for a passing youth and wasted powers, responsive rather than suggestive (if there be such monstrous anomaly on the whole face of God's creation), nothing being wasted, and all pronounced good, that comes direct from the Divine Hand. To follow fresh tracks when the record of the years had left nothing but the traces of the chariot-wheels of daily monotonous duties that dragged-heavily, when summer and winter and seed-time and harvest found Mildred still through those seven revolving courses of seasons within the walls of that quiet sickroom.

It is given to some women to look back on these long level blanks of life; on mysteries of waiting, that intervene between youth and work, when the world's noise comes dimly to them, like the tumult of city's streets through closed shutters; when pain and hardship seem preferable to their death-in-life, and they long to prove the armour that has grown rusted with disuse.

How many a volume could be written, and with profit, on the watchers as well as the workers of life, on the bystanders as well as the sufferers. 'Patient hearts their pain to see.' Well has this thought been embodied in the words of a nineteenth-century Christian poet; while to many a pallid malcontent, wearied with inaction and panting for strife, might the Divine words still be applied: 'Could ye not have watched with Me one hour?'

Mildred Lambert's life for eight-and-twenty years might be summed up in a few sentences. A happy youth, scarcely clouded by the remembrance of a dead father and the graves of the sisters that came between her infancy and the maturer age of her only brother; and then the blurred brightness when Arnold, who had married before he had taken orders, became the hard-working vicar of a remote Westmorland parish—and he and his wife and children passed out of Milly's daily life.

Milly was barely nineteen when this happened; but even then her mother—who had always been ailing—was threatened with a chronic complaint involving no ordinary suffering; and now began the long seven years' watching which faded Milly's youth and roses together.

Milly had never known how galling had been the strain to the nerves—how intense her own tenacity of will and purpose, till she had folded her mother's pale hands together; and with a lassitude too great for tears, felt as she crept away that her work was finished none too soon, and that even her firm young strength was deserting her.

Trouble had not come singly to Mildred. News of her sister-in-law's unexpected death had reached her, just before her mother's last brief attack, and her brother had been too much stunned by his own loss to come to her in her loneliness.

Not that Milly wondered at this. She loved Arnold dearly; but he was so much older, and they had grown necessarily so apart. He and his wife had been all in all to each other; and the family in the vicarage had seemed so perfected and completed that the little petted Milly of old days might well plead that she was all but forgotten.

But Betha's death had altered this; and Arnold's letter, written as good men will write when their heart is well-nigh broken, came to Mildred as she sat alone in her black dress in her desolate home.

New work—unknown work—and that when youth's elasticity seemed gone, and spirits broken or at least dangerously quieted by the morbid atmosphere of sickness and hypochondria. They say the prisoner of twenty years will weep at leaving his cell. The tears that Mildred shed that night were more for the mother she had lost and the old safe life of the past, than pity for the widowed brother and motherless children.

Do we ever outlive our selfishness? Do we ever cease to be fearful for ourselves?

And yet Mildred was weary of solitude. Arnold was her own, her only brother; and Aunt Milly—well, perhaps it might be pleasant.

'Say yes, Milly—for Betha's sake—for my darling's sake (she was so fond of you), if not for mine. Think how her children miss her! Matters are going wrong already. It is not their fault, poor things; but I am so helpless to decide. I used to leave everything to her, and we are all so utterly lost.

'I could not have asked you if our mother had lingered; but your faithful charge, my poor Milly, is over—your martyrdom, as Betha called it. She was so bright, and loved to have things so bright round her, that your imprisonment in the sickroom quite oppressed her. It was "poor Milly," "our dear good Milly," to the last. I wish her girls were more like her; but she only laughed at their odd ways, and told me I should live to be proud of them.

'Olive is as left-handed as ever, and Chrissy little better. Richard is mannish, but impracticable, and a little difficult to understand. We should none of us get on at all but for Roy : he has his mother's heart-sunshine and loving smile ; but even Roy has his failures.

'We want a woman among us, Milly—a woman with head and hands, and a tolerable stock of patience. Even Heriot is in difficulties, but that will keep till you come—for you will come, will you not, my dear ?'

'Come ! how could you doubt me, Arnold ?' replied Mildred, as she laid down the letter ; but 'God help me and them' followed close on the sigh.

'After all, it is a clear call to duty,' she soliloquised. 'It is not my business to decide on my fitness or unfitness, or to measure myself to my niche. We are not promised strength before the time, and no one can tell before he tries whether he be likely to fail. Richard's mannishness, and Olive's left-handed ways, and Chrissy's poorer imitation, shall not daunt me. Arnold wants me. I shall be of use to some one again, and I will go.'

But Mildred, for all her bravery, grew a little pale over her brother's second letter :—'You must come at once, and not wait to summer and winter it, or, as some of our old women say, "to bide the bitterment on't." Shall I send Richard to help you about your house business, and to settle your goods and chattels ? Let the old furniture go, Milly ; it has stood a fair amount of wear and tear, and you are young yet, my dear. Shall I send Dick ? He was his mother's right hand. The lad's mannish for his nineteen years.' Mannish again ! This Richard began to be formidable. He was a bright well-looking lad of thirteen when Mildred had seen him last. But she remembered his mother's fond descriptions of Cardie's cleverness and goodness. One sentence had particularly struck her at the time. Betha had been comparing her boys, and dwelling on their good points with a mother's partiality. 'As to Roy, he needs no praise of mine ; he stands so well in every one's estimation—and in his own, too—that a little fault-finding would do him good. Cardie is different : his diffidence takes the form of pride ; no one understands him but I—not even his father. The one speaks out too much, and the other too little ; but one of these days he will find out his son's good heart.'

'I wonder if Arnold will recognise me,' thought Mildred, sorrowfully, that night, as she sat by her window, looking out on her little strip of garden, shimmering in the moonlight. 'I feel so old and changed, and have grown into such quiet ways. Are there some women who are never young, I wonder? Am I one of them? Is it not strange,' she continued, musingly, 'that such beautiful lives as Betha's are struck so suddenly out of the records of years, while I am left to take up the incompleted work she discharged so lovingly? Dear Betha! what a noble heart it was! Arnold reverenced as much as he loved her. How vain to think of replacing, even in the faintest degree, one of the sweetest women this earth ever saw : sweet, because her whole life was in exact harmony with her surroundings.' And there rose before Mildred's eyes a faint image that often haunted her—of a face with smiling eyes, and brown hair just touched with gold—and the small firm hand that, laid on unruly lips, could hush coming wrath, and smooth the angry knitting of baby brows.

It was strange, she thought, that neither Olive nor Chrissy were like their mother. Roy's fairness and steady blue eyes were her sole relics—Roy, who was such a pretty little fellow when Mildred had seen him last.

Mildred tried to trace out a puzzled thought in her head before she slept that night. A postscript in Arnold's letter, vaguely worded, but most decidedly mysterious, gave rise to a host of conjectures.

'I have just found out that Heriot's business must be settled long before the end of next month—when you come to us. You know him by name and repute, though not personally. I have given him your address. I think it will be better for you both to talk the matter over, and to give it your full consideration, before you start for the north. Make any arrangements you like about the child. Heriot's a good fellow, and deserves to be helped ; he has been everything to us through our trouble.'

What could Arnold mean? Betha's chatty letters—thoroughly womanly in their gossip—had often spoken of Arnold's friend, Dr. Heriot, and of his kindness to their boys. She had described him as a man of great talents, and an undoubted acquisition to their small society. 'Arnold (who was her universal referee) wondered that a man like Dr. Heriot should bury himself in a Westmorland valley. Some one had told them that he had given up a large West End practice. There was some mystery about him ; his wife made him miserable. No one knew the

rights or the wrongs of it ; but they would rather believe anything than that he was to blame.'

And in another letter she wrote : 'A pleasant evening has
just been sadly interrupted. The Bishop was here and one or
two others, Dr. Heriot among them ; but a telegram summoning
him to his wife's deathbed had just reached him.

'Arnold, who stood by him, says he turned as pale as death
as he read it ; but he only put it into his hand without a word,
and left the room. I could not help following him with a word
of comfort, remembering how good he was to us when we had
nearly lost Chrissy last year ; but he looked at me so strangely
that the words died on my lips. "When death only relieves us
of a burden, Mrs. Lambert, we touch on a sorrow too great for
any ordinary comfort. You are sorry for me, but pray for her."
And wringing my hand, he turned away. She must have been
a bad wife to him. He is a good man ; I am sure of it.'

How strange that Dr. Heriot should be coming to see her,
and on private business, too ! It seemed so odd of Arnold to
send him ; and yet it was pleasant to feel that she was to be
consulted and her opinion respected. 'Mildred, who loves to
help everybody, must find some way of helping poor Heriot,'
had been her brother's concluding words.

Mildred Lambert's house was one of those modest suburban
residences lying far back on a broad sunny road bordering on
Clapham Common ; but on a May afternoon even Laurel Cottage,
unpretentious as it was, was not devoid of attractions, with its
trimly cut lawn and clump of sweet-scented lilac and yellow
drooping laburnum, stretching out long fingers of gold in the
sunshine.

Mildred was sitting alone in her little drawing-room, ostensibly
sorting her papers, but in reality falling into an occasional
reverie, lulled by the sunshine and the silence, when a brisk
footstep on the gravel outside the window made her start.
Visitors were rare in her secluded life, and, with the exception
of the doctor and the clergyman, and perhaps a sympathising
neighbour, few ever invaded the privacy of Laurel Cottage ; the
light, well-assured footstep sounded strange in Mildred's ears,
and she listened with inward perturbation to Susan's brief
colloquy with the stranger.

'Yes, her mistress was disengaged ; would he send in his
name and business, or would he walk in ?' And the door was
flung open a little testily by Susan, who objected to this innova-
tion on their usual afternoon quiet.

'Forgive me, if I am intruding, Miss Lambert, but your brother told me I might call.'

'Dr. Heriot?'

'Yes; he has kept his promise then, and has written to inform you of my intended visit? We have heard so much of each other that I am sure we ought to need no special introduction.' But though Dr. Heriot, as he said this, held out his hand with a frank smile, a grave, penetrating look accompanied his words; he was a man rarely at fault, but for the moment he seemed a little perplexed.

'Yes, I expected you; will you sit down?' replied Mildred, simply. She was not a demonstrative woman, and of late had grown into quiet ways with strangers. Dr. Heriot's tone had slightly discomposed her; instinctively she felt that he failed to recognise in her some given description, and that a brief embarrassment was the result.

Mildred was right. Dr. Heriot was trying to puzzle out some connection between the worn, soft-eyed woman before him, and the fresh girlish face that had so often smiled down on him from the vicarage wall, with shy, demure eyes, and the roses in her belt not brighter than the pure colouring of her bloom. The laughing face had grown sad and quiet—painfully so, Dr. Heriot thought—and faint lines round mouth and brow bore witness to the strain of a wearing anxiety and habitual repression of feeling; the skin of the forehead was too tightly stretched, and the eyes shone too dimly for health; while the thin, colourless cheek, seen in juxtaposition to the black dress, told their own story of youthful vitality sacrificed to the inexorable demand of hypochondria.

But it was a refined, womanly face, and one that could not fail to interest; a kind patient soul looked through the quiet eyes; youth and its attractions had faded, but a noble unconsciousness had replaced it; in talking to her you felt instinctively that the last person of whom Mildred thought was herself. But if Dr. Heriot were disappointed in the estimate he had formed of his friend's sister, Mildred on her side was not the less surprised at his appearance.

She had imagined him a man of imposing aspect—a man of height and inches, with iron-gray hair. The real Dr. Heriot was dark and slight, rather undersized than otherwise, with a dark moustache, and black, closely-cropped hair, which made him look younger than he really was. It was not a handsome face; at first sight there was something stern and forbidding about it, but the lines round the mouth relaxed pleasantly when he smiled, and the eyes had a clear, straightforward look ; while about the whole man there was a certain indefinable air of good-breeding, as of one long accustomed to hold his own amongst men who were socially his superiors.

Mildred had taken her measurement of Dr. Heriot in her own quiet way long before she had exhausted her feminine budget of conversation : the fineness of the weather, the long dusty journey, his need of refreshment, and inquiries after her brother's health and spirits.

'He is not a man to be embarrassed, but his business baffles him,' she thought to herself ; 'he is ill at ease, and unhappy. I must try and meet him half-way.' And accordingly Mildred began in her straightforward manner.

'It is a long way to come up on business, Dr. Heriot. Arnold told me you had difficulties, though he did not explain their nature. Strange to say, he spoke as though I could be of some assistance to you !'

'I have no right to burden you,' he returned, somewhat incoherently ; 'you look little fit now to cope with such responsibilities as must fall to your share. Would not rest and change be beneficial before entering on new work ?'

'I am not talking of myself,' returned Mildred, with a faint smile, though her colour rose at the unmistakable tone of sympathy in Dr. Heriot's voice. 'My time for rest will come presently. Is it true, Dr. Heriot, that I can be of any service to you ?'

'You shall judge,' was the answer. 'I will meet your kindness with perfect frankness. My business in London at the present moment concerns a little girl—a distant relative of my poor wife's—who has lost her only remaining parent. Her father and I were friends in our student days ; and in a weak moment I accepted a presumptive guardianship over the child. I thought Philip Ellison was as likely as not to outlive me, and as he had some money left him there seemed very little risk about the whole business.'

Mildred gave him a glance full of intelligence. It was clear to her now wherein Dr. Heriot's difficulty lay. He was still too young a man to have the sole guardianship of a motherless orphan.

'Philip was but a few years older than myself, and, as he explained to me, it was only a purely business arrangement, and that in case of his death he wished to have a disinterested person to look after his daughter's interest. Things were different with me then, and I had no scruples in acceding to his wish. But Philip Ellison was a bad manager, and on an evil day was persuaded to invest his money in some rotten company—heaven knows what !—and as a natural consequence lost every penny. Since then I have heard little about him. He was an artist, but not a rising one ; he travelled a great deal in France and Germany, and now and then he would send over pictures to be sold, but I am afraid he made out only a scanty subsistence for himself and his little daughter. A month ago I received news of his death, and as she has not a near relation living, except some cousins in Australia, I find I have the sole charge of a girl of fourteen ; and I think you will confess, Miss Lambert, that the position has its difficulties. What in the world'—here Dr. Heriot's face grew a little comical—'am I to do with a raw school-girl of fourteen ?'

'What does Arnold suggest ?' asked Mildred, quietly. In her own mind she was perfectly aware what would be her brother's first generous thought.

'It was my intention to put the child at some good English school, and have her trained as a governess; but it is a dreary prospect for her, poor little soul, and somehow I feel as though I ought to do better for Philip Ellison's daughter. He was one of the proudest men that ever lived, and was so wrapped up in his child.'

'But my brother has negatived that, and proposed another plan,' interrupted Mildred, softly. She knew her brother well.

'He was generous enough to propose that she should go at once to the vicarage until some better arrangement could be made. He assured me that there was ample room for her, and that she could share Olive's and Chrissy's lessons ; but he begged me to refer it to you, as he felt he had no right to make such an addition to the family circle without your full consent.'

'Arnold is very good, but he must have known that I could have no objection to offer to any plan of which he approves. He is so kind-hearted, that one could not bear to damp his enthusiasm.'

'Yes, but think a moment before you decide,' returned Dr. Heriot, earnestly. 'It is quite true that I was bound to your brother and his wife by no ordinary ties of friendship, and that they would have done anything for me, but this ought not to be allowed to influence you. If I accept Mr. Lambert's offer, at least for the present, I shall be adding to your work,

increasing your responsibilities. Olive and Chrissy will tax
your forbearance sufficiently without my bringing this poor
little waif of humanity upon your kindness ; and you look so
far from strong,' he continued, with a quick change of tone.

'I am quite ready for my work,' returned Mildred, firmly ;
'looks do not always speak the truth, Dr. Heriot. Please let
me have the charge of your little ward; she will not be a
greater stranger to me than Olive and Chrissy are. Why,
Chrissy was only nine when I saw her last. Ah,' continued
Mildred, folding her hands, and speaking almost to herself,
'if you knew what it will be to me to see myself surrounded by
young faces, to be allowed to love them, and to try to win their
love in return—to feel I am doing real work in God's world,
with a real trust and talent given to me—ah ! you must let me
help you in this, Dr. Heriot; you were so good to Betha, and
it will make Arnold happy.' And Mildred stretched out her
hand to him with a new impulse, so unlike the composed
manner in which she had hitherto spoken, that Dr. Heriot,
surprised and touched, could find no response but 'God bless
you for this, Miss Lambert !'

Mildred's gentle primness was thawing visibly under Dr.
Heriot's pleasant manners. By and by, as she presided at the
sunny little tea-table, and pressed welcome refreshment on her
weary guest, she heard more about this strange early friendship
of his, and shared his surmises as to the probable education and
character of his ward.

'She must be a regular Bohemian by this time,' he observed.
'From what I can hear they were never long in one place. It
must be a strange training for a girl, living in artists' studios,
and being the sole companion of a silent, taciturn man such as
Philip was.'

'She will hardly have the characteristics of other girls,'
observed Mildred.

'She cannot possibly be more out of the common than Olive.
Olive has all sorts of absurd notions in her head. It is odd
Mrs. Lambert's training should have failed so signally in her
girls. I am afraid your preciseness will be sometimes offended,'
he continued, looking round the room, which, with all its
homeliness, had the little finishes that a woman's hand always
gives. 'Olive might have arranged those flowers, but she
would have forgotten to water them, or to exclude their presence
when dead.'

'You are a nice observer,' returned Mildred, smiling. 'Do

not make me afraid of my duties beforehand, as though I do not exactly know how all the rooms look! Betha's pretty drawing-room trampled by dirty boots, Arnold's study a hopeless litter of books, not a corner of the writing-table clear. Chrissy used them as bricks,' she continued, laughing. 'Roy and she had a mighty Tower of Babel one day. You should have seen Arnold's look when he found out that *The Seven Lamps of Architecture* laid the foundation; but Betha only laughed, and told him it served him right.'

'But she kept them in order, though. In her quiet way she was an excellent disciplinarian. Well, Miss Lambert, I am trespassing overmuch on your goodness. To-morrow I am to make my ward's acquaintance—one of the clique has brought her over from Dieppe—and I am·to receive her from his hands. Would it be troubling you too much if I ask you to accompany me?—the poor child will feel so forlorn with only men round her.'

'I will go with you and bring her home. No, please, do not thank me, Dr. Heriot. If you knew how lonely I am here ——' and for the first time Mildred's eyes filled with tears.

CHAPTER II

'O, my Father's hand,
Stroke heavily, heavily the poor hair down,
Draw, press the child's head closer to thy knee—
I'm still too young, too young, to sit alone.'—AURORA LEIGH.

So this was Polly.

It was only a shabby studio, where poverty and art fought a hand-to-hand struggle for the bare maintenance, but among the after scenes of her busy life Mildred never forgot the place where she first saw Dr. Heriot's ward; it lingered in her memory, a fair, haunting picture as of something indescribably sweet and sad.

Its few accessories were so suggestive of a truer taste made impossible by paucity of success; an unfinished painting all dim grays and pallid, watery blues; a Cain fleeing out of a blurred outline of clouds; fragmentary snatches of colour warming up pitiless details; rickety chairs and a broken-down table; a breadth of faded tapestry; a jar of jonquils, the form pure Tuscan, the material rough earthenware, a plaster Venus, mutilated but grand, shining out from the dull red background of a torn curtain. A great unfurnished room, full of yellow light and warm sunshine, and, standing motionless in a ladder of motes and beams, with brown eyes drinking in the twinkling glory like a young eagle, was a girl in a shabby black dress, with thin girlish arms clasped across her breast. For a moment Dr. Heriot paused, and he and Mildred exchanged glances; the young figure in its forlornness came to them like a mournful revelation; the immobility was superb, the youthful languor pitiful. As Dr. Heriot touched her, she turned on them eyes full of some lost dream, and a large tear that had been gathering unconsciously brimmed over and splashed down on his hand.

'My child, have we startled you? Mr. Fabian told us to come up.' For a moment she looked bewildered. Her thoughts had evidently travelled a long way, but with consciousness came a look of relief and pleasure.

'Oh, I knew you would come—papa told me so. Oh, why have you been so long?—it is three months almost since papa died. Oh, poor papa! poor papa!' and the flush of joy died out of her face as, clasping her small nervous hands round Dr. Heriot's arm, she laid her face down on them and burst into a passion of tears.

'I sent for you directly I heard; they kept me in ignorance —have they not told you so? Poor child, how unkind you must have thought me!' and a grieved look came over Dr. Heriot's face as he gently stroked the closely-cropped head, that felt like the dark, soft plumage of some bird.

'No, I never thought you that,' she sobbed. 'I was only so lonely and tired of waiting; and then I got ill, and Mr. Fabian was good to me, and so were the others. But papa had left me to you, and I wanted you to fetch me. You have come to take me home, have you not?'

She looked up in his face pleadingly as she said this; she spoke in a voice sweet, but slightly foreign, but with a certain high-bred accent, and there was something unique in her whole appearance that struck her guardian with surprise. The figure was slight and undeveloped, with the irregularity of fourteen; but the ordinary awkwardness of girlhood was replaced by dignity, almost grace, of movement. She was dark-complexioned, but her face was a perfect oval, and the slight down on the upper lip gave a characteristic but not unpleasing expression to the mouth, which was firm but flexible; the hair had evidently been cut off in recent illness, for it was tucked smoothly behind the ears, and was perfectly short behind, which would have given her a boyish look but for the extreme delicacy of the whole contour.

'You have come to take me home, have you not?' she repeated anxiously.

'This lady has,' he replied, with a look at Mildred, who had stood modestly in the background. 'I wish I had a home to offer you, my dear; but my wife is dead, and——'

'Then you will want me all the more,' she returned eagerly. 'Papa and I have so often talked about you; he told me how good you were, and how unhappy.'

'Hush, Mary,' laying his hand lightly over her lips; but

Mildred could see his colour changed painfully. But she interrupted him a little petulantly—

'Nobody calls me Mary, and it sounds so cold and strange.'

'What then, my dear ?'

'Why, Polly, of course !' opening her brown eyes widely ; 'I have always been Polly—always.'

'It shall be as you will, my child.'

'How gently you speak ! Are you ever irritable, like papa, I wonder ?—he used to be so ill and silent, and then, when we tried to rouse him, he could not bear it. Who is this lady, and why do you say you have no home for me ?'

'She means to be our good friend, Polly—there, will that do ? But you are such a dignified young lady, I should never have ventured to call you that unasked.'

'Why not ?' she repeated, darting at him a clear, straightforward glance. Evidently his reticence ruffled her ; but Dr. Heriot skilfully evaded the brief awkwardness.

'This lady is Miss Lambert, and she is the sister of one of my best friends ; she is going to take charge of his girls and boys, who have lost their mother, and she has kindly offered to take charge of you too.'

'She is very good,' returned Polly, coldly ; 'very, very good, I mean,' as though she had repented of a slight hauteur. 'But I have never had anything to do with children. Papa and I were always alone, and I would much rather live with you ; you have no idea what a housekeeper I shall make you. I can dress salad and cook *omelettes,* and Nanette taught me how to make *potage.* I used to take a large basket myself to the market when we lived at Dresden, when Nanette was so bad with rheumatism.'

'What an astonishing Polly !'

'Ah ! you are laughing at me,' drawing herself up proudly, and turning away so that he should not see the tears in her eyes.

'My dear Polly, is that a "crime" ?'

'It is when people are in earnest. I have said nothing that deserves laughing at—have I, Miss Lambert ?' with a sweet, candid glance that won Mildred's heart.

'No, indeed ; I was wishing that my nieces were like you.'

'I did not mean that—I was not asking for praise,' stammered Polly, turning a vivid scarlet. 'I only wanted my guardian to know that I should not be useless to him. I can do much more than that. I can mend and darn better than Annette, who was three years older. You are smiling still.'

'If I smile, it is only with pleasure to know my poor friend had such a good daughter. Listen to me, Polly—how old are you?'

'Fourteen last February.'

'What a youthful Polly!—too young, I fear, to comprehend the position. And then with such Bohemian surroundings— that half-crazed painter, Fabian,' he muttered, 'and a purblind fiddler and his wife. My poor child,' he continued, lay- ing his hand on her head lightly, and speaking as though moved in spite of himself, 'as long as you want a friend, you will never find a truer one than John Heriot. I will be your guardian, adopted father, what you will; but,' with a firmness of voice that struck the girl in spite of herself, 'I cannot have you to live with me, Polly.'

'Why not?' she asked, pleadingly.

'Because it would be placing us both in a false position; be- cause I could not incur such a responsibility; because no one is so fit to take charge of a young girl as a good motherly woman, such as you will find in Miss Lambert.' And as the girl looked at him bewildered and disappointed, he continued kindly, 'You must forget this pleasant dream, Polly; perhaps some day, when your guardian is gray-haired, it may come to pass; but I shall often think how good my adopted daughter meant to be to me.'

'Shall I never see you then?' asked Polly mournfully.

If these were English ways, the girl thought, what a cold, heartless place it must be! Had not Mr. Fabian promised to adopt her if the English guardian should not be forthcoming? Even Herr Schreiber had offered to keep her out of his poor salary, when her father's death had left her dependent on the little community of struggling artists and musicians. Polly was having her first lesson in the troublesome *convenances* of life, and to the affectionate, ardent girl it was singularly unpalatable.

'I am afraid you will see me every day,' replied her guardian, with much gravity. 'I shall not be many yards off—just round the corner, and across the market-place. No, no, Miss Polly; you will not get rid of me so easily. I mean to direct your studies, haunt your play-time, and be the cross old Mentor, as Olive calls me.'

'Oh, I am so glad!' returned the girl earnestly, and with a sparkle of pleasure in her eyes. 'I like you so much already that I could not bear you to do wrong.'

It was Heriot's turn to look puzzled.

'Would it not be wrong,' she returned, answering the look, 'when papa trusted me to you, and told me on his deathbed that you would be my second father, if you were to send me right away from you, and take no notice of me at all ?'

'I should hardly do that in any case,' returned her guardian, seriously. 'What a downright, unconventional little soul you are, Polly ! You may set your mind at rest ; your father's trust shall be redeemed, his child shall never be neglected by me. But come—you have not made Miss Lambert's acquaintance. I hope you mean to tell her next you like her.'

'She looks good, but sad—are you sad ?' touching Mildred's sleeve timidly.

'A little. I have been in trouble, like you, and have lost my mother,' replied Milly, simply ; but she was not prepared for the suddenness with which the girl threw her arms round her neck and kissed her.

'I might have thought—your black dress and pale face,' she murmured remorsefully. 'Every one is sad, every one is in trouble—myself, my guardian, and you.'

'But you are the youngest—it falls heaviest on you.'

'What am I to call you ? I don't like Miss Lambert, it sounds stiff,' with a little shrug and movement of the hands, rather graceful than otherwise.

'I shall be Aunt Milly to the others, why not to you ?' returned Mildred, smiling.

'Ah, that sounds nice. Papa had a sister, only she died ; I used to call her Aunt Amy. Aunt Milly ! ah, I can say that easily ; it makes me feel at home, somehow. Am I to come home with you to-day, Aunt Milly ?'

'Yes, my dear.' Milly absolutely blushed with pleasure at hearing herself so addressed. 'I am not going to my new home for three weeks, but I shall be glad of your company, if you will come and help me.'

'Poor Mr. Fabian will be sorry, but he is expecting to lose me. There is one thing more I must ask, Aunt Milly.'

'A dozen if you will, dear.'

'Oh, but this is a great thing. Oh, please, dear Aunt Milly, may I bring Rag and Tatters ?' And as Mildred looked too astonished for reply, she continued, hurriedly : 'Tatters never left papa for an instant, he was licking his hand when he died ; and Rag is such a dear old thing. I could not be happy any-where without my pets.' And without waiting for an answer she left the room ; and the next instant the light, springy tread was heard in company with a joyous scuffling and barking; then a large shaggy terrier burst into the room, and Polly followed with a great tortoise-shell cat in her arms.

'Isn't Rag handsome, except for this?' touching the animal where a scrap of fur had been rudely mauled off, and presented a bald appearance; 'he has lost the sight of one eye too. Veteran Rag, we used to call him. He is so fond of me, and follows me like a dog; he used to go out with me in Dresden, only the dogs hunted him.'

'You may bring your pets, Polly,' was Mildred's indulgent answer; 'I think I can answer for my brother's goodwill.'

Dr. Heriot shook his head at her laughingly.

'I am afraid you are no rigid disciplinarian, Miss Lambert; but it is "Love me, love my dog" with Polly, I expect. Now, my child, you must get ready for the flitting, while I go in search of Mr. Fabian. From the cloud of tobacco-smoke that met us on entering, I fancy he is on the next story.'

'He is with the Rogers, I expect. His model disappointed him, and he is not working to-day. If you will wait a moment, I will fetch him.'

'What an original character!' observed Dr. Heriot as the door closed.

'A loveable one,' was Mildred's rejoinder. She was interested and roused by the new phase of life presented to her to-day. She looked on amused, yet touched, when Polly returned, leading by the hand her pseudo-guardian—a tall old man, with fiery eyes and scanty gray hair falling down his neck, in a patched dressing-gown that had once been a gorgeous Turkey-red. It was the first time that the simple woman had gazed on genius down-at-heel, and faring on the dry crust of unrequited self-respect.

'There is my Cain, sir; a new conception—unfinished, if you will—but you may trace the idea I am feebly striving to carry out. Sometimes I fancy it will be my last bit of work. Look at that dimly-traced figure beside the murderer—that is his good angel, who is to accompany the branded one in his lifelong exile. I always believed in Cain's repentance—see the remorse in his eyes. I caught that expression on a Spanish sailor's face when he had stabbed his mate in a drunken brawl. I saw my Cain then.'

Needy genius could be garrulous, as Mildred found. The old man warmed at Polly's open-eyed admiration and Mildred's softly-uttered praise; appreciation was to him what meat and drink would be to more material natures. He looked almost majestic as he stood before them, in his ragged dressing-gown, descanting on the merits of his Tobit, that had sold for an old song. 'A Neapolitan fisher-boy had sat for my angel ; every one paints angels with yellow hair and womanish faces, but I am not one of those that must follow the beaten track—I formed my angel on the loftiest ideal of Italian beauty, and got sneered at for my pains. One ought to coin a new proverb nowadays, Dr. Heriot—Originality moves contempt. People said the subject was not a taking one ; Tobit was too much like an old-clothes man, or a veritable descendant of Moses and Sons. There was no end to the quips and jeers ; even our set had a notion it would not do, and I sold it to a dealer at a sum that would hardly cover a month's rent,' finished the old man, with a mixture of pathos and dignity.

'After all, public taste is a sort of lottery,' observed Dr. Heriot ; 'true genius is not always requited in this world, if it offends the tender prejudices of preconceived ideas.'

'The worship of the golden image fills up too large a space in the market-place,' replied Mr. Fabian, solemnly, 'while the blare of instruments covers the fetish-adoration of its votaries. The world is an eating and drinking and money-getting world, and art, cramped and stifled, goes to the wall.'

'Nay, nay ; I have not so bad an opinion of my generation as all that,' interposed Dr. Heriot, smiling. 'I have great faith in the underlying goodness of mankind. One has to break through a very stiff outer-crust, I grant you ; but there are soft places to be found in most natures.' And, as the other shook his head—'Want of success has made you a little down-hearted on the subject of our human charities, Mr. Fabian ; but there is plenty of reverence and art-worship in the world still. I predict a turn of the wheel in your case yet. Cain may still glower down on us from the walls of the Royal Academy.'

'I hope so, before the hand has lost its cunning. But I am too egotistical. And so you are going to take Polly from me— from Dad Fabian, ay ?'—looking at the young girl fondly.

'Indeed, Mr. Fabian, I must thank you for your goodness to my ward. Poor child ! she would have fared badly without it. Polly, you must ask Miss Lambert to bring you to see this kind friend again.'

'Nay, nay ; this is a poor place for ladies to visit,' replied the other, hastily, as he brushed away the fragment of a piece of snuff with a trembling hand ; but he looked gratified, not-

withstanding. 'Polly has been a good girl—a very good girl—
and weathered gallantly through a very ticklish illness, though
some of us thought she would never reach England alive.'

'Were you so ill, Polly?' inquired her guardian anxiously.

'Dad Fabian says so; and he ought to know, for he and
Mrs. Rogers nursed me. Oh, he was so good to me,' continued
Polly, clinging to him. 'He used to sit up with me part of the
night and tell me stories when I got better, and go without his
dinner sometimes to buy me fruit. Mrs. Rogers was good-
natured, too; but she was noisy. I like Dad Fabian's nursing
best.'

'You see she fretted for her father,' interposed the artist.
'Polly's one of the right sort—never gives way while there is
work to be done; and so the strain broke her down. She has
lost most of her pretty hair. Ellison used to be so proud of
her curls; but it suits her, somehow. But you must not keep
your new friends waiting, my child. There, God bless you!
We shall be seeing you back again here one of these days, I
dare say.'

Mildred felt as though her new life had begun from the
moment the young stranger crossed her threshold. Polly bade
her guardian good-bye the next day with unfeigned regret. 'I
shall always feel I belong to him, though he cannot have me to
live with him,' she said, as she followed Mildred into the house.
'Papa told me to love him, and I will. He is different, somehow, from what I expected,' she continued. 'I thought he
would be gray-haired, like papa. He looks younger, and is not
tall. Papa was such a grand-looking man, and so handsome;
but he has kind eyes—has he not, Aunt Milly?—and speaks so
gently.'

Mildred was quite ready to pronounce an eulogium on Dr.
Heriot. She had already formed a high estimate of her brother's
friend; his ready courtesy and highly-bred manners had given
her a pleasing impression, while his gentleness to his ward, and
a certain lofty tone of mind in his conversation, proved him a
man of good heart and of undoubted ability. There was a
latent humour at times discernible, and a certain caustic wit,
which, tinged as it was with melancholy, was highly attractive.
She felt that a man who had contrived to satisfy Betha's somewhat fastidious taste could not fail to be above the ordinary
standard, and, though she did not quite echo Polly's enthusiasm,
she was able to respond sympathetically to the girl's louder
praise.

Before many days were over Polly had transferred a large portion of loving allegiance to Mildred herself. Women—that is, ladies—had not been very plentiful in her small circle. One or two of the artists' wives had been kind to her; but Polly, who was an aristocrat by nature, had rather rebelled against their want of refinement, and discovered flaws which showed that, young as she was, she had plenty of discernment.

'Mrs. Rogers was noisy, and showed all her teeth when she laughed, and tramped as she walked—in this way;' and Polly brought a very slender foot to prove the argument. And Mrs. Hornby? Oh, she did not care for Mrs. Hornby much—'she thought of nothing but smart dresses, and dining at the restaurant, and she used such funny words—that men use, you know. Papa never cared for me to be with her much; but he liked Mrs. Rogers, though she fidgeted him dreadfully.'

Mildred listened, amused and interested, to the girl's prattle. The young creature on the stool at her feet was conversant with a life of which she knew nothing, except from books. Polly would chatter for hours together of picture-galleries and museums, and little feasts set out in illuminated gardens, and of great lonely churches with swinging lamps, and little tawdry shrines. Monks and nuns came familiarly into her reminiscences. She had had *gateau* and cherries in a convent-garden once, and had swung among apple-blossoms in an orchard belonging to one.

'I used to think I should like to be a nun once,' prattled Polly, 'and wear a great white flapping cap, as they did in Belgium. Sœur Marie used to be so kind. I shall never forget that long, straight lime-walk, where the girls used to take their recreation, or sit under the cherry-trees with their lace-work, while Sœur Marie read the lives of the saints. Do you like reading the lives of the saints, Aunt Milly? I dont. They are glorious, of course; but it pains me to know how uncomfortable they made themselves.'

'I do not think I have ever read any, Polly.'

'Have you not?'—with a surprised arching of the brows. 'Sœur Marie thought them the finest books in the world. She used to tell me stories of many of them; and her face would flush and her eyes grow so bright, I used to think she was a saint herself.'

Mildred rarely interrupted the girl's narratives; but little bits haunted her now and then, and lingered in her memory with tender persistence. What sober prose her life seemed in contrast to that of this fourteen-years' old girl! How bare and

empty seemed her niche compared to Polly's series of pictures!
How clearly Mildred could see it all! The wandering artist-
life, in search of the beautiful, poverty oppressing the mind less
sadly when refreshed by novel scenes of interest; the grave,
taciturn Philip Ellison, banishing himself and his pride in a
self-chosen exile, and training his motherless child to the same
exclusiveness.

The few humble friends, grouped under the same roof, and
sharing the same obscurity; stretching out the right hand of
fellowship, which was grasped, not cordially, but with a certain
protest, the little room which Polly described so graphically being
a less favourite resort than the one where Dad Fabian was painting his Tobit.

'It was only after papa got so ill that Mrs. Rogers would
bring up her work and sit with us. Papa did not like it much;
but he was so heavy that I could not lift him alone, and, noisy
as she was, she knew how to cheer him up. Dad suited papa
best: they used to talk so beautifully together. You have no
idea how Dad can talk, and how clever he is. Papa used to
say he was one of nature's gentlemen. His father was only a
working man, you know;' and Polly drew herself up with a
gesture Mildred had noticed before, and which was to draw
upon her later the *soubriquet* of 'the princess.'

'I think none the less of him for that,' returned Mildred,
with gentle reproof.

'You are not like papa then,' observed Polly, with one of her
pretty gestures of dissent. 'It fretted him so being with people
not nice in their ways. The others would call him milord, and
laugh at his grand manners; but all the same they were afraid
of him; every one feared him but I; and I only loved him,'
finished Polly, with one of her girlish outbursts of emotion,
which could only be soothed by extra petting on Mildred's part.

Mildred's soft heart was full of compassion for the lonely girl.
Polly, who cried herself to sleep every night for the longing for
her lost father, often woke to find Mildred sitting beside her bed
watching her.

'You were sleeping so restlessly, I thought I would look in
on you,' was all she said; but her motherly kiss spoke volumes.

'How good you are to me, Aunt Milly,' Polly would say to
her sometimes. 'I am getting to love you more every day; and
then your voice is so soft, and you have such nice ways. I
think I shall be happy living with you, and seeing my guardian
every day; but we don't want Olive and Chrissy, do we?'—for

Mildred had described the vicarage and its inhabitants—'It will feel as though we were in a beehive after this quiet little nest,' as she observed once. Mildred smiled, as she always did over Polly's quaint speeches, which were ripe at times with an old-fashioned wisdom, gathered from the stored garner of age. She would ponder over them sometimes in her slow way, when the girl was sleeping her wet-eyed sleep.

Would it come to her to regret the quietness of life which she was laying by for ever as a garment that had galled and fretted her ?—that life she had inwardly compared to a dead mill-stream, flecked only by the shadow and sunlight of per-petually recurring days ? Would there come a time when the burden and heat of the day would oppress her ?—when the load of existence would be too heavy to bear, and even this retrospect of faint gray distances would seem fair by contrast ?

Women who lead contemplative and sedentary lives are over-much given to this sort of morbid self-questioning. They are for ever examining the spiritual mechanism of their own natures, with the same result as though one took up a feeble and growing plant by the root to judge of its progress. They spend labour for that which is not bread. By and by, out of the vigour of her busy life, Mildred learnt the wholesome sweetness of a motto she ever afterwards cherished as her favourite : *Laborare est orare.* Polly's questions, direct or indirect, sometimes ruffled the elder woman's tranquillity, however gently she might put them by. 'Were you ever a girl, Aunt Milly ?—a girl like me, I mean ?' And as Mildred bit her lip and coloured slightly at a question that would have galled any woman of eight-and-twenty, she continued, caressingly, 'You are so nice ; only just a trifle too solemn. I think, after all, I would rather be Polly than you. You seem to have had no pictures in your life.'

'My dear child, what do you mean ?' returned Mildred ; but she spoke with a little effort.

'I mean, you don't seem to have lived out pretty little bits, as I have. You have walked every day over that common and down those long white sunny roads, where there is nothing to imagine, unless one stares up at the clouds—just clouds and dust and wheel-ruts. You have never gone through a forest by moonlight, as I have, and stopped at a little rickety inn, with a dozen *Jäger* drinking *lager-bier* under the linden-trees, and the peasants dancing in their *sabots* on a strip of lawn. You have never——' continued Polly breathlessly ; but Mildred inter-rupted her.

'Stop, Polly; I love your reminiscences; but I want to ask you a question. Is that all you saw in our walk to-day—clouds and dust and wheel-ruts?'

'I saw a hand-organ and a lazy monkey, and a brass band, driving me frantic. It made me feel—oh, I can't tell you how I felt,' returned Polly, with a grimace, and putting up her hands to her delicate little ears.

'The music was bad, certainly; but I found plenty to admire in our walk.'

Polly opened her eyes. 'You are not serious, Aunt Milly.'

'Let me see: we went across the common, and then on. My pictures are very humble ones, Polly; but I framed at least half-a-dozen for my evening's refreshment.'

Polly drew herself up a little scornfully. 'I don't admire monkeys, Aunt Milly.'

'What sort of eyes have you, child?' replied Mildred, who had recovered her cheerfulness. 'Do you mean that you did not see that old blind man with the white beard, and, evidently, his little grand-daughter, at his knees, just before we crossed the common?'

'Yes; I noticed she was a pretty child,' returned Polly, with reluctant candour.

'She and her blue hood and tippet, and the great yellow mongrel dog at her feet, made a pretty little sketch, all by themselves; and then, when we went on a little farther, there was the old gipsy-woman, with a handsome young ne'er-do-weel of a boy. Let me tell you, Polly, Mr. Fabian would have made something of his brown skin and rags. Oh, what rags!'

'She was a horrid old woman,' put in Polly, rather crossly.

'Granted; but, with a clump of fir-trees behind her, and a bit of sunset-clouds, she made up a striking picture. After that we came on a flock of sheep. One of them had got caught in a furze-bush, and was bleating terribly. We stood looking at it for full a minute before the navvy kindly rescued it.'

'I was sorry for the poor animal, of course. But, Aunt Milly, I don't call that much of a picture.'

'Nevertheless, it reminded me of the one that hangs in my room. To my thinking it was highly suggestive; all the more, that it was an old sheep, and had such a foolish, confiding face. We are never too old to go astray,' continued Mildred, dreamily.

'Three pictures, at least we have finished now,' asked Polly, impatiently.

'Finished! I could multiply that number threefold! Why,

there was the hay-stack, with the young heifers round it ; and
that red-tiled cottage, with the pigeons tumbling and wheeling
round the roof, and the flower-girl asleep on my own doorstep,
with the laburnum shedding its yellow petals on her lap, to the
great delight of the poor sickly baby.   Come, Polly ; who made
the most of their eyes this evening ?   Only clouds, dust, and
wheel-ruts, eh ?'

'You are too wise for me, Aunt Milly.   Who would have
thought you could have seen all that ?   Dad Fabian ought to
have heard you talk !   We must go out to-morrow evening,
and you shall show me some more pictures.   But doesn't it
strike you, Aunt Milly'—leaning her dimpled chin on her
hand—'that you have made the most of very poor material ?
After all'—triumphantly—'there is not much in your pictures !'

CHAPTER III

VIÂ TEBAY

'All the land in flowing squares.
Beneath a broad and equal blowing wind,
Smelt of the coming summer, as one large cloud
Drew downward ; but all else of heaven was pure
Up to the sun, and May from verge to verge,
And May with me from head to heel.

·   ·   ·

To left and right
The cuckoo told his name to all the hills,
The mellow ouzel fluted in the elm,
The redcap whistled, and the nightingale
Sung loud, as though he were the bird of day.'—TENNYSON.

'AUNT MILLY, I can breathe now. Oh, how beautiful!' and Polly clapped her hands with girlish glee, as the train slowly steamed into Tebay Junction, the gray old station lying snugly among the green Westmorland hills.

'Oh, my dear, hush! who is that tall youth taking off his hat to us? not Roy, surely, it must be Richard. Think of not knowing my own nephews!' and Mildred looked distressed and puzzled.

'Now, Aunt Milly, don't put yourself out; if this stupid door would only open, I would get out and ask him myself. Oh, thank you,' as the youth in question hurried forward to perform that necessary service, looking at her, at the same time, rather curiously. 'If you please, Aunt Milly wants to know if you are Roy or Richard.'

'Roy,' was the prompt answer. 'What, are you Polly, and is that Aunt Milly behind you? For shame, Aunt Milly, not to know me when I took my hat off to you at least three minutes ago;' but Roy had the grace to blush a little over this audacious statement as he helped Mildred out, and returned her warm grasp of the hand.

'My dear boy, how could you have known us, and Polly, a perfect stranger, too?'

Roy burst into a ringing laugh.

'Why you see, Aunt Milly, one never loses by a little extra attention; it always pays in the long run. I just took off my hat at random as the train came in sight, and there, as it happened, was Polly's face glued against the window. So I was right, and you were gratified!'

'Now I am sure it is Roy.'

'Roy, Rex, or Sauce Royal, as they called me at Sedbergh. Well, Miss Polly,' with another curious look, 'we are *bonâ fide* adopted cousins, as Dr. John says, so we may as well shake hands.'

'Humph,' was Polly's sole answer, as she gave her hand with the air of a small duchess, over which Roy grimaced slightly; and then with a cordial inflection of voice, as he turned to Mildred—

'Welcome to Westmorland, Aunt Milly—both of you, I mean; and I hope you will like us, as much as we shall like you.'

'Thank you, my boy; and to think I mistook you for Richard! How tall you have grown, Royal.'

'Ah, I was a bit of a lad when you were down here last. I am afraid I should not have recognised you, Aunt Milly, but for Polly. Well, what is it? you look disturbed; there is a vision of lost boxes in your eyes; there, I knew I was right; don't be afraid, we are known here, and Barton will look after all your belongings.'

'But how long are we to remain? Polly is tired, poor child, and so am I.'

'You should have come by York, as Richard told you; always follow Richard's advice, and you will never do wrong, so he thinks; now you have two hours to wait, and yourself to thank, and only my pleasing conversation to while away the time.'

'You hard-hearted boy; can't you see Aunt Milly is ready to drop?' broke in Polly, indignantly; 'how were we to know you lived so near the North Pole? My guardian ought to have met us,' continued the little lady, with dignity; 'he would have known what to have done for Aunt Milly.'

Roy stared, and then burst into his ready, good-humoured laugh.

'Whew! what a little termagant! Of course you are tired—

women always are ; take my arm, Aunt Milly ; lean on me ;
now we will go and have some tea ; let us know when the train
starts, Barton, and look us out a comfortable compartment;'
and, so saying, Roy hurried his charges away ; Mildred's tired
eyes resting admiringly on the long range of low, gray buildings,
picturesque, and strangely quiet, backed by the vivid green of
the great circling hills, which, to the eyes of southerners, invested Tebay Junction with unusual interest.

The refreshment-room was empty ; there was a pleasant
jingling of cups and spoons behind the bar ; in a twinkling the
spotless white table-cloth was covered with home-made bread,
butter, and ham, and even Polly's brow cleared like magic as
she sipped her hot tea, and brought her healthy girlish appetite
to bear on the tempting Westmorland cakes.

'There, Dr. John or Dick himself couldn't be a better squire
of dames,' observed Roy, complacently. 'Aunt Milly, when
you have left off admiring me, just close your eyes to your
surroundings a little while—it will do you no end of good.'

Roy was rattling on almost boisterously, Mildred thought ;
but she was right in attributing much of it to nervousness.
Roy's light-heartedness was assumed for the time ; in reality,
his sensitive nature was deeply touched by this meeting with
his aunt; his four-months'-old trouble was still too recent to
bear the least allusion. Betha's children were not likely to forget her, and Roy, warmly as he welcomed his father's sister,
could not fail to remember whose place it was she would try so
inadequately to fill. Jokes never came amiss to Roy, and he
had the usual boyish dislike to show his feelings ; but he was
none the less sore at heart, and the quick impatient sigh that
was now and then jerked out in the brief pauses of conversation
spoke volumes to Mildred.

'You are so like your mother,' she said, softly ; but the boy's lip
quivered, and he turned so pale, that Mildred did not venture
to say more ; she only looked at him with the sort of yearning
pride that women feel in those who are their own flesh and blood.

'He is not a bit like Arnold, he is Betha's boy,' she thought
to herself ; 'her "long laddie," as she used to call him. I dare
say he is weak and impulsive. Those sort of faces generally
tell their own story pretty correctly ;' and the thought crossed
her, that perhaps one of Dad Fabian's womanish angels might
have had the fair hair, long pale face, and sleepy blue eyes,
which were Roy's chief characteristics, and which were striking
enough in their way.

Polly, who had soon got over her brief animosity, was now chattering to him freely enough.

'I think you will do, for a country boy,' she observed, patronisingly ; 'people who live among the mountains are generally free and easy, and not as polished as those who live in cities,' continued Polly, uttering this sententious plagiarism as innocently as though it were the product of her own wisdom.

'Such kind of borrowing as this, if it be not bettered by the borrower, among good authors, is accounted plagiary ; see Milton,' said the boy, fresh from Sedbergh, with a portentous frown, assumed for the occasion. 'Name your reference. I repel such vile insinuations, Miss Polly, as I am a Westmorland boy.'

'I learnt that in my dictation,' returned Polly, vexed, but too candid for reticence ; 'but Dad Fabian used to say the same thing ; please don't stroke Veteran Rag the wrong way, he does not like it.'

'Poor old Veteran, he has won some scars, I see. I am afraid you are a character, Polly. Rag and Tatters, and copy-book wisdom, well-thumbed and learnt, and then retailed as the original article. I wish Dr. John could hear you ; he would put you through your paces.'

'Who is Dr. John ?' asked Polly, coming down a little from her stilts, and evidently relenting in favour of Roy's handsome face.

'Oh, Dr. John is Dr. John, unless you choose to do as the world does, and call him Dr. Heriot ; he is Dr. John to us ; after all, what's in a name ?'

'I like my guardian to be called Dr. Heriot best ; the other sounds disrespectful and silly.'

'We did not know your opinion before, you see,' returned Roy, with a slight drawl, and almost closing his eyes ; 'if you could have telegraphed your wish to us three or four years ago it might have been different ; but with the strict conservative feeling prevalent at the vicarage, I am afraid Dr. John it will remain, unless,' meditating deeply ; 'but no, he might not like it.'

'What ?'

'Well, we might make it Dr. Jack, you know.'

'After all, boys are nothing but plagues,' returned Polly, scornfully.

' "Playa, plagua, plague, *et cetera, et cetera*, that which smites or wounds ; any afflictive evil or calamity ; a great trial or vexation ; also an acute malignant febrile disease, that often prevails in Egypt, Syria, and Turkey, and that has at times prevailed in the large cities of Europe, with frightful mortality ; hence any pestilence." Have you swallowed Webster's *Diction-ary*, Polly ? '

'My dears, I hope you do not mean to quarrel already ? '

'We are only sounding the depths of each other's wisdom. Polly is awfully shallow, Aunt Milly ; the sort of person, you know, who utilises all the scraps. Wait till she sits at the feet of Gamaliel—Dr. John, I mean ; he is the one for finding out "all is not gold that glitters." '

Mildred smiled. 'Let them fight it out,' she thought ; 'no one can resist long the charm of Polly's perfect honesty, and her pride is a little too thin-skinned for daily comfort ; good-natured raillery will be a wholesome tonic. What a clever boy he is ! only seventeen, too,' and she shook her head indulgently at Roy.

'Kirkby Stephen train starts, sir ; all the luggage in ; this way for the ladies.'

'Quick-march ; down with you, Tatters ; lie there, good dog. Don't let the grass grow under your feet, Aunt Milly ; there's a providential escape for two tired and dusty Londoners. Next compartment, Andrews,' as the red-coated guard bore down on their carriage. 'There, Aunt Milly,' with an exquisite considera-tion that would have become Dr. John himself, 'I have deferred an introduction to the squire himself.'

'My dear Roy, how thoughtful of you. I am in no mood for introductions, certainly,' returned Mildred, gratefully.

'Women never are unless they have on their best bonnets ; and, to tell you the truth,' continued the incorrigible Roy, 'Mr. Trelawny is the sort of man for whom one always furbishes up one's company manners. As Dr. John says, there is nothing slip-shod, or in *deshabille*, in him. Everything about him is so terribly perfect.'

'Roy, Roy, what a quiz you are ! '

'Hush, there they come ; the Lady of the Towers herself, Ethel the Magnificent ; the weaver of yards of flimsy verse, patched with rags and shreds of wisdom, after Polly's fashion. Did you catch a glimpse of our notabilities, Aunt Milly ? '

Mildred answered yes ; she had caught a glimpse over Roy's shoulder of a tall, thin, aristocratic-looking man ; but the long sweep of silk drapery and the outline of a pale face were all that she could see of the lady with him.

She began to wish that Roy would be a little less garrulous as the train moved out of Tebay station, and bore them swiftly to their destination; she was nerving herself for the meeting with her brother, and the sight of the vicarage without the presence of its dearly-loved mistress, while the view began to open so enchantingly before them on either side, that she would willingly have enjoyed it in silence. But Polly was less reticent, and her enthusiasm pleased Roy.

'You see we are in the valley of the Lune,' he explained, his grandiloquence giving place to boyish earnestness. 'Ours is one of the loveliest spots in the whole district. Now we are at the bottom of Ravenstone-dale, out of which it used to be said that the people would never allow a good cow to go, or a rich heiress to be taken; and then we shall come to Smardale Gill. Is it not pretty, with its clear little stream running at the bottom, and its sides covered with brushwood? Now we are in my father's parish,' exclaimed Roy, eagerly, as the train swept over the viaduct. 'And now look out for Smardale Hall on the right; once the residents were grand enough to have a portion of the church to themselves, and it is still called Smardale Chapel; the whole is now occupied by a farmhouse. Ah, now we are near the station. Do you see that castellated building? that is Kirkleatham House, the Trelawnys' place. Now look out for Dick, Aunt Milly. There he is! I thought so, he has spotted the Lady of the Towers.'

'My dear, is that Richard?' as a short and rather square-shouldered young man, but decidedly good-looking, doffed his straw hat in answer to some unseen greeting, and then peered inquiringly into their compartment.

'Ah, there you are, Rex. Have you brought them? How do you do, Aunt Milly? Is that young lady with you Miss Ellison?' and he shook hands rather formally, and without looking at Polly. 'I hope you did not find your long stay at Tebay very wearisome. Did you give them some tea, Rex? That's right. Please come with me, Aunt Milly; our waggonette is waiting at the top of the steps.'

'Oh, Richard, I wish you were not all such strangers to me!' Mildred could not have helped that involuntary exclamation which came out of the fulness of her heart. Her elder nephew was walking gravely by her side, with slow even strides; he looked up a little surprised.

'I suppose we must be that. After seven years' absence you will find us all greatly changed of course. I remember you perfectly, but then I was fourteen when you paid your last visit.'

'You remember me? I hardly expected to hear you say that,'

and Mildred felt a glow of pleasure which all Roy's friendliness had not called forth.

'You are looking older—and as Dr. Heriot told us, somewhat ill; but it is the same face of course. My father will be glad to welcome you, Aunt Milly.'

'And you?'

His dark face flushed, and he looked a little discomfited. Mildred felt sorry she had asked the question, it would offend his reticence.

'It is early days for any of us to be glad about anything,' he returned with effort. 'I think for my father's and the girls' sake, your coming could not be too soon; you will not complain of our lack of welcome I hope, though some of us may be a little backward in acting up to it.'

'He is speaking of himself,' thought Mildred, and she answered the unspoken thought very tenderly. 'You need not fear my misunderstanding you, Richard; if you will let me be your friend as well as the others', I shall be glad: but no one can fill her place.'

He started, and drew his straw hat nervously over his brow. 'Thank you, Aunt Milly,' was all he said, as he placed her in the waggonette, and took the driver's seat on the box.

'There are changes even here, Aunt Milly,' observed Roy, who had seated himself opposite to her for the purpose of making pertinent observations on the various landmarks they passed, and he pointed to the long row of modern stuccoed and decidedly third-class villas springing up near the station. 'The new line brings this. We are in the suburbs of Kirkby Stephen, and I dare say you hardly know where you are;' a fact which Mildred could not deny, though recognition dawned on her senses, as the low stone houses and whitewashed cottages came in sight; and then the wide street paved with small blue cobbles out of the river, and small old-fashioned shops, and a few gray bay-windowed houses bearing the stamp of age, and well-worn respectability. Ah, there was the market-place, with the children playing as usual round the old pump, and the group of loiterers sunning themselves outside the Red Lion. Through the grating and low archway of the empty butter-market Mildred could see the grass-grown paths and gleaming tombstones and the gray tower of the grand old church itself. The approach to the vicarage was singularly ill-adapted to any but pedestrians. It required a steady hand and eye to guide a pair of spirited horses round the sharp angles of the narrow winding alley, but the little country-bred browns knew their work. The vicarage gates were wide open, and two black figures were shading their eyes in the porch. But Richard, instead of driving in at the gate, reined in his horses so suddenly that he nearly brought them on their haunches, and leaning backward over the box, pointed with his whip across the road.

'There is my father taking his usual evening stroll—never mind the girls, Aunt Milly. I dare say you would rather meet him alone.'

Mildred stood up and steadied herself by laying a hand on Richard's shoulder. The sun was setting, and the gray old church stood out in fine relief in the warm evening light, blue breadths of sky behind it, and shifting golden lines of sunny clouds in the distance; while down the quiet paths, bareheaded and with hands folded behind his back, was a tall stooping figure, with scanty gray hair falling low on his neck, walking to and fro, with measured, uneven tread.

The hand on Richard's shoulder shook visibly; Mildred was trembling all over.

'Arnold! Oh, how old he looks! How thin and bowed! Oh, my poor brother.'

'You must make allowance for the shock he has had—that we have all had,' returned Richard in a soothing tone. 'He always walks like this, and at the same time. Go to him, Aunt Milly, it does him good to be roused.'

Mildred obeyed, though her limbs moved stiffly; the little gate swung behind her; a tame goat browsing among the tombs bleated and strained at its tether as she passed; but the figure she followed still continued its slow, monotonous walk.

Mildred shrunk back for a moment into the deep church porch to pause and recover herself. At the end of the path there were steps and an unused gate leading to the market; he must turn then.

How quiet and peaceful it all looked! The dark range of school buildings buried in shadow, the sombre line of houses closing in two sides of the churchyard. Behind the vicarage the purple-rimmed hills just fading into indistinctness. Up and down the stone alley some children were playing, one wee toddling mite was peeping through the railings at Mildred. The goat still bleated in the distance; a large blue-black terrier swept in hot pursuit of his master.

'Ah, Pupsie, have you found me? The evenings are chilly still; so, so, old dog, we will go in.'

Mildred waited for a moment and then glided out from the porch—he turned, saw her, and held out his arms without a word.

Mr. Lambert was the first to recover himself; for Mildred's tears, always long in coming, were now falling like rain.

'A sad welcome, my dear; but there, she would not have us grieving like this.'

'Oh, Arnold, how you have suffered! I never realised how much, till Richard stopped the horses, and then I saw you walking alone in the churchyard. The dews are falling, and you are bareheaded. You should take better care of yourself, for the children's sake.'

'Ay, ay; just what she said; but it has grown into a sort of habit with me. Cardie comes and fetches me in, night after night; the lad is a good lad; his mother was right after all.

'Dear Betha; but you have not laid her here, Arnold?'

He shook his head.

'I could not, Mildred, though she wished it as much as I did. She often said she would like to lie within sight of the home where she had been so happy, and under the shadow of the church porch. She liked the thought of her children's feet passing so near her on their way to church, but I had no power to carry out her wish.'

'You mean the churchyard is closed?'

'Yes, owing to the increase of population, the influx of railway labourers, and the union workhouse, deaths in the parish became so numerous that there was danger of overcrowding. She lies in the cemetery.'

'Ah! I remember.'

'I do not think her funeral will ever be forgotten; people came for miles round to pay their last homage to my darling. One old woman over eighty came all the way from Castlesteads to see her last of "the gradely leddy," as she called her. You should have seen it, to know how she was loved.'

'She made you very happy while she lived, Arnold!'

'Too happy!—look at me now. I have the children, of course, poor things; but in losing her, I feel I have lost the best of everything, and must walk for ever in the shadow.'

He spoke in the vague musing tone that had grown on him of late, and which was new to Mildred—the worn, set features and gray hair contrasted strangely with the vivid brightness of his eyes, at once keen and youthful; he had been a man in the prime of life, vigorous and strong, when Mildred had seen him last ; but a long illness and deadly sorrow had wasted his energy, and bowed his upright figure, as though the weight were physical as well as mental.

'But this is a poor welcome, Milly ; and you must be tired and starved after your day's journey. You are not looking robust either, my dear—not a trace of the old blooming Milly' (touching her thin cheek sorrowfully). 'Well, well, the children must take care of you, and we'll get Dr. Heriot to prescribe. Has the child come with you after all ?'

Mildred signified assent.

'I am glad of it. Thank you heartily for your ready help, Milly ; we would do anything for Heriot ; the boys treat him as a sort of elder brother, and the girls are fond of him, though they lead him a life sometimes. He is very grateful to you, and says you have lifted a mountain off him. Is the girl a nice girl, eh ?'

'I must leave you to judge of that. She has interested me, at any rate ; she is thoroughly loveable.'

'She will shake down among the others, and become one of us, I hope. Ah ! well, that will be your department, Mildred. I am not much to be depended on for anything but parish matters. When a man loses hope and energy it is all up with him.'

The little gate swung after them as he spoke ; the flower-bordered courtyard before the vicarage seemed half full of moving figures as they crossed the road ; and in another moment Mildred was greeting her nieces, and introducing Polly to her brother.

'I cannot be expected to remember you both,' she said, as Olive timidly, and Christine rather coldly, returned her kiss. 'You were such little girls when I last saw you.'

But with Mildred's tone of benevolence there mingled a little dismay. Betha's girls were decidedly odd.

Olive, who was a year older than Polly, and who was quite a head taller, had just gained the thin ungainly age, when to the eyes of anxious guardians the extremities appear in the light of afflictive dispensations ; and premature old age is symbolised by the rounded and stooping shoulders, and sunken chest ; the age of trodden-down heels and ragged finger-ends, when the glory of the woman, as St. Paul calls it, instead of being coiled into smooth knots, or swept round in faultless plaits, of coroneted beauty, presents a vista of frayed ends and multitudinous hair-pins. Olive's loosely-dropping hair and dark cloudy face gave Mildred a shock ; the girl was plain too, though the irregular features beamed at times with a look of intelligence. Christine, who was two years younger, and much better-looking, in spite of a rough, yellowish mane, had an odd, original face, a pert nose, argumentative chin, and restless dark eyes, which already looked critically at persons and things. 'Contradiction Chriss,' as the boys called her, was certainly a character in her way.

'Are you tired, aunt ? Will you come in ?' asked Olive, in a low voice, turning a dull sort of red as she spoke. 'Cardie thinks you are, and supper is ready, and——'

'I am very tired, dear, and so is Polly,' answered Mildred, cheerfully, as she followed Olive across the dimly-lighted hall, with its old-fashioned fireplace and settles ; its tables piled up with coats and hats, which had found their way to the harmonium too.

They went up the low, broad staircase Mildred remembered so well, with its carved balustrades and pretty red and white drugget, and the great blue China jars in the window recesses.

The study door stood open, and Mildred had a glimpse of the high-backed chair, and table littered over with papers, before she began ascending again, and came out into the low-ceiled passage, with deep-set lattice windows looking on the court and churchyard.

'Chrissy and I sleep here,' explained Olive, panting slightly from nervousness, as Mildred looked inquiringly at her. 'We thought—at least Cardie thought—this little room next to us would do for Miss Ellison.'

Polly peeped in delightedly. It was small, but cosy, with a curiously-shaped bedstead—the head having a resemblance to a Latin cross, with three pegs covered with white dimity. The room was neatly arranged—a decided contrast to the one they had just passed ; and there was even an effort at decoration, for the black bars of the grate were entwined with sprays of honesty—the shining, pearly leaves grouped also in a tall red jar, on the mantelpiece.

'That is a pretty idea. Was it yours, Olive ?'

Olive nodded. 'Father thought you would like your old room, aunt—the one he and mother always called yours.'

The tears came again in Mildred's eyes. Somehow it seemed but yesterday since Betha welcomed her so warmly, and showed her the room she was always to call hers. There was the tiny dressing-room, with its distant view, and the quaint old-fashioned rooin, with an oaken beam running across the low ceiling, and its wide bay-window.

There was the same heartsease paper that Mildred remembered seven years ago, the same flowery chintz, the curious old quilt, a hundred years old, covered with twining carnations. The very fringe that edged the beam spoke to her of a brother's thoughtfulness, while the same hand had designed the motto which from henceforth was to be Mildred's own—'*Laborare est orare.*'

'The lines are fallen to me in pleasant places,' whispered Mildred as she drew near the window, and stood there spellbound by the scene, which, though well-remembered, seemed to come before her with new beauty.

Underneath her lay the vicarage garden, with its terrace walk and small, trim lawn; and down below, half hidden by a steep wooded bank, flowed the Eden, its pebbly beach lying dry under the low garden wall, but farther on plashing with silvery gleams through the thick foliage.

To the right was the foot-bridge leading to the meadows, and beyond that the water-mill and the weir; and as far as eye could reach, green uplands and sweeps of pasturage, belted here and there with trees, and closing in the distance soft ranges of fells, ridge beyond ridge, fading now into gray indistinctness, but glorious to look upon when the sun shone down upon their 'paradise of purple and the golden slopes atween them,' or the storm clouds, lowering over them, tinged them with darker violet.

'A place to live in and die in,' thought Mildred, solemnly, as the last thing that night she stood looking out into the moonlight.

The hills were invisible now, but gleams of watery brightness shone between the trees, and the garden lay flooded in the silver light. A light wind stirred the foliage with a soft soughing movement, and some animal straying to the river to drink trod crisply on the dry pebbles.

'A place where one should think good thoughts and live out one's best life,' continued Mildred, dreamily. A sigh, almost a groan, from beneath her open window seemed to answer her unspoken thought; and then a dark figure moved quietly away. It was Richard!

CHAPTER IV

MILDRED'S NEW HOME

'Half drowned in sleepy peace it lay,
As satiate with the boundless play
Of sunshine on its green array.
And clear-cut hills of gloomy blue,
To keep it safe, rose up behind,
As with a charmèd ring to bind
The grassy sea, where clouds might find
A place to bring their shadows to.'—JEAN INGELOW.

'AUNT MILLY, I have wakened to find myself in Paradise,' were the first words that greeted Mildred's drowsy senses the next morning; and she opened her eyes to find the sun streaming in through the great uncurtained window, and Polly in her white dressing-gown, curled up on the low chair, gazing out in rapturous contemplation.

'It must be very early,' observed Mildred, wearily. She was fatigued with her journey and the long vigil she had kept the preceding night, and felt a little discontented with the girl's birdlike activity.

'One ought not to be tired in Paradise,' returned Polly, reprovingly. 'Do people have aches and pains and sore hearts here, I wonder—in the valley of the Eden, as he called it—and yet Mr. Lambert looks sad enough, and so does Richard. Do you like Richard, Aunt Milly?'

'Very much,' returned Mildred, with signs of returning animation in her voice.

'Well, he is not bad—for an icicle,' was Polly's quaint retort; 'but I like Roy best; he is tiresome, of course—all boys are—but oh, those girls, Aunt Milly!'

'Well, what of them?' asked Mildred, in an amused voice. 'I am sure you could not judge of them last night, poor things; they were too shy.'

'They were dreadful. Oh, Aunt Milly, don't let us talk of them !'

'I am sure Olive is clever, Polly ; her face is full of intelligence. Christine is a mere child.'

Polly shrugged her shoulders. She did not care to argue on such an uninteresting question. The little lady's dainty taste was offended by the somewhat uncouth appearance of the sisters. She changed the subject deftly.

'How the birds are singing ! I think the starlings are building their nests under the roof, they are flying in and out and chirping so busily. How still it is on the fells ! There is an old gray horse feeding by the bridge, and some red and white cattle coming over the side of the hill. This is better than your old Clapham pictures, Aunt Milly.'

Mildred smiled ; she thought so too.

'Roy says the river is a good way below, and that it is rather a dangerous place to climb. He thinks nothing of it—but then he is a boy ! How blue the hills are this morning ! They look quite near. But Roy says they are miles away. That long violet one is called the Nine Standards, and over there are Hartley Fells. We were out on the terrace last night, and he told me their names. Roy is very fond of talk, I think ; but Richard stood near us all the time, and never said a word, except to scold Roy for chattering so much.'

'Richard was afraid the sound of your voices would disturb my brother.'

'That is the worst of it, as Roy says, Richard is always in the right. I don't think Roy is unfeeling, but he forgets sometimes ; he told me so himself. We had quite a long talk when the others went in.'

'You and he seem already very good friends.'

'Yes, he is a tolerably nice boy,' returned Polly, condescendingly ; 'and we shall get on very well together, I dare say. Now I will leave you in peace, Aunt Milly, to finish dressing ; for I mean to make acquaintance with that big green hill before breakfast.'

Mildred was not sorry to be left in peace. It was still early. So, while Polly wetted her feet in the grass, Mildred went softly downstairs to refresh her eyes and memory with a quiet look at the old rooms in their morning freshness.

The door of her brother's study stood open, and she ventured in, almost holding her breath, lest her step should reach his ear in the adjoining room.

There was the chair where he always sat, with his gray head against the light, the one narrow old-fashioned window framing only a small portion of the magnificent prospect. There were the overflowing waste-paper baskets, as usual, brimming over their contents on the carpet—the table a hopeless chaos of documents, pamphlets, and books of reference.

There were some attempts at arrangement in the well-filled bookcases that occupied two sides of the small room, but the old corner behind the mother's chair and work-table still held the débris of the renowned Tower of Babel, and a family tendency to draw out the lower books without removing the upper ones had resulted in numerous overthrows, so that even Mr. Lambert objected to add to the dusty confusion.

Books and papers were everywhere; they littered even the couch—that couch where Betha had lain for so many months, only tired, before they discovered what ailed her—the couch where her husband had laid the little light figure morning after morning, till she had grown too ill to be moved even that short distance.

Looking round, Mildred could understand the growing helplessness of the man who had lost his right hand and helpmeet; the answer and ready sympathy that never failed him were wanting now; the comely, bright presence had gone from his sight; the tones that had always vibrated so sweetly in his ear were silent for ever. With his lonely broodings there must ever mix a bitter regret, and the dull, perpetual anguish of a yearning never to be satisfied. Earth is full of these desolations, which come alike on the evil and the good—mysteries of suffering never to be understood here, but which, to such natures as Arnold Lambert's, are but as the Refiner's furnace, purging the dross of earthly passion and centring them on things above.

Instinctively Mildred comprehended this, as her eye fell on the open pages of the Bible—the Bible that had been her husband's wedding gift to Betha, and in which she had striven to read with failing eyes the very day before her death.

Mildred touched it reverently and turned away.

She lingered for a moment in the dining-room, where a buxom North-countrywoman was laying the table for breakfast. Everything here was unchanged.

It was still the same homely, green, wainscotted room, with high, narrow windows looking on to the terrace. There was the same low, old-fashioned sideboard and silk-lined chiffonnier; the same leathern couch and cumbrous easy-chair; the same picture of 'Virtue and Vice,' smiling and glaring over the high wooden mantelpiece. Yes, the dear old room, as Mildred had fondly termed it in her happy three months' visit, was exactly the same ; but Betha's drawing-room was metamorphosed into fairyland.

All Arnold's descriptions had not prepared her for the pleasant surprise. Behind the double folding-doors lay a perfect picture-room, its wide bay looking over the sunny hills, and a glass door opening on the beck gravel of the courtyard.

Outside, the long levels of green, with Cuyp-like touches of brown and red cattle, grouped together on the shady bank, tender hints of water gleaming through the trees, and the soft billowy ridges beyond ; within, the faint purple and golden tints of the antique jars and vases, and shelves of rare porcelain, the rich hues of the china harmonising with the high-backed ebony chairs and cabinet, and the high, elaborately-finished mantelpiece, curiously inlaid with glass, and fitted up with tiny articles of *vertu;* the soft, blue hangings and Sèvres table and other dainty finishes giving a rich tone of colour to the whole. Mr. Lambert was somewhat of a *dilettante,* and his accurate taste had effected many improvements in the vicarage, as well as having largely aided in the work nearest his heart—the restoration of his church.

The real frontage of the vicarage looked towards the garden terrace and Hillsbottom, the broad meadow that stretched out towards Hartley Fells, with Hartley Fold Farm and Hartley Castle in the distance ; from its upper window the Nine Standards and Mallerstang, and to the south Wild-boar Fells, were plainly visible. But the usual mode of entrance was at the back. The gravelled sweep of courtyard, with its narrow grass bordering and flower-bed, communicated with the out-houses and stable-yard by means of a green door in the wall. The part of the vicarage appropriated to the servants' use was very old, dating, it is said, from the days of Henry VIII, and some of the old windows were still remaining. Mildred remembered the great stone kitchen and rambling cellarage and the cosy housekeeper's room, where Betha had distilled her fragrant waters and tied up her preserves. As she passed down the long passage leading to the garden-door she could see old Nan, bare-armed and bustling, clattering across the stones in her country clogs, the sunny backyard distinctly visible. Some hens were clucking round a yellow pan ; the goat bleated from the distance ; the white tombstones gleamed in the morning

sun ; a scythe cut crisply through the wet grass ; a fleet step
on the gravel behind the little summer-house lingered and then
turned.

'You are early, Aunt Milly—at least, for a Londoner, though
we are early people here, as you will find. I hope you have
slept well.'

'Not very well ; my thoughts were too busy. Is it too
early to go over to the church yet, Richard ?'

'The bells will not ring for another half-hour, if that is
what you mean ; but the key hangs in my father's study. I
can take you over if you wish.'

'No, do not let me hinder you,' glancing at the Greek lexi-
con he held in his hand.

'Oh, my time is not so valuable as that,' he returned, good-
humouredly. 'Of course you must see the restoration ; it is
my father's great work, and he is justly proud of it. If you go
over, Aunt Milly, I will be with you in a minute.'

Mildred obeyed, and waited in the grand old porch till
Richard made his appearance, panting, and slightly disturbed.

'It was mislaid, as usual. When you get used to us a little
more, Aunt Milly, you will find that no one puts anything in
its proper place. It used not to be so,' he continued, in a suppressed voice ; 'but we have got into sad ways lately ; and
Olive is a wretched manager.'

'She is so young, Richard. What can you expect from a
girl of fifteen ?'

'I have seen little women and little mothers at that age,' he
returned, with brusque quaintness. 'Some girls, placed as she is,
would be quite different ; but Livy cares for nothing but books.'

'She is clever then ?'

'I suppose so,' indifferently. 'My father says so, and so did
——' (he paused, as though the word were difficult to utter)—
'but—but she was always trying to make her more womanly.
Don't you think clever women are intolerable, Aunt Milly ?'

'Not if they have wise heads and good hearts ; but they
need peculiar training. Oh, how solemn and beautiful !' as
Richard at last unlocked the door ; and they entered the vast
empty church, with the morning sun shining on its long aisles
and glorious arcades.

Richard's querulous voice was hushed in tender reverence
now, as he called Mildred to admire the highly-decorated roof
and massive pillars, and pointed out to her the different parts
that had been restored.

'The nave is Early English, and was built in 1220; the north aisle is of the original width, and was restored in Perpendicular style; the window at the eastern end is Early English too. The south aisle was widened about 1500, and has been restored in the Perpendicular; and the transepts are Early English, in which style the chancel also has been rebuilt. Nothing of the original remains except the Sedilia, probably late Early English, or perhaps the period sometimes called Wavy, or Decorated.'

'You know it all by heart, Richard. How grand those arches are; the church itself is almost cathedral-like in its vast size.'

'We are very fond of it,' he returned, gravely. 'Do you recollect this chapel? It is called the Musgrave Chapel. One of these tombs belonged to Sir Thomas Musgrave, who is said to have killed the last wild boar seen in these parts, about the time of Edward III.'

'Ah! I remember hearing that. You are a capital guide, Richard.'

'Since my father has been ill, I have always taken strangers over the church, and so one must be acquainted with the details. This is the Wharton Chapel, Aunt Milly; and here is the tomb of Lord Thomas Wharton and his two wives; it was built as a mortuary chapel, in the reign of Elizabeth, so my father says. Ah! there is the bell, and I must go into the vestry and see if my father be ready.'

'You have not got a surpliced choir yet, Richard?'

He shook his head.

'We have to deal with northern prejudices; you have no idea how narrow and bigoted some minds can be. I could tell you of a parish, not thirty miles from here, where a sprig of holly in the church at Christmas would breed a riot.'

'Impossible, Richard!'

'You should hear some of the Squire's stories about twenty years ago; these are enlightened times compared to them. We are getting on tolerably well, and can afford to wait; our daily services are badly attended. There is the vicarage pew, Aunt Milly; I must go now.'

Only nineteen—Richard's mannishness was absolutely striking; how wise and sensible he seemed, and yet what underlying bitterness there was in his words as he spoke of Olive. 'His heart is sore, poor lad, with missing his mother,' thought Mildred, as she watched the athletic figure, rather strong than graceful, cross the broad chancel ; and then, as she sat admiring the noble pulpit of Shap granite and Syenetic marble, the vicarage pew began slowly to fill, and two or three people took their places.

Mildred stole a glance at her nieces : Olive looked heavy-eyed and absent ; and Chriss more untidy than she had been the previous night. When service had begun she nudged her aunt twice, once to say Dr. Heriot was not there, and next that Roy and Polly had come in late, and were hiding behind the last pillar. She would have said more, but Richard frowned her into silence. It was rather a dreary service ; there was no music, and the responses, with the exception of Richard's, were inaudible in the vast building ; but Mildred thought it restful, though she grieved to see that her brother's worn face looked thinner and sadder in the morning light, and his tall figure more bowed and feeble.

He waited for her in the porch, where she lingered behind the others, and greeted her with his old smile ; and then he took Richard's arm.

'We have a poor congregation you see, Mildred ; even Heriot was not there.'

'Is he usually ?' she asked, somewhat quickly.

'I have never known him miss, unless some bad case has kept him up at night. He joined us reluctantly at first, and more to please us than himself ; but he has grown into believing there is no fitter manner of beginning the day ; his example has infected two or three others, but I am afraid we rarely number over a dozen. We do a little better at six o'clock.'

'It must be very disheartening to you, Arnold.'

'I do not permit myself to feel so ; if the people will not come, at least they do not lack invitation—twice a day the bells ring out their reproachful call. I wish Christians were half as devout as Mahometans.'

'Mrs. Sadler calls it new-fangled nonsense, and says she has not time to be always in church,' interrupted Chrissy, in her self-sufficient treble.

'My little Chriss, it is not good to repeat people's words. Mrs. Sadler has small means and a large family, and the way she brings them up is highly creditable.' But his gentle reproof fell unheeded.

'But she need not have told Miss Martingale that she knew you were a Ritualist at heart, and that the daily services were unnecessary innovations,' returned Chrissy, stammering slightly over the long words.

'Now, Contradiction, no one asked for this valuable piece of information,' exclaimed Roy, with a warning pull at the rough tawny mane ; 'little girls like you ought not to meddle in parish matters. You see Gregory has been steadily at work this morning, father,' pointing to the long swathes of cut grass under the trees ; 'the churchyard will be a credit to us yet.'

But Roy's good-natured artifice to turn his father's thoughts into a pleasanter channel failed to lift the cloud that Chrissy's unfortunate speech had raised.

'Innovations ! new-fangled ideas !' he muttered, in a grieved voice, 'simple obedience—that I dare not, on the peril of a bad conscience, withhold, to the rules of the Church, to the loving precept that bids me gather her children into morning and evening prayer.'

'Contradiction, you deserve half-a-dozen pinches for this,' whispered Roy ; 'you have set him off on an old grievance.'

'Never sacrifice principles, Cardie, when you are in my position,' continued Mr. Lambert. 'If I had listened to opposing voices, our bells would have kept silence from one Sunday to another. Ah, Milly ! I often ask myself, "Can these dry bones live ?" The husks and tares that choke the good seed in these narrow minds that listen to me Sunday after Sunday would test the patience of any faithful preacher.'

'Aunt Milly looks tired, and would be glad of her breakfast,' interposed Richard.

Mildred thanked him silently with her eyes ; she knew her brother sufficiently of old to dread the long vague self-argument that would have detained them for another half-hour in the porch had not Richard's dexterous hint proved effectual. Mildred learnt a great deal of the habits of the family during the hour that followed ; the quiet watchful eyes made their own observation—and though she said little, nothing escaped her tender scrutiny. She saw her brother would have eaten nothing but for the half-laughing, half-coaxing attentions of Roy, who sat next him. Roy prepared his egg, and buttered his toast, and placed the cresses daintily on his plate, unperceived by Mr. Lambert, who was opening his letters and glancing over his papers.

When he had finished—and his appetite was very small—he pushed away his plate, and sat looking over the fells, evidently lost in thought. But his children, as though accustomed to his

silence, took no further notice of him, but carried on the conversation among themselves, only dropping their voices when
a heavier sigh than usual broke upon their ears.   The table was
spread with a superabundance of viands that surprised Mildred ;
but the cloth was not over clean, and was stained with coffee in
several places.   Mildred fancied that it was to obviate such a
catastrophe for the future that Richard sat near the urn.   A
German grammar lay behind the cups and saucers, and Olive
munched her bread and butter very ungracefully over it, only
raising her head when querulous or reproachful demands for
coffee roused her reluctant attention, and it evidently needed
Richard's watchfulness that the cups were not returned unsweet-
ened to their owner.

'There, you have done it again,' Mildred heard him say in a
low voice.   'The second clean cloth this week disfigured with
these unsightly brown patches.'

'Something must be the matter with the urn,' exclaimed
Olive, looking helplessly with regretful eyes at the mischief.

'Nonsense, the only fault is that you will do two things at a
time.   You have eaten no breakfast, at least next to none, and
made us all uncomfortable.   And pray how much German have
you done ? '

'I can't help it, Cardie ; I have so much to do, and there
seems no time for things.'

'I should say not, to judge by this,' interposed Roy, wickedly,
executing a pirouette round his sister's chair, to bring a large
hole in his sock to view.   'Positively the only pair in my
drawers.   It is too hard, isn't it, Dick ? '

But Richard's disgust was evidently too great for words, and
the unbecoming flush deepened on Olive's sallow cheeks.

'I was working up to twelve o'clock at night,' she said, looking ready to cry, and appealing to her silent accuser.   'Don't
laugh, Chriss, you were asleep ; how could you know ? '

'Were you mending this ? ' asked her brother gravely, holding
up a breadth of torn crape for her inspection, fastened by pins,
and already woefully frayed out.

'I had no time,' still defending herself heavily, but without
temper.   'Please leave it alone, Cardie, you are making it
worse.   I had Chriss's frock to do ; and I was hunting for your
things, but I could not find them.'

'I dare say not.   I dare not trust myself to your tender
mercies.   I took a carpet-bagful down to old Margaret.   If Rex
took my advice, he would do the same.'

'No, no, I will do his to-day. I will indeed, Rex. I am so sorry about it. Chriss ought to help me, but she never does, and she tears her things so dreadfully,' finished Olive, reproachfully.

'What can you expect from a contradicting baby,' returned Roy, with another pull at the ill-kempt locks as he passed. Chriss gave him a vixenish look, but her aunt's presence proved a restraining influence. Evidently Chriss was not a favourite with her brothers, for Roy teased, and Richard snubbed her pertness severely. Roy, however, seemed to possess a fund of sweet temper for family use, which was a marked contrast to Richard's dictatorial and somewhat stern manner, and he hastened now to cover poor Olive's discomfiture.

'Never mind, Lily, a little extra ventilation is not unhealthy, and is a somewhat wholesome discipline; you may cobble me up a pair for to-morrow if you like.'

'You are very good, Roy, but I am sorry all the same, only Cardie will not believe it,' returned Olive. There were tears in the poor girl's voice, and she evidently felt her brother's reproof keenly.

'Actions are better than words,' was the curt reply. 'But this is not very amusing for Aunt Milly. What are you and Miss Ellison going to do with yourselves this morning?'

'Bother Miss Ellison; why don't you call her Polly?' burst in Roy, irreverently.

'I have not given him leave,' returned the little lady haughtily. 'You were rude, and took the permission without asking.'

'Nonsense, don't be dignified, Polly; it does not suit you. We are cousins, aren't we? brothers and sisters once removed?'

'I am Aunt Milly's niece; but I am not to call him Uncle Arnold, am I?' was Polly's unexpected retort. But the shout it raised roused even Mr. Lambert.

'Call me what you like, my dear; never mind my boy's mischief,' laying his hand on Roy's shoulder caressingly. 'He is as skittish and full of humour as a colt; but a good lad in the main.'

Polly contemplated them gravely, and pondered the question; then she reached out a little hand and touched Mr. Lambert timidly.

'No! I will not call you Uncle Arnold; it does not seem natural. I like Mr. Lambert best. But Roy is nice, and may call me what he likes; and Richard, too, if he will not be so cross.'

'Thanks, my princess,' answered Roy, with mocking reverence. 'So you don't approve of Dick's temper, eh ?'

'I think Olive stupid to bear it; but he means well,' returned Polly composedly. And as Richard drew himself up
affronted at the young stranger's plain speaking, she looked in
his face, in her frank childish way, 'Cardie is prettier than
Richard, and I will call you that if you like, but you must not
frown at me and tell me to do things as you tell Olive. I am
not accustomed to be treated like a little sheep,' finished Polly,
naïvely; and Richard, despite his vexed dignity, was compelled
to join in the laugh that greeted this speech.

'Polly and I ought to unpack,' suggested Mildred, in her
wise matter-of-fact way, hoping to restore the harmony that
every moment seemed to disturb.

'No one will invade your privacy to-day, Aunt Milly; it
would be a violation of county etiquette to call upon strangers
till they had been seen at church. You and Miss——' Richard
paused awkwardly, and hurried on—'You will have plenty of
time to settle yourself and get rested.'

'Fie, Dick—what a blank. You are to be nameless now, Polly.'

'Don't be so insufferably tiresome, Rex; one can never
begin a sensible conversation in this house, what with Chriss's
contradictions on one side and your jokes on the other.'

'Poor old Issachar between two burdens,' returned Roy,
patting him lightly. 'Cheer up; don't lose heart; try again,
my lad. Aunt Milly, when you have finished with Polly, I
want to show her Podgill, our favourite wood; and Olive and
Chriss shall go too.'

'Wait till the afternoon, Roy, and then we can manage it,'
broke in Chriss, breathlessly.

'You can go, Christine, but I have no time,' returned Olive
wearily; but as Richard seemed on the point of making some
comment, she gathered up her books, and, stumbling heavily
over her torn dress in her haste, hurried from the room.

Mildred and Polly shut themselves in their rooms, and were
busy till dinner-time. Once or twice when Mildred had occasion
to go downstairs she came upon Olive; once she was standing
by the hall table jingling a basket of keys, and evidently in
weary argument on domestic matters with Nan—Nan's broad
Westmorland dialect striking sharply against Olive's feeble
refined key.

'Titter its dune an better, Miss Olive—t' butcher will send
fleshmeat sure enough, but I maun gang and order it mysel'.'

'Very well, Nan, but it must not be that joint ; Mr. Richard does not like it, and——'

'Eh ! I cares lile for Master Richard,' grumbled Nan, crossly. 'T'auld maister is starved amyast—a few broth will suit him best.'

'But we can have the broth as well,' returned Olive, with patient persistence. 'Mamma always studied what Richard liked, and he must not feel the difference now.'

'Nay, then I maun just gang butcher's mysel', and see after it.'

But Mildred heard no more. By and by, as she was sorting some books on the window seat, she saw Chrissy scudding across the courtyard, and Olive following her with a heavy load of books in her arms ; the elder girl was plodding on with down-cast head and stooping shoulders, the unfortunate black dress trailing unheeded over the rough beck gravel, and the German grammar still open in her hand.

CHAPTER V

OLIVE

' The yearnings of her solitary spirit, the out-gushings of her shrinking sensibility, the cravings of her alienated heart, are indulged only in the quiet holiness of her solitude. The world sees not, guesses not the conflict, and in the ignorance of others lies her strength.'—BETHMONT.

DINNER was hardly a sociable meal at the vicarage. Olive was in her place looking hot and dusty when Mildred came downstairs, and Chriss tore in and took her seat in breathless haste, but the boys did not make their appearance till it was half over. Richard immediately seated himself by his aunt, and explained the reason of their delay in a low tone, though he interrupted himself once by a few reproachful words to Olive on the comfortless appearance of the room.

'It is Chriss's fault,' returned Olive. 'I have asked her so often not to bring all that litter in at dinner-time; and, Chriss, you have pulled down the blind too.'

Richard darted an angry look at the offender, which was met defiantly, and then he resumed the subject, though with a perturbed brow. Roy and he had been over to Musgrave to read classics with the vicar. Roy had left Sedbergh, and since their trouble their father had been obliged to resign this duty to another. 'He was bent on preparing me for Oxford himself, but since his illness he has occupied himself solely with parish matters. So Mr. Wigram offered to read with us for a few months, and as the offer was too good a one to be refused, Roy and I walk over three or four times a week.'

'Have you settled to take Holy Orders then, Richard?' asked Mildred, a little surprised.

'It has been settled for me, I believe,' he returned, a slight hardness perceptible in his voice; 'at least it is my father's great wish, and I have not yet made up my mind to disappoint him, though I own there is a probability of my doing so.'

'And Roy?'

4

Richard smiled grimly. 'You had better ask him; he is looked upon in the light of a sucking barrister, but he is nothing but a dabbler in art at present; he has been under a hedge most of the morning, taking the portrait of a tramp that he chose to consider picturesque. Where is your Zingara, Roy?' But Roy chose to be deaf, and went on eagerly with his plans for the afternoon's excursion to Podgill.

Mildred watched the party set out, Polly and Chriss in their broad-brimmed hats, and Roy with a sketch-book under his arm. Richard was going over to Nateby with his father. Olive looked after them longingly.

'My dear, are you not going too? it will do you good; and I am sure you have a headache.'

'Oh, it is nothing,' returned Olive, putting her hair back with her hands; 'it is so warm this afternoon, and——'

'And you were up late last night,' continued Mildred in a sympathising voice.

'Not later than usual. I often work when the others go to bed; it does not hurt me,' she finished hastily, as a dissenting glance from Mildred met her. 'Indeed, I am quite strong, and able to bear much more.'

'We must not work the willing horse, then. Come, my dear, put on your hat; or let me fetch it for you, and we will over- take the Podgill party.'

'Oh no,' returned Olive, shrinking back, and colouring nervously. 'You may go, aunt; but Rex does not want me, or Chriss either; nobody wants me—and I have so much work to do.'

'What sort of work, mending?'

'Yes, all the socks and things. I try to keep them under, but there is a basketful still. Roy and Chriss are so careless, and wear out their things; and then you heard Richard say he could not trust me with his.'

'Richard is particular; many young men are. You must not be so sensitive, Olive. Well, my dear, I shall be very glad of your help, of course; but these things will be my business now.'

Olive contracted her brow in a puzzled way. 'I do not understand.'

'Not that I have come to be your father's housekeeper, and to save your young shoulders from being quite weighed down with burdens too heavy for them? There, come into my room, and let us talk this matter over at our leisure. Our fingers can be busy at the same time;' and drawing the girl gently to a low seat by the open window, Mildred placed herself beside her, and was soon absorbed in the difficulties of a formidable rent.

'You must be tired too, aunt,' observed Olive presently, with an admiring glance at the erect figure and nimble fingers.

'Not too tired to listen if you have anything to tell me,' returned Mildred with a winning smile. 'I want to hear where all those books were going this morning, and why Chriss was running on empty-handed.'

'Chriss does not like carrying things, and I don't mind,' replied Olive. 'We go every morning, and in the afternoon too when we are able, to study with Mrs. Cranford; she is so nice and clever. She is a Frenchwoman, and has lived in Germany half her life; only she married an Englishman.'

'And you study with her?'

'Yes, Dr. Heriot recommended her; she was a great friend of his, and after her husband's death—he was a lawyer here— she was obliged to do something to maintain herself and her three little girls, so Dr. Heriot proposed her opening a sort of school; not a regular one, you know, but just morning and afternoon classes for a few girls.'

'Have you many companions?'

'No; only Gertrude Sadler and the two Misses Northcote. Polly is to join us, I believe.'

'So her guardian says. I hope you like our young *protégée* Olive.'

'I shall not dislike her, at least, for one reason,' and as Mildred looked up in surprise, she added more graciously, 'I mean we are all so fond of Dr. Heriot that we will try to like her for his sake.'

'Polly deserves to be loved for her own sake,' replied Mildred, somewhat piqued at Olive's coldness. 'I was wrong to ask you such a question. Of course you cannot judge of any one in so short a time.'

'Oh, it is not that,' returned Olive, eager, and yet stammering. 'I am afraid I am slow to like people always, and Polly seems so bright and clever, that I am sure never to get on with her.'

'My dear Olive, you must not allow yourself to form such morbid ideas. Polly is very original, and will charm you into liking her, before many days are over; even our fastidious Richard shows signs of relenting.'

'Oh, but he will never care for her as Roy seems to do already. Cardie cares for so few people ; you don't half know how particular he is, and how soon he is offended ; nothing but perfection will ever please him,' she finished with a sigh.

'We must not be too hard in our estimate of other people. I am half inclined to find fault with Richard myself in this respect ; he does not make sufficient allowance for a very young housekeeper,' laying her hand softly on Olive's dark hair ; and as the girl looked up at her quickly, surprised by the caressing action, Mildred noticed, for the first time, the bright intelligence of the brown eyes.

'Oh, you must not say that,' she returned, colouring painfully. 'Cardie is very good, and helps me as much as he can ; but you see he was so used to seeing mamma do everything so beautifully.'

'It is not worse for Richard than for the others.'

'Oh yes, it is ; she made so much of him, and they were always together. Roy feels it dreadfully ; but he is lighthearted, and forgets it at times. I don't think Cardie ever does.'

'How do you know ; does he tell you so ?' asked Mildred, with kindly scrutiny.

Olive shook her head mournfully. 'No, he never talks to me, at least in that way ; but I know it all the same ; one can tell it by his silence and pained look. It makes him irritable too. Roy has terrible breaks-down sometimes, and so has Chriss ; but no one knows what Cardie suffers.'

Mildred dropped her work, and regarded the young speaker attentively. There was womanly thoughtfulness, and an underlying tenderness in the words of this girl of fifteen ; under the timid reserve there evidently beat a warm, affectionate heart. For a moment Mildred scanned the awkward hunching of the shoulders, the slovenly dress and hair, and the plain, cloudy face, so slow to beam into anything like a smile ; Olive's normal expression seemed a heavy, anxious look, that furrowed her brow with unnatural lines, and made her appear years older than her actual age ; the want of elasticity and the somewhat slouching gait confirming this impression.

'If she were not so plain ; if she would only dress and hold herself like other people, and be a little less awkward,' sighed Mildred. 'No wonder Richard's fastidiousness is so often offended ; but his continual fault-finding makes her worse. She is too humble-minded to defend herself, and too generous to resent his interference. If I do not mistake, this girl has a fine nature, though it is one that is difficult to understand ; but to think of this being Betha's daughter !' and a vision rose before Mildred of the slight, graceful figure and active movements of the bright young house-mother, so strangely contrasted with Olive's clumsy gestures.

The silence was unbroken for a little time, and then Olive raised her head. 'I think I must go down now, the others will be coming in. It has been a nice quiet time, and has done my head good ; but,' a little plaintively, 'I am afraid I have not done much work.'

Mildred laughed. 'Why not ? you have not looked out of the window half so often as I have. I suppose you are too used to all that purple loveliness ; your eyes have not played truant once.'

'Yes, it is very beautiful ; but one seems to have no time now to enjoy,' sighed the poor drudge. 'You work so fast, aunt ; your fingers fly. I shall always be awkward at my needle ; mamma said so.'

'It is a pity, of course ; but perhaps your talents lie in another direction,' returned her aunt, gravely. 'You must not lose heart, Olive. It is possible to acquire ordinary skill by persevering effort.'

'If one had leisure to learn—I mean to take pains. But look, how little I have done all this afternoon.' Olive looked so earnest and lugubrious that Mildred bit her lip to keep in the amused smile.

'My dear,' she returned quaintly, 'there is a sin not mentioned in the Decalogue, but which is a very common one among women, nevertheless, "the lust of finishing." We ought to love work for the work's sake, and leave results more than we do. Over-hurry and too great anxiety for completion has a great deal to do with the overwrought nerves of which people complain nowadays. "In quietness and in confidence shall be your strength."'

Olive looked up with something like tears in her eyes. 'Oh, aunt, how beautiful. I never thought of that.'

'Did you not ? I will illuminate the text for you and hang it in your room. So much depends on the quietness we bring to our work ; without being exactly miserly with our eyes and hands, as you have been this afternoon, one can do so much with a little wise planning of our time, always taking care not to resent interference by others. You will think I deal in proverbial philosophy, if I give you another maxim, "Man's importunity is God's opportunity."'

'I will always try to remember that when Chriss interrupts me, as she does continually,' answered Olive, thoughtfully. 'People say there are no such things as conflicting duties, but I have often such hard work to decide—which is the right thing to be done.'

'I will give you an infallible guide then : choose that which seems hardest, or most disagreeable ; consciences are slippery things ; they always give us such good reasons for pleasing ourselves.'

'I don't think that would answer with me,' returned Olive doubtfully. 'There are so many things I do not like, the disagreeable duties quite fill one's day. I like hearing you talk very much, aunt. But there is Cardie's voice, and he will be disappointed not to find the tea ready when he comes in from church.'

'Then I will not detain you another moment ; but you must promise me one thing.'

'What is that ?'

'There must be no German book behind the urn to-night. Better ill-learnt verbs than jarring harmony, and a trifle that vexes the soul of another ceases to be a trifle. There, run along, my child.'

Mildred had seen very little of her brother that day, and after tea she accompanied him for a quiet stroll in the churchyard. There was much that she had to hear and tell. Arnold would fain know the particulars of his mother's last hours from her lips, while she on her side yearned for a fuller participation in her brother's sorrow, and to gather up the treasured recollections of the sister she had loved so well.

The quiet evening hour—the scene—the place—fitted well with such converse. Arnold was less reticent to-night, and though his smothered tones of pain at times bore overwhelming testimony to the agony that had shattered his very soul, his expressions of resignation, and the absence of anything like bitterness in the complaint that he had lost his youth, the best and brightest part of himself, drew his sister's heart to him in endearing reverence.

'I was dumb, and opened not my mouth, because Thou didst it,' seemed to be the unspoken language of his thoughts, and every word breathed the same mournful submission to what was felt to be the chastisement of love.

'Dear, beautiful Betha ; but she was ready to go, Arnold ?'

'None so ready as she—God forbid it were otherwise—but I do not know. I sometimes think the darling would have been glad to stay a little longer with me. Hers was the nature that saw the sunny side of life. Heriot could never make her share in his dark views of earthly troubles. If the cloud came she was always looking for the silver lining.'

'It is sad to think how rare these natures are,' replied Mildred. 'What a contrast to our mother's sickbed !'

'Ah, then we had to battle with the morbidity of hypochondria, the sickness of the body aggravated by the diseased action of the mind, the thickening of shadows that never existed except in one weary brain. My darling never lost her happy smile except when she saw my grief. I think that troubled the still waters of her soul. In thinking of their end, Mildred, one is reminded of Bunyan's glorious allegory—glorious, inspired, I should rather say. That part where the pilgrims make ready for their passage across the river. My darling Betha entered the river with the sweet bravery of Christiana, while, according to your account, my poor mother's sufferings only ceased with her breath.'

'Yet she was praying for the end to come, Arnold.'

'Yes, but the grasshopper was ever a burden to her. Do you remember what stout old Bunyan says ? "The last words of Mr. Despondency were : Farewell night ! Welcome day ! His daughter (Much-afraid) went through the river singing, but no one could understand what she said." '

'As no one could tell the meaning of the sweet solemn smile that crossed our mother's face at the last ; she had no fears then, Arnold.'

'Just so. If she could have spoken she would have doubtless told you that such was the case, or used such words as Mr. Despondency leaves as his dying legacy. Do you remember them, Mildred ? They are so true of many sick souls,' and he quoted in a low sweet voice, ' "My will and my daughter's is (that tender, loving Much-afraid, Milly), that our desponds and slavish fears be by no man ever received from the day of our departure for ever, for I know after my death they will offer themselves to others. For, to be plain with you, they are ghosts which we entertained when we first began to be pilgrims, and could never throw them off after ; and they will walk about and seek entertainment of the pilgrims ; but, for our sakes, shut the doors upon them." '

'It is a large subject, Arnold, and a very painful one.'

'It is one on which you should talk to Heriot ; he has a fine benevolence, and is very tender in his dealings with these self-tormentors. He is always fighting the shadows, as he calls them.'

'I have often wondered why women are so much more morbid than men.'

'Their lives are more to blame than they ; want of vigour and action, a much-to-be-deplored habit of incessant introspection and a too nice balancing of conscientious scruples, a lack of large-mindedness, and freedom of principle. All these things lie at the root of the mischief. As John Heriot has it, " The thinking machine is too finely polished." '

'I fancy Olive is slightly bitten with the complaint,' observed Mildred, wishing to turn her brother's thought to more practical matters.

'Indeed ! her mother never told me so. She once said Olive was a noble creature in a chrysalis state, and that she had a mind beyond the generality of girls, but she generally only laughed at her for a bookworm, and blamed her for want of order. I don't profess to understand my children,' he continued mournfully ; 'their mother was everything to them. Richard often puzzles me, and Olive still more. Roy is the most transparent, and Christine is a mere child. It has often struck me lately that the girls are in sad need of training. Betha was over-lenient with them, and Richard is too hard at times.'

'They are at an angular age,' returned his sister, smiling. 'Olive seems docile, and much may be made of her. I suppose you wish me to enter on my new duties at once, Arnold ?'

'The sooner the better, but I hope you do not expect me to define them ?'

'Can a mother's duties be defined ?' she asked, very gravely.

'Sweetly said, Milly. I shall not fear to trust my girls to you after that. Ah, there comes Master Richard to tell us the dews are falling.'

Richard gave Mildred a reproachful look as he hastened to his father's side.

'You have let him talk too much ; he will have no sleep to-night, Aunt Milly. You have been out here more than two hours, and supper is waiting.'

'So late, Cardie ? Well, well ; it is something to find time can pass otherwise than slowly now. You must not find fault with your aunt ; she is a good creature, and her talk has refreshed me. I hope, Milly, you and my boy mean to be great friends.'

' Do you doubt it, sir ?' asked Richard gravely.

'I don't doubt your good heart, Cardie, though your aunt may not always understand your manner,' answered his father gently. 'Youth is sometimes narrow-minded and intolerant, Milly. One graduates in the school of charity later in life.'

'I understand your reproof, sir. I am aware you consider me often overbearing and dogmatical, but in my opinion petty worries would try the temper of a saint.'

' Pin-pricks often repeated would be as bad as a dagger-thrust, and not nearly so dignified. Never mind, Cardie, many people find toleration a very difficult duty.'

'I could never tolerate evils of our own making, and what is more, I should never consider it my duty to do so. I do not know that you would have to complain of my endurance in greater matters.'

' Possibly not, Cardie. This boy of mine, Milly,' pressing the strong young arm on which he leant, 'is always leading some crusade or other. He ought to have lived centuries ago, and belted on his sword as a Red Cross Knight. He would have brought us home one of the dragon's heads at last.'

' You are jesting,' returned Richard, with a forced smile.

' A poor jest, Cardie, then ; only clothing the truth in alle-gory. After all, you are right, my boy, and I am somewhat weary ; help me to my study. I will not join the others to-night.'

Richard's face so plainly expressed 'I told you so,' that Mildred felt a warm flush come to her face, as though she had been discovered in a fault. It added to her annoyance also to find on inquiry that Olive had been shut up in her room all the evening, ' over Roy's socks,' as Chrissy explained, while the others had been wandering over the fells at their own sweet will.

'This will never do ; you will be quite ill, Olive,' exclaimed Mildred, impatiently ; but as Richard entered that moment, to fetch some wine for his father, she forbore to say any more, only entering a mental resolve to kidnap the offending basket and lock it up safely from Olive's scrupulous fingers.

'I am coming into your room to have a talk,' whispered Polly when supper was over ; 'I have hardly seen you all day. How I do miss not having my dear Aunt Milly to myself.'

' I don't believe you have missed me at all, Polly,' returned

Mildred, stroking the short hair, and looking with a sort of relief into the bright piquant face, for her heart was heavy with many sad thoughts.

'Roy and I have been talking about you, though; he has found out you have a pretty hand, and so you have.'

'Silly children.'

'He says you are awfully jolly. That is the schoolboy jargon he talks; but he means it too; and even Chriss says you are not so bad, though she owned she dreaded your coming.'

Mildred winced at this piece of unpalatable intelligence, but she only replied quietly, 'Chrissy was afraid I should prove strict, I suppose.'

'Oh, don't let us talk of Chriss,' interrupted Polly, eagerly; 'she is intolerable. I want to tell you about Roy. Do you know, Aunt Milly, he wants to be an artist.'

'Richard hinted as much at dinner time.'

'Oh, Richard only laughs at him, and thinks it is all nonsense; but I have lived among artists all my life,' continued Polly, drawing herself up, 'and I am quite sure Roy is in earnest. We were talking about it all the afternoon, while Chrissy was hunting for bird-nests. He told me all his plans, and I have promised to help him.'

'It appears his father intends him to be a barrister.'

'Yes; some old uncle left him a few hundred pounds, and Mr. Lambert wished him to go to the University, and, as he had no vocation for the Church, to study for the bar. Roy told me all about it; he cannot bear disappointing his father, but he is quite sure that he will make nothing but an artist.'

'Many boys have these fancies. You ought not to encourage him in it against his father's wish.'

'Roy is seventeen, Aunt Milly; as he says, he is no child, and he draws such beautiful pictures. I have told him all about Dad Fabian, and he wants to have him here, and ask his advice about things. Dad could look after Roy when he goes to London. Roy and I have arranged everything.'

'My dear Polly,' began Mildred, in a reproving tone; but her remonstrance was cut short, for at that instant loud sobs were distinctly audible from the farthest room, where the girls slept.

Mildred rose at once, and softly opened the door; at the same moment there was a quick step on the stairs, and Richard's low, admonishing voice reached her ear; but as the loud sobbing sounds still continued, Mildred followed him in unperceived.

'Hush, Chrissy. What is all this about? You are disturbing my father; but, as usual, you only think of yourself.'

'Please don't speak to her like that, Cardie,' pleaded Olive. 'She is not naughty; she has only woke up in a fright; she has been dreaming, I think.'

'Dreaming!—I should think so, with that light full in her eyes, those sickening German books as usual,' with a glance of disgust at the little round table, strewn with books and work, from which Olive had evidently that moment risen. 'There, hush, Chrissy, like a good girl, and don't let us have any more of this noise.'

'No, I can't. Oh, Cardie, I want mamma—I want mamma!' cried poor Chrissy, rolling on her pillow in childish abandonment of sorrow, but making heroic efforts to stifle her sobs. 'Oh, mamma—mamma—mamma!'

'Hush!—lie silent. Do you think you are the only one who wants her?' returned Richard, sternly; but the hand that held the bedpost shook visibly, and he turned very pale as he spoke. 'We must bear what we have to bear, Chrissy.'

'But I won't bear it,' returned the spoilt child. 'I can't bear it, Cardie; you are all so unkind to me. I want to kiss her, and put my arms round her, as I dreamt I was doing. I don't love God for taking her away, when she didn't want to go; I know she didn't.'

'Oh, hush, Chriss—don't be wicked!' gasped out Olive, with the tears in her eyes; but, as though the child's words had stung him beyond endurance, Richard turned on her angrily.

'What is the good of reasoning with a child in this state? can't you find something better to say? You are of no use at all, Olive. I don't believe you feel the trouble as much as we do.'

'Yes, she does. You must not speak so to your sister, Richard. Hush, my dear—hush;' and Mildred stooped with sorrowful motherly face over the pillow, where Chrissy, now really hysterical, was stuffing a portion of the sheet in her mouth to resist an almost frantic desire to scream. 'Go to my room, Olive, and you will find a little bottle of sal-volatile on my table. The child has been over-tired. I noticed she looked pale at supper.' And as Olive brought it to her with shaking hand and pallid face, Mildred quietly measured the drops, and, beckoning to Richard to assist her, administered the stimulating draught to the exhausted child. Chrissy tried to push it away, but Mildred's firm, 'You must drink it, my dear,' overcame her resistance, though her painful choking made swallowing difficult.

'Now we will try some nice fresh water to this hot face and these feverish hands,' continued Mildred, in a brisk, cheerful tone ; and Chrissy ceased her miserable sobbing in astonishment at the novel treatment. Every one but Dr. Heriot had scolded her for these fits, and in consequence she had used an unwholesome degree of restraint for a child : an unusually severe breakdown had been the result.

'Give me a brush, Olive, to get rid of some of this tangle. I think we look a little more comfortable now, Richard. Let me turn your pillow, dear—there, now ;' and Mildred tenderly rested the child's heavy head against her shoulder, stroking the rough yellowish mane very softly. Chrissy's sobs were perceptibly lessening now, though she still gasped out 'mamma' at intervals.

'She is better now,' whispered Mildred, who saw Richard still near them. 'Had you not better go downstairs, or your father will wonder ?'

'Yes, I will go,' he returned ; yet he still lingered, as though some visitings of compunction for his hardness troubled him. 'Good-night, Chrissy ;' but Chrissy, whose cheek rested comfortably against her aunt's shoulder, took no notice. Possibly want of sympathy had estranged the little sore heart.

'Kiss your brother, my dear, and bid him good-night. All this has given him pain.' And as Chrissy still hesitated, Richard, with more feeling than he had hitherto shown, bent over them, and kissed them both, and then paused by the little round table.

'I am very sorry I said that, Livy.'

'There was no harm in saying it, if you thought it, Cardie. I am only grieved at that.'

'I ought not to have said it, all the same ; but it is enough to drive one frantic to see how different everything is.' Then, in a whisper, and looking at Mildred, 'Aunt Milly has given us all a lesson ; me, as well as you. You must try to be like her, Livy.'

'I will try ;' but the tone was hopeless.

'You must begin by plucking up a little spirit, then. Well, good-night.'

'Good-night, Cardie,' was the listless answer, as she suffered him to kiss her cheek. 'It was only Olive's ordinary want of demonstration,' Richard thought, as he turned away, a little relieved by his voluntary confession ; 'only one of her cold, tiresome ways.'

Only one of her ways !

Long after Chrissy had fallen into a refreshing sleep, and Mildred had crept softly away to sleepy, wondering Polly, Olive sat at the little round table with her face buried in her arms, both hid in the loosely-dropping hair.

'I could have borne him to have said anything else but this,' she moaned. 'Not feel as they do, not miss her as much, my dear, beautiful mother, who never scolded me, who believed in me always, even when I disappointed her most;—oh, Cardie, Cardie, how could you have found it in your heart to say that!'

CHAPTER VI

CAIN AND ABEL

'There was a little stubborn dame
Whom no authority could tame ;
Restive by long indulgence grown,
No will she minded but her own.'—WILKIE.

CHRISSY was sufficiently unwell the next day to make her aunt's
petting a wholesome remedy. In moments of languor and
depression even a whimsical and erratic nature will submit to
a winning power of gentleness, and Chriss's flighty little soul
was no exception to the rule : the petting, being a novelty,
pleased and amused her, while it evidently astonished the others.
Olive was too timid and awkward, and Richard too quietly matter-
of-fact, to deal largely in caresses, while Roy's demonstrations
somehow never included Contradiction Chriss.

Chriss unfortunately belonged to the awkward squad, whose
manœuvres were generally held to interfere with every one else.
People gave her a wide berth ; she trod on their moral corns
and offended their tenderest prejudices ; she was growing up
thin-lipped and sharp-tongued, and there was a spice of venom
in her words that was not altogether childlike.

'My poor little girl,' thought Mildred, as she sat beside her
working ; 'it is very evident that the weeds are growing up fast
for lack of attention. Some flowers will only grow in the sunshine ; no child's nature, however sweet, will thrive in an
atmosphere of misunderstanding and constant fault-finding.'

Chrissy liked lying in that cool room, arranging Aunt Milly's
work-box, or watching her long white fingers as they moved so
swiftly. Without wearying the overtasked child, Mildred kept
up a strain of pleasant conversation that stimulated curiosity
and raised interest. She had even leisure and self-denial
enough to lay aside a half-crossed darn to read a story when
Chriss's nerves seemed jarring into fretfulness again, and was

rather pleased than otherwise when, at a critical moment, long-drawn breaths warned her that she had fallen into a sound sleep.

Mildred sat and pondered over a hundred new plans, while tired Chriss lay with the sweet air blowing on her and the bees humming underneath the window. Now and then she stole a glance at the little figure, recumbent under the heartsease quilt. 'She would be almost pretty if those sharp lines were softened and that tawny tangle of hair arranged properly ; she has nice long eyelashes and a tolerably fair skin, though it would be the better for soap and water,' thought motherly Mildred, with the laudable anxiety of one determined to make the best of everything, though a secret feeling still troubled her that Chrissy would be the least attractive to her of the four.

Chrissy's sleep lengthened into hours ; that kindly foster-nurse Nature often taking restorative remedies of forcible narcotics into her own hands. She woke hungry and talkative, and after partaking of the tempting meal her aunt had provided, submitted with tolerable docility when Mildred announced her intention of making war with the tangles.

'It hurts dreadfully. I often wish I were bald—don't you, Aunt Milly ?' asked Chrissy, wincing in spite of her bravery.

'In that case you will not mind if I thin some of this shagginess,' laughed Mildred, at the same time arming herself with a formidable pair of shears. 'I wonder you are not afraid of Absalom's fate when you go bird-nesting.'

'I wish you would cut it all off, like Polly's,' pleaded Chriss, her eyes sparkling at the notion. 'It makes my head so hot, and it is such a trouble. It would be worth anything to see Cardie's face when I go downstairs, looking like a clipped sheep ; he would not speak to me for a week. Do please, Aunt Milly.'

'My dear, do you think that such a desirable result ?'

'What, making Cardie angry ? I like to do it of all things. He never gets into a rage like Roy—when you have worked him up properly—but his mouth closes as though his lips were iron, as though it would never open again ; and when he does speak, which is not for a very long time, his words seem to clip as sharp as your scissors—"Christine, I am ashamed of you !"'

'Those were the very words I wanted to use myself.'

'What ?' and Chrissy screwed herself round in astonishment to look in her aunt's grave face. 'I am quite serious, I assure you, Aunt Milly. I sha'n't mind if I look like a singed pony, or a convict; Rex is sure to call me both. Shall I fetch a pudding-basin and have it done—as Mrs. Stokes always does little Jem's?'

'Hush, Chrissy; this is pure childish nonsense. There! I've trimmed the refractory locks: you look a tidy little girl now. You have really very pretty hair, if you would only keep it in order,' continued Mildred, trying artfully to rouse a spark of womanly vanity; but Chriss only pouted.

'I would rather be like the singed pony.'

'Silly child!'

'Rex was in quite a temper when Polly said she hoped hers would never grow again. You have spoiled such a capital piece of revenge, Aunt Milly; I have almost a mind to do it myself.' But Chriss's mischief-loving nature—always a dangerous one—was quelled for the moment by the look of quiet contempt with which Mildred took the scissors from her hand.

'I did not expect to find you such a baby at thirteen, Chriss.'

Chriss blazed up in a moment, with a great deal of spluttering and incoherence. 'Baby! I a baby! No one shall call me that again!' tossing her head and elevating her chin in childlike disdain.

'Quite right; I am glad you have formed such a wise determination, it would have been babyish, Chriss,' wilfully misunderstanding her. 'None but very wicked and spiteful babies would ever scheme to put another in a rage. Do you know,' continued Mildred cheerfully, as she took up her work, apparently regardless that Chrissy was eyeing her with the same withering wrath, 'I always had a notion that Cain must have tried to put Abel in a passion, and failed, before he killed him!'

Chrissy recoiled a little.

'Perhaps he wanted him to fight, as men and boys do now, you know, only Abel's exceeding gentleness could not degenerate into such strife. To me there is something diabolical in the idea of trying to make any one angry. Certainly the weapons with which we do it are forged for us, red-hot, and put into our hands by the evil one himself.'

'Aunt Milly!' Chrissy's head was quiescent now, and her chin in its normal position: the transition from anger to solemnity bewildered her. Mildred went on in the same quiet tone.

'You cannot love Cardie very much, when you are trying to make him angry, can you, Chrissy?'

'No—o—at least, I suppose not,' stammered Chriss, who had no want of truth among her other faults.

'Well, what is the opposite of loving?'

'Hating. Oh, Aunt Milly, you can't think so badly of me as that! I don't hate Cardie.'

'God forbid, my child! You know what the Bible says— 'He who hateth his brother is a murderer.' But, Chrissy, does it ever strike you that Cain could not always have been quite bad? He had a childhood too.'

'I never thought of him but as quite grown up,' returned Chriss, with a touch of stubbornness, arising from an uneasy and awakened conscience. 'How fond you are of Cain, Aunt Milly.'

'He is my example, my warning beacon, you see. He was the first-begotten of Envy, that eldest-born of Hell—a terrible incarnation of unresisted human passion. Had he first learned to restrain the beginnings of evil, it would not have overwhelmed him so completely. Possibly in their young, hard-working life he would have loved to be able to make Abel angry.'

'Aunt Milly!' Chrissy was shedding a few indignant tears now.

'Well, my dear?'

'It is too bad. You have no right to compare me with Cain,' sobbing vengefully.

'Did I do so? Nay, Chriss, I think you are mistaken.'

'First to be called a baby, and then a murderer!'

'Hush! hush!'

'I know I am wicked to try and make them angry, but they tease me so; they call me Contradiction, and the Barker, and Pugilist Pug, and lots of horrid names, and it was only like playing at war to get one's revenge.'

'Choose some fairer play, my little Chriss.'

'It is such miserable work trying to be proper and good; I don't think I've got the face for it either,' went on Chriss, a subtle spirit of fun drying up her tears again, as she examined her features curiously in Mildred's glass. 'I don't look as though I could be made good, do I, Aunt Milly'—frowning fiercely at herself—'not like a young Christian?'

'More like a long-haired kitten,' returned Mildred, quaintly.

The epithet charmed Chriss into instant good-humour; for a moment she looked half inclined to hug Mildred, but the effort was too great for her shyness, so she contented herself with a look of appreciation. 'You can say funny things then—how

5

nice ! I thought you were so dreadfully solemn—worse than Cardie. Cardie could not say a funny thing to save his life, except when he is angry, and then, oh ! he is droll,' finished incorrigible Chriss, as she followed her aunt downstairs, skipping three steps at a time.

Richard met them in the hall, and eyed the pseudo-invalid a little dubiously.

'So you are better, eh, Chriss ? That's right. I thought there was not much that ailed you after all,' in a tone rather amiable than unfeeling.

'Not much to you, you mean. Perhaps you don't mind having a log in your head,' began Chrissy, indignantly, but seeing visionary Cains in her aunt's glance, she checked herself. 'If I am better it is all thanks to Aunt Milly's nursing, but she spoilt everything at the last.'

'Why ?' asked Richard, curiously, detecting a lurking smile at the corner of Mildred's mouth.

'Why, I had concocted a nice little plan for riling you— putting you in a towering passion, you know—by coming down looking like a singed pony, or like Polly, in fact ; but she would not let me, took the scissors away, like the good aunt in a story-book.'

'What nonsense is she talking, Aunt Milly ? She looks very nice, though quite different to Chrissy somehow.'

'We have only shorn a little of the superabundant fleece,' returned Mildred, wondering why she felt so anxious for Richard's approval, and laughing at herself for being so.

'But I wanted it to be clipped just so, half an inch long, like Jemmy Stokes, and offered to fetch Nan's best pudding-basin for the purpose ; but Aunt Milly would not hear of it. She said such dreadful things, Cardie !' And as Richard looked at her, with puzzled benevolence in his eyes, she raised herself on tip-toe and whispered into his ear, 'She said—at least she almost implied, but it is all the same, Cardie—that if I did I should go on from bad to worse, and should probably end by murdering you, as Cain did Abel.'

The following day was Sunday, and Mildred, who for her own reasons had not yet actively assumed the reins of govern-ment, had full leisure and opportunity for studying the family ways at the vicarage. In one sense it was certainly not a day of rest, for, with the exception of Roy and Chrissy, the young people seemed more fully engrossed than on any other day.

Richard and Olive were both at the early service, and

Mildred, who, as usual, waited for her brother in the porch, was distressed to find Olive still with her hat on, snatching a few mouthfuls of food at the breakfast-table while she sorted a packet of reward cards.

'My dear Olive, this is very wrong; you must sit down and make a proper meal before going to the Sunday School.'

'Indeed I have not a moment,' returned Olive, hurriedly, without looking up. 'My class will be waiting for me. I have to go down to old Mrs. Stevens about her grandchildren. I had no time last night. Richard always makes the breakfast on Sunday morning.'

'Yes,' returned Richard, in his most repressive tone, as he poured out a cup of coffee and carried it round to Olive, and then cut her another piece of bread and butter. 'I believe Livy would like to dispense with her meals altogether or take them standing. I tell her she is comfortless by nature. She would go without breakfast often if I did not make a fuss about it. There you must stay till you have eaten that.' But Mildred noticed, though his voice was decidedly cross, he had cut the bread *à la tartine* for his sister's greater convenience.

Morning service was followed by the early dinner. Mr. Lambert, who was without a curate, the last having left him from ill-health, was obliged to accept such temporary assistance as he could procure from the neighbouring parishes. To-day Mr. Heath, of Brough, had volunteered his services, and accompanied the party back to the vicarage. Mildred, who had hoped to hear her brother preach, was somewhat disappointed. She thought Mr. Heath and his sermon very commonplace and uninteresting. Ideas seemed wanting in both. The conversation during dinner turned wholly on parish matters, and the heinous misdemeanours of two or three ratepayers who had made a commotion at the last vestry meeting. The only sentence that seemed worthy of attention was at the close of the meal, just as the bell was ringing for the public catechising.

'Where is Heriot? I have not set eyes on him yet!'

Richard, who was just following Olive out of the room, paused with his hand on the door to answer.

'He has come back from Penrith. I met him by the Brewery after Church, coming over from Hartly. He promised if he had time to look in after service as usual.'

Polly's eyes sparkled, and she almost danced up to Richard, 'Heriot! Is that my Dr. Heriot?' with a decided stress on the possessive pronoun.

'Oh, that's Heriot's ward, is it, Lambert? Humph, rather a queer affair, isn't it, leaving that child to him? Heriot's a comparatively young man, hardly five-and-thirty I should say,' and Mr. Heath's rosy face grew preternaturally solemn.

'Polly is our charge now,' returned Mr. Lambert, with one of his kind, sad smiles, stretching out a hand to the girl. 'Mildred has promised to look after her; and she will be Olive's and Chrissy's companion. You are one of my little girls now, are you not, Polly?' Polly shook her head, her face had lengthened a little over Mr. Lambert's words.

'I like you, of course, and I like to be here. Aunt Milly is so nice, and so is Roy; but I can only belong to my guardian.'

'Hoity-toity, there will be some trouble here, Lambert. You must put Heriot on his guard,' and Mr. Heath burst out laughing; Polly regarding him the while with an air of offended dignity.

'Did I say anything to make him laugh? there is nothing laughable in speaking the truth. Papa gave me to my guardian, and of course that means I belong to him.'

'Never mind, Polly, let Mr. Heath laugh if he likes. We know how to value such a faithful little friend—do we not, Mildred?'—and patting her head gently, he bade her fetch him a book he had left on his study table, and to Mildred's relief the conversation dropped, and Mr. Heath shortly afterwards took his departure.

Later on in the afternoon Mildred set out for a quiet walk to the cemetery. Polly and Chriss were sunning themselves on the terrace, while Roy was stretched in sleepy enjoyment on the grass at their feet, with his straw hat pulled over his face. Richard had walked up to Kirkleatham on business for his father. No one knew exactly what had become of Olive.

'She will turn up at tea-time, she always does,' suggested Roy, in a tone of dreamy indifference. 'Go on, Polly, you have a sweet little voice for reading as well as singing. We are reading Milton, Aunt Milly, only Polly sometimes stops to spell the long words, which somehow breaks the Miltonic wave of harmony. Can't you fancy I am Adam, and you are Eve, Polly, and this is a little bit of Paradise—just that delicious dip of green, with the trees and the water; and the milky mother of the herd coming down to the river to drink; and the rich golden streak of light behind Mallerstang? If it were not Sunday now,' and Roy's fingers grasped an imaginary brush.

'Roy and Polly seem to live in a Paradise of their own,'

thought Mildred, as she passed through the quiet streets. 'They have only known each other for two days, and yet they are always together and share a community of interest—they are both such bright, clever, affectionate creatures. I wonder where Olive is, and whether she ever knows what a real idle hour of *dolce far niente* means. That girl must be taught positively how to enjoy ;' and Mildred pushed the heavy swinging cemetery gates with a sigh, as she thought how joyless and weary seemed Olive's life compared to that of the bright happy creature they had laid there. Betha's nature was of the heartsease type ; it seemed strange that the mother had transmitted none of her sweet sunshiny happiness to her young daughter ; but here Mildred paused in her wonderings with a sudden start. She was not alone as she supposed. She had reached a shady corner behind the chapel, where there was a little plot of grass and an acacia tree ; and against the marble cross under which Betha Lambert's name was written there sat, or rather leant—for the attitude was forlorn even in its restfulness—a drooping, black figure easily recognised as Olive.

'This is where she comes on Sunday afternoons ; she keeps it a secret from the others ; none of them have discovered it,' thought Mildred, grieved at having disturbed the girl's sacred privacy, and she was quietly retracing her steps, when Olive suddenly raised her head from the book she was reading. As their eyes met, there was a start and a sudden rush of sensitive colour to the girl's face.

'I did not know ; I am so sorry to disturb you, my love,' began Mildred, apologetically.

'It does not disturb me—at least, not much,' was the truthful answer. 'I don't like the others to know I come here— because—oh, I have reasons—but this is your first visit, Aunt Milly,' divining Mildred's sympathy by some unerring instinct.

'Yes—may I stay for a moment ? thank you, my dear,' as Olive willingly made room for her. 'How beautiful and simple ; just the words she loved,' and Mildred read the inscription and chosen text—'His banner over me is love.'

'Do you like it ? Mamma chose it herself ; she said it was so true of her life.'

'Happy Betha !' and in a lower voice, 'Happy Olive !'

'Why, Aunt Milly ?'

'To have had such a mother, though it be only to lose her. Think of the dear bright smiles with which she will welcome you all home.'

Olive's eyes glistened, but she made no answer. Mildred was struck with the quiet repose of her manner; the anxious careworn look had disappeared for the time, and the soft intelligence of her face bore the stamp of some lofty thought.

'Do you always come here, Olive? At this time I mean.'

'Yes, always—I have never missed once; it seems to rest me for the week. Just at first, perhaps, it made me sad, but now it is different.'

'How do you mean, my dear?'

'I don't know that I can put it exactly in words,' she returned, troubled by a want of definite expression. 'At first it used to make me cry, and wish I were dead, but now I never feel so like living as when I am here.'

'Try to make me understand. I don't think you will find me unsympathising,' in Mildred's tenderest tones.

'You are never that, Aunt Milly. I find myself telling you things already. Don't you see, I can come and pour out all my trouble to her, just as I used to? and sometimes I fancy she answers me, not in speaking, you know, but in the thoughts that come as I sit here.'

'That is a beautiful fancy, Olive.'

'Others might laugh at it—Cardie would, I know, but it is impossible to believe mamma can help loving us wherever she is; and she always liked us to come and tell her everything, when we were naughty, or if we had anything nice happening to us.'

'Yes, dear, I quite understand. But you were reading.'

'That was mamma's favourite book. I generally read a few pages before I go. One seems to understand it all so much better in this quiet place, with the sun shining, and all those graves round. One's little troubles seem so small and paltry by comparison.'

Mildred did not answer. She took the book out of Olive's hand—it was *Thomas à Kempis*—and a red pencil line had marked the following passage :—

'Thou shalt not long toil here, nor always be oppressed with griefs.

'Wait a little while, and thou shalt see a speedy end of thy evils.

'There will come a time when all labour and trouble shall cease.

'Poor and brief is all that passeth away with time.

'Do [in earnest] what thou doest; labour faithfully in My vineyard : I will be thy recompense.

'Write, read, chant, mourn, keep silence, pray, endure crosses manfully ; life everlasting is worth all these conflicts, and greater than these.

'Peace shall come in one day, which is known unto the Lord; and it shall not be day nor night (that is at this present time), but unceasing light, infinite brightness, stedfast peace, and secure rest.'

'Don't you like it?' whispered Olive, timidly; but Mildred still made no answer. How she had wronged this girl! Under the ungainly form lay this beautiful soul-coinage, fresh from God's mint, with His stamp of innocence and divinity fresh on it, to be marred by a world's use or abuse.

Mildred's clear instinct had already detected unusual intelligence under the clumsiness and awkward ways that were provocative of perpetual censure in the family circle. The timidity that seemed to others a cloak for mere coldness had not deceived her. But she was not prepared for this faith that defied dead matter, and clung about the spirit footsteps of the mother, bearing in the silence—that baffling silence to smaller natures—the faint perceptive whispers of deathless love.

'Olive, you have made me ashamed of my own doubts,' she said at last, taking the girl's hand and looking on the unlovely face with feelings akin to reverence. 'I see now, as I never have done before, how a thorough understanding robs even death of its terror—how "perfect love casteth out fear."'

'If one could always feel as one does now,' sighed Olive, raising her dark eyes with a new yearning in them. 'But the rest and the strength seem to last for such a little time. Last Sunday,' she continued, sadly, 'I felt almost happy sitting here. Life seemed somehow sweet, after all, but before evening I was utterly wretched.'

'By your own fault, or by that of others?'

'My own, of course. If I were not so provoking in my ways —Cardie, I mean—the others would not be so hard on me. Thinking makes one absent, and then mistakes happen.'

'Yes, I see.' Mildred did not say more. She felt the time was not come for dealing with the strange idiosyncrasies of a peculiar and difficult character. She was ignorant as yet what special gifts or graces of imagination lay under the comprehensive term of 'bookishness,' which had led her to fear in Olive the typical bluestocking. But she was not wrong in the supposition that Olive's very goodness bordered on faultiness; over-conscientiousness, and morbid scrupulosity, producing a sort of mental fatigue in the onlooker—restfulness being always more highly prized by us poor mortals than any amount of struggling and perceptible virtue.

Mildred was a true diplomatist by nature—most womanly

women are. It was from no want of sympathy, but an exercise of real judgment, that she now quietly concluded the conversation by the suggestion that they should go home.

Mildred had the satisfaction of hearing her brother preach that evening, and, though some of the old fire and vigour were wanting, and there were at times the languid utterances of failing strength, still it was evident that, for the moment, sorrow was forgotten in the deep earnestness of one who feels the immensity of the task before him—the awful responsibility of the cure of souls.

The text was, 'Why halt ye between two opinions?' and afforded a rich scope for persuasive argument ; and Mildred's attention never wavered but once, when her eyes rested for a moment accidentally on Richard. He and Roy, with some other younger members of the congregation, occupied the choir-stalls, or rather the seats appropriated for the purpose, the real choir-stalls being occupied by some of the neighbouring farmers and their families—an abuse that Mr. Lambert had not yet been able to rectify.

Roy's sleepy blue eyes were half closed ; but Richard's forehead was deeply furrowed with the lines of intense thought, a heavy frown settled over the brows, and the mouth was rigid ; the immobility of feature and fixed contraction of the pupils bespeaking some violent struggle within.

The sunset clouds were just waning into pallor and blue-gray indistinctness, with a lightning-like breadth of gold on the outermost edges, when Mildred stepped out from the dark porch, with Polly hanging on her arm.

'Is that Jupiter or Venus, Aunt Milly?' she asked, pointing to the sky above them. 'It looks large and grand enough for Jupiter ; and oh, how sweet the wet grass smells !'

'You are right, my little astronomer,' said a voice close behind them. 'There is the king of planets in all his majesty. Miss Lambert, I hope you recognise an old acquaintance as well as a new friend. Ah, Polly ! Faithful, though a woman ! I see you have not forgotten me.' And Dr. Heriot laughed a low amused laugh at feeling his disengaged hand grasped by Polly's soft little fingers.

The laugh nettled her.

'No, I have not forgotten, though other people have, it seems,' she returned, with a little dignity, and dropping his hand. 'Three whole days, and you have never been to see us or bid us welcome ! Do you wonder Aunt Milly and I are offended ?'

Mildred coloured, but she had too much good sense to disclaim a share in Polly's childish reproaches.

'I will make my apology to Miss Lambert when she feels it is needed ; at present she might rather look upon it in the light of a liberty,' observed Dr. Heriot, coolly. 'Country practitioners are not very punctual in paying mere visits of ceremony. I hope you have recovered from the fatigues of settling down in a new place, Miss Lambert ?'

Mildred smiled. 'It is a very bearable sort of fatigue. Polly and I begin to look upon ourselves as old inhabitants. Novelty and strangeness soon· wear off.'

'And you are happy, Polly ?'—repossessing himself of the little hand, and speaking in a changed voice, at once grave and gentle.

'Very—at least, when I am not thinking of papa' (the last very softly). 'I like the vicarage, and I like Roy—oh, so much !—almost as much as Aunt Milly.'

'That is well'—with a benign look, that somehow included Mildred—'but how about Mr. Lambert and Richard and Olive ? I hope my ward does not mean to be exclusive in her likings.'

'Mr Lambert is good, but sad—so sad !' returned Polly, with a solemn shake of her head. 'I try not to look at him ; he makes me ache all over. And Olive is dreadful ; she has not a bit of life in her ; and she has got a stoop like the old woman before us in church.'

'Some one would be the better for some of Olive's charity, I think,' observed her guardian, laughing. 'You must take care of this little piece of originality, Miss Lambert ; it has a trifle too much keenness. "The pungent grains of titillating dust," as Pope has it, perceptible in your discourse, Polly, have a certain sharpness of flavour. So handsome Dick is under the lash, eh ?'

Polly held her peace.

'Come, I am curious to hear your opinion of Mentor the younger, as Rex calls him.'

' "Sternly he pronounced the rigid interdiction" *vide* Milton. Don't go away, Dick ; it will be wholesome discipline on the score of listeners hearing no good of themselves.'

'What, are you behind us, lads ? Polly's discernment was not at fault, then.'

'It was not that,' she returned, indifferently. 'Richard knows I think him cross and disagreeable. He and Chrissy put me in mind sometimes of the Pharisees and Sadducees.'

The rest laughed ; but her guardian ejaculated, half-seriously, 'Defend me from such a Polly ! '

'Well, am I not right ?' she continued, pouting. 'Chrissy never believes anything, and Richard is always measuring out rules for himself and other people. You know you are tiresome sometimes,' she continued, facing round on Richard, to the great amusement of the others ; but the rigid face hardly relaxed into a smile. He was in no mood for amusement to-night.

'Come, I won't have fault found with our young Mentor. I am afraid my ward is a little contumacious, Miss Lambert,' turning to her, as she stood with the little group outside the vicarage.

'I don't understand your long words ; but I see you are all laughing at me,' returned Polly, in a tone of such pique that Dr. Heriot very wisely changed the conversation.

CHAPTER VII

A MOTHER IN ISRAEL

' Of marvellous gentleness she was unto all folk, but specially unto her
own, whom she trusted and loved right tenderly. Unkind she
would not be unto no creature, nor forgetful of any kindness or
service done to her before, which is no little part of nobleness.
. . . Merciful also and piteous she was unto such as was grieved and
troubled, and to them that were in poverty or sickness, or any other
trouble.'—FISHER, Bishop of Rochester.

MILDRED was not slow in perceiving that Dr. Heriot had im-
ported a new element of cheerfulness into the family circle ;
they were all seated cosily round the supper-table when she came
downstairs. Olive, who had probably received some hint to that
effect, had placed herself between her father and Richard.

Mildred looked at the vacant place at the head of the table a
little dubiously.

'Never hesitate in claiming abrogated authority,' observed
Dr. Heriot, gravely, as he placed the chair for her.

Mildred gave him a puzzled glance : ' Does my brother—does
Olive wish it ? '

' Can you doubt it ? ' he returned, reproachfully. ' Have you
not found out how wearily those young shoulders bear the
weight of any responsibility ! ' with a pitying glance in Olive's
direction, which seemed hardly needed, for she looked brighter
than usual. ' Give them time to gain strength, and she will
thank you for the mercy shown her. To-night she will eat her
supper with some degree of enjoyment, now this joint is off her
mind,' and, quietly appropriating the carving-knife, he was soon
engaged in satisfying the young and healthy appetites round
him ; while answering at the same time the numerous questions
Roy and Chrissy were pleased to put to him.

Dr. Heriot, or Dr. John, as they called him, seemed the family
referee. A great stress was laid on the three days' absence,
which it was averred had accumulated a mass of plans to be
decided.

Richard wanted to consult him about the mare. Mr. Lambert had some lengthy document from the Bounty Office to show him. Chrissy begged for an invitation for herself and Polly for the following evening, and Olive pleaded to be allowed to come too, as she wanted to refer to some books in his library.

Polly looked from one to the other only half-pleased with all this familiarity. 'He might be every one's guardian,' she remarked *sotto voce* to Roy ; but Dr. Heriot soon found means to allay the childish jealousy, which he was quick enough to perceive.

Mildred thought he looked younger and happier to-night, with all those young aspirants for his notice pressing round him. She was startled to hear a soft laugh from Olive once, though it was checked immediately, as though duty put a force on inclination.

Mr. Lambert retired to his study after supper, and Olive, at Dr. Heriot's request, went to the piano. Mildred had heard she had no taste for music ; but to her surprise she played some hymns with accuracy and feeling, the others joining in as they pleased. Richard pleaded fatigue and a headache, and sat in the farthest corner, looking over the dark fells, and shading his eyes from the lamplight ; but Dr. Heriot sang in a rich, full voice, Polly sitting at his feet and sharing his hymn-book, while Chrissy looked over his shoulder. Mildred was enjoying the harmony, and wondering over Roy's beautiful tenor, when she was startled to see him turn suddenly very pale, and leave off singing ; and a moment afterwards, as though unable to contain himself, he abruptly left the room.

Olive glanced uneasily round, and then, under cover of the singing, whispered to Mildred—

'I forgot. Oh, how careless !—how wrong of me ! Aunt Milly, will you please go after him ?'

Mildred obeyed. She found him leaning against the open garden door—white, and almost gasping.

'My dear boy, you are ill. Shall I call Dr. Heriot to you ?' but he shook his head impatiently.

'Nonsense—I am all right ; at least, I shall be in a moment. Don't stay, Aunt Milly. I would not have Cardie see me for worlds ; he would be blaming Olive, and I know she forgot.'

'The hymn we were singing, do you mean ?'

'Yes ; she—mamma—was so fond of it. We used to have it every night in her room. She asked for it almost at the last. *Sun of my soul ;* the hymn of hymns, she called it. It was just like Livy to forget. I can stand any but that one—it beats me. Ah, Aunt Milly!' his boyish tones suddenly breaking beyond control.

'Dear Rex, don't mind; these feelings do you honour. I love you the better for them;' pressing the fair head tenderly to her shoulder, as she had done Chrissy's. She was half afraid he might resent the action, but for the moment his manhood was helpless

'That is just what she used to do,' he said, with a half sob. 'You remind me of her somehow, Aunt Milly. There's some one coming after us. Please—please let me go,'—the petulant dignity of seventeen years asserting itself again,—but he seemed still so white and shaken that she ventured to detain him.

'Roy, dear, it is only Olive. There is nothing of which to be ashamed.'

'Livy, oh, I don't mind her. I thought it was Dick or Heriot. Livy, how could you play that thing when you know —you know——' but the rest of the speech was choked somehow.

'Oh, Rex, I am so sorry.'

'Well, never mind; it can't be helped now. Only Aunt Milly has seen me make an ass of myself.'

'You are too good to scold me, Rex, I know, but I am grieved—I am indeed. I am so fond of that hymn for her sake, that I always play it to myself; and I forgot you could not bear it,' continued poor Olive, humbly.

'All right; you need not cover yourself with dust and ashes,' interrupted Roy, with a nervous laugh. 'Ah, confound it, there's Richard! What a fellow he is for turning up at the wrong time. Good-night, Livy,' he continued, with a pretence at cheerfulness; 'the dews are unwholesome. Pleasant dreams and sweet repose;' but Olive still lingered, regardless of Roy's good-humoured attempts to save an additional scolding.

'Well, what's all this about?' demanded Richard, abruptly.

'It is my fault, as usual, Cardie,' returned Olive, courting her fate with clumsy bravery. 'I upset him by playing that hymn. Of course I ought to have remembered.'

'Culprit, plaintiff, defendant, and judge in one,' groaned Roy. 'Spare us the rest, Dick, and prove to our young minds that honesty is the best policy.'

But Richard's brow grew dark. 'This is the second time it has happened; it is too bad, Olive. Not content with harass-ing us from morning to night with your shiftless, unwomanly ways, you must make a blunder like this. One's most sacred feelings trampled on mercilessly,—it is unpardonable.'

'Oh, draw it mild, Dick;' but Roy's lip still quivered; his sensitive nature had evidently received a shock.

'You are too good-natured, Rex. Such cruel heedlessness deserves reproof, but it is all lost on Livy; she will never understand how we feel about these things.'

'Indeed, Cardie——' but Richard sternly checked her.

'There is no use in saying anything more about it. If you are so devoid of tact and feeling, you can at least have the grace to be ashamed of yourself. Come, Roy, a turn in the air will do you good; my head still aches badly. Let us go down over Hillsbottom for a stroll;' and Richard laid his hand persuasively on Roy's shoulder.

Roy shook off his depression with an effort. Mildred fancied his brother's well-meant attempt at consolation jarred on him; but he was of too easy a nature to contend against a stronger will; he hesitated a moment, however.

'We have not said good-night to Livy.'

'Be quick about it, then,' returned Richard, turning on his heel; then remembering himself, 'Good-night, Aunt Milly. I suppose we shall not see you on our return?' but he took no notice of Olive, though she mutely offered her cheek as he passed.

'My dear, you will take cold, standing out here with uncovered head,' Mildred said, passing her arm gently through the girl's to draw her to the house; but Olive shook her head, and remained rooted to the spot.

'He never bade me good-night,' she said at last, and then a large tear rolled slowly down her face.

'Do you mean Richard? He is not himself to-night; something is troubling him, I am sure.' But Mildred felt a little indignation rising, as she thought of her nephew's hardness.

'Rex kissed me, though; and he was the one I hurt. Rex is never hard and unkind. Oh, Aunt Milly, I think Cardie begins to dislike me;' the tears falling faster over her pale cheeks.

'My dear Olive, this is only one of your morbid fancies. It is wrong to say such things—wrong to Richard.'

'Why should I not say what I think? There, do you see them'—pointing to a strip of moonlight beyond the bridge— 'he has his arm round Roy, and is talking to him gently. I know his way; he can be, oh so gentle when he likes. He is only hard to me; he is kinder even to Chrissy, who teases him from morning to night; and I do not deserve it, because I love him so;' burying her face in her hands, and weeping convulsively, as no one had ever seen Olive weep before.

'Hush, dear—hush; you are tired and overstrained with the long day's work, or you would not fret so over an impatient word. Richard does not mean to be unkind, but he is domineering by nature, and——'

'No, Aunt Milly, not domineering,' striving to speak between her sobs; 'he thinks so little of himself, and so much of others. He is vexed about Roy's being upset; he is so fond of Roy.'

'Yes, but he has no right to misunderstand his sister so completely.'

'I don't think I am the right sort of sister for him, Aunt Milly. Polly would suit him better; she is so bright and winning; and then he cares so much about looks.'

'Nonsense, Olive; men don't think if their sisters have beauty or not. I mean it does not make any difference in their affection.'

'Ah, it does with Cardie. He thinks Chriss will be pretty, and so he takes more notice of her. He said once it was very hard for a man not to be proud of his sisters; he meant me, I know. He is always finding fault with my hair and my dress, and telling me no woman need be absolutely ugly unless she likes.'

'I can see a gleam in the clouds now. We will please our young taskmaster before we have done.'

Olive smiled faintly, but the tears still came. It was true: she was worn in body and mind. In this state tears are a needful luxury, as Mildred well knew.

'It is not this I mind. Of course one would be beautiful if one could; but I should think it paltry to care,' speaking with mingled simplicity and resignation.

'Mamma told us not to trouble about such things, as it would all be made up to us one day. What I really mind is his thinking I do not share his and Roy's feelings about things.'

'People have different modes of expressing them. You could play that hymn, you see.'

'Yes, and love to do it. When Roy left the room I had forgotten everything. I thought mamma was singing it with us, and it seemed so beautiful.'

'Richard would call that visionary.'

'He would never know;' her voice dropping again into its

hopeless key. 'He thinks I am too cold to care much even about that; he does indeed, Aunt Milly:' as Mildred, shocked and distressed, strove to hush her. 'Not that I blame him, because Roy thinks the same. I never talk to any of them as I have done to you these two days.'

'Then we have something tangible on which to lay the blame. You are too reserved with your brothers, Olive. You do not let them see how much you feel about things.' She winced.

'No, I could not bear to be repulsed. I would rather—much rather—be thought cold, than laughed at for a visionary. Would not you, Aunt Milly? It hurts less, I think.'

'And you can hug yourself in the belief that no one has discovered the real Olive. You can shut yourself up in your citadel, while they batter at the outworks. My poor girl, why need you shroud yourself, as though your heart, a loving one, Olive, had some hidden deformity? If Richard had my eyes, he would think differently.'

Olive shook her head.

'My child, you depreciate yourself too much. We have no right to look down on any piece of God's handiwork. Separate yourself from your faults. Your poor soul suffers for want of cherishing. It does not deserve such harsh treatment. Why not respect yourself as one whom God intends to make like unto the angels?'

'Aunt Milly, no one has said such things to me before.'

'Well, dear!'

'It is beautiful—the idea, I mean—it seems to heal the sore place.'

'I meant it to do so. It is not more beautiful than the filial love that can find rest by a mother's grave. Cardie would never think of doing that. When his paroxysms of pain come on him, he vents himself in long solitary walks, or shuts himself up in his room.'

'Aunt Milly, how did you know that? who told you?'

'My own intuition,' returned Mildred, smiling. 'Come, child, it is long past ten. I wonder what Polly and Dr. Heriot have been doing with themselves all this time. Go to sleep and forget all about these troubles;' and Mildred kissed the tear-stained face tenderly as she spoke.

She found Dr. Heriot alone when she entered the drawing-room. He looked up at her rather strangely, she thought. Could he have overheard any of their conversation?

'I was just coming out to warn you of imprudence,' he said, rising and offering her his chair. 'Sit there and rest yourself a little. Do mothers in Israel generally have such tired faces?' regarding her with a grave, inscrutable smile.

He had heard then. Mildred could not help the rising colour that testified to her annoyance.

'Forgive me,' he returned, leaning over the back of her chair, and speaking with the utmost gentleness. 'I did not mean to annoy you, far from it. Your voices just underneath the window reached me occasionally, and I only heard enough to——'

'Well, Dr. Heriot?'

Mildred sat absolutely on thorns.

'To justify the name I just called you. I cannot help it, Miss Lambert, you so thoroughly deserve it.'

Mildred grew scarlet.

'You ought to have given us a hint. Olive had no idea, neither had I. I thought—we thought, you were talking to the girls.'

'So I was; but I sent them away long ago. My dear Miss Lambert, I believe you are accusing me in your heart of listening,' elevating his eyebrows slightly, as though the idea was absurd. 'Pray dismiss such a notion from your mind. I was in a brown study, and thinking of my favourite Richard, when poor Olive's sobs roused me.'

'Richard your favourite!'

'Yes, is he not yours?' with an inquisitive glance. 'All Dick's faults, glaring as they are, could not hide his real excellence from such observing eyes.'

'He interests me,' she returned, reluctantly ; 'but they all do that of course.' Somehow she was loath to confess to a secret predilection in Richard's favour. 'He does not deserve me to speak well of him to-night,' she continued, with her usual candour.

Dr. Heriot looked surprised.

'He has been captious and sharp with Olive again, I suppose. I love to see a woman side with her sex. Well, do you know, if I were Richard, Olive would provoke me.'

'Possibly,' was Mildred's cool reply, for the remembrance of the sad tear-stained face made any criticism on Olive peculiarly unpalatable at that moment.

Dr. Heriot was quick to read the feeling.

'Don't be afraid, Miss Lambert. I don't mean to say a

word against your adopted daughter, only to express my thankfulness that she has fallen into such tender hands,' and for a moment he looked at the slim, finely-shaped hands lying folded in Mildred's lap, and which were her chief beauty. 'I only want you to be lenient in your judgment of Richard, for in his present state she tries him sorely.'

'One can see he is very unhappy.'

'People are who create a Doubting Castle for themselves, and carry Giant Despair, as a sort of old man of the mountains, on their shoulders,' he returned, drily. '"The perfect woman nobly planned" is rather an inconvenient sort of burden too. Well, it is growing late, and I must go and look after those boys.'

'Wait a minute, Dr. Heriot. You know his trouble, perhaps?'

He nodded.

'Troubles, you mean. They are threefold, at least, poor Cardie! Very few youths of nineteen know how to arrange their life, or to like other people to arrange it for them.'

'I want to ask you something; you know them all so well. Do you think I shall ever win his confidence?'

'You,' looking at her kindly; 'no one deserves it more, of course; but——' pausing in some perplexity.

'You hesitate.'

'Well, Cardie is peculiar. His mother was his sole confidant, and, when he lost her, I verily believe the poor fellow was as near heart-break as possible. I have got into his good graces lately, and now and then he lets off the steam; but not often. He is a great deal up at Kirkleatham House; but I doubt the wisdom of an adviser so young and fair as Miss Trelawny.'

'Miss Trelawny! Who is she?'

'What, have you not heard of "Ethel the Magnificent"? The neighbourhood reports that Richard and I have both lost our hearts to her, and are rivals. Only believe half you hear in Kirkby Stephen, Miss Lambert.'

'But Richard is only nineteen.'

'True; and I was accused of wearing her hair in a locket at my watch-guard. Miss Trelawny's hair is light brown, and this is bright auburn. I don't trouble myself to inform people that I may possibly be wearing my mother's hair.'

'Then you don't think my task will be easy?' asked Mildred, ignoring the bitterness with which he had spoken.

'What task—that of winning Cardie's confidence? I hope

you don't mean to be an anxious mother, and grow gray before your time.' Then, as though touched by Mildred's yearning look, 'I wish I could promise you would have no difficulty; but facts are stubborn things. Richard is close and somewhat impracticable; but as you seem an adept in winning, you may soften down his ruggedness sooner than we expect. Come, is that vaguely encouraging?'

One of Mildred's quaint smiles flitted over her face as she answered—

'Not very; but I mean to try, however. If I am to succeed I must give Miss Trelawny a wide berth.'

'Why so?' looking at her in surprise.

'If your hint be true, Richard's mannishness would never brook feminine interference.'

Dr. Heriot laughed.

'I was hardly prepared for such feminine sagacity. You are a wise woman, Miss Lambert. If you go on like this, we shall all be afraid of you. The specimen is rare enough in these parts, I assure you. Well, good-night.'

It was with mingled feelings that Mildred retired to rest that night. The events of the day, with its jarring interests and disturbed harmony, had given her deep insight into the young lives around her.

Three days!—she felt as though she had been three months among them. She was thankful that Olive's confidence seemed already won—thankful and touched to the heart; and though her conversation with Dr. Heriot had a little damped her with regard to Richard, hers was the sort of courage that gains strength with obstacles; and, before she slept that night, the fond prayer rose to her lips, that Betha's sons might find a friend in her.

She woke the next morning with a consciousness that duty lay ready to hand, opening out before her as the dawn brightened into day. On her way downstairs she came upon Olive, looking heavy-eyed and unrefreshed, as though from insufficient sleep. She was hunting among her father's papers for a book she had mislaid.

'Have you seen it, Aunt Milly?'

'Do you mean this?' holding out a dilapidated *Wilhelm Tell* for her inspection. 'I picked it up in the court, and placed it on the shelf for safety. Wait a moment, dear,' as Olive was rushing away, 'I want to speak to you. Was it by yours or your father's wish that you gave up your seat at supper to me?'

'Oh, it was Dr. John—at least—I mean I would much rather you always had it, Aunt Milly,' returned Olive, in her usual incoherent fashion. 'Please, do take it; it was such a load off my mind to see you sitting there.'

'But, my dear,' remonstrated Mildred; but Olive interrupted her with unusual eagerness.

'Oh, you must; you look so much nicer; and I hate it so. Dr. John arranged it all, and papa said "Yes," as he always does. He put it so kindly, that one could not mind; he told papa that with my disposition—timidity he meant, and absence of mind—it would be better for everybody's comfort if you assumed the entire management of everything at once; and that it would be better for me to learn from you for a few years, until you had made me a capable woman. Cardie heard him, I know; for he gave quite a sigh of relief.'

'Perhaps they are right; but it seems strange for Dr. Heriot to interfere in such a matter,' returned Mildred, in a puzzled tone.

'Oh, Dr. John always settles things; nobody calls it interference from him,' explained Olive, in her simple matter-of-fact way. 'It is such a relief to be told what to do. Papa only thanked him, and begged me to put myself entirely under your direction. You are to have the keys, and I am to show you the store cupboards and places, and to introduce you to Nan. We are afraid you will find her a little troublesome at first, Aunt Milly;' but Mildred only smiled, and assured her she was not afraid of Nan, and as the bells were ringing the brief colloquy ceased.

Mildred was quite aware Dr. Heriot was in church, as his fine voice was distinctly audible, leading the responses. To her surprise he joined them after service, and without waiting for an invitation, announced his intention of breakfasting with them.

'Nan's rolls are especially tempting on Monday morning,' he observed, coolly; 'but to-day that is not my inducement. Is teaching one's ward the catechism included in the category of a guardian's duty, Miss Lambert?'

'I was not aware that such was the case,' returned Mildred, laughing. 'Do you mean to teach Polly hers?'

Polly drew herself up affronted.'

'I am not a little girl; I am fourteen.'

'What a great age, and what a literal Polly!' taking her hands, and looking at her with an amused twinkle in his eyes.

'Last night you certainly looked nothing but a good little girl, singing hymns at my feet; but to-day you are bridling like a young princess; you are as fond of transformation as Proteus.'

'Who is Proteus?'

'A sea-god—but there is your breakfast; the catechism must wait till afterwards. I mean to introduce you to Mrs. Cranford in proper style. Miss Lambert, is your coffee always so good? I trust not, or my presence may prove harassing at the breakfast-table.'

'It is excellent, Aunt Milly:' the last from Richard.

Mildred hoped the tone of hearty commendation would not reach Olive's ear, as her German grammar lay by her plate as usual; but she only looked up and nodded pleasantly.

'I never could make coffee nicely; you must teach me, Aunt Milly,' and dropped her eyes on her book again.

'No paltry jealousy there,' thought Mildred; and she sat behind her urn well pleased, for even Arnold had roused himself once to ask for his cup to be replenished. Mildred had been called away on some household business, and on her return she found Dr. Heriot alone, reading the paper. He put it down as she entered.

'Well, is Nan formidable?'

'Her dialect is,' returned Mildred, smiling; 'I am afraid she looks upon me in the light of an interloper. I hope she does not always mean to call me "t'maister's sister."'

'Probably. Nan has her idiosyncrasies, but they are rather puzzling than dangerous; she is a type of the old Daleswoman, sturdy, independent, and sharp-tongued; but she is a good creature in the main, though a little contemptuous on "women-foaks." I believe Dick is her special favourite, though she told him once "he's niver off a grummle, and that she was fair stot t' deeth wi't' sound on't," if you know what that means.'

Mildred shook her head.

'You must not expect too much respect to a southerner at first. I did battle on your behalf before you came, Miss Lambert, and got terribly worsted. "Bless me, weel, Doctor!" says Nan, "what's the matter that t'maister's sister come here? I can do verra weel by messel', and Miss Olive can fend for hersel'; it's nought but daftness, but it's ne'er my business; if they please themselves they please me. I must bide t' bittermcnt."'

Mildred gave one of her quiet laughs.

'Nan and I will be great friends soon; we must learn to

respect each other's prejudices. Poor Olive had not a chance of putting in a word. Nan treated her as though she were a mere infant.'

'She has known her ever since she was one, you see, Miss Lambert. I have been putting Polly through her paces, and find she has plenty to learn and unlearn.'

'I suppose she has been tolerably well educated ?'

'Pretty fairly, but after a desultory fashion. I fancy she has picked up knowledge somehow, as a bird picks up crumbs ; her French accent is perfect, and she knows a little German. She is mostly deficient in English. I must have a long talk with Mrs. Cranford.'

'I understood Polly was to take lessons from her ?'

'You must take an early opportunity of making her acquaintance ; she is truly excellent ; the girls are fortunate in having such an instructress. Do you know, Chrissy is already a fair Latin scholar.'

'Chrissy ! you mean Olive, surely ?'

'No, Chriss is the bluestocking—does Euclid with the boys, and already develops a taste for mathematics. Mr. Lambert used to direct her severer studies. I believe Richard does it now. Olive's talents lie in quite another direction.'

'I am anxious to know—is she really clever ?' asked Mildred, astonished at this piece of information.

'I believe she is tolerably well read for a girl of her age, and is especially fond of languages—the modern ones I mean— though her father has taught her Latin. I have always thought myself, that under that timid and lethargic exterior there is a vast amount of imaginative force—certain turns of speech in her happier moments prove it to me. I should not be surprised if we live to discover she has genius.'

'I am convinced that hers is no ordinary mind,' returned Mildred, seriously ; 'but her goodness somehow pains one.'

Dr. Heriot laughed.

'Have you ever heard Roy's addition to the table of weights and measures, "How many scruples make an olive ?"' he asked. 'My dear Miss Lambert, that girl is a walking conscience ; she has the sort of mind that adds, subtracts, divides, and multiplies duties, till the grasshopper becomes a burden ; she is one of the most thoroughly uncomfortable Christians I ever knew. It is a disease,' he continued, more gravely, 'a form of internal and spiritual hyperclimacteric, and must be treated as such.'

'I wish she were more like your ward,' replied Mildred,

anxiously; 'Polly is so healthy and girlish—she lives too much to have time for always probing her feelings.'

'You are right,' was the answer. 'Polly is just the happy medium, neither too clever nor too stupid—a loving-hearted child, who will one of these days develop into a loving-hearted woman. Is she not delicious with her boyish head and piquante face—pretty too, don't you think so?' And as the sound of the girls' voices reached them at this moment, Dr. Heriot rose, and a few minutes afterwards Mildred saw him cross the court, with Polly and Chrissy hanging on each arm.

CHAPTER VIII

'ETHEL THE MAGNIFICENT'

'A maid of grace and complete majesty.'

LATER on in the morning Mildred was passing by the door of her brother's study, when she heard his voice calling to her. He was sitting in his usual chair, with his back to the light, reading, but he laid down his book directly.

'Are you busy, Mildred?'

'Not if you want me,' she returned, brightly. 'I was just thinking I had hardly spoken to you to-day.'

'The same thought was lying heavy on my conscience. Heriot tells me you are looking better already. I hope you are beginning to feel at home with us, my dear.'

'With you, Arnold—do you need to ask?' Mildred returned, reproachfully. But the tears started to her eyes.

'And the children are good to you?' he continued, a little anxiously.

'They are everything I can wish. Cardie is most thoughtful for my comfort, and Olive is fast losing her shyness. The only thing I regret is that I manage to see so little of you, Arnold.'

He patted her hand gently. 'It is better so, my dear. I am poor company, I fear, and have grown into strangely unsociable ways. They are good children; but you must not let them spoil me, Mildred. Sometimes I think I ought to rouse myself more for their sakes.'

'Indeed, Arnold, their conduct is most exemplary. Neither Cardie nor Roy ever seem to let you go out alone.'

'Ay, ay,' he muttered; 'his mother was right. The lad is beyond his years, and has a wise head on young shoulders. Heriot tells me I must be looking out for a curate. I had some notion of waiting for Richard, but he will have it the work is beyond me.'

Mildred was silent. She thought any work, however

exhausting, was better than the long lonely hours passed in the study—hours during which his children were denied admittance, and for which all Richard's mannishness was not allowed to find a remedy ; and yet, as she looked at the wan, thin face, and weary stoop of the figure, might it not be that Dr. Heriot was right ?

'Heriot has heard of some one at Durham who is likely to suit me, he thinks ; he wants me to have him down. By the bye, Mildred, how do you get on with Heriot ?'

'He is very nice,' she returned, vaguely, rather taken aback by the suddenness of the question. 'Such a general favourite could not fail to please,' she continued, a little mischievously.

'Ah, you are laughing at us. Well, Heriot is our weak point, I confess. Cardie is not given to raptures, but he has not a word to say against him, and Trelawny is always having him up at Kirkleatham. Kirkby Stephen could not do without Heriot now.'

'He is clever in his profession, then ?'

'Very. And then so thoroughly unselfish ; he would go twenty miles to do any one a service, and take as much pains to hide it afterwards. I shall be disappointed, indeed Mildred, if you and he do not become good friends.'

'Dear Arnold, he is a perfect stranger to me yet. I like him quite well enough to wish to see more of him. There seems some mystery about him,' she continued, hesitating ; for Mildred, honest and straightforward by nature, was a foe to all mysteries.

'Only the mystery of a disappointed life. He has no secrets with us—he never had. We knew him when we lived at Lambeth, and even then his story was well known to us.'

'Betha told me he had given up a large West End practice in consequence of severe domestic trouble. She hinted once that he had a bad wife.'

'She was hardly deserving of the name. I have heard that she was nine years older than he, and a great beauty ; a woman, too, of marvellous fascination, and gifted beyond the generality of her sex, and that he was madly in love when he married her.'

'Perhaps the love was only on his side ?'

'Alas ! yes. He found out, when it was too late, that she had accepted him out of pique, and that his rival was living. The very first days of their union were embittered by the discovery that jealousy had forged these life-long fetters for them, and that already remorse was driving his unhappy bride almost frantic. Can you conceive the torment for poor Heriot ? He could not set her free, though he loved her so that he would willingly have laid down his life to give her peace. She had no mother living, or he would have sent her away when he saw how distasteful his presence was to her ; but, though she had murdered his happiness as well as her own, he was bound to be her protector.'

'He was right,' returned Mildred, in a low voice.

'Ay, and he acted nobly. Instead of overwhelming her with reproaches that could have done no good, or crushing her still more with his coldness, he forgave her, and set himself to win the heart that proved itself so unworthy of his forbearance. Any other husband would have thought himself injured beyond reparation, but not so Heriot. He hid his wretchedness, and by every means in his power tried to lighten the burden of his domestic misery.'

'But people must have seen it ?'

'Not through his complaint, for he ever honoured her. I have been told by those who knew him at the time, that his conduct to her was blameless, and that they marvelled at the gentleness with which he bore her wayward fits. After the birth of their only child there was an interval of comparative comfort ; in her weakness there was a glimmering of compassion for the man she had injured, and who was the father of her boy. Heriot was touched by the unusual kindness of her manner ; there were even tears in her eyes when he took the little creature in his arms and noticed the long eyelashes, so like his mother's.'

'But the child died ?'

'Yes—"the little peacemaker," as Heriot fondly called it. But certainly all peace was buried in its little grave ; for it was during the months that followed her child's loss that Margaret Heriot developed that unwholesome craving for stimulants which afterwards grew to absolute disease, and which was to wear out her husband's patience into slow disgust and then into utter weariness of life.'

'Oh, Arnold, I never suspected this !'

'It was just then we made his acquaintance, and, as a priest, he sought my help and counsel in ministering to what was indeed a diseased mind ; but, poor misguided woman ! she would not see me. In her better moments she would cling to Heriot, and beg him to save her from the demon that seemed to possess her. She even knelt and asked his forgiveness once ; but no remedy that he could recommend could be effectual in the case of one who had never been taught to deny herself a moment's gratification. I shudder to think of the scenes to which she subjected him, of the daily torture and uncertainty in which he lived : his was the mockery of a home. Her softer feelings had in time turned to hate ; she never spoke to him at last but to reproach him with being the cause of her misery.'

'Then it was this that induced him to give up his London practice ?'

'Yes. It was a strange act of his ; but I verily believe the man was broken-hearted. He had grown to loathe his life, and the spectacle of her daily degradation made him anxious to shake off friends and old belongings. I believe, too, she had contracted serious debts, and he was anxious to take her out of the way of temptation. Heriot was always a creature of impulse ; his chief motive in following us here was to bury himself socially, though I think our friendship had even then become necessary to him. At one time he trusted, too, that the change might be beneficial for her ; but he soon found out his mistake.'

'They say that women who have contracted this fatal habit are so seldom cured,' sighed Mildred.

'God help their husbands !' ejaculated Mr. Lambert. 'I always thought myself that the poor creature was possessed, for her acts certainly bordered on frenzy. He found at last that he was fighting against mental disease, but he refused all advice to place her under restraint. "I am her husband," he said once to me ; "I have taken her for better and worse. But there will be no better for her, my poor Margaret ; she will not be long with me—there is another disease at work ; let her die in her husband's home."'

'But did she die there ? I thought Betha told me she was away from him.'

'Yes, he had sent her with her nurse to the sea, meaning to join them, when news reached him that she was rapidly failing. The release came none too soon. Poor creature ! she had suffered martyrdom ; it was by her own wish that he was called, but he arrived too late—the final attack was very sudden. And so, as he said, the demon that had tormented her was cast out for ever. "Anything more grandly beautiful than she looked could not be imagined." But what touched him most was to find among the treasures she had secretly hidden about her, an infant's sock and a scrap of downy hair ; and faintly, almost illegibly, traced on the paper by her dying hand, " My little son's hair, to be given to his father." Ah, Mildred, my dear, you look ready to weep ; but, alas ! such stories are by no means rare, and during my ministry I have met with others almost as sad as Heriot's. His troubles are over now, poor fellow, though doubtless they have left lifelong scars. Grieved as he has been, he may yet see the fruit of his noble forbearance in that tardy repentance and mute prayer for forgiveness. Who knows but that the first sight that may meet his eyes in the other world may be Margaret, "sitting clothed and in her right mind at her Master's feet"?'

Never had Mildred seen her brother more roused and excited than during the recital of his friend's unhappy story, while in herself it had excited a degree of emotion that was almost painful.

'It shows how carefully we should abstain from judging people from their outward appearance,' she remarked, after a short interval of silence. 'When I first saw Dr. Heriot I thought there was something a little repellent in that dark face of his, but when he spoke he gave me a more pleasing impression.'

'He has his bitter moods at times ; no one could pass through such an ordeal quite unscathed. I am afraid he will never marry again ; he told me once that the woman did not live whom he could love as he loved Margaret.'

'She must have been very beautiful.'

'I believe her chief charm lay in her wonderful fascination of manner. Heriot is a severe critic in feminine beauty ; he is singularly fastidious ; he will not allow that Miss Trelawny is handsome, though I believe she is generally considered to be so. But I must not waste any more time in gossiping about our neighbours. By the bye, Mildred, you must prepare for an inundation of visitors this afternoon.'

Mr. Lambert was right. Mildred, to her great surprise, found herself holding a reception, which lasted late into the afternoon ; at one time there was quite a block of wagonettes and pony carriages in the courtyard ; and but for her brother's kindness in remaining to steer her through the difficulties of numerous introductions, she might have found her neighbours' goodwill a little perplexing.

She had just decided in her own mind that Mrs. Sadler was disagreeable, and the Northcotes slightly presuming and in bad style, and that Mrs. Heath was as rosy and commonplace as her husband, when they took their leave, and another set of visitors arrived who were rather more to Mildred's taste.

These were the Delameres of Castlesteads. The Reverend Stephen Delamere was a tall, ascetic-looking man, with quiet,

well-bred manners, in severe clerical costume. His wife had a
simple, beautiful face, and was altogether a pleasant, comely-
looking creature, but her speech was somewhat homely ; and
Mildred thought her a little over-dressed : the pink cheeks and
smiling eyes hardly required the pink ribbons and feathers to
set them off. Their only child, a lad of ten years, was with
them, and Mildred, who was fond of boys, could not help
admiring the bold gipsy face and dark eyes.

' I am afraid Claude is like me, people say so,' observed Mrs.
Delamere, turning her beaming face on Mildred. ' I would much
rather he were like his father ; the Delameres are all good-
looking ; old Mr. Delamere was ; Stephen called him after his
grandfather ; I think Claude such a pretty name ; Claude
Lorraine Delamere : Lorraine is a family name, too ; not mine,
you know,' dimpling more than ever at the idea ; ' good gracious,
the Greysons don't own many pretty names among them.'

' Susie, I have been asking our friend Richard to take an
early opportunity of driving his aunt over to Castlesteads,'
interrupted her husband, with an uneasy glance, ' and we must
make Miss Lambert promise to bring over her nieces to the
Rush-bearing.'

Mrs. Delamere clapped her plump hands together joyously,
showing a slit in her pink glove as she did so.

' I am so glad you have mentioned that, Stephen, I might
have forgotten it. Miss Lambert, you must come to us ; you
must indeed. The Chestertons of the Hall are sure to ask
you ; but you must remember you are engaged to us.'

' The Rush-bearing,' repeated Mildred, somewhat perplexed.

' It is an old Westmoreland custom,' explained Mr. Delamere ;
' it is kept on St. Peter's Day, and is a special holiday with us.
I believe it was revived in the last century at Great Musgrave,'
he continued, looking at Mr. Lambert for confirmation of the
statement.

' Yes, but it did not long continue ; it has been revived
again of late ; it is a pretty sight, Mildred, and well worth
seeing ; the children carry garlands instead of rushes to the
church, where service is said ; and afterwards there is a dance
in the park, and sports, such as wrestling, pole-leaping, and
trotting matches, are carried on all the afternoon.'

' But what is the origin of such a custom, Arnold ? '

' It dates from the time when our forefathers used green
rushes instead of carpets, the intention being to bless the
rushes on the day of the patron saint.'

'You must permit me to contradict you in one particular, Lambert, as our authorities slightly differ. The real origin of the custom was that, on the day of the patron saint, the church was strewn with fresh rushes, the procession being headed by a girl dressed in white, and wearing a crown ; but Miss Lambert looks impressed,' he continued, with a serious smile ; 'you must come and see it for yourself. Chrissy tells me she is too old to wear a crown this year. Some of our ladies show great taste in the formation of their garlands.'

'May Chesterton's is always the prettiest. Do you mean to dance with May on the green this year, Claude ?' asked Mrs. Delamere, turning to her boy.

Claude shook his head and coloured disdainfully.

'I am going in for the foot-race ; father says I may,' he returned, proudly.

'May is his little sweetheart ; he has been faithful to her ever since he was six years old. Uncle Greyson says——'

'Susie, we must be going,' exclaimed her husband, hastily. 'You must not forget the Chestertons and Islip are dining with us to-night. Claude, my boy, bid Miss Lambert good-bye. My wife and I hope to see you very soon at the vicarage.'

'Yes, come soon,' repeated Mrs. Delamere, with a comfortable squeeze of her hand and more smiles. 'Stephen is always in such a hurry ; but you must pay us a long visit, and bring that poor girl with you. Yes, I am ready, Stephen,' as a frown of impatience came over her husband's face. 'You know of old what a sad gossip I am ; but there, what are women's tongues given them for if they are not to be used ?' and Susie looked up archly at the smooth, blue-shaven face, that was slow to relax into a smile.

Mildred hoped that these would be her last visitors, but she was mistaken, for a couple of harmless maiden ladies, rejoicing in the cognomen of Ortolan, took their places, and chirruped to Mildred in shrill little birdlike voices. Mildred, who had plenty of quiet humour of her own, thought they were not unlike a pair of love-birds Arnold had once given her, the little sharp faces, and hooked noses, and light prominent eyes were not unlike them ; and the bright green shawls, bordered with yellow palm-leaves, completed the illusion. They were so wonderfully alike, too, the only perceptible difference being that Miss Tabitha had gray curls, and a velvet band, and talked more ; and Miss Prissy had a large miniature of an officer, probably an Ortolan too, adorning her small brown wrist.

They talked to Mildred breathlessly about the mothers' meeting, and the clothing-club, and the savings' bank.

'Such a useful institution of dear Mr. Lambert's,' exclaimed Miss Prissy.

'The whole parish is so well conducted,' echoed her sister with a tremulous movement of the head and curls ; 'we think ourselves blessed in our pastor, Miss Lambert,' in a perfectly audible whisper ; 'such discourses, such clear doctrine and Bible truth, such resignation manifested under such a trying dispensation. Oh dear, Prissy,' interrupting herself, as a stanhope, with a couple of dark brown horses, was driven into the court with some little commotion, 'here is the squire, and what will he say at our taking the precedence of him, and making bold to pay our respects to Miss Lambert ?'

'He would say you are very kind neighbours, I hope,' returned Mildred, trying not to smile, and wondering when her ordeal would be over. Her brother had not effected his escape yet, and his jaded face was a tacit reproach to her. Richard, who had ushered in their previous visitors, and had remained yawning in the background, brightened up visibly.

'Here are the Trelawnys, sir; it is very good of them to call so soon.'

'It is only what I should have expected, Cardie,' returned his father, with mild indifference. 'Mr. Trelawny is a man of the world, and knows what is right, that is all.'

And Richard for once looked crestfallen.

'Dear now, but doesn't she look a beauty,' whispered Miss Tabitha, ecstatically, as Miss Trelawny swept into the room on her father's arm, and greeted Mildred civilly, but without effusion, and then seated herself at some little distance, where Richard immediately joined her, the squire meanwhile taking up a somewhat lofty attitude on the hearthrug, directly facing Mildred.

Mildred thought she had never seen a finer specimen of an English gentleman ; the tall, well-knit figure, the clear-cut face, and olive complexion, relieved by the snow-white hair, made up a very striking exterior ; perhaps the eyes were a little cold and glassy-looking, but on the whole it could not be denied that Mr. Trelawny was a very aristocratic-looking man.

His manners were easy and polished, and he was evidently well read on many subjects. Nevertheless a flavour of condescension in his tone gave Mildred an uneasy conviction that she was hardly appearing to her best advantage. She was painfully aware once or twice of a slight hesitation marring a more than usually well-worded sentence, and could see it was at once perceived.

Mildred had never considered herself of great consequence, but she had a certain wholesome self-respect which was grievously wounded by the patronising indulgence that rectified her harmless error.

'I felt all at once as though I were nobody, and might be taken up for false pretensions for trying to be somebody,' as she expressed it to Dr. Heriot afterwards, who laughed and said—

'Very true.'

Mildred would have risen to seat herself by Miss Trelawny, but the squire's elaborate observations allowed her no reprieve. Once or twice she strove to draw her into the conversation ; but a turn of the head, and a brief answer, more curt than agreeable, was all that rewarded her efforts. Nevertheless Mildred liked her voice ; it had a pleasant crispness in it, and the abruptness was not unmusical.

Mildred only saw her full face when she rose to take leave : her figure was very graceful, but her features could hardly be termed beautiful ; though the dead brown hair, with its waves of ripples, and the large brilliant eyes, made her a decidedly striking-looking girl.

Mildred, who was somewhat Quaker-like in her taste, thought the cream-coloured silk, with its ruby velvet facings, somewhat out of place in their homely vicarage, though the Rubens hat was wonderfully picturesque ; it seemed less incongruous when Miss Trelawny remarked casually that they were on their way to a garden-party.

'Do you like archery ? Papa is thinking of getting up a club for the neighbourhood,' she said, looking at Mildred as she spoke. In spite of their dark brilliancy there was a sad, wistful look in her eyes that somehow haunted Mildred. They looked like eyes that were demanding sympathy from a world that failed to understand them.

It was not to be expected that Mildred would be prepossessed by Miss Trelawny in a first visit. Not for weeks, nor for long afterwards, did she form a true estimate of her visitor, or learn the idiosyncrasies of a character at once peculiar and original.

People never understood Ethel Trelawny. There were subtle difficulties in her nature that baffled and repelled them. 'She was odd,' they said, 'so unusual altogether, and said such queer things;' a few even hinted that it was possible that a part might sometimes be acted.

Miss Trelawny was nineteen now, and had passed through two London seasons with indifferent success, a fact somewhat surprising, as her attractions certainly were very great. Without being exactly beautiful, she yet gave an impression of beauty, and certain tints of colour and warm lights made her at times almost brilliant. In a crowded ballroom she was always the centre of observation; but one by one her partners dropped off, displeased and perplexed by the scarifying process to which they had been subjected.

'People come to dance and not to think,' observed one young cornet, turning restive under such treatment, and yet obstinate in his admiration of Ethel. He had been severely scorched during a previous dance, but had returned to the charge most gallantly; 'the music is delicious; do take one more turn with me; there is a clear space now.'

'Do people ever think; does that man, for example?' returned Ethel, indicating a tall man before them, who was pulling his blonde moustache with an expression of satisfied vacuity. 'What sort of dwarfed soul lives in that six feet or so of human matter?'

'Miss Trelawny, you are too bad,' burst out her companion with an expression of honest wrath that showed him not far removed from boyhood. 'That fellow is the bravest and the kindest-hearted in our regiment. He nursed me, by Jove, that he did, when I was down with fever in the hunting-box last year. Not think—Robert Drummond not think,' and he doubled his fist with an energy that soon showed a gash in the faultless lavender kid glove.

'I like you all the better for your defence of your friend,' returned Ethel calmly, and she turned on him a smile so frank and sweet that the young man was almost dazzled. 'If one cannot think, one should at least feel. If I give you one turn more, I dare say you will forgive me,' and from that moment she and Charlie Treherne were firm friends.

But others were not so fortunate, and retired crestfallen and humiliated. One of Charlie's brother-officers whom he introduced to Ethel in a fit of enthusiasm as 'our major, and a man every inch of him, one of the sort who would do the charge at Balaclava again,' subsided into sulkiness and total inanity on finding that instead of discussing Patti and the last opera, Ethel was bent on discovering the ten missing tribes of Israel.

'How hot this room is. They don't give us enough ventilation, I think,' gasped the worthy major at length.

'I was just thinking it was so cool. You are the third partner I have had who has complained of the heat. If you are tired of this waltz, let us sit down in that delightful conservatory;' but as the major, with a good deal of unnecessary energy, declared he could dance till daybreak without fatigue, Ethel quietly continued her discourse.

'I have a theory, I forget from whom I first gathered it, that we shall be discovered to be the direct descendants of the tribe of Gad. Look round this room, Major Hartstone, you will find a faint type of Jewish features on many a face; that girl with the dark *crêpé* hair especially. I consider we shall play a prominent part in the millennium.'

'Millennium—aw; you are too droll, Miss Trelawny. I can see a joke as well as most people, but you go too deep for me. Fancy what Charlie will say when I tell him that he belongs to the tribe of Gad—tribe of Gad—aw—aw—' and as the major, unable to restrain his hilarity any longer, burst into a fit of hearty laughter, Ethel, deeply offended, desired him to lead her to her place.

It was no better in the Row, where Miss Trelawny rode daily with her father, her beautiful figure and superb horsemanship attracting all eyes. At first she had quite a little crowd of loungers round her, but they dispersed by degrees.

'Do you see that girl—Miss Boville?' asked one in a languid drawl, as Ethel reined her horse up under a tree, and sat looking dreamily over the shifting mass of carriages and gaily-dressed pedestrians; 'she is awfully handsome; don't you think so?'

'I don't know. I have not thought about it,' she returned, abstractedly; 'the question is, Captain Ellison, has she a beautiful mind?'

'My dear Miss Trelawny, you positively startle me; you are so unlike other people. I only know she has caught Medwin and his ten thousand a year.'

'Poor thing,' was the answer, leaning over and stroking her horse's neck thoughtfully. 'Touched—quite touched,' observed the young man, significantly tapping his forehead, as Ethel rode by—'must be a little queer, you know, or she would not say such things—sort of craze or hallucination—do you know if it be in the family?'

'Nonsense, it is only an ill-arranged mind airing its ideas;

she is delightfully young and fresh,' returned his companion, a clever barrister, who had the wit to read a girl's vagarisms aright as the volcanic eruptions of an undisciplined and unsatisfied nature.

But it would not do ; people passed over Ethel for other girls who were comparatively plain and ordinary, but whose thinking powers were more under control. One declaration had indeed been made, but it was received by such sad wonder on Ethel's part, that the young man looked at her in reproachful confusion.

'Surely you cannot have mistaken my attentions, Miss Trelawny ? As a man of honour, I thought it right to come to a clear understanding ; if I have ventured to hope too much, I trust you will tell me so.'

'Do you mean you wish to marry me ?' asked Ethel, in a tone of regret and dismay.

Arthur Sullivan had been a special favourite with her ; he had listened to her rhapsodies good-humouredly, and had forborne to laugh at them ; he was good-looking too, and possessed of moderate intelligence, and they had got on very well together during a whole season. It was with a sensation of real pain that she heard him avow his intentions.

'There is some mistake. I have never led you to believe that I would ever be your wife,' she continued, turning pale, and her eyes filling with tears.

'No, Miss Trelawny—never,' he answered, hurriedly ; 'you are no flirt. If any one be to blame, it is I, for daring to hope I could win you.'

'Indeed it is I who do not deserve you,' she returned, sadly ; 'but it is not your fault that you cannot give me what I want. Perhaps I expect too much ; perhaps I hardly know what it is I really do want.'

'May I wait till you find out ?' he asked, earnestly ; 'real love is not to be despised, even though it be accompanied with little wisdom.'

The white lids dropped heavily over the eyes, and for a moment she made no answer; only as he rose from her side, and walked up and down in his agitation, she rose too, hurriedly.

'It cannot be—I feel it—I know it—you are too good to me, Mr. Sullivan ; and I want something more than goodness—but—but—does my father know ?'

'Can you doubt it ?'

'Then he will never forgive me for refusing you. Oh, what

a hard thing it is to be a woman, and to wait for one's fate, instead of going out to seek it. Now I have lost my friend in finding a lover, and my father's anger will be bitter against me.'

Ethel was right; in refusing Arthur Sullivan she had refused the presumptive heir to a baronetcy, and Mr. Trelawny's ambitious soul was sorely vexed within him.

'You have never been of any use or comfort to me, Ethel, and you never will,' he said, harshly; 'just as I was looking to you to redeem matters, you are throwing away this chance. What was the fault with the young fellow? you seemed fond enough of him at one time; he is handsome and gentlemanly enough to please any girl; but it is just one of your fads.'

'He is very amiable, but his character wants backbone, papa. When I marry, my husband must be my master; I have no taste for holding the reins myself.'

'When you marry: I wish you would marry, Ethel, for all the comfort you are to me. If my boys had lived—but what is the use of wishing for anything?'

'Papa,' she returned with spirit, 'I cannot help being a girl; it is my misfortune, not my fault. I wish I could satisfy you better,' she continued, softly, 'but it seems as though we grow more apart every day.'

'It is your own fault,' he returned, morosely. 'Marry Arthur Sullivan, and I will promise to think better of your sense.'

'I cannot, papa. I am not going to marry any one,' she answered, in the suppressed voice he knew so well. And then, as though fearful the argument might be continued, she quietly left the room.

CHAPTER IX

KIRKLEATHAM

'And on we went ; but ere an hour had pass'd,
We reach'd a meadow slanting to the North ;
Down which a well-worn pathway courted us
To one green wicket in a privet hedge ;
This, yielding, gave into a grassy walk
Through crowded lilac-ambush trimly pruned ;
And one warm gust, full-fed with perfume, blew
Beyond us, as we enter'd in the cool.
The garden stretches southward.'—TENNYSON.

THE next few days passed quietly enough. Mildred, who had now assumed the entire management of the household, soon discovered that Olive's four months of misrule and shiftlessness had entailed on her an overplus of work, and, though she was never idle, she soon found that even her willing hands could hardly perform all the tasks laid on them, and that scarcely an interval of leisure was available throughout the day.

'It will not be always so,' she remarked, cheerfully, when Richard took upon himself to remonstrate with her. 'When I have got things a little more into order, I mean to have plenty of time to myself. Polly and I have planned endless excursions to Podgill and the out-wood, to stock the new fernery Roy is making for us, and I hope to accompany your father sometimes when he goes to Nateley and Winton.'

'Nevertheless, I mean to drive you over to Brough to-day. You must come, Aunt Milly. You are looking pale, Dr. John says, and the air will do you good. Huddle all those things into the basket,' he continued, in a peremptory voice that amused Mildred, and, acting on his words, he swept the neat pile of dusters and tea-cloths that lay beside her into Olive's unlucky mending-basket, and then faced round on her with his most persuasive air. 'It is such a delicious day, and you have been working like a galley-slave ever since you got up this morning,' he said, apologetically. 'My father would be quite troubled if he knew how hard you work. Do you know Dr. John threatens to tell him ?'

'Dr. John had better mind his own business,' returned Mildred, colouring. 'Very well, Richard, you shall have your way as usual ; my head aches rather, and a drive will be refreshing. Perhaps you could drop me at Kirkleatham on our way home. I must return Miss Trelawny's visit.'

Richard assented with alacrity, and then bidding Mildred be ready for him in ten minutes, he hastened from the room.

Mildred had noticed a great change in Richard during the last week ; he seemed brighter, and was less carping and disagreeable in his manners to Olive ; and though he still snubbed her at times, there was an evident desire to preserve harmony in the family circle, which the others were not slow to appreciate.

In many little ways he showed Mildred that he was grateful to her for the added comfort of her presence ; any want of regularity and order was peculiarly trying to him ; and now that he was no longer aggravated by Olive's carelessness and left-handed ways, he could afford even to be gracious to her, especially as Mildred had succeeded in effecting some sort of reformation in the offending hair and dress.

'There, now you look nice, and Cardie will say so,' she said, as she fastened up the long braids, which now looked bright and glossy, and then settled the collar, which was as usual somewhat awry, and tied the black ribbon into a natty bow. 'A little more time and care would not be wasted, Olive. We have no right to tease other people by our untidy ways, or to displease their eyes ; it is as much an act of selfishness as of indolence, and may be encouraged until it becomes a positive sin.'

'Do you think so, Aunt Milly ?'

'I am sure of it. Chrissy thinks me hard on her, but so much depends on the habits we form when quite young. I believe with many persons tidiness is an acquired virtue ; it requires some sort of education, and certainly not a little discipline.'

'But, Aunt Milly, I thought some people were always tidy ; from their childhood, I mean. Chriss and I never were,' she continued, sorrowfully.

'Some people are methodical by nature ; Cardie, for example. They early see the fitness and beauty of order. But, Olive, for your comfort, I am sure it is to be acquired.'

'Not by me, Aunt Milly.'

'My dear—why not ? It is only a question of patience and

discipline. If you made the rule now of never going to a drawer in a hurry. When Chrissy wants anything, she jerks the contents of the whole drawer on the floor; I have found her doing it more than once.'

'She could not find her gloves, and Cardie was waiting,' returned Olive, always desirous of screening another's fault.

'Yes; but she left it to you to pick up all the things again. If Chriss's gloves were in their right place, no one need have been troubled. I could find my gloves blindfold.'

'I am always tidying my own and Chrissy's drawers, Aunt Milly; but in a few days they are as bad as ever,' returned Olive, helplessly.

'Because you never have time to search quietly for a thing. Did you look in the glass, Olive, while you were doing your hair this morning?'

'I don't know. I think so. I was learning my German verses, I believe.'

'So Cardie had a right to grumble over your crooked parting and unkempt appearance. You should keep your duties like the contents of your drawers, neatly piled on the top of each other. No lady can arrange her hair properly and do German at the same time. Tell me, Olive, you have not so many head-aches since I got your father to forbid your sitting up so late at night.'

'No, Aunt Milly; but all the same I wish you and he had not made the rule; it used to be such a quiet time.'

'And you learn all the quicker since you have had regular walks with Polly and Chriss.'

'I am less tired after my lessons, certainly. I thought that was because you took away the mending-basket; the stooping made my back ache, and——'

'I see,' returned Mildred, with a satisfied smile.

Olive's muddy complexion was certainly clearer, and there was less heaviness in her gait, since she had judiciously insisted that the hours of rest should be kept intact. It had cost Olive some tears, however, for that quiet time when the household were sleeping round her was very precious to the careworn girl.

Richard gave vent to an audible expression of pleasure when he noticed his sister's altered appearance, and his look of approbation was most pleasant to Mildred.

'If you would only hold yourself up, and smile sometimes, you would really look as well as other people,' was the qualified praise he gave her.

'I am glad you are pleased,' returned Olive, simply. 'I never expect you to admire me, Cardie. I am plainer than any one else, I know.'

'Yes; but you have nice eyes, and what a quantity of hair,' passing his hand over the thick coils in which Mildred had arranged it. 'She looks a different girl, does she not, Aunt Milly?'

'It is very odd, but I believe Cardie does not dislike me so much to-day,' Olive said, when she wished her aunt good-night.

She and Polly took turns every night in coming into Mildred's room with little offers of service, but in reality to indulge in a cosy chat. It was characteristic of the girls that they never came together. Olive was silent and reserved before Polly, and Polly was at times a little caustic in her wit. 'We mix as badly as oil and water,' she said once. 'I shall always think Olive the most tiresome creature in the world. Chriss is far more amusing.'

'Why do you think so?' asked Mildred, gently. She was always gentle with Olive; these sort of weary natures need much patience and delicacy of handling, she thought.

'He speaks more kindly, and he has looked at me several times, not in his critical way, but as if he were not so much displeased at my appearance; but, Aunt Milly, it is so odd, his caring, I mean.'

'Why so, my dear?'

'If I loved a person very much, I should not care how they looked; they might be ugly or deformed, but it would make no difference. Cardie's love seems to vary somehow.'

'Anything unsightly is very grievous to him, but not in the way you mean, Olive. He is peculiarly tender over any physical infirmity. I liked his manner so to little Cathy Villers to-day.'

'But all the same he attaches too much importance to merely outward things,' returned Olive, who sometimes showed tenacity in her opinions; 'not that I blame him,' she continued, as though she feared she had been uncharitable, 'only that it is so odd.'

Mildred was in a somewhat gladsome mood as she prepared for her drive. Richard's thoughtfulness pleased her; on the whole things were going well with her. Under her judicious management, the household had fallen into more equable and tranquil ways. There were fewer jars, and more opportunity for Roy's lurking spirit of fun to develop itself. She had had two or three stormy scenes with Chriss ; but the little girl had already learned to respect the gentle firmness that would not abate one iota of lawful authority.

'We are learning our verbs from morning to night,' grumbled Chriss, in a confidential aside to Roy ; 'that horrid one, "to tidy," you know. Aunt Milly is always in the imperative mood. I declare I am getting sick of it. Hannah or Rachel used to mend my gloves and things, and now she insists on my doing it myself. I broke a dozen needles one afternoon to spite her, but she gave me the thirteenth with the same sweet smile. It is so tiresome not to be able to provoke people.'

But even Chrissy was secretly learning to value the kind forbearance that bore with her wayward fancies, and the skilfulness that helped her out of many a scrape. Mildred had made the rule that after six o'clock no lesson-books were to be opened. In the evening they either walked or drove, or sat on the lawn working, while Richard or Roy read aloud, Mildred taking the opportunity to overlook her nieces' work, and to remonstrate over the giant strides that Chriss's needle was accustomed to take. Even Olive owned these quiet times were very nice, while Mr. Lambert had once or twice been drawn into the charmed circle, and had paced the terrace in lieu of the churchyard, irresistibly attracted by the pleasant spectacle.

Mildred was doing wonders in her quiet way ; she had already gained some insight into parish matters ; she had accompanied her brother in his house-to-house visitation, and had been much struck by the absence of anything like distress. Poverty was there, but not hard-griping want. As a general rule the people were well-to-do, independent, and fairly respectable. One village had a forlorn and somewhat neglected appearance ; but the generality of Mr. Lambert's parishioners struck Mildred as far superior to the London poor whom she had visited.

As yet she had not seen the darker side of the picture ; she was shocked to hear Mr. Lambert speak on future occasions of the tendency to schism, and the very loose notions of morality that prevailed even among the better sort of people. The clergy had uphill work, he said. The new railway had brought a large influx of navvies, and the public-houses were always full.

' The commandments are broken just as easily in sight of God's hills as they are in the crowded and fetid alleys of our metropolis,' he said once. ' Human nature is the same everywhere, even though it be glossed over by outward respectability.

Mildred had already come in contact with the Ortolans more than once, and had on many occasions seen the green and yellow shawls flitting in and out of the cottages.

'They do a great deal of good, and are really very worthy creatures, in spite of their oddities,' observed Mr. Lambert once. 'They live over at Hartley. There is a third one, an invalid, Miss Bathsheba, who is very different from the others, and is, I think, quite a superior person. When I think of the gallant struggle they have carried on against trouble and poverty, one is inclined to forgive their little whims: it takes all sorts of people to make up a world, Mildred.'

Mildred thoroughly enjoyed her drive. Richard was in one of his brightest moods, and talked with more animation than usual, and seeing that his aunt was really interested in learning all about their surroundings, he insisted on putting up the pony-carriage, and took Mildred to see the church and the castle.

The vicarage and churchyard were so pleasantly situated, and the latter looked so green and shady, that she was disappointed to find the inside of the church very bare and neglected-looking, while the damp earthy atmosphere spoke of infrequent services.

There were urgent need of repairs, and a general shabbiness of detail that was pitiable: the high wooden pews looked comfortless, ordinary candles evidently furnished a dim and insufficient light. Mildred felt quite oppressed as she left the building.

'There can be no true Church-spirit here, Richard. Fancy worshipping in that damp, mouldy place; are there no zealous workers here, who care to beautify their church?'

Richard shook his head. 'We cannot complain of our want of privileges after that. I have been speaking to my father, and I really fancy we shall acquire a regular choir next year, and if so we shall turn out the Morrisons and Gunnings. My father is over-lenient to people's prejudices; it grieves him to disturb long-rooted customs.'

'Where are we going now, Richard?'

'To Brough Castle; the ruin stands on a little hill just by; it is one of the celebrated Countess of Pembroke's castles. You know the legend, Aunt Milly?'

'No, I cannot say that I do.'

'She seems to have been a strong-minded person, and was always building castles. It was prophesied that as long as she went on building she would not die, and in consequence her rage for castle-building increased with her age; but at last there was a severe frost, during which no work could be carried on, and so the poor countess died.'

'What a lovely view there is from here, Richard.'

'Yes, that long level of green to our left is where the celebrated Brough fair is held. The country people use it as a date, "last Brough Hill," as they say—the word "Brough" comes from "Brugh," a fortification. My father has written a very clever paper on the origin of the names of places; it is really very interesting.'

'Some of the names are so quaint'—"Smardale," for example.'

'Let me see, that has a Danish termination, and means Butter-dale—"dale" from "dal," a valley; Garsdale, grass-dale; Sleddale, from "slet," plain, the open level plain or dale, and so on. I recollect my father told us that "Kirkby," on the contrary, is always of Christian origin, as "Kirkby Stephen," and "Kirkby Kendal;" but perhaps you are not fond of etymology, Aunt Milly.'

'On the contrary, it is rather a favourite study of mine; go on, Richard. I want to know how Kirkby Stephen got its name.'

'I must quote my father again, then. He thinks the victorious Danes found a kirk with houses near it, and called the place Kirkby, and they afterwards learnt that the church was dedicated to St. Stephen, the proto-martyr, and then added his name to distinguish it from the other Kirkbys.'

'It must have been rather a different church, Richard.'

'I see I must go on quoting. He says, "We can almost picture to ourselves that low, narrow, quaint old church, with its rude walls and thatched roof." But, Aunt Milly, we must be thinking of returning, if we are to call on the Trelawnys. By the bye, what do you think of them?'

'Of Mr. Trelawny, you mean, for I certainly did not exchange three words with his daughter.'

'I noticed she was very silent; she generally is when he is present. What a pity it is they do not understand each other better.'

He seemed waiting for her to speak, but Mildred, who was taking a last lingering look at the ruin, was slow to respond.

'He seems very masterful,' she said at last when they had entered the pony-carriage, and were driving homewards.

'Yes, and what is worse, so narrow in his views. He is very kind to me, and I get on with him tolerably well,' continued Richard, modestly; 'but I can understand the repressing influence under which she lives.'

'It seems so strange for a father not to understand his daughter.'

'I believe he is fond of her in his own way; he can hardly help being proud of her. You see, he lost his two boys when they were lads in a dreadful way; they were both drowned in bathing, and he has never got over their loss; it is really very hard for him, especially as his wife died not very long afterwards. They say the shock killed her.'

'Poor man, he has known no ordinary trouble. I can understand how lonely it must be for her.'

'Yes, it is all the worse that she does not care for the people about here. With the exception of us and the Delawares, she has no friends—no intimate friends, I mean.'

'Her exclusiveness is to blame, then; our neighbours seem really very kind-hearted.'

'Yes, but they are not her sort. I think you like the Delawares yourself, Aunt Milly?'

'Very much. I was just going to ask you more about them. Mrs. Delaware is very nice, but it struck me that she is not equal to her husband.'

'No; he is a fine fellow. You see, she was only a yeoman's daughter, and he educated her to be his wife.'

'That accounts for her homely speech.'

'My father married them. She was a perfect little rustic beauty, he says. She ran away from school twice, and at last told Mr. Delaware that he might marry her or not as he pleased, but she would have no more of the schooling; if she were not nice enough for him, she was for Farmer Morrison of Wharton Hall, and of course that decided the question.'

I hope she makes him a good wife.'

'Very, and he is exceedingly fond of her, though she makes him uneasy at times. Her connections are not very desirable, and she can never be made to understand that they are to be kept in the background. I have seen him sit on thorns during a whole evening, looking utterly wretched, while she dragged in Uncle Greyson and Brother Ben every other moment.'

'I wish she would dress more quietly; she looks very unlike a clergyman's wife.'

Richard smiled. 'Miss Trelawny is very fond of driving over to Warcop Vicarage. She enjoys talking to Mr. Delaware, but I have noticed his wife looks a little sad at not being able to join in their conversation; possibly she regrets the schooling;' but here Richard's attention was diverted by a drove of oxen, and as soon as the road was clear he had started a new topic, which lasted till they reached their destination.

Kirkleatham was a large red castellated building built on a slight eminence, and delightfully situated, belted in with green meadows, and commanding lovely views of soft distances; that from the terrace in front of the house was especially beautiful, the church and town of Kirkby Stephen distinctly visible, and the grouping of the dark hills at once varied and full of loveliness.

As they drove through the shrubbery Richard had a glimpse of a white dress and a broad-brimmed hat, and stopping the pony-carriage, he assisted Mildred to alight.

'Here is Miss Trelawny, sitting under her favourite tree; you had better go to her, Aunt Milly, while I find some one to take the mare;' and as Mildred obeyed, Miss Trelawny laid down her book, and greeted her with greater cordiality than she had shown on the previous visit.

'Papa is somewhere about the grounds; you can find him,' she said when Richard came up to them, and as he departed somewhat reluctantly, she led Mildred to a shady corner of the lawn, where some basket-chairs, and a round table strewn with work and books, made up a scene of rustic comfort.

The blue curling smoke rose from the distant town into the clear afternoon air, the sun shone on the old church tower, the hills lay in soft violet shadow.

'I hope you admire our view?' asked Miss Trelawny, with her full, steady glance at Mildred; and again Mildred noticed the peculiar softness, as well as brilliancy, of her eyes. 'I think it is even more beautiful than that which you see from the vicarage windows. Mr. Lambert and I have often had a dispute on that subject.'

'But you have not the river—that gives such a charm to ours. I would not exchange those snatches of silvery brightness for your greater distances. What happiness beautiful scenery affords! hopeless misery seems quite incompatible with those ranges of softly-tinted hills.'

A pensive—almost a melancholy—look crossed Miss Trelawny's face.

'The worst of it is, that our moods and Nature's do not always harmonise; sometimes the sunshine has a chilling brightness when we are not exactly attuned to it. One must be really susceptible—in fact, an artist—if one could find happiness in the mere circumstance of living in a beautiful district like ours.'

'I hope you do not undervalue your privileges,' returned Mildred, smiling.

'No, I am never weary of expatiating on them ; but all the same, one asks a little more of life.'

'In what way ?'

'In every possible way,' arching her brows, with a sort of impatience. 'What do rational human beings generally require ?—work—fellowship—possible sympathy.'

'All of which are to be had for the asking. Nay, my dear Miss Trelawny,' as Ethel's slight shrug of the shoulders testified her dissent, 'where human beings are more or less congregated, there can be no lack of these.'

'They may possibly differ in the meaning we attach to our words. I am not speaking of the labour market, which is already glutted.'

'Nor I.'

'The question is,' continued the young philosopher, wearily, 'of what possible use are nine-tenths of the unmarried women ? half of them marry to escape from the unbearable routine and vacuum of their lives.'

Ethel spoke with such mournful candour, that Mildred's first feeling of astonishment changed into pity—so young and yet so cynical—and with such marginal wastes of unfulfilled purpose.

'When there is so much trouble and faultiness in the world,' she answered, 'there must be surely work enough to satisfy the most hungry nature. Have you not heard it asserted, Miss Trelawny, that nature abhors a vacuum ?'

To her surprise, a shade crossed Miss Trelawny's face.

'You talk so like our village Mentor, that I could almost fancy I were listening to him. Are there no duties but the seven corporal works of mercy, Miss Lambert ? Is the intellect to play no part in the bitter comedy of women's lives ?'

'You would prefer tragedy ?' questioned Mildred, with a slight twitching of the corner of her mouth. It was too absurdly incongruous to hear this girl, radiant with health, and glorying in her youth, speaking of the bitter comedy of life. Mildred began to accuse her in her own mind of unreal sentiment, and the vaporous utterings of girlish spleen ; but Ethel's intense earnestness disarmed her of this suspicion.

'I have no respect for the people ; they are utterly brutish and incapable of elevation. I am horrifying you, Miss Lambert, but indeed I am not speaking without proof. At one time I took great interest in the parish, and used to hold mothers' meetings—pleasant evenings for the women. I used to give them tea, and let them bring their needlework, on condition they listened to my reading. Mr. Lambert approved of my plan; he only stipulated that as I was so very young—in age, I suppose, he meant—that Miss Prissy Ortolan should assist me.'

'And it was an excellent idea,' returned Mildred, warmly.

'Yes, but it proved an utter failure,' sighed Ethel. 'The women liked the tea, and I believe they got through a great deal of needlework, only Miss Prissy saw after that; but they cared no more for the reading than Minto would,' stooping down to pat the head of a large black retriever that lay at her feet. 'I had planned a course of progressive instruction, that should combine information with amusement; but I found they preferred their own gossip. I asked one woman, who looked more intelligent than the others, how she had liked Jean Ingelow's beautiful poem, "Two Brothers and a Sermon," which I had thought simple enough to suit even their comprehensions, and she replied, "Eh, it was fine drowsy stuff, and would rock off half-a-dozen crying babies."'

Mildred smiled.

'I gave it up after that. I believe Miss Tabitha and Miss Prissy manage it. They read little tracts to them, and the women do not talk half so much; but it's very disheartening to think one's theory had failed.'

'You soared a little beyond them, you see.'

'I suppose so; but I thought their life was prosaic enough; but here comes my father and Richard. I see they have Dr. Heriot with them.'

Ethel spoke quietly, but Mildred thought there was a slight change in her manner, which became less animated.

Dr. Heriot looked both surprised and pleased when he saw Mildred; he placed himself beside her, and listened with great interest to the account of their afternoon's drive. On this occasion, Mildred's quiet fluency did not desert her.

Mr. Trelawny was less stiff and ceremonious in his own house; he insisted, with old-fashioned politeness, that they should remain for some refreshment, and he himself conducted Mildred to the top of the tower, from which there was an extensive view.

On their return, they found a charming little tea-table set out under the trees; and Ethel, in her white gown, with pink May blossoms in her hair, was crossing the lawn with Richard. Dr. Heriot was still lounging complacently in his basket-chair.

Ethel made a charming hostess; but she spoke very little to any one but Richard, who hovered near her, with a happy boyish-looking face. Mildred had never seen him to such advantage; he looked years younger, when the grave restraint of his manners relaxed a little; and she was struck by the unusual softness of his dark eyes. In his best moods, Richard was undoubtedly attractive in the presence of elder men. He showed a modest deference to their opinions, and at the same time displayed such intelligence, that Mildred felt secretly proud of him. He was evidently a great favourite with Mr. Trelawny and his daughter. Ethel constantly appealed to him, and the squire scolded him for coming so seldom.

The hour was a pleasant one, and Mildred thoroughly enjoyed it. Just as they were dispersing, and the pony-carriage was coming round, Dr. Heriot approached Ethel.

'Well, have you been to see poor Jessie?' he asked, a little anxiously.

Miss Trelawny shook her head.

'You know I never promised,' she returned, as though trying to defend herself.

'I never think it fair to extort promises—people's better moods so rapidly pass away. If you remember, I only advised you to do so. I thought it would do you both good.'

'You need not rank us in the same category,' she returned, proudly; 'you are such a leveller of classes, Dr. Heriot.'

'Forgive me, but when you reach Jessie's standard of excellence, I would willingly do so. Jessie is a living proof of my theory—that we are all equal—and the education and refinement on which you lay such stress are only adventitious adjuncts to our circumstances. In one sense—we are old friends, Miss Trelawny; and I may speak plainly, I know—I consider Jessie greatly your superior.'

A quick sensitive colour rose to Ethel's face. They were walking through the shrubbery; and for a moment she turned her long neck aside, as though to hide her pained look; but she answered, calmly—

'We differ so completely in our estimates of things; I am quite aware how high I stand in Dr. Heriot's opinion.'

'Are you sure of that?' answering her with the sort of amused gentleness with which one would censure a child. 'I am apt to keep my thoughts to myself, and am not quite so easy to read as you are, Miss Trelawny. So you will not go and see my favourite Jessie?' with a persuasive smile.

'No,' she said, colouring high; 'I am not in the mood for it.'

'Then we will say no more about it; and my remedy has failed.' But though he talked pleasantly to her for the remainder of the way, Mildred noticed he had his grave look, and that Ethel failed to rally her spirits.

CHAPTER X

THE RUSH-BEARING

' Heigho ! daises and buttercups,
  Fair yellow daffodils, stately and tall,
  A sunshiny world full of laughter and leisure,
  And fresh hearts unconscious of sorrow and thrall !
  Send down on their pleasure smiles passing its measure,
  God that is over us all.'—JEAN INGELOW.

MILDRED soon became accustomed to Dr. Heriot's constant presence about the house, and the slight restraint she had at first felt rapidly wore off.

She soon looked upon it as a matter of course to see him at least three evenings in the week ; loneliness was not to his taste, and in consequence, when he was not otherwise engaged, he generally shared their evening meal at the vicarage, and remained an hour afterwards, talking to Mr. Lambert or Richard. Mildred ceased to start with surprise at finding him in the early morning turning over the books in her brother's study, or helping Polly and Chriss in their new fernery. Polly was made happy by frequent invitations to her guardian's house, where she soon made herself at home, coming back to Mildred with delightful accounts of how her guardian had allowed her to dust his books and mend his gloves ; and how he had approved of the French coffee she had made him.

One afternoon Chriss and she had been in the kitchen, concocting all sorts of delicious messes, which Dr. Heriot, Cardie, and Roy were expected to eat afterwards.

Dr. Heriot gave an amusingly graphic account of the feast afterwards to Mildred, and his old housekeeper's astonishment at ' them nasty and Frenchified dishes.'

Polly had carried in the omelette herself, and placed it with a flushed, triumphant face before him, her dimpled elbows still whitened with flour ; the dishes were all charmingly garlanded with flowers and leaves—tiny breast-knots of geranium and heliotrope lay beside each plate. Polly had fastened a great cream-coloured rose into Olive's drooping braids, which she wore reluctantly.

'I wish you could have seen it all, Miss Lambert; it was the prettiest thing possible; they had transformed my bachelor's den into a perfect bower. Roy must have helped them, and given some of his artistic touches. There were great trailing sprays of ivy, and fern-fronds in my terra-cotta vases, and baskets of wild roses and ox-eyed daisies; never was my *fête* day so charmingly inaugurated before. The worst of it was that Polly expected me to taste all her dishes in succession; and Chriss insisted on my eating a large slice of the frosted cake.'

Mildred was not present at Dr. Heriot's birthday party; she had preferred staying with her brother, but she found he had not forgotten her; the guests were surprised in their turn by finding a handsome gift beside each plate, a print that Roy had long coveted, Trench on *Parables* for Richard, Schiller's works for Olive, a neat little writing-desk for Polly, and a silk-lined work-basket for Chriss, who coloured and looked uncomfortable over the gift. Polly had orders to carry a beautiful book on Ferns to Aunt Milly, and a slice of the iced-cake with Dr. Heriot's compliments, and regrets that she had not tasted the omelette—a message that Polly delivered with the utmost solemnity.

'Oh, it was so nice, Aunt Milly; Dr. Heriot is so good and indulgent. I think he is the best man living—just to please us he let us serve up the coffee in those beautiful cups without handles, that he values so, and that have cost I don't know how much money; and Olive dropped hers because she said it burnt her fingers, and broke it all to fragments. Livy looked ready to cry, but Dr. Heriot only laughed, and would not let Cardie scold her.'

'That was kind of Dr. Heriot.'

'He is never anything but kind. I am sure some of the things disagreed with him, but he would taste them all; and then afterwards—oh, Aunt Milly, it was so nice—we sang glees in the twilight, and when it got quite dark, he told us a splendid ghost-story—only it turned out a dream—which spoilt it rather; and laughed at Chrissy and me because we looked a little pale when the lamp came in. I am sure Richard enjoyed it as well as us, for he rubbed his hands and said, "Excellent," when he had finished.'

Mildred looked at her book when the girls had retired, fairly wearied with chattering. It was just what she had wanted

How thoughtful of Dr. Heriot. Her name was written in full ; and for the first time she had a chance of criticising the bold, clear handwriting. 'From a family friend—John Heriot,' was written just underneath. After all, had it not been a little churlish of her to refuse going with the children ? The evening had gone very heavily with her ; her brother had been in one of his taciturn moods and had retired to his room early ; and finding the house empty, and somewhat desolate, she had betaken herself to the moonlighted paths of the churchyard, and had more than once wished she could peep in unseen on the party.

It was not long afterwards that Mildred was induced to partake of Dr. Heriot's hospitality.

It was the day before the Castlesteads Rush-bearing. Mildred was in the town with Olive and Polly, when, just as they were turning the corner by the King's Arms, a heavy shower came on ; and Dr. Heriot, who was entering his own door, beckoned to them to run across and take shelter.

Dr. Heriot's house stood in a secluded corner of the market-place, behind the King's Arms ; the bank was on the left-hand side, and from the front windows there was a good view of the market-place, the town pump, and butter market, and the quaint, old-fashioned shops.

The shops of Kirkby Stephen drove a brisk trade, in spite of the sleepy air that pervaded them, and the curious intermixture of goods that they patronised.

The confectioner's was also a china shop, and there was a millinery room upstairs, while the last new music was only procurable at the tin shop. Jams and groceries could be procured at the druggist's, while the fashionable milliner of the town was also the postmistress. On certain days the dull little butcher's shop, with its picturesque gable and overhanging balcony, was guileless of anything but its chopping-blocks, and perhaps the half-carcase of a sheep ; beef was not always to be had for the asking, a fact which London housekeepers were slow to understand.

On Mondays the town wore a more thriving appearance ; huge wagons blocked up the market-place, stalls containing all sorts of wares occupied the central area, the countrywomen sold chickens and eggs, and tempting rolls of fresh butter, the gentlemen farmers congregated round the King's Arms ; towards afternoon, horse-dealers tried their horses' paces up and down the long street, while the village curs made themselves conspicuous barking at their heels.

'I hope you will always make use of me in this way,' said
Dr. Heriot, as he shook Mildred's wet cloak, and ushered them
into the hall ; 'the rain has damped you already, but I hope it
is only a passing shower for the little rush-bearers' sakes to-
morrow.'

'The barometer points to fair,' observed Polly, anxiously.

'Yes, and this shower will do all the good in the world, lay
the dust, and render your long drive enjoyable. Ah! Miss
Lambert, you have found out why Olive honours me by so many
visits,' as Mildred glanced round the large handsome hall, fitted
up by glass bookcases ; and with its carpeted floor and round
table, and brackets of blue dragon china looking thoroughly
comfortable.

'This is my dining-room and consulting-room ; my surgery
is elsewhere,' continued Dr. Heriot. 'My drawing-room is so
little used, that I am afraid Marjory often forgets to draw up
the blinds.' And he showed Mildred the low-ceiled pleasant
rooms, well-furnished, and tastefully arranged ; but the drawing-
room having the bare disused air of a room that a woman's footstep seldom enters. Mildred longed to droop the curtain into
less stiff folds, and to fill the empty vases with flowers.

Polly spoke out her thought immediately afterwards.

'I mean to come in every morning on my way to school,
and pull up the blinds, and fill that china bowl with roses.
Marjory won't mind anything I do.'

'Your labour will be wasted, Polly,' returned her guardian,
rather sadly. 'No one but Mrs. Sadler, or Miss Ortolan, or
perhaps Mrs. Northcote, ever sits on that yellow couch. Your
roses would waste their sweetness on the desert air ; no one
would look at them, or smell them ; but it is a kind thought,
little one,' with a gentle, approving smile.

'Which room was the scene of Polly's feast ?' asked Mildred,
curiously.

'Oh, the den—I mean the room I generally inhabit ; it is
snug, and opens into the conservatory ; and I have grown to
like it somehow. Now, Polly, you must make us some tea ;
but the question is, will you favour the yellow couch and the
empty rose-bowls, Miss Lambert, or do you prefer the dining-
room ?'

'Dr. Heriot, what do you mean by treating Aunt Milly so
stiffly ? of course we shall have tea in the den, as usual.' But
he interrupted her by a brief whisper in her ear, which made
her laugh and clap her hands. Evidently there was some

delightful secret between them, for Polly's eyes sparkled as she stood holding his arm with both hands; and even Dr. Heriot's twinkled with amusement.

'Miss Lambert, Polly wants to know if you can keep a secret? I don't think you look dangerous, so you shall be shown the mystery of the den.'

'Does Olive know?' asked Mildred, looking at the girl as she sat hunching her shoulders, as usual, over a book.

'Yes, but she does not approve. Olive never approves of anything nice,' returned Polly, saucily. 'Let us go very quietly; he generally whistles so loudly that he never hears anything;' and as Polly softly opened the door, very clear, sweet whistling was distinctly audible.

There was a little glass-house beyond the cosy room they were entering; and there, amongst flowers and canaries, and gaily-striped awning, in his old blue cricketing coat, was Roy painting.

Dr. Heriot beckoned Mildred to come nearer, and she had ample leisure to admire the warm sunshiny tints of a small landscape, to which he was putting finishing touches, until the melodious whistling ceased, and an exclamation of delight from Polly made him turn round.

'Aunt Milly, this is too bad; you have stolen a march on me;' and Roy's fair face was suffused for a moment. 'I owe Dr. John a grudge for this,' threatening him with his palette and brush.

Polly could not resist the pleasure of showing her aunt the mysteries of Bluebeard's den. 'When you miss your boy, you will know where to find him in future, Miss Lambert.'

'Roy, dear, you must not be vexed. I had no idea Polly's secret had anything to do with you,' said Mildred, gently. 'Dr. Heriot is very good to allow you to make use of this pleasant studio.'

Roy's brow cleared like magic.

'I am glad you think so. I was only afraid you would talk nonsense, as Livy does, about waste of time, and hiding talents under a bushel. Holloa, Livy, I did not know you were there; no offence intended; but you do talk an awful quantity of rubbish sometimes.'

'I only said it was a pity you did not tell papa about it; your being an artist, I mean,' answered Olive, mildly; but Roy interrupted her impatiently.

'You know I cannot bear disappointing him, but of course

it has to be told.   Aunt Milly, do you think my father would ask Dad Fabian down to see Polly ?   I should so like to have a talk with him.   You see, Dr. John is only an amateur ; he cannot tell me if I am ever likely to be an artist,' finished Roy, a little despondingly.

'I am not much of a critic, but I like your picture, Roy ; it looks so fresh and sunny.   I could almost feel as though I were sitting down on that mossy bank ; and that little girl in her red cloak is charming.'

Roy coloured bashfully over the praise.

'I tell him that with his few advantages he does wonders ; he has only picked up desultory lessons here and there,' observed Dr. Heriot.

'That old fellow at Sedbergh taught me to grind colours, and I fell in with an artist at York once.   I don't mind you knowing a bit, Aunt Milly ; only'—lowering his voice so as not to be heard by the others—'I want to get an opinion worth having, and be sure I am not only the dabbler Dick thinks me, before I bother the Padre about it ; but I shall do no good at anything else, let Dick say what he will ;' a touch of defiance and hopelessness in his voice, very different from his ordinary saucy manners.   Evidently Roy was in earnest for once in his life.

'You are quite right, Roy ; it is the most beautiful life in the world,' broke in Polly, enthusiastically.   'It is nobler to try at that and fail, than to be the most successful lawyer in the world.'

'The gentlemen of the robe would thank you, Polly.   Do you know, I have a great respect for a learned barrister.'

'All that Polly knows about them is, they wear a wig and carry a blue bag,' observed Roy, with one of his odd chuckles.

'What a Bohemian you are, Polly.'

'I like what is best and brightest and most loveable in life,' returned Polly, undauntedly.   'I think you are an artist by nature, because you care so much for beautiful scenery, and are so quick to see different shades and tints of colouring.   Dad Fabian is older, and grander, far—but you talk a little like him, Roy ; your words have the same ring, somehow.'

'Polly is a devout believer in Roy's capabilities,' observed Dr. Heriot, half-seriously and half-laughing.   'You are fortunate, Roy, to have inspired so much faith already ; it must warm up your landscapes and brighten your horizons for you.   After all, there is nothing like sympathy in this world,' with a scarcely audible sigh.

'Dr. Heriot, tea is ready,' broke in Polly, with one of her quick transitions from enthusiasm to matter-of-fact reality, as she moved as though by right to her place at the head of the table, and looked as though she expected her guardian to seat himself as usual beside her; while Dr. Heriot drew up a comfortable rocking-chair for Mildred.   Certainly the den presented a cheerful aspect to-night; the little glass-house, as Dr. Heriot generally termed it, with its easel and flowers, and its pleasant glimpse of the narrow garden and blue hills behind, looked picturesque in the afternoon light; the rain had ceased, the canaries burst into loud song, there was a delicious fragrance of verbena and heliotrope; Roy stretched his lazy length on the little red couch, his fair head in marked contrast with Mildred's brown coils; a great crimson-hearted rose lay beside her plate.

Dr. Heriot's den certainly lacked no visible comfort; there were easy-chairs for lounging, small bookcases filled with favourite books, a writing-table, and a marble stand, with a silver reading-lamp, that gave the softest possible light; one or two choice prints enlivened the walls.   Dr. Heriot evidently kept up a luxurious bachelor's life, for the table was covered with good things; and Mildred ventured to praise the excellent Westmorland cakes.

'Marjory makes better girdle-cakes than Nan,' observed Polly. 'Do you know what my guardian calls them, Aunt Milly?'

'You should allow Miss Lambert to finish hers first,' remonstrated Dr. Heriot.

'He calls them "sudden deaths."'

'Miss Lambert is looking quite pale, and laying down hers. I must help myself to some to reassure her;' and Dr. Heriot suited his action to his words.   'I perfectly scandalise Marjory by telling her they are very unwholesome, but she only says, "Hod tongue o' ye, doctor; t' kyuks are au weel enuff; en'ill hurt nin o' ye; if y'ill tak 'em i' moderation."'

'I think Marjory is much of a muchness with Nan in point of obstinacy.'

'Nan's habits bewilder me,' observed Mildred.   'She eats so little flesh meat, as she calls it; and whatever time I go into the kitchen, she seems perpetually at tea.'

'Ay, four o'clock tea is the great meal of the day; the servants certainly care very little for meat here.   I am often surprised, when I go into the cottages, to see the number of cakes just freshly baked; it is the most tempting meal they have. The girdle-cakes, and the little black teapot on the hob, and not

unfrequently a great pile of brown toast, have often struck me
as so appetising after a cold, wet ride, that I have often shared
a bit and a sup with them.   Have you ever heard of Kendal
wigs, Miss Lambert?'

Mildred shook her head.

'They are very favourite cakes.   Many a farmer's wife on a
market-day thinks her purchases incomplete without bringing
home a goodly quantity of wigs.   I am rather fond of them myself.   All my oat-bread, or havre-bread as they call it, is sent
me by an old patient who lives at Kendal.   Do you know there
is a quaint proverb, very much used here, "as crafty as a Kendal
fox"?'

'What is the origin of that?' asked Mildred, much amused.

'Well, it is doubtful.   It may owe its origin to some sly old
Reynard who in days long since "escaped the hunter many times
and oft;" or it might possibly originate in some family of the
name of Fox living at Kendal, and noted for their business
habits and prudence.   There are two proverbs peculiar to this
country.'

'You mean the Pendragon one,' observed Roy.

'Yes.'

> 'Let Uter Pendragon do what he can,
> Eden will run where Eden ran.'

'You look mystified, Miss Lambert; but at Pendragon Castle
in Mallerstang there may still be seen traces of an attempt
to turn the waters of Eden from their natural and wonted
channel, and cause them to flow round the castle and fill the
moat.'

'How curious!'

'Proverbs have been rightly defined "as the wisdom of the
many and the wit of one."   In one particular I believe this
saying has a deep truth hidden in it.   One who has studied the
Westmorland character, says that its meaning is, that the
people living on the banks of the Eden are as firm and persevering in their own way as the river itself; and that when they
have once made up their minds as to what is their duty, all
attempts to turn them aside from walking in the right way and
doing their duty are equally futile.'

'Hurrah for the Edenites!' exclaimed Roy, enthusiastically.
'I don't believe there is a county in England to beat Westmorland.'

'I must tell you what a quaint old writer says of it.   "Here is cold comfort from nature," he writes, "but somewhat of warmth from industry : that the land is barren is God's good pleasure ; the people painful (*i.e.* painstaking), their praise." But I am afraid I must not enlighten your minds any more on proverbial philosophy, as it is time for me to set off on my evening round.   A doctor can use scant ceremony, Miss Lambert.'

'It is time you dismissed us,' returned Mildred, rising ; ' we have trespassed too long on your time already ;' but, in spite of her efforts, she failed to collect her party.   Only Olive accompanied her home.   Roy returned to his painting and whistling, and Polly stayed behind to water the flowers and keep him company.

The next day proved fine and cloudless, and at the appointed time the old vicarage wagonette started off, with its bevy of boys and girls, with Mildred to act as *chaperone.*

Mildred was loath to leave her brother alone for so long a day, but Dr. Heriot promised to look in on him, and bring her a report in the afternoon.

The drive to Castlesteads was a long one, but Roy was in one of his absurd moods, and Polly and he kept up a lively exchange of *repartee* and jest, which amused the rest of the party.   On their way they passed Musgrave, the church and vicarage lying pleasantly in the green meadows, on the very banks of the Eden ; but Roy snorted contemptuously over Mildred's admiring exclamation—

'It looks very pretty from this distance, and would make a tolerable picture ; and I don't deny the walk by the river-bank is pleasant enough in summer-time, but you would be sorry to live there all the year round, Aunt Milly.'

'Is the vicarage so comfortless, then ?'

'Vicarage ! It is little better than a cottage.   It is positively bare, and mean, miserable little wainscoted rooms looking on a garden full of currant-bushes and London-pride.   In winter the river floods the meadows, and comes up to the sitting-room window ; just a place for rheumatism and agues and low fevers. I wonder Mr. Wigram can endure it !'

'There are the Northcotes overtaking us, Cardie,' interrupted Chriss, eagerly ; 'give the browns a touch-up ; I don't want them to pass us.'

Richard did as he was requested, and the browns evidently resenting the liberty, there was soon a good distance between the two wagonettes ; and shortly afterwards the pretty little village of Castlesteads came in sight, with its beeches and white cottages and tall May-pole.

'There is no time to be lost, Cardie. I can hear the band already. We must make straight for the park.'

'We had better get down and walk, then, while George sees to the horses, or we shall lose the procession. Come, Aunt Milly, we are a little late, I am afraid ; and we must introduce you to Mrs. Chesterton of the Hall in due form.'

Mildred obeyed, and the little party hurried along the road, where knots of gaily-dressed people were already stationed to catch the first glimpse of the rush-bearers. The park gates were wide open, and a group of ladies, with a tolerable sprinkling of gentlemen, were gathered under the shady trees.

Mr. Delaware came striding across the grass in his cassock, with his college cap in his hand.

'You are only just in time,' he observed, shaking hands cordially with Mildred ; 'the children are turning the corner by the schools. I must go and meet them. Susie, will you introduce Miss Lambert to these ladies ?'

Mrs. Chesterton of the Hall was a large, placid-looking woman, with a motherly, benevolent face ; she was talking to a younger lady, in very fashionable attire, whom Mrs. Delaware whispered was Mrs. de Courcy, of the Grange : her husband, Major de Courcy, was at a little distance, with Mr. Chesterton and the Trelawnys.

Mildred had just time to bow to Ethel, when the loud, inspiriting blare of brazen instruments was heard outside the park gates. There was a burst of joyous music, and a faint sound of cheering, and then came the procession of children, with their white frocks and triumphant crowns.

The real garland used for the rush-bearing is of the shape of the old coronation crowns, and was formerly so large that it was borne by each child on a cushion ; and even at the present time it was too weighty an ornament to be worn with comfort.

One little maiden had recourse to her mother's support, and many a little hand went up to steady the uneasy diadem.

Mildred, who had never seen such a sight, was struck with the beauty and variety of the crowns. Some were of brilliant scarlet and white, such as covered May Chesterton's fair curls ; others were of softer violet. One was of beautifully-shaped roses ; and another and humbler one of heliotrope and large-eyed pansies. Even the cottage garlands were woven with taste and fancy. One of the poorest children, gleaning in lanes and fields, had formed her crown wholly of buttercups and ox-eyed daisies, and wore it proudly.

A lame boy, who had joined the procession, carried his garland in the shape of a large cross, which he held aloft. Mildred watched the bright colours of moving flowers through the trees, and listened to the music half-dreamily, until Richard touched her arms.

'Every one is following the procession. You will lose the prettiest part of the whole, if you stand here, Aunt Milly; the children always have a dance before they go into church.' And so saying, he piloted her through the green park in the direction of the crowd.

By and by, they came to a little strip of lawn, pleasantly shaded by trees, and here they found the rush-bearers drawn up in line, with the crowns at their feet; the sun was shining, the butterflies flitted over the children's heads, the music struck up gaily, the garlands lay in purple and crimson splashes of colour on the green sward.

'Wouldn't it make a famous picture?' whispered Roy, eagerly. 'I should like to paint it, and send it to the Royal Academy—"The Westmorland Rush-bearing." Doesn't May look a perfect fairy in her white dress, with her curls falling over her neck? That rogue of a Claude has chosen her for his partner. There, they are going to have lemonade and cake, and then they will "trip on the light, fantastic toe," till the church bells ring;' but Mildred was too much absorbed to answer. The play of light and shadow, the shifting colours, the children's innocent faces and joyous laughter, the gaping rustics on the outside of the circle, charmed and interested her. She was sorry when the picture was broken up, and Mr. Delaware and the other clergy formed the children into an orderly procession again.

Mildred and Richard were the last to enter the church, but Miss Trelawny made room for them beside her. The pretty little church was densely crowded, and there was quite an inspiring array of clergy and choristers when the processional hymn was sung. Mr. Delaware gave an appropriate and very eloquent address, and during a pause in the service the church-wardens collected the garlands from the children, which were placed by the officiating priest and the assistant clergy on the altar-steps, or on the sloping sills of the chancel windows, or even on the floor of the sanctuary itself, the sunshine lighting up with vivid hues the many-coloured crowns.

These were left until the following day, when they were placed on a frame made for the purpose at the other end of the church, and there they hung until the next rush-bearing day ; the brown drooping leaves and faded flowers bearing solemn witness of the mutability and decay of all earthly things.

But as Mildred looked at the altar-steps, crowded with the fragrant and innocent offerings of the children, so solemnly blessed and accepted, and heard the fresh young voices lifted up in the crowning hymn of praise, there came to her remembrance some lines she had heard sung in an old city church, when the broidered bags, full of rich offerings, had been laid on the altar :—

> ' Holy offerings rich and rare,
> Offerings of praise and prayer,
> Purer life and purpose high,
> Claspèd hands and lifted eye,
> Lowly acts of adoration
> To the God of our salvation.
> On His altar laid we leave them,
> Christ present them !   God receive them ! '

CHAPTER XI

AN AFTERNOON IN CASTLESTEADS

'The fields were all i' vapour veil'd
  Till, while the warm, breet rays assail'd,
    Up fled the leet, grey mist.
The flowers expanded one by one,
  As fast as the refreshing sun
    Their dewy faces kiss'd.

'And pleasure danced i' mony an e'e
  An' mony a heart, wi' mirth and glee
    Thus flutter'd and excited—
An' this was t' cause, ye'll understand
Some friends a grand picnic had plann'd,
    An' they had been invited.'
      Tom Twisleton's Poems in the Craven Dialect.

It had been arranged that Mildred should form one of the luncheon-party at the vicarage, and that Richard should accompany her, while the rest of the young people were regaled at the Hall, where pretty May Chesterton held a sort of court.

The pleasant old vicarage was soon crowded with gaily-dressed guests—amongst them Mr. Trelawny and his daughter, and the Heaths of Brough.

Mildred, who had a predilection for old houses, found the vicarage much to her taste ; she liked the quaint dimly-lighted rooms, with their deep embrasures, forming small inner rooms —while every window looked on the trim lawn and churchyard.

At luncheon she found herself under Mr. Delaware's special supervision, and soon had abundant opportunity of admiring the straightforward common sense and far-seeing views that had gained him universal esteem ; he was evidently no mean scholar, but what struck Mildred was the simplicity and reticence that veiled his vast knowledge and made him an appreciative listener.

Miss Trelawny, who was seated at his right hand, monopolised the greater share of his attentions, and Mildred fancied that her *naïveté* and freshness were highly attractive, as every now and then an amused smile crossed his face.

Mrs. Delaware bloomed at them from the end of the table. She was rather more quietly dressed and looked prettier than ever, but Mildred noticed that the uneasy look, of which Richard had spoken, crossed her husband's face, as her voice, by no means gently modulated, reached his ears ; evidently he had a vexed sort of affection for the happy dimpling creature, who offended all his pet prejudices, wounded his too sensitive refinement, and disturbed the established *régime* of his scholarly life.

Susie's creams and roses were unimpeachable, and her voice had the clear freshness of a lark, but dearly as he might love her, she could hardly be a companion to her husband in his higher moods—the keynote of sympathy must be wanting between this strangely-assorted couple, Mildred thought, and she wondered if any vague regrets for that youthful romance of his marred the possible harmonies of the present.

Would not a richly-cultivated mind like Ethel Trelawny's, for example, with strong original bias and all kinds of motiveless asceticism, have accorded better with his notions of womanly perfection, the classic features and low-pitched voice gaining by contrast with Susie's loud tuneful key and waste of bloom ?

By an odd coincidence Mildred found herself alone with Mrs. Delaware after luncheon ; the other ladies had already gone over to the park with the vicar, but his wife, who had been detained by some unavoidable business, had asked Mildred to wait for her.

Presently she appeared flushed and radiant.

'It is so good of you to wait, Miss Lambert ; Stephen is so particular, and I was afraid things might go wrong as they did last year ; I suppose he has gone on with the others.'

'Yes.'

'And Miss Trelawny ?'

'I believe so.'

Mrs. Delaware's bright face fell a little.

'Miss Trelawny is a rare talker, at least Stephen says so ; but I never understand whether she is in fun or earnest ; she must be clever, though, or Stephen would not say so much in her praise.'

'I think she amuses him.'

'Stephen does not care for amusement, he is always so terribly in earnest. Sometimes they talk for hours, till my head quite aches with listening to them. Do you think women ought to be so clever, Miss Lambert?' continued Susie, a little wistfully; and Mildred thought what a sweet face she had, and wondered less over Mr. Delaware's choice—after all, blue eyes, when they are clear and loving, have a potent charm of their own.

'I do not know that Miss Trelawny is so very clever,' she returned; 'she is original, but not quite restful; I could understand that she would tire most men.'

'But not men like my Stephen,' betraying in her simplicity some hidden irritation.

'Possibly not for an hour or two, only by continuance. The cleverest man I ever knew,' continued Mildred artfully, 'married a woman without an idea beyond housekeeping; he was an astronomer, and she used to sit working beside him, far into the night, while he carried on his abstruse calculations; he was a handsome man, and she was quite ordinary-looking, but they were the happiest couple I ever knew.'

'Maybe she loved him dearly,' returned Susie simply, but Mildred saw a glittering drop or two on her long eyelashes; and just then they reached the park gates, where they found Mr. Delaware waiting for them.

The park now presented a gay aspect, the sun shone on the old Hall and its trimly-kept gardens, its parterres blazing with scarlet geraniums, and verbenas, and heliotropes, and its shady winding walks full of happy groups.

On the lawn before the Hall the band was playing, and rustic couples were already arranging themselves for the dance, tea was brewing in the great white tent, with its long tables groaning with good cheer, children were playing amongst the trees; in the meadow below the sports were held—the hound trail, pole-leaping, long-leaping, trotting-matches and wrestling filling up the afternoon.

Mildred was watching the dancers when she heard herself accosted by name; there was no mistaking those crisp tones, they could belong to no other than Ethel Trelawny.

Miss Trelawny was looking remarkably well to-day, her cheeks had a soft bloom, and the rippling dark-brown hair strayed most becomingly from under the little white bonnet; she looked brighter, happier, more animated.

'I thought you were busy in the tent, Miss Trelawny.'

Ethel laughed.

'I gave up my place to Mrs. Cooper; it is too much to expect any one to remain in that stiffling place four mortal hours; just fancy, Miss Lambert, tea commences at 2 P.M. and goes on till 6.'

'I pity the tea-makers; Mrs. Delaware is one of course.'

'She is far from cool, but perfectly happy. Mrs. Delaware's table is always crowded, mine was so empty that I gave it up to Mrs. Cooper in disgust. Mr. Delaware will give me a scolding for deserting my post, but I daresay I shall survive it. How cool it is under these trees; shall we walk a little?'

'If you like; but I enjoy watching those dancers.'

'Distance will lend enchantment to the view—there is no poetry of movement there;' pointing a little disdainfully to a clumsy bumpkin who was violently impelling a full-blown rustic beauty through the mazes of a waltz.

'What is lost in grace is made up in heartiness,' returned Mildred, bent on defending her favourite pastime. 'Look how lightly and well that girl in the lilac muslin is dancing; she would hardly disgrace a ballroom.'

'She looks very happy,' returned Ethel, a little enviously; 'she is one of Mr. Delaware's favourite scholars, and I think she is engaged to that young farmer with whom she is dancing; by the bye, have you seen Dr. Heriot?'

'No. I did not know he was here.'

'He was in the tent just now looking for you. He said he had promised to report himself as soon as he arrived. He found fault with the cup of tea I gave him, and then he and Richard went off together.'

Mildred smiled; she thought she knew the reason why Miss Trelawny looked so animated. She knew Dr. Heriot was a great favourite up at Kirkleatham, in spite of the many battles that were waged between him and Ethel; somehow she felt glad herself that Dr. Heriot had come.

Following Miss Trelawny's lead, they had crossed the park and the pleasure garden, and were now in a little grove skirting the fields, which led to a lonely summer-house, set in the heart of the green meadows, with an enchanting view of the blue hills beyond.

'What a lovely spot,' observed Mildred.

'Here would my hermit spirit dwell apart,' laughed Ethel. 'What a sense of freedom those wide hills give one. I am glad

9

you like it,' she continued, more simply. 'I brought you here because I saw you cared for these sort of things.'

'Most people care for a beautiful prospect.'

'Yes; but theirs is mere surface admiration—yours goes deeper. Do you know, Miss Lambert, I was wondering all luncheon time why you always look so restful and contented?'

'Perhaps because I am so,' returned Mildred, smiling.

'Yes, but you have known trouble; your face says so plainly; there are lines that have no business to be there; in some things you are older than your age.'

'You are a keen observer, Miss Trelawny.'

'Do not answer me like that,' she returned, a little hurt; 'you are so earnest yourself that you ought to allow for earnestness in others. I knew directly I heard your voice that I should like you; does my frankness displease you?' turning on her abruptly.

'On the contrary, it pleases me!' replied Mildred, but she blushed a little under the scrutiny of this strange girl.

'You are undemonstrative, so am I to most people; but directly I saw your face and heard you speak I knew yours was a true nature, and I was anxious to win you for my friend; you do not know how sadly I want one,' she continued, her voice trembling a little. 'One cannot live without sympathy.'

'It is not meant that we should do so,' returned Mildred, softly.

'I believe mine to be an almost isolated case,' returned Ethel. 'No mother, no ——' she checked herself, turned pale and hurried on, 'with only a childlike memory of what brother-love really is, and a faint-off remembrance of a little white wasted face resting on a pillow strewn with lilies. I was very young then, but I remember how I cried when they told me my baby-sister was an angel in heaven.'

'How old were you when your brothers died?' asked Mildred, gently. Ethel's animation had died away, and a look of deep sadness now crossed her face.

'I was only ten, Rupert was twelve, and Sidney fourteen; such fine manly boys, Sid. especially, and so good to me. Mamma never got over their death; and then I lost her; it seems so lonely their leaving me behind. Sometimes I wonder for what purpose I am left, and if I have much to suffer before I am allowed to join them?' and Ethel's eyes grew fixed and dreamy, till Mildred's sympathetic voice roused her.

'I should think nothing can replace a brother. When I

was young I used to wish I were one of a large family. I
remember envying a girl who told me she had seven sisters.'

Ethel looked up with a melancholy smile.

'I wonder what it would be like to have a sister? I mean
if Ella had lived—she would be sixteen now. I used to have
all sorts of strange fancies about her when I was a child.
Mamma once read me Longfellow's poem of *Resignation*, and it
made a great impression on me. You remember the words,
Miss Lambert?' and Ethel repeated in her fresh sweet voice—

> ' "Not as a child shall we again behold her,
>   For when with raptures wild,
>   In our embraces we again enfold her,
>   She will not be a child.
>
> "But a fair maiden in her Father's mansion,
>   Clothed with celestial grace,
>   And beautiful with all the soul's expansion
>   Shall we behold her face."

That image of progressive beatitude and expanding youth
seized strongly upon my childish imagination.' Mildred's
smile was a sufficient answer, and Ethel went on in the same
dreamy tone, 'After a time the little dead face became less
distinct, and in its place I became conscious of a strange
feeling, of a new sort of sister-love. I thought of Ella growing
up in heaven, not learning the painful lessons I was so wearily
learning here, but schooled by angels in the nobler mysteries of
love; and so strong was this belief, that when I was naughty
or had given way to temper, I would cry myself to sleep,
thinking that Ella would be disappointed in me, and often I
did not dare look up at the stars for fear her eyes should be
sorrowfully looking down on me. You will think me a fanciful
visionary, Miss Lambert, but this childish thought has been my
safeguard in many an hour of temptation.'

'I would all our fancies were as pure. You need not fear
that I should laugh at you as visionary, my dear Miss
Trelawny; after all you may have laid your grasp on a great
truth—there can be nothing undeveloped and imperfect in
heaven, and infancy is necessarily imperfect.'

'I never sympathised with the crude fancies of the old
masters,' returned Miss Trelawny; 'the winged heads of their
bodiless cherubs are as unsatisfactory and impalpable as Homer's
flitting shades and shivering ghosts; but your last speech has
chilled me somehow.'

Mildred looked up in surprise; but Ethel's smile reassured her.

'No one but my father ever calls me Ethel—to the world I am Miss Trelawny, even Olive and Chriss are ceremonious, and latterly Mr. Lambert has dropped the old familiar term; somehow it adds to one's feeling of loneliness.'

'Do you mean that you wish me to drop such ceremony?' returned Mildred, laughing a little nervously. 'Ethel! it is a quaint name, hardly musical, and with a suspicion of a lisp, but full of character; it suits you somehow.'

'Then you will use it!' exclaimed Ethel impulsively. 'We are strangers, and yet I have talked to you this afternoon as I have never done to any one before.'

'There you pay me a compliment.'

'You have such a motherly way with you, Mildred—Miss Lambert, I mean.'

Mildred blushed, 'Please do not correct yourself.'

'What! I may call you Mildred? how nice that will be; I shall feel as though you are some wise elder sister, you have got such tender old-fashioned ways, and yet they suit you somehow. I like you better, I think, because there seems nothing young about you.'

Ethel's speech gave Mildred a little pang—unselfish and free from vanity as her nature was, she was still only a woman, and regret for her passing youth shadowed her brightness for a moment. Until her mother's death she had never given it a thought. Why did Ethel's fresh beauty and glorious young vitality raise the faint wish, now heard for the first time, that she were more like the youthful and fairer Mildred of long ago? but even before Ethel had finished speaking, the unworthy thought was banished.

'I believe a wearing and long-continued trouble ages more than years; women have no right to grow sober before thirty, I know. Some lighter natures go haymaking between the tombs, she went on quaintly, and as Ethel looked up astonished at the strange simile—'I have borrowed my metaphor from a homely circumstance, but as I sat working in the cool lobby yesterday they were making hay in the sunny churchyard, and somehow the idea seemed incongruous—the idea of gleaning sweetness and nourishment from decay. But does it not strike you we are becoming very philosophical—what are the little rush-bearers doing now I wonder?'

'After all, your human sympathies are less exclusive than

mine,' returned her companion, regretfully. 'I like this cool
retreat better than the crowded park ; but we are not to be left
any longer in peace,' she continued, with a slight access of colour,
' there are Dr. Heriot and Richard bearing down on us.' Mildred
was not sorry to be disturbed, as she thought it was high time
to look after Olive and Chriss, an intention that Dr. Heriot
instantly negatived by placing himself at her side.

'There is not the slightest necessity—they are under Mrs.
Chesterton's wing,' he remarked coolly ; 'we have been searching
the park and grounds fruitlessly for an hour, till Richard hit on
this spot ; the hiding-place is worthy of Miss Trelawny.'

'You mean it is romantic enough ; your words have a double
edge, Dr. Heriot.'

'Pax,' he returned, laughingly, 'it is too hot to renew the
skirmish we carried on in the tent. I have brought you a
favourable report of your brother, Miss Lambert ; Mr. Warden,
an old college chum of his, had arrived unexpectedly, and he
was showing him the church.'

One of Mildred's sweet smiles flitted over her face.

'How good you are to take all this trouble for me, Dr.
Heriot.'

Dr. Heriot gave her an inscrutable look in which drollery
came uppermost.

'Are you given to weigh fractional kindnesses in your
neighbour ? Most people give gratitude in grains for whole
ounces of avoirdupois weight ; what a grateful soul yours is,
Miss Lambert.'

'The moral being that Dr. Heriot dislikes thanks, Mildred.'

Dr. Heriot gave a low exclamation of surprise, which evidently
irritated Miss Trelawny. 'It has come to that already, has it,'
he said to himself with an inward chuckle, but Mildred could
make nothing of his look of satisfaction and Ethel's aggravated
colour.

'Why don't you deliver us one of your favourite tirades
against feminine caprice and impulse ?' observed Miss Trelawny,
in a piqued voice.

'When caprice and impulse take the form of wisdom,' was
the answer in a meaning tone, 'Mentor's office of rebuke fails.'

Ethel arched her eyebrows slightly, 'Mentor approves
then ?'

'Can you doubt it ?' in a more serious tone. 'I feel we
may still have hopes of you ;' then turning to Mildred, with
the play of fun still in his eyes, 'Our aside baffles you, Miss

Lambert. Miss Trelawny is good enough to style me her Mentor, which means that she has given me a right to laugh at her nonsense and talk sense to her sometimes.'

'You are too bad,' returned Ethel in a low voice ; but she was evidently hurt by the raillery, gentle as it was.

'Miss Trelawny forms such extravagant ideals of men and women, that no one but a moral Anak can possibly reach to her standard ; the rest of us have to stand tiptoe in the vain effort to raise ourselves.'

'Dr. Heriot, how can you be so absurd ?' laughed Mildred.

'It must be very fatiguing to stand on tiptoe all one's life ; perhaps we might feel a difficulty of breathing in your rarer atmosphere, Miss Trelawny—fancy one's ideas being always in full dress, from morning to night. When you marry, do you always mean to dish up philosophy with your husband's breakfast ?'

The hot colour mounted to Ethel's forehead.

'I give you warning that he will yawn over it sometimes, and refresh himself by talking to his dogs ; even Bayard, that peerless knight, *sans peur* and *sans reproche*, could be a little sulky at times, you may depend on it !'

'Bayard is not my hero now,' she returned, trying to pluck up a little spirit with which to answer him. 'I have decided lately in favour of Sir Philip Sidney, as my beau-ideal of an English gentleman.'

'Rex and I chose him for our favourite ages ago,' observed Richard eagerly, who until now had remained silent.

'Yes,' continued Ethel, enthusiastically, 'that one act of unselfishness has invested him with the reverence of centuries ; can you not fancy the awful temptation, Mildred—the death thirst under the scorching sun, the unendurable agony of untended wounds, the cup of cold water, just tasted and refused for the sake of the poor wretch lying beside him ; one could lay down one's life for such a man as that !'

'Yes, it was a gentlemanly action,' observed Dr. Heriot, coolly ; and as Ethel's face expressed resentment at the phrase, 'have you ever thought how much is comprehended under the term gentleman ? To me the word is fuller and more comprehensive than that of hero ; your heroes are such noisy fellows ; there is always a sound of the harp, sackbut, psaltery, and dulcimer about them ; and they pass their life in fitting their attitudes to their pedestal.'

'Dr. John is riding one of his favourite hobbies,' observed

Richard, in a low voice. 'Never mind, he admires Sir Philip as much as we do !' .

'True, Cardie ; but though I do not deny the heroism of the act, I maintain that many a man in his place would do the same thing. Have we no stories of heroism in our Crimean annals ? Amongst the hideous details of the Indian mutiny were there no deeds that might match that of the dying soldier at Zutphen ?'

'Perhaps so ; but all the same I have a right to my own ideal.'

A mocking smile swept over Dr. Heriot's face.

'Virtue in an Elizabethan ruff surpasses virtue clad in nineteenth century broadcloth and fustian. I suspect even in your favourite Sir Philip's case distance lends enchantment to the view ; he wrote very sweetly on Arcadia, but who knows but a twinge of the gout may not have made him cross ?'

'How you persist in misunderstanding me,' returned Ethel, with a touch of feeling in her voice. 'I suppose as usual I have brought this upon myself, but why will you believe that I am so hard to please ? After all you are right ; Bayard and Sir Philip Sidney are only typical characters of their day ; there must be great men even in this generation.'

'There are downright honest men—men who are not ashamed to confess to flaws and inconsistencies, and possible twinges of gout.'

'There you spoil all,' said Mildred, with an amused look ; but Dr. Heriot's mischievous mood was not to be restrained.

'One of these honest fellows with a tolerably tough will, and not an ounce of imagination in his whole composition—positively of the earth, earthy—will strike the right chord that is to bring Hermione from off her pedestal—don't frown, Miss Trelawny ; you may depend upon it those old Turks were right, and there is a fate in these things.' .

Ethel curved her long neck superbly, and turned with a . slightly contemptuous expression to Richard : her patience was exhausted.

'I think my father will be wondering what has become of me ; will you take me to him ?'

'There they go, Ethel and her knight ; how little she knows that perhaps her fate is beside her ; they are too much of an age, but that lad has the will of half a dozen men.'

'Why do you tease her so ?' remonstrated Mildred. Dr. Heriot still retained his seat comfortably beside her. 'She is very girlish and romantic, but she hardly deserved such biting sarcasms.'

'Was I sarcastic?' he asked, evidently surprised. 'Poor child! I would not have hurt her for the world. And these luxuriant fancies need pruning; hers is a fine nature run to seed for want of care and proper nurture.'

'I think she needs sympathy,' returned gentle Mildred.

'Then she has sought it in the right quarter,' with a look she could hardly misunderstand, 'and where the supply is always equal to the demand; but I warn you she is somewhat of an egotist.'

'Oh no!' warmly. 'I am sure Miss Trelawny is not selfish.'

'That depends how you interpret the phrase. She would give you all her jewels without a sigh, but you must allow her to talk out all her fine feeling in return. After all, she is only like others of her sex.'

'You are in one of your misanthropical moods.'

'Men are not always feeling their own pulse and detailing their moral symptoms, depend upon it; it is quite a feminine weakness, Miss Lambert. I think I know one woman tolerably free from the disease, at least outwardly;' and as Mildred blushed under the keen, yet kindly look, Dr. Heriot somewhat abruptly changed the subject.

CHAPTER XII

THE WELL-MEANING MISCHIEF-MAKER

'And in that shadow I have pass'd along,
    Feeling myself grow weak as it grew strong ;
Walking in doubt and searching for the way,
    And often at a stand—as now to-day.

    .   .   .   .

Perplexities do throng upon my sight
    Like scudding fogbanks, to obscure the light ;
Some new dilemma rises every day,
    And I can only shut my eyes and pray.'—ANON.

MILDRED had been secretly reproaching herself for allowing Dr. Heriot's pleasing conversation so completely to monopolise her, and even her healthy conscience felt a pang something like remorse when, half an hour later, they came upon Olive sitting alone on a tree-trunk, having evidently stolen apart from her companions to indulge unobserved in one of her usual reveries.

She was too much absorbed to notice them till addressed by name, and then, to Mildred's surprise, she started, coloured from chin to brow, and, muttering some excuse, seemed only anxious to effect her escape.

'I hope you are not composing an Ode to Melancholy,' observed Dr. Heriot, with one of his quizzical looks. 'You look like a forsaken wood-nymph, or a disconsolate Chloe, or Jacques' sobbing deer, or any other uncomfortable image of loneliness. What an unsociable creature you are, Olive.'

'Why are you not with Chrissy and the Chestertons ? I hope we have not all neglected you,' interposed Mildred in her soft voice, for she saw that Olive shrank from Dr. Heriot's good-humoured raillery. 'Are you tired, dear ? Roy has not ordered the carriage for another hour, I am afraid.'

'No, I am not tired ; I was only thinking. I will find Chriss,' returned Olive, stammering and blushing still more under her aunt's affectionate scrutiny. 'Don't come with me, please,

Aunt Milly. I like being alone.' And before Mildred could answer, she had disappeared down a little side-walk, and was now lost to sight.

Dr. Heriot laughed at Mildred's discomposed look.

'You remind me of the hen when she hatched the duckling and found it taking kindly to the unknown element. You must get used to Olive's odd ways; she is decidedly original. I should not wonder if we disturbed her in the first volume of some wonderful scheme-book, where all the heroines are martyrs and the hero is a full-length portrait of Richard. I warn you all her *dénouements* will be disastrous. Olive does not believe in happiness for herself or other people.'

'How hard you are on her!' returned Mildred, finding it impossible to restrain a smile; but in reality she felt a little anxious. Olive had seemed more than usually absorbed during the last few days; there was a concentrated gravity in her manner that had struck Mildred more than once, but all questioning had been in vain. 'I am not unhappy—at least, not more than usual. I am only thinking out some troublesome thoughts,' she had said when Mildred had pressed her the previous night. 'No, you cannot do anything for me, Aunt Milly. I only want to help myself and other people to do right.' And Mildred, who was secretly weary of this endless scrupulosity, and imagined it was only a fresh attack of Olive's troublesome conscience, was fain to rest content with the answer, though she reproached herself not a little afterwards for a selfish evasion of a manifest duty.

The remainder of the day passed over pleasantly enough. Dr. Heriot had contrived to make his peace with Miss Trelawny, for she had regained her old serenity of manner when Mildred saw her again. She came just as they were starting, to beg that Mildred would spend a long day at Kirkleatham House.

'Papa is going over to Appleby, to the Sessions Court, and I shall be alone all day to-morrow. Do come, Mildred,' she pleaded. 'You do not know what a treat it will be to me.' And though Mildred hesitated, her objections were all overruled by Richard, who insisted that nobody wanted her, and that a holiday would do her good.

Richard's arguments prevailed, and Mildred thoroughly enjoyed her holiday. Some hours of unrestrained intercourse only convinced her that Ethel Trelawny's faults lay on the surface, and were the result of a defective education and disadvantageous circumstances, while the real nobility of her character revealed itself in every thought and word. She had laid aside the slight hauteur and extravagance that marred simplicity and provoked the just censure of men like Dr. Heriot ; lesser natures she delighted to baffle by an eccentricity that was often ill-timed and out of place, but to-day the stilts, as Dr. Heriot termed them, were out of sight. Mildred's sincerity touched the right keynote, her brief captiousness vanished, unconsciously she showed the true side of her character. Gentle, though unsatisfied ; childishly eager, and with a child's purity of purpose ; full of lofty aims, unpractical, waiting breathless for mere visionary happiness for which she knew no name ; a sweet, though subtle egotist, and yet tender - hearted and womanly ;—no wonder Ethel Trelawny was a fascinating study to Mildred that long summer's day.

Mildred listened with unwearied sympathy while Ethel dwelt pathetically on her lonely and purposeless life, with its jarring gaieties and absence of congenial fellowship.

'Papa is dreadfully methodical and business-like. He always finds fault with me because I am so unpractical, and will never let me help him, or talk about what interests him ; and then he cares for politics. He was so disappointed because he failed in the last election. His great ambition is to be a member of parliament. I know they got him to contest the Kendal borough ; but he had no chance, though he spent I am afraid to say how much money. The present member was too popular, and was returned by a large majority. He was very angry because I did not sympathise with him in his disappointment ; but how could I, knowing it was for the honour of the position that he wanted it, and not for the highest motives ? And then the bribery and corruption were so sickening.'

'I do not think we ought to impute any but the highest motives until we know to the contrary,' returned Mildred, mildly.

Ethel coloured. 'You think me disloyal ; but papa knows my sentiments well ; we shall never agree on these questions— never. I fancy men in general take a far less high standard than women.'

'You are wrong there,' returned practical Mildred, firing up at this sweeping assertion, which had a taint of heresy in her ears. 'Because men live instead of talk their opinions, you misjudge them. Do you think the single eye and the steady aim is not a necessary adjunct of all real manhood ? Look at my brother, look at Dr. Heriot, for example ; they are no mere worldlings, leading purposeless existences ; they are both hard workers and deep thinkers.'

'We will leave Dr. Heriot out of the question; I see he has begun to be perfection in your eyes, Mildred. Nay,'—and Mildred drew herself up with a little dignity and looked annoyed,—'I meant nothing but the most platonic admiration, which I assure you he reciprocates in an equal degree. He thinks you a very superior person—so well-principled, so entirely unselfish; he is always quoting you as an example, and——'

'I agree with you that we should leave personalities in the background,' returned Mildred, hastily, and taking herself to task for feeling aggrieved at Dr. Heriot calling her a superior person. The argument waxed languid at this point; Ethel became a little lugubrious under Mildred's reproof, and relapsed into pathetic egotism again, pouring out her longings for vocation, work, sympathy, and all the disconnected iota of female oratory worked up into enthusiasm.

'I want work, Mildred.'

'And yet you dream dreams and see visions.'

'Hush! please let me finish. I do not mean make-believes, shifts to get through the day, fanciful labours befitting rank and station, but real work, that will fill one's heart and life.'

'Yours is a hungry nature. I fear the demand would double the supply. You would go starved from the very place where we poor ordinary mortals would have a full meal.'

Ethel pouted. 'I wish you would not borrow metaphors from our tiresome Mentor. I declare, Mildred, your words have always more or less a flavour of Dr. Heriot's.'

Mildred quietly took up her work. 'You know how to reduce me to silence.'

But Ethel playfully impeded the sewing by laying her crossed hands over it.

'Dr. Heriot's name seems an apple of discord between us, Mildred.'

'You are so absurd about him.'

'I am always provoked at hearing his opinions second-hand. I have less comfort in talking to him than to any one else; I always seem to be airing my own foolishness.'

'At least, I am not accountable for that,' returned Mildred, pointedly.

'No,' returned Ethel, with her charming smile, which at once disarmed Mildred's prudery. 'You wise people think and talk much alike; you are both so hard on mere visionaries. But I can bear it more patiently from you than from him.'

'I cannot solve riddles,' replied Mildred, in her old sensible manner. 'It strikes me that you have fashioned Dr. Heriot into a sort of bugbear—a *bête noir* to frighten naughty, prejudiced children ; and yet he is truly gentle.'

'It is the sort of gentleness that rebukes one more than sternness,' returned Ethel in a low voice. 'How odd it is, Mildred, when one feels compelled to show the worst side of oneself, to the very people, too, whom one most wishes to propitiate, or, at least—but my speech threatens to be as incoherent as Olive's.'

'I know what you mean ; it comes of thinking too much of a mere expression of opinion.'

'Oh no,' she returned, with a quick blush ; 'it only comes from a rash impulse to dethrone Mentor altogether—the idea of moral leading reins are so derogatory after childhood has passed.'

'You must give me a hint if I begin to lecture in my turn. I shall forget sometimes you are not Olive or Chriss.'

The soft, brilliant eyes filled suddenly with tears.

'I could find it in my heart to wish I were even Olive, whom you have a right to lecture. How nice it would be to belong to you really, Mildred—to have a real claim on your time and sympathy.'

'All my friends have that,' was the soft answer. 'But how dark it is growing—the longest day must have an end, you see.'

'That means—you are going,' she returned, regretfully. 'Mother Mildred is thinking of her children. I shall come down and see you and them soon, and you must promise to find me some work.'

Mildred shook her head. 'It must not be my finding if it is to satisfy your exorbitant demands.'

'We shall see ; anyhow you have left me plenty to think about—you will leave a little bit of sunshine behind you in this dull, rambling house. Shall you go alone ? Richard or Royal ought to have walked up to meet you.'

'Richard half promised he would, but I do not mind a lonely walk.' And Mildred nodded brightly as she turned out of the lodge gates. She looked back once ; the moon was rising, a star shone on the edge of a dark cloud, the air was sweet with the breath of honeysuckles and roses, a slight breeze stirred Ethel's white dress as she leaned against the heavy swing-gate, the sound of a horse's hoofs rang out from the distance, the next moment she had disappeared into the shrubbery, and Dr. Heriot walked his horse all the way to the town by the side of Mildred.

Mildred's day had refreshed and exhilarated her; congenial society was as new as it was delightful. 'Somehow I think I feel younger instead of older,' thought the quiet woman, as she turned up the vicarage lane and entered the courtyard; 'after all, it is sweet to be appreciated.'

'Is that you, Aunt Milly? You look ghost-like in the gloaming.'

'Naughty boy, how you startled me! Why did not you or Richard walk up to Kirkleatham House?'

'We could not,' replied Roy, gravely. 'My father wanted Richard, and I—I did not feel up to it. Go in, Aunt Milly; it is very damp and chilly out here to-night.' And Roy resumed his former position of lounging against the trellis-work of the porch. There was a touch of despondency in the lad's voice and manner that struck Mildred, and she lingered for a moment in the porch.

'Are you not coming in too?'

'No, thank you, not at present,' turning away his face.

'Is there anything the matter, Roy?'

'Yes—no. One must have a fit of the dumps sometimes; life is not all syrup of roses'—rather crossly for Roy.

'Poor old Royal—what's amiss, I wonder? There, I will not tease you,' touching his shoulder caressingly, but with a half-sigh at the reticence of Betha's boys. 'Where is Richard?'

'With my father—I thought I told you;' then, mastering his irritability with an effort, 'please don't go to them, Aunt Milly, they are discussing something. Things are rather at sixes and sevens this evening, thanks to Livy's interference; she will tell you all about it. Good-night, Aunt Milly;' and as though afraid of being further questioned, Roy strode down the court, where Mildred long afterwards heard him kicking up the beck gravel, as a safe outlet and vent for pent-up irritability.

Mildred drew a long breath as she went upstairs. 'I shall pay dearly for my pleasant holiday,' she thought. She could hear low voices in earnest talk as she passed the study, but as she stole noiselessly down the lobby no sound reached her from the girls' room, and she half hoped Olive was asleep.

As she opened her own door, however, there was a slight sound as of a caught breath, and then a quick sob, and to her dismay she could just see in the faint light the line of crouching shoulders and a bent figure huddled up near the window that could belong to no other than Olive. It must be confessed that Mildred's heart shrank for a moment from the weary task that lay before her; but the next instant genuine pity and compassion banished the unworthy thought.

'My poor child, what is this?'

'Oh, Aunt Milly,' with a sort of gasp, 'I thought you would never come.'

'Never mind; I am here now. Wait a moment till I strike a light,' commenced Mildred, cheerfully; but Olive interrupted her with unusual fretfulness.

'Please don't; I can talk so much better in the dark. I came in here because Chrissy was awake, and I could not bear her talk.'

'Very well, my dear, it shall be as you wish,' returned Mildred, gently; and the soft warm hands closed over the girl's chill, nervous fingers with comforting pressure. A strong restful nature like Mildred's was the natural refuge of a timid despondent one such as Olive's. The poor girl felt a sensation something like comfort as she groped her way a little nearer to her aunt, and felt the kind arm drawing her closer.

'Now tell me all about it, my dear.'

Olive began, but it was difficult for Mildred to follow the long rambling confession; with all her love for truth, Olive's morbid sensitiveness tinged most things with exaggeration. Mildred hardly knew if her timidity and incoherence were not jumbling facts and suppositions together with a great deal of intuitive wisdom and perception. There was a sad amount of guess-work and unreality, but after a few leading questions, and by dint of allowing Olive to tell her story in her own way, she contrived to get tolerably near the true state of the case.

It appeared that Olive had for a long time been seriously unhappy about her brothers. Truthful and uncompromising herself, there had seemed to her a want of integrity and a blamable lack of openness in their dealings with their father. With the best intentions, they were absolutely deceiving him by leaving him in such complete ignorance of their wishes and intentions. Royal especially was making shipwreck of his father's hopes concerning him, devoting most of his time and energies to a secret pursuit; while his careless preparation for his tutor was practical, if not actual, dishonesty.

'At least Cardie works hard enough,' interrupted Mildred at this point.

'Yes, because it will serve either purpose ; but, Aunt Milly, he ought to tell papa how he dreads the idea of being ordained ; it is not right ; he is unfit for it ; it is worse than wrong—absolute sacrilege ;' and Olive poured out tremblingly into her aunt's shocked ear that she knew Cardie had doubts, that he was unhappy about himself. No—no one had told her, but she knew it ; she had watched him, and heard him talk, and she burst into tears as she told Mildred that once he absolutely sneered at something in his father's sermon which he declared obsolete, and not a matter of faith at all.

'But, my dear,' interrupted the elder woman, anxiously, 'my brother ought to know. I—some one—must speak to Richard.'

'Oh, Aunt Milly, you will hear—it is I—who have done the mischief ; but you told me there were no such things as conflicting duties ; and what is the use of a conscience if it be not to guide and make us do unpleasant things ?'

'You mean you spoke to Richard ?'

'I have often tried to speak to him, but he was always angry, and muttered something about my interference ; he could not bear me to read him so truly. I know it was all Mr. Macdonald. Papa had him to stay here for a month, and he did Cardie so much harm.'

'Who is he—I never heard of him ?' And Olive explained, in her rambling way, that he was an old college friend of her father's and a very clever barrister, and he had come to them to recruit after a long illness. According to her accounts, his was just the sort of character to attract a nature like Richard's. His brilliant and subtle reasoning, his long and interesting disquisitions on all manner of subjects, his sceptical hints, conveying the notion of danger, and yet never exactly touching on forbidden ground, though they involved a perilous breadth of views, all made him a very unsafe companion for Richard's clever, inquisitive mind. Olive guessed, rather than knew, that things were freely canvassed in those long country walks that would have shocked her father ; though, to his credit be it said, Henry Macdonald had no idea of the mischievous seed he had scattered in the ardent soil of a young and undeveloped nature.

Mildred was very greatly dismayed too when she heard that Richard had read books against which he had been warned, and which must have further unsettled his views. 'I think mamma guessed he had something on his mind, for she was always trying to make him talk to papa, and telling him papa could help him; but I heard him say to her once that he could not bear to disappoint him so, that he must have time, and battle through it alone. I know mamma could not endure Mr. Macdonald; and when papa wanted to have him again, she said, once quite decidedly, "No, she did not like him, and he was not good for Richard." I noticed papa seemed quite surprised and taken aback.'

'Well, go on, my dear;' for Olive sighed afresh at this point, as though it were difficult to proceed.

'Of course you will think me wrong, Aunt Milly. I do myself now; but if you knew how I thought about it, till my head ached and I was half stupid!—but I worked myself up to believe that I ought to speak to papa.'

'Ah!' Mildred checked the exclamation that rose to her lips, fearing lest a weary argument should break the thread of Olive's narrative, which now showed signs of flowing smoothly.

'I half made up my mind to ask your advice, Aunt Milly, on the rush-bearing day, but you were tired, and Polly was with you, and——'

'Have I ever been too tired to help you, Olive?' asked Mildred, reproachfully; all the more that an uncomfortable sensation crossed her at the remembrance that she had noticed a wistful anxiety in Olive's eyes the previous night, but had nevertheless dismissed her on the plea of weariness, feeling herself unequal to one of the girl's endless discussions. 'I am sorry—nay, heartily grieved—if I have ever repelled your confidence.'

'Please don't talk so, Aunt Milly; of course it was my fault, but' (timidly) 'I am afraid sometimes I shall tire even you;' and Mildred's pangs of conscience were so intense that she dared not answer; she knew too well that Olive had of late tired her, though she had no idea the girl's sensitiveness had been wounded. A kind of impatience seized her as Olive talked on; she felt the sort of revolt and want of realization that borders the pity of one in perfect health walking for the first time through the wards of a hospital, and met on all sides by the spectacle of mutilated and suffering humanity.

'How shall I ever deal with all these moods of mind?' she thought hopelessly, as she composed herself to listen.

'So you spoke to your father, Olive? Go on; I will tell you afterwards what I think.'

There was a little sternness in the low tones, from which

10

the girl shrank. Of course Aunt Milly thought her wrong and interfering. Well, she had been wrong, and she went on still more humbly :

'I thought it was my duty ; it made me miserable to do it, because I knew Cardie would be angry, though I never knew how angry ; but I got it into my head that I ought to help him, in spite of himself, and because Rex was so weak. You have no idea how weak and vacillating Rex is when it comes to disappointing people, Aunt Milly.'

'Yes, I know ; go on,' was all the answer Mildred vouch-safed to this.

'I brooded over it all St. Peter's day, and at night I could not sleep. I thought of that verse about cutting off the right hand and plucking out the right eye ; it seemed to me it lay between Cardie and speaking the truth, and that no pain ought to hinder me ; and I determined to speak to papa the first opportunity ; and it came to-day. Cardie and Rex were both out, and papa asked me to walk with him to Winton, and then he got tired, and we sat down half-way on a fallen tree, and then I told him.'

'About Richard's views ?'

'About everything. I began with Rex ; I told papa how his very sweetness and amiability made him weak in things ; he so hated disappointing people, that he could not bring himself to say what he wished ; and just now, after his illness and trouble, it seemed doubly hard to do it.'

'And what did he say to that ?'

'He looked grieved ; yes, I am sure he was grieved. He does not believe that Roy knows his own mind, or will ever do much good as an artist ; but all he said was, "I understand— my own boy—afraid of disappointing his father. Well, well, the lad knows best what will make him happy."'

'And then you told him about Richard ?'

'Yes,' catching her breath as though with a painful thought ; 'when I got to Cardie, somehow the words seemed to come of themselves, and it was such a relief telling papa all I thought. It has been such a burden all this time, for I am sure no one but mamma ever guessed how unhappy Cardie really was.'

'You, who know him so well, could inflict this mortification on him—no, I did not mean to say that, you have suffered enough, my child ; but did it not occur to you that you were betraying a sacred confidence ?'

'Confidence, Aunt Milly !'

'Yes, Olive; your deep insight into your brother's character, and your very real affection for him, ought to have guarded you from this mistake. If you had read him so truly as to discover all this for yourself, you should not have imparted this knowledge without warning, knowing how much it would wound his jealous reticence. If you had waited, doubtless Richard's good sense would have induced him at last to confide in his father.'

'Not until it was too late—until he had worn himself out. He gets more jaded and weary every day, Aunt Milly.'

Mildred shook her head.

'The golden rule holds good even here, "To do unto others as we would they should do unto us." How would you like Richard to retail your opinions and feelings, under the impression he owed you a duty?'

'Aunt Milly, indeed I thought I was acting for the best.'

'I do not doubt it, my child; the love that guided you was clearer than the wisdom; but what did Arnold—what did your father say?'

'Oh, Aunt Milly, he looked almost heart-broken; he covered his face with his hands, and I think he was praying; and yet he seemed almost as though he were talking to mamma. I am sure he had forgotten I was there. I heard him say something about having been selfish in his great grief; that he must have neglected his boy, or been hard and cruel to him, or he would never have so repelled his confidence. "Betha's boy, her darling," he kept saying to himself; "my poor Cardie, my poor lad," over and over again, till I spoke to him to rouse him; and then he said,'—here Olive faltered,—' "that I had been a good girl—a faithful little sister,—and that I must try and take her place, and remind them how good and loving she was." And then he broke down. Oh, Aunt Milly, it was so dreadful; and then I made him come back.'

'My poor brother! I knew he would take it to heart.'

'He said it was like a stab to him, for he had always been so proud of Cardie; and it was his special wish to devote his first-born to the service of the Church; and when I asked if he wished it now, he said, vehemently, "A half-hearted service, reluctantly made—God forbid a son of mine should do such wrong!" and then he was silent for a long time; and just at the beginning of the town we met Rex, and papa whispered to me to leave them together.'

'My poor Olive, I can guess what a hard day you have had,' said Mildred, caressingly, as the girl paused in her recital.

'The hardest part was to come;' and Olive shivered, as though suddenly chilled. 'I was not prepared for Rex being so angry; he is so seldom cross, but he said harder things to me than he has said in his life.'

Mildred thought of the harmless kicks on the beck gravel, and the irritability in the porch, and could not forbear a smile. She could not imagine Roy's wrath could be very alarming, especially as Olive owned her father had been very lenient to him, and had promised to give the subject his full consideration. In this case, Olive's interference had really worked good; but Roy's manhood had taken fire at the notion of being watched and talked over; his father's mild hints of moral weakness and dilatoriness had affronted him; and though secretly relieved, the difficulty of revelation had been spared him, he had held his head higher, and had crushed his sister by a tirade against feminine impertinence and interference; and, what hurt her most, had declared his intention of never confiding in such a 'meddlesome Matty again.'

Mildred was thankful the darkness hid her look of amusement at this portion of Olive's lugubrious story, though the girl herself was too weak and cowed to see the ludicrous side of anything; and her voice changed into the old hopeless key as she spoke of Richard's look of withering scorn.

'He was almost too angry to speak to me, Aunt Milly. He said he never would trust me again. I had better not know what he thought of me. I had injured him beyond reparation. I don't know what he meant by that, but Roy told me that he would not have had his father troubled for the world; he could manage his own concerns, spiritual as well as temporal, for himself. And then he sneered; but oh, Aunt Milly, he looked so white and ill. I am sure now that for some reason he did not want papa to know; perhaps things were not so bad as I thought, or he is trying to feel better about it all. Do you think I have done wrong, Aunt Milly?'

And Olive wrung her hands in genuine distress and burst into fresh tears, and sobbed out that she had done for herself now; no one would believe she had said it for the best; even Rex was angry with her—and Cardie, she was sure Cardie would never forgive her.

'Yes, when this has blown over, and he and his father have

come to a full understanding. I have better faith in Cardie's good heart than that.'

But Mildred felt more uneasy than her cheerful words implied. She had seen from the first that Richard had persistently misunderstood his sister ; this fresh interference on her part, as he would term it, touching on a very sore place, would gall and irritate him beyond endurance. He had no conception of the amount of unselfish affection that was already lavished upon him ; in fact he thought Olive provokingly cold and undemonstrative, and chafed at her want of finer feelings. It needed some sort of shock or revelation to enable him to read his sister's character in a truer light, and any kind of one-sided reconciliation would be a very warped and patched affair.

Mildred's clear-sightedness was fully alive to these difficulties ; but it was expedient to comfort Olive, who had relapsed into her former state of agitation. There was clearly no wrong in the case ; want of tact and mistaken kindness were the heaviest sins to be laid to poor Olive's charge ; yet Mildred now found her incoherently accusing herself of wholesale want of principle, of duty, and declaring that she was unworthy of any one's affections.

'I shall call you naughty for the first time, Olive, if I hear any more of this,' interrupted her aunt ; and by infusing a little judicious firmness into her voice, and by dint of management, though not without difficulty, and representing that she herself was in need of rest, she succeeded in persuading the worn-out girl to seek some repose.

Unwilling to trust her out of her sight, she made her share her own bed ; nor did she relax her vigil until the swollen eyelids had closed in refreshing sleep, and the sobbing breaths were drawn more evenly. Once, at an uneasy movement, she started from the doze into which she had fallen, and put aside the long dark hair with a fondling hand ; the moon was then shining from behind the hill, and the beams shone full through the uncurtained windows ; the girl's hands were crossed upon her breast, folded over the tiny silver cross she always wore, a half-smile playing on her lips—

'Cardie is always a good boy, mamma,' she muttered, drowsily, at Mildred's disturbing touch. Olive was dreaming of her mother.

CHAPTER XIII

A YOUTHFUL DRACO AND SOLON

' But thoughtless words may bear a sting
  Where malice hath no place,
  May wake to pain some secret sting
  Beyond thy power to trace.
  When quivering lips, and flushing cheek,
  The spirit's agony bespeak,
  Then, though thou deem thy brother weak,
  Yet soothe his soul to peace.'—S. A. STORRS.

THINGS certainly seemed at sixes and sevens, as Roy phrased it, the next morning. The severe emotions of the previous night had resulted in Olive's case in a miserable sick headache, which would not permit her to raise her head from the pillow. Mildred, who had rightly interpreted the meaning of the wistful glance that followed her to the door, had resolved to take the first opportunity of speaking to her nephews separately, and endeavouring to soften their aggrieved feelings towards their sister; by a species of good fortune she met Roy coming out of his father's room.

Roy had slept off his mighty mood, and kicked away his sullenness, and an hour of Polly's sunshiny influence had restored him to good humour; and though his brow clouded a little at his aunt's first words, and he broke into a bar of careless whistling in a low and displeased key at the notion of her meditation, yet his better feelings were soon wrought upon by a hint of Olive's sufferings, and he consented, though a little condescendingly, to be the bearer of his own embassage of peace.

Olive's heavy eyes filled up with tears when she saw him.

'Dear Rex, this is so kind.'

'I am sorry your head is so bad, Livy,' was the evasive answer, in a sort of good-natured growl. Roy thought it would not do to be too amiable at first. '"You do look precious bad to be sure," as the hangman said to the gentleman he afterwards throttled.   Take my advice, Livy,' seating himself astride the rocking-chair, and speaking confidentially, ' medlars, spelt with either vowel, are very rotten things, and though I would not joke for worlds on such an occasion, it behoves us to stick to our national proverbs, and, as you know as well as I, a burnt child dreads the fire.'

'I will try to remember, Rex ; I will, indeed ; but please make Cardie think I meant it for the best.'

' It was the worst possible best,' replied Roy, gravely, 'and shows what weak understandings you women have—part of the present company excepted, Aunt Milly.   " Age before honesty," and all that sort of thing, you know.'

'You incorrigible boy, how dare you be so rude ?'

' Don't distress the patient, Aunt Milly.   What a weak-eyed sufferer you look, Livy—regularly down in the doleful doldrums. You must have a strong dose of Polly to cheer you up—a grain of quicksilver for every scruple.'

Olive smiled faintly.   ' Oh, Rex, you dear old fellow, are you sure you forgive me ?'

'Very much, thank you,' returned Roy, with a low bow from the rocking-chair.   ' And shall be much obliged by your not mentioning it again.'

'Only one word, just——— '

' Hush,' in a stentorian whisper, ' on your peril not an utterance—not the ghostly semblance of a word.   Aunt Milly, is repentance always such a painful and distressing disorder ? Like the immortal Rosa Dartle, "I only ask for information." I will draw up a diagnosis of the symptoms for the benefit of all the meddlesome Matties of futurity—No, you are right, Livy,' as a sigh from Olive reached him ; ' she was not a nice character in polite fiction, wasn't Matty—and then show it to Dr. John.   Let me see ; symptoms, weak eyes and reddish lids, a pallid exterior, with black lines and circles under the eyes, not according to Euclid—or Cocker—a tendency to laugh nervously at the words of wisdom, which, the conscience reprobating, results in an imbecile grin.'

' Oh, Rex, do—please don't—my head does ache so—and I don't want to laugh.'

'All hysteria, and a fresh attack of scruples—that quicksilver must be administered without delay, I see—hot and cold fits—aguish symptoms, and a tendency to incoherence and extravagance, not to say lightheadedness—nausea, excited by

the very thought of Dr. Murray—and a restless desire to mis-
place words—"do—please don't," being a fair sample. I
declare, Livy, the disease is as novel as it is interesting.'

Mildred left Olive cheered in spite of herself, but with a
fresh access of pain, and went in search of Richard.

He was sitting at the little table writing. He looked up
rather moodily as his aunt entered.

'Breakfast seems late this morning, Aunt Milly. Where is
Rex ?'

'I left him in Olive's room, my dear ;' and as Richard
frowned, 'Olive has been making herself ill with crying, and
has a dreadful headache, and Roy was kind enough to go and
cheer her up.'

No answer, only the scratching of the quill-pen rapidly
traversing the paper.

Mildred stood irresolute for a moment and watched him ;
there was no softening of the fine young face. Chriss was right
when she said Richard's lips closed as though they were iron.

'I was sorry to hear what an uncomfortable evening you all
had last night, Richard. I should hardly have enjoyed myself,
if I had known how things were at home.'

'Ignorance is bliss, sometimes. I am glad you had a pleasant
evening, Aunt Milly. I was sorry I could not meet you. I
told Rex to go.'

'I found Rex kicking up his heels in the porch instead.
Never mind,' as Richard looked annoyed. 'Dr. Heriot brought
me home. But, Richard, dear, I am more sorry than I can say
about this sad misunderstanding between you and Olive.'

'Aunt Milly, excuse me, but the less said about that the
better.'

'Poor girl ! I know how her interference has offended you ; it
was ill-judged, but, indeed, it was well meant. You have no
conception, Richard, how dearly Olive loves you.'

The pen remained poised above the paper a moment, and
then, in spite of his effort, the pent-up storm burst forth.

'Interference ! unwarrantable impertinence ! How dare she
betray me to my father ?'

'Betray you, Richard ?'

'The very thing I was sparing him ! The thing of all others
I would not have had him know for worlds ! How did she
know ? What right had she to guess my most private feelings ?
It is past all forbearance ; it is enough to disgust one.'

'It is hard to bear, certainly ; but, Richard, the fault is after

all a trifling one; the worst construction one can put on it is
error of judgment and a simple want of tact; she had no idea
she was harming you.'

'Harming me!' still more stormily; 'I shall never get over
it. I have lost caste in my father's opinion; how will he be
ever able to trust me now? If she had but given me warning of
her intention, I should not be in this position. All these months
of labour gone for nothing. Questioned, treated as a child—but,
were he twenty times my father, I should refuse to be catechised;'
and Richard took up his pen again, and went on writing, but
not before Mildred had seen positive tears of mortification had
sprung to his eyes. They made her feel softer to him—such a
lad, too—and motherless—and yet so hard and impracticable—
mannish, indeed!'

She stooped over him, even venturing to lay a hand on his
shoulder. 'Dear Cardie, if you feel she has injured you so
seriously, there is all the greater need of forgiveness. You
cannot refuse it to one so truly humble. She is already
heart-broken at the thought she may have caused mischief.'

'Are you her ambassadress, Aunt Milly?'

'No; you know your sister better. She would not have
ventured—at least——'

'I thought not,' he returned coldly. 'I wish her no ill, but,
I confess, I am hardly in the mood for true forgiveness just now.
You see I am no saint, Aunt Milly,' with a sneer, that sat ill on
the handsome, careworn young face, 'and I am above playing the
hypocrite. Tender messages are not in my line, and I am sorry
to say I have not Roy's forgiving temper.'

'Dear Rex, he is a pattern to us all,' thought Mildred, but
she wisely forbore making the irritating comparison; it would
certainly not have lightened Richard's dark mood. With an
odd sort of tenacity he seemed dwelling on his aunt's last words.

'You are wrong in one thing, Aunt Milly. I do not know
my sister. I know Rex, and love him with all my heart; and
I understand the foolish baby Chriss, but Olive is to me simply
an enigma.'

'Because you have not attempted to solve her.'

'Most enigmas are tiresome, and hardly worth the trouble of
solving,' he returned calmly.

'Richard! your own sister! for shame!' indignantly from
Mildred.

'I cannot help it, Aunt Milly; Olive has always been
perfectly incomprehensible to me. She is the worst sister, and,

as far as I can judge, the worst daughter I ever knew. In my opinion she has simply no heart.'

'Perhaps I had better leave you, Richard ; you are not quite yourself.'

The quiet reproof in Mildred's gentlest tones seemed to touch him.

'I am sorry if I grieve you, Aunt Milly. I wish myself that we had never entered on this subject.'

'I wish it with all my heart, Richard ; but I had no idea my own nephew could be so hard.'

'Unhappiness and want of sympathy make a man hard, Aunt Milly. But, all the same,' speaking with manifest effort, 'I am making a bad return for your kindness.'

'I wish you would let me be kind,' she returned, earnestly. 'Nay, my dear boy,' as an impatient frown crossed his face, 'I am not going to renew a vexed subject. I love Olive too well to have her unjustly censured, and you are too prejudiced and blinded by your own troubles to be capable of doing her justice. I only want'—here Mildred paused and faltered—'remember the bruised reed, Richard, and the mercy promised to the merciful. When we come to our last hour, Cardie, and our poor little life-torch is about to be extinguished, I think we shall be thankful if no greater sins are written up against us than want of tact and the error of judgment that comes from over-conscientiousness and a too great love ;' and without looking at his face, or trusting herself to say more, Mildred turned to the breakfast-table, where he shortly afterwards joined her.

Olive was in such a suffering condition all the morning that she needed her aunt's tenderest attention, and Mildred did not see her brother till later in the day.

The reaction caused by 'the Royal magnanimity,' as Mildred phrased it to Dr. Heriot afterwards, had passed into subsequent depression as the hours passed on, and no message reached her from the brother she loved but too well. Mildred feigned for a long time not to notice the weary, wistful looks that followed her about the room, especially as she knew Olive's timidity would not venture on direct questioning, but the sight of tears stealing from under the closed lids caused her to relent. Roy's prescription of quicksilver had wholly failed. Polly, saddened and mystified by the sorrowful spectacle of three-piled woe, forgot all her saucy speeches, and blundered over her sympathising ones. And Chrissy was even worse ; she clattered about

the room in her thick boots, and talked loudly in the crossest
possible key about people being stupid enough to have feelings
and make themselves ill about nothing. Chriss soon got her
dismissal, but as Mildred returned a little flushed from the
summary ejectment which Chriss had playfully tried to dispute,
she stooped over the bed and whispered—

'Never mind, dear, it could not be helped ; has it made
your head worse ? '

'Only a little. Chriss is always so noisy.'

'Shall we have Polly back ? she is quieter and more accustomed to sickrooms.'

'No, thank you ; I like being alone with you best, Aunt
Milly, only—' here a large tear dropped on the coverlid.

'You must not fret then, or your nurse will scold. No,
indeed, Olive. I know what you are thinking about, but I
don't know that having you ill on my hands will. greatly mend
matters.'

'Cardie,' whispered Olive, unable to endure the suspense any
longer, 'did you give him my message ? '

'I told him you were far from well ; but you know as well
as I do, Olive, that there is no dealing with Cardie when he is
in one of these unreasonable moods ; we must be patient and
give him time.'

'I know what you mean, Aunt Milly—you think he will
never forgive me.'

'I think nothing of the kind ; you must not be so childish,
Olive,' returned Mildred, with a little wholesome severity. 'I
wish you would be a good sensible girl and go to sleep.'

'I will try,' she returned, in a tone of languid obedience ;
'but I have such an ache here,' pressing her hand to her heart,
'such an odd sort of sinking, not exactly pain. I think it is
more unhappiness and——'

'That is because the mind acts and reacts on the body ; you
must quiet yourself, Olive, and put this unlucky misunderstanding out of your thoughts. Remember, after all, who it is
"who maketh men to be of one mind in a house ; " you have
acted for the best and without any selfish motives, and you may
safely leave the disentangling of all this difficulty to Him. No,
you must not talk any more,' as Olive seemed eager to speak ;
'you are flushed and feverish, and I mean to read you to sleep
with my monotonous voice ; ' and in spite of the invalid's incredulous look Mildred so far kept her word that Olive first
lost whole sentences, and then vainly tried to fix her attention

on others, and at last thought she was in Hill-beck woods and that some doves were cooing loudly to her, at which point Mildred softly laid down the book and stole from the room.

As she stood for a moment by the lobby window she saw her brother was taking his evening's stroll in the churchyard, and hastened to join him. He quickened his steps on seeing her, and inquired anxiously after Olive.

'She is asleep now, but I have not thought her looking very well for the last two or three days,' answered his sister. 'I do not think Olive is as strong as the others—she flags sadly at times.'

'All this has upset her; they have told you, I suppose, Mildred?'

'Olive told me last night.'

'I do not know that I have ever received a greater shock except one. I hardly had an idea myself how much my hopes were fixed upon that boy, but I am doomed to disappointment.'

'It seems to me he is scarcely to be blamed; think how young he is, only nineteen, and with such abilities.'

'Poor lad; if he only knew how little I blame him,' returned his father with a groan. 'It only shows the amount of culpable neglect of which I have been guilty, throwing him into the society of such a man; but indeed I was not aware till lately that Macdonald was little better than a free-thinker.'

Mildred looked shocked—things were even worse than she thought.

'I fancy he has drifted into extremes during the last year or two, for though always a little slippery in his Church views, he had not developed any decided rationalistic tendency; but Betha, poor darling, always disliked him; she said once, I remember, that he was not a good companion for our boys. I do not think she mentioned Richard in particular.'

'Olive told me she had.'

'Perhaps so; she was always so keenly alive to what concerned him. He was my only rival, Milly,' with a sad smile. 'No mother could have been prouder of her boy than she was of Cardie. I am bound to say he deserved it, for he was a good son to her; at least,' with a stifled sigh, 'he did not withhold his confidence from his mother.'

'You found him impracticable then, Arnold?'

He shook his head sadly.

'The sin lies on my own head, Milly. I have neglected my children, buried myself in my own pursuits and sorrow, and now I am sorely punished. My son refuses the confidence which his father actually stooped to entreat,' and there was a look of such suppressed anguish on Mr. Lambert's face that Mildred could hardly refrain from tears.

' Richard is always so good to you,' she said at last.

' Do I not tell you I blame myself and not the boy that there is this barrier between us ! but to know that my son is in trouble which he will not permit me to share, it is very hard, Mildred.'

' It is wrong, Arnold.'

' Where has the lad inherited his proud spirit ? his mother was so very gentle, and I was always alive to reason. I must confess he was perfectly respectful, not to say filial in his manner, was grieved to distress me, would have suffered anything rather than I should have been so harassed ; but it was not his fault that people had meddled in his private concerns ; you would have thought he was thirty at least.'

' I am sure he meant what he said ; there is no want of heart in Richard.'

' He tried to smoothe me over, I could see, hoped that I should forget it, and would esteem it a favour if I would not make it a matter of discussion between us. He had been a little unsettled, how much he refused to say. He could wish with me that he had never been thrown so much with Macdonald, as doubts take seed as rapidly as thistledown ; but when I urged and pressed him to repose his doubts in me, as I might possibly remove them, he drew back and hesitated, said he was not prepared, he would rather not raise questions for which there might not be sufficient reply ; he thought it better to leave the weeds in a dark corner where they could trouble no one ; he wished to work it out for himself—in fact, implied that he did not want my help.'

' I think you must have misunderstood him, Arnold. Who could be better than his own father, and he a clergyman ? '

' Many, my dear ; Heriot, for example. I find Heriot is not quite so much in the dark as I supposed, though he treats it less seriously than we do ; he says it is no use forcing confidence, and that Cardie is peculiar and resents being catechised, and he advises me to send him to Oxford without delay, that he may meet men on his own level and rub against other minds; but I feel loath to do so, I am so in the dark about him. Heriot may be right, or it may be the worst possible thing.'

' What did Richard say himself ? '

'He seemed relieved at my proposing it, thanked me, and jumped at the idea, begged that he might go after Christmas; he was wasting his time here, looked pleased and dubious when I proposed his reading for the bar, and then his face fell—I suppose at the thought of my disappointment, for he coloured and said hurriedly that there was no need of immediate decision; he must make up his mind finally whether he should ever take holy orders. At present it was more than probable that——'

'"Say at once it is impossible," I interrupted, for the thought of such sacrilege made me angry. "No, father, do not say that," he returned, and I fancied he was touched for the moment. "Don't make up your mind that we are both to disappoint you. I only want to be perfectly sure that I am no hypocrite—that at any rate I am true in what I do. I think she would like that best, father," and then I knew he meant his mother.'

'Dear Arnold, I am not sure after all that you need be unhappy about your boy.'

'I do not distrust his rectitude of purpose; I only grieve over his pride and inflexibility—they are not good bosom-companions to a young man. Well, wherever he goes he is sure of his father's prayers, though it is hard to know that one's son is a stranger. Ah, there comes Heriot, Milly. I suppose he thinks we all want cheering up, as it is not his usual night.'

Mildred had already guessed such was the case, and was very grateful for the stream of ready talk that, at supper-time, carried Polly and Chriss with it. Roy had recovered his spirits, but he seemed to consider it a duty to preserve a subdued and injured exterior in his father's presence; it showed remorse for past idleness, and was a delicate compliment to the absent Livy; while Richard sat by in grave taciturnity, now and then breaking out into short sentences when silence was impossible, but all the time keenly cognisant of his father's every look and movement, and observant of his every want.

Dr. Heriot followed Mildred out of the room with a half-laughing inquiry how she had fared during the family gale.

'It is no laughing matter, I assure you; we are all as uncomfortable as possible.'

'When Greek meets Greek, you know the rest. You have no idea how dogmatical and disagreeable Mr. Lambert can make himself at times.'

This was a new idea to Mildred, and was met with unusual indignation.

'Parents have a notion they can enforce confidence—that the

very relationship instils it.   Here is the vicar groaning over his
son's unfilial reticence and breaking his heart over a fit of very
youthful stubbornness which calls itself manly pride, and
Richard all the while yearning after his father, but bitter at
being treated and schooled like a child.   I declare I take
Richard's part in this.'

'You ought not to blame my brother,' returned Mildred in
a low voice.

'He blames himself, and rightly too.   He had no business
to have such a man about the house.   Richard is a cantanker-
ous puppy not to confide in his father.   But what's the good of
leading a horse to the water ?—you can't make him drink.'

'I begin to think you are right about Richard,' sighed
Mildred ; 'one cannot help being fond of him, but he is very
unsatisfactory.   I am afraid I shall never make any impression.'

'Then no one will.   Fie ! Miss Lambert, I detect a whole
world of disappointment in that sigh.   What has become of
your faith ?   Half Dick's faultiness comes from having an old
head on young shoulders ; in my opinion he's worth half a dozen
Penny-royals rolled in one.'

'Dr. Heriot, how can you !   Rex has the sweetest disposition in the world.   I strongly suspect he is his father's favourite.'

'Have you just found that out ?   It would have done you
good to have seen the vicar gloating over Roy's daubs this afternoon, as though they were treasures of art ; the rogue actually
made him believe that his coffee-coloured clouds, with ragged
vermilion edges, were sublime effects.   I quite pleased him
when I assured him they were supernatural in the truest sense
of the word.   He wiped his eyes actually, over the gipsy sibyl
that I call Roy's gingerbread queen.   What a rage the lad put
himself in when I said I had never seen such a golden complexion except at a fair booth or in very bad cases of jaundice.'

'How you do delight to tease that boy ! '

'Isn't it too bad—ruffling the wings of my "sweet Whistler,"
as I call him.   He is the sort of boy all you women spoil.   He
only wants a little more petting to become as effeminate as heart
can wish.   I am half afraid that I shall miss his bright face
when a London studio engulfs him.'

'You think my brother will give him his way, then ? '

'He has no choice.   Besides, he quite believes he has an
unfledged Claude Lorraine or Salvator Rosa on his hands.   I
believe Polly's Dad Fabian is to be asked, and the matter
regularly discussed.   Poor Lambert ! he will suffer a twinge or

two before he delivers the boy into the hands of the Bohemians. He turned quite pale when I hinted a year in Rome ; but there seems no reason why Roy should not have a regular artistic education ; and, after all, I believe the lad has some talent— some of his smaller sketches are very spirited.'

'I thought so myself,' replied Mildred ; and the subject of their conversation appearing at this moment, the topic was dropped.

CHAPTER XIV

RICHARD CŒUR-DE-LION

'What is life, father?'
       'A battle, my child,
Where the strongest lance may fail;
Where the wariest eyes may be beguiled,
And the stoutest heart may quail;
Where the foes are gathered on every hand
And rest not day or night,
And the feeble little ones must stand
In the thickest of the fight.'—ADELAIDE ANNE PROCTER.

THE next day the vicarage had not regained its wonted atmosphere of quiet cheerfulness, which had been its normal condition since Mildred's arrival.

In vain had 'the sweet Whistler' haunted the narrow lobby outside Olive's room, where, with long legs dangling from the window-seat, he had warbled through the whole of 'Bonnie Dundee' and 'Comin' thro' the Rye;' after which, helping himself *ad libitum* from the old-fashioned bookcase outside Mildred's chamber, he had read through the whole index of the *Shepherd's Guide* with a fine nasal imitation of Farmer Tallentire.

'Roy, how can you be so absurd?'

'Shut up, Contradiction; don't you see I am enlightening Aunt Milly's mind—clearing it of London fogs? Always imbibe the literature of your country. People living on the fellside will find this a useful handbook of reference, containing "a proper delineation of the usual horn and ear-marks of all the members' sheep, extending from Bowes and Wensleydale to Sedbergh in Yorkshire, from Ravenstone-dale and Brough to Gillumholme in Westmorland, from Crossfell and Kirkoswold—— "'

Here, Chriss falling upon the book, the drawling monotone was quenched, and a sharp scuffle ensued, in which Royal made his escape, betaking himself during the remainder of the day to his glass studio and the society of congenial canaries.

11

The day was intensely hot ; Olive's headache had yielded at last to Mildred's treatment, but she seemed heavy and languid and dragged herself with difficulty to the dinner-table, shocking every one but Richard with her altered appearance.

Richard had so far recovered his temper that he had made up his mind with some degree of magnanimity to ignore (at least outwardly) what had occurred. He kissed Olive coolly when she entered, and hoped, somewhat stiffly, that her head was better ; but he took no notice of the yearning look in the dark eyes raised to his, though it haunted him long afterwards, neither did he address her again ; and Mildred was distressed to find that Olive scarcely touched her food, and at last crept away before half the meal was over, with the excuse that her head was aching again, but in reality unable to bear the chill restraint of her brother's presence.

Mildred found her giddy and confused, and yet unwilling to own herself anything but well, and with a growing sense of despondency and hopelessness that made her a trying companion for a hot afternoon. She talked Mildred and herself into a state of drowsiness at last, from which the former was roused by hearing Ethel Trelawny's voice on the terrace below.

Mildred was thankful for any distraction, and the sight of the tall figure in the riding-habit, advancing so gracefully to meet her, was especially refreshing, though Ethel accosted her with unusual gravity, and hoped she would not be in the way.

'Papa has ridden over to Appleby, and will call for me on his return. I started with the intention of going with him, but the afternoon is so oppressive that I repented of my determination ; will you give me a cup of tea instead, Mildred ?'

'Willingly,' was the cheerful answer ; and as she gave the order, Ethel seated herself on the steps leading down to the small smooth-shaven croquet-lawn, and, doffing her hat and gauntlets, amused herself with switching the daisy-heads with her jewelled riding-whip until Mildred returned.

'Is Olive better ?' she asked abruptly, as Mildred seated herself beside her with needlework.

Mildred looked a little surprised as she answered, but a delicately-worded question or two soon showed her that Ethel was not entirely ignorant of the state of the case. She had met Richard in the town on the previous day, and, startled at his gloomy looks, had coaxed him, though with great difficulty, to accompany her home.

'It was not very easy to manage him in such a mood,

continued Ethel, with her crisp laugh. 'I felt, as we were going up the Crofts, as though I were Una leading her lion. He was dumb all the way; he contrived a roar at the end, though—we were very nearly having our first quarrel.'

'I am afraid you were hard on your knight then.'

Ethel coloured a little disdainfully, but she coloured nevertheless.

'Boys were not knighted in the old days, Mildred—they had to win their spurs, though,' hesitating, 'few could boast of a more gallant exploit perhaps;' but with a sudden sparkle of fun in her beautiful eyes, 'a lionised Richard, not a Cœur-de-Lion, but the horrid, blatant beast himself, must be distressful to any one but a Una.'

'Poor Richard! you should have soothed instead of irritated him.'

'Counter-irritants are good for some diseases; besides, it was his own fault. He did not put me in possession of the real facts of the case until the last, and then only scantily. When I begged to know more, he turned upon me quite haughtily; it might have been Cœur-de-Lion himself before Ascalon, when Berengaria chose to be inquisitive. Indeed he gave me a strong hint that I could have no possible right to question him at all. I felt inclined half saucily to curtsey to his mightiness, only he looked such a sore-hearted Cœur-de-Lion.'

'I like your choice of names; it fits Cardie somehow. I believe the lion-hearted king could contrive to get into rages sometimes. If I were mischievous, which I am not, I would not let you forget you have likened yourself to Berengaria.'

It was good to see the curl of Ethel's lips as she completely ignored Mildred's speech.

'I suppressed the mocking reverence and treated him to a prettily-worded apology instead, which had the effect of bringing him 'off the stilts,' as a certain doctor calls it. I tell him sometimes, by way of excuse, that the teens are a stilted period in one's life.'

'Do you mean that you are younger than Richard?'

'I am three months his junior, as he takes care to remind me sometimes. Did you ever see youth treading on the heels of bearded age as in Richard's case, poor fellow? I am really very sorry for him,' she continued, in a tone of such genuine feeling that Mildred liked her better than ever.

'I hope you told him so.'

'Yes, I was very good to him when I saw my sarcasms hurt.

I gave him tea with my own fair hands, and was very plentiful in the matter of cream, which I know to be his weakness; and I made Minto pet him and Lassie jump up on his knee, and by and by my good temper was rewarded, and " Richard was himself again ! " '

' Did he tell you he is going to Oxford after Christmas ? '

' Yes; I am thankful to hear it. What is the good of his rusting here, when every one says he has such wonderful abilities ? I hope you do not think me wrong, Mildred,' blushing slightly, ' but I strongly advocated his reading for the Bar.' ·

Mildred sighed.

' There is no doubt he wishes it above all things; he quite warmed into eagerness as we discussed it. My father has always said that his clear logical head and undoubted talents would be invaluable as a barrister. He has no want of earnestness, but he somehow lacks the persuasive eloquence that ought to be innate in the real priest; and yet when I said as much he shook his head, and relapsed into sadness again, said there was more than that, hinted at a rooted antipathy, then turned it off by owning that he disliked the notion of talking to old women about their souls; was sure he would be a cypher at a sickbed, good for nothing but scolding the people all round, and thought writing a couple of sermons a week the most wearisome work in the world—digging into one's brains for dry matter that must not be embellished even by a few harmless Latin and Greek quotations.'

Mildred looked grave. ' I fear he dislikes the whole thing.'

But Ethel interposed eagerly. ' You must not blame him if he be unfit by temperament. He had far better be a rising barrister than a half-hearted priest.'

' I would sooner see him anything than that—a navvy rather.'

' That is what I say,' continued Miss Trelawny, triumphant; ' and yet when I hinted as much he threw up his head with quite. a Cœur-de-Lion look, and said, " Yes, I know, but you must not tempt me to break through my father's wishes. If it can be done without sacrilege—— " And then he stopped, and asked if it were only the Westmorland old women were so trying. I do call it very wrong, Mildred, that any bias should have been put on his wishes in this respect, especially as in two more years Richard knows he will be independent of his father.' And as Mildred looked astonished at this piece of information, Ethel modestly returned that she had been intimate so many years at the vicarage—at least with the vicar and his wife and

Richard—that many things came to her knowledge. Both she and her father knew that part of the mother's money had, with the vicar's consent, been settled on her boy, and Mildred, who knew that a considerable sum had a few years before been left to Betha by an eccentric uncle whom Mr. Lambert had inadvertently offended, and that he had willed it exclusively for the use of his niece and her children, was nevertheless surprised to hear that while a moderate portion had been reserved to her girls, Roy's share was only small, while Richard at one-and-twenty would be put in possession of more than three hundred a year.

'Between three and four, I believe Mr. Lambert told my father. Roy is to have a hundred a year, and the girls about two thousand apiece. Richard will have the lion's share. I believe this same uncle took a fancy to Roy's saucy face, and left a sum of money to be appropriated to his education. Richard says there will be plenty for a thorough art education and a year at Rome ; he hinted too that if Roy failed of achieving even moderate success in his profession, there was sufficient for both. Anything rather than Roy should be crossed in his ambition ! I call that generous, Mildred.'

'And I ; but I am a little surprised at my brother making such a point of Richard being a clergyman ; he is very reticent at times. Come, Ethel, you look mysterious. I suppose you can explain even this ?'

'I can ; but at least you are hardly such a stranger to your own nephews and nieces as not to be aware of the worldly consideration there is involved.'

'You forget,' returned Mildred, sadly, 'what a bad correspondent my brother is ; Betha was better, but it was not often the busy house-mother could find leisure for long chatty letters. You are surely not speaking of what happened when Richard was fourteen ?'

Ethel nodded and continued :

'That accounts of course for his being in such favour at the Palace. They say the Bishop and Mrs. Douglas would do anything for him—that they treat him as though he were their own son ; Rolf and he are to go to the same college—Magdalen, too, though Mr. Lambert wanted him to go to Queen's ; they say, if anything happened to Mr. Lambert, that Richard would be sure of the living ; in a worldly point of view it certainly sounds better than a briefless barrister.'

'Ethel, you must not say such things. I cannot allow that

my brother would be influenced by such worldly considerations, tempting as they are,' replied Mildred, indignantly.

But Ethel laid her hand softly on her arm.

'Dear Mildred, this is only one side of the question ; that something far deeper is involved I know from Richard himself ; I heard it years ago, when Cardie was younger, and had not learned to be proud and cold with his old playmate,' and Ethel's tone was a little sad.

'May I know ?' asked Mildred, pleadingly ; 'there is no fear of Richard ever telling me himself.'

Ethel hesitated slightly.

'He might not like it ; but no, there can be no harm ; you ought to know it, Mildred ; until now it seemed so beautiful— Richard thought so himself.'

'You mean that Betha wished it as well as Arnold ?'

'Ah ! you have guessed it. What if the parents, in the fulness of their fresh young happiness, desired to dedicate their firstborn to the priesthood, would not this better fit your conception of your brother's character, always so simple and unconventional ?'

A gleam of pleasure passed over Mildred's face, but it was mixed with pain. A fresh light seemed thrown on Richard's difficulty ; she could understand the complication now. With Richard's deep love for his mother, would he not be tempted to regard her wishes as binding, all the more that it involved sacrifice on his part ?

'It might be so, but Richard should not feel it obligatory to carry out his parents' wish if there be any moral hindrance,' she continued thoughtfully.

'That is what I tell him. I have reason to know that it was a favourite topic of conversation between the mother and son, and Mrs. Lambert often assured me, with tears in her eyes, that Richard was ardent to follow his father's profession. I remember on the eve of his confirmation that he told me himself that he felt he was training for the noblest vocation that could fall to the lot of man. Until two years ago there was no hint of repugnance, not a whisper of dissent ; no wonder all this is a blow to his father ! '

'No, indeed ! ' assented Mildred.

Can you guess what has altered him so ? ' continued Ethel, with a scrutinising glance. 'I have noticed a gradual change in him the last two or three years ; he is more reserved, less candid in every way. I confess I have hardly understood him of late.'

'He has not recovered his mother's death,' returned Mildred, evasively ; it was a relief to her that Ethel was in ignorance of the real cause of the change in Richard. She herself was the only person who held the full clue to the difficulty ; Richard's reserve had baffled his father. Mr. Lambert had no conception of the generous scruples that had hindered his son's confidence, and prevented him from availing himself of his tempting offer ; and as she thought of the Cœur-de-Lion look with which he had repelled Ethel's glowing description, a passionate pity woke in her heart, and for the moment she forgave the chafed bitter temper, in honest consideration for the noble struggle that preceded it.

'What were you telling me about Richard and young Douglas ?' she asked, after a minute's pause, during which Ethel, disappointed by her unexpected reserve, had relapsed into silence. 'Betha was ill at the time, or I should have had a more glowing description than Arnold's brief paragraph afforded me. I know Richard jumped into the mill-stream and pulled one of the young Douglases out ; but I never heard the particulars.'

'You astonish me by your cool manner of talking about it. It was an act of pure heroism not to be expected in a boy of fourteen ; all the county rang with it for weeks afterwards. He and Rolf were playing down by the mill, at Dalston, a few miles from the Palace, and somehow Rolf slipped over the low parapet : you know the mill-stream : it has a dangerous eddy, and there is a dark deep pool that makes you shudder to look at : the miller's man heard Richard's shout of distress, but he was at the topmost story, and long before he could have got to the place the lad must have been swept under the wheel. Richard knew this, and the gallant little fellow threw off his jacket and jumped in. Rolf could not swim, but Richard struck out with all his might and caught him by his sleeve just as the eddy was sucking him in. Richard was strong even then, and he would have managed to tow him into shallow water but for Rolf's agonised struggles ; as it was, he only just managed to keep his head above water, and prevent them both from sinking until help came. Braithwaite had not thrown the rope a moment too soon, for, as he told the Bishop afterwards, both the boys were drifting helplessly towards the eddy. Richard's strength was exhausted by Rolf's despairing clutches, but he had drawn Rolf's head on his breast and was still holding him up ; he fainted as they were hauled up the bank, and as it was, his heroism cost him a long illness. I have called him Cœur-de-Lion ever since.'

'Noble boy!' returned Mildred, with sparkling eyes; but they were dim too.

'There, I hear the horses! how quickly time always passes in your company, Mildred. Good-bye; I must not give papa time to get one foot out of the stirrup, or he will tell me I have kept him waiting;' and leaving Mildred to follow her more leisurely, Ethel gathered up her long habit and quickly disappeared.

Later that evening as Dr. Heriot passed through the dusky courtyard, he found Mildred waiting in the porch.

'How late you are; I almost feared you were not coming to-night,' she said anxiously, in answer to his cheery 'good evening.'

'Am I to flatter myself that you were watching for me then?' he returned, veiling a little surprise under his usual light manner. 'How are all the tempers, Miss Lambert? I hope I am not required to call spirits blue and gray from the vasty deep, as I am not sure that I feel particularly sportive to-night.'

'I wanted to speak to you about Olive,' returned Mildred, quietly ignoring the banter. 'She does not seem well. The headache was fully accounted for yesterday, but I do not like the look of her to-night. I felt her pulse just now, and it was quick, weak, and irregular, and she was complaining of giddiness and a ringing in her ears.'

'I have noticed she has not looked right for some days, especially on St. Peter's day. Do you wish me to see her?' he continued, with a touch of professional gravity.

'I should be much obliged if you would,' she returned, gratefully; 'she is in my room at present, as Chriss's noise disturbs her. Your visit will put her out a little, as any questioning about her health seems to make her irritable.'

'She will not object to an old friend; anyhow, we must brave her displeasure. Will you lead the way, Miss Lambert?'

They found Olive sitting huddled up in her old position, and looking wan and feverish. She shaded her eyes a little fretfully from the candle Mildred carried, and looked at Dr. Heriot rather strangely and with some displeasure.

'How do you feel to-night, Olive?' he asked kindly, possessing himself with some difficulty of the dry languid hand, and scrutinising with anxiety the sunken countenance before him. Two days of agitation and suppressed illness had quite altered the girl's appearance.

'I am well—at least, only tired—there is nothing the matter with me. Aunt Milly ought not to have troubled you,' still irritably.

'Aunt Milly knows trouble is sometimes a pleasure. You are not well, Olive, or you would not be so cross with your old friend.'

She hesitated, put up her hand to her head, and looked ready to burst into tears.

'Come,' he continued, sitting down beside her, and speaking gently as though to a child, 'you are ill or unhappy—or both, and talking makes your head ache.'

'Yes,' she returned, mechanically, 'it is always aching now, but it is nothing.'

'Most people are not so stoical. You must not keep things so much to yourself, Olive. If you would own the truth I daresay you have felt languid and disinclined to move for several days?'

'I daresay. I cannot remember,' she faltered; but his keen, steady glance was compelling her to rouse herself.

'And you have not slept well, and your limbs ache as though you were tired and bruised, and your thoughts get a little confused and troublesome towards evening.'

'They are always that,' she returned, heavily; but she did not refuse to answer the few professional questions that Dr. Heriot put. His grave manner, and the thoughtful way in which he watched Olive, caused Mildred some secret uneasiness; it struck her that the girl was a little incoherent in her talk.

'Well—well,' he said, cheerfully, laying down the hand, 'you must give up the fruitless struggle and submit to be nursed well again. Get her to bed, Miss Lambert, and keep her and the room as cool as possible. She will remain here, I suppose,' he continued abruptly, and as Mildred assented, he seemed relieved. 'I will send her some medicine at once. I shall see you downstairs presently,' he finished pointedly; and Mildred, who understood him, returned in the affirmative. She was longing to have Dr. Heriot's opinion; but she was too good a nurse not to make the patient her first consideration. Supper was over by the time the draught was administered, and Olive left fairly comfortable with Nan within earshot. The girls had already retired to their rooms, and Dr. Heriot was evidently waiting for Mildred, for he seemed absent and slightly inattentive to the vicar's discourse. Richard, who was at work over some of his father's papers, made no attempt to join in the conversation.

Mr. Lambert interrupted himself on Mildred's entrance.

'By the bye, Milly, have you spoken to Heriot about Olive ?'

'Yes, I have seen her, Mr. Lambert ; her aunt was right ; the girl is very far from well.'

'Nothing serious, I hope,' ejaculated the vicar, while Richard looked up quickly from his writing. Dr. Heriot looked a little embarrassed.

'I shall judge better to-morrow ; the symptoms will be more decided ; but I am afraid—that is, I am nearly certain—that it is a touch of typhoid fever.'

The stifled exclamation came not from the vicar, but from the farthest corner of the room. Mr. Lambert merely turned a little paler, and clasped his hands.

'God forbid, Heriot ! That poor child !'

'We shall know in a few hours for certain—she is ill, very ill I should say.'

'But she was with us, she dined with us to-day,' gasped Richard, unable to comprehend what was the true state of the case.

'It is not uncommon for people who are really ill of fever to go about for some days until they can struggle with the feelings of illness no longer. To-night there is slight confusion and incoherence, and the ringing in the ears that is frequently the forerunner of delirium ; she will be a little wandering to-night,' he continued, turning to Mildred.

'You must give me your instructions,' she returned, with the calmness of one to whom illness was no novelty ; but Mr. Lambert interrupted her.

'Typhoid fever ; the very thing that caused such mortality in the Farrer and Bales' cottages last year.'

'I should not be surprised if we find Olive has been visiting there of late, and inhaling some of the poisonous gases. I have always said this place is enough to breed a fever ; the water is unwholesome, too, and she is so careless that she may have forgotten how strongly I condemned it. The want of water-works, and the absence of the commonest precautions, are the crying evils of a place like this.' And Dr. Heriot threw up his head and began to pace the room, as was his fashion when roused or excited, while he launched into bitter invectives against the suicidal ignorance that set health at defiance by permitting abuses that were enough to breed a pestilence.

The full amount of the evil was as yet unknown to Mildred; but sufficient detail was poured into her shrinking ear to justify Dr. Heriot's indignation, and she was not a little shocked to find the happy valley was not exempt from the taint of fatal ignorance and prejudice.

'Your old hobby, Heriot,' said Mr. Lambert, with a faint smile; 'but at least the Board of Guardians are taking up the question seriously now.'

'How could they fail to do so after the last report of the medical officer of health? We shall get our waterworks now, I suppose, through stress of hard fighting; but——'

'But my poor child——' interrupted Mr. Lambert, anxiously.

Dr. Heriot paused in his restless walk.

'Will do well, I trust, with her youth, sound constitution, and your sister's good nursing. I was going to say,' he continued, turning to Mr. Lambert, 'that with your old horror of fevers, you would be glad if the others were to be removed from any possible contagion that might arise; though, as I have already told you, that I cannot pronounce decidedly whether it be the *typhus mitior* or the other; in a few hours the symptoms will be decided. But anyhow it is as well to be on the safe side, and Polly and Chriss can come to me; we can find plenty of room for Richard and Royal as well.'

'You need not arrange for me—I shall stay with my father and Aunt Milly,' returned Richard abruptly, tossing back the wave of dark hair that lay on his forehead, and pushing away his chair.

'Nay, Cardie, I shall not need you; and your aunt will find more leisure for her nursing if you are all off her hands. I shall be easier too. Heriot knows my old nervousness in this respect.'

'I shall not leave you, father,' was Richard's sole rejoinder; but his father's affectionate and anxious glance was unperceived as he quickly gathered up the papers and left the room.

'I think Dick is right,' returned Dr. Heriot, cheerfully. 'The vicarage need not be cleared as though it were the pestilence. Now, Miss Lambert, I will give you a few directions, and then I must say good-night.'

When Mildred returned to her charge, she found Richard standing by the bedside, contemplating his sister with a grave, impassive face. Olive did not seem to notice him; she was moving restlessly on her pillow, her dark hair unbound and falling on her flushed face. Richard gathered it up gently and looked at his aunt.

'We may have to get rid of some of it to-morrow,' she whispered; 'what a pity, it is so long and beautiful; but it will prevent her losing all. You must not stay now, Richard; I fancy it disturbs her,' as Olive muttered something drowsily, and flung her arms about a little wildly; 'leave her to me to-night, dear; I will come to you first thing to-morrow morning, and tell you how she is.'

'Thank you,' he replied, gratefully.

Mildred was not wrong in her surmises that something like remorse for his unkindness made him stoop over the bed with the softly uttered 'Good-night, Livy.'

'Good-night,' she returned, drowsily. 'Don't trouble about me, Cardie;' and with that he was fain to retire.

Things continued in much the same state for days. Dr. Heriot's opinion of the nature of the disease was fully confirmed. There was no abatement of fever, but an increase of debility. Olive's delirium was never violent—it was rather a restlessness and confusion of thought; she lay for hours in a semi-somnolent state, half-muttering to herself, yet without distinct articulation. Now and then a question would rouse her, and she would give a rational answer; but she soon fell back into the old drowsy state again.

Her nights were especially troubled in this respect. In the day she was comparatively quiet; but for many successive nights all natural sleep departed from her, and her confused and incoherent talk was very painful to hear.

Mildred fancied that Richard's presence made her more restless than at other times; but when she hinted this, he looked so pained that she could not find it in her heart to banish him, especially as his ready strength and assistance were a great comfort to her. Mildred had refused all exterior help. Nan's watchful care was always available during her hours of necessary repose, and Mildred had been so well trained in the school of nursing, that a few hours' sound sleep would send her back to her post rested and refreshed. Dr. Heriot's admiration of his model nurse, as he called her, was genuine and loudly expressed; and he often assured Mr. Lambert, when unfavourable symptoms set in, that if Olive recovered it would be mainly owing to her aunt's unwearied nursing.

Mildred often wondered what she would have done without Richard, as Olive grew weaker, and the slightest exertion brought on fainting, or covered her with a cold, clammy sweat. Richard's strong arms were of use now to lift her into easier positions.

Mildred never suffered him to share in the night watches, for which she and Nan were all-sufficient; but the last thing at night, and often before the early dawn, his pale anxious face would be seen outside the door; and all through the day he was ever at hand to render valuable assistance. Once Mildred was surprised to hear her name softly called from the far end of the lobby, and on going out she found herself face to face with Ethel Trelawny.

'Oh, Ethel! this is very wrong. Your father——'

'I told her so,' returned Richard, who looked half grateful and half uneasy; 'but she would come—she said she must see you. Aunt Milly looks pale,' he continued, turning to Ethel; 'but we cannot be surprised at that—she gets so little sleep.'

'You will be worn out, Mildred. Papa will be angry, I know; but I cannot help it. I mean to stay and nurse Olive.'

'My dear Ethel!' Richard uttered an incredulous exclamation; but Miss Trelawny was evidently in earnest; her fine countenance looked pale and saddened.

'I can and must; do let me, Mildred. I have often stayed up all night for my own pleasure.'

'But you are so unused to illness—it cannot be thought of for a moment,' ejaculated Richard in alarm.

'Women nurse by instinct. I should look at Mildred—she would soon teach me. Why do you all persist in treating me as though I were quite helpless? Papa is wrong; typhoid fever is not infectious, and if it were, what use am I to any one? My life is not of as much consequence as Mildred's.'

'There is always the risk of contagion, and—and—why will you always speak of yourself so recklessly, Miss Trelawny?' interposed Richard in a pained voice, 'when you know how precious your life is to us all;' but Ethel turned from him impatiently.

'Mildred, you will let me come?'

'No, Ethel, indeed I cannot, though I am very grateful to you for wishing it. Your father is your first consideration, and his wishes should be your law.'

'Papa is afraid of everything,' she pleaded; 'he will not let me go into the cottages where there is illness, and——'

'He is right to take care of his only child,' replied Mildred, calmly.

Richard seemed relieved.

'I knew you would say so, Aunt Milly; we are grateful—

more grateful than I can say, dear Miss Trelawny ; but I knew it ought not to be.'

'And you must not come here again without your father's permission,' continued Mildred, gently, and taking her hands ; 'we have to remember sometimes that to obey is better than sacrifice, dear Ethel. I am grieved to disappoint your generous impulse,' as the girl turned silently away with the tears in her eyes.

'Dr. Heriot said I should have no chance, and Richard was as bad. Well, good-bye,' trying to rally her spirits as she saw Mildred looked really pained. 'I envy you your labour of love, Mildred ; it is sweet—it must be sweet to be really useful to some one ;' and the sigh that accompanied her words evidently came from a deep place in Ethel Trelawny's heart.

CHAPTER XV

THE GATE AJAR

'Oh, live !
So endeth faint the low pathetic cry
Of love, whom death hath taught, love cannot die.'
Poems by the Author of 'John Halifax.'

'His dews drop mutely on the hill,
His cloud above it saileth still,
Though on its slope men sow and reap :
More softly than the dew is shed,
Or cloud is floated overhead,
He giveth His beloved sleep.'—E. B. BROWNING.

THE fever had run its course,—never virulent or excessive, there had still been no abatement in the unfavourable symptoms, and, as the critical days approached, Mildred's watchfulness detected an increased gravity in Dr. Heriot's manner. Always assiduous in his attentions, they now became almost unremitting ; his morning and evening visits were supplemented by a noonday one ; by and by every moment he could snatch from his other patients was spent by Olive's bedside.

A silent oppression hung over the vicarage ; anxious footsteps crept stealthily up to the front door at all hours, with low-whispered inquiries. Every morning and evening Mildred telegraphed signals to Roy and Polly as they stood on the other side of the beck in Hillsbottom, watching patiently for the white fluttering pendant that was to send them away in comparative tranquillity. Sometimes Roy would climb the low hill in Hillsbottom, and lie for hours, with his eyes fixed on the broad projecting window, on the chance of seeing Mildred steal there for a moment's fresh air. Roy, contrary to his usual light-heartedness, had taken Olive's illness greatly to heart ; the remembrance of his hard words oppressed and tormented him. Chriss often kept him company—Chriss, who grew crosser day by day with suppressed unhappiness, and who vented her uncomfortable feelings in contradicting everything and everybody from morning to night.

One warm sunshiny afternoon, Mildred, who was sensible of unusual languor and oppression, had just stolen to the window to refresh her eyes with the soft green of the fellsides, when Dr. Heriot, who had been standing thoughtfully by the bedside, suddenly roused himself and followed her.

'Miss Lambert, do you know I am going to assert my authority?'

Mildred looked up inquiringly, but there was no answering smile on her pale face.

'I am going to forbid you this room for the next two hours. Indeed,' as Mildred shook her head incredulously, 'I am serious in what I say ; you have just reached the limit of endurance, and an attack of faintness may possibly be the result, if you do not follow my advice. An hour's fresh air will send you back fit for your work.'

'But Olive ! indeed I cannot leave Olive, Dr. Heriot.'

'Not in my care ?' very quietly. 'Of course I shall remain here until you return.'

'You are very kind ; but indeed—no—I cannot go ; please do not ask me, Dr. Heriot ;' and Mildred turned very pale.

'I do not ask, I insist on it,' in a voice Mildred never heard before from Dr. Heriot. 'Can you not trust me ?' he continued, relapsing into his ordinary gentle tone. 'Believe me, I would not banish you but for your own good. You know '—he hesitated ; but the calm, quiet face seemed to reassure him— 'things can only go on like this for a few hours, and we may have a very trying night before us. You will want all your strength for the next day or two.'

'You apprehend a change for the worse ?' asked Mildred, drawing her breath more quickly, but speaking in a tone as low as his, for Richard was watching them anxiously from the other end of the room.

'I do not deny we have reason to fear it,' he returned, evasively ; 'but there will be no change of any kind for some hours.'

'I will go, then, if Richard will take me,' she replied, quietly ; and Richard rose reluctantly.

'You must not bring her back for two hours,' was Dr. Heriot's parting injunction, as Mildred paused by Olive's bedside for a last lingering look. Olive still lay in the same heavy stupor, only broken from time to time by the imperfect muttering. The long hair had all been cut off, and only a dark lock or two

escaped from under the wet cloths ; the large hollow eyes looked
fixed and brilliant, while the parched and blackened lips spoke
of low, consuming fever. As Mildred turned away, she was
startled by the look of anguish that crossed Richard's face ; but
he followed her without a word.

It was a lovely afternoon in July, the air was full of the
warm fragrance of new-mown hay, the distant fells lay in purple
shadow. As they walked through Hillsbottom, Mildred's eyes
were almost dazzled by the soft waves of green upland shining
in the sunshine. Clusters of pink briar roses hung on every
hedge ; down by the weir some children were wading among
the shallow pools ; farther on the beck widened, and flowed
smoothly between its wooded banks. By and by they came to
a rough footbridge, leading to a little lane, its hedgerows
bordered with ferns, and gay with rose-campion and soft blue
harebells, while trails of meadow-sweet scented the air ; beyond,
lay a beautiful meadow, belting Podgill, its green surface gemmed
with the starry eyebright, and golden in parts with yellow trefoil
and ragwort.

Mildred stooped to gather, half mechanically, the blue-eyed
gentian that Richard was crushing under his foot ; and then a
specimen of the soft-tinted campanella attracted her, its cluster
of bell-shaped blossoms towering over the other wildflowers.

'Shall we go down into Podgill, Aunt Milly, it is shadier
than this lane ?' and Mildred, who was revolving painful
thoughts in her mind, followed him, still silent, through the
low-hanging woods, with its winding beck and rough stepping-
stones, until they came to a green slope, spanned by the viaduct.

'Let us sit down here, Richard ; how quiet and cool it is !'
and Mildred seated herself on the grass, while Richard threw
himself down beside her.

'How silent we have been, Richard. I don't think either of us
cared to talk ; but Dr. Heriot was right——I feel refreshed already.'

'I am glad we came then, Aunt Milly.'

'I never knew any one so thoughtful. Richard, I want to
speak to you ; did you ever find out that Olive wrote poetry ?'

Richard raised himself in surprise.

'No, Aunt Milly.'

'I want to show you this ; it was written on a stray leaf,
and I ventured to capture it ; it may help you to understand
that in her own way Olive has suffered.'

Richard took the paper from her without a word ; but
Mildred noticed his hand shook. Was it cruel thus to call his

12

hardness to remembrance ? For a moment Mildred's soft heart wavered over the task she had set for herself.

It was scrawled in Olive's schoolgirl hand, and in some parts was hard to decipher, especially as now and then a blot of teardrops had rendered it illegible ; but nevertheless Richard succeeded in reading it.

'How speed our lost in the Unknown Land,
Our dear ones gone to that distant strand !
  Do they know that our hearts are sore
With longing for faces that never come,
With longing to hear in our silent home
  The voices that sound no more !
There's a desolate look by the old hearth-stone,
That tells of some light of the household gone
  To dwell with the ransomed band ;
But none may follow their upward track,
And never, ah ! never, a word comes back
  To tell of the Unknown Land !

'We know by a gleam on the brow so pale,
When the soul bursts forth from its mortal veil,
  And the gentle and good departs,
That the dying ears caught the first faint ring
Of the songs of praise that the angels sing ;
  But back to our yearning hearts
Comes never, ah ! never, a word to tell
That the purified spirit we love so well
  Is safe on the heavenly strand ;
That the Angel of Death has another gem
To set in the star-decked diadem
  Of the King of the Unknown Land !

'How speed our lost in the realms of air
We would ask—we would ask, Do they love us there ?
  Do they know that our hearts are sore,
That the cup of sorrow oft overflows,
And our eyes grow dim with weeping for those—
  For those who shall "weep no more" ?
And when the Angel of Death shall call,
And earthly chains from about us fall,
  Will they meet us with clasping hand ?
But never, ah ! never a voice replies
From the "many mansions" above the skies
  To tell of the Unknown Land !'[1]

'Aunt Milly, why did you show me this ?' and Richard's eyes, full of reproachful pain, fixed themselves somewhat sternly on her face.

'Because I want you to understand. Look, there is another on the next leaf ; see, she has called it "A little while" and

[1] H. M. B.

"for ever." My poor girl, every word is so true of her own earnest nature.'

    '"For ever," they are fading,
      Our beautiful, our bright ;
    They gladden us "a little while,"
      Then pass away from sight ;
    "A little while " we're parted
      From those who love us best,
    Who gain the goal before us
      And enter into rest.

    'Our path grows very lonely,
      And still those words beguile,
    And cheer our footsteps onward ;
      'Tis but a little while.
    "A little while " earth's sorrow,—
      Its burdens and its care,
    Its struggles 'neath the crosses,
      Which we of earth must bear.

    'There's time to do and suffer—
      To work our Master's will,
    But not for vain regretting
      For thoughts or deeds of ill.
    Too short to spend in weeping
      O'er broken hopes and flowers,
    For wandering and wasting,
      Is this strange life of ours.

    'Though, when our cares oppress us,
      Earth's "little while " seems long,
    If we would win the battle
      We must be brave and strong.
    And so with humble spirit,
      But highest hopes and aim,
    The goal so often longed for
      We may perhaps attain.

    '"For ever " and "for ever "
      To dwell among the blest,
    Where sorrows never trouble
      The deep eternal rest ;
    When one by one we gather
      Beneath our Father's smile,
    And Heaven's sweet "for ever "
      Drowns earth's sad "little while."' [1]

'Well, Richard ?'

But there was no answer ; only the buzzing of insects in giddy circles broke the silence, mingled with the far-off twitter of birds. Only when Mildred again looked up, the paper had fluttered to their feet, and Richard had covered his face with his shaking hands.

           [1] H. M. B.

'Dear Cardie, forgive me; I did not mean to pain you like this.'

'Aunt Milly,' in a voice so hoarse and changed that Mildred quite started, 'if she die, if Olive die, I shall never know a moment's peace again;' and the groan that accompanied the words wrung Mildred's tender heart with compassion.

'God forbid we should lose her, Richard,' she returned, gently.

'Do not try to deceive me,' he returned, bitterly, in the same low, husky tones. 'I heard what he said—what you both said—that it could not go on much longer; and I saw his face when he thought he was alone. There is no hope—none.'

'Oh, Richard, hush,' replied Mildred, in uncontrollable agitation; 'while there is life, there is hope. Think of David, "While the child was yet alive I fasted and wept;" he could not tell whether God meant to be gracious to him or not. We will pray, you and I, that our girl may be spared.'

But Richard recoiled in positive horror.

'I pray, Aunt Milly? I, who have treated her so cruelly? I, who have flung hard words to her, who have refused to forgive her? I——' and he hid his pale, convulsed face in his hands again.

'But you have forgiven her now, you do her justice. You believe how truly she loved, she will ever love you.'

'Too late,' he groaned. 'Yes, I see it now, she was too good for us; we made her unhappy, and God is taking her home to her mother.'

'Then you will let her go, dear Cardie. Hush, it would break her heart to see you so unhappy;' and Mildred knelt down on the grass beside him, and stroked back the dark waves of hair tenderly. She knew the pent-up anguish of weeks must have its vent, now that his stoical manhood had broken down. Remorse, want of rest, deadly conflict and anxiety, had at last overcome the barrier of his reserve; and, as he flung himself down beside her, with his face hidden in the bracken, she knew the hot tears were welling through his fingers.

For a long time she sat beside him, till his agitation had subsided; and then, in her low, quiet voice, she began to talk to him. She spoke of Olive's purity and steadfastness of purpose, her self-devotedness and power of love; and Richard raised his head to listen. She told him of those Sunday afternoons spent by her mother's grave, that quiet hour of

communion bracing her for the jars and discords of the week.
And she hinted at those weary moods of perpetual self-torture
and endless scruple, which hindered all vigorous effort and
clouded her youth.

'A diseased sensibility and overmuch imagination have
resulted in the despondency that has so discouraged and
annoyed you, Richard.   She has dwelt so long among shadows
of her own raising, that she has grown a weary companion to
healthier minds ; her very love is so veiled by timidity that it
has given you an impression of her coldness.'

'Blind fool that I was,' he ejaculated.   'Oh, Aunt Milly,
do you think she can ever forgive me ? '

'There can be no question of forgiveness at all ; do not
distress her by asking for it, Richard.   Olive's heart is as
simple as a little child's ; it is not capable of resentment.   Tell
her that you love her, and you will make her happy.'

Richard did not answer for a minute, his thoughts had
suddenly taken a new turn.

'I never could tell how it was she read me so correctly,'
he said at last ; 'her telling my father, and not me, was so
incomprehensible.'

'She did not dare to speak to you, and she was so unhappy ;
but, Richard, even Olive does not hold the clue to all this
trouble.'

He started nervously, changed colour, and plucked the
blades of grass restlessly.   But in his present softened mood,
Mildred knew he would not repulse her ; trouble might be near
at hand, but at least he would not refuse her sympathy any
longer.

'Dear Cardie, your difficulty is a very real one, and only
time and prayerful consideration can solve it ; but beware how
you let the wishes of your dead mother, dear and binding as
they may be to you, prove a snare to your conscience.   Richard,
I knew her well enough to be sure that was the last thing she
would desire.'

The blood rushed to Richard's face, eager words rose to his
lips, but he restrained them ; but the grateful gleam in his eyes
spoke volumes.

'That is your real opinion, Aunt Milly.'

'Indeed it is.   Unready hands, an unprepared heart, are not
fit for the sanctuary.   I may wish with you that difficulties had
not arisen, that you could carry out your parents' dedication and
wish ; but vocation cannot be forced, neither must you fall into

Olive's mistake of supposing self-sacrifice is the one thing need-ful.   After all, our first duty is to be true to ourselves.'

'Aunt Milly, how wise you are!' he exclaimed in involun-tary admiration.   'No one, not even my father, put it so clearly. You are right, I do not mean to sacrifice myself unless I can feel it my duty to do so.   But it is a question I must settle with myself.'

'True, dear, only remember the brave old verse—

> " Stumbleth he who runneth fast ?
> Dieth he who standeth still ?
> Not by haste or rest can ever
> Man his destiny fulfil."

"Never hasting, never resting," a fine life-motto, Cardie ; but our time is nearly at an end, we must be going now.'

As they walked along, Richard returned of his own accord to the subject they had been discussing, and owned his inde-cision was a matter of great grief to him.

'Conscientious doubts will find their answer some day,' re-plied Mildred ; 'but I wish you had not refused to confide them to your father.'

Richard bit his lip.

'It was wrong of me ; I know it, Aunt Milly ; but it would have been so painful to him, and so humiliating to myself.'

'Hardly so painful as to be treated like a stranger by his own son.   You have no idea how sorely your reserve has fretted him.'

'It was cowardly of me ; but indeed, Aunt Milly, the whole question was involved in difficulty.   My father is sometimes a little vague in his manner of treating things ; he is more scholarly than practical, and I own I dreaded complication and disappointment.'

Mildred sighed.   Perhaps after all he was right.   Her brother was certainly a little dreamy and wanting in concentra-tion and energy just now ; but little did Richard know the depth of his father's affection.   Just as the old war-horse will neigh at the sound of the battle, and be ready to rush into the midst of the glittering phalanx, so would Arnold Lambert have warred with the grisly phantoms of doubt and misbelief that were leagued against Richard's boyish faith, ready to lay down his life if need be for his boy ; but as he sat hour after hour in his lonely study, the sadness closed more heavily round him—sadness for his lost love in heaven, his lost confidence on earth.

Dr. Heriot gave Mildred and Richard a searching glance as

they re-entered the room. Both looked worn and pale, but a softened and subdued expression was on Richard's face as he stood by the bedside, looking down on his sister.

'No change,' whispered Mildred.

'None at present ; but there may be a partial rally. Where is Mr. Lambert, I want to speak to him ;' and, as though to check further questioning, Dr. Heriot reiterated a few instructions, and left the room.

The hours passed on. Richard, in spite of his aunt's whispered remonstrances, still kept watch beside her ; and Mr. Lambert, who as usual had been praying by the side of his sick child, and had breathed over her unconsciousness his solemn benediction, had just left the room, when Mildred, who was giving her nourishment, noticed a slight change in Olive, a sudden gleam of consciousness in her eyes, perhaps called forth by her father's prayer, and she signed to Richard to bring him back.

Was this the rally of which Dr. Heriot spoke ? the brief flicker of the expiring torch flaming up before it is extinguished ? Olive seemed trying to concentrate her drowsy faculties, the indistinct muttering became painfully earnest, but the unhappy father, though he placed his ear to the lips of the sinking girl, could connect no meaning with the inarticulate sounds, until Mildred's greater calmness came to his help.

'Home. I think she said home, Arnold ;' and then with a quick intuitive light that surprised herself, 'I think she wishes to know if God means to take her home.'

Olive's restlessness a little abated. This time the parched and blackened lips certainly articulated 'home' and 'mother.' They could almost fancy she smiled.

'Oh, do not leave me, my child,' ejaculated Mr. Lambert, stretching out his arms as though to keep her. 'God is good and merciful ; He will not take away another of my darlings ; stay a little longer with your poor father ;' and Olive understood him, for the bright gleam faded away.

'Oh, father, she will surely stay if we ask her,' broke in Richard in an agitated voice, thrusting himself between them and speaking with a hoarse sob ; 'she is so good, and knows we all love her and want her. You will not break my heart, Livy, you will forgive me and stay with us a little ?' and Richard flung himself on his knees and buried his head on the pillow.

Ah, the bright gleam had certainly faded now ; there was a wandering, almost a terrified expression in the hollow, brilliant eyes. Were those gates closing on her ? would they not let her go ?

'Cardie, dear Cardie, hush, you are agitating her ; look how her eyelids are quivering and she has no power to speak. Arnold, ask him to be calm,' and Mr. Lambert, still holding his seemingly dying child, laid his other hand on Richard's bent head.

'Hush, my son, we must not grieve a departing spirit. I was wrong. His will be done even in this. He has given, and He must take away ; be silent while I bless my child again, my child whom I am giving back to Him and to her mother,' but as he lifted up his hands the same feeble articulation smote on their ear.

'Cardie wants me—poor Cardie—poor papa—not my will.'

Did Mildred really catch those words, struggling like broken breaths ?—was it the cold sweat of the death-damp that gathered on the clammy brow ?—were the fingers growing cold and nerveless on which Richard's hot lips were pressed ?—were those dark eyes closing to earth for ever ?

'Mildred—Richard—what is this ?'

' " Lord, if he sleep he shall do well ! " exclaimed the disciples.'

'Hush ; thank God, this is sleep, natural sleep,—the crisis is passed, we shall save her yet,' and Dr. Heriot, who had just entered, beckoned the father and brother gently from the room.

CHAPTER XVI

COMING BACK

'If Thou shouldst bring me back to life,
　　More humble I should be,
More wise, more strengthened for the strife,
　　More apt to lean on Thee.
Should death be standing at the gate,
　　Thus should I keep my vow,
But, Lord ! whatever be my fate,
　　Oh, let me serve Thee now ! '—ANNE BRONTË.

'THIS sickness is not unto death.'

The news that the crisis had passed, and that the disease that had so long baffled the physician's skill had taken a favourable turn, soon spread over the town like wildfire ; the shadow of death no longer lingered on the threshold of the vicarage ; there were trembling voices raised in the *Te Deum* the next morning ; the vicar's long pause in the Thanksgiving was echoed by many a throbbing heart ; Mildred's book was wet with her tears, and even Chrissy looked softened and subdued.

There were agitated greetings in the church porch afterwards. Olive's sick heart would have been satisfied with the knowledge that she was beloved if she had seen Roy's glistening eyes and the silent pressure of congratulation that passed between her father and Richard.

'Heriot, we feel that under Providence we owe our girl's life to you.'

'You are equally beholden to her aunt's nursing ; but indeed, Mr. Lambert, I look upon your daughter's recovery as little less than a miracle. I certainly felt myself justified to prepare you for the worst last night ; at one time she appeared to be sinking.'

'She has been given back to us from the confines of the grave,' was the solemn answer ; and as he took his son's arm and they walked slowly down the churchyard, he said, half to himself—'and a gift given back is doubly precious.'

The same thought seemed in his mind when Richard entered the study late that night with the welcome tidings that Olive was again sleeping calmly.

'Oh, Cardie, last night we thought we should have lost our girl; after all, God has been good to me beyond my deserts.'

'We may all say that, father.'

'I have been thinking that we have none of us appreciated Olive as we ought; since she has been ill a hundred instances of her unselfishness have occurred to me; in our trouble, Cardie, she thought for others, not for herself. I never remember seeing her cry except once, and yet the dear child loved her mother.'

Richard's face paled a little, but he made no answer; he remembered but too well the time to which his father alluded—how, when in his jealous surveillance he had banished her from her father's room, he had found her haunting the passages with her pale face and black dress, or sitting on the stairs, a mute image of patience.

No, there had been no evidence of her grief; others beside himself had marvelled at her changeless and monotonous calm; she had harped on her mother's name with a persistency that had driven him frantic, and he had silenced the sacred syllables in a fit of nervous exasperation; from the very first she had troubled and wearied him, she whom he was driven to confess was immeasurably his superior. Yes, the scales had fallen from his eyes, and as his father spoke a noble spirit pleaded in him, and the rankling confession at last found vent in the deep inward cry—

'Father, I have sinned against heaven and before Thee, in that I have offended one of Thy little ones,' and the *Deo gratias* of an accepted repentance and possible atonement followed close upon the words.

'Father, I want to speak to you.'

'Well, Cardie.'

'I know how my silence has grieved you; Aunt Milly told me. I was wrong—I see it now.'

Richard's face was crimsoning with the effort, but the look in his father's eyes as he laid his thin hand on his arm was sufficient reward.

'Thank God for this, my boy, that you have spoken to me at last of your own accord; it has lifted a heavy burden from my heart.'

'I ought not to have refused my confidence ; you were too good to me. I did not deserve it.'

'You thought you were strong enough to remove your own stumbling-blocks ; it is the fault of the young generation, Cardie; it would fain walk by its own lights.'

'I must allow my motives were mixed with folly, but the fear of troubling you was predominant.'

'I know it, I know it well, my son, but all the same I have yearned to help you. I have myself to blame in this matter, but the thought that you would not allow me to share your trouble was a greater punishment than even I could bear ; no, do not look so sorrowful, this moment has repaid me for all my pain.'

But it was not in Richard's nature to do anything by halves, and in his generous compunction he refused to spare himself ; the barrier of his reserve once broken down, he made ample atonement for his past reticence, and Mr. Lambert more than once was forced to admit that he had misjudged his boy.

Late into the night they talked, and when they parted the basis of a perfect understanding was established between them ; if his son's tardy confidence had soothed and gratified Mr. Lambert, Richard on his side was equally grateful for the patience and loving forbearance with which his father strove to disentangle the webs that insidious argument had woven in his clear young brain ; there was much lurking mischief, much to clear away and remove, difficulties that only time and prayerful consideration could surmount ; but however saddened Mr. Lambert might feel in seeing the noxious weeds in that goodly vineyard, he was not without hope that in time Richard's tarnished faith might gleam out brightly again.

During the weeks that ensued there were many opportunities for hours of quiet study and talk between the father and son ; in his new earnestness Mr. Lambert became less vague, this fresh obstacle roused all his energy ; there was something pathetic in the spectacle of the worn scholar and priest buckling on his ancient armour to do battle for his boy ; the old flash came to his eye, the ready vigour and eloquence to his speech, gleams of sapient wisdom startled Richard into new reverence, causing the young doubter to shrink and feel abashed.

'If one could only know, if an angel from heaven might set the seal to our assurance !' he exclaimed once. 'Father, only to know, to be sure of these things.'

'Oh, Cardie, what is that but following the example of the

affectionate but melancholy Didymus; "Blessed are they that have not seen and yet have believed"; the drowning mariner cannot see the wind that is lashing the waves that threaten to engulf his little bark, cannot "tell whence it comes or whither it goes," yet faith settles the helm and holds the rudder, and bids him cling to the spar when all seems over.'

'But he feels it beyond and around him; he feels it as we feel the warmth of the latent sunshine or the permeating influences of light; we can see the light, father,' he continued eagerly, 'we can lift our eyes eagle-wise to the sun if we will; why should our inner light be quenched and clouded?'

'To test our faith, to make us hold on more securely; after all, Cardie, the world beyond—truth revealed—religion—look to us often through life like light seen from the bottom of a well—below us darkness, then space, narrowed to our perception, a glimmering of blue sky sown thick with stars—light, keen and arrowy, shining somewhere in the depths; some of us rise to the light, drawn irresistibly to it, a few remain at the bottom of the well all their lives.'

'And some are born blind.'

'Let us leave them to the mercy of the Great Physician; in our case scales may fall from our eyes, and still with imperfect vision we may look up and see men as trees walking, but we must grope on still. Ah, my boy, when in our religious hypochondria whole creeds desert us, and shreds and particles only remain of a fragmentary and doubtful faith, don't let us fight with shadows, which of their very nature elude and fade out of our grasp; let us fall on our knees rather, Cardie, and cry—"Lord, I believe—I will believe; help Thou my unbelief."'

Many and many such talks were held, the hours and days slipping away, Mildred meanwhile devoting herself to the precious work of nursing Olive back to convalescence.

It was a harder task than even Dr. Heriot expected; slowly, painfully, almost unwillingly, the girl tottered back to life; now and then there were sensible relapses of weakness; prostration, that was almost deathlike, then a faint flicker, followed by a conscious rally, times when they trembled and feared and then hoped again; when the shadowy face and figure filled Mildred with vague alarm, and the blank despondency in the large dark eyes haunted her with a sense of pain.

In vain Mildred lavished on her the tenderest caresses; for days there was no answering smile on the pallid face, and yet no invalid could be more submissive.

Unresistingly, uncomplainingly, Olive bore the weakness that was at times almost unendurable ; obediently she took from their hands the nourishment they gave her ; but there seemed no anxiety to shake off her illness ; it was as though she submitted to life rather than willed it, nay, as though she received it back with a regret and reluctance that caused even her unselfishness a struggle.

Was the cloud returning ? Had they been wrong to pray so earnestly for her life ? Would she come back to them a sadder and more weary Olive, to tax their forbearance afresh, instead of winning an added love ; was she who had been as a little child set in their midst for an example of patient humility, to carry this burden of despondent fear about with her from the dark valley itself ?

Mildred was secretly trembling over these thoughts ; they harassed and oppressed her ; she feared lest Richard's new reverence and love for his sister should be impaired when he found the old infirmity still clinging to her ; even now the sad look in her eyes somewhat oppressed him.

'Livy, you look sometimes as though you repented getting well,' he said affectionately to her one day, when her languor and depression had been very great.

'Oh no, please don't say so, Cardie,' she returned faintly, but the last trace of colour forsook her face at his words ; 'how can—how can you say that, when you know you wanted me ?' and as the tears began to flow, Richard, alarmed and perplexed, soothed and comforted her.

Another day, when her father had been sitting by her, reading and talking to her, he noticed that she looked at him with a sort of puzzled wonder in her eyes.

'What is it, my child ?' he asked, leaning over her and stroking her hair with caressing hand. 'Do you feel weary of the reading, Olive ?'

'No, oh no ; it was beautiful,' she returned, with a trembling lip ; 'I was only thinking—wondering why you loved me.'

'Love you, my darling ! do not fathers love their children, especially when they have such good affectionate children ?'

'But I am not good,' she returned, with something of her old shrinking. 'Oh, papa, why did you and Cardie want me so, your poor useless Olive ; even Cardie loves me now, and I have done nothing but lie here and give trouble to you all ; but you are all so good—so good,' and Olive buried her pale face in her father's shoulder.

The old self-depreciation waking up to life, the old enemy leaguing with languor and despondency to mar the sweet hopefulness of convalescence. Mildred in desperation determined to put her fears to the proof when Olive grew strong enough to bear any conversation.

The opportunity came sooner than she hoped.

One day the cloud lifted a little. Roy had been admitted to his sister's room, and his agitation and sorrow at her changed appearance and his evident joy at seeing her again had roused Olive from her wonted lethargy. Mildred found her afterwards lying exhausted but with a smile on her face.

'Dear Roy,' she murmured, 'how good he was to me. Oh, Aunt Milly,' clasping Mildred's hands between her wasted fingers, 'I don't deserve for them to be so dear and good to me, it makes me feel as though I were wicked and ungrateful not to want to get well.'

'I dreaded to hear you say this, Olive,' returned Mildred. As she sat down beside her, her grieved look seemed a reproach to Olive.

'It was not that I wanted to leave you all,' she said, laying her cheek against the hand she held, 'but I have been such a trouble to every one as well as to myself; it seemed so nice to have done with it all—all the weariness and disappointment I mean.'

'You were selfish for once in your life then, Olive,' returned Mildred, trying to smile, but with a heavy heart.

'I tried not to be,' she whispered. 'I did not want you to be sorry, Aunt Milly , but I knew if I lived it would all come over again. It is the old troublesome Olive you are nursing,' she continued softly, 'who will try and disappoint you as she has always done. I can't get rid of my old self, and that is why I am sorry.'

'Sorry because we are glad ; it is Olive and no other that we want.'

'Oh, if I could believe that,' returned the girl, her eyes filling with tears ; 'but it sounds too beautiful to be true, and yet I know it was only Cardie's voice that brought me back, he wanted me so badly, and he asked me to stay. I heard him—I heard him sob, Aunt Milly,' clutching her aunt with weak, nerveless fingers.

'Are you sure, Olive ? You were fainting, you know.'

'Yes, I was falling—falling into dark, starry depths, full of living creatures, wheels of light and flame seemed everywhere, and then darkness. I thought mamma had got me in her arms, she seemed by me through it all, and then I heard Cardie say I should break his heart, and then he sobbed, and papa blessed me. I heard some gate close after that, and mamma's arms seemed to loosen from me, and I knew then I was not dying.'

'But you were sorry, Olive.'

'I tried not to be ; but it was hard, oh, so hard, Aunt Milly. Think what it was to have that door shut just as one's foot was on the threshold, and when I thought it was all over and I had got mamma back again ; but it was wrong to grieve. I have not earned my rest.'

'Hush, my child, you must not take up a new lease of life so sadly ; this is a gift, Olive, a talent straight from the Master's hands, to be received with gratitude, to be used joyfully ; by and by, when you are stronger, you will find more beautiful work your death would have left unfinished.'

A weary look crossed Olive's face.

'Shall I ever be strong enough to work again ?'

'You are working now ; nay, my child,' as Olive looked up with languid surprise, 'few of us are called upon to do a more difficult task than yours ; to take up life when we would choose death, to bear patiently the discipline of suffering and inaction, to wait till He says "work."'

'Dear Aunt Milly, you always say such comforting things. I thought I was only doing nothing but give you trouble.'

'There you were wrong, Olive ; every time you suppress an impatient sigh, every time you call up a smile to cheer us, you are advancing a step, gaining a momentary advantage over your old enemy ; you know my favourite verses—

> "Broadest streams from narrowest sources,
> Noblest trees from meanest seeds,
> Mighty ends from small beginnings,
> From lowly promise lofty deeds.
>
> "Acorns which the winds have scattered,
> Future navies may provide ;
> Thoughts at midnight, whispered lowly,
> Prove a people's future guide."

I am a firm believer in little efforts, Olive.'

Olive was silent for a few minutes, but she appeared thinking deeply ; but when she spoke next it was in a calmer tone.

'After all, Aunt Milly, want of courage is my greatest fault.'

'I cannot deny it, dear.'

'I am so afraid of responsibility that it seemed easier to die than to face it. You were right; I was selfish to want to leave you all.'

'You must try to rejoice with us that you are spared.'

'Yes, I will try,' with a sigh; but as she began to look white and exhausted, Mildred thought it wiser to drop the conversation.

The family circle was again complete in the vicarage, and in the evenings a part of the family always gathered in the sick-room. This was hailed as a great privilege by the younger members—Roy, Polly, and Chriss eagerly disputing it. It was an understood thing that Richard should be always there; Olive seemed restless without him. Roy was her next favourite; his gentleness and affection seemed to soothe her; but Mildred noticed that Polly's bright flow of spirits somewhat oppressed her, and it was not easy to check Chriss's voluble tongue.

One evening Ethel was admitted. She had pleaded so hard that Richard had at last overcome Olive's shrinking reluctance to face any one outside the family circle; but even Olive's timidity was not proof against Ethel's endearing ways; and as Miss Trelawny, shocked and distressed at her changed appearance, folded the girl silently in her arms, the tears gathered to her eyes, and for a moment she seemed unable to speak.

'You must not be so sorry,' whispered Olive, gratefully; 'Aunt Milly will soon nurse me quite well.'

'But I was not prepared for such a change,' stammered Ethel. 'Dear Olive, to think how you must have suffered! I should hardly have known you; and yet,' she continued, impulsively, 'I never liked the look of you so well.'

'We tell her she has grown,' observed Richard, cheerfully; 'she has only to get fat to make a fine woman. Aunt Milly has contrived such a bewitching head-dress that we do not regret the loss of all that beautiful hair.'

'Oh, Cardie, as though that mattered;' but Olive blushed under her brother's affectionate scrutiny. Ethel Trelawny was right when she owned Olive's appearance had never pleased her more, emaciated and changed as she was. The sad gentleness of the dark, unsmiling eyes was infinitely attractive. The heavy sallowness was gone; the thin white face looked fair and transparent; little rings of dark hair peeped under the lace cap; but what struck Ethel most was the rapt and elevated expression of the girl's face—a little dreamy, perhaps, but suggestive of another and nobler Olive.

'Oh, Olive, how strange it seems, to think you have come back to us again, when Mildred thought you had gone!' ejaculated Ethel, in a tone almost of awe.

'Yes,' returned Olive, simply; 'I know what death means now. When I come to die, I shall feel I know it all before.'

'But you did not die, dear Olive!' exclaimed Ethel, in a startled voice. 'No one can know but Lazarus and the widow's son; and they have told us nothing.'

'Aunt Milly says they were not allowed to tell; she thinks there is something awful in their silence; but all the same I shall always feel that I know what dying means.'

Ethel looked at her with a new reverence in her eyes. Was this the stammering, awkward Olive?

'Tell me what you mean,' she whispered gently; 'I cannot understand. One must die before one can solve the mystery.'

'And was I not dying?' returned Olive, in the same dreamy tone. 'When I close my eyes I can bring it all back; the faintness, the dizziness, the great circles of light, the deadly, shuddering cold creeping over my limbs, every one weeping round me, and yet beyond a great silence and darkness; we begin to understand what silence means then.'

'A great writer once spoke of "voices at the other end of silence,"' returned Ethel, in a stifled tone. This strange talk attracted and yet oppressed her.

'But silence itself—what is silence?—one sometimes stops to think about it, and then its grandeur seems to crush one. What if silence be the voice of God!'

'Dear Livy, you must not excite yourself,' interrupted Richard; but his tone was awestruck too.

'Great thoughts do not excite,' she returned, calmly. She had forgotten Ethel—all of them. From the couch where she lay she could see the dark violet fells, the soft restful billows of green, silver splashes of light through the trees. How peaceful and quiet it all looked. Ah! if it had only been given her to walk in those green pastures and 'beside the still waters of the Paradise of God;' if that day which shall be known to the Lord 'had come to her when "at eventide it shall be light;"'—eventide!—alas! for her there still must remain the burden and heat of the day—sultry youth, weariness of premature age, 'light that shall neither be clear nor dark,' before that blessed

13

eventide should come, 'and she should pass through the silence into the rest beyond.'

'Aunt Milly, if you or Cardie would read me something,' she said at last, with a wonderful sadness in her voice; and as they hastened to comply with her wish, the brief agitation vanished from her face. What if it were not His will! what if some noble work stood ready to her faltering hand, "content to fill a little space, if Thou be glorified!" 'Oh, I must learn to say that,' she whispered.

'Are you tired, Livy?' asked Richard at last, as he paused a moment in his reading; but there was no answer. Olive's eyes were closed. One thin hand lay under her cheek, a tear hung on the eyelashes; but on the sleeping face there lay an expression of quiet peace that was almost childlike.

It was noticed that Olive mended more rapidly from that evening. Dr. Heriot had recommended change of air; and as Olive was too weak to bear a long journey, Mildred took her to Redcar for a few weeks. Richard accompanied them, but did not remain long, as his father seemed unwilling to lose him during his last few months at home.

During their absence two important events took place at the vicarage. Dad Fabian paid his promised visit, and the new curate arrived. Polly's and Chriss's letter brimmed over with news. 'Every one was delighted with her dear old Dad,' Polly wrote; 'Richard was gracious, Mr. Lambert friendly, and Roy enthusiastically admiring.'

Dad had actually bought a new coat and had cut his hair, which Polly owned was a grief to her; 'and his beard looked like everybody else's beard,' wrote the girl with a groan. If it had not been for his snuff-box she would hardly have known him. Some dealer had bought his *Cain*, and the old man's empty pockets were replenished.

It was a real joy to Olive's affectionate heart to know that Roy's juvenile efforts were appreciated by so great a man. Mildred, who was almost as simple in worldly matters as her niece, was also a devout believer in Dad Fabian's capabilities. The dark-lined picture of Cain fleeing from his avenging conscience, with his weeping guardian angel by his side, had made a great impression on her.

Olive and she had long talks over Polly's rapid scrawls. Roy had genius, and was to be an artist after all. He was to enter a London studio after Christmas. Dad Fabian knew the widow of an artist living near Hampstead who would board and lodge

him, and look after him as though he were a son of her own ;
and Dad Fabian himself was to act as his sponsor, art-guide, and
chaperon.

'My guardian thinks very highly of Dad,' wrote Polly, in her
pretty, childish handwriting. 'He calls him an unappreciated
genius, and says Roy will be quite safe under his care. Dad is a
little disappointed Roy's forte is landscape painting ; he wanted
him to go in for high art ; but Roy paints clouds better than faces.'

'Dear Roy, how we shall miss him !' sighed Olive, as she
laid the letter down.

'Polly more than any one,' observed Mildred, thinking how
strange it would be to see one bright face without the other close
to it.

The new curate was rather a tame affair after this.

'His name is Hugh Marsden, and he is to live at Miss
Farrer's, the milliner,' announced Olive one day, when she had
received a letter from Richard. 'Miss Farrer has two very nice
rooms looking over the marketplace. Her last lodger was a
young engineer, and it made a great difference to her income
when he left her. Richard says he is a "Queen's man, and a
very nice fellow ;" he is only in deacon's orders.'

'Let us see what Chriss has to say about him in her letter,'
returned Mildred ; but she contemplated a little ruefully the
crabbed, irregular writing, every word looking like a miniature
edition of Contradiction Chriss herself.

'Mr. Marsden has arrived,' scrawled Chriss, 'and has just had
tea here. I don't think we shall like him at all. Roy says he is
a jolly fellow, and is fond of cricket and fishing, and those sort of
things, but he looks too much like a big boy for my taste ; I
don't like such large young men ; and he has big hands and feet
and a great voice, and his laugh is as big as the rest of him. I
think him dreadfully ugly, but Polly says "No, he has nice honest
eyes."

'He tried to talk to Polly and me ; only wasn't it rude,
Aunt Milly ? He called me my dear, and asked me if I liked
dolls. I felt I could have withered him on the spot, only he
was so stupid and obtuse that he took no notice, and went on
about his little sister Sophy, who had twelve dolls, whom she
dressed to represent the twelve months in the year, and how she
nearly broke her heart when he sat down on them by accident
and smashed July.'

Roy gave a comical description of the whole thing and Chriss's
wrathful discomfiture.

'We have just had great fun,' he wrote; 'the Rev. Hugh has just been here to tea; he is a capital fellow—up to larks, and with plenty of go in him, and with a fine deep voice for intoning; he is wild about training the choir already. He talked a great deal about his mother and sisters; he is an only son. I bet you anything, you women will be bored to death with Dora, Florence, and Sophy. If they are like him they are not handsome. One thing I must tell you, he riled Contradiction awfully by asking her if she liked dolls; she was Pugilist Pug then and no mistake. You should have seen the air with which she drew herself up. "I suppose you take me for a little girl," quoth she. Marsden's face was a study. "I am afraid you will take her for a spoilt one," says Dad, patting her shoulder, which only made matters worse. "I think your sister must be very silly with her twelve seasons," bursts out Chriss. "I would sooner do algebra than play with dolls; but if you will excuse me, I have my Cæsar to construe;" and she walked out of the room with her chin in the air, and every curl on her head bristling with wrath. Marsden sat open-mouthed with astonishment, and Dad was forced to apologise; and there was Polly all the time "behaving like a little lady."'

'As though Polly could do wrong,' observed Mildred with a smile, as she finished Roy's ridiculous effusion.

It was the beginning of October when they returned home. Olive had by this time recovered her strength, and was able to enjoy her rambles on the sand; and though Mr. Lambert found fault with the thin cheeks and lack of robustness, his anxiety was set at rest by Mildred, who declared Olive had done credit to her nursing, and a little want of flesh was all the fault that could be found with her charge.

The welcome home was sweet to the restored invalid. Richard's kiss was scarcely less fond than her father's. Roy pinched her cheek to be sure that this was a real, and not a make-believe, Olive; while Polly followed her to her room to assure herself that her hair had really grown half an inch, as Aunt Milly declared it had.

Nor was Mildred's welcome less hearty.

'How good it is to see you in your old place, Aunt Milly,' said Richard, with an affectionate glance, as he placed himself beside her at the tea-table.

'We have missed you, Milly!' exclaimed her brother a moment afterwards. 'Heriot was saying only last night that the vicarage did not seem itself without you.'

'Nothing is right without Aunt Milly!' cried Polly, with a squeeze; and Roy chimed in, indignantly, 'Of course not; as though we could do without Aunt Milly!'

The new curate was discussed the first evening. Mr. Lambert and Richard were loud in their praises; and though Chriss muttered to herself in a surly undertone, nobody minded her.

His introduction to Olive happened after a somewhat amusing fashion.

He was crossing the hall the next day, on his way to the vicar's study, when Roy bade him go into the drawing-room and make acquaintance with Aunt Milly.

It happened that Mildred had just left the room, and Olive was sitting alone, working.

She looked up a little surprised at the tall, broad-shouldered young man who was making his way across the room.

'Royal told me I should find you here, Miss Lambert. I hope your niece has recovered the fatigue of her journey.'

'I am not Aunt Milly; I am Olive,' returned the girl, gravely, but not refusing the proffered hand. 'You are my father's new curate, Mr. Marsden, I suppose?'

'Yes; I beg your pardon, I have made a foolish mistake I see,' returned the young man, confusedly, stammering and flushing over his words. 'Royal sent me in to find his aunt, and—and—I did not notice.'

'What does it matter?' returned Olive, simply. The curate's evident nervousness made her anxious to set him at his ease. 'You could not know; and Aunt Milly looks so young, and my illness has changed me. It was such a natural mistake, you see,' with the soft seriousness with which Olive always spoke now.

'Thank you; yes, of course,' stammered Hugh, twirling his felt hat through his fingers, and looking down at her with a sort of puzzled wonder. The grave young face under the quaint head-dress, the soft dark hair just parted on the forehead, the large earnest eyes, candid, and yet unsmiling, filled him with a sort of awe and reverence.

'You have been very ill,' he said at last, with a pitying chord in his voice. 'People do not look like that who have not suffered. You remind me,' he continued, sitting down beside her, and speaking a little huskily, 'of a sister whom I lost not so very long ago.'

Olive looked up with a sudden gleam in her eyes.

'Did she die?'

'Yes. You are more fortunate, Miss Lambert; you were permitted to get well.'

'You are a clergyman, and you say that,' she returned, a little breathlessly. 'If it were not wrong I should envy your sister, who finished her work so young.'

'Hush, Miss Lambert, that is wrong,' replied Hugh. His brief nervousness had vanished; he was quite grave ·now; his round, boyish face, ruddy and brown with exercise, paled a little with his earnestness and the memory of a past pain.

'Caroline wanted to live, and you want to die,' he said, in a voice full of rebuke. 'She cried because she was young, and did not wish to leave us, and because she feared death; and you are sorry to live.'

'I have always found life so hard,' sighed Olive. It did not seem strange to her that she should be talking thus to a stranger; was he not a clergyman—her father's curate—in spite of his boyish face? 'St. Paul thought it was better, you know; but indeed I am trying to be glad, Mr. Marsden, that I have all this time before me.'

'Trying to be glad for the gift of life!' Here was a mystery to be solved by the Rev. Hugh Marsden, he who rejoiced in life with the whole strength of his vigorous young heart; who loved all living things, man, woman, and child—nay, the very dumb animals themselves; who drank in light and vigour and cheerfulness as his daily food; who was glad for mere gladness' sake; to whom sin was the only evil in the world, and suffering a privilege, and not a punishment; who measured all things, animate and inanimate, with a merciful breadth of views, full of that 'charity that thinketh no evil,'—he to be told by this grave, pale girl that she envied his sister who died.

'What is the matter—have I shocked you?' asked Olive, her sensitiveness taking alarm at his silence.

'Yes—no; I am sorry for you, that is all, Miss Lambert. I am young, but I am a clergyman, as you say. I love life, as I love all the good gifts of my God; and I think,' hesitating and dropping his voice, 'your one prayer should be, that He may teach you to be glad.'

CHAPTER XVII

' And still I changed—I was a boy no more ;
My heart was large enough to hold my kind,
And all the world. As hath been apt before
With youth, I sought, but I could never find
Work hard enough to quiet my self-strife,
And the strength of action craving life.
She, too, was changed.'—JEAN INGELOW.

IN the histories of most families there are long even pauses
during which life flows smoothly in uneventful channels, when
there are few breaks and fewer incidents to chronicle ; times
when the silent ingathering of individual interests deepens and
widens imperceptibly into an under-current of strength ready
for the crises of emergency. Times of peace alternating with
the petty warfare which is the prerogative of kinsmanship, a
blessed routine of daily duty misnamed by the young monotony,
but which in reality is to train them for the rank and file in
the great human army hereafter ; quiescent times during
which the memory of past troubles is mercifully obliterated
by present ease, and ' the cloud no bigger than a man's hand '
does not as yet obscure the soft breadth of heaven's blue.

Such a time had come to the Lamberts. The three years
that followed Olive's illness and tardy convalescence were quite
uneventful ones, marked with few incidents worthy of note ;
outwardly things had seemed unchanged, but how deep and
strong was the under-current of each young individual life ;
what rapid developments, what unfolding of fresh life and
interests in the budding manhood and womanhood within the
old vicarage walls.

Such thoughts as these came tranquilly to Mildred as she sat
alone one July day in the same room where, three years before,
the Angels of Life and Death had wrestled over one frail girl,

in the room where she had so patiently and tenderly nursed
Olive's sick body and mind back to health.

For once in her life busy Mildred was idle, the work lay unfolded beside her, while her eyes wandered dreamily over the
fair expanse of sunny green dotted with browsing sheep and
tuneful with the plaintive bleating of lambs ; there was a crisp
crunching of cattle hoofs on the beck gravel below, a light wind
touched the elms and thorns and woke a soft soughing, the tall
poplar swayed drowsily with a flicker of shaking leaves ; beyond
the sunshine lay the blue dusk of the circling hills, prospect fit
to inspire a day-dream, even in a nature more prosaic than
Mildred Lambert's.

It was Mildred's birthday ; she was thirty to-day, and she
was smiling to herself at the thoughts that she felt younger and
brighter and happier than she had three years before.

They had been such peaceful years, full of congenial work
and blessed with sympathetic fellowship ; she had sown so
poorly, she thought, and had reaped such rich harvests of
requited love ; she had come amongst them a stranger three years
ago, and now she could number friends by the score ; even her
poorer neighbours loved and trusted her, their northern reserve
quite broken down by her tender womanly graces.

'There are two people in Kirkby Stephen that would be
sorely missed,' a respectable tradesman once said to Miss Trelawny, 'and they are Miss Lambert and Dr. Heriot, and I don't
know which is the greater favourite. I should have lost my
wife last year but for her ; she sat up with her three nights
running when that fever got hold of her.'

And an old woman in the workhouse said once to Dr. Heriot
when he wished her to see the vicar :

'Nae thanks to ye, doctor ; ye needn't bother yersel' about
minister, Miss Lambert has sense enough. I wudn't git mair
gude words nir she gi'es ; she's terrible gude, bless her ;' and
many would have echoed old Sally Bates's opinion.

Mildred's downright simplicity and unselfishness were winning all hearts.

'Aunt Milly has such a trustworthy face, people are obliged
to tell their troubles when they look at her,' Polly said once,
and perhaps the girl held the right clue to the secret of Mildred
Lambert's influence.

Real sympathy, that spontaneity of vigorous warm feeling
emanating from the sight of others' pain, is rarer than we
imagine. Without exactly giving expression to conventional

forms of condolence, Mildred conveyed the most delicate sympathy in every look and word ; by a rapid transit of emotion, she seemed to place herself in the position of the bereaved ; to feel as they felt—the sacred silence of sorrow ; her few words never grazed the outer edge of that bitter irritability that trenches on great pain, and so her mere presence seemed to soothe them.

Her perfect unconsciousness added to this feeling ; there were times when Mildred's sympathy was so intense that she absolutely lost herself. 'What have I done that you should thank me ?' was a common speech with her ; in her own opinion she had done absolutely nothing ; she had so merged her own individual feelings into the case before her that gratitude was a literal shock to her, and this same simplicity kept her quiet and humble under the growing idolatry of her nephews and nieces.

'My dear Miss Lambert, how they all love you,' Mrs. Delaware said to her once ; 'even that fine grown young man Richard seems to lay himself out to please you.'

'How can they help loving me,' returned Mildred, with that shy soft smile of hers, ' when I love them so dearly, and they see it ? Of course I do not deserve it ; but it is the old story, love begets love ;' and the glad, steady light in her eyes spoke of her deep content.

Yes, Mildred was happy ; the quiet woman joyed in her life with an intense appreciation that Olive would have envied. Mildred never guessed that there were secret springs to this fountain of gladness, that the strongly-cemented friendship between herself and Dr. Heriot added a fresh charm to her life, investing it with the atmosphere of unknown vigour and strength. Mildred had always been proud of her brother's intellect and goodness, but she had never learnt to rely so entirely on his sagacity as she now did on Dr. Heriot.

If any one had questioned her feelings with respect to the vicarage Mentor, Mildred would have assured them with her sweet honesty that her brother's friend was hers also, that she did full justice to his merits, and was ready to own that his absence would leave a terrible gap in their circle ; but even Mildred did not know how much she had learnt to depend on the sympathy that never failed her and the quick appreciation that was almost intuitive.

Mildred knew that Dr. Heriot liked her ; he had found her trustworthy in time of need, and he showed his gratitude by making fresh demands on her time and patience most unblushingly : in his intercourse with her there had always been a curious mixture of reverence and tenderness which was far removed from any warmer feeling, though in one sense it might be called brotherly.

Perhaps Mildred was to blame for this; in spite of her appreciation of Dr. Heriot, she had never broken through her habit of shy reserve, which was a second nature with her—the old girlish Mildred was hidden out of sight. Dr. Heriot only saw in his friend's sister a gentle, soft-eyed woman, seeming older than she really was, and with tender, old-fashioned ways, always habited in sober grays and with a certain staidness of mien and quiet precision of speech, which, with all its restfulness, took away the impression of youth.

Yes, good and womanly as he thought her, Dr. Heriot was ignorant of the real Mildred. Aunt Milly alone with her boys, blushing and dimpling under their saucy praise, would have shattered all his ideas of primness ; just as those fits of wise eloquence, while Olive and Polly lingered near her in the dark, the sweet impulse of words that stirred them to their hearts' core, would have roused his latent enthusiasm to the utmost.

Dr. Heriot's true ideal of womanly beauty and goodness passed his door daily, disguised in Quaker grays and the large shady black hat that was for use and not for ornament, but he did not know it; when he looked out it was to note how fresh and piquant Polly looked in her white dress and blue ribbons as she tripped beside Mildred, or how the Spanish hat with its long black feather suited Olive's sombre complexion.

Olive had greatly improved since her illness; she was still irredeemably plain in her own eyes, but few were ready to endorse this opinion ; her figure had rounded and filled out into almost majestic proportions, her shoulders had lost their ungainly stoop, and her slow movements were not without grace.

Her complexion would always be sallow, but the dark abundant hair was now arranged to some advantage, and the large earnest eyes were her redeeming features, while a settled but soft seriousness had replaced the old absorbing melancholy.

Olive would never look on the brighter side of life as a happier and more sanguine temperament would ; she still took life seriously, almost solemnly, though she had ceased to repine that length of days had been given her ; with her, conscientiousness was still a fault, and she would ever be given to weigh herself carefully and be found wanting ; but there were times when even Olive owned herself happy, when the grave face would relax into smiles and the dark eyes grow bright and soft.

And there were reasons for this ; Olive no longer suffered the pangs of passionate and unrequited love, and her heart was at rest concerning Richard.

For two years the sad groping after truth, the mute search for vocation, the conflict between duty and inclination, had continued, and still the grave, stern face, kindly but impressive, has given no clue to his future plans. 'I will tell you when I know myself, father,' was his parting speech more than once. 'I trust you, Cardie, and I am content to wait,' was ever his father's answer.

But deliverance came at last, when the fetters fell off the noble young soul, when every word in the letter that reached Mr. Lambert spoke of the new-born gladness that filled his son's heart ; there was no reticence.

'You trusted me and you were content to wait then ; how often I have repeated these words to myself, dear father ; you have waited, and now your patience shall be rewarded.

'Father, at last I know myself and my own mind ; the last wave of doubt and fear has rolled off me ; I can see it all now, I feel sure. I write it tremblingly. I feel sure that it is all true.

'Oh, how good God has been to me ! I feel almost like the prodigal ; only no husks could have satisfied me for a moment ; it was only the truth I wanted—truth literal and divine ; and, father, you have no reason to think sadly of me any longer, for "before eventide my light has come." '

'I am writing now to tell you that it is my firm and unalterable intention to carry out your and my mother's wishes with respect to my profession ; will you ask my friends not to seek to dissuade me, especially my friends at Kirkleatham ? You know how sorely inclination has already tempted me ; believe me, I have counted the cost and weighed the whole matter calmly and dispassionately. I have much to relinquish—many favourite pursuits, many secret ambitions—but shall I give what costs me nothing ? and after all I am only thankful that I am not considered too unworthy for the work.'

It was this letter, so humble and so manly, that filled Olive's brown eyes with light and lifted the weight from her heart. Cardie had not disappointed her ; he had been true to himself

and his own convictions. Mildred alone had her misgivings ;
when she next saw Richard, she thought that he looked worn
and pale, and even fancied his cheerfulness was a little forced ;
and his admission that he had slept badly for two or three
nights so filled her with alarm that she determined to speak to
him at all costs.

His composed and devout demeanour at service next morning, however, a little comforted her, and she was hesitating
whether the change in him might be her own fancy, when
Richard himself broke the ice by an abrupt question as they
were walking towards Musgrave that same afternoon.

' What is all this about Ethel Trelawny, Aunt Milly ? '

And Mildred absolutely started at his tone, it was suppressed
and yet so eager.

' She will not return to Kirkleatham for some weeks, Richard ;
she and her father are visiting in Scotland.'

Richard turned very pale.

' It is true, then, Aunt Milly ? '

' What is true ? '

' That she is engaged to that man ? '

' To Sir Robert Ferrers ?   What I have you heard of that ?
No, indeed, Richard, she has refused him most decidedly ; why
he is old enough to be her father I '

' That is no objection with ome women.   Are you sure ?
They are not in Renfrewshire, then

' They have never been there ; they are staying with friends
near Ballater.   Why, Richard, what is this ? ' as Richard stopped
as though he were giddy and covered his face with his hands.

' I never meant you or any one to know,' he gasped at length,
while Mildred watched his varying colour with alarm ; ' but I
have not been able to sleep since I heard, and the suddenness
of the relief—oh I are you quite sure, Aunt Milly ? ' with a
painful eagerness in his tone very strange to hear in grave, self-
contained Richard.

' Dear Cardie, let there be full confidence between us ; you
see you have unwittingly betrayed yourself.'

' Yes, I have betrayed myself,' he muttered with increasing
agitation ; ' what a fool you must think me, Aunt Milly, and
all because I could not put a question quietly ; but I was not
prepared for your answer ; what a consummate——'

' Hush, don't call yourself names.   I knew your secret
long ago, Cardie.   I knew what friends you and Ethel Trelawny
were.'

A boyish flush suffused his face.

'Ethel is very fond of her old playmate.'

He winced as though with sudden pain.

'Ah, that is just it, Aunt Milly; she is fond of me and nothing else.'

'I like her name for you, Cœur-de-Lion, it sounds so musical from her lips; you are her friend, Richard; she trusts you implicitly.'

'I believe—I hope she does;' but drawing his hand again before his eyes, 'I am too young, Aunt Milly. I was only one-and-twenty last month.'

'True, and Sir Robert was nearly fifty; she refused a fine estate there.'

'Was her father angry with her?'

'Not so terribly incensed as he was about Mr. Cathcart the year before. Mr. Cathcart had double his fortune and was a young, good-looking man. I was almost afraid that in her misery she should be driven to marry him.'

'He has no right to persecute her so; why should he be so anxious to get rid of his only child?'

'That is what we all say. Poor Ethel, hers is no light cross. I am thankful she is beginning to take it patiently; the loss of a father's love must be dreadful, and hers is a proud spirit.'

'But not now; you said yourself, Aunt Milly, how nobly she behaved in that last affair.'

'True,' continued Mildred in a sorrowful tone; 'all the more that she was inclined to succumb to a momentary fascination; but I am certain that with all his intellect Mr. Cathcart would have been a most undesirable husband for her; Sir Robert Ferrers is far preferable.'

'Aunt Milly!'

'Yes, Richard, and I told her so; but her only answer was that she would not marry where she could not love. I am afraid this will widen the breach between her and her father; her last letter was very sad.'

'It is tyranny, downright persecution; how dares he. Oh, Aunt Milly!' in a tone of deep despondency, 'if I were only ten years older.'

'I am afraid you are very young, Cardie. I wish you had not set your heart on this.'

'Yes, we are too much of an age; but she need not fear, I am older in everything than she; there is nothing boyish about me, is there, Aunt Milly?'

'Not in your love for Ethel, I am afraid ; but, Cardie, what would her father say if he knew it ?'

'He will know it some day. Look here, Aunt Milly, I am one-and-twenty now, and I have loved Ethel, Miss Trelawny I mean, since I was a boy of twelve ; people may laugh, but I felt for my old playmate something of what I feel now. She was always different from any one else in my eyes. I remember telling my mother when I was only ten that Ethel should be my wife.'

'But, Richard——'

'I know what you are going to say—that it is all hopeless moonshine, that a curate with four or five hundred a year has no right to presume to Mr. Trelawny's heiress ; that is what he and the world will tell me ; but how am I to help loving her ?'

'What am I to say to you, Cardie ? Long before you are your father's curate Ethel may have met the man she can love.'

'Then I shall bear my trouble, I hope, manfully. Don't you think this is my one dread, that and being so young in her eyes ? How little she knew how she tempted me when she told me I ought to distinguish myself at the Bar ; I felt as though it were giving her up when I decided on taking orders.'

'She would call you a veritable Cœur-de-Lion if she knew. Oh ! my poor boy, how hardly this has gone with you,' as Richard's face whitened again with emotion.

'It has been terribly hard,' he returned, almost inaudibly ; 'it was not so much at last reluctance and fear of the work as the horrible dread of losing her by my own act. I thought—it was foolish and young of me, I daresay—but I thought that as people spoke of my capabilities I might in time win a position that should be worthy even of her. Oh, Aunt Milly ! what a fool you must think me.'

Richard's clear glance was overcast with pain as he spoke, but Mildred's affectionate smile spoke volumes.

'I think I never loved you so well, Cardie, now I know how nobly you have acted. Have you told your father of this ?'

'No, but I am sure he knows ; you have no idea how much he notices ; he said something to me once that showed me he was aware of my feelings ; we have no secrets now ; that is your doing, Aunt Milly.'

Mildred shook her head.

'Ah, but it was ; you were the first to break down my reserve ; what a churl I must have been in those days. You all think too well of me as it is. Livy especially puts me in a bad humour with myself.'

'I wanted to speak to you of Olive, Richard; are you not thankful that she has found her vocation at last?'

'Indeed I am. I wrote my congratulations by return of post. Fancy Kirke and Steadman undertaking to publish those poems, and Livy only eighteen!'

'Dr. Heriot always told us she had genius. Some of them are really very beautiful. Dear Olive, you should have seen her face when the letter came.'

'I know; I would have given anything to be there.'

'She looked quite radiant, and yet so touchingly humble when she held it out to her father, and then without waiting for us to read it she left the room. I know she was thanking God for it on her knees, Richard, while we were all gossiping to Dr. Heriot on Livy's good fortune.'

Richard looked touched.

'What an example she is to us all; if she would only believe half the good of herself that we do, Aunt Milly.'

'Then she would lose all her childlike humility. I think she gets .less morbidly self-conscious year by year; there is no denying she is brighter.'

'She could not help it, brought into contact with such a nature as Marsden's; that fellow gives one the impression of perfect mental and bodily health. Dr. John told me it was quite refreshing to look at him.'

'Chriss amuses me, she will have it he is so noisy.'

'He has a loud laugh certainly, and his voice is not exactly low-pitched, but he is a splendid fellow. Roy keeps up a steady correspondence with him. By the bye, I have not shown you my last letter from Rome;' and Richard, who had regained his tranquillity and ordinary manner, pulled the thin, foreign-looking envelope from his breast-pocket and entertained Mildred for the remainder of the way with an amusing account cf some of Roy's Roman adventures.

That night, as Richard sat alone with his father in the study, Mr. Lambert placed his hand affectionately on his son's broad shoulder with a look that was rather more scrutinising than usual.

'So the last cloud has cleared away; that is right, Cardie.'

'I do not understand you, father;' but the young man faltered a little under his father's quiet glance.

'Nay, it is for you to explain; only last night you seemed

as though you had some trouble on your mind, you were anxious and absorbed, and this evening the oppression seems removed.'

For a moment Richard hesitated, and the old boyish flush came to his face, and then his determination was taken.

'Father,' he said, speaking in a quick, resolute tone, and tossing back his wave of dark hair as he spoke, always a trick of his when agitated, 'there shall be no half-confidence between us ; yesterday I was heavy at heart because I thought Ethel Trelawny would marry Sir Robert Ferrers ; to-day I hear she has refused him and the weight is gone.'

Mr. Lambert gave a low, dismayed exclamation, and his hand dropped from his son's shoulder.

'Ah, is it so, my poor boy?' he said at last, and there was no mistaking the sorrowful tone.

'Yes, it is so, father,' he returned firmly ; 'you may call me a fool for my pains—I do not know, perhaps I am one—but it is too late to help it now ; the mischief is of too long standing.'

In spite of his very real sympathy a smile crossed his father's lips, and yet as he looked at Richard it somehow died away. Youthful as he was, barely one-and-twenty, there was a set determination, a staid manliness, in his whole mien that added five years at least to his age.

Even to a disinterested eye he seemed a son of whom any father might be proud ; not tall—the massive, thick-set figure seemed made for strength more than grace—but the face was pre-eminently handsome, the dark eyes beamed with intelligence, the forehead was broad and benevolent, the lips still closed with the old inflexibility, but the hard lines had relaxed : firm and dominant, yet ruled by the single eye of integral principle ; there was no fear that Richard Lambert would ever overstep the boundaries of a clearly-defined right.

'That is my brave boy,' murmured his father at last, watching him with a sort of wistful pain ; 'but, Cardie, I cannot but feel grieved that you have set your heart on this girl.'

'What ! do you doubt the wisdom or the fitness of my choice ?' demanded the young man hotly.

'Both, Cardie ; the girl is everything that one could wish ; dear to me almost as a daughter of my own, but Trelawny—ah, my poor boy, do you dream that you can satisfy her father's ambition ?'

'I shall not try to do so,' returned Richard, speaking with set lips ; 'I know him too well ; he would sell her to the highest bidder, sell his own flesh and blood ; but she is too noble for his corrupting influence.'

'You speak bitterly, Cardie.'

'I speak as I feel. Look here, father, foolishly or wisely, it does not matter now, I have set my heart on this thing ; I have grown up with this one idea before me, the hope of one day, however distant, calling Ethel Trelawny my wife. I do not think I am one to change.'

Mr. Lambert shook his head.

'I fear not, Cardie.'

'I am as sure of the faithfulness of my own heart as I am that I am standing here ; young as I am, I know I love her as you loved my mother.'

His father covered his face with his hand.

'No, no ; do not say that, Cardie.'

'I must say what is true ; you would not have me lie to you.'

'Surely not ; but, my boy, this is a hard hearing.'

'You are thinking of Mr. Trelawny,' returned Richard, quietly ; 'that is not my worst fear ; my chief obstacle is Ethel herself.'

'What ! you doubt her returning your affection ?' asked his father.

'Yes, I doubt it,' was the truthful answer ; but it was made with quivering lips. 'I dread lest I should not satisfy her exacting fastidiousness ; but all the same I mean to try ; you will bid me Godspeed, father ?'

'Yes, yes ; but, Cardie, be prudent, remember how little you have to offer—a few hundreds a year where she has thousands, not even a curacy !'

'You think I ought to wait a little ; another year—two perhaps ?'

'That is my opinion, certainly.'

Richard crossed the room once or twice with a rapid, disordered stride, and then he returned to his father's side.

'You are right ; I must not do anything rashly or impulsively just because I fear to lose her. I ought not to speak even to her until I have taken orders ; and yet if I could only make her understand how it is without speaking.'

'You must be very prudent, Cardie ; remember my son has no right to aspire to an heiress.'

Richard's face clouded.

'That dreadful money ! There is one comfort—I believe she

14

hates it as much as I do; but it is not entailed property—he can leave it all away from her.'

'Yes, if she displeases him. Mildred tells me he holds this threat perpetually over her; poor girl, he makes her a bad father.'

'His conduct is unjustifiable in every way,' returned Richard in a stifled voice; 'any one less noble would be tempted to make their escape at all hazards, but she endures her wretchedness so patiently. Sometimes I fancy, father, that when she can bear her loneliness no longer my time for speaking will come, and then——'

But Richard had no time to finish his sentence, for just then Dr. Heriot's knock sounded at the door, and with a mute handshake of perfect confidence the father and son separated for the night.

This conversation had taken place nearly a year before, but from that time it had never been resumed; sacredly did Mr. Lambert guard his boy's confidence, and save that there was a deferential tenderness in his manner to Ethel Trelawny and a wistful pain in his eyes when he saw Richard beside her, no one would have guessed how heavily his son's future weighed on his heart. Richard's manner remained unchanged; it was a little graver, perhaps, and indicative of greater thoughtfulness, but there was nothing lover-like in his demeanour, nothing that would check or repel the warm sisterly affection that Ethel evidently cherished for him; only at times Ethel wondered why it was that Richard's opinions seemed to influence her more than they used, and to marvel at her vivid remembrance of past looks and speeches.

Somehow every time she saw him he seemed less like her old playmate, Cœur-de-Lion, and transformed into an older and graver Richard; perhaps it might be that the halo of the future priesthood already surrounded him; but for whatever reason it might be, Ethel was certainly less dictatorial and argumentative in her demeanour towards him, and that a very real friendship seemed growing up between them.

Richard was more than two-and-twenty now, and Roy just a year younger; in another eight months he would be ordained deacon; as yet he had made no sign, but as Mildred sat pondering over the retrospect of the three last years in the golden and dreamy afternoon, she was driven to confess that her boys were now men, doing men's work in the world, and to wonder, with womanly shrinkings of heart, what the future might hold out to them of good and evil.

CHAPTER XVIII

OLIVE'S WORK

' Read from some humbler poet,
Whose songs gushed from his heart,
As showers from the clouds of summer,
Or tears from the eyelids start ;

' Who through long days of labour
And nights devoid of ease,
Still heard in his soul the music
Of wonderful melodies.

' Such songs have power to quiet
The restless pulse of care,
And come like the benediction
That follows after prayer.'—LONGFELLOW.

' AUNT MILLY, the book has come !'

Chriss's impetuous young voice roused Mildred from her
reverie. Chriss's eager footsteps, her shrill tone, broke in upon
the stillness, driving the gossamer threads of fancy hither and
thither by the very impetus of youthful noise and movement.
Mildred's folded hands dropped apart—she turned soft bewildered looks on the girl.

' What has come ? I do not understand you,' she said,
with a little laugh at her own bewilderment.

' Aunt Milly, what are you thinking about ? are you asleep
or dreaming ?' demanded Chriss, indignantly ; ' why the book
—Olive's book, to be sure.'

' Has it come ? My dear Chriss, how you startled me ; if
you had knocked, it would have been different, but bursting in
upon me like that.'

' One can't knock for ever,' grumbled Chriss, in an aggrieved
voice. ' Of course I thought you were asleep this hot afternoon ; but to see you sitting smiling to yourself, Aunt Milly,
in that aggravating way and not understanding when one
speaks.'

'Hush! I understand you now,' returned Mildred, colouring; 'one gets thinking sometimes, and——'

'Your thoughts must have been miles off, then,' retorted Chriss, with an inquisitive glance that seemed to embarrass Mildred, 'if it took you all that time to travel to the surface. Polly told me to fetch you, because tea is ready, and then the books came—such a big parcel!—and Olive's hand shook so that she could not undo the knots, and so she cut the string, and Cardie scolded her.'

'It was not much of a scolding, I expect.'

'Quite enough to bring Mr. Marsden to the rescue. "How can you presume to reprimand a poetess," he said, quite seriously; you should have heard Dr. John laugh. Look here, he has sent you these roses, Aunt Milly,' drawing from under her little silk apron a delicious bouquet of roses and maidenhair fern.

A pretty pink colour came into Mildred's cheeks.

'What beautiful roses! He must have remembered it was my birthday; how kind of him, Chriss. I must come down and thank him.'

'You must wear some in honour of the occasion—do, Aunt Milly; this deep crimson one will look so pretty on your gray silk dress; and you must put on the silver locket, with the blue velvet, that we all gave you.'

'Nonsense,' returned Mildred, blushing; but Chriss was inexorable.

Dr. Heriot looked up for the minute fairly startled when Mildred came in with her pink cheeks and her roses. Chriss's artful fingers, bent on mischief, had introduced a bud among the thick braids; the pretty brown hair looked unusually soft and glossy; the rarely seen dimple was in full play.

'You have done honour to my roses, I see,' he said, as Mildred thanked him, somewhat shyly, and joined the group round Olive.

The drawing-room table was heaped over with the new-smelling, little green volumes. As Mildred approached, Olive held out one limp soft copy with a hand that shook perceptibly.

'It has come at last, and on your birthday too; I am so glad,' she whispered as Mildred kissed her.

A soft light was in the girl's eyes, two spots of colour burnt in her usually pale cheeks, her hand closed and unclosed nervously on the arm of her chair.

'There, even Marsden says they are beautiful, and he does

not care much for poetry,' broke in Richard, triumphantly.
'Livy, it has come to this, that I am proud of my sister.'

'Hush, please don't talk so, Cardie,' remonstrated Olive with
a look of distress.

The spots of colour were almost hectic now, the smooth
forehead furrowed with anxiety; she looked ready to cry. This
hour was full of sweet torment to her. She shrank from this
home criticism, so precious yet so perilous: for the first time
she felt afraid of the utterance of her own written voice: if she
only could leave them all and make her escape. She looked up
almost pleadingly at Hugh Marsden, whose broad shoulders
were blocking up the window, but he misunderstood her.

'Yes, I think them beautiful; but your brother is right,
and I am no judge of poetry: metrical thoughts always appear
so strange, so puzzling to me—it seems to me like a prisoned
bird, beating itself against the bars of measurement and metres,
as though it tried to be free.'

'Why, you are talking poetry yourself,' returned Richard;
'that speech was worthy of Livy herself.'

Hugh burst into one of his great laughs; in her present
mood it jarred on Olive. Aunt Milly had left her, and was
talking to her father. Dr. John was at the other end of the
room, busy over his copy. Why would they talk about her so?
it was cruel of Cardie, knowing her as he did. She made a
little gesture, almost of supplication, looking up into the curate's
broad, radiant face, but the young man again misunderstood her.

'You must forgive me, I am sadly prosaic,' he returned,
speaking now in a lower key; 'these things are beyond me.
I do not pretend to understand them. That people should take
the trouble to measure out their words and thoughts—so many
feet, so many lines, a missed adjective, or a halting rhyme—it
is that that puzzles me.'

'Fie, man, what heresy; I am ashamed of you!' broke in
Richard, good-humouredly; 'you have forfeited Livy's good
opinion for ever.'

'I should be sorry to do that,' returned Hugh, seriously,
'but I cannot help it if I am different from other people.
When I was at college I used to take my sisters to the opera,
poor Caroline especially was fond of it: do you know it gave me
the oddest feeling. There was something almost ludicrous to
me in hearing the heroine of the piece trilling out her woes with
endless roulades; in real life people don't sing on their death-
beds.'

'Listen to him,' returned Richard, taking him by the shoulders; 'what is one to do with such a literal, matter-of-fact fellow? You ought to talk to him, Livy, and bring him to a better frame of mind.'

But Hugh was not to be silenced; he stood up manfully, with his great square shoulders blocking up the light, beaming down on Olive's shrinking gravity like a gentle-hearted giant; he was one to make himself heard, this big, clumsy young man. In spite of his boyish face and loud voice, people were beginning to speak well of Hugh Marsden; his youthful vigour and energy were waking up northern lethargy and fighting northern prejudice. Was not the surpliced choir owing mainly to his persevering efforts? and were not the ranks of the Dissenters already thinned by that loud-voiced but persuasive eloquence of his?

Olive absolutely cowered under it to-night. Hugh had no idea how his noisy vehemence was jarring on that desire for quiet, and a nice talk with Aunt Mildred, for which she was secretly longing; and yet she and Hugh were good friends.

'One can't help one's nature,' persisted Hugh, fumbling over the pages of one of the little green books with his big hands as he spoke. 'In the days of the primitive Church they had the gift of unknown tongues. I am sure much of our modern poetry needs interpretation.'

'Worse and worse. He will vote your "Songs of the Hearth" a mass of unintelligible rubbish directly.'

'You are too bad,' returned the young man with an honest blush; 'you will incense your sister against me. What I really mean is,' sitting down beside Olive and speaking so that Richard should not hear him, 'that poetry always seems to me more ornament than use. You cannot really have felt and experienced all you have described in that poem—"Coming Back," for example.'

'Hush, don't show it me,' returned Olive, hurriedly. 'I don't mind your saying this, but you do not know—the feeling comes, and then the words; these are thoughts too grand and deep for common forms of expression; they seem to flow of themselves into the measure you criticise. Oh! you do not understand——'

'No, but you can teach me to do so,' returned Hugh, quite gravely. He had laid aside his vehemence at the first sound of Olive's quiet voice; he had never lost his first impression of her, —he still regarded her with a sort of puzzled wonder and reverence. A poetess was not much in his line he told himself,—the only poetry he cared for was the Psalms, and perhaps Homer and Shakespeare. Yes, they were grand fellows, he thought; they could never see their like again. True, the 'Voices of the Hearth' were very beautiful, if he could only understand them.

'One cannot teach these things,' replied Olive, with her soft, serious smile.

As she answered Hugh she felt almost sorry for him, that this beautiful gift had come to her, and that he could not understand—that he who revelled in the good things of this life should miss one of its sweetest comforts.

She wondered vaguely over the young clergyman's denseness all the evening. Hugh had a stronger developed passion for music, and was further endowed with a deep rich baritone voice. As Olive heard him joining in the family glees, or beating time to Polly's nicely-executed pieces, she marvelled all the more over this omitted harmony in his nature. She had at last made her escape from the crowded, brilliantly-lighted room, and was pacing the dark terrace, pondering over it still when Mildred found her.

'Are you tired of us, Olive?'

'Not tired of you, Aunt Milly. I have scarcely spoken to you to-day, and it is your birthday, too,' putting her arm affectionately round Mildred, and half leaning against her. In her white dress Olive looked taller than ever. Richard was right when he said Livy would make a fine woman; she looked large and massive beside Mildred's slight figure. 'Dear Aunt Milly, I have so wanted to talk to you all the evening, but they would not let me.'

Mildred smiled fondly at her girl; during the last three years, ever since her illness, she had looked on Olive as a sacred and special charge, and as care begets tenderness as surely as love does love, so had Olive's ailing but noble nature gained a larger share of Mildred's warm affections than even Polly's brightness or Chriss's saucy piquancy could win.

'Have you been very happy to-night, dear?' she asked, softly. 'Have you been satisfied with Olive's ovation?'

'Oh, Aunt Milly! it has made me too glad; did you hear what Cardie said? it made me feel so proud and so ashamed. Do you know there were actually tears in papa's eyes when he kissed me.'

'We are all so proud of our girl, you see.'

'They almost make me cry between them. I wanted to get away and hide myself, only Mr. Marsden would go on talking to me.'

'Yes, I heard him; he was very amusing; he is full of queer hobbies.'

'I cannot help being sorry for him, he must lose so much, you know; poetry is a sort of sixth sense to me.'

'Darling, you must use your sweet gift well.'

'That is what I have been thinking,' laying her burning face against her aunt's shoulders, as they both stood looking down at a glimmer of shining water below them. 'Aunt Milly, do you remember what you said to comfort me when I was so wickedly lamenting that I had not died?'

Mildred shook her head.

'I only know I lectured you soundly.'

'Oh! Aunt Milly, and they were such dear, wise words that you spoke, too; you told me that perhaps God had some beautiful work for me to do that my death would leave unfinished. Do you think' (speaking softly and slowly) 'that I have found my work?'

'Dear, I cannot doubt it; no one who reads those lovely verses of yours can dispute the reality of your gift. You have genius, Olive; why should I seek to hide it?'

'Thank you, Aunt Milly. Your telling me will not make me proud; you need not be afraid of that, dear. I am only so very, very grateful that I have found my voice.'

'Your voice, Olive!'

'Ah, I have made you smile; but can you fancy what a dumb person would feel if his tongue were suddenly loosed from its paralysis of silence, what a flow and a torrent of words there would be?'

'Yes, the thought has often struck me when I have read the Gospels.'

'Aunt Milly, I think I have something of the same feeling. I have always wanted to find expression for my thoughts—an outlet for them; it is a new tongue, but not an unknown one, as Mr. Marsden half hinted.'

'Three years ago this same Olive who talks so sweetly to-night was full of trouble at the thought of a new lease of life.'

'It was all my want of faith; it was weak, cowardly. I know it well after all,' in a low voice; 'to-night was worth living for. I am not sorry now, Aunt Milly.'

'What are you two talking about? I am come to pay my tribute to the heroines of the night, and find them star-gazing, broke in a familiar voice.

A tall figure in shining raiment bore down upon them—a confused vision of soft white draperies and gleaming jewels under a cashmere cloak.

'Ethel, is it you?' exclaimed Mildred, in an astonished voice.

'Yes, it is I, dear Mildred,' replied the crisp tones, while two soft arms came out from the cloak and enveloped her. 'I suppose I ought to be on the road to Appleby Castle, but I determined to snatch half an hour to myself first, to offer my congratulations to you and this dear girl' (kissing Olive). 'You are only a secondary light to-night, Mildred.'

'What! have you seen it?'

'Yes; my copy came last night. I sat up half the night reading it. You have achieved a success, Olive, that no one else has; you have absolutely drawn tears from my eyes.'

'I thought you never cried over books, Ethel,' in a mischievous tone from Mildred.

'I am usually most strong-hearted, but the "Voices of the Hearth" would have melted a flint. Olive, I never thought it would come to this, that I should be driven to confess that I envied you.'

'Oh no, Ethel, not that, surely!'

'Ah, but I do! that this magnificent power should be given you to wield over all our hearts, that you should sing to us so sweetly, that we should be constrained to listen, that this girlish head should speak to us so wisely and so well,' touching Olive's thick coils with fingers that glittered in the moonlight.

'You must not praise her, or she will make her escape,' laughed Mildred, with a glance at Olive's averted face; 'we have overwhelmed her already with the bitter-sweet of home criticism, and by and by she will have to run the gauntlet of severer, and it may be adverse, reviews.'

'Then she will learn to prize our appreciation. Olive, I am humiliated when I think how utterly I have misunderstood you.'

'Why?' asked Olive, shyly, raising those fathomless dark eyes of hers to Ethel's agitated face.

'I have always looked upon you as a gloomy visionary who held impossible standards of right and wrong, and who vexed herself and others by troublesome scruples; but I see now that Mildred was right.'

'Aunt Mildred always believes the best of every one,' interrupted Olive, softly.

She was flattered and yet pleased by Ethel's evident agitation—why would they all think so much of her? What had she done? The feelings had always been there—the great aching of unexpressed thoughts; and now a voice had been given her with which to speak them. It was all so simple to Olive, so sacred, so beautiful. Why would they spoil it with all this talk?

'Well, perhaps I had better not finish my sentence,' went on Ethel, with a sigh; after all, it was a pity to mar that unconscious simplicity—Olive would never see herself as others saw her; no fatal egotism wrapped her round. She turned to Mildred with a little movement of fondness as she dropped Olive's hand, and they all turned back into the house.

'If I have nothing else, I have you,' she whispered, with a thrill of mingled envy and grief that went to Mildred's heart.

The music and the conversation stopped as the door opened on the dazzling apparition in the full light. Ethel looked pale, and there was a heavy look round her eyes as though of unshed tears; her manner, too, was subdued.

People said that Ethel Trelawny had changed greatly during the last few years; the old extravagance and daring that had won such adverse criticism had wholly gone. Ethel no longer scandalised and repelled people; her vivacity was tempered with reserve now. A heavy cloud of oppression, almost of melancholy, had quenched the dreamy egotism that had led her to a one-sided view of things; still quaint and original, she was beginning to learn the elastic measurement of a charity that should embrace a fairer proportion of her fellow-creatures.

But the lesson was a hard one to her fastidiousness. It could not be said even now that Ethel Trelawny had found her work in life, but notwithstanding she worked hard. Under Mildred's loving tuition she no longer looked upon her poorer neighbours with aversion or disgust, but set herself in many ways to aid them and ameliorate their condition. True the task was uncongenial and the labour hard, and the reward by no means adequate, but at least she need no longer brand herself with being a dreamer of dreams, or sigh that no human being had reason to bless her existence.

A great yearning took possession of her as she stood in her gleaming silks, looking round that happy domestic circle. Mr. Lambert had not as yet stolen back to his beloved study, but sat in the bay-window, discussing parish affairs with Dr. Heriot. Richard had challenged the curate to a game of chess, and Chriss had perched herself on the arm of her brother's chair, and was watching the game. Polly, in her white dress, was striking plaintive chords with one hand and humming to herself in a sweet, girlish voice.

'Check-mate; you played that last move carelessly, Marsden. Your knight turned traitor!' cried Richard. His handsome profile cut sharply against the lamplight, he looked cool, on the alert, while Hugh's broad face was puckered and wrinkled with anxiety.

'Please do not let me interrupt you!' exclaimed Ethel, hurriedly, 'you look all so comfortable. I only want to say good-night, every one,' with a wave of her slim hand as she spoke.

Richard gave a start, and rose to his feet, as he regarded the queenly young creature with her pale cheeks and radiant dress. A sort of perfumy fragrance seemed to pervade him as she brushed lightly past him; something subtle seemed to steal away his faculties. Had he ever seen her look so beautiful?

Ethel stopped and gave him one of her sad, kind smiles.

'You do not often come to see us now, Richard. I think my father misses you,' was all she said.

'I will come—yes—I will come to-morrow,' he stammered. 'I did not think—you would miss me,' he almost added, but he remembered himself in time.

His face grew stern and set as he watched her in the lamplight, gliding from one to another with a soft word or two. Why was it her appearance oppressed him to-night? he thought. He had often seen her dressed so before, and had gloried in her loveliness; to-night it seemed incongruous, it chilled him—this glittering apparition in the midst of the family circle.

She looked more like the probable bride of Sir Robert Ferrers than the wife of a poor curate, he told himself bitterly, as he watched her slow lissom movements, the wavy undulating grace that was Ethel's chief charm, and yet as he thought it he knew he wronged her. For the man she could love, Ethel would pull off all her glistening gewgaws, put away from her all the accessories that wealth could give her. Delighting in luxury, revelling in it, it was in her to renounce it all without a sigh.

Richard knew this, and paid her nobleness its just tribute even while he chafed in his own moodiness. She would do all this, and more than this, for the man she loved; but could she, would she, ever be brought to do it for him?

When alone again with Mildred, Ethel threw her arms round her friend.

'Oh, Mildred ! it seems worse than ever.'

'My poor dear.'

'Night after night he sits opposite to me, and we do not speak, except to exchange commonplaces, and then he carps at every deviation of opinion.'

'I know how dreadful it must be.'

'And then to be brought into the midst of a scene like that,' pointing to the door they had just closed; 'to see those happy faces and to hear all that innocent mirth,' as at that moment Polly's girlish laughter was distinctly audible, with Hugh's pealing 'Ha, ha' following it; 'and then to remember the room I have just left.'

'Hush, try to forget it, or the Sigourneys will wonder at your pale face.'

'These evenings haunt me,' returned Ethel, with a sort of shudder. 'I think I am losing my nerve, Mildred ; but I feel positively as though I cannot bear many more of them— the great dimly-lighted room ; you know my weakness for light ; but he says it makes his head bad, and those lamps with the great shades are all he will have ; the interminable dinner which Duncan always seems to prolong, the difficulty of finding a subject on which we shall not disagree, and the dread of falling into one of those dreadful pauses which nothing seems to break. Oh, Mildred, may you never experience it.'

'Poor Ethel, I can understand it all so well.'

Ethel dried her eyes.

'It seems wrong to complain of one's father, but I have not deserved this loss of confidence ; he is trying my dutifulness too much.'

'It will not fail you. "Let patience have her perfect work," Ethel.'

'No, you must only comfort me to-night ; I am beyond even your wise maxims, Mildred. I wish I had not come, it makes me feel so sore, and yet I could not resist the longing to see you on your birthday. See, I have brought you a gift,' showing her a beautifully-chased cross in her hand.

'Dear Ethel, how wrong ; I have asked you so often not to overwhelm me with your presents.'

'How selfish to deny me my one pleasure. I have thought about this all day. We have had visitors, a whole bevy from Carlisle, and I could not get away ; and now I must go to that odious party at the Castle.'

'You must indeed not wait any longer, your friends will be wondering,' remonstrated Mildred.

'Oh no, Mrs. Sigourney is always late. You are very unsociable to-night, Mildred, just when I require so much.'

'I only wish I knew how to comfort you.'

'It comforts me to look into your face and hold your hand. Listen, Mildred—to-night I was so hungry and desolate for want of a kind word or look, that I grew desperate ; it was foolish of me, but I could have begged for it as a hungry dog will beg for a crumb.'

'What did you say ?' asked Mildred, breathlessly.

'I went and stood by his chair when I ought to have left the room ; that was a mistake, was it not ?' with a low, bitter laugh. 'I think I touched his sleeve, for he drew it away with a look of surprise. "Papa, I said ; I cannot bear this any longer. I do not feel as though I were your child when you never look at me voluntarily."'

'And what was his answer ?'

' "Ethel, you know I hate scenes, they simply disgust me." '

'Only that !'

'No. I was turning away when he called me back in his sternest manner.'

' "Your reproach is unseemly under the circumstances, but it shall be answered," he said, and his voice was so hard and cold. "It is my misfortune that you are my child, for you have never done anything but disappoint me. Now, do not interrupt me," as I made some faint exclamation. " I have not withheld my confidence ; you know my ambition, and also that I have lately sustained some very heavy losses ; in default of a son I have looked to you to retrieve our fortunes, but "—in such a voice of withering scorn—" I have looked in vain." '

'Bitter words, my poor Ethel ; my heart aches for you. What could such a speech mean ? Can it be true that he is really embarrassed ?'

'Only temporarily ; you know he dabbles in speculations, and he lost a good deal by those mining shares last year ; that was the reason why we missed our usual London season. No, it is not that. You see he has never relinquished the secret ambition of a seat in Parliament. I know him so well ; nothing can turn him from anything on which he has set his heart, and either of those men would have helped him to compass his end.'

'He has no right to sacrifice you to his ambition.'

'You need not fear, I am no Iphigenia. I could not marry Sir Robert, and I would not marry Mr. Cathcart. Thank Heaven, I have self-respect enough to guard me from such humiliation. The worst is,' she hesitated, 'papa is so quick that he found out how his intellect fascinated me; it was the mere fascination of the moment, and died a natural death; but he will have it I was not indifferent to him, and it is this that makes him so mad. He says it is obstinacy, and nothing else.'

'Mr. Cathcart has not renewed his offer? forgive me,' as Ethel drew herself up, and looked somewhat offended. 'You know I dread that man—so sceptical—full of sophistry. Oh, my dear! I cannot help fearing him.'

'You need not,' with a sad smile; 'my heart is still in my own keeping. No,' as Mildred's glance questioned her archly, 'I have been guilty of nothing but a little hero-worship, but nevertheless,' she averred, 'intellect and goodness must go hand-in-hand before I can call any man my master.'

'I shall not despair of you finding them together; but come, I will not let you stay any longer, or your pale cheeks will excite comment. Let me wrap this cloak round you—come.'

But Ethel still lingered.

'Don't let Richard know all this; he takes my unhappiness too much to heart already; only ask him to come sometimes and break the monotony.'

'He will come.'

'Things always seem better when he is with us; he makes papa talk, and much of the restraint seems removed. Well, good-night; this is sad birthday-talk, but I could not keep the pain in.'

As Mildred softly closed the door she saw Richard beside her.

'What have you been talking about all this time?' he asked, anxiously.

'Only on the old sore subject. She is very unhappy, Richard; she wants you to go oftener. You do her father good.'

'But she looked pale to-night. She is not in fresh trouble, is she, Aunt Milly?'

'No, only the misunderstanding gets more every day; we must all do what we can to lighten her load.'

Richard made no answer, he seemed thinking deeply; even after Mildred left him he remained in the same place.

'One of these days she must know it, and why not now?' he said to himself, and there was a strange concentrated light in his eyes as he said it.

CHAPTER XIX

THE HEART OF CŒUR-DE-LION

' At length, as suddenly become aware
Of this long pause, she lifted up her face,
And he withdrew his eyes—she looked so fair
And cold, he thought, in her unconscious grace.
Ah ! little dreams she of the restless care,
He thought, that makes my heart to throb apace :
Though we this morning part, the knowledge sends
No thrill to her calm pulse—we are but Friends ! '

JEAN INGELOW.

MILDRED pondered long and sorrowfully that night over her friend's trouble.

She knew it was no fancied or exaggerated recital of wrongs. The inmates of the vicarage had commented openly on the Squire's changed looks and bearing. His cordiality had always savoured more or less of condescension, but latterly he had held himself aloof from his neighbours, and there had been a gloomy reserve in his manner that had made him well-nigh unapproachable.

Irritable and ready to take offence, and quick to resent even a difference of opinion, he was already on bad terms with more than one of his neighbours. Dr. Heriot's well-deserved popularity, and his plainness of speech, had already given umbrage to his jealous and haughty temperament. It was noticed on all sides that the Doctor was a less frequent visitor at Kirkleatham House, and that Mr. Trelawny was much given to carp at any expressed opinion that emanated from that source.

This was incomprehensible, to say the least of it, as he had always been on excellent terms with both father and daughter ; but little did any one guess the real reason of so inexplicable a change.

Ethel was right when she acknowledged that ambition was her father's besetting sin ; the petty interests of squirearchal life had never satiated his dominant passion and thirst for power. Side by side with his ambition and narrow aims there was a vacuum that he would fain have filled with work of a broader type, and with a pertinacity that would have been noble but for its subtle egotism, he desired to sit among the senators of his people.

Twice had he essayed and twice been beaten, and it had been whispered that his hands were not quite clean, with the cleanness of a man to whom corruption is a hideous snare ; and still, with a dogged resolution that ought to have served him, he determined that one day, and at all costs, his desire should be accomplished.

Already there were hints of a coming election, and whispered reports of a snug borough that would not be too severely contested ; but Mr. Trelawny had another aim. The Conservative member for the next borough had given offence to his constituents by bringing in a Bill for the reformation of some dearly-loved abuse. The inhabitants were up in arms ; there had been much speechifying and a procession, during which sundry well-meaning flatterers had already whispered that the right man in the right place would be a certain lord of beeves and country squire, to whom the township and people were as dear as though he had first drawn breath in their midst.

Parliament would shortly be dissolved, it was urged, and Mr. Trelawny's chances would be great ; already his friends were canvassing on his behalf, and among them Mr. Cathcart, of Broadlands.

The Cathcarts were bankers and the most influential people, and commanded a great number of votes, and it was Edgar Cathcart who had used such strong language against the aforesaid member for meddling with an abuse which had been suffered for at least two hundred years, and was respectable for its very antiquity.

Ethel's refusal of Edgar Cathcart had inflicted a deadly blow to her father's interests, and one that he was never likely to forgive, all the more that he was shrewd enough to suspect that she had not been altogether indifferent to his fascination of manner.

Now above all things he had coveted this man for his son-in-law. Broadlands and its hereditary thousands would have been no mean match for the daughter of a country squire. With Edgar Cathcart to back him he could have snapped his fingers at the few loyal voters who would have still rallied round their erring townsman, and from a hint that had been lately dropped, he knew the banker was ready at any moment to renew his offer ; but Ethel had persisted in her refusal, and bitterly and loudly did her father curse the folly of a girl who could renounce such a position for a mere whim or fancy.

'If you do not love him, whom do you love ?' he had said to her, and, courageous as she was, she had quailed before the sneer that had accompanied his words.

But she never guessed the thought that rose in his mind as he said them. 'She has some infatuation that makes her proof against other men's addresses,' he argued angrily with himself. 'No girl in her senses could be blind to the attraction of a man like Edgar Cathcart unless she has already given away her heart. I am not satisfied about this fellow Heriot. He comes here far too often, and she encourages him. I always thought he meant to marry Lambert's prim sister ; but he is so deep there is no reading him. I shall have to pick a quarrel to get rid of him, for if he once gets an influence over Ethel, all Cathcart's chances are gone.'

Like many other narrow-minded men, Mr. Trelawny brooded over an idea until it became fixed and ineradicable. Ethel's warm reception of Dr. Heriot, and her evident pleasure in his society, were construed as so many evidences of his own sagacity and her guilt. His only child and heiress, for whom he had planned so splendid a future, intended to throw herself away on a common country practitioner ; she meant to disgrace herself and him.

The wound rankled and became envenomed, steeping his whole soul in bitterness and discontent. He was a disappointed man, he told himself—disappointed in his ambition and in his domestic affections. He had loved his wife, as such men love, next to himself ; he had had a certain pride in the possession of her, and though he had ever ruled her with a rod of iron, he had mingled much fondness with his rule. But she had left him, and the sons, who had been to him as the twin apples of his eyes, had gone likewise. He had groaned and humbled himself beneath that terrible stroke, and had for a little time walked softly as one who has been smitten justly ; and the pathos of his self-pity had been such that others had been constrained to feel for him, though they marvelled that his daughter, with the mother's eyes, had so little power to comfort him.

There were times when he wondered also, when his veiled coldness showed rents in it, and he owned to a certain pride in her that was not devoid of tenderness.

15

For it was only of late that he had fallen into such carping ways, and that the real breach was apparent. It was true Ethel had her mother's eyes, but she lacked her mother's submissive gentleness ; never a meek woman, she had yet to learn the softness that disarms wrath. Her open-eyed youth found flaws in everything that was not intrinsically excellent. She canvassed men and manners with the warm injudiciousness of undeveloped wisdom ; acts were nothing, motives everything, and no cleanness available that had a stain on its whiteness.

In place of the plastic girlhood he expected, Mr. Trelawny found himself confronted by this daring and youthful Argus. He soon discovered Ethel's inner sympathies were in open revolt against his. It galled him, even in his pride, to see those clear, candid eyes measuring, half unconsciously and half incredulously, the narrow limits of his nature. Whatever he might seem to others, he knew his own child had weighed him in the balance of her harsh-judging youth, and found him wanting.

It was not that her manner lacked dutifulness, or that she ever failed in the outward acts of a daughter ; below the surface of their mutual reserve there was, at least on Ethel's part, a deep craving for a better understanding ; but even if he were secretly fond of her, there was no denying that Mr. Trelawny was uneasy in her presence ; conscience often spoke to him in her indignant young voice ; under those shining blue eyes ambition seemed paltry, and the stratagems and manœuvres of party spirit little better than mere truckling and the low cunning of deceit.

It would not be too much to say that he almost feared her ; that there were times when this sense of uncongeniality was so oppressive that he would gladly have got rid of her, when he would rather have been left alone than endure the silent rebuke of her presence. Of late his anger had been very great against her ; the scorn with which she had defended herself against his tenacious will had rankled deeply in his mind, and as yet there was no question of forgiveness.

If he could not bend her to his purpose he would at least treat her as one treats a contumacious child. She had spoken words—rash, unadvisable, but honest words—which even his little soul had felt deeply. No, he would not forgive her ; there should be no confidence, no loving intercourse between them, till she had given up this foolish fancy of hers, or at least had brought herself to promise that she would give it up ; and yet, strange to say, though Dr. Heriot had become a thorn in his side, though the dread of him drove all comfort from his pillow, he yet lacked courage openly to accuse her ; some latent sense of honour within him checked him from so insulting his motherless child.

It so happened that on the evening after Mildred's birthday, Dr. Heriot called up at Kirkleatham House to speak to Mr. Trelawny on some matter of business.

Richard was dining there, and Ethel's careworn face had relaxed into smiles at the sight of her favourite ; the gloomy room seemed brightened somehow, dinner was less long and oppressive, no awful pauses of silence fell between the father and daughter to be bridged over tremblingly. Richard's cheerful voice and ready flow of talk—a little forced, perhaps—went on smoothly and evenly ; enthusiasm was not possible under the chilling restraint of Mr. Trelawny's measured sentences, but at least Ethel saw the effort and was grateful for it.

Richard was holding forth fluently on a three days' visit to London that he had lately paid, when a muttered exclamation from Mr. Trelawny interrupted him, and a moment afterwards the door-bell rang.

A shade of angry annoyance passed over the Squire's handsome face—his thin lips closed ominously.

'What does he want at this time of night ?' he demanded, darting a suspicious glance at Ethel, whose quick ears had recognised the footsteps ; her bright flush of pleasure faded away at that wrathful look ; she heaved a little petulant sigh as her father left the room, closing the door sharply after him.

'It is like everything else,' she murmured. 'It used to be so pleasant his dropping in of an evening, but everything seems spoiled somehow.'

'I do not understand. I thought Dr. Heriot was so intimate here,' returned Richard, astonished and shocked at this new aspect of things. Mr. Trelawny's look of angry annoyance had not been lost on him—what had come to him ? would he quarrel with them all ? 'I do not understand ; I have been away so long, you know,' and unconsciously his voice took its softest tone.

'There is nothing to understand,' replied Ethel, wearily ; 'only papa and he are not such good friends now ; they have disagreed in politics—gentlemen will, you know—and lately Dr. Heriot has vexed him by insisting on some sanitary reforms in some of the cottages. Papa hates any interference with his tenants, and it is not easy to silence Dr. Heriot when he thinks it is his duty to speak.'

'And sanitary reform is Dr. John's special hobby. Yes, I see ; it is a grievous pity,' assented Richard, and then he resumed the old topic. It was not that he was unsympathising, but he could not forget the happiness of being alone with Ethel ; the opportunity had come for which he had longed all last night. As he talked on calmly and rapidly his temples beat and ached with excitement. Once or twice he stole a furtive glance as she sat somewhat absently beside him. Could he venture it ? would not his lips close if he essayed a subject at once so sweet and perilous ? As he talked he noted every trick, every gesture ; the quaint fashion of her dress, made of some soft, clinging material ; it had a Huguenot sleeve, he remembered—for she had told him it was designed from a French picture—and was trimmed with old Venetian point ; an oddly-shaped mosaic ring gleamed on one of her long taper fingers and was her only ornament. He had never seen her look so picturesque and yet so sweet as she did that night, but as he looked the last particle of courage seemed to desert him. Ethel listened only absently as he talked ; she was straining her ears to catch some sound from the adjoining room. For once Richard's talk wearied her. How loudly the birds were chirping their good-night—would he come in and wish her good-bye as he used to do, and then linger for an hour or so over his cup of coffee ? Hark ! that was his voice. Was he going ? And, oh ! surely that was not her father's answering him.

'Hush ! oh, please hush !' she exclaimed, holding out a hand as though to silence him, and moving towards the door. 'Oh, Richard, what shall we do ? I knew it would come to this.'

'Come to what ? Is there anything the matter ? Please do not look so pale over it.' What had she heard—what new vexation was this ? But as he stood beside her, even he caught the low, vehement tones of some angry discussion. There was no denying Ethel's paleness ; she almost wrung her hands.

'Of course ; did I not tell you ? Oh, you do not know papa ! When he is angry like this, he will say things that no one can bear. Dr. Heriot will never come here again—never ! He is quarrelling with all his friends. By and by he will with you, and then you will learn to hate us.'

'No, no—you must not say that,' replied Richard, soothingly. With her distress all his courage had returned. He even ventured to touch her hand, but she drew it quickly away. She

was not thinking of Richard now, but of a certain kind friend
whose wise counsels she had learnt to value.

At least he should not go without bidding her good-bye.
Ethel never thought of prudence in these moments of hot indignation. To Richard's dismay she caught her hand away from
him and flung open the door.

'Why is Dr. Heriot going, papa?' she asked, walking up to
them with a certain majesty of gait which she could assume at
times. As she asked the question she flashed one of her keen,
open-eyed looks on her father. The Squire's olive complexion
had turned sallow with suppressed wrath, the veins on his
forehead were swollen like whipcord; as he answered her, the
harshness of his voice grated roughly on her ear.

'You are not wanted, Ethel; go back to young Lambert.
I cannot allow girls to interfere in my private business.'

'You have quarrelled with Dr. Heriot, papa,' returned
Ethel, in her ringing tones, and keeping her ground unflinchingly, in spite of Richard's whispered remonstrance.

'Come away—you will only make it worse,' he whispered;
but she had turned her face impatiently from him.

'Papa, it is not right—it is not fair. Dr. Heriot has done
nothing to deserve such treatment; and you are sending him
away in anger.'

'Ethel, how dare you!' returned the Squire. 'Go back into
that room instantly. If you have no self-respect, and cannot
control your feeling, it is my duty to protect you.'

'Will you protect me by quarrelling with all my friends?'
returned Ethel, in her indignant young voice; her delicate
nostrils quivered, the curve of her long neck was superb. 'Dr.
Heriot has only told you the truth, as he always does.'

'Indeed, you must not judge your father—after all, he has a
right to choose his own friends in his own house—you are very
good, Miss Trelawny, to try and defend me, but it is your
father's quarrel, not yours.'

'If you hold intercourse with my daughter after this, you
are no man of honour——' began the Squire with rage, but Dr.
Heriot quietly interrupted him.

'As far as I can I will respect your strange caprice, Mr.
Trelawny; but I hope you do not mean to forbid my addressing
a word to an old friend when we meet on neutral ground;'
and the gentle dignity of his manner held Mr. Trelawny's
wrath in abeyance, until Ethel's imprudence kindled it
afresh.

'It is not fair—I protest against such injustice!' she exclaimed ; but Dr. Heriot silenced her.

'Hush, it is not your affair, Miss Trelawny ; you are so generous, but, indeed, your father and I are better apart for a little.　When he retracts what he has said, he will not find me unforgiving.　Now, good-bye.'　The brief sternness vanished from his manner, and he held out his hand to her with his old kind smile, his eyes were full of benignant pity as he looked at her pale young face ; it was so like her generosity to defend her friends, he thought.

Richard followed him down the long carriage road, and they stood for a while outside the lodge gates.　If Dr. Heriot held the clue to this strange quarrel, he kept his own counsel.

'He is a narrow-minded man with warped views and strong passions; he may cool down, and find out his mistake one day,' was all he said to Richard.　'I only pity his daughter for being his daughter.'

He might well pity her.　Richard little thought, as he hurried after his friend, what an angry hurricane the imprudent girl had brought on herself ; with all her courage, the Squire made her quail and tremble under his angry sneers.

'Papa! papa!' was all she could say, when the last bitter arrow was launched at her.　'Papa, say you do not mean it— that he cannot think that.'

'What else can a man think when a girl is fool enough to stand up for him ?　For once—yes, for once—I was ashamed of my daughter!'

'Ashamed of me?'—drawing herself up, but beginning to tremble from head to foot—that she, Ethel Trelawny, should be subjected to this insult !

'Yes, ashamed of you ! that my daughter should be absolutely courting the notice of a beggarly surgeon—that——'

'Papa, I forbid you to say another word,'—in a voice that thrilled him—it was so like her mother's, when she had once— yes, only once—risen against the oppression of his injustice— 'you have gone too far ; I repel your insinuation with scorn. Dr. Heriot does not think this of me.'

'What else can he think ?' but he blenched a little under those clear innocent eyes.

'He will think I am sorry to lose so good a friend,' she returned, and her breast heaved a little ; 'he will think that Ethel Trelawny hates injustice even in her own father ; he will think what is only true and kind,' her voice dropping into sadness; and with that she walked silently from the room.

She was hard hit, but she would not show it; her step was as proud as ever till she had left her father's presence, and then it faltered and slackened, and a great shock of pain came over her face.

She had denied the insinuation with scorn, but what if he really thought it? What if her imprudent generosity, always too prone to buckle on harness for another, were to be construed wrongly—what if in his eyes she should already have humiliated herself?

With what sternness he had rebuked her judgment of her father; with him, want of dutifulness and reverence were heinous sins that nothing could excuse; she remembered how he had ever praised meekness in women, and how, when she had laughingly denied all claim to that virtue, he had answered her half sadly, 'No, you are not meek, and never will be, until trouble has broken your spirit: you are too aggressive by nature to wear patiently the "ornament of a meek and quiet spirit;"' and she remembered how that half-jesting, half-serious speech had troubled her.

Ethel's feeling for Dr. Heriot had been the purest hero-worship; she had been proud of his friendship, and the loss of it under any circumstances would have troubled her sadly; she had never blinded herself to the fact that more than this would be impossible.

Already her keen eyes had lighted on his probable choice, some one who should bring meekness in lieu of beauty, and fill his home with the sunshiny sweetness of her smile. 'She will be a happy woman, whoever she is,' thought Ethel, with a sigh, not perfectly free from envy; there were so few men who were good as well as wise, 'and this was one,' she said to herself, and a flood of sadness came over her as she remembered that speech about her lack of meekness.

If he could only think well of her—if she had not lost caste in his eyes, she thought, it might still be well with her, and in a half-sad, half-jesting way she had pictured her life as Ethel Trelawny always, 'walking in maiden meditation fancy free,' a little solitary, perhaps, a trifle dull, but wiser and better when the troublesome garb of youth was laid aside, and she could— as in very honesty she longed to do now—call all men her brothers. But the proud maidenly reserve was stabbed at all points; true, or untrue, Ethel was writhing under those sneering words. Richard found her, on his return, standing white and motionless by the window ; her eyes had a plaintive look in them as of a wild animal too much hurt to defend itself ; her pale cheeks alarmed him.

'Why do you agitate yourself so ? there is no cause ! Dr. Heriot has just told me it is a mere quarrel that may be healed any time.'

'It is not that—it is those bitter cruel words,' she returned, in a strange, far-away voice ; 'that one's own father should say such things,' and then her lip quivered, and two large tears welled slowly to her eyes. Ah, there was the secret stab—her own father !

'My dear Miss Trelawny—Ethel—I cannot bear to see you like this. You are overwrought—all this has upset you. Come into the air and let us talk a little.'

'What is there to talk about ?' she returned dreamily.

He had called her Ethel for the first time since their old childish days, and she had not noticed it. She offered no resistance as he brought a soft fleecy shawl and wrapped it round her, and then gently removed the white motionless fingers that were clutching the window-frame ; as they moved hand in hand over the grassy terrace, she was quite unconscious of the firm, warm pressure ; somewhere far away she was thinking of a forlorn Ethel, whose father had spoken cruel words to her. Richard was always good to her—always ; there was nothing new in that. Only once she turned and smiled at her favourite, with a smile so sad and sweet that it almost broke his heart.

'How kind you are ; you always take such care of me, Richard.'

'I wish I could—I wish I dare try,' he returned, in an odd, choked voice. 'Let us go to your favourite seat, Ethel ; the sun has not set yet.'

'It has set for me to-night,' she replied, mournfully.

The creeping mists winding round the blue bases of the far-off hills suited her better, she thought. She followed Richard mechanically into the quaint kitchen garden ; there was a broad terrace-walk, with a seat placed so as to command the distant view ; great bushes of cabbage-roses and southernwood scented the air ; gilly-flowers, and sweet-williams, and old-fashioned stocks bloomed in the borders ; below them the garden sloped steeply to the crofts, and beyond lay the circling hills. In the distance they could hear the faint pealing of the curfew bell, and the bleating of the flocks in the crofts.

Ethel drew a deep sigh; the sweet calmness of the scene seemed to soothe her.

'You were right to bring me here,' she said at last, gratefully.

'I have brought you here—because I want to speak to you,' returned Richard, with the same curious break in his voice.

His temples were beating still, but he was calm, strangely calm, he remembered afterwards. How did it happen? were the words his own or another's? How did it come that she was shrinking away from him with that startled look in her eyes, and that he was speaking in that low, passionate voice? Was it this he meant when he called her Ethel?

'No, no! say you do not mean it, Richard! Oh, Richard, Richard!' her voice rising into a perfect cry of pain. What, must she lose him too?

'Dear, how can I say it? I have always meant to tell you —always; it is not my fault that I have loved you, Ethel; the love has grown up and become a part of myself ever since we were children together!'

'Does Mildred—does any one know?' she asked, and a vivid crimson mantled in her pale cheeks as she asked the question.

'Yes, my father knows—and Aunt Milly. I think they all guessed my secret long ago—all but you,' in a tenderly reproachful voice; 'why should they not know? I am not ashamed of it,' continued the young man, a little loftily.

Somehow they had changed characters. It was Ethel who was timid now.

'But—but—they could not have approved,' she faltered at last.

'Why should they not approve? My father loves you as a daughter—they all do; they would take you into their hearts, and you would never be lonely again. Oh, Ethel, is there no hope? Do you mean that you cannot love me?'

'I have always loved you; but we are too young, yes, that is it, we are too young—too much of an age. If I marry, I must look up to my husband. Indeed, indeed, we are too young, Richard!'

'I am, you mean;' how calm he was growing; why his very voice was under his control now. 'Listen to me, dear: I am only six months older than you, but in a love like mine age does not count; it is no boyish lover you are dismissing, Ethel; I am older in everything than you; I should not be afraid to take care of you.'

No, he was not afraid ; as she looked up into that handsome resolute face, and read there the earnestness of his words, Ethel's eyes dropped before that clear, dominant glance as they had never done before. It was she that was afraid now—afraid of this young lover, so grave, so strong, so self-controlled ; this was not her old favourite, this new, quiet-spoken Richard. She would fain have kept them both, but it must not be.

'May I speak to your father?' he pleaded. 'At least you will be frank with me ; I have little to offer, I know—a hard-working curate's home, and that not yet.'

'Hush ! I will not have this from you,' and for a moment Ethel's true woman's soul gleamed in her eyes ; 'if you were penniless it would make no difference; I would give up anything, everything for the man I loved. For shame, Richard, when you know I loathe the very name of riches.'

'Yes, I know your great soul, Ethel ; it is this that I love even more than your beauty, and I must not tell you what I think of that ; it is not because I am poor and unambitious that you refuse me ?'

'No, no,' she returned hurriedly ; 'you know it is not.'

'And you do not love any one else ?'

'No, Richard,' still more faintly.

'Then I will not despair,' and as he spoke there rushed upon him a sudden conviction, from whence he knew not, that one day this girl whom he was wooing so earnestly, and who was silencing him with such brief sweet replies, should one day be his wife ; that the beauty, and the great soul, and the sad yearning heart should be his and no other's ; that one day—a long distant day, perhaps—he should win her for his own.

And with the conviction, as he told Mildred long afterwards, there came a settled calm, and a wonderful strength that he never felt before ; the world, his own world, seemed flooded over with this great purpose and love of his ; and as he stood there before her, almost stooping over, and yet not touching her, there came a vivid brightness into his eyes that scared Ethel.

'Of what are you thinking, Richard ?' she said almost tremblingly.

'Nay, I must not tell you.'

Should he tell her ? would she credit this strange prophecy of his ? dimly across his mind, as he stood there before her, there came the thought of a certain shepherd, who waited seven years for the Rachel of his love.

'No, I will not tell you ; dear, give me your hand,' and as she gave it him—wondering and yet fearful—he touched it lightly and reverently with his lips.

'Now I must go. Some day—years hence, perhaps—I shall speak of this again ; until then we are friends still, is it not so ? '

'Yes—yes,' she returned eagerly ; 'we must try to forget this. I cannot lose you altogether, Richard.'

'You will never lose me ; perhaps—yes it will be better—I may go away for a little time ; you must promise me one thing, to take care of yourself, if only for the sake of your old friend Richard.'

'Yes, I will promise,' she returned, bursting into tears. Oh, why was her heart so hard ; why could she not love him ? As she looked after him, walking with grave even strides down the garden path, a passionate pity and yearning seemed to wake in her heart. How good he was, how noble, how true. 'Oh, if he were not so young, and I could love him as he ought to be loved,' she said to herself as the gate clanged after him, and she was left alone in the sunset.

CHAPTER XX

WHARTON HALL FARM

'A dappled sky, a world of meadows,
  Circling above us the black rooks fly
Forward, backward ; lo, their dark shadow
  Flits on the blossoming tapestry.

Bare grassy slopes, where kids are tethered
  Round valleys like nests all ferny-lined,
Round hills, with fluttering tree-tops feathered,
  Swell high in their freckled robes behind.'

JEAN INGELOW.

MR. LAMBERT was soon made acquainted with his son's disappointment ; but his sympathy was somewhat chilled by Richard's composed tranquillity of bearing. Perhaps it might be a little forced, but the young man certainly bore himself as though he had sustained no special defeat ; the concentrated gravity of purpose which had scared Ethel was still apparent.

'You need not be so anxious about me, father,' he said, with almost a smile, in return to Mr. Lambert's look of questioning sadness. 'I have climbed too high and have had a fall, that is all. I must bear what other and better men have borne before me.'

'My brave boy ; but, Cardie, is there no hope of relenting ; none ?'

'She would not have me, that is all I can tell you,' returned Richard, in the same quiet voice. 'You must not take this too much to heart ; it is my fate to love her, and to go on loving her ; if she refused me a dozen times, it would be the same with me, father.'

Mr. Lambert shook his head ; he was greatly troubled ; for the moment his heart was a little sore against this girl, who was the destroyer of his son's peace.

'You may hide it from me, but you will eat out your heart with sadness and longing,' he said, with something of a groan. Richard was very dear to him, though he was not Benjamin.

He was more like Joseph, he thought, a little quaintly, as he looked up at the noble young face. 'Yes, Joseph, the ruler among his brethren. Ah, Cardie, it is not to be, I suppose ; and now you will eat out your heart and youth with the longing after this girl.'

'Do not think so meanly of me,' returned the young man with a flush. 'You loved my mother for three years before you married her, and I only pleaded my cause yesterday. Do you think I should be worthy of loving the noblest, yes, the noblest of women,' he continued, his gray eyes lighting up with enthusiasm, 'if I were so weakly to succumb to this disappointment. *Laborare est orare*—that shall be my motto, father. We must leave results in higher hands.'

'God bless and comfort you, my son,' returned Mr. Lambert, with some emotion. He looked at Richard with a sort of tender reverence ; would that all disappointed lovers could bear themselves as generously as his brave boy, he thought ; and then they sat for a few minutes in silence.

'You do not mind my going away for a little while ? I think Roy would be glad to have me ?' asked Richard presently.

'No, Cardie ; but we shall be sorry to lose you.'

'If I were only thinking of myself, I would remain ; but it will be better for her,' he continued, hesitating ; 'she could not come here, at least, not yet ; but if I were away it would make no difference. I want you all to be kinder than ever to her, father,' and now his voice shook a little for the first time. 'You do not know how utterly lonely and miserable she is,' and the promise given, Richard quietly turned the conversation into other channels.

But he was less reticent with Mildred, and to her he avowed that his pain was very great.

'I can bear to live without her ; at least I could be patient for years, but I cannot bear leaving her to her father's sorry protection. If my love could only shield her in her trouble, I think I could be content,' and Mildred understood him.

'We will all be so good to her for your sake,' she returned, with a nice womanly tact, not wearying him with effusion of sympathy, but giving him just the comforting assurance he needed. Richard's fortitude and calmness had deceived his father, but Mildred knew something of the silence of exceeding pain.

'Thank you,' he said in a low voice ; and Mildred knew she had said the right thing.

But as he was bidding them good-bye two days afterwards, he beckoned her apart from the others.

'Aunt Milly, I trust her to you,' he said, hurriedly; 'remember all my comfort lies in your goodness to her.'

'Yes, Richard, I know; as far as I can, I will be her friend. You shall hear everything from me,' and so she sent him away half-comforted.

Half-comforted, though his heart ached with its mighty burden of love; and though he would have given half his strong young years to hear her say, 'I love you, Richard.' Could older men love better, nay, half as well as he did, with such self-sacrificing purity and faith?

Yes, his pain was great, for delay and uncertainty are bitter to the young, and they would fain cleave with impatient hand the veiled mystery of life; but nevertheless his heart was strong within him, for though he could not speak of his hope, for fear that others might call it visionary, yet it stirred to the very foundation of his soul; for so surely as he suffered now, he knew that one day he should call Ethel Trelawny his wife.

When Richard was gone, and the household unobservant and occupied in its own business, Mildred quietly fetched her shady hat, and went through the field paths, bordered by tall grasses and great shining ox-eyed daises, which led to the shrubberies of Kirkleatham.

The great house was blazing in the sunshine; Ethel's doves were cooing from the tower; through the trees Mildred could see the glimmer of a white gown; the basket-work chair was in its old place, under her favourite acacia tree; the hills looked blue and misty in the distance.

Ethel turned very pale when she saw her friend, and there was visible constraint in her manner.

'I did not expect you; you should not have come out in all this heat, Mildred.'

'I knew you would scold me; but I have not seen you for nearly a week, so I came through the tropics to look after you,' returned Mildred, playfully. 'You are under my care now. Richard begged me to be good to you,' she continued, more seriously.

A painful flush crossed Ethel's face; her eyelids dropped.

'You must not let this come between us, Ethel; it will make him more unhappy than he is, and I fear,' speaking still more gravely, 'that though he says so little about himself, that he must be very unhappy.'

Ethel tried ineffectually to control her emotion.

'I could not help it. You have no right to blame me, Mildred,' she said in a low voice.

'No, you could not help it! Who blames you, dear?—not I, nor Richard. It was not your fault, my poor Ethel, that you could not love your old playmate. It is your misfortune and his, that is all.'

'I know how good he is,' returned Ethel, with downcast eyes. Yes, it was her misfortune, she knew; was he not brave and noble, her knight, *sans peur* and *sans reproche*, her lion-hearted Richard? Could any man be more worthy of a woman's love? —and yet she had said him 'nay.' 'I know he is good, too good,' she said, with a little spasm of fury against her own hardness of heart, 'and I was a churl to refuse his love.'

'Hush; how could you help it? we cannot control these things, we women,' returned Mildred, still anxious to soothe. She looked at the pale girl before her with a feeling of tender awe, not unmixed with envy, that she should have inspired such passionate devotion, and yet remained untouched by it. This was a puzzle to gentle Mildred. 'You must try to put it all out of your mind, and come to us again,' she finished, with an unconscious sigh. 'Richard wished it; that is why he has gone away.'

'Has he gone away?' asked Ethel with a startled glance, and Mildred's brief resentment vanished when she saw how heavy the once brilliant eyes looked. Richard would have been grieved as well as comforted if he had known how many tears Ethel's hardness of heart had caused her. She had been thinking very tenderly of him until Mildred came between her and the sunshine; she was sorry and yet relieved to hear he was gone; the pain of meeting him again would be so great, she thought.

'It was wise of him to go, was it not?' returned Mildred. 'It was just like his kind consideration. Oh, you do not know Richard.'

'No, I do not know him,' replied Ethel, humbly. 'When he came and spoke to me, I would not believe it was he, himself; it seemed another Richard, so different. Oh, Mildred, tell me that you do not hate me for being so hard, not as I hate myself.'

'No, no, my poor child,' returned Mildred fondly. Ethel had thrown herself on the grass beside her friend, and was looking up in her face with great pathetic eyes. With her white gown and pale cheeks she looked very young and fair. Mildred was thankful Richard could not see her. 'No, whatever happens, we shall always be the same to each other. I shall only love you a little more because Richard loves you.'

There was not much talk after that. Ethel's shyness was not easily to be overcome. The sweet dreamy look had come back to her eyes. Mildred had forgiven her; she would not let this pain come between them; she might still be with her friends at the vicarage; and as she thought of this she blessed Richard in her heart for his generosity.

But Mildred went back a little sadly down the croft, and through the path with the great white daisies. The inequality of things oppressed her; the surface of their little world seemed troubled and disturbed as though with some impending changes. They were girls and boys no longer, but men and women, with full-grown capacities for joy and sorrow, with youthful desires stretching hither and thither.

'Most men work out their lot in life. After all, Cardie may get his heart's desire; it is only women who must wait till their fate comes to them, sometimes with empty hands,' thought Mildred, a little rebelliously, looking over the long level of sunshine that lay before her; and then she shook off the thought as though it stung her, and hummed a little tune as she filled her basket with roses. 'Roses and sunshine; a golden paradise hiding somewhere behind the low blue hills; the earth, radiant under the Divine glittering smile; a fragrant wind sweeping over the sea of grass, till it rippled with green light; "and God saw that it was good," this beautiful earth that He had made, yes, it is good; it is only we who cloud and mar its brightness with our repinings,' thought Mildred, preaching to herself softly, as she laid the white buds among her ferns. 'A jarring note, a missing chord, and we are out of harmony with it all; and though the sun shines, the midges trouble us.'

It was arranged that on the next day Mr. Marsden was to escort Mildred and her nieces to Wharton Hall, that the young curate might have an opportunity of witnessing a Westmorland clipping.

It was an intensely hot afternoon, but neither Polly nor Chriss were willing to give up the expedition. So as Mildred was too good-natured to plead a headache as an excuse, and as Olive was always ready to enact the part of a martyr on an emergency, neither of them owned how greatly they dreaded the hot, shadeless roads.

'It is a long lane that has no turning,' gasped Hugh, as

they reached the little gate that bounded the Wharton Hall property. 'It is a mercy we have escaped sunstroke.'

'Providence is kinder than you deserve, you see,' observed a quiet voice behind him.

And there was Dr. Heriot leading his horse over the turf.

'Miss Lambert, have you taken leave of your usual good sense, or have you forgotten to consult your thermometer ?'

'I was unwilling to disappoint the. girls, that was all,' returned Mildred ; 'they were so anxious that Mr. Marsden should be initiated into the mysteries of sheep-clipping. Mrs. Colby has promised us some tea, and we shall have a long rest, and return in the cool of the evening.'

'I think I shall get an invitation for tea too. My mare has lamed herself, and I wanted Michael Colby's head man to see her ; he is a handy fellow. I was here yesterday on business ; they were clipping then.'

'Mr. Marsden ought to have been here two years ago,' interposed Polly eagerly. 'Mr. Colby got up a regular old-fashioned clipping for Aunt Milly. Oh, it was such fun.'

'What ! are there fashions in sheep-shearing ?' asked Hugh, in an amused tone. They were still standing by the little gate, under the shade of some trees ; before them were the farm-buildings and outhouses ; and the great ivied gateway, which led to the courtyard and house. Under the gray walls were some small Scotch oxen ; a peacock trailed its feathers lazily in the dust. The air was resonant with the bleating of sheep and lambs ; the girls in their white dresses and broad-brimmed hats made a pretty picture under the old elms. Mildred looked like a soft gray shadow behind them.

'There are clippings and clippings,' returned Dr. Heriot, sententiously, in answer to Hugh's half-amused and half-contemptuous question. 'This is a very ordinary affair compared with that to which Polly refers.'

'How so ?' asked Hugh, curiously.

'Owners of large stocks, I have been told, often have their sheep clipped in sections, employ a certain number of men from day to day, and provide a certain number of sheep, each clipper turning off seven or eight sheep an hour.'

'Well, and the old-fashioned clipping ?'

'Oh, that was another affair, and involved feasting and revelry. The owner of a farm like this, for example, sets apart a special day, and bids his friends and neighbours for miles round to assist him in the work. It is generally con-

16

sidered that a man should clip threescore and ten sheep in a day, a good clipper fourscore.'

'I thought the sheep-washing last month a very amusing sight.'

'Ah, Sowerby tells me that sheep improve more between washing and clipping than at any other period of equal length. Have you ever seen Best's *Farming Book*, two hundred years old? If you can master the old spelling, it is very curious to read. It says there "that a man should always forbear clipping his sheep till such time as he find their wool indifferently well risen from the skin ; and that for divers reasons."'

'Give us the reasons,' laughed Hugh. 'I believe if I were not in holy orders I should prefer farming to any other calling.' And Dr. Heriot drew out a thick notebook.

'I was struck with the quaintness, and copied the extract out verbatim. This is what old Best says :—

' "I. When the wool is well risen from the skin the fleece is as it were walked together on the top, and underneath it is but lightly fastened to the undergrowth ; and when a fleece is thus it is called a mattrice coat.

' "II. When wool is thus risen there is no waste, for it comes wholly off without any bits or locks.

' "III. Fleeces, when they are thus, are far more easy to wind up, and also more easy for the clippers, for a man may almost pull them off without any clipping at all.

' "IV. Sheep that have their wool thus risen have, without question, a good undergrowth, whereby they will be better able to endure a storm than those that have all taken away to the very skin."

'You will notice, Marsden, as I did when I first came here, that the sheep are not so clearly shorn as in the south. They have a rough, almost untidy look ; but perhaps the keener climate necessitates it. An old proverb says :—

> "The man that is about to clip his sheepe
> Must pray for two faire dayes and one faire weeke."'

'That needs translation, Dr. Heriot. Chriss looks puzzled.'

'I must annotate Best, then. And here Michael Sowerby is my informant. Don't you see, farmers like a fine day beforehand, that the wool may be dry—the day he clips, and the ensuing week—that the sheep may be hardened, and their wool somewhat grown before a storm comes.' .

'They shear earlier in the south,' observed Hugh. He was curiously interested in the whole thing.

.'According to Best it used to be here in the middle of June, but it is rarely earlier than the end of June or beginning of July. There is an old saying, and a very quaint one, that you

should not clip your sheep till you see the 'grasshopper sweat,"
and it depends on the nature of the season—whether early or
late—when this phenomenon appears in the pastures.'

'I see no sort of information comes amiss to Dr. Heriot,' was
Hugh's admiring aside to Olive.

Olive smiled, and nodded. The conversation had not
particularly interested her, but she liked this idle lingering in
the shade ; the ivied walls and gateway, and the small blue-
black cattle, with the peacock strutting in the sun, made up a
pretty picture. She followed almost reluctantly, when Dr.
Heriot stretched himself, and called to his mare, who was feeding beside them, and then led the way to the sheep-pens.
Here there was blazing sunshine again, hoarse voices and laughing, and the incessant bleating of sheep, and all the bustle
attendant on a clipping.

Mr. Colby came forward to meet them, with warm welcome.
He was a tall, erect man, with a pleasant, weatherbeaten face,
and a voice with the regular Westmorland accent. Hugh, as
the newcomer, was treated with marked attention, and regret
was at once manifested that he should only witness such a very
poor affair.

But Hugh Marsden, who had been bred in towns, thought it
a very novel and amusing sight. There were ten or twelve
clippers at work, each having his stool or creel, his pair of
shears, and a small cord to bind the feet of the victims.

The patient creatures lay helplessly under the hands that
were so skilfully denuding them of their fleece. Sometimes
there was a struggling mass of wool, but in most instances there
was no resistance, and it was impossible to help admiring the
skill and rapidity of some of the clippers.

The flock was penned close at hand ; boys caught them when
wanted, and brought them to the clippers, received them when
shorn, and took them to the markers, who also applied the tar
to the wounded.

In the distance the lambs were being dipped, and filled the
air with their distressful bleatings, refusing to recognise in the
shorn, miserable creatures that advanced to meet them the
comfortable fleecy parents they had left an hour ago.

Olive watched the heartrending spectacle till her heart grew
pitiful. The poor sheep themselves were baffled by the noxious
sulphur with which the fleece of the lambs were dripping. In
the pasture there was confusion, a mass of white shivering
bodies, now and then ecstasies, recognition, content. To her

the whole thing was a living poem—the innocent faces, the unrest, the plaintive misery, were intact with higher meanings.

'This miserable little lamb, dirty and woebegone, cannot find its mother,' she thought to herself. 'It is even braving the terrors of the crowded yard to find her; even with these dumb, unreasoning creatures, love casteth out fear.'

'Mr. Colby has been telling us such a curious thing,' said Hugh, coming to her side, and speaking with his usual loud-voiced animation. 'He says that in the good old times the Fell clergy always attended these clippings, and acted the part of "doctor;" I mean applied the tar to the wounded sheep.'

'Colby has rather a racy anecdote on that subject,' observed Dr. Heriot, overhearing him. 'Let's have it, Michael, while your wife's tea is brewing. By the bye, I have not tasted your "clipping ale" yet.'

'All right, doctor, it is to the fore. If the story you mean concerns the election of a minister, I think I remember it.'

'Of course you do; two of the electors were discussing the merits of the rival candidates, one of whom had preached his trial sermon that day.'

Michael Colby rubbed his head thoughtfully.

'Ay, ay; now I mind.'

'"Ay," says one, "a varra good sarmon, John; I think he'll du."'

'"Du," says John; "ay, fer a Sunday priest, I'll grant ye, he's aw weel enugh; byt fer clippens en kirsnens toder 'ill bang him aw't nowt."'

Mildred was no longer able to conceal that her head ached severely, and, at a whispered request from Polly, Dr. Heriot led the way to the farmhouse.

Strangers, seeing Wharton Hall for the first time, are always struck by the beauty of the old gateway, mantled in ivy, through which is the trim flower-bordered inclosure, with its comfortable dwelling-house and low, long dairy, and its picturesque remnant of ruins, the whole forming three sides of a quadrangle.

Wharton Hall itself was built by Thomas Lord Wharton about the middle of the sixteenth century, and is a good specimen of a house of the period. Part of it is now in ruins, a portion of it occupied as a farmhouse.

Mrs. Colby, a trim, natty-looking little body, was bustling about the great kitchen with her maids. Tea was not quite ready, and there was a short interval of waiting, in a long, narrow room upstairs, with a great window, looking over the dairy and garden, and the beautiful old gateway.

'I call this my ideal of a farmhouse!' cried Hugh enthusiastically, as they went down the old crazy staircase, having peeped into a great empty room, which Polly whispered would make a glorious ballroom.

The sunshine was streaming into the great kitchen through the narrow windows. July as it was, a bright fire burnt in the huge fireplace; the little round table literally groaned under the dainties with which it was spread; steel forks and delicate old silver spoons lay side by side, the great clock ticked, the red-armed maids went clattering through the flagged passages and dairies, a brood of little yellow chickens clucked and pecked outside in the dust.

'What a picture it all is,' said Olive; and Dr. Heriot laughed. The white dresses and the girls' fresh faces made up the principal part of the picture to him. The grand old kitchen, the sunshine, and the gateway outside were only the background, the accessories of the whole.

Polly wore a breast-knot of pale pinky roses; she had laid aside her broad-brimmed hat; as she moved hither and thither in her trailing dress, with her short, almost boyishly-cropped hair, she looked so graceful and piquante that Dr. Heriot's eyes followed her everywhere with unconscious pleasure.

Polly was more than eighteen now, but her hair had never grown properly—it was still tucked behind the pretty little ears, and the smooth glossy head still felt like the down of an unfledged bird; 'there was something uncommon about Polly Ellison's style,' as people said, and as Mildred sometimes observed to Dr. Heriot—'Polly is certainly growing very pretty.'

He thought so now as he watched the delicate, high-bred face, the cheeks as softly tinted as the roses she wore. Polly's gentle fun always made her the life of the party; she was busily putting in the sugar with the old-fashioned tongs—she carried the cups to Dr. Heriot and Hugh with saucy little speeches.

How well Mildred remembered that evening afterwards. Dr. Heriot had placed her in the old rocking-chair beside the open window, and had thrown himself down on the settle beside her. Chriss, who was a regular salamander, had betaken herself to the farmer's great elbow-chair; the other girls and Hugh had gathered round the little table; the sunshine fell full on Hugh's beaming face and Olive's thoughtful profile; how peaceful and bright it all was, she thought, in spite of her aching head; the girlish laughter pealed through the room, the sparrows and martins chirped from the ivy, the sheep bleating sounded musically from the distance.

'It is an ill wind that blows no one any good,' laughed Dr. Heriot; 'my mare's lameness has given me an excuse for idleness. Look at that fellow Marsden; it puts one into a good temper only to look at him; he reminds one of a moorland breeze, so healthy and so exuberant.'

'We are going to see the dairy!' cried Polly, springing up; 'Chriss and I and Mr. Marsden. Olive is too lazy to come.'

'No, I am only tired,' returned Olive, a little weary of the mirth and longing for quiet.

When the others had gone she stole up the crazy stairs and stood for a long time in the great window looking at the old gateway. They all wondered where she was, when Hugh found her and brought her down, and they walked home through the gray glimmering fields.

'I wonder of what you were thinking when I came in and startled you?' asked Hugh presently.

'I don't know—at least I cannot tell you,' returned Olive, blushing in the dusky light. Could she tell any one the wonderful thoughts that sometimes came to her at such hours; would he understand it if she could?

The young man looked disconcerted—almost hurt.

'You think I should not understand,' he returned, a little piqued, in spite of his sweet temper; 'you have never forgiven me my scepticism with regard to poetry. I thought you did not bear malice, Miss Olive.'

'Neither do I,' she returned, distressed. 'I was only sorry for you then, and I am sorry now you miss so much; poetry is like music, you know, and seems to harmonise and go with everything.'

'Nature has made me prosaic and stupid, I suppose,' returned Hugh, almost sorrowfully. He did not like to be told that he could not understand; he had a curious notion that he would like to know the thoughts that had made her eyes so soft and shining; it seemed strange to him that any girl should dwell so apart in a world of her own. 'How you must despise me,' he said at last, with a touch of bitterness, 'for being what I am.'

'Hush, Mr. Marsden, how can you talk so?' returned Olive, in a voice of rebuke.

The idea shocked her. What were her beautiful thoughts compared to his deeds—her dreamy, contemplative life contrasted with his intense working energies? As she looked up at the great broad-shouldered young fellow striding beside her, with swinging arms and great voice, and simple boyish face, it came upon her that perhaps his was the very essence of poetry, the entire harmony of mind and will with the work that was planned for him.

'Oh, Mr. Marsden, you must never say that again,' she said earnestly, so that Hugh was mollified.

And then, as was often the case with the foolish-fond fellow, when he could get a listener, he descanted eagerly about his little Croydon house and his mother and sisters. Olive was always ready to hear what interested people ; she thought Hugh was not without a certain homely poetry as she listened—perhaps the moonlight, the glimmering fields, or Olive's soft sympathy inspired him ; but he made her see it all.

The little old house, with its faded carpet and hangings, and its cupboards of blue dragon-china—'bogie-china' as they had called it in their childhood—the old-fashioned country town, the gray old almshouses, Church Street, steep and winding, and the old church with its square tower, and four poplar trees—yes, she could see it all.

Olive and Chriss even knew all about Dora and Florence and Sophy ; they had seen their photographs at least a dozen times, large, plain-featured women, with pleasant kindly eyes, Dora especially.

Dora was an invalid, and wrote little books for the Christian Knowledge Society, and Florence and Sophy gave lessons in the shabby little parlour that looked out on Church Street ; through the wire blinds the sisters' little scholars looked out at the old-fashioned butcher's shop and the adjoining jeweller's. At the back of the house there was a long narrow garden, with great bushes of lavender and rosemary.

The letters that came to Hugh were all fragrant with lavender, great bunches of it decked the vases in his little parlour at Miss Farrer's ; antimacassars, knitted socks, endless pen - wipers and kettle-holders, were fashioned for Hugh in the little back room with its narrow windows looking over the garden, where Dora always lay on her little couch.

'She is such a good woman—they are all such good women,' he would say, with clumsy eloquence that went to Olive's heart ; 'they are never sad and moping, they believe the best of everybody, and work from morning till night, and they are so good to the poor, Sophy especially.'

'How I should like to know them,' Olive would reply simply; she believed Hugh implicitly when he assured her that Florence was the handsomest woman he knew; love had beautified those plain-featured women into absolute beauty, divine kindness and goodness shone out of their eyes, devotion and purity had transformed them.

'That is what Dora says, she would so like to know you; they have read your book and they think it beautiful. They say you must be so good to have such thoughts!' cried Hugh, with sudden effusion.

'What are you two young people talking about?' cried Dr. Heriot's voice in the darkness. 'Polly has quarrelled with me, and Chriss is cross, and Miss Lambert is dreadfully tired.'

'Are you tired, Aunt Milly? Mr. Marsden has been telling me about his sisters, and—and—I think we have had a little quarrel too.'

'No, it was I that was cross,' returned Hugh, with his big laugh; 'it always tries my temper when people talk in an unknown tongue.'

Olive gave him a kind look as she bade him good-night.

'I have enjoyed hearing about your sisters, so you must never call yourself prosaic and stupid again, Mr. Marsden,' she said, as she followed the others into the house.

CHAPTER XXI

UNDER STENKRITH BRIDGE

' I never felt chill shadow in my heart
Until this sunset.'—GEORGE ELIOT.

A FEW days after the Wharton Hall clipping, Mildred went
down to the station to see some friends off by the train to Penrith. A party of bright-faced boys and girls had invaded the
vicarage that day, and Mildred, who was never happier than
when surrounded by young people, had readily acceded to their
petition to walk back with them to the station.

It was a lovely July evening, and as Mildred waved her last
adieu, and ascended the steps leading to the road, she felt
tempted to linger, and, instead of turning homewards, to direct her
steps to a favourite place they often visited—Stenkrith Bridge.

Stenkrith Bridge lies just beyond the station, and carries
the Nateby road across the river and the South Durham railway.
On either side of the road there are picturesque glimpses of this
lovely spot. Leaning over the bridge, one can see huge fragmentary boulders, deep shining pools, and the spray and froth
of a miniature cascade.

There is an interesting account of this place by a con-
temporary which is worthy of reproduction.

He says, 'Above the bridge the water of Eden finds its way
under, between, or over some curiously-shaped rocks, locally
termed "brockram," in which, by the action of pebbles driven
round and round by the water in times of flood, many curious
holes have been formed. Just as it reaches the bridge, the
water falls a considerable depth into a round-shaped pool or
"lum," called Coop Kernan Hole : the word hole is an
unnecessary repetition. The place has its name from the fact
that by the action of the water it has been partly hollowed out
between the rock ; at all events, is cup or coop-shaped, and the

water which falls into it is churned and agitated like cream in an old-fashioned churn, before escaping through the fissures of the rocks.

'After falling into Coop Kernan Hole, the water passes through a narrow fissure into another pool or lum at the low side of the bridge, called "Spandub," which has been so named because the distance of the rocks between which the river ran, and which overshadow it, could be spanned by the hand.

'We doubt not that grown men and adventurous youths had many a time stretched their hands across the narrow chasm, and remembered and talked about it when far away from their native place; and when strangers came to visit our town, and saw the beautiful river, on the banks of which it stands, they would be hard to convince that half a mile higher up it was only a span wide. But William Ketching came lusting for notoriety, stretched out his evil hand across the narrow fissure, declared he would be the last man to span Eden, and with his walling-hammer broke off several inches from that part of the rock where it was most nearly touching. "It was varra bad," says an old friend of ours who remembers the incident; "varra bad on him; he sudn't hev done it. It was girt curiosity to span Eden."'

Mildred had an intense affection for this beautiful spot. It was the scene of many a merry gipsy tea; and in the summer Olive and she often made it their resort, taking their work or books and spending long afternoons there.

This evening she would enjoy it alone, 'with only pleasant thoughts for company,' she said to herself, as she strolled contentedly down the smooth green glade, where browsing cattle only broke the silence, and then made her way down the bank to the river-side.

Here she sat down, rapt for a time by the still beauty of the place. Below her, far as she could see, lay the huge gray and white stones through which the water worked its channel. Low trees and shrubs grew in picturesque confusion—dark lichen-covered rocks towered, jagged and massive, on either side of the narrow chasm. Through the arch of the bridge one saw a vista of violet-blue sky and green foliage. The rush of the water into Coop Kernan Hole filled the ear with soft incessant sound. Some one beside Mildred seemed rooted to the spot.

'This is a favourite place with you, I know,' said a voice in her ear; and Mildred, roused from her dreams, started, and turned round, blushing with the sudden surprise.

'Dr. Heriot, how could you? You have startled me dreadfully!'

'Did you not see me coming?' he returned, jumping lightly from one rock to the other, and settling himself comfortably a little below her. 'I saw you at the station and followed you here. Do I intrude on pleasanter thoughts?' he continued, giving her the benefit of one of his keen, quiet glances.

'No; oh no,' stammered Mildred. All at once she felt ill at ease. The situation was novel—unexpected. She had often encountered Dr. Heriot in her walks and drives, but he had never so frankly sought her out as on this evening. His manner was the same as usual—friendly, self-possessed—but for the first time in her life Mildred was tormented with a painful self-consciousness. Her slight confusion was unnoticed, however, for Dr. Heriot went on in the same cool, well-assured voice—

'You are such a comfortable person, Miss Lambert, one can always depend on hearing the truth, the whole truth, and nothing but the truth from you. I confess I should have been grievously disappointed if you had sent me about my own business.'

'Am I given to dismiss you in such a churlish manner, Dr. Heriot?' returned Mildred, with a little nervous laugh; but she only thought, 'How strange of him to follow me here!'

'You are the soul of courtesy itself; you have a benevolent forehead, Miss Lambert. "Entertainment for Pilgrims" ought to be bound round it as a sort of phylactery. Why are women so much more unselfish than men, I wonder?'

'They need something to compensate them for their weakness,' she returned, softly.

'Their weakness is strength sometimes, and masters our brute force. I am in the mood for moralising, you see. Last Sunday evening I was reading my *Pilgrim's Progress*. I have retained my old childish penchant for it. Apollyon with his darts was my favourite nightmare for years. When I came to the part about Charity and the Palace Beautiful, I thought of you.'

Mildred raised her eyes in surprise, and again the sensitive colour rose to her face. Dr. Heriot was given to moralising, she knew, but it was a little forced this evening. In spite of his coolness a suppressed excitement bordered the edge of his words; he looked like a man on the brink of a resolution.

'The damsel Discretion would suit me better,' she said at last, with assumed lightness.

'Yes, Discretion is your handmaid, but my name fits you more truly,' he returned, with a kind look which somehow made her heart beat faster. 'Your sympathy offers such a soft pillow for sore hearts, and aches and troubles—have you a ward for incurables, as well as for the sick and maimed waifs and strays of humanity, I wonder?'

'Dr. Heriot, what possesses you this evening?' returned Mildred, with troubled looks. How strangely he was talking! —was he in fun or earnest? Ought she to stay there and listen to him, or should she gently hint to him the expediency of returning home? A dim instinct warned her that this hour might be fraught with perilous pleasure; a movement would break its spell. She rose hastily.

'You are not going?' he exclaimed, raising himself in some surprise; 'it is still early. This is an ungrateful return for the compliment I have just paid you. I am certain it is Discretion now, and not Charity, that speaks.'

'They will be expecting me,' she returned. Dr. Heriot had risen to his feet, and now stretched out his hand to detain her.

'They do not want you,' he said, with a persuasive smile; 'they can exist an hour without Aunt Milly. Sit down again, Charity, I entreat you, for I have followed you here to ask your advice. I really need it,' he continued, seriously, as Mildred still hesitated; but a glance at the grave, kind face decided her. 'Perhaps, after all, he had some trouble, and she might help him. It could be no harm; it was only too pleasant to be sitting there monopolising his looks and words, usually shared with others. The opportunity might never occur again. She would stop and hear all that he had to say. Was he not her brother's friend, and hers also?'

Dr. Heriot seemed in no hurry to explain himself; he sat throwing pebbles absently into the watery fissures at their feet, while Mildred watched him with some anxiety. Time had dealt very gently with Dr. Heriot; he looked still young, in the prime of life. A close observer might notice that the closely-cropped hair was sprinkled with gray, but the lines that trouble had drawn were almost effaced by the kindly hand of time. There was still a melancholy shade in the eyes, an occasional dash of bitterness in the kind voice, but the trouble lay far back and hidden; and it could not be denied that Dr. Heriot was visibly happier than he had been three years ago. Yes, it was true, sympathy had smoothed out many a furrow; kindly fellowship and close intimacy had brightened the life of the lonely man ; little discrepancies and angles had vanished under beneficent treatment.   The young fresh lives around him, with their passionate interests, their single-eyed pursuits, lent him new interests, and fostered that superabundant benevolence ; and Hope and its twin-sister Desire bloomed by the side of his desolate hearth.

Dr. Heriot had ever told himself that passion was dead within him, slain by that deadly disgust and terror of years. 'A man cannot love twice as I loved Margaret,' he had said to his friend more than once ; and the two men, drawn together by a loss so similar, and yet so diverse, had owned that in their case, and with their faithful tenacity, no second love could be possible.

'But you are a comparatively young man ; you are in the very prime of life, Heriot ; you ought to marry,' his friend had said to him once.

'I do not care to marry for friendship and companionship,' he had answered.   'My wife must be everything or nothing to me.   I must love with passion or not at all.'   And there had risen up before his mind the dreary spectacle of a degraded beauty that he once had worshipped, and which had power to charm him to the very last.

It was three years since Dr. Heriot had uttered his bitter protest against matrimony, and since then there had grown up in his heart a certain sweet fancy, which had emanated first out of pure benevolence, but which, while he cherished and fostered it, had grown very dear to him.

He was thinking of it now, as the pebbles splashed harmlessly in the narrow rivulets, while Mildred watched him, and thought with curious incongruity of the dark, sunless pool lying behind the gray rocks, and of the wild churning and seething of foamy waters which seemed to deaden their voices ; would he ever speak, she wondered.   She sat with folded hands, and a soft, perplexed smile on her face, as she waited, listening to the dreamy rush of the water.

He roused himself at last in earnest.

'How good you are to me, Miss Lambert.   After all, I have no right to tax your forbearance.'

'All friends have a right,' was the low answer.

'All friends, yes.   I wonder what any very special friend dare claim from you ?   I could fancy your goodness without stint or limit then ; it would bear comparison with the deep waters of Coop Kernan Hole itself.'

'Then you flatter me;' but she blushed, yes, to her sorrow, as Mildred rarely blushed.

'You see I am disposed to shelter myself beside it. Miss Lambert, I need not ask you—you know my trouble.'

'Your trouble? Oh yes; Arnold told me.'

'And you are sorry for me?'

'More than I can say,' and Mildred's voice trembled a little, and the tears came to her eyes. With a sort of impulse she stretched out her hand to him—that beautiful woman's hand he had so often admired.

'Thank you,' he returned, gratefully, and holding it in his. 'Miss Lambert, I feel you are my friend; that I dare speak to you. Will you give me your advice to-night, as though—as though you were my sister?'

'Can you doubt it?' in a voice so low that it was almost inaudible. A slight, almost imperceptible shiver passed over her frame, but her mild glance still rested on his averted face; some subtle sadness that was not pain seemed creeping over her; somewhere there seemed a void opened, an empty space, filled with a dying light. Mildred never knew what ailed her at that moment, only, as she sat there with her hands once more folded in her lap, she thought again of the dark, sunless pool lying behind the gray rocks, and of the grewsome cavern, where the churned and seething waters worked their way to the light.

Somewhere from the distance Dr. Heriot's voice seemed to rouse her.

'You are so good and true yourself, that you inspire confidence. A man dare trust you with his dearest secret, and yet feel no dread of betrayal; you are so gentle and so unselfish, that others lay their burdens at your feet.'

'No, no—please don't praise me. I have done nothing—nothing—that any other woman would not have done,' returned Mildred, in a constrained tone. She shrank from this praise. Somehow it wounded her sensibility. He must talk of his trouble and not her, and then, perhaps, she would grow calm again, more like the wise, self-controlled Mildred he thought her.

'I only want to justify the impulse that bade me follow you just now,' he returned, with gentle gravity. 'You shall not lose the fruit of your humility through me, Miss Lambert. I am glad you know my sad story, it makes my task an easier one.'

'You must have suffered greatly, Dr. Heriot.'

'Ah, have I not?' catching his breath quickly. 'You do

not know, how can you, how a man of my nature loves the
woman he has made his wife.'

'She must have been very beautiful.' The words escaped
from Mildred before she was aware.

'Beautiful,' he returned, in a tone of gloomy triumph. 'I
never saw a face like hers, never ; but it was not her beauty
only that I loved ; it was herself—her real self—as she was to
others, never to me. You may judge the power of her fascination, when I tell you that I loved her to the last in spite of all
—ay, in spite of all—and though she murdered my happiness.
Oh, the heaven our home might have been, if our boy had
lived,' speaking more to himself than to her, but her calm voice
recalled him.

'Time heals even these terrible wounds.'

'Yes, time and the kindness of friends. I was not ungrateful, even in my loneliness. Since Margaret died, I have been
thankful for moderate blessings, but now they cease to content
me : in spite of my resolve never to call another woman my
wife, I am growing strangely restless and lonely.'

'You have thought of some one ; you want my advice, my
assistance, perhaps.' Would those churning waters never be
still ? A fine trembling passed through the folded fingers, but
the sweet, quiet tones did not falter. Were there two Mildreds,
one suffering a new, unknown pain ; the other sitting quietly
on a gray boulder, with the water lapping to her very feet.

'Yes, I have thought of some one,' was the steady answer.
'I have thought of my ward.'

'Polly !' Ah, surely those seething waters must burst their
bounds now, and overwhelm them with a noisy flood. Was she
dreaming ? Did she hear him aright ?

'Yes, Polly—my bright-faced Polly. Miss Lambert, you
must not grow pale over it ; I am not robbing Aunt Milly of
one of her children. Polly belongs to me.'

'As thy days so shall thy strength be ;' the words seemed
to echo in her heart. Mildred could make nothing of the pain
that had suddenly seized on her ; some unerring instinct warned
her to defer inquiry. Aunt Milly !—yes, she was only Aunt
Milly, and nothing else.

'You are right ; Polly belongs to you,' she said, looking at
him with wistful eyes, out of which the tender, shining light
seemed somehow faded, 'but you must not sacrifice yourself for
all that,' she continued, with the old-fashioned wisdom he had
ever found in her.

'There you wrong me; it will be no sacrifice,' he returned, eagerly. 'Year by year Polly has been growing very dear to me. I have watched her closely; you could not find a sweeter nature anywhere.'

'She is worthy of a good man's love,' returned Mildred, in the same calm, impassive tone.

'You are so patient that I must not stint my confidence!' he exclaimed. 'I must tell you that for the last two years this thought has been growing up in my heart, at first with reluctant anxiety, but lately with increasing delight. I love Polly very dearly, Miss Lambert; all the more, that she is so dependent on me.'

Mildred did not answer, but evidently Dr. Heriot found her silence sympathetic, for he went on in the same absorbed tone—

'I do not deny that at one time the thought gave me pain, and that I doubted my ability to carry out my plan, but now it is different. I love her well enough to wish to be her protector; well enough to redeem her father's trust. In making this young orphan my wife, I shall console myself; my conscience and my heart will be alike satisfied.'

'She is very young,' began Mildred, but he interrupted her a little sadly.

'That is my only remaining difficulty—she is so young. The discrepancy in our ages is so apparent. I sometimes doubt whether I am right in asking her to sacrifice herself.'

A strange smile passed over Mildred's face. 'Are you sure she will regard it in that light, Dr. Heriot?'

'What do you think?' he returned, eagerly. 'It is there I want your advice. I am not disinterested. I fear my own selfishness, my hearth is so lonely. Think how this young girl, with her sweet looks and words, will brighten it. Dare I venture it? Is Polly to be won?'

'She is too young to have formed another attachment,' mused Mildred. 'As far as I know, she is absolutely free; but I cannot tell, it is not always easy to read girls.' A fleeting thought of Roy, and a probable childish entanglement, passed through Mildred's mind as she spoke, but the next moment it was dismissed as absurd. They were on excellent terms, it was true, but Polly's frank, sisterly affection was too openly expressed to excite suspicion, while Roy's flirtations were known to be legion. A perfectly bewildering number of Christian names were carefully entered in Polly's pocket-book, annotated by Roy himself.

Polly was cognisant of all his love affairs, and alternately coaxed and scolded him out of his secrets.

'And you think she could be induced to care for her old guardian ?' asked Dr. Heriot, and there was no mistaking the real anxiety of his tone.

'Why do you call yourself old ?' returned Mildred, almost brusquely. 'If Polly be fond of you, she will not find fault with your years. Most men do not call themselves old at eight-and-thirty.'

'But I have not led the life of most men,' was the sorrowful reply. 'Sometimes I fear a bright young girl will be no mate for my sadness.'

'It has not turned you into a misanthrope ; you must not be discouraged, Dr. Heriot ; trouble has made you faint-hearted. The best of your life lies before you, you may be sure of that.'

'You know how to comfort, Miss Lambert. You lull fears to sleep so sweetly that they never wake again. You will wish me success, then ?'

'Yes, I will wish you success,' she returned, with a strange melancholy in her voice. Was it for her to tell him that he was deceiving himself ; that benevolence and fancy were painting for him a future that could never be verified ?

He would take this young girl into the shelter of his honest heart, but would he satisfy her, would he satisfy himself ?

Would his hearth be always warm and bright when she bloomed so sweetly beside it ; would her innocent affection content this man, with his deep, passionate nature, and yearning heart ; would there be no void that her girlish intellect could not fill ?

Alas ! she knew him too well to lay such flattering unction to her soul ; and she knew Polly too. Polly would be no child-wife, to be fed with caresses. Her healthy woman's nature would crave her husband's confidence without stint and limit ; there must be response to her affection, an answer to every appeal.

'I will wish you success,' she had said to him, and he had not detected the sadness of her tone, only as he turned to thank her she had risen quickly to her feet.

'Is it so late ? I ought not to have kept you so long,' he exclaimed, as he followed her.

'Yes, the sun has set,' returned Mildred hurriedly ; but as they walked along side by side she suddenly hesitated and stopped. She had an odd fancy, she told him, but she wanted

17

to see the dark pool on the other side of the gray rock, Coop Kernan Hole she thought they called it, for through all their talk it had somehow haunted her.

'If you will promise me not to go too near,' he had answered, 'for the boulders are apt to be slippery at times.'

And Mildred had promised.

He was a little surprised when she refused all assistance and clambered lightly from one huge boulder to another, and still more at her quiet intensity of gaze into the black sullen pool. It was so unlike Mildred—cheerful Mildred—to care about such places.

The sunset had quite died away, but some angry, lurid clouds still lingered westward; the air was heavy and oppressed, no breeze stirred the birches and aspens; below them lay Coop Kernan Hole, black and fathomless, above them the pent-up water leaped over the rocks with white resistless force.

'We shall have a storm directly; this place looks weird and uncanny to-night; let us go.'

'Yes, let us go,' returned Mildred, with a slight shiver. 'What is there to wait for?' What indeed?

She did not now refuse the assistance that Dr. Heriot offered her; her energy was spent, she looked white and somewhat weary when they reached the little gate. Dr. Heriot noticed it.

'You look as if you had seen a ghost. I shall not bring you to this place again in the gloaming,' he said lightly; and Mildred had laughed too.

What had she seen?

Only a sunless pool, with night closing over it; only gray rocks, washed evermore with a foaming torrent; only a yawning chasm, through which churning waters seethed and worked their way, where a dying light could not enter; and above thunder-clouds, black with an approaching storm.

'Yes, I shall come again; not now, not for a long time, and you shall bring me,' she had answered him, with a smile so sweet and singular that it had haunted him.

True prophetic words, but little did Mildred know when and how she would stand beside Coop Kernan Hole again.

CHAPTER XXII

DR. HERIOT'S WARD

'I can pray with pureness
For her welfare now—
Since the yearning waters
Bravely were pent in.
God—He saw me cover,
With a careless brow,
Signs that might have told her
Of the work within.'—PHILIP STANHOPE WORSLEY.

THE pretty shaded lamps were lighted in the drawing-room ; a large gray moth had flown in through the open windows and brushed round them in giddy circles. Polly was singing a little plaintive French air, Roy's favourite. *Tra-la-la, Qui va la,* it went on, with odd little trills and drawn-out chords. Olive's book had dropped to her lap, one long braid of hair had fallen over her hot cheek. Mildred's entrance had broken the thread of some quiet dream,—she uttered an exclamation and Polly's music stopped.

'Dear Aunt Milly, how late you are, and how tired you look !'

'Yes, I am tired, children. I have been to Stenkrith, and Dr. Heriot found me, and we have had a long talk. I think I have missed my tea, and——'

'Aunt Milly, you look dreadful,' broke in Polly, impulsively ; 'you must sit there,' pushing her with gentle force into the low chair, 'and I shall go and bring you some tea, and you are not to talk.'

Mildred was only too thankful to submit ; she leant back wearily upon the cushions Polly's thoughtfulness had provided, with an odd feeling of thankfulness and unrest ;—how good her girls were to her. She watched Polly coming across the room, slim and tall, carrying the little tea-tray, her long dress flowing out behind her with gentle undulating movement. The lamplight shone on the purple cup, and the softly-tinted peach lying beside it, placed there by Polly's soft little fingers; she carried a little filagree-basket, a mere toy of a thing, heaped up with queen's cakes; a large creamy rose detached itself from her dress and fell on Mildred's lap.

'This is the second time you have shivered, and yet your hands are warm—oh, so warm,' said the girl anxiously, as she hung over her.

Mildred smiled and roused herself, and tried to do justice to the little feast.

'They had all had a busy day,' she said with a yawn, and stretching herself.

The vicarage had been a Babel since early morning, with all those noisy tongues. Yes, the tea had refreshed her, but her head still ached, and she thought it would be wiser to go to bed.

'Please do go, Aunt Milly,' Olive had chimed in, and when she had bidden them good-night, she heard Polly's flute-like voice bursting into *Tra-la-la* again as she closed the door; *Qui va la* she hummed to herself as she crept wearily along.

The storm had broken some miles below them, and only harmless summer lightning played on the ragged edges of the clouds as they gleamed fitfully, now here, now there; there were sudden glimpses of dark hills and a gray, still river, with some cattle grouped under the bridge, and then darkness.

'How strange to shiver in such heat,' thought Mildred, as she sat down by the open window. She scarcely knew why she sat there—'Only for a few minutes just to think it all out,' she said to herself, as she pressed her aching forehead between her hands; but hours passed and still she did not move.

Years afterwards Mildred was once asked which was the bitterest hour of her life, and she had grown suddenly pale and the answer had died away on her lips; the remembrance of this night had power to chill her even then.

A singular conflict was raging in Mildred's gentle bosom, passions hitherto unknown stirred and agitated it; the poor soul, dragged before the tribunal of inexorable womanhood, had pleaded guilty to a crime that was yet no crime—the sin of having loved unsought.

Unconsciousness could shield her no longer, the beneficent cloak of friendship could not cover her; mutual sympathy, the united strength of goodness and intellect, her own pitying woman's heart, had wrought the mischief under which she was now writhing with an intolerable sense of terror and shame.

And how intolerable can only be known by any pure-minded woman under the same circumstances! It would not be too much to say that Mildred absolutely cowered under it; tranquillity was broken up; the brain, calm and reasonable no longer, grew feverish with the effort to piece together tormenting fragments of recollection.

Had she betrayed herself? How had she sinned if she had so sinned? What had she done that the agony of this humiliation had come upon her—she who had thought of others, never of herself?

Was this the secret of her false peace? was her life indeed robbed of its sweetest illusion—she who had hoped for nothing, expected nothing? would she now go softly all her days as one who had lost her chief good?

And yet what had she desired—but to keep him as her friend? was not this the sum and head of her offending?

'Oh, God, Thou knowest my integrity!' she cried from the depths of her suffering soul.

Alas! was it her fault that she loved him? was it only her fancy that some sympathy, subtle but profound, united them? was it not he who deceived himself? Ah, there was the stab. She knew now that she was nothing to him and he was everything to her.

Her very unconsciousness had prepared this snare for her. She had called him her friend, but it had come to this, that his step was as music in her ear, and the sunshine of his presence had glorified her days. How she had looked for his coming, with what quiet welcoming smiles she had received her friend; his silence had been as sweet to her as his words; the very seat where he sat, the very reels of cotton on her little work-table with which he had played, were as sacred as relics in her eyes.

How she had leant on his counsel; his yea was yea to her, and his nay, nay. How wise and gentle he had ever been with her; once she had been ill, and the tenderness of his sympathy had made her almost love her illness. 'You must get well; we cannot spare you,' he had said to her, and she had thanked him with her sweetest smiles.

How happy they had been in those days: the thought of any change had terrified her; sometimes she had imagined herself twenty years older, but Mildred Lambert still, with a grayhaired friend coming quietly across in the dusk to sit with her and Arnold when all the young ones were gone—her friend, always her friend!

How pitiable had been her self-deception; she must have loved him even then. The thought of Margaret's husband marrying another woman, and that woman the girl that she had cherished as her own daughter, tormented her with a sense of impossibility and pain. Good heavens, what if he deceived himself! What if for the second time in his life he worked out his own disappointment, passion and benevolence leading him equally astray.

Sadness indescribable and profound steeped the soul of this noble woman; pitiful efforts after prayer, wild searching for light, for her lost calmness, for mental resolve and strength, broke the silence of her anguish; but such a struggle could not long continue in one so meek, so ordinarily self-controlled; then came the blessed relief of tears; then, falling on her knees and bowed to the very dust, the poor creature invoked the presence of the Great Sufferer, and laid the burden of her sorrow on the broken heart of her Lord.

One who loved Mildred found, long afterwards, a few lines copied from some book, and marked with a red marginal line, with the date of this night affixed :—

> 'So out in the night on the wide, wild sea,
> When the wind was beating drearily,
> And the waters were moaning wearily,
> I met with Him who had died for me.'

Had she met with Him? 'Had the wounded Hand touched hers in the dark?' Who knows?

The lightnings ceased to play along the edges of the cloud, the moon rose, the long shadows projected from the hills, the sound of cattle hoofs came crisply up the dry channel of the beck, and still Mildred knelt on, with her head buried on her outstretched arms. ' I will not go unless Thou bless me '—was that her prayer?

Not in words, perhaps; but as the day broke, with faint gleams and tints of ever-broadening glory, Mildred rose from her knees, and looked over the hills with sad, steadfast eyes.

The conflict had ceased, the conqueror was only a woman— a woman no longer young, with pale cheeks, with faded, weary eyes—but never did braver hands gird on the cross that must henceforth be carried unflinchingly.

' Mine be the pain, and his the happiness,' she whispered. Her knees were trembling under her with weakness, she looked wan and bloodless, but her soul was free at last. 'I am innocent; I have done no wrong. God is my witness!' she cried in her inmost heart. 'I shall fear to look no man in the face. God bless him—God bless them both! He is still my friend, for I have done nothing to forfeit his friendship. God will take care of me. I have duty, work, blessings innumerable, and a future heaven when this long weariness is done.'

And again: 'He will never know it. He will never know that yesterday, as I stood by his side, I longed to be lying at the bottom of the dark, sunless pool. It was a wicked wish—God forgive me for it. I saw him look at me once, and there was surprise in his eyes, and then he stretched out his kind hand and led me away.'

And then once more: 'There is no trouble unendurable but sin, and I thank my God that the shame and the terror has passed, and left me, weak indeed, but innocent as a little child. If I had known—but no, His Hand has been with me through it all. I am not afraid; I have not betrayed myself; I can bear what God has willed.'

She had planned it all out. There must be no faltering, no flinching; not a moment must be unoccupied. Work must be found, new interests sought after, heart-sickness subdued by labour and fatigue; there was only idleness to be dreaded, so she told herself.

It has been often said by cynical writers that women are better actors than men; that they will at times play out a part in the dreary farce of life that is quite foreign to their real character, dressing their face with smiles while their heart is still sore within them.

But Mildred was not one of these; she had been taught in no ordinary school of adversity. In the dimness of that seven years' seclusion she had learnt lessons of fortitude and endurance that would have baffled the patience of weaker women. Flesh and blood might shrink from the unequal combat, but her courage would not fail; her strength, fed from the highest sources, would still be found sufficient.

Henceforth for Mildred Lambert there should shine the light of a day that was not 'clear nor dark;' she knew that for her no dazzling sunrise of requited love should flood her woman's kingdom with brightness; happiness must be replaced by duty, by the quiet contentment of a heart 'at leisure from itself.'

'There is no trouble unendurable but sin,' she had said to herself. Oh, that other poor sufferers—sufferers in heart, in this world's good things—would lay this truth to their souls! It would rob sorrow of its sting, it would lift the deadly mists from the charnel-house itself. For to the Mildreds of life religion is no Sunday garb, to be laid aside when the week-day burdens press heaviest; no garbled mixture of sentiment and symbolic rites, of lip-worship and heart freedom, tolerated by 'the civilised heathenism' of the present day, for in their heart they know that to the Christian, suffering is a privilege, not a punishment; that from the days of Calvary 'Take up thy cross and follow Me' is the literal command literally obeyed by the true followers of the great Master of suffering.

Mildred was resolved to tolerate no weakness; she dressed herself quickly, and was down at the usual time. 'How old and faded I look,' she thought, as she caught the reflection of herself in the glass.

Her changed looks would excite comment, she knew, and she braced herself to meet it with tolerable equanimity; a sleepless night could be pleaded as an excuse for heavy eyes and swollen eyelids. Polly indeed seemed disposed to renew her soft manipulations and girlish officiousness, but Mildred contrived to put them aside. 'She was going down to the schools, and after that there were the old women at the workhouse and at Natcby,' she said, with the quiet firmness which always made Aunt Milly's decrees unalterable. 'Her girls must take care of themselves until she returned.'

'Charity begins at home, Aunt Milly. I am sure Olive and I are worth a score of old women,' grumbled Polly, who in season and out of season was given to clatter after Mildred in her little high-heeled shoes.

Dr. Heriot's ward was becoming a decidedly fashionable young lady; the pretty feet were set off by silver buckles, Polly's heel's tapped the floor endlessly as she tripped hither and thither; Polly's long skirts, always crisp and rustling, her fresh dainty muslins, her toy aprons and shining ribbons, were the themes of much harmless criticism; the little hands were always faultlessly gloved; London-marked boxes came to her perpetually, with Roy's saucy compliments; wonderful ruby and cream-coloured ribbons were purchased with the young artist's scanty savings. Nor was Dr. Heriot less mindful of the innocent vanity that somehow added to Polly's piquancy. The little watch that ticked at her waist, the gold chain and locket, the girlish ring with its turquoise heart, were all the gifts of the kind guardian and friend.

Dr. Heriot's bounty was unfailing. The newest books found their way to Olive's and Mildred's little work-tables; Chriss was made happy by additions to her menagerie of pets; a gray parrot, a Skye terrier whose shaggy coat swept the ground, even pink-eyed rabbits found their way to the vicarage; the grand silk dresses that Dr. Heriot had sent down on Polly's last birthday for her and Olive were nothing in Chriss's eyes compared to Fritter-my-wig, who could smoke, draw corks, bark like a dog, and reduce Veteran Rag to desperation by a vision of concealed cats on the stable wall. Chriss's oddities were not disappearing with her years—indeed she was still the same captious little person as of old; with her bright eyes and tawny-coloured mane she was decidedly picturesque, though stooping shoulders, and the eye-glass her short-sight required, detracted somewhat from her good looks.

On any sunny afternoon she could be seen sitting on the low step leading to the lawn, her parrot, Fritter-my-wig, on her shoulder, and Tatters and Witch at her feet, and most likely a volume of Euripides on her lap. The quaint little figure, the red-brown touzle of curls, the short striped skirt, and gold eye-glasses, struck Roy on one of his rare visits home; one of his most charming pictures was painted from the recollection. 'There was an Old Woman,' it was called. Chriss objected indignantly to the dolls that were introduced, though Roy gravely assured her that he had adhered to Hugh's beautiful idea of the twelve months.

Polly had some reason for her discontent and grumbling. The weather had changed, and heavy summer rains seemed setting in, and Mildred's plan for her day did not savour of prudence. It suited Mildred's sombre thoughts better than sunshine; she went upstairs almost cheerfully, and took out a gray cloak that was Polly's favourite aversion on the score that it reminded her of a Sister-of-Charity cloak. 'Not that I do not love and honour Sisters,' she had added by way of excuse, 'but I should not like you to be one, Aunt Milly,' and Mildred had hastened to assure her that she had never felt it to be her vocation.

She remembered Polly's speech now as she shook out the creases; the straight, long folds, the unobtrusive colour, somehow suited her. 'I think people who are not young ought always to dress in black or gray,' she said to herself; 'butterfly colours are only fit for girls. I should like nothing better than to be allowed to hide all this hair under a cap and Quaker's bonnet.' And yet, as she said this, Mildred remembered with a sudden pang that Dr. Heriot had once observed in her hearing that she had beautiful hair.

She went on bravely through the day—no work came amiss to her ; after a time she ceased even to feel fatigue. Once the crowded schoolroom would have made her head ache after the first hour or so, but now she sat quite passive, with the girls sewing round her, and the boys spelling out their tasks with incessant buzz and movement.

The old women in the workhouse did not tire her with their complaints ; she sat for a long time by the side of one old creature who was bedridden and palsied ; the idiot girl—alas ! she was forty years old—blinked at her with small dazed eyes, as she showed her the gaily-coloured pictures she had pasted on rag for her amusement, and followed her contentedly up and down the long whitewashed wards.

In the cottages she was as warmly welcomed as ever ; one sick child, whom she had often visited, held out his little arms and ceased crying with pain when he saw her. Mildred laid aside her damp cloak, and walked up and down the flagged kitchen for a long time with the boy's head on her shoulder ; singing to him with her low sweet voice.

' Ay, but he's terrible fond of you, poor thing !' exclaimed the mother gratefully. She was an invalid too, and lay on a board beside the empty fireplace, looking out of the low latticed window crowded with flower-pots. The other children gathered round her, plucking her skirt shyly, and listening to Mildred's cooing voice ; the little fellow's blue eyes seemed closing drowsily, one small blackened hand stole very near Mildred's neck.

> 'There's a home for little children
> Above the bright blue sky,'

sang Mildred.

' Ay, Jock ; but, thoo lile varment, thoo'll nivver gang oop if thou bealst like a bargeist,' whispered the woman to a white-headed urchin beside her, who seemed disposed for a roar.

' I cares lile—nay, I dunn't,' muttered Jock, contumaciously ; to Jock's unregenerated mind the white robes and the palms seemed less tempting than the shouts of his little companions outside. ' There's lile Geordie and Dawson's Sue,' he grumbled, rubbing his eyes with his dirty fists.

' Gang thee thy ways, or I'll fetch thee a skelp wi' my stick,' returned the poor mother, weary of the discussion, and Jock scampered off, nothing loth.

Mildred sang her little hymn all through as the boy's head drooped heavily on her shoulder ; as she walked up and down, her dreamy eyes had a far-off look in them, and yet nothing escaped her notice. She saw the long rafter over her head, with the Sunday boots and shoes neatly arranged on it, with bunches of faint-smelling herbs hanging below them ; the adjoining door was open, the large bare room, with its round table and bedstead, and heaped up coals on the floor, was plainly visible to her, as well as its lonely occupant darning black stockings in the window.

'After all, was she as lonely,' she thought, 'as Bett Hutchinson, who lived by herself, with only a tabby cat for company, and kept her coal-cellar in her bedroom ? and yet, though Bett had weak eyes and weak nerves, and was clean out of her wits on the subject of the boggle family, from the "boggle with twa heeds" down to Jock's "bargheist ahint the yat-stoop."'

Bett's superstition was a household word with her neighbours, 'daft Bett and her boggles' affording a mine of entertainment to the gossips of Nateby. Mildred, and latterly Hugh Marsden, had endeavoured to reason Bett out of her fancies, but it was no use. 'I saw summut—nay, nay, I saw summut,' she always persisted. 'I was a'most daft—'twas t'boggle, and nought else,' she murmured.

Mildred was no weak girl, to go moaning about the world because her heart must be emptied of its chief treasure. Bett's penurious loneliness read her a salutary lesson ; her own life, saddened as it was, grew rich by comparison. '"If in mercy Thou wilt spare joys that yet are mine,"' she whispered, as she laid the sleeping child down in the wooden cot and spread the patched quilt lovingly over him.

Jock grinned at her from behind an oyster-shell and mud erection ; lile Geordie and Dawson's Sue were with him. 'Aw've just yan hawpenny left,' she heard him say as she passed.

Mildred had finished the hardest day's work that she had ever done in her life, but she knew that it was not yet over. Dr. Heriot was not one to linger over a generous impulse ; 'If it is worth doing at all, one should do it at once,' was a favourite maxim of his.

Mildred knew well what she had to expect. She was only thankful that the summer's dusk allowed her to slip past the long French window that always stood open. They were lighting the lamp already—some one, probably Olive, had asked for it. A voice, that struck Mildred cold with a sudden anguish, railed playfully against bookworms who could not afford a blind-man's holiday.

'He is here; of course I knew how it would be,' she murmured, as she groped her way a little feebly up the stairs. She would have given much for a quiet half-hour in her room, but it was not to be; the tapping sound she dreaded already struck upon her ear, the crisp rustle of garments in the passage, then the faint knock and timid entrance. 'I knew it was Polly. Come in; do you want me, my dear?' the tired voice striving bravely after cheerfulness.

'Aunt Milly—oh, Aunt Milly!—I thought you would never come;' and in the dark two soft little hands clasped her tight, and a burning face hid itself in her neck. 'Oh,' with a sort of gasp, 'I have wanted my Aunt Milly so badly!'

Then the noble, womanly heart opened with a great rush of tenderness, and took in the girl who had so unconsciously become a rival.

'What is this, my pet—not tears, surely?' for Polly had laid her head down, and was sobbing hysterically with excitement and relief.

'I cannot help it. I was longing all the time for papa to know; and then it was all so strange, and I thought you would never come. I shall be more comfortable now,' sobbed Polly, with a girlish abandon of mingled happiness and grief. 'Directly I heard your step outside the window I made an excuse to get away to you.'

'I ought not to have left you—it was wrong; but, no, it could not be helped,' returned Mildred, in a low voice. She pressed the girl to her, and stroked the soft hair with cold, trembling fingers. 'Are those happy tears, my pet? Hush, you must not cry any more now.'

'They do me good. I felt as though I were some one else downstairs, not Polly at all. Oh, Aunt Milly, can you believe it?—do you think it is all real?'

'What is real? You have told me nothing yet, remember. Shall I guess, Polly? Is it a great secret—a very great secret, my darling?'

'Aunt Milly, as though you did not know, when he told me that you and he had had a long talk about it yesterday!'

'He—Dr. Heriot, I suppose you mean?'

'He says I must call him something else now,' returned the girl in a whisper, 'but I have told him I never shall. He will always be Dr. Heriot to me—always. I don't like his other name, Aunt Milly; no one does.'

'John—I think it beautiful!' with a certain sharp pain in her voice. She remembered how he had once owned to her that no one had called him by this name since he was a boy. He had been christened John Heriot—John Heriot Heriot—and his wife had always called him Heriot. 'Only my mother ever called me John,' he had said in a regretful tone, and Mildred had softly repeated the name after him.

'It has always been my favourite name,' she had owned with that simplicity that was natural to her; and his eyes had glistened as though he were well-pleased.

'It is beautiful; it reminds one of St. John. I have always liked it,' she said a little quickly.

'His wife called him Heriot; yes, I know, he told me—but I am so young, and he—well, he is not exactly old, Aunt Milly, but——'

'Do you love him, Polly?—child, do you really love him?' and for a moment Mildred put the girl from her with a sort of impatience and irritation of suspense. Polly's pretty face was suffused with hot blushes when she came back to her place again.

'He asked me that question, and I told him yes. How can one help it, and he so good? Aunt Milly, you have no idea how kind and gentle he was when he saw he frightened me.'

'Frightened you, my child?'

'The strangeness of it all, I mean. I could not understand him for a long time. He talked quite in his old way, and yet somehow he was different; and all at once I found out what he meant.'

'Well?'

'And then I got frightened, I suppose. I thought how could I satisfy him, and he so much older and cleverer. He is so immeasurably above all my girlish silliness, and so I could not help crying a little.'

'Poor little Polly! but he comforted you.'

'Oh yes,' with more blushes, 'he talked to me so beautifully that I could not be afraid any more. He said that for years this had been in his mind, that he had never forgotten how I had wanted to live with him and take care of him, and how he had always called me "his sweet little heartsease" ever since. Oh, Aunt Milly, I know he wants me. It was so sad to hear him talk about his loneliness.'

'You will not let him be lonely any longer. I have lost my Polly, I see.'

'No, no, you must not say so,' throwing her arm round her, only with a sort of bashful pride, very new in Polly; 'he has no one to take care of him but me.'

'Then he shall have our Sunbeam—God bless her!' and Mildred kissed her proudly. 'I hope you did not tell him he was old, Polly.'

'He asked me if I thought him so, and of course I said it was only I who was too young.'

'And what did he say to that?'

'He laughed, and said it was a fault that I should soon mend, but that he meant to be very proud as well as fond of his child-wife. Do you know, he actually thinks me pretty, Aunt Milly.'

'He is right; you are pretty—very pretty, Polly,' she repeated, absently. She was saying in her own heart 'Dr. Heriot's wife—John Heriot's child-wife'—over and over again.

'Roy never would tell me so, because he said it would make me vain. Roy will be glad about this, will he not, Aunt Milly?'

'I do not know; nay, I hope so, my darling.'

'And Richard, and all of them; they are so fond of Dr. Heriot. Do you remember how often they have joked him about Heriot's Choice?'

'Yes, I remember.'

A sudden spasm crossed Mildred's gentle face, but she soon controlled herself. She must get used to these sharp pangs, these recollections of the happy, innocent past; she had misunderstood her friend, that was all.

'Dear Aunt Milly, make me worthier of his love,' whispered the girl, with tears in her eyes; 'he is so noble, my benefactor, my almost father, and now he is going to make me his wife, and I am so young and childish.'

And she clung to Mildred, quivering with vague irrepressible emotion.

'Hush, you will be his sunbeam, as you have been ours. What did he call you—his heartsease? You must keep that name, my pet.'

'But—but you will teach me, he thinks so much of you; he says you are the gentlest, and the wisest, and the dearest friend he has ever had. Where are you going, Aunt Milly?' for Mildred had gently disengaged herself from the girl's embrace.

'Hush, we ought to go down; you must not keep me any

longer, dear Polly; he will expect—it is my duty to see him.'

Mildred was adjusting her hair and dress with cold, shaking fingers, while Polly stood by and shyly helped her.

'It does not matter how you look,' the girl had said, with innocent unconscious sarcasm; 'you are so tired, the tumbled gray alpaca will do for to-night.'

'No, it does not matter how I look,' replied Mildred, calmly.

A colourless weary face and eyes, with an odd shine and light in them, were reflected between the dimly-burning candles. Polly stood beside her slim and conscious; she had dried her tears, and a sweet honest blush mantled her young cheeks. The little foot tapped half impatiently on the floor.

'You have no ribbons or flowers, but perhaps after all it will not be noticed,' she said, with pardonable egotism.

'No, he will have only eyes for you to-night. Come, Polly, I am ready;' and as the girl turned coy and seemed disposed to linger, Mildred quietly turned to the door.

'I thought I was to be dismissed without your saying good-night to me,' was Dr. Heriot's greeting as he advanced to meet them. He was holding 'Mildred's cold hand tightly, but his eyes rested on Polly's downcast face as he spoke.

'We ought to have come before, but I knew you would understand.'

'Yes, I understand,' he returned, with an expression of proud tenderness. 'You will give your child to me, Miss Lambert?'

'She has always seemed to belong to you more than to me,' and then she looked up at him for a moment with her old beautiful smile. 'I need not ask you to be good to her—you are good to every one; but she is so young, little more than a child.'

'You may trust me,' he returned, putting his arm gently round the young girl's shoulders; 'there shall not a hair of her head suffer harm if I can prevent it. Polly is not afraid of me, is she?'

'No,' replied Polly, shyly; but the bright eyes lifted themselves with difficulty.

She looked after him with a sort of perplexed pride, half-conscious, half-confused, as he released her and bade them all good-night. When he was gone she hovered round Mildred in the old childish way and seemed unwilling to leave her.

'I have done the right thing. Bless her sweet face. I

know I shall make her happy,' thought Dr. Heriot as he walked with rapid strides across the market-place ; 'a man cannot love twice in his life as I loved my Margaret, but the peaceful affection such as I can give my darling will satisfy her I know. If only Philip could see into my heart to-night I think he would be comforted for his motherless child.' And then again—'How sweetly Mildred Lambert looked at me to-night ; she is a good woman, there are few like her. Her face reminded me of some Madonna I have seen in a foreign gallery as she stood with the girl clinging to her. I wonder she has never married ; these ministering women lead lonely lives sometimes. Sometimes I have fancied she knew what it is to love, and suffered. I thought so yesterday and again to-day, there was such a ring of sadness in her voice. Perhaps he died, but one cannot tell— women never reveal these things.'

And so the benevolent heart sunned itself in pleasant dreams. The future looked fair and peaceful, no brooding complications, no murky clouds threatened the atmosphere, passion lay dormant, rest was the chief good to be desired. Could benevolence play him false, could affection be misplaced, would he ever come to own to himself that delusion had cheated him, that husks and not bread had been given him to eat, that his honest yearning heart had again betrayed him, that a kindly impulse, a protecting tenderness, had blinded him to his true happiness?

'How good he is,' thought the young girl as she laid her head on the pillow ; 'how dearly I must love him : I ought to love him. I never imagined any one could be half so gentle. I wonder if Roy will be glad when I tell him—oh yes, I wonder if Roy will be glad?'

CHAPTER XXIII

'AND MAIDENS CALL IT LOVE-IN-IDLENESS'

> ' Is there within thy heart a need
> That mine cannot fulfil ?
> One chord that any other hand
> Could better wake or still ?
> Speak now, lest at some future day
> My whole life wither and decay.'
>
> ADELAIDE ANNE PROCTER.

THE news of Dr. Heriot's engagement soon spread fast ; he was amused, and Polly half frightened, by the congratulations that poured upon them. Mr. Trelawny, restored to something like good humour by the unexpected tidings, made surly overtures of peace, which were received on Dr. Heriot's part with his usual urbanity. The Squire imparted the news to his daughter after his own ungracious fashion.

' Do you hear Heriot's gone and made a fool of himself ? ' he said, as he sat facing her at table ; ' he has engaged himself to that ward of his ; why, he is twenty years older than the girl if he is a day ! '

' Papa, do you know what you are saying ? ' expostulated Ethel ; the audacity of the statement bewildered her ; she would have scorned herself for her credulity if she had believed him. Dr. Heriot—their Dr. Heriot ! No, she would not so malign his wisdom.

The quiet scepticism of her manner excited Mr. Trelawny's wrath.

' You women all set such store by Heriot,' he returned, sneeringly ; ' everything he did was right in your eyes ; you can't believe he would be caught like other men by a pretty face, eh ? '

' No, I cannot believe it,' she returned, still firmly.

' Then you may go into the town and hear it for yourself,' he continued, taking up his paper with a pretence of indifference, but his keen eyes still watched her from beneath it. Was

18

it only her usual obstinacy, or was she really incredulous of his tidings? 'I had it from Davidson, who had congratulated the Doctor himself that morning,' he continued, sullenly; 'he said he never saw him look better in his life; the girl was with him.'

'But not Polly—you cannot mean Polly Ellison?' and now Ethel turned strangely white. 'Papa, there must be some mistake about it all. I—I will go and see Mildred.'

'You may spare yourself that trouble,' returned Mr. Trelawny, gloomily.

Ethel's changing colour, her evident pain, were not lost upon him. 'There may be a chance for Cathcart still,' was his next thought; 'women's hearts as well as men are often caught at the rebound; she'll have him out of pique—who knows?' and softened by this latter reflection he threw down his paper, and continued almost graciously—

'Yes, you may spare yourself that trouble, for I met Miss Lambert myself this afternoon.'

'And you spoke to her?' demanded Ethel, with almost trembling eagerness.

'I spoke to her, of course; we had quite a long talk, till she said the sun was in her eyes, and walked on. She seemed surprised that I had heard the news already, said it was so like Kirkby Stephen gossip, but corroborated it by owning that they were all as much in the dark as we were; but Miss Ellison being such a child, no one had thought of such a thing.'

'Was that all she said? Did she look as well as usual? I have not seen her for nearly a fortnight, you know,' answered Ethel, apologetically.

'I can't say I noticed. Miss Lambert would be a nice-looking woman if she did not dress so dowdily; but she looked worse than ever this morning,' grumbled the Squire, who was a *connoisseur* in woman's dress, and had eyed Mildred's brown hat and gray gingham with marked disfavour. 'She said the sun made her feel a little faint, and then she sent her love to you and moved away. I think we might as well do the civil and call at the vicarage this afternoon; we shall see the bride-elect herself then,' and Ethel, who dared not refuse, agreed very unwillingly.

The visit was a trying ordeal for every one concerned. Polly indeed looked her prettiest, and blushed very becomingly over the Squire's laboured compliments, though, to do him justice, they were less hollow than usual; he was too well pleased at the match not to relapse a little from his frigidity.

'You must convince my daughter—she has chosen to be very sceptical,' he said, with a side-long look at Ethel, who just moved her lips and coloured slightly. She had kissed Polly in her ordinary manner, with no special effusion, and added a quiet word or two, and then she had sat down by Mildred.

'Polly looks very pretty and very happy, does she not?' asked Mildred after a time, lifting her quiet eyes to Ethel.

'I beg your pardon—yes, she looks very nice,' returned Ethel, absently. 'I suppose I ought to say I am glad about this,' she continued with some abruptness as Mildred took up her work again, and sewed with quick even stitches, 'but I cannot; I am sorry, desperately sorry. She is a dear little soul, I know, but all the same I think Dr. Heriot has acted foolishly.'

'My dear Ethel,—hush, they will hear you!' The busy fingers trembled a little, but Mildred did not again raise her eyes.

'I do not care who hears me; he is just like other men. I am disappointed in him; I will have no Mentor now but you, Mildred.'

'Dr. Heriot has done nothing to deserve your scorn,' returned Mildred, but her cheek flushed a little. Did she know that instinctively Ethel had guessed her secret, that her generous heart throbbed with sympathy for a pain which, hidden as it was, was plainly legible to her clear-sightedness? 'We ought all to be glad that he has found comfort at last,' she said, a little unsteadily.

Ethel darted a singular look at her, admiring, yet full of pain.

'I am not so short-sighted as you. I am sorry for a good man's mistake—for it is a mistake, whatever you may say, Mildred. Polly is pretty and good, but she is not good enough for him. And then, he is more than double her age!'

'I thought that would be an additional virtue in your eyes,' returned Mildred, pointedly. She was sufficiently mistress of herself and secure enough in her quiet strength to be able to retaliate in a gentle womanly way. Ethel coloured and changed her ground.

'They have nothing in common. She is nice, but then she is not clever; you know yourself that her abilities are not above the average, Mildred.'

'Dr. Heriot does not like clever women, he has often said so; Olive would not suit him at all.'

'I never thought of Olive,' in a piqued voice. Ethel was losing her temper over Mildred's calmness. 'I am aware plain people are not to his taste.'

'No, Polly pleases him there ; and then, she is so sweet.'

'I should have thought him the last man to care for insipid sweetness,' began Ethel, stormily, but Mildred stopped her with unusual warmth.

'You are wrong there ; there is nothing insipid about Polly ; she is bright, and good, and true-hearted ; you undervalue his choice when you say such things, Ethel. Polly's extreme youthfulness and gaiety of spirits have misled you.'

'How lovingly you defend your favourite, Mildred ; you shall not hear another word in her disparagement. What does he call her ? Mary ?'

'No, Polly ; but I believe he has plenty of pet names for her.'

'Yes, he will pet her—ah, I understand, and I am not to scorn him. I am not to call him foolish, Mildred ?'

'Of course not. Why should you ?'

'Ah, why should I ? Papa, it is time for us to be going ; you have talked to Miss Ellison long enough. My pretty bird,' as Polly stole shyly up to them, 'I have not wished you joy yet, but it is not always to be had for the wishing.'

'I wish every one would not be so kind,' stammered Polly. Mr. Trelawny's condescension and elaborate compliments had almost overwhelmed the poor little thing.

'How the child blushes ! I wonder you are not afraid of such a grave Mentor, Polly.'

'Oh, no, he is too kind for that—is he not, Aunt Milly ?'

'I hope you do not make Mildred the umpire,' replied Ethel, watching them both. 'Oh these men !' she thought to herself, as she dropped the girl's hand ; her eyes grew suddenly dim as she stooped and kissed Mildred's pale cheek. 'Good—there is no one worthy of you,' she said to herself ; 'he is not—he never will be now.'

'People are almost too kind ; I wish they would not come and talk to me so,' Polly said, with one of her pretty pouts, as she walked with Dr. Heriot that evening. He was a little shy of courting in public, and loved better to have her with him in one of their quiet walks ; this evening he had come again to fetch her, and Mildred had given him some instruction as to the length and duration of their walk.

'Had you not better come with us ?' he had said to her, as though he meant it ; but Mildred shook her head with a slight

smile. 'We shall all meet you at Ewbank Scar ; it is better for
you to have the child to yourself for a little,' she had replied.

Polly wished that Aunt Milly had come with them after all.
Dearly as she loved her kind guardian and friend, she was still
a little shy of him ; a consciousness of girlish incompleteness, of
undeveloped youth, haunted her perpetually. Polly was sufficiently quick-witted to feel her own deficiencies. How should
she ever be able to satisfy him ? she thought. Aunt Milly could
talk so beautifully to him, and even Olive had brief spasms of
eloquence. Polly felt sometimes as she listened to them as
though she were craning her neck to look over a wall at some
unknown territory with strange elevations and giddy depths, and
wide bridgeless rivers meandering through it.

Suppositions, vague imaginations, oppressed her ; Polly could
talk sensibly in a grave matter-of-fact way, and at times she had
a pretty *piquante* language of her own ; but Chriss's erudition,
and Olive's philosophy, and even Mildred's gentle sermonising,
were wearying to her. 'I can talk about what I have seen and
what I have heard and read,' she said once, 'but I cannot play
at talk—make believe—as you grown-up children do. I think
it is hard,' continued practical Polly, 'that Aunt Milly, who has
seen nothing, and has been shut up in a sickroom all the best
years of her life, can spin yards of talk where I cannot say a
word.' But Dr. Heriot found no fault with his young companion ;
on the contrary, Polly's *naïveté* and freshness were infinitely refreshing to the weary man, who, as he told himself, had lived
out the best years of his life. He looked at her now as she
uttered her childish complaint. One little gloved hand rested
on his arm, the other held up the long skirts daintily, under the
broad-brimmed hat a pretty oval face dimpled and blushed with
every word.

'If people would only not be so kind—if they would let me
alone,' she grumbled.

'That is a singular grievance, Polly,' returned Dr. Heriot,
smiling ; 'happiness ought not to make us selfish.'

'That is what Aunt Milly says. Ah, how good she is !'
sighed the girl, enviously ; 'almost a saint. I wish I were
more like her.'

'I am satisfied with Polly as she is, though she is no saint.'

'No, are you really ?' looking up at him brightly. 'Do you
know, I have been thinking a great deal since—you know when
——' her colour giving emphasis to her unfinished sentence.

'Indeed ? I should like to know some of those thoughts,'

with a playful glance at her downcast face. 'I must positively hear them, Polly. How sweet and still it is this evening. Suppose we sit and rest ourselves for a little while, and you shall tell me all about them.'

Polly shook her head. 'They are not so easy to tell,' she said, looking very shy all at once. Dr. Heriot had placed her on a stile at the head of the little lane that skirted Podgill ; the broad sunny meadow lay before them, gemmed with trefoil and Polly's favourite eyebright ; blue gentian, and pink and white yarrow, and yellow ragwort, wove straggling colours in the tangled hedgerows ; the graceful campanula, with its bell-like blossoms, gleamed here and there, towering above the lowlier rose-campion, while meadowsweet and trails of honeysuckle scented the air.

Dr. Heriot leant against the fence with folded arms ; his mood was sunny and benignant. In his gray suit and straw hat he looked young, almost handsome. Under the dark moustache his lip curled with an amused, undefinable smile.

'I see you will want my help,' he said, with a sort of compassion and amusement at her shyness. Whatever she might own, his little fearless Polly was certainly afraid of him.

'I have tangled them dreadfully,' blushed Polly ; 'the thoughts, I mean. Every night when I go to bed I wish—I wish I were as wise as Aunt Milly, and then perhaps I should satisfy you.'

'My dear child!' and then he stopped a little, amazed and perplexed. Why was Mildred Lambert's goodness to be ever thrust on him, he thought, with a man's natural impatience ? He had not bent his neck to her mild sway ; her friendship was very precious to him—one of the good things for which he daily thanked God ; but this innocent harping on her name fretted him with a vague sense of injury. 'Polly, who has put this in your head ?' he said ; and there was a shadow of displeasure in his tone, quiet as it was.

'No one,' she returned, in surprise ; 'the thought has often come to me. Are you never afraid,' she continued, timidly, but her young face grew all at once sweet and earnest—'are you not afraid that you will be tired—dreadfully tired—when you have only me to whom to talk ?'

Then his gravity relaxed : the speech was so like Polly,—so like his honest, simple-minded girl.

'And what if I were ?' he repeated, playing with her fears.

'I should be so sorry,' she returned, seriously. 'No, I should be more than sorry ; I think it would make me unhappy. I

should always be trying to get older and wiser for your sake ;
and if I did not succeed I should be ready to break my heart.
No, do not smile,' as she caught a glimpse of his amused face ;
'I was never more serious in my life.'

'.Why, Mary, my little darling, what is this ?' he said, lifting
the little hand to his lips ; for the bright eyes were full of tears
now.

'No, call me Polly—I like that best,' she returned, hurriedly.
'Only my father called me Mary ; and from you——'

'Well, what of me, little one ?'

'I do not know. It sounds so strange from your lips. It
makes me feel afraid, somehow, as though I were grown up and
quite old. I like the childish Polly best.'

'You shall be obeyed, dear—literally and entirely, I mean ;'
for he saw her agitation needed soothing. 'But Polly is not quite
herself to-night ; these fears and scruples are not like her.   Let
me hear all these troublesome thoughts, dearest ; you know I
am a safe confidant.'   And encouraged by the gentleness of his
tone, Polly crept close into the shelter of the kind arm that had
been thrown round her.

'I don't think it hurts one to have fears,' she said, in her
simple way ; 'they seem to grow out of one's very happiness.
You must not mind if I am afraid at times that I shall not
always please you ; it will only be because I want to do it so
much.'

'There, you wound and heal in one breath,' he replied, half-
laughing, and half-touched.

'It has come into my mind more than once that when we
are alone together ; when I come to take care of you ; you know
what I mean.'

'When you are my own sweet wife—I understand, Polly ;'
and now nothing could exceed the grave tenderness of his voice.

'Yes, when you bring me home to the fireside, which you say
has been so lonely,' she returned, with touching frankness, at
once childlike and womanly.   'When you have no one but me
to comfort you, what if you find out too late that I am so young
—so very young—that I have not all you want ?'

'Polly—my own Polly !'

'Ah, you may call me that, and yet the disappointment may
be bitter. You have been so good to me, I love you so dearly,
that I could not bear to see a shade on your face, young as I am.
I do not feel like a child about this.'

'No, you are not a child,' he returned, looking at her with

new reverence in his eyes. In her earnestness she had forgotten her girlish shyness ; her hands were clasped fearlessly on his arm, truth was written on her guileless face, her words rang in his ear with mingled pathos and purity.

'No, you are not a child,' he repeated, and then he stopped all of a sudden ; his wooing had grown difficult to him. He had never liked her so well, he had never regarded her with such proud fondness, as now, when she pleaded with him for toleration of her undeveloped youth. For one swift instant a consciousness of the truth of her words struck home to him with a keen sense of pain, marring the pleasant harmony of his dream ; but when he looked at her again it was gone.

And yet how was he to answer her ? It was not petting fondness she wanted—not even ordinary love-speeches—only rest from an uneasy fear that harassed her repose—an assurance, mute or otherwise, that she was sufficient for his peace. If he understood her aright, this was what she wanted.

'Polly, I do not think you need to be afraid,' he said at last, hesitating strangely over his words. 'I understand you, my darling ; I know what you mean ; but I do not think you need be afraid.'

'Ah, if I could only feel that!' she whispered.

'I will make you feel it ; listen to me, dear. We men are odd, unaccountable beings ; we have moods, our work worries us, we have tired fits now and then, nothing is right, all is vanity of vanity, disgust, want of success, blurred outlines, opaque mist everywhere—then it is I shall want my little comforter. You will be my veritable Sunbeam then.'

'But if I fail you ?'

'Hush, you will never fail me. What heresy, what disbelief in a wife's first duty ! Do you know, Polly, it is just three years since I first dreamt of the beneficent fairy who was to rise up beside my hearth.'

'You thought of me three years ago ?'

'Thought of you ? No, dreamt of you, fairy. You know you came to me first in a ladder of motes and beams. Don't you remember Dad Fabian's attic, and the picture of Cain, and the strange guardian coming in through the low doorway ?'

'Yes, I remember ; you startled me.'

'Polly is a hundred times prettier now ; but I can recognise still in you the slim creature in the rusty black frock, with thin arms, and large dark eyes, drinking in the sunlight. It was such a forlorn Polly then.'

'And then you were good to me.'

'I am afraid I must have seemed stern to you, poor child, repelling your young impulse in such a manner. I remember, while you were pleading in your innocent fashion, and Miss Lambert was smiling at you, that a curious fancy came into my head. Something hardly human seemed to whisper to me, "John Heriot, after all, you may have found a little comforter."'

'I am so glad. I mean that you have thought of me for such a time.' Polly was dimpling again; the old happy light had come back to her eyes.

'You see it is no new idea. I have watched my Polly growing sweeter and brighter day by day. How often you have confided in me; how often I have shared your innocent thoughts. You were not afraid to show me affection then.'

'I am not now,' she stammered.

'Perhaps not now, my bright-eyed bird; you have borrowed courage and eloquence for the occasion, inciting me to all manner of lover-like and foolish speeches. What do you say, little one—do you think I play the lover so badly, after all?'

'Yes—no—it does not suit you, somehow,' faltered Polly, truthful still.

'What, am I too old?' but Dr. Heriot's tone was piqued in spite of its assumed raillery.

'No, you know you are not; but I like the old ways and manners best. When you talk like this I get shy and stupid, and do not feel like Polly at all.'

'You are the dearest and sweetest Polly in the world,' he returned, with a low, satisfied laugh; 'the most delightful combination of quaintness and simplicity. I wonder what wise Aunt Milly would say if she heard you.'

'That reminds me that she will be expecting us,' returned Polly, springing off the stile without waiting for his hand. She had shaken off her serious mood, and chatted gaily as they hurried along the upper woodland path; her hands were full of roses and great clusters of campanula by the time they reached Mildred, who was sitting on a little knoll that overlooked the Scar. In winter-time the beck rushed noisily down the high rocky face of the cliff, but now the long drought had dried up its sources, and with the exception of a few still pools the river-bed was dry.

Mildred sat with her elbow on her knee, looking dreamily at the gray scarped rock and overhanging vegetation; while Olive and Chriss scrambled over the slippery boulders in search of ferns. Behind the dark woods the sunset clouds were flaming with breadths of crimson and yellow glory. Over the barren rocks a tiny crescent moon was rising ; Mildred's eyes were riveted on it.

'We have found some butterwort and kingcups ; Dr. Heriot declares it is the same that Shakespeare calls " Winking Marybuds." You must add it to your wild-flower collection, Aunt Milly.'

'Are you tired of waiting for us, Miss Lambert ? Polly has been giving me some trouble, and I have had to lecture her.'

'Not very severely, I expect,' returned Mildred. She looked anxiously from one to another, but Polly's gaiety reassured her as she flung a handful of flowers into her lap, and then proceeded to sort and arrange them.

'You might give us Perdita's pretty speech, Polly,' said Dr. Heriot, who leant against a young thorn watching her.

Polly gave a mischievous little laugh. She remembered the quotation ; Roy had so often repeated it. He would spout pages of Shakespeare as they walked through the wintry woods. 'You have brought it upon yourself,' she cried, holding up to him a long festoon of gaudy weeds, and repeating the lines in her fresh young voice.

> 'Here's flowers for you !
> Hot lavender, mints, savory, marjoram ;
> The marigold, that goes to bed with the sun,
> And with him rises weeping: these are flowers
> Of middle summer, and I think they are given
> To men of middle age. You are very welcome.'

'Oh, Polly—Polly—fie !'

'Little Heartsease, do you know what you deserve ?' but Dr. Heriot evidently enjoyed the mischief. 'After all, I brought it on myself. I believe I was thinking of the crazy Danish maid, Ophelia, all the time.'

'You have had your turn,' answered Polly, with her prettiest pout ; 'my next shall be for Aunt Milly. I am afraid I don't look much like Ophelia, though. There, Aunt Milly—there's rosemary, that's for remembrance—pray you, love, remember ; and there is pansies, that's for thoughts.'

'Make them as gay as your own, Heartease ;' then—

'Hush, don't interrupt me ; I am making Aunt Milly shiver. "There's fennel for you and columbines ; there's rue for you, and here's some for me. We may call it herb of grace o' Sundays. You may wear your rue with a difference."'

'You are offering me a sorry garland;' and Mildred forced a smile over the girl's quaint conceit. 'Mints, savory, marjoram, all the homeliest herbs you could find in your garden. I shall not forget the compliment to my middle age,' grumbled Dr. Heriot, who was unusually tickled at the goodness of the *repartee*. Polly was never so thoroughly at her ease as when she was under Aunt Milly's wing. Just then Mildred rose to recall Olive and Chriss; as she went down the woody hillock a quick contraction of pain furrowed her brow.

'There's rue for you,' she said to herself; 'ah, and rosemary, that's for remembrance. Oh, Polly, I felt tempted to use old Polonius's words, and say, "there's a method in madness"; how little you know the true word spoken in jest; never mind, if I can only take it as "my herb of grace o' Sundays," it will be well yet.'

Mildred found herself monopolised by Chriss during their homeward walk. Polly and Dr. Heriot were in front, and Olive, as was often her custom, lingering far behind.

'Let them go on, Aunt Milly,' whispered Chriss; 'lovers are dreadfully poor company to every one but themselves. Polly will be no good at all now she is engaged.'

'What do you know about lovers, a little girl like you?' returned Mildred, amused in spite of herself.

'I am not a little girl, I am nearly sixteen,' replied Chriss, indignantly. 'Romeo and Juliet were all very well, and so were Ferdinand and Miranda, but in real life it is so stupid. I have made up my mind that I shall never marry.'

'Wait until you are asked, puss.'

'Ah, as to that,' returned the young philosopher, calmly, 'as Dr. John says, it takes all sorts of people to make up a world, and I daresay some one will be found who does not object to eye-glasses.'

'Or to blue stockings,' observed Mildred, rather slyly.

'You forget we live in enlightened days,' remarked Chriss, sententiously; 'this sort of ideas belonged to the Dark Ages. Minds are not buried alive now because they happen to be born in the feminine gender,' continued Chriss, with a slight confusion of metaphor.

Mildred smiled. Chriss's odd talk distracted her from sad thoughts. The winding path had already hidden the lovers from her; unconsciously she slackened her pace.

'I should not mind a nice gray professor, perhaps, if he knew lots of languages, and didn't take snuff. But they all do;

it clears the brain, and is a salutary irritant,' went on Chriss, who had only seen one professor in her life, and that one a very dingy specimen. 'I should like my professor to be old and sensible, and not young and silly, and he must not care about eating and drinking, or expect me to sew on his buttons, or mend his gloves. Some one ought to invent a mending-machine. I am sure these things take away half the pleasure of living.'

'My little Chriss, do you mean to be head without hands ? You will be a very imperfect woman, I am afraid, and I hope in that case you will not find your professor.'

'I would rather be without him, after all,' replied Chriss, discontentedly. 'Men are so stupid ; they want their own way, and every one has to give in to them. I would rather live in lodgings like Roy, somewhere near the British Museum, where I could go and read every day, and in the evening I would go to lectures and concerts, or stop at home and play with Fritter-my-wig : that is just the sort of life I should like, Aunt Milly.'

'What is to become of your father and me ? Perhaps Olive may marry.'

'Olive ? not a bit of it. She always says nothing would induce her to leave papa. You don't want me to stop all my life in this little corner of the world, where everything is behind the times, and there is not a creature to whom one cares to speak ?'

'Chriss, Chriss, what a Radical you are,' returned Mildred. She was a little weary of Chriss's childish chatter. They were in the deep lane skirting Podgill now ; just beyond the foot-bridge Polly and Dr. Heriot were standing waiting for them.

'Is the tangle all gone ?' he asked presently. 'Are you quite happy again, Heartsease ?'

'Yes, very happy,' she assured him, with a bright smile, and he felt a pressure of the hand that rested on his arm.

'What a darling she is,' he thought to himself somewhat later that night, as he walked across the market-place, now shining in the moonlight. 'Little witch, how prettily she acted that speech of Perdita, her eyes imploring forgiveness all the time for her mischief. The child has deep feelings too. Once or twice she made me feel oddly. But I need not fear ; she will make a sweet wife, I know, my innocent Polly.'

But the little scene haunted his fancy, and he had an odd dream about it that night. He thought that they were in the grassy knoll again looking over the Scar, and that some one pushed some withered herbs into his hands. 'Here's rue for you, and there's some for me ; you may wear your rue with a difference,' said a voice.

'Unkind Polly !' he returned, dropping them, and stretched out his arms to imprison the culprit ; but Polly was not there, only Mildred Lambert was there, with her elbow on her knee, looking sadly over the Scar.

CHAPTER XXIV

> Hey the green ribbon ! we kneeled beside it,
> We parted the grasses dewy and sheen ;
> Drop over drop, there filtered and slided
> A tiny bright beck that trickled between.
> Tinkle, tinkle, sweetly it sung to us,
> Light was our talk as of faëry bells—
> Faëry wedding-bells faintly rung to us
> Down in their fortunate parallels.—JEAN INGELOW.

RICHARD came home for a few days towards the end of the long vacation. He was looking pale and thin in spite of his enforced cheerfulness, and it was easy to see that the inaction of the last few weeks had only induced restlessness, and a strong desire for hard, grinding work, as a sedative for mental unrest. His brotherly congratulations to Polly were mixed with secret amusement.

'So you are "Heriot's choice," are you, Polly ?' he said, taking her hand kindly, and looking at the happy, blushing face.

'Are you glad, Richard ?' she whispered, shyly.

'I can hardly tell,' he returned, with a curiously perplexed expression. 'I believe overwhelming surprise was my first sensation on hearing the wonderful intelligence. I gave such an exclamation that Roy turned quite pale, and thought something had happened at home, and then he got in a temper, and carried off the letter to read by himself ; he would have it I was chaffing him.'

Polly pouted half-seriously. 'You are not a bit nice to me, Richard, or Roy either. Why has he never written to me himself ? He must have got my two letters.'

'You forget ; I have never seen anything of him for the last six weeks. Fancy my finding him off on the tramp when I returned that night, prosecuting one of his art pilgrimages, as he calls them, to some shrine of beauty or other. He had not even the grace to apologise for his base desertion till a week afterwards. However, Frognal without Rex was not to be borne; so I started off to Cornwall in search of our reading party, and then got inveigled by Oxenham, who carried me off to Ilfracombe.'

'It was very wrong of Rex to leave you; he is not generally so thoughtless,' returned Polly, who had been secretly chagrined by this neglect on the part of her old favourite. 'Is there no letter from Rex?' had been a daily question for weeks.

'Rex is a regular Bohemian since he took to wearing a moustache and a velvet coat. All the Hampstead young ladies are breaking their hearts over him. He looks so handsome and picturesque; if he would only cut his hair shorter, and open his sleepy eyes, I should admire him myself.'

Polly sighed.

'I wish he would come home, dear old fellow. I long to see him; but I am dreadfully angry with him, all the same; he ought to have written to Dr. Heriot, if not to me. It is disrespectful—unkind—not like Rex at all.' And Polly's bright eyes swam with tears of genuine resentment.

'I shall tell Roy how you take his unkindness to heart.'

She shook her head.

'It is very ungrateful of him, to say the least of it. You have spoiled him, Polly.'

'No,' she returned, very gravely. 'Rex is too good to be spoiled: he must have some reason for his silence. If he had told me he was going to be married—to—to any of those young ladies you mention, I would have gone to London to see his wife. I know,' she continued, softly, 'Rex was fonder of me than he was of Olive and Chriss. I was just like a favourite sister, and I always felt as though he were my own—own brother. Why there is nothing that I would not do for Rex.'

'Dear Polly, we all know that; you have been the truest little sister to him, and to us all.'

'Yes, and then for him to treat me like this—to be silent six whole weeks. Perhaps he did not like Aunt Milly writing. Perhaps he thought I ought to have written to him myself; and I have since—two long letters.'

'Dr. Heriot will be angry with Rex if he sees you fretting.'

'I am not fretting; I never fret,' she returned, indignantly; 'as though that foolish boy deserved it. I am happier than I can tell you. Oh, Richard, is he not good?'

And there was no mistaking the sweet earnestness with which she spoke of her future husband.

'Ah, that he is.'

'How grave you look, Richard! Are you really glad—really and truly, I mean?'

'Why, Polly, what a little Jesuit you are, diving into people's secret thoughts in this way.' And there was a shadow of embarrassment in Richard's cordial manner. 'Of course I am glad that you should be happy, dear, and not less so that Dr. John's solitary days are over.'

'Yes, but you don't think me worthy of him,' she returned, plaintively, and yet shrewdly.

'I don't think you really grown up, you mean; you wear long dresses, you are quite a fashionable young lady now, but to me you always seem little Polly.'

'Rude boy,' she returned, with a charming pout, 'one would think you had gray hairs, to listen to you. I can't be so very young or so very silly, or he would not have chosen me, you know.'

'I suppose you have bewitched him,' returned Richard, smiling; but Polly refused to hear any more and ran away laughing.

Richard's face clouded over his thoughts when he was left alone. Whatever they were he kept them locked in his own breast; during the few days he remained at home, he was observant of all that passed under his eyes, and there was a deferential tenderness in his manner to Mildred that somewhat surprised her; but neither to her nor to any other person did he hint that he was disappointed by Dr. Heriot's choice.

During the first day there had been no mention of Kirkleatham or Ethel Trelawny, but on the second day Richard had himself broken the ice by suggesting that Mildred should contrive some errand that should take her thither, and that in the course of her visit she should mention his arrival at the vicarage.

'I must think of her, Aunt Milly; we are neither of us ready to undergo the awkwardness of a first meeting. Perhaps in a few months things may go on much as usual. I always meant to write to her before my ordination. Tell her that I shall only be here for a few days—that Polly wants me to wait over her birthday, but that I have no intention of intruding on her.'

'Are you so sure she will regard it as an intrusion?' asked Mildred, quietly.

'There is no need to debate the question,' was the somewhat

hasty reply. 'I must not deviate from the rule I have laid down for myself, to see as little as possible of her until after my ordination.'

'And that will be at Whitsuntide ?'

'Yes,' he returned, with an involuntary sigh ; 'so, Aunt Milly, you will promise to go after dinner ?'

Mildred promised, but fate was against her. Olive and Polly had driven over to Appleby with Dr. Heriot, and relays of callers detained her unwillingly all the afternoon ; she saw Richard was secretly chafing, as he helped her to entertain them with the small talk usual on such occasions. He was just bidding a cheerful good-bye to Mrs. Heath and her sister, when horses' hoofs rung on the beck gravel of the courtyard, and Ethel rode up to the door, followed by her groom. ·

Mildred grew pale from sympathy when she saw Richard's face, but there was no help for it now ; she saw Ethel start and flush, and then quietly put aside his assistance, and spring lightly to the ground ; but she looked almost as white as Richard himself when she came into the room, and not all her dignity could hide that she was trembling.

'I did not know, I thought you were alone,' she faltered, as Mildred kissed her ; but Richard caught the whisper.

'You shall be alone if you wish it,' he returned, trying to speak in his ordinary manner, but failing miserably.

Poor lad, this unexpected meeting with his idol was too much even for his endurance. 'I was not prepared for it,' as he said afterwards. He thought she looked sweeter than ever under the influence of that girlish embarrassment. He watched her anxiously as she stood still holding Mildred's hand.

'You shall not be made uncomfortable, Miss Trelawny ; it is my fault, not yours, that I am here. I told Aunt Milly to prevent this awkwardness. I will go, and then you two will be alone together ;' and he was turning to the door, but Ethel's good heart prompted her to speak, and prevented months of estrangement.

'Why should you go, Richard ? this is your home, not mine ; Mildred, ask him not to do anything so strange—so unkind.'

'But if my presence embarrasses you ?' he returned, with an impetuous Cœur-de-Lion look that made Ethel blush.

She could not answer.

'It will not do so if you sit down and be like yourself,' said Mildred, pleadingly. She looked at the two young

19

creatures with half-pitying, half-amused eyes. Richard's out-raged boyish dignity and Ethel's yearning overture of peace to her old favourite—it was beautiful and yet sad to watch them, she thought. 'Richard, will you ring that bell, please?' continued the wary woman; 'Ethel has come for her afternoon cup of tea, and she does not like to be kept waiting. Tell Etta to be quick, and fetch some of her favourite seed-cake from the dining-room sideboard.'

Mildred's common sense was rarely at fault; to be matter-of-fact at such a crisis was invaluable. It restored Richard's calmness as nothing else could have done; it gave him five minutes' grace, during which he hunted for the cake and his mislaid coolness together; that neither could be found at once mattered little. Richard's overcharged feelings had safe vent in scolding Etta and creating commotion and hubbub in the kitchen, where the young master's behests were laws fashioned after the Mede and Persian type.

When he re-entered the room Mildred knew she could trust him. He found Ethel sitting by the open window with her hat and gauntlets off, enjoying the tea Mildred had provided. He carried the cake gravely to her, as though it were a mission of importance, and Ethel, who could not have swallowed a mouthful to save her life, thanked him with a sweet smile and crumbled the fragments on her plate.

By and by Mildred was called away on business. She obeyed reluctantly when she saw Ethel's appealing look.

'I shall only be away a few minutes. Give her some more tea, Richard,' she said as she closed the door.

Richard did as he was bid; but either his hand shook or Ethel's, though neither owned to the impeachment, and the cup slipped, and some of the hot liquid was spilt on the blue cloth habit.

The laugh that followed was a very healing one. Richard was on his knees trying to undo the mischief and blaming himself in no measured terms for his awkwardness. When he saw the sparkle in Ethel's eye his brow cleared like magic.

'You are not angry with me, then?'

'Angry with you! What an idea, Richard; such a trifling accident as that. Why it has not even hurt the cloth.'

'No, but it has scalded your hand; let me look.' And as Ethel tried to hide it he held it firmly in his own.

'You see it is nothing, hardly a red spot!' but he did not let it go.

'Ethel, will you promise me one thing? No, don't draw your hand away, I shall say nothing to frighten you. I was a fool just now, but then one is a fool sometimes when one comes suddenly upon the woman one loves. But will you promise not to shun me again, not as though you hated me, I mean?'

'Hated you! For shame, Richard.'

'Well, then, as though you were afraid of me. You disdained my assistance just now, you would not let me lift you from your horse. How often have I done so before, and you never repulsed me!'

'You ought not to have noticed it, you ought to have understood,' returned Ethel, with quivering lips. It was very sweet to be talking to him again if only he would not encroach on his privilege.

'Then let things be between us as they always have been,' he pleaded. 'I have done nothing to forfeit your friendship, have I? I have humbled myself, not you,' with a flavour of bitterness which she could not find it in her heart to resent. 'Let me see you sitting here sometimes in my father's house; such a sight will go far to soothe me. Shall it be so, Ethel?'

'Yes, if you wish it,' she returned, almost humbly.

Her only thought was how she should comfort him. Her womanly eyes read signs of conflict and suffering in the pale, wan face; when she had assented, he relinquished her hand with a mute clasp of thanks. He looked almost himself when Mildred came back, apologising for her long delay. Had she really been gone half-an-hour—neither of them knew it. Ethel looked soothed, tranquillised, almost happy, and Richard not graver than his wont.

Mildred was relieved to find things on this agreeable footing, but she was not a little surprised when two days afterwards Richard announced his intention of going up to Kirkleatham, and begged her to accompany him.

'I will promise not to make a fool of myself again; you shall see how well I shall behave,' he said, anticipating her remonstrance. 'Don't raise any objection, please, Aunt Milly. I have thought it all over, and I believe I am acting for the best,' and of course Richard had his way.

Ethel's varying colour when she met them testified to her surprise, and for a little while her manner was painfully constrained, but it could not long remain so. Richard seemed determined that she should be at her ease with him. He talked well and freely, only avoiding with the nicest tact any subject that might recall the conversation in the kitchen garden.

Mildred sat by in secret admiration and wonder; the simple woman could make nothing of the young diplomatist. That Richard could talk well on grave subjects was no novelty to her; but never had he proved himself so eloquent; rather terse than fluent, addicted more to correctness than wit, he now ranged lightly over a breadth of subjects, touching gracefully on points on which he knew them to be both interested, with an admirable choice of words that pleased even Ethel's fastidiousness.

Mildred saw that her attention was first attracted, and then that she was insensibly drawn to answer him. She seemed less embarrassed, the old enthusiasm woke. She contradicted him once in her old way, he maintained his opinion with warm persistence;—they disagreed. They were still in the height of the argument when Mildred looked at her watch and said they must be going.

It was Ethel's turn now to proffer hospitality, but to her surprise Richard quietly refused it. He would come again and bid her good-bye, he said gravely, holding her hand; he hoped then that Mr. Trelawny would be at home.

His manner seemed to trouble Ethel. She had stretched out her hand for her garden-hat. It had always been a custom with her to walk down the croft with Mildred, but now she apparently changed her mind, for she replaced it on the peg.

'You are right,' said Richard, quietly, as he watched this little by-play, 'it is far too hot in the crofts, and to-day Aunt Milly has my escort. Old customs are sometimes a bore even to a thorough conservative such as you, Miss Trelawny.'

'I will show you that you are wrong,' returned Ethel, with unusual warmth, as the broad-brimmed hat was in her hand again. There was a pin-point of sarcasm under Richard's smooth speech that grazed her susceptibility.

Perhaps Richard had gained his end, for an odd smile played round his mouth as he walked beside her. He did not seem to notice that she did not address him again, but confined her attention to Mildred. Her cheeks were very pink, possibly from the heat, when she parted from them at the gate, and Richard got only a very fleeting pressure of the hand.

'Richard, I do not know whether to admire or to be afraid of you,' said Mildred, half in jest, as they crossed the road.

A flash of intelligence answered her.

'Did I behave well? It is weary work, Aunt Milly; it will

make an old man of me before my time, but she shall reverence me yet,' and his mouth closed with the old determined look she knew so well.

Dr. Heriot had planned a picnic to Hillbeck in honour of Polly's eighteenth birthday, the vicarage party and Mr. Marsden being the only guests.

Hillbeck Wood was a very favourite place of resort on hot summer days. To-day dinner was to be spread in the deep little glen lying behind an old disused cotton-mill, a large dilapidated building that Polly always declared must be haunted, and to please this fancy of hers Dr. Heriot had once fabricated a weird plot of a story which was so charmingly terrible, as Chriss phrased it, that the girls declared nothing would induce them to remain in the glen after sundown.

There was certainly something weird and awesome in the very silence and neglect of the place, but the glen behind it was a lovely spot. The hillsides were thickly wooded ; through the bottom of the glen ran a sparkling little beck ; the rich colours of the foliage, wearing now the golden and red livery of autumn, were warm and harmonious ; while a cloudless sky and a soft September air brightened the scene of enjoyment.

Mildred, who, as usual on such occasions, was doomed to rest and inaction, amused herself with collecting a specimen of *ruta muraria* for her fernery, while Polly and Chriss washed salad in the running stream, and Richard and Hugh Marsden unpacked the hampers, and Olive spread the tempting contents on dishes tastefully adorned with leaves and flowers under Dr. Heriot's supervision, while Mr. Lambert sat by, an amused spectator of the whole.

There was plenty of innocent gaiety over the little feast. Hugh Marsden's blunders and large-handed awkwardness were always provocative of mirth, and he took all in such good part. Polly and Chriss waited on everybody, and even washed the plates in the beck, Polly tucking up her fresh blue cambric and showing her little high-heeled shoes as she tripped over the grass.

When the meal was over the gentlemen seemed inclined to linger in the pleasant shade ; Chriss was coaxing Dr. Heriot for a story, but he was too lazy to comply, and only roused himself to listen to Richard and Hugh Marsden, who had got on the subject of clerical work and the difficulty of contesting northern prejudice.

'Their ignorance and hard-headedness are lamentable,'

groaned Hugh; 'dissent has a terrible hold over their mind; but to judge from a few of the stories Mr. Delaware tells us, things are better than they were.'

'My father met with a curious instance of this crass ignorance on the part of one of his parishioners about fifteen years ago,' returned Richard. 'I have heard him relate it so often. You remember old W——, father?'

'I am not likely to forget him,' replied Mr. Lambert, smiling. 'It was a very pitiful case to my mind, though one cannot forbear a smile at the quaintness of his notion. Heriot has often heard me refer to it.'

'We must have it for Marsden's benefit then.'

'I think Richard was right in saying that it was about fifteen years ago that I was called to minister to an old man in his eighty-sixth year, who had been blind from his birth, I believe, and was then on his deathbed. I read to him, prayed for him, and talked to him; but though his lips moved I did not seem to gain his attention. At last, in despair, I said good-afternoon, and rose to go, but he suddenly caught hold of me.

'"Stop ye, parson," he said; "stop ye a bit, an' just hear me say my prayers, will ye?" I thought it a singular request, but I remained, and he began repeating the Lord's Prayer, the Creed, the collect "Lighten our darkness," and finished up with the quaint old couplet beginning—

> "Matthew, Mark, Luke, and John,
> Bless the bed that I lie on,"

and after he had finished he said triumphantly, "Hoo d'ye think I've deean? I said 'em gay weel. D'ye think I'll pass?"

'Of course I said something appropriate in reply; but his attention seemed wholly fixed on the fact that he could say his prayers correctly, as he had been probably taught in his early childhood, and when I had noticed his lips moving he had been conning the prayers over to himself before repeating them for my judgment.'[1]

A lugubrious shake of the head was Hugh's only answer.

'I grant you such a state of things seems almost incredible in our enlightened nineteenth century,' continued Mr. Lambert, 'but many of my older brethren have curious stories to tell of their parishioners, all of them rather amusing than otherwise. Your predecessor, Heriot—Dr. Bailey—had a rare

---

[1] Taken from fact.

stock of racy anecdotes, with which he used to entertain us on winter evenings over a glass of hot whisky toddy.'

'To which he was slightly too much addicted,' observed Dr. Heriot.

'Well, well, we all have our faults,' replied the vicar, charitably. 'We will not speak against poor Bailey, who was in the main a downright honest fellow, though he was not without his weakness. Betha used to remonstrate with him sometimes, but it was no use ; he said he was too old to break off a habit. I don't think, Heriot, he ever went to great lengths.'

'Possibly not,' was the somewhat dry reply, 'but we are willing to be amused by the old doctor's reminiscences.'

'You know the old Westmorland custom for giving names ; well, some forty years ago George Bailey, then a young doctor new to practice, was sent for to visit a man named John Atkinson, who lived in a house at the head of Swale-dale.

'Having reached the place, he knocked at the door, and asked if John Atkinson lived there.

' "Nay," says the woman, "we've naebody ev that nyam hereaboots."

' "What ?" says Bailey, "nobody of the name in the dale ?"

' "Nyah," was the reply, made with the usual phlegm and curtness of the genuine Daleswoman. "There's naebody ev that nyam."

' "Well, it is very odd," returned Bailey, in great perplexity. "This looks like the house to which I was directed. Is there any one ill in the dale ?"

' "Bless me, bairn," exclaimed the woman, "ye'll mean lile Geordie John. He's my man ; en's liggen en theyar," pointing to an inner room, "varra badly. Ye'll be t'doctor, I warn't. Cum, cum yer ways in en see him. Noo I think on't, his reet nyam is John Atkinson, byt he allus gas by lile Geordie John. His fad'r was Geordie, ye kna, an' nobbut a varra lile chap." '

'Capital !' observed Dr. Heriot, as he chuckled and rubbed his hands over this story. 'Bailey told it with spirit, I'll be bound. How well you have mastered the dialect, Mr. Lambert.'

'I made it my study when I first came here. Betha and I found a fund of amusement in it. Have you ever noticed, Heriot, there is a dry, heavy sort of wit—a certain richness and appropriateness of language—employed by some of these Dalesmen, if one severs the grain from the rough husk ?'

'They are not wanting in character or originality certainly, though they are often as rugged as their own hills. I fancy

Bailey had lived among them till he had grown to regard them as the finest people and the best society in the world.'

'I should not wonder. I remember he told me once that he was called to a place in Orton to see an elderly man who was sick. "Well, Betty," he said to the wife, "how's Willy?"

'"Why," says Betty, "I nau'nt; he's been grumbling for a few days back, and yesterday he tyak his bed. I thout I'd send for ye. He mebbe git'nt en oot heat or summat; byt gang ye in and see him." The doctor having made the necessary examination came out of the sickroom, and Betty followed him.

'"Noo, doctor, hoo div ye find him?'

'"Well, Betty, he's very bad.'

'"Ye dunnot say he's gangen t'dee?'

'"Well,' returned Bailey, reluctantly, 'I think it is not unlikely; to my thinking he cannot pull through.'

'"Oh, dear me,' sighed Betty, "poor auld man. He's ben a varra good man t'me, en I'll be wa to looes him, byt we mun aw gang when oor time cums. Ye'll cum agen, doctor, en deeah what ye can for hym. We been lang t'gither, Willy an me, that ha' we."

'Well, Bailey continued his visits every alternate day, giving no hope, and on one Monday apprising her that he thought Willy could not last long.

'Tuesday was market-day at Penrith, and Betty, who thought she would have everything ready, sent to buy meat for the funeral dinner.

'On Wednesday Bailey pronounced Willy rather fresher, but noticed that Betty seemed by no means glad; and this went on for two or three visits, until Betty's patience was quite exhausted, and in answer to the doctor's opinion that he was fresher than he expected to have seen him and might live a few days longer, she exclaimed—

'"Hang leet on him! He allus was maist purvurse man I ivver knew, an wad nobb't du as he wod! Meat 'll aw be spoilt this het weather."

'"Never mind," said Bailey, soothingly, "you can buy some more."

'"Buy mair, say ye?" she returned indignantly. "I'll du nowt o't mack; he mud ha deet when he shapt on't, that mud he, en hed a dinner like other fok, but noo I'll just put him by wi' a bit breead an cheese."

'As a matter of fact, the meat was spoilt, and had to be buried a day or two before the old man died.'

Hugh Marsden's look of horror at the conclusion of the vicar's anecdote was so comical that Dr. Heriot could not conceal his amusement ; but at this moment a singular incident put a check to the conversation.

For the last few minutes Polly had seemed unusually restless, and directly Mr. Lambert had finished, she communicated in an awe-stricken whisper that she had distinctly seen the tall shadow of a man lurking behind the wall of the old cotton-mill, as though watching their party.

'I am sure he is after no good,' continued Polly. 'He looks almost as tall and shadowy as Leonard in Dr. Heriot's story ; and he was crouching just as Leonard did when the phantom of the headless maiden came up the glen.'

Of course this little sally was received with shouts of laughter, but as Polly still persisted in her incredible story, the young men declared their intention of searching for the mysterious stranger, and as the girls wished to accompany them, the little party dispersed across the glen.

Mildred, who was busy with one of the maids in clearing the remnants of the feast and choosing a place where they should boil their gipsy kettle, heard every now and then ringing peals of laughter mixed with odd braying sounds.

Chriss was the first to reappear.

'Oh, Aunt Milly,' she exclaimed breathlessly, 'what do you think Polly's mysterious Leonard has turned out to be ? Nothing more or less than an old donkey browsing at the head of the glen. Polly will never hear the last of it.'

'Leonard-du-Bray "In a bed of thistles,"' observed Richard, mischievously. 'Oh, Polly, what a mare's nest you have made of it.'

Polly looked hot and discomposed ; the laugh was against her, and to put a stop to their teasing, Mildred proposed that they should all go up to the Fox Tower as they had planned, while she stayed behind with her brother.

'We will bring you back some of the shield and bladder fern,' was Chriss's parting promise. Mildred watched them climbing up the wooded side of the glen, Dr. Heriot and Polly first, hand-in-hand, and Olive following more slowly with Richard and Hugh Marsden ; and then she went and sat by her brother, and they had one of their long quiet talks, till he proposed strolling in the direction of the Fox Tower, and left her to enjoy a solitary half-hour.

The little fire was burning now. Etta, in her picturesque

red petticoat and blue serge dress, was gathering sticks in the thicket ; the beck flowed like a silver thread over the smooth gray stones ; the sunset clouds streaked the sky with amber and violet ; the old cotton-mill stood out gray and silent.

Mildred, who felt strangely restless, had strolled to the mill, and was trying to detach a delicate spray of ivy frond that was strongly rooted in the wall, when a footstep behind her made her start, and in another moment a shadow drew from a project-ing angle of the mill itself.

Mildred rose to her feet with a smothered exclamation half of terror and surprise, and then turned pale with a vague presentiment of trouble. The figure behind her had a velvet coat and fair moustache, but could the white haggard face and bloodshot eyes belong to Roy ?

‘ Rex, my dear Roy, were you hiding from us ? ’

‘ Hush, Aunt Milly, I don’t want them to see me. I only want you.’

CHAPTER XXV

ROYAL

'This would plant sore trouble
  In that breast now clear,
And with meaning shadows
  Mar that sun-bright face.
See that no earth-poison
  To thy soul come near !
Watch ! for like a serpent
  Glides that heart-disgrace.'
                    PHILIP STANHOPE WORSLEY.

'My dear boy, were you hiding from us ? '

Mildred had recovered from her brief shock of surprise ; her heart was heavy with all manner of foreboding as she noted Royal's haggard and careworn looks, but she disguised her anxiety under a pretence of playfulness.

'Have you been masquerading under the title of Leonard-du-Bray, my dear ?' she continued, with a little forced laugh, holding his hot hands between her own, for Rex was still Aunt Milly's darling ; but he drew them irritably, almost sullenly, away. There was a lowering look on the bright face, an expression of restless misery in the blue eyes, that went to Mildred's heart.

'I am in no mood for jests,' he returned, bitterly ; 'do I look as though I were, Aunt Milly ? Come a little farther with me behind this wall where no one will spy upon us.'

'They have all gone to the Fox Tower, they will not be back for an hour yet. Look, the glen is quite empty, even Etta has disappeared ; come and let me make you some tea ; you look worn out—ill, and your hands are burning. Come, my dear, come,' but Roy resisted.

'Let me alone,' he returned, freeing himself angrily from her soft grasp, 'I am not going to make one of the birthday party, not even to please the queen of the feast. Are you coming, Aunt Milly, or shall I go back the same way I came ?'

Roy spoke rudely, almost savagely, and there was a sneer on the handsome face.

'Yes, I will follow you, Rex,' returned Mildred, quietly.

What had happened to their boy—to their Benjamin? She walked by his side without a word, till he had found a place that suited him, a rough hillock behind a dark angle of the wall ; the cotton-mill was between them and the glen.

'This will do,' he said, throwing himself down on the grass, while Mildred sat down beside him. 'I had to make a run for it before. Dick nearly found me out though. I meant to have gone away without speaking to one of you, but I thought you saw me.'

'Rex, dear, have you got into trouble ?' she asked, gently. 'No, do not turn from me, do not refuse to answer me ; there must be some reason for this strange behaviour, or you would not shun your best friends.'

He shook his head, but did not answer.

'It cannot be anything very wrong, but we must look it in the face, Roy, whatever it is. Perhaps your father or Richard could help you better than I could, or even—' she hesitated slightly—'Dr. Heriot.'

Roy started convulsively.

'He ! don't mention his name. I hate—I hate him,' clenching his hand, his white artist hand, as he spoke.

Mildred recoiled. Was he sane ? had he been ill and they had not known it ? His fevered aspect, the restless brilliancy of his eyes, his incoherence, filled her with dismay.

'Roy, you frighten me,' she said, faintly. 'I believe you are ill, dear—that you do not know what you are saying ;' but he laughed a strange, bitter laugh.

'Ill ! I wish I were ; I vow I should be glad to have done with it. The life I have been leading for the last six weeks has been almost unbearable. Do you recollect you once told me that I should take trouble badly, that I was a moral coward and should give in sooner than other men ? Well, you were a true prophet, Aunt Milly.'

'Dear Roy, I am trying to be patient, but do you know, you are torturing me with this suspense.'

He laughed again, and patted her hand half-kindly, half-carelessly.

'You need not look so alarmed, mother Milly,' his pet name for her ; 'I have not forged a cheque, or put my name to a bill, or got into any youthful scrape. The trouble is none of my making. I am only a coward, and can't face it as Dick would if he were in my place, and so I thought I would come and have a look at you all before I went away for a long, long time. I was pretty near you all the time you were at dinner, and heard all Dad's stories. It is laughable, isn't it, Aunt Milly ?' but the poor lad's face contracted with a look of hopeless misery as he spoke.

'My dear, I am so glad,' returned Mildred in a reassured tone; 'never mind the trouble; trouble can be borne, so that you have done nothing wrong. But I feared I hardly know what, you looked and spoke so mysteriously; and then, remember we have heard nothing about you for so long—even Polly's letters have been unanswered.'

'Did she say so ? did she mind it ? What does she think, Aunt Milly ?'

'She has not complained, at least to me, but she has looked very wistful I notice at post-time ; once or twice I fancied your silence a little damped her happiness.'

'She is happy then ? what an ass I was to doubt it,' he groaned; 'as though she could be proof against the fascinations of a man like Dr. Heriot; but oh ! Polly, Polly, I never could have believed you would have thrown me over like this,' and Roy buried his face in his hands with a hoarse sob as he spoke.

Mildred sat almost motionless with surprise. Strange to say, she had not in the least realised the truth ; perhaps her own trouble had a little deadened her quick instinct of sympathy, or Roy's apparently brotherly affection had deceived her, but she had never guessed the secret of his silence. He had seemed such a boy too, so light-hearted, that she could hardly even now believe him the victim of a secret and hopeless attachment.

And then the complication. Mildred smiled again, a little smile ; there was something almost ludicrous, she thought, in the present aspect of affairs. Was it predestined that in the Lambert family the course of true love would not run smooth ? Richard, refused by the woman he had loved from childhood, she herself innocent, but self-betrayed, wasting strangely under the daily torture she bore with such outward patience, and now Roy, breaking his heart for the girl he had never really wooed.

'Rex, dear, I have been very stupid, but I never guessed this,' waking up from her bitter reverie as another and another hoarse sob smote upon her ear. Poor lad, he had been right in asserting himself morally unfit to cope with any great trouble ; weak and yet sensitive, he had succumbed at once to the blow that had shattered his happiness. 'Hush, you must bear this like a man for her sake—for Polly's sake,' she whispered, bending over him and trying to unclench his fingers. 'Rex, there is more than yourself to think about.'

'Is that all you have to say to me?' he returned, starting up; 'is that how you comfort people whose hearts are broken, Aunt Milly? How do you know what I feel, what I suffer, or how I hate him who has robbed me of my Polly? for she is mine—she is—she ought to be by every law, human and divine,' he continued, in the same frenzied voice.

'Hush, this is wrong, you must not talk so,' replied Mildred, in the firm soothing voice with which she would have controlled a passionate child. 'Sit down by me again, Rex, and we will talk about this,' but he still continued his restless strides without heeding her.

'Who says she loves him? Let him give me my fair chance and see which she will choose. It will not be he, I warrant you. Polly's heart is here—here,' striking himself on the breast, 'but she is too young to know it, and he has taken a mean advantage of her ignorance. You have all been against me, every one of you,' continued the poor boy, in a tone so sullen and despairing that it wrung Mildred's heart. 'You knew I loved her, that I always loved her, and yet you never gave me a hint of this; you have been worse than any enemy to me; it was cruel—cruel!'

'For shame, Rex, how dare you speak to Aunt Milly so!'— and Richard suddenly turned the angle of the wall and confronted his brother.

'I heard your voice and the last sentence, and—and I guess the rest, Rex,' and Richard's wrathful voice softened, and he laid his hand on Roy's shoulder.

The other looked at him piteously.

'Are they all with you? have you brought them to gloat over my misery? Speak out like a man, Dick, is Dr. Heriot behind that wall? I warn you, I am in a dangerous mood.'

'No one is with me,' returned Richard, in a tone of forced composure, 'they are in the woods a long way off still; I came back to see what had become of Aunt Milly. You are playing us a sorry trick, Rex, to be hiding away like this; it is childish, unmanly to the last degree.'

'Ah, you nearly found me out once before, Dick; Polly was with you. I had a good sight of her sweet face then, the little traitor. I saw the diamonds on her finger. You little knew

who Leonard was. Ah, ha!' and Roy wrenched himself from
his brother's grasp as he had done from Mildred's, and resumed
his restless walk.

'We must get him away,' whispered Mildred.

Richard nodded, and then he went up and spoke very gently
to Roy.

'I know all about it, Rex; we must think what must be
done. But we cannot talk here; some one else will be sure to
find us out, and you are not in a fit state for any discussion;
you must come home with me at once.'

'Why so?'

Richard hesitated and coloured as though with shame. Rex
burst again into noisy laughter.

'You think I am not myself, eh! that I have had a little of
the devil's liquor,' but Richard's grave pitying glance subdued
him. 'Don't be hard on me, Dick, it was the first time, and I
was so horribly weak and had dragged myself for miles, and I
wanted strength to see her again. I hated it even as I took it,
but it has answered its purpose.'

'Richard, oh, Richard!' and at Mildred's tone of anguish
Richard went up to her and put his arms round her.

'You must leave him to me, Aunt Milly. I must take him
home; he has excited himself and taken what is not good for
him, and so he cannot control himself as well as usual. Of
course it is wrong, but he did not mean it, I am sure. Poor
Rex, he will repent of it bitterly to-morrow if I can only
persuade him to leave this place.'

But Mildred's tears had already sobered Roy; his manner as
he stood looking at them was half ashamed and half resentful.

'Why are you both so hard on me?' he burst out at last;
'when a fellow's heart is broken he is not always as careful as
he should be. I felt so deadly faint climbing the hill in the
sun that I took too much of what they offered as a restorative;
only Dick is such a saint that he can't make allowances for
people.'

'I will make every allowance if you will only come home
with me now,' pleaded his brother.

'Where—home? Oh, Dick, you should not ask it,' returned Roy, turning very pale; 'I cannot, I must not go home
while she is there. I should betray myself—it would be worse
than madness.'

'He is right,' assented Mildred; 'he must go back to
London, but you cannot leave him, Richard.'

'Yes, back to London—Jericho if you will; it is all one and the same to me since I have lost my Polly. I left my traps at an inn five miles from here where I slept, or rather woke, last night. I shouldn't wonder if you have to carry me on your back, Dick, or leave me lying by the roadside, if that faintness comes on again.'

'I must get out the wagonette,' continued Richard, in a sorely perplexed voice, 'there's no help for it. Listen to me, Rex. You do not wish to bring unhappiness to two people besides yourself; you are too good-hearted to injure any one.'

'Is not that why I am hiding?' was the irritable answer, 'only first Aunt Milly and then you come spying on me. If I could have got away I should have done it an hour ago, but, as ill-luck would have it, I fell over a stone and hurt my foot.'

'Thank Heaven that we are all of the same mind! that was spoken like yourself, Rex. Now we have not a moment to lose, they cannot be much longer; I must get out the horses myself, as Thomas will be at his sister's, and it will be better for him to know nothing. Follow me to the farm as quickly as you can, while Aunt Milly goes back to the glen.'

Roy nodded, his violence had ebbed away, and he was far too miserable and subdued to dispute his brother's will. When Richard left them he lingered a moment by Mildred's side.

'I was a brute to you just now, Aunt Milly, but I know you will forgive me.'

'It was not you, my dear, it was your misery that spoke;' and as a faint gleam woke in his eyes, as though her kindness touched him, she continued earnestly—'Be brave, Rex, for all our sakes; think of your mother, and how she would have counselled you to bear this trouble.'

They were standing side by side as Mildred spoke, and she had her hand on his shoulder, but a rustling in the steep wooded bank above them arrested all further speech—her fingers closed nervously on his coat-sleeve.

'Hush! what was that! not Richard?'

Roy shook his head, but there was no time to answer or to draw back into the shelter of the old wall; they were even now perceived. Light footsteps crunched over the dead leaves, there was the shimmer of a blue dress, a bright face peeped at them between the branches, and then with a low cry of astonishment Polly sprang down the bank.

'Be brave, Rex, and think only of her.'

Mildred had no time to whisper more, as the girl ran up to

them and caught hold of Roy's two hands with an exclamation of pleasure.

'Dear Roy, this is so good of you, and on my birthday too. Was Aunt Milly in your secret? did she contrive this delightful surprise? I shall scold you both presently, but not now. Come, they are all waiting; how they will enjoy the fun,' and she was actually trying to drag him with gentle force, but the poor lad resisted her efforts.

'I can't—don't ask me, Polly; please let me go. There, I did not mean to hurt your soft, pretty hand, but you must not detain me. Aunt Milly will tell you; at least there is nothing to tell, only I must go away again,' finished Roy, turning away, not daring to look at her, the muscles of his face quivering with uncontrollable emotion.

Polly gave a terrified glance at both; even Aunt Milly looked strangely guilty, she thought.

'Yes, let him go, Polly,' pleaded Mildred.

'What does it all mean, Aunt Milly? is he ill, or has something happened? Why does he not look at me?' cried the girl, in a pained voice.

Roy cast an appealing glance at Mildred to help him; the poor fellow's strength was failing under the unexpected ordeal, but Mildred's urgent whisper, 'Go by all means, leave her to me,' reached Polly's quick ear.

'Why do you tell him to go?' she returned resentfully, interposing herself between them. 'You shall not go, Roy, till you have looked at me and told me what has happened. Why, his hand is cold and shaking, just as yours did that hot night, Aunt Milly,' and Polly held it in both hers in her simple affectionate way. 'Have you been ill, Roy? no one has told us;' but her lips quivered as though she had found him greatly changed.

'Yes—no; I believe I must be ill;' but Mildred, truthful woman, interposed—

'He has not been ill, Polly, but something has occurred to vex him, and he is not quite himself just now. He has told Richard and me, and we think the best thing will be for him to go away a little while until the difficulty lessens.' Mildred was approaching dangerously near the truth, but she knew how hard it would be for Polly's childish mind to grasp it, unless Roy were weak enough to betray himself. His working features, his strange incoherence, had already terrified the girl beyond measure.

20

'What difficulty, Aunt Milly? If Roy is in trouble we must help him to bear it. It was wrong of you and Richard to tell him to go away. He looks ill enough for us to nurse and take care of him. Rex, dear, you will come home with us, will you not?'

'No, she says right; I must go,' he returned, hoarsely. 'I was wrong to come here at all, but I could not help myself. Dear Polly, indeed—indeed I must; Dick is waiting for me.'

'And when will you come again?'

'I cannot tell—not yet.'

'And you will go away; you will leave me on my birthday without a kind word, without wishing me joy? and you never even wrote to me.' And now the tears seemed ready to come.

'This is past man's endurance,' groaned Roy. 'Polly, if you cared for me you would not torture me like this.' And he turned so deadly pale that even Mildred grew alarmed. 'I will say anything you like if you will only let me go.'

'Tell me you are glad, that you are pleased; you know what I mean,' stammered Polly. She had hung her head, and the strange paleness and excitement were lost on her, as well as the fierce light that had come in Roy's eyes.

'For shame, Polly! after all, you are just like other women —I believe you like to test your power. So I am to wish you joy of your John Heriot, eh?'

'Yes, Rex. I have so missed your congratulation.'

'Well, you shall have it now. How do people wish each other joy on these auspicious occasions? We are not sister and brother—not even cousins. I have never kissed you in my life, Polly—never once.; but now I suppose I may.' He snatched her to him as he spoke with an impetuous, almost violent movement, but as he stooped his head over her he suddenly drew back. 'No, you are Heriot's now, Polly—we will shake hands.' And as she looked up at him, scared and sorely perplexed, his lips touched her bright hair, softly, reverently. 'There, he will not object to that. Bless you, Polly! Don't forget me—don't forget your old friend Roy. Now I must go, dear.' And as she still held him half unconsciously, he quickly disengaged himself and limped painfully away.

Mildred watched till he had disappeared, and then she came up to the girl, who was standing looking after him with blank, wide-open eyes.

'Come, Polly, they will be waiting for us, you know.' But there was no sign of response.

'They will be seeking us everywhere,' continued Mildred. 'The sun has set, and my brother will be faint and tired with his long day. Come, Polly, rouse yourself; we shall have need of all our wits.'

'What did he mean?—I do not understand, Aunt Milly. Why was it wrong for him to kiss me?—Richard did. What made him so strange? He frightened me; he was not like Roy at all.'

'People are not like themselves when something is troubling them. I know all about Roy's difficulty; it will not always harass him. Perhaps he will write to us, and then we shall feel happier.'

'Why did he not tell me himself?' returned the girl, plaintively. 'No one has ever come between us before. Roy tells me everything; I know all his fancies, only they never come to anything. It is very hard that I am to be less to him now.'

'It is the way of the world, little one,' returned Mildred, gravely. 'Roy cannot expect to monopolise you, now that another has a claim on your time and thoughts.'

'But Dr. Heriot would not mind. You do not know him, Aunt Milly. He is so good, so above all that sort of thing. He always said that he thought our friendship for each other so unique and beautiful—he understood me so well when I said Roy was just like my own, own brother.'

'Dear Polly, you must not fret if Roy does not see it in quite the same light at first,' continued Mildred, hesitating. 'He may feel—I do not say he does—as though he has lost a friend.'

'I will write and undeceive him,' she returned, eagerly. 'He shall not think that for a moment. But no, that will not explain all his sorrowful looks and strangeness. He seemed as though he wanted to speak, and yet he shunned me. Oh, Aunt Milly, what shall I do? How can I be happy and at ease now I know Roy is in trouble?'

'Polly, you must listen to me,' returned Mildred, taking her hand firmly, but secretly at her wits' end; even now she could hear voices calling to them from the farther side of the glen. 'This little complication—this difficulty of Roy's—demands all our tact. Roy will not like the others to know he has been here.'

'No! Are you sure of that, Aunt Milly?' fixing her large dark eyes on Mildred.

'Quite sure—he told me so himself; so we must guard his confidence, you and I. I must make some excuse for Richard, who will be back presently ; and you must help me to amuse the others, and make time pass till he comes back.'

'Will he be long gone? What is he doing with Roy?' pushing back her hair with strangely restless fingers—a trick of Polly's when in trouble or perplexity ; but Mildred smoothed the thick wild locks reprovingly.

'He will drive him for a mile or two until they meet some vehicle ; he will not be longer than he can help. Roy has hurt his foot, and cannot walk well, and is tired besides.'

'Tired ! he looks worn out ; but perhaps we had better not talk any more now, Aunt Milly,' continued Polly, brushing some furtive tears from her eyes ; there is Dr. Heriot coming to find us.'

'We were just going to scour the woods for you two,' he observed, eyeing their discomposed faces, half comically and half anxiously. 'Were you still looking for Leonard-du-Bray?' But as Polly faltered and turned crimson under his scrutinising glance, Mildred answered for her.

'Polly was looking for me, I believe. We have been sad truants, I know, and shall be punished by cold tea.'

'And Richard—have you not seen Richard?' he demanded in surprise.

'Yes, but he left me before Polly made her appearance ; he has gone farther on, and will be back presently. Polly is dreadfully tired, I am afraid,' she continued, as she saw how anxiously he was eyeing the girl's varying colour ; but Polly, weary and over-anxious, answered with unwonted irritability—

'Every one is tired, more or less ; these days are apt to become stupid in the end.'

'Well, well,' he returned, kindly, 'you and Aunt Milly shall rest and have your tea, and I will walk up to the farm and order the wagonette ; it is time for us to be going.'

'No, no !' exclaimed Polly, in sudden fright at the mistake she had made. 'Have you forgotten your promise to show us the glen in the moonlight?'

'But, my child, you are so tired.' But she interrupted him.

'I am not tired at all,' she said, contradicting herself. 'Aunt Milly, make him keep his promise. One can only have one birthday in a year, and I must have my own way in this.'

'I shall take care you have it very seldom,' he returned, fondly. But she only shivered and averted her face in reply.

During the hour that followed, while they waited in suspense for Richard, Polly continued in the same variable mood. She laughed and talked feverishly ; a moment's interval in the conversation seemed to oppress her ; when, in the twilight, Dr. Heriot's hand approached hers with a caressing movement, she drew herself away almost petulantly, and then went on with her nonsense.

Mildred's brow furrowed with anxiety as she watched them. She could see Dr. Heriot was perplexed as well as pained by the girl's fitful mood, though he bore it with his usual gentleness. After her childish repulse he had been a little silent, but no one but Mildred had noticed it.

The others were talking merrily among themselves. Olive and Mr. Marsden were discussing the merits and demerits of various Christian names which according to their ideas were more or less euphonious. The subject seemed to interest Dr. Heriot, and during a pause he turned to Polly, and said, in a half-laughing, half-serious tone—

'Polly, when we are married, do you always mean to call me Dr. Heriot ?'

For a moment she looked up at him with almost a scared expression. ' Yes, always,' she returned at last, very quietly.

'But why so, my child,' he replied, gravely, amusing himself at her expense, ' when John Heriot is my name ? '

'Because—because—oh, I don't know,' was the somewhat distressed answer. ' Heriot is very pretty, but John—only Aunt Milly likes John ; she says it is beautiful—her favourite name.'

It was only one of Polly's random speeches, and at any other time would have caused Mildred little embarrassment ; but anxious, jaded, and weary as she was, her feelings were not so well under control, and as Dr. Heriot raised his eyes with a pleased expression as though to hear it corroborated by her own lips, a burning blush, that seemed to scorch her, suddenly rose to her face.

'Polly, how can you be so foolish ?' she began, with a trace of real annoyance in her clear tones ; but then she stopped, and corrected herself with quiet good sense. ' I believe, after all, it is my favourite name. You know it belonged to the beloved disciple.'

'Thank you,' was Dr. Heriot's low reply, and the subject dropped ; but Mildred, sick at heart, wondered if her irritability had been noticed. The pain of that dreadful blush seemed to scorch her still. What would he think of her ?

Her fears were not quite groundless. Dr. Heriot had noticed her sudden embarrassment, and had quickly changed the subject ; but more than once that night he went over the brief conversation, and questioned himself as to the meaning of that strange sudden flush on Mildred Lambert's face.

Most of the party were growing weary of their enforced stay, when Richard at last made his appearance in the glen. The moon had risen, the heavy autumnal damps had already saturated the place, the gipsy fire had burnt down to its last ember, and Etta sat shivering beside it in her red cloak.

Richard's apologies were ample and sounded sincere, but he offered no explanation of his strange desertion. The wagonette was waiting, he said, and they had better lose no time in packing up. He thought even Polly must have had enough of her beloved cotton-mill.

Polly made no answer; with Richard's reappearance her forced spirits seemed to collapse; she stood by listlessly while the others lifted the hampers and wraps; when the little cavalcade started she followed with a step so slow and flagging that Dr. Heriot paused more than once.

'Oh, Heartsease, how tired you are!' he said, pityingly, 'and I have not a hand to give you. Wrap yourself in my plaid, darling. I have seen you shiver more than once.' But she shook her head, and the plaid still trailed from her arm over the dewy grass.

But Mildred noticed one thing. She saw, when the wagonette had started along the dark country road, that Dr. Heriot had taken the plaid and wrapped it round the weary girl; but she saw something else—she saw Polly steal timidly closer to the side of her betrothed husband, saw the kind arm open to receive her, and the little pale face suddenly lay itself down on it with a look of weariness and grief that went to her heart.

CHAPTER XXVI

'When dark days have come, and friendship
  Worthless seemed, and life in vain,
That bright friendly smile has sent me
  Boldly to my task again ;

It has smiled on my successes,
  Raised me when my hopes were low,
And by turns has looked upon me
  With all the loving eyes I know.'
                    ADELAIDE ANNE PROCTER.

THERE was a long troubled talk between Mildred and Richard
that night. Richard, who had borne his own disappointment
so bravely, seemed utterly downcast on his brother's account.

'I would rather have had this happen to any of us but
Roy,' he said, walking up and down Mildred's room that night.

'Hush, Richard, she will hear us,' returned Mildred,
anxiously; and then he came and rested his elbow on the
sill beside her, and they talked in a low subdued key, looking
over the shadowy fells and the broad level of moonlight that
lay beneath them.

'You do not know Roy as well as I do. I believe he is
physically as well as morally unfit to cope with a great sorrow ;
where other men fight, he succumbs too readily.'

'You have your trouble too, Cardie; he should remember
that.'

'I have not lost hope, Aunt Milly,' he returned, gravely.
'I am happier than Rex—far happier ; for it is no wrong for
me to love Ethel. I have a right to love her, so long as no
one else wins her. Roy will have it Polly has jilted him for
Heriot.'

'Jilted him ! that child !'

'Yes, he maintains that she loves him best, only that she is
unconscious of her own feelings. He declares that to his belief

she has never really given her heart to Heriot. I am afraid he is right in declaring the whole thing has been patched up too hastily. It has always seemed to me as though Polly were too young to know her own mind.'

'Some girls are married at eighteen.'

'Yes, but not Polly; look what a child she is, and how quiet a life she has led for the last three years; she has seen no one but ourselves, Marsden, and Heriot; do you know, gentle as he is, she seems half afraid of him.'

'That is only natural in her position.'

'You think it does not augur want of love? Well, you may be right; I only profess to understand one girl,'—with a sigh —'and I can read her like a book; but Roy, Aunt Milly— what must we do about Roy?'

Mildred shook her head dejectedly.

'He must not come here under the circumstances, it would not be possible or right; he has done mischief enough already.'

'Surely he did not betray himself?' in Richard's sternest voice; 'he assured me over and over again that he had not said a word which Dr. Heriot might not hear.'

'No; he commanded himself wonderfully; he only forgot himself once, and then, poor lad, he recollected himself in time, —but she must have noticed how badly it went with him— there was heart-break in his face.'

'I had sad work with him for the first two miles,' returned Richard. 'I was half afraid of leaving him at all, he looked and spoke so wildly, only my threat of telling my father brought him to reason; he begged—he implored me to keep his secret, and that no one but you and I should ever know of his madness.'

'There would be nothing gained by telling my brother,' returned Mildred.

'Certainly not; it would be perfectly useless, and fret him beyond measure; he would take Roy's trouble to heart, and have no pleasure in anything. How thankful I am, Aunt Milly, that I have already planned my London journey for the day after to-morrow.'

'Yes, indeed, I shall feel easier when he is under your care.'

'I must invent some excuse for being absent most of the day to-morrow; I cannot bear to think of him shut up in that wretched inn, and unable to stir out for fear of being recognised. He was very lame, I remember; I must find out if he has really injured his foot.'

'Do you think I might go with you, Cardie?' for Mildred was secretly yearning to comfort her boy, but Richard instantly put a veto on her proposal.

'It would not be safe, Aunt Milly; it will excite less questioning if I go alone; you must be content to trust him to me. I will bring you a faithful report to-morrow evening;' and as Mildred saw the wisdom of the reasoning she resolved to abide by it.

But she passed a miserable night. Roy's haggard face and fierce reckless speeches haunted her. She dreaded to think of the time when Richard would be obliged to return to Oxford, and leave Roy to battle alone with his misery. She wondered what Richard would think if she were to propose going up to him for a month or two; she was becoming conscious herself of a need of change,—a growing irritability of the nerves chafed her calm spirit, daily suffering and suppression were wearing the brave heart sadly. Mildred, who ailed nothing ordinarily, had secret attacks of palpitation and faintness, which would have caused alarm if any one had guessed it, but she kept her own counsel.

Once, indeed, Dr. Heriot had questioned her. 'You do not look as well as you used, Miss Lambert; but I suppose I am not to be consulted?' and Mildred had shaken her head laughingly. But here was work for the ministering woman—to forget her own strange sorrow in caring for another;—Roy needed her more than any one; Olive could be safely left in charge of the others. Mildred fell asleep at last planning long winter evenings in the young artist's studio.

The next day seemed more than usually long. Polly, who looked as though she had not slept all night, spent her time in listlessly wandering about the house and garden, much to Olive's mild wonder.

'I do wish you would get something to do, Polly,' she said more than once, looking up from her writing-table at the sound of the tapping heels; 'you have not practised those pieces Dr. John ordered from London.'

'Olive is right; you should try and occupy yourself, my dear,' observed Mildred, looking up from her marking; piles of socks lay neatly beside her, Mr. Lambert's half-stitched wristband was in her lap. She looked with soft reproving eyes at poor restless Polly, her heart all the time very full of pity.

'How can you ask me to play?' returned Polly, in a resentful tone. Play when Roy was ill or in some dreadful trouble—

was that their love for him? When Mildred next looked up the girl was no longer standing watching her with sad eyes; across the beck, through the trees, she could see the shimmer of a blue dress; a forlorn young figure strolled aimlessly down the field path and paused by the weir. Of what was she thinking? Were her thoughts at all near the truth—'Don't forget me; think of your old friend Roy!'—were those words, said in the saddest voice she had ever heard, still ringing in her ears.

It was late in the evening when Richard returned, and he beckoned Mildred softly out of the room. Polly, who was sitting beside Dr. Heriot, followed them with wistful eyes, but neither of them noticed her.

Richard gave a very unsatisfactory report. He found Roy looking ill in body as well as in mind, and suffering great pain from his foot, which was severely contused, though he obstinately refused to believe anything was really the matter, and had firmly declared his intention of accompanying his brother to London. His excitement had quite subsided, but the consequent depression was very great. Richard believed he had not slept, from the pain of his foot and mental worry, and being so near home only made his desolation harder to bear.

He had pencilled a little line to Polly, which he had begged Richard to bring with his love, and at the same time declared he would never see her again when she was once Dr. Heriot's wife; and, when Richard had remonstrated against the weakness and moral cowardice of adopting such a line of action, had flamed up into his old fierceness; she had made him an exile from his home and all that he loved, he had no heart now for his profession, he knew his very hand had lost its cunning; but not for that could he love her the less or wish her ill. 'She is Polly after all,' he had finished piteously, 'the only girl I ever loved or cared to love, and now she is going near to spoil my whole life!'

'It was useless to argue with him,' Richard said; 'everything like advice seemed to irritate him, and no amount of sympathy could lull the intolerable pain; he found it answer better to remain silent and let him talk out his trouble, without trying to stem the bitter current.' It went to Mildred's heart to hear how the poor lad at the last had broken down utterly at bidding his brother good-bye.

'Don't leave me, Dick; I am not fit to be left,' he had said; and then he had thrown himself down on the miserable couch, and had hidden his face in his arms.

'And the note, Richard?'

'Here it is; he said you might read it, that there was not a word in it that the whole world might not see—she could show it to Heriot if she liked.'

'All the same, I wish he had not written it,' returned Mildred, doubtfully, as she unfolded the slip of paper.

'Dear Polly,' it began, 'I fear you must have thought me very strange and unkind last evening—your reproachful eyes are haunting me now. I cannot bear you to misunderstand me. "No one shall come between us." Ah, I remember you said that; it was so like you, dear—so like my Polly! Now you must try not to think hardly of me—a great trouble has befallen me, as Aunt Milly and Richard know, and I must go away to bear it; no one can help me to bear it; your little fingers cannot lighten it, Polly—your sympathy could not avail me; it is my own burden, and I must bear it alone. You must not fret if we do not meet for some time—it is better so, far better. I have my work; and, dear, I pray that you may be very happy with the man you love (if he be the one you love, Polly).'

'Oh, Richard, he ought not to have said that!'

'She will not understand; go on, Aunt Milly.'

'But there can be no doubt of that, he is a good man, almost worthy of my Polly; but I must not say that any longer, for you are Heriot's Polly now, are you not? but whose ever you are, God bless you, dear.—Roy.'

Mildred folded the letter sadly.

'He has betrayed himself in every line,' she said, slowly and thoughtfully. 'Richard, it will break my heart to do it, but I think Polly ought not to see this; we must keep it from her, and one day we must tell Roy.'

'I was afraid you might say so, but if you knew how he pleaded that this might be given to her; he seemed to think it would hinder her fretting. "She cares for me more than any of you know—more than she knows herself,' he said, as he urged me to take it."

'What must we do? It will set her thinking. No, Richard, it is too venturesome an experiment.'

But Mildred's wise precautions were doomed to be frustrated, for at that moment Polly quietly opened the door and confronted them.

The two conspirators moved apart somewhat guiltily.

'Am I interrupting you? I knocked, but no one answered. Aunt Milly looks disconcerted,' said Polly, eyeing them both with keen inquisitive glance. 'I—I only wanted to know if Richard has brought me a message or note from Roy ?'

Richard hesitated and looked at Mildred. This business was making him anxious; he would fain wash his hands of it.

'Why do you not answer ?' continued the girl, palpitating a little. 'Is that letter for me, Aunt Milly ?' and as Mildred reluctantly handed it to her, a reproachful colour overspread Polly's face.

'Were you keeping this from me ? I thought people's letters were sacred property,' continued the little lady, proudly. 'I did not think you could do such a thing, Aunt Milly.'

'Dear Polly !' remonstrated Richard ; but Mildred interposed with quiet dignity—

'Polly should be just, even though she is unhappy. Roy wished me to read his letter, and I have done so.'

'Forgive me !' returned Polly, almost melting into tears. 'I know I ought not to have spoken so, but it has been such a miserable day,' and she leant against Mildred as she read the note.

She read it once—twice—without comment, and then her features began to work.

'Dear Aunt Milly, how unhappy he is—he—Roy ; he cannot have done anything wrong ?'

'No, no, my precious ; of course not !'

'Then why must we not help him to bear it ?'

'We can pray for him, Polly.'

'Yes, yes, but I cannot understand it,' piteously. 'I have always been Roy's friend—always, and now he has made Richard and you his confidants.'

'We are older and wiser, you see,' began Richard, with glib hypocrisy, which did not become him.

Polly stamped her little foot with impatience.

'Don't, Richard. I will not have you talk to me as though I were a child. I have a right to know this ; you are all treating me badly. Roy would have told me, I know he would, if Aunt Milly had not come between us !' and she darted a quick reproachful look at Mildred.

'It is Polly who is hard on us, I think,' returned Mildred, putting her arm gently round the excited girl ; and at the fond tone Polly's brief wrath evaporated.

'I cannot help it,' she returned, hiding her face on Mildred's shoulder ; 'it is all so wretched, everything is spoiled. Roy is not pleased that I am going to be married, he seems angry—put out about it ; it is not that—it cannot be that that is the matter with him ? Why do you not answer ?' she continued, impatiently, looking at them both with wide-open innocent eyes. 'Roy cannot be jealous ?'

Mildred would have given worlds to have been able to answer No, but, unused to evasion of any kind, the prudent falsehood died a natural death upon her lips.

'My dear Polly, what makes you so fanciful ?' she began with difficulty ; but it was enough,—Mildred's face could not deceive, and that moment's hesitating silence revealed the truth to the startled girl ; her faithful friend was hurt, jealous.

'You see yourself that Rex wants you to be happy,' continued Mildred, somewhat inconsequently.

'I shall be happy if he be so—not unless,' replied the girl, a little sadly.

Her pretty pink colour had faded, her hands dropped from Mildred's shoulder ; she stood for a long time quiet with her lips apart, her young head drooping almost to her breast.

'Shall you answer his letter, Polly ?' asked Richard at last, trying to rouse her.

'Yes—no,' she faltered, turning very pale. 'Give my love to him, Richard—my dear love. I—I will write presently,' and so saying, she slowly and dejectedly left the room.

'Aunt Milly, do you think she guesses ?' whispered Richard, when she had gone.

'Heaven only knows, Richard ! This is a wretched business ; there seems nothing but trouble everywhere,' and Mildred almost wrung her hands. Richard thought he had never seen her so agitated—so unlike herself.

The days and weeks that followed tried Mildred sorely ; heavy autumnal rains had set in ; wet grass, dripping foliage, heaps of rotting leaves saturated with moisture, met her eyes daily. A sunless, lurid atmosphere surrounded everything ; by and by the rain ceased, and a merciless wind drove across the fells, drying up the soddened pools, whirling the last red leaves from the bare stems, and threatening to beat in the vicarage windows.

A terrible scarping wind, whose very breath was bitterness to flesh and blood, blatant and unresting, filled the valley with a strange voice and life.

The river was full to the brim now ; the brown water that rushed below the terrace carried away sticks and branches, and light eddying leaves ; great fires roared up the vicarage chimneys, while the girls sat and shivered beside them.

Those nights were terrible to Mildred—the wild stir and tumult, the fury of the great rushing wind, fevered her blood with strange excitement, and drove sleep from her pillow, or, when weariness overcame her, haunted her brain with painful images.

Never had the tranquil soul so lacked tranquillity, never had daily life, never had the many-folded hours, held such torture for her.

'I must have change, or I shall be ill,' she thought, as she contemplated her wan and bloodless exterior morning after morning. 'Anything but that—anything but having him pitying me.'

Relief by his hand might be sweet indeed ; but a doubt of her own power of self-control, should weakness seize upon her, oppressed her like a nightmare, and the longing to escape from her daily ordeal of suffering amounted to actual agony.

Morning after morning she opened Richard's letters, in the hope that her proposal had been accepted, but each morning some new delay or object fretted her.

Richard had remained in London up to the last possible moment. Roy's injured foot had rendered him dependent on his brother's nursing ; his obstinacy had led to a great deal of unnecessary delay and suffering ; wakeful and harassed nights had undermined his strength, and made him so nervous and irritable by day, that only patience and firm management could effect any improvement ; he was so recklesss that it required coaxing to induce him to take the proper remedies, or to exert himself in the least ; he had not yet roused himself, or resumed his painting, and all remonstrances were at present unavailing.

Mildred sighed over this fresh evidence of Roy's weakness and instability of purpose, and then she remembered that he was suffering, perhaps ill. No one knew better than herself the paralysing effects on will and brain caused by anxiety and want of sleep ; some stimulus, stronger than she or Richard could administer, was needful to rouse Roy's dormant energies.

Help came when they had least looked for it.

'Is Roy painting anything now?' asked Polly suddenly, one day, when she was alone with Mildred.

[Mildred was writing to Richard ; his last letter lay open beside her on the table. Polly had glanced at it once or twice, but she had not questioned Mildred concerning its contents. Polly had fallen into very quiet ways lately ; the pretty pink colour had never returned to her face, the light footstep was slower now, the merry laugh was less often heard, a sweet wistful smile had replaced it; she was still the same busy active Polly, gentle and affectionate, as of old, but some change, subtle yet undefinable, had passed over the girl. Dr. Heriot liked the difference, even though he marvelled at it. 'Polly is looking quite the woman,' he would say presently. Mildred paused, a little startled over Polly's abrupt question.]

'Richard does not say; it is not in his letter, my dear,' she stammered.

'Not in this one, perhaps, but in his last,' persisted Polly. 'Try to remember, Aunt Milly; how does Richard say that Rex occupies himself?'

'I am afraid he is very idle,' returned Mildred, reluctantly. Polly coloured, and looked distressed.

'But his foot is better; he is able to stand, is he not?'

'I believe so. Richard certainly said as much as that.'·

'Then it is very wrong for him to be losing time like this; he will not have his picture in the Academy after all. Some one ought to write and remind him,' faltered Polly, with a little heat.

'I have done so more than once, and Richard is for ever lecturing. Roy is terribly desultory, I am afraid.'

'Indeed you are wrong, Aunt Milly,' persisted the girl earnestly. 'Roy loves his work—dearly—dearly—it is only his foot, and—' she broke down, recovered herself, and hurried on—

'I think it would be a good thing if Dad Fabian were to go and talk to him. I will write to him—yes, and I will write to Roy.'

Mildred did not venture to dissuade her; she had a notion that perhaps Polly's persuasion might be more efficacious than Richard's arguments. She took it quite as a matter of course, when, half an hour later, Polly laid the little note down beside her.

'There, you may read it,' she said, hurriedly. 'Let it go in Richard's letter; he may read it too, if he likes.'

It was very short, and covered the tiniest sheet of note-paper; the pretty handwriting was not quite so steady as usual.

'My dearest brother Roy,' it began—never had she called him that before—'I have never written to thank you for your note. It was a dear, kind note, and I love you for writing it; do not be afraid of my misunderstanding or thinking you

unkind; you could not be that to any one. I am so thankful
your poor foot is better; it has been terrible to think of your
suffering all this time. I am so afraid it must have interfered
with your painting, and that you have not got on well with the
picture you began when you were here. Roy, dear, you must
promise to work at it harder than ever, and as soon as you are
able. I am sure it will be the best picture you have ever done,
and I have set my heart on seeing it in the Academy next year;
but unless you work your hardest, there will be no chance of
that. I have asked Dad Fabian to come and lecture you.
You and he must have one of your clever art-talks, and then
you must get out your palette and brushes, and set to work on
that pretty little girl's red cloak.

'Do, Roy—do, my dear brother. Your loving friend, POLLY.

'Be kind to Dad Fabian. Make much of the dear old man.
Remember he is Polly's friend.'

It was the morning after the receipt of this letter, so Richard
informed Mildred, that Roy crept languidly from the sofa, where
he spent most of his days, and sat for a long time fixedly regarding the unfinished canvas before him.

Richard made no observation, and shortly left the room.
When he returned an hour afterwards, Roy was working at a
child's drapery, with compressed lips and frowning brow.

He tossed back his fair hair with the old irritable movement
as his brother smiled approval.

'Well done, Roy; there is nothing like making a beginning
after all.'

'I hate it as much as ever,' was the sullen answer. 'I am
only doing it because—she told me—and I don't mean to disappoint her. I am her slave; she might put her pretty foot
on my neck if she liked. Ah, Polly, Polly, what a poor fool
you have made of me.' And Roy put his head on the easel,
and fairly groaned.

But there was no shirking labour after that. Roy spent
long moody hours over his work, while Richard sat by with his
books. An almost unbroken silence prevailed in the young
artist's studio. 'The sweet whistler' in Dr. Heriot's little glass-
house no longer existed; a half-stifled sigh, or an ejaculation of
impatience, only reached Richard's ears from time to time; but
Roy seemed to have no heart for conversation,—nothing
interested him, his attention flagged after the first few minutes.

Richard was obliged to go back to Oxford at the beginning
of the term; but Dad Fabian took his place. Mildred learnt

to her dismay that the old man was located at the cottage, at Roy's own wish, and was likely to remain for some weeks. How Mildred's heart sank at the news; her plan had fallen to the ground; the change and quiet for which she was pining were indefinitely postponed.

No one but Dr. Heriot guessed how Mildred's strength was failing; but his well-meant inquiries were evidently so unpalatable that he forbore to press them. Only once or twice he hinted to Mr. Lambert that he thought his sister was looking less strong than usual, and wanted change of air.

'Heriot tells me that you are not looking well—that you want a change, Mildred,' her brother said to her one day, and, to his surprise, she looked annoyed, and answered more hastily than her wont—

'There is nothing the matter with me, at least nothing of consequence. I am not one of those who are always fancying themselves ill.'

'But you are thinner. Yes, I am sure he is right; you are thinner, Mildred.'

'What nonsense, Arnold; he has put that in your head. By and by I shall be glad of a little change, I daresay. When Mr. Fabian leaves Roy, I mean to take his place.'

'A good idea,' responded Mr. Lambert, warmly; 'it will be a treat for Rex, and will do you good at the same time. I was thinking of running up myself after Christmas. One sees so little of the boy, and his letters are so short and unsatisfactory; he seems a little dull, I fancy.'

'Mr. Fabian will cheer him up,' replied Mildred, evasively. She was thankful when her brother went back to his study. She felt more than usually oppressed and languid that day, though she would not own it to herself; her work wearied her, and the least effort to talk jarred the edge of her nerves.

'How dreadful it is to feel so irritable and cross, as I have done lately,' she thought. 'Perhaps after all he is right, and I am not so strong as usual; but I cannot have them all fancying me ill. The bare idea is intolerable. If I am going to be ill, I hope I may know it, that I may get away somewhere, where his kindness will not kill me.'

She shivered here, partly from the thought, and partly from the opening of the door. A keen wind whistled through the passage, a rush of cold air followed Polly as she entered. Dr. Heriot was with her.

His cordial greeting was as hearty as ever.

21

'All alone, and in the dark, and positively doing nothing; how unlike Aunt Milly,' he said, in his cheerful quizzical voice ; and kneeling down on the rug, he stirred the fire, and threw on another log, rousing a flame that lighted up the old china and played on the ebony chairs and cabinet.

The shadows had all fled now, the firelight gleamed warmly on the couch, where Mildred was sitting in her blue dress, and on Dr. Heriot's dark face as he threw himself down in the easy-chair that, as he said, looked so inviting.

'Polly is tired, and so am I. We have been having an argument that lasted us all the way from Appleby.' And he leant back his head on the cushions, and looked up lazily at Polly as she stood beside him in her soft furs, swinging her hat in her hand and gazing into the fire. 'Polly, do be reasonable and sit down ! he exclaimed, coaxingly.

'I cannot, I shall be late for tea ; I—I—do not wish to say anything more about it,' she panted, somewhat unsteadily.

'Nay, Heartsease,' he returned, gravely, 'this is hardly using me well ; let us refer the case to Aunt Milly. This naughty child,' he continued, imprisoning her hand, as she still stood beside him—and Mildred noticed now that she seemed to lean against the chair for support—'this naughty Polly of ours is giving me trouble ; she will have it she is too young to be married.'

Mildred put her hand suddenly to her heart ; a troublesome palpitation oppressed her breathing. Polly hung her head, and then a sudden resolution seized her.

'Let me go to Aunt Milly. I want to speak to her,' she said, wrenching herself gently from his hold ; and as he set her free, she dropped on the rug at Mildred's side.

'You must not come to me to help you, Polly,' said Mildred, with a faint smile ; 'you must be guided in this by Dr. Heriot's wishes.'

'Ah, I knew you would be on my side, Miss Lambert ; but you have no idea how obstinate she is. She declares that nothing will induce her to marry until her nineteenth birthday.'

'A whole year !' repeated Mildred, in surprise. She felt like a prisoner, to whom the bitterness of death was past, exposed to the torturing suspense of a long reprieve.

'Oh, Aunt Milly, ask him not to press me,' pleaded the girl ; 'he is so good and patient in everything else, but he will not listen to me in this ; he wants me to go home to him now, this Christmas.'

'Why should we wait?' replied Dr. Heriot, with an unusual touch of bitterness in his voice. 'I shall never grow younger; my home is solitary enough, Heaven knows; and in spite of all my kind friends here, I have to endure many lonely hours. Polly, if you loved me, I think you would hardly refuse.'

'He says right,' whispered Mildred, laying her cold hand on the girl's head. 'It is your duty; he has need of you.'

'I cannot,' replied Polly, in a choked voice; but as she saw the cloud over her lover's brow, she came again to his side, and knelt down beside him.

'I did not mean to grieve you, dear; but you will wait, will you not?'

'For what reason, Polly?' in a sterner voice than she had ever heard from him before.

'For many reasons; because—because—' she hesitated, 'I am young, and want to grow older and wiser for your sake; because—' and now a low sob interrupted her words, 'though I love you—dearly—ah, so dearly—I want to love you more, as I know I shall every day. You must not be angry with me if I try your patience a little.'

'I am not angry,' he repeated, slowly, 'but your manner troubles me. Are you sure you do not repent our engagement —that you love me, Polly?'

'Yes, yes; please do not say such things,' clinging to him, and crying as though her heart would break.

They had almost forgotten Mildred, shrinking back in the corner of her couch.

'Hush! Heartsease, my darling—hush! you distress me,' soothing her with the utmost tenderness. 'We will talk of this again; you shall not be hampered or vexed by me. I am not so selfish as that, Polly.'

'No, you are goodness itself,' she replied, remorsefully; and now she kissed his hand—oh, so gratefully. 'But you must never say that again—never—never.'

'What?'

'That I do not love you; it is not the truth; it cannot be, you know. You do not think it?' looking up fearfully into his face.

'I think you love me a little,' he answered, lightly—too lightly, Mildred thought, for the gloomy look had not passed away from his eyes.

'He is disappointed; he thinks as I do, that perfect love ought to cast out fear,' she said to herself.

But whatever were his thoughts, he did not give utterance to them, but only seemed bent on soothing Polly's agitation. When he had succeeded, he sent her away, to get rid of all traces of tears, as he said, but as the door closed on her, Mildred noticed a weary look crossed his face.

How her heart yearned to comfort him!

'Right or wrong, I suppose I must abide by her decision,' he said at last, speaking more to himself than to her. That roused her.

'I do not think so,' she returned, speaking with her old energy. 'Give her a little time to get used to the idea, and then speak to her again. The thought of Christmas has startled her. Perhaps Easter would frighten her less.'

'That is just it. Why should it frighten her?' he returned, doubtfully. 'She has known me now for three years. I am no stranger to her; she has always been fond of me; she has told me so over and over again. No,' he continued, decidedly, 'I will not press her to come till she wishes it. I am no boy that cannot bear a disappointment. I ought to be used to loneliness by this time.'

'No, no; she shall not treat you so, Dr. Heriot. I will not have it. I—some one will prevent it; you shall not be left lonely for another year—you, so good and so unselfish.' But here Mildred's excitement failed; a curious numb feeling crept over her; she fancied she saw a surprised look on Dr. Heriot's face, that he uttered an exclamation of concern, and then she knew no more.

CHAPTER XXVII

COOP KERNAN HOLE

' The great and terrible Land
Of wilderness and drought
Lies in the shadows behind me—
For the Lord hath brought me out.

' The great and terrible river
I stood that night to view
Lies in the shadows before me—
But the Lord will bear me through.'—Poems by R. M.

MILDRED felt a little giddy and confused when she opened her eyes.

'Is anything the matter? I suppose I have been a little faint; but it is nothing,' she said, feebly. Her head was on a soft pillow; her face was wet with cold, fragrant waters; Polly was hanging over her with a distressed expression; Dr. Heriot's hand was on her wrist.

'Hush, you must not talk,' he said, with a grave, professional air, 'and you must drink this,' so authoritatively that Mildred could not choose but to obey. 'It is nothing of consequence,' he continued, noticing an anxious look on her face; 'the room was hot, and our talk wearied you. I noticed you were very pale when we came in.' And Mildred felt relieved, and asked no more questions.

She was very thankful for the kindness that shielded her from all questioning and comment. When Dr. Heriot had watched the reviving effects of the cordial, and had satisfied himself that there would be no return of the faintness, he quietly but peremptorily desired that Polly should leave her. 'You would like to be perfectly alone for a little while, would you not?' he said, as he adjusted the rug over her feet and placed the screen between her and the firelight, and Mildred thanked him with a grateful glance. How could he guess that silence was what her exhausted nerves craved more than anything?

But Dr. Heriot was not so impervious as he seemed. He was aware that some nervous malady, caused by secret anxiety or hidden care, was wasting Mildred's fine constitution. The dilated pupils of the eyes, the repressed irritability of manner, the quick change of colour, with other signs of mental disturbance, had long ago attracted his professional notice, and he had racked his brains to discover the cause.

'She has over-exerted herself, or else she has some trouble,' he said to himself that night, as he sat beside his solitary fire. She had crept away to her own room during the interval of peace that had been allowed her, and he had not suffered them to disturb her. 'I will come and see her to-morrow,' he had said to Olive ; 'let her be kept perfectly quiet until then ;' and Olive, who knew from experience the soothing effects of his pre-scription, mounted guard herself over Mildred's room, and forbade Polly or Chriss to enter.

Dr. Heriot had plenty of food for meditation that night. In spite of his acquiescence in Polly's decision, he felt chilled and saddened by the girl's persistence.

For the first time he gravely asked himself, Had he made a mistake ? Was she too young to understand his need of sym-pathy ? Would it come to this, that after all she would dis-appoint him ? As he looked round the empty room a strange bitterness came over him.

'And it is to this loneliness that she will doom me for another year,' he said, and there was a heavy cloud on his brow as he said it. 'If she really loved me, would she abandon me to another twelvemonth of miserable retrospection, with only Margaret's dead face to haunt me with its strange beauty ?' But even as the thought passed through him came the remem-brance of those clinging arms and the dark eyes shining through their tears.

'I love you dearly—dearly—but I want to love you more.'

'Oh, Heartsease,' he groaned, 'I fear that the mistake is mine, and that I have not yet won the whole of your innocent heart. I have taken it too much as a matter of course. Perhaps I have not wooed you so earnestly as I should have wooed an older woman, and yet I hardly think I have failed in either devotion or reverence. Ah,' he continued, with an involuntary sigh, 'what right have I to complain if she withhold her fresh young love—am I giving her all that is in me to give ?' But here he stopped, as though the reflection pained him.

He remembered with what sympathy Mildred had advocated

his cause. She had looked excited—almost indignant—as Polly had uttered her piteous protest for time. Had her clear eyes noticed any signs of vacillation or reluctance? Could he speak to her on the subject? Would she answer him frankly? And then, for the first time, he felt as though he could not so speak to her.

'Every one takes their troubles to her, but she shall not be harassed by me,' he thought. 'She is sinking now under the burdens which most likely other people have laid upon her. I will not add to their weight.' And a strange pity and longing seized him to know what ailed the generous creature, who never thought of herself, but of others.

Mildred felt as though some ordeal awaited her when she woke the next morning. She looked so ill and weak that Olive was in despair when she insisted on rising and dressing herself. 'It will bring on the faintness again to a certainty,' she said, in a tone of unusual remonstrance; but Mildred was determined.

But she was glad of Olive's assistance before she had finished, and the toilet was made very slowly and wearily. At the drawing-room door Dr. Heriot met her with a reproachful face; he looked a little displeased.

'So you have cast my prescription to the wind,' he said, drily, 'and are determined not to own yourself ill.' But Mildred coloured so painfully that he cut short his lecture and assisted her to the couch in silence.

'There you may stop for the next two or three days,' he continued, somewhat grimly. 'Mr. Lambert has desired me to look after you, and I shall take good care that you do not disobey my orders again. I have made Olive head nurse, and woe be to her if there be a single infringement of my rules.'

Mildred looked up at him timidly. He had been so gentle with her the preceding evening that this change of manner disturbed her. This was not his usual professional gravity; on such occasions he had ever been kindness itself. He must be put out—annoyed—the idea was absurd, but could she have displeased him? She was too weak to bear the doubt.

'Have I vexed you, Dr. Heriot, by coming down?' she asked, gently. 'I should be worse if I fancied myself ill. I— I have had these attacks before; they are nothing.'

'That is your opinion, is it? I must say I thought better of your sense, Miss Lambert,' still gruffly.

Mildred's eyes filled with tears.

'Yes, I am vexed,' he continued, sitting down by her; but

his tone was more gentle now. 'I am vexed that you are hiding from us that you are suffering. You keep us all in the dark; you deny you are ill. I think you are treating us all very badly.'

'No—no,' she returned, with difficulty. 'I am not ill—you must not tell me so.' And her cheek paled perceptibly.

'Have you turned coward suddenly?' he replied, with a keen look at her. 'I have heard you say more than once that the dread of illness was unknown to you; that you could have walked a fever hospital without a shudder. What has become of your courage, Miss Lambert?'

'I am not afraid, but I do not want to be ill,' she returned, faintly.

'That is more unlike you than ever. Impatience, want of submission, do not certainly belong to your category of faults. Well, if you promise to follow my prescription, I think I can undertake that you shall not be ill.'

Mildred drew a long sigh of relief; the sigh of an oppressed heart was not lost on Dr. Heriot.

'But you must get rid of what is on your mind,' he went on, quickly. 'If other people's burdens lie heavily, you must shift them to their own shoulders and think only of yourself. Now I want to ask you a few questions.'

Mildred looked frightened again, but something in Dr. Heriot's manner this morning constrained her to obey. His inquiries were put skilfully, and needed only a yea and nay, as though he feared she would elude him. Mildred found herself owning to loss of appetite and want of sleep; to languor and depression, and a tendency to excessive irritation; noises jarred on her; a latent excitement took the place of strength. She had lost all pleasure in her duties, though she still fulfilled them.

'And now what does this miserable state of the nerves mean?' was his next question. Mildred said nothing.

'You have suffered no shock—nothing has alarmed you?' She shook her head.

'You cannot eat or sleep; when you speak you change colour with every word; you are wasted, getting thinner every day, and yet there is no disease. This must mean something, Miss Lambert—excuse me; but I am your friend as well as your doctor. I cannot work in the dark.'

Mildred's lips quivered. 'I want change—rest. I have had anxieties—no one can be free in this world. I am getting too weak for my work.' What a confession from Mildred! At another time she would have died rather than utter it; but his quiet strength of will was making evasion impossible. She felt as though this friend of hers was reading her through and through. She must escape in some measure by throwing herself upon his mercy.

He looked uneasy at that; his eyes softened, then suffused.

'I thought as much,' he muttered; 'I could not be deceived by that face.' And a great pity swelled up in his heart.

He would like to befriend this noble woman, who was always so ready to sacrifice herself to the needs of others. He would ask her to impart her trouble, whatever it was; he might be able to help her. But Mildred, who read his purpose in his eyes, went on breathlessly—

'It is the rest I want, and the change; I am not ill. I knew you would say so; but the nerves get strained sometimes, and then worries will come.'

'Tell me your trouble,' he returned abruptly, but it was the abruptness of deep feeling. 'I have not forgotten your kindness to me on more than one occasion. I have debts of gratitude to pay, and they are heavy. Make me your friend—your brother, if you will; you will find I am to be trusted.' But the poor soul only shrank from him.

'It cannot be told—there are reasons against it. I have more than one trouble—anxiety,' she faltered. 'Dr. Heriot, indeed—indeed, you are very good, but there are some things that cannot be told.'

'As you will,' he returned, very gently; but Mildred saw he was disappointed. In what a strange complication she was involved! She could not even speak to him of her fear on Roy's behalf. He took his leave soon after that, and Mildred fancied a slight reserve mingled with the kindness with which he bade her good-bye.

He seemed conscious of it, for he came back again after putting on his coat, thereby preventing a miserable afternoon of fanciful remorse on Mildred's part.

'I will think what is to be done about the change,' he said, drawing on his driving-gloves. 'I am likely to be busy all day, and shall not see you again this evening. Keep your mind at rest as well as you can. You don't need to be told in what spirit all trials must be borne—the darker the cloud the more need of faith.' He held out his hand to her again with one of his bright, genial smiles, and Mildred felt braced and comforted

Mildred was obliged to allow herself to be treated as an invalid for the next few days; but when Dr. Heriot saw how the inaction and confinement fretted her, he withdrew a few of his restrictions, even at times going against his better judgment, when he saw how cruelly she chafed under her own restlessness.

This was the case one chill, sunless afternoon, when he found her standing by the window looking out over the fells, with a sad wistfulness that went to his heart.

As he went up to her he was shocked to see the marks of recent tears upon her face.

'What is this—you are not worse to-day?' he asked, in a tone of vexed remonstrance.

'No—oh no,' she returned, holding out her hand to him with a misty smile, the thin blue-veined hand, with its hot dry palm; 'you will think me a poor creature, Dr. Heriot, but I could not help fretting over my want of strength just now.'

'Rome was not built in a day,' he responded, cheerily; 'and people who indulge in fainting fits cannot expect to feel like Hercules. Who would have thought that such an inexorable nurse as Miss Lambert should prove such a fractious invalid?' and there was a tone of reproof under the light raillery.

'I do not mean to be impatient,' she answered, sighing; 'but I am so weary of this room and my own thoughts, and then there are my poor people.'

'Don't trouble your head about them; they will do very well without you,' with pretended roughness.

She shook her head.

'You are wrong; they miss me dreadfully; Olive has brought me several messages from them already.'

'Then Olive ought to be ashamed of herself, and shall be deposed from her office of nurse, and Polly shall reign in her stead.'

But Mildred was too much depressed and in earnest to heed his banter.

'There is poor Rachel Sowerby up at Stenkrith; her mother has been down this morning to say that she cannot last very much longer.'

'I am just going up to see her now. I fear it is only a question of days,' he replied, gravely.

Mildred clasped her hands with an involuntary movement of pain.

'Rachel is very dear to me; she is the model girl and the

favourite of the whole school, and her mother says she is pining to see me. Oh, Dr. Heriot—' but here she stopped.

'Well,' he returned, encouragingly; and for the second time he noticed the exceeding beauty of Mildred's eyes, as she fixed them softly and beseechingly on his face.

'Do you think it would hurt me to go that little distance, just to see Rachel?'

'What, in this bitter wind!' he remonstrated. 'Wait until to-morrow, and I will drive you over.'

'There may be no to-morrows for Rachel,' she returned, with gentle persistence. 'I am afraid I shall fret sadly if I do not see her again; she was my best Sunday scholar. The wind will not hurt me; if you knew how I long to be out in it; just before you came in I was wishing I were on the top of one of those fells, feeling it sweep over me.'

'Ministers of grace defend me from the soft pleading of a woman's tongue!' exclaimed Dr. Heriot, impatiently, but he laughed too; 'you are a most troublesome patient, Miss Lambert; but I suppose you must have your way; but you must take the consequences of your own wilfulness.'

Mildred quietly seated herself.

'No, I am not wilful; I have no wish to disobey you,' she returned, in a low voice.

He drew near and questioned her face; evidently it dissatisfied him.

'If I do not let you go, you will only worry yourself the whole day, and your lungs are sound enough,' he continued, brusquely; but Mildred's strange unreasonableness tried him. 'Wrap yourself up well. Polly is going with me, but there is plenty of room for both. I will pay my visit, and leave you with Rachel for an hour, while I get rid of some of my other patients.'

Mildred lost no time in equipping herself, and though Dr. Heriot pretended to growl the greater part of the way, he could not help noticing how the wind—bleak and boisterous as it was —seemed to freshen his patient, and bring back the delicate colour to her cheeks.

'What a hardy north-country woman you have become,' he said, as he lifted her down from the phaeton, and they went up the path to the house.

'I feel changed already; thank you for giving me my way in this,' was the grateful answer.

When Dr. Heriot had taken his departure, she went up to

the sickroom, and sat for a long time beside her old favourite, reading and praying with her, until Rachel had fallen into a doze.

'She will sleep maybe for an hour or two; she had a terrible night of pain,' whispered Mrs. Sowerby, 'and she will sleep all the sweeter for your reading to her. Poor thing! she was set on seeing her dear Miss Lambert, as she always calls you.'

'I will come again and see her to-morrow, if Dr. Heriot permits it,' she replied.

When Mrs. Sowerby had gone back to her daughter's room, she went and sat by herself at a window looking over Stenkrith; the rocks and white foaming pools were distinctly visible through the leafless trees; a steep flight of steps led down to the stream and waterfall; the steps were only a few yards from the Sowerbys' house. As Mildred looked, a strange longing to see the place again took possession of her.

For a moment she hesitated, as Dr. Heriot's strictures on her imprudence recurred to her memory, but she soon repelled them.

'He does not understand—how can he—that this confinement tries me,' she thought, as she crept softly down the stairs, so as not to disturb Rachel. 'The wind was delicious. I feel ten times better than I did in that hot room; he will not mind when I tell him so.'

Mildred's feverish restlessness, fed by bitter thought, was getting the better of her judgment; like the skeleton placed at Egyptian feasts to remind the revellers that they were mortal, so Mildred fancied her courage would be strengthened, her resolution confirmed, by a visit to the very spot where her bitterest wound had been received; she remembered how the dark churning waters had mingled audibly with her pain, and for the moment she had wished the rushing force had hurried her with it, with her sweet terrible secret undisturbed, to the bottom of that deep sunless pool.

And now the yearning to see it again was too strong to be resisted. Polly had accompanied Dr. Heriot. Mrs. Sowerby was in her daughter's room; there was no one to raise a warning voice against her imprudence.

The whole place looked deserted and desolate; the sun had hidden its face for days; a dark moisture clung to the stones, making them slippery in places; the wind was more boisterous than ever, wrapping Mildred's blue serge more closely round her feet, and entangling her in its folds, blowing her hair wildly about her face, and rendering it difficult with her feeble force to keep her footing on the slimy rocks.

'I shall feel it less when I get lower down,' she panted, as she scrambled painfully from one rock to another, often stopping to take breath. A curious mood—gentle, yet reckless—was on her. 'He would be angry with her,' she thought. Ah, well! his anger would only be sweet to her; she would own her fault humbly, and then he would be constrained to forgive her; but this longing for freedom, for the strong winds of heaven, for the melody of rushing waters, was too intense to be resisted; the restlessness that devoured her still led her on.

'I see something moving down there,' observed Polly, as Dr. Heriot's phaeton rolled rapidly over the bridge—'down by the steps, I mean; it looked almost like Aunt Mildred's blue serge dress.'

'Your eyes must have deceived you, then,' he returned coolly, as he pulled up again at the little gate.

Polly made no answer, but as she quickened her steps towards the place, he followed her, half vexed at her persistence.

'My dear child, as though your Aunt Milly would do anything so absurd,' he remonstrated. 'Why, the rocks are quite unsafe after the rain, and the wind is enough to cut one in halves.'

'It is Aunt Milly. I told you so,' returned Polly, triumphantly, as she descended the step; 'there is her blue serge and her beaver hat. Look! she sees us; she is waving her hand.'

Dr. Heriot suppressed the exclamation that rose to his lips.

'Take care, Polly, the steps are slippery; you had better not venture on the stones,' he said, peremptorily. 'Keep where you are, and I will bring Miss Lambert back.'

Mildred saw him coming; her heart palpitated a little.

'He will think me foolish, little better than a child,' she said to herself; 'he will not know why I came here;' and her courage evaporated. All at once she felt weak; the rocks were certainly terribly slippery.

'Wait for me; I will help you!' he shouted, seeing her indecision; but either Mildred did not hear, or she misunderstood him; the stone was too high for her unassisted efforts; she tried one lower; it was wet; her foot slipped, she tried to recover herself, fell, and then, to the unspeakable horror of the two watching her above, rolled from rock to rock and disappeared.

Polly's wild shriek of dismay rang through the place, but Dr. Heriot never lost his presence of mind for a moment.

'Stay where you are; on your peril disobey me!' he cried, in a voice of thunder, to the affrighted girl; and then, though with difficulty, he steered his way between the slippery stones, and over the dangerous fissures.   He could see her now; some merciful jag in the rocks had caught part of her dress, and arrested her headlong progress.   The momentary obstacle had enabled her, as she slipped into one of the awful fissures that open into Coop Kernan Hole, to snatch with frantic hands at the slimy rock, her feet clinging desperately to the narrow slippery ledge.

'John, save me!' she screamed, as she felt herself slipping into the black abyss beneath.

'John!'

John Heriot heard her.

'Yes, I am coming, Mildred; hold on—hold on, another minute.'   The drops of mortal agony stood on his brow as he saw her awful peril, but he dared not, for both their sakes, venture on reckless haste; already he had slipped more than once, but had recovered himself.   It seemed minutes to both of them before Polly saw him kneeling on one knee beside the hole, his feet hanging over the water.

'Hush! do not struggle so, Mildred,' he pleaded, as he got his arm with difficulty round her, and she clung to him almost frantically; the poor soul had become delirious from the shock, and thought she was being dashed to pieces; her face elongated and sharpened with terror, as she sank half fainting against his shoulder.   The weight on his arm was terrible.

'Good Heavens! what can I do?' he ejaculated, as he felt his strength insufficient to lift her.   His position was painful in the extreme; his knee was slipping under him; and the dripping serge dress, heavy with water, increased the strain on the left arm; a false movement, the slightest change of posture, and they must both have gone.   He remembered how he had heard it said that Coop Kernan Hole was of unknown depth under the bridge; the dark sluggish pool lay black and terrible between the rocks; if she slipped from his hold into that cruel water, he knew he could not save her, for he had ever been accounted a poor swimmer, and yet her dead-weight was already numbing his arm.

'Mildred, if you faint we must both die!' he cried in despair.

His voice seemed to rouse her; some instinct of preservation prompted her to renewed effort ; and as he held her more firmly, she managed to get one hand round his neck—the other still clutched at the rock ; and as Polly's cries for help reached a navvy working at some distance, she saw Dr. Heriot slowly and painfully lift Mildred over the edge of the rock.

'Thank God !' he panted, and then he could say no more ; but as he felt the agonised shuddering run through Mildred's frame, as, unconscious of her safety, she still clung to him, he half-pityingly and half-caressingly put back the unbound hair from the pale face, as he would have done to a child.

But he looked almost as ghastly as Mildred did, when, aided by the navvy's strong arms, they lifted her over the huge masses of rocks and up the steep steps.

Polly ran to meet them ; her lover's pale and disordered appearance alarmed her almost as much as Mildred's did.

'Oh, Heriot !' cried the young girl, 'you are hurt ; I am sure you are hurt.'

'A strain, nothing else,' he returned, quickly ; 'run on, dear Polly, and open the door for us. Mrs. Sowerby must take us in for a little while.'

When Mildred perfectly recovered consciousness, she was lying on the old-fashioned couch in Mrs. Sowerby's best room ; but she was utterly spent and broken, and could do nothing for a little while but weep hysterically.

Polly lent over her, raining tears on her hands.

'Oh, Aunt Milly,' sobbed the faithful little creature, 'what should we have done if we had lost you ? Darling—darling, how dreadful it would have been.'

'I wished to die,' murmured Mildred, half to herself ; 'but I never knew how terrible death could be. Oh, how sinful— how ungrateful I have been.' And she covered her face with her hands.

'Oh, Heriot ; ask her not to cry so,' pleaded poor Polly. 'I have never seen her cry before, never—and it hurts me so.'

'It will do her good,' he returned, hastily ; but he went and stood by the window, until Polly joined him.

'She is better now,' she said, timidly glancing up into his absorbed face.

Upon that he turned round.

'Then we must get her home, that she may change her wet things as soon as possible. Do you feel as though you can move ?' he continued, in his ordinary manner, though perhaps it was a trifle grave. 'You are terribly bruised, I fear, but I trust not otherwise injured.'

She looked up a little surprised at the calmness of his tone, and then involuntarily she stretched out her hands to him—

'Let me thank you first—you have saved my life,' she whispered.

'No,' he returned, quietly. 'It is true your disobedience placed us both in jeopardy ; but it was your obedience at the last that really saved your life. If you had fainted, you must inevitably have been lost. I could not have supported you much longer in my cramped position.'

'Your arm—did I hurt it ?' she asked, anxiously, noticing an expression of pain pass over his face.

'I daresay I have strained it slightly,' he answered, indifferently ; 'but it does not matter. The question is, do you think you can bear to be moved ?'

'Oh, I can walk. I am better now,' she replied, colouring slightly.

His coolness disappointed her ; she was longing to thank him with the full fervour of a grateful heart. It was sweet, it was good in spite of everything to receive her life back through his hands. Never—never would she dare to repine again, or murmur at the lot Providence had appointed her ; so much had the dark lesson of Coop Kernan Hole taught her.

'Well, what is it ?' he asked, reading but too truly the varying expressions of her eloquent face.

'If you will only let me thank you,' she faltered, 'I shall never forget this hour to my dying day.'

'Neither shall I,' he returned, abruptly, as he wrapped her up in his dry plaid and assisted her to rise. His manner was as kind and considerate as ever during their short drive, but Mildred felt as though his reserve were imposing some barrier on her.

Consternation prevailed in the vicarage at the news of Mildred's danger. Olive, who seldom shed tears, became pale and voiceless with emotion, while Mr. Lambert pressed his sister to his heart with a whispered thanksgiving that was audible to her alone.

It was good for Mildred's sore heart to feel how ardently she was beloved. A great flood of gratitude and contrition swept over her as she lay, bruised and shaken, with her hand in Arnold's, looking at the dear faces round her. 'It has come to me not in the still, small voice, but in the storm,' she thought.

'He has brought me out of the deep waters to serve Him more faithfully—to give a truer account of the life restored to me.'

The clear brightness of her eyes surprised Dr. Heriot as he came up to her to take leave; they reminded him of the Mildred of old. 'You must promise to sleep to-night. Some one must be with you—Olive or Polly—you might get nervous alone,' he said, with his usual thoughtfulness; but she shook her head.

'I think I am cured of my nervousness for ever,' she returned, in a voice that was very sweet. The soft smiling eyes haunted him. Had an angel gone down and troubled the pool? What healing virtues had steeped the dark waters that her shuddering feet had pressed? Could faith, full-formed, spring from such parentage of deadly anguish and fear? Mildred could have answered in the verse she loved so well—

> 'He never smiled so sweet before
> Save on the Sea of Sorrow, when the night
> Was saddest on our heart. We followed him
> At other times in sunshine. Summer days
> And moonlight nights He led us over paths
> Bordered with pleasant flowers; but when His steps
> Were on the mighty waters, when we went
> With trembling hearts through nights of pain and loss,
> His smile was sweeter, and His love more dear;
> And only Heaven is better than to walk
> With Christ at midnight over moonless seas.'

CHAPTER XXVIII

DR. HERIOT'S MISTAKE

'In the cruel fire of sorrow
Cast thy heart, do not faint or wail ;
Let thy hand be firm and steady,
Do not let thy spirit quail :
But wait till the trial is over,
And take thy heart again ;
For as gold is tried by fire,
So a heart must be tried by pain !'

ADELAIDE ANNE PROCTER.

MILDRED slept soundly that night in spite of her bruises. It was Dr. Heriot who waked.

What nightmare of oppression was on him? What light, scorching and illuminating, was shining on him through the gloom? Was he losing his senses?—had he dreamt it? Had he really heard it? 'John, save me, John!' as of a woman in mortal anguish calling on her mate, as Margaret had once—but once—called him, when a glimpse of the dark valley had been vouchsafed her, and she had bidden him, with frenzied eye and tongue, arrest her downward course : 'I cannot die—at least, not like this—you must save me, John!' and that time he had saved her.

And now he had heard it again, at the only time when conventionality lays aside its decorous disguise, and the souls of men are bare to their fellows—at the time of awful peril on the brink of a momentarily expected death : so had she called to him, and so, with the sudden waking response of his soul, he had answered her.

He could see it all now. Never, to his dying hour, could he forget that scene—the prostrate figure crashing among the rocks, as though to an immediate and terrible death; the agonised struggle in the dark pit, the white face pressed heavily like death to his shoulder, the long unbound hair streaming across his arm ; never before had he owned to himself that this woman was fair, until he had put back the blinding hair with his hand, as she clung to him in suffering helplessness.

'I wished to die, but I never knew how terrible death could be,' he had heard her whisper between her quivering lips ; and the knowledge that her secret was his had bidden him turn away his eyes from her—his own suffused with tears.

'Fool ! blind fool that I was !' he groaned. 'Fool ! never to guess how dear she was until I saw death trying to snatch her from me ; never to know the reason why her presence inspired me with such comfort and such rest ! And I must needs call it friendship. Was it friendship that brought me day after day with such a sore heart to minister to her weakness ?—was it only friendship and pity, and a generous wish to succour her distress ?'

'Oh, fool ! miserable fool ! for ever fated to destroy my own peace of mind !' But we need not follow the bitter self-communing of that generous spirit through that long night of doubt and pain from which he rose a sadder and a better man.

Alas ! he had grasped the truth too late. The true woman, the true mate, the very nature akin to his own, had been beside him all these years, and he had not recognised her, blind in his pitiful worship of lesser lights.

And as he thought of the innocent girl who had pledged her faith to him, he groaned again within himself. Polly was not less dear to him in the misery that had befallen him, yet he knew, and shuddered at the knowledge, that all unwittingly he had deceived himself and her ; he would love his child-wife dearly, he knew, but not as he could love a woman like Mildred.

'If she had been less reserved, less unapproachable in her gentle dignity, it might have been better for both of us,' he said to himself. 'The saint has hidden the woman ; one cannot embrace a halo !' and he thought with sharp anguish how well this new phase of weakness had become her. When she had claimed his indulgence for her wayward and nervous fancies, he had felt even then a sort of pride that she should appeal to him in her helplessness.

But these were vain thoughts. It might have been better for both of them if she were lying now under the dark waters of Coop Kernan Hole, her angel soul in its native heaven. Yes, it might be far better ; he did not know—he had not Mildred's faith ; for as long as they must dwell together, and yet apart, in this mortal world, life could only be a bitter thing for him ; but not for that should he cease to struggle.

'I have more than myself to consider,' he continued, as he rose and drew back the curtain, and looked out on the rich harvest of the sky-glittering sheaves of stars, countless worlds beyond worlds, stretching out into immensity. 'God do so to me and more also if my unkindness or fickleness cloud the clear mirror of that girlish soul. It is better, far better, for me to suffer—ay, for her too—than to throw off a responsibility at once so sacred and so pure.'

How Mildred would have gloried in this generous victory if she had witnessed it ! The knowledge that the tardy blessing of his love had been vouchsafed her, though too late and in vain, would have gladdened her desolate heart, and the honour and glory of it would have decked her lonely life with infinite blossom.

But now she could only worship his goodness from afar. None but Mildred had ever rightly read him, or knew the unselfishness that was so deeply ingrained in this man's nature. Loving and impulsive by nature, he had patiently wooed and faithfully held to the woman who had scorned his affection and provoked his forbearance ; he had borne his wrecked happiness, the daily spectacle of his degradation, with a resignation that was almost sublime ; he had comforted the poor sinner on her deathbed with assurances of forgiveness that had sunk into her soul with strange healing ; when at last she had left him, he had buried his dead out of his sight, covering with thick sods, and heaping the earth with pious hands over the memory of her past sins.

It was this unselfishness that had first taught him to feel tenderly to the poor orphan ; he had schemed out of pure benevolence to make her his wife, until the generous fancy had grown dear to him, and he had believed his own happiness involved in it.

And now that it had resulted in a bitter awakening to himself and disappointment to another, no possibility of eluding his fate ever came into his mind. Polly already belonged to him ; she was his, made his own by a distinct and plighted troth ; he could no more put her away from him than he would have turned away the half-frozen robin that sought refuge from the inclement storm. Mildred had betrayed her love too late ; it was his lot to rescue her from death, but not to bid her welcome to a heart that should in all honour belong to another. True, it was a trial most strange and bitter—an ordeal from which flesh and blood might well shrink ; but long before this he had looked into the burning fiery furnace of affliction, and he knew, as such men know, that though he might be cast therein bound and helpless, that even there the true heart could discern the form most like unto the Son of God.

It was with some such feeling as this that he lingered by Polly's side, as though to gain a minute's strength before he should be ushered into Mildred's presence.

'How tired you look, Heriot,' she said, as he stood beside her ; the word had involuntarily slipped from her in her gladness yesterday, and as she timidly used it again his lips touched her brow in token of his thanks.

'We are improving, Heartsease. I suppose you begin to find out that I am not as formidable as I look—that Dr. Heriot had a very chilling sound, it made me feel fifty at least.'

'I think you are getting younger, or I am getting older,' observed Polly, quaintly ; 'to be sure you look very pale this morning, and your forehead is dreadfully wrinkled. I am afraid your arm has been troubling you.'

'Well, it has been pretty bad,' he returned, evasively ; 'one does not get over a strain so easily. But, now, how is Mildred ?'

The word escaped from him involuntarily, but he did not recall it. Polly did not notice his slight confusion.

'She is down in the drawing-room. I think she expects you,' she replied. 'Olive said she had a beautiful night, but of course the bruises are very painful ; one of her arms is quite blackened, she cannot bear it touched.'

'I will see what can be done,' was his answer.

As he crossed the lobby his step was as firm as ever, his manner as gravely kind as he stood by Mildred's side ; the delicacy of her aspect smote him with dull pain, but she smiled in her old way as she gave him her left hand.

'The other is so much bruised that I cannot bear the lightest touch,' she said, drawing it out from her white shawl, and showing him the cruel black marks ; 'it is just like that to my shoulder.'

He looked at it pityingly.

'And yet you slept ?'

'As I have not slept for weeks ; no terrible dreams haunted me, no grim presentiments of evil fanned my pillow with black wing ; you must have exorcised the demon.'

'That is well,' he returned, sitting down beside her, and trying to speak with his old cheerfulness ; 'reality has beaten off hypochondriacal fancies. Coop Kernan Hole has proved a stern mentor.'

'I trust I may never forget the lesson it has taught me,' she returned, with a slight shudder at the remembrance, and then they were both silent for a moment. 'Dr Heriot,' she continued, presently, 'yesterday I wanted to thank you—I ought rather to have craved your forgiveness.'

He smiled at that; in spite of himself the old feeling of rest had returned to him with her presence; her sweet looks, her patience, her brave endurance of what he knew would be keen suffering to other women, won the secret tribute of his admiration; he would lay aside his heavy burden for this one hour, and enjoy this brief interval of peace.

'I do not wonder that you refused my thanks,' she went on, earnestly; 'to think that my foolish act of disobedience should have placed your life as well as mine in such deadly peril; indeed, you must assure me of your forgiveness, or I shall never be happy again,' and Mildred's lip trembled.

He took the bruised hand in his, but so tenderly that she did not wince at his touch; the blackened fingers lay on his palm as restfully as the little bird he had once warmed in his hands one snowy day. How he loved this woman who was suing to him with such sweet lips for forgiveness;—the latent flame just kindled burned with an intensity that surprised himself.

'Ah!' she said, mistaking his silence, and looking up into his dark face—and it looked strangely worn and harassed in the clear morning light—'you do not answer, you think I am much to blame. I have tried your patience too far—even yours!'

'I was angry with you, certainly, when I saw you down on those rocks jeopardising your precious life,' he replied, slowly. 'Such foolhardiness was unlike you, and I had reserved certain vials of wrath at my disposal—but now——'

He finished with his luminous smile.

'You think I have been punished sufficiently?'

'Yes, first stoned and then half submerged. I forgave you directly you called on me for help,' he returned, making believe to jest, but watching her intently all the time. Would she understand his vague allusion? But Mildred, unconscious that she had betrayed herself, only looked relieved.

'Besides, there can be no question of forgiveness between friends, and whatever happens we are friends always,' relinquishing her hand a little abruptly.

He rose soon after that.

Mildred was uneasy ; he was evidently suffering severely from his arm,. but he continued to evade her anxious inquiries, assuring her that it was nothing to the pain of her bruises, and that a wakeful night, more or less, mattered little to him.

But as he went out of the room, he told himself that these interviews were perilously sweet, and must be avoided at all hazards ; either he must wound her with his coldness, or his tenderness would inevitably betray itself in some unguarded look or word. Twice, already, had her name lingered on his tongue, and more than one awkward pause had brought her clear glances questioning to his face.

What right had he to hold the poor blackened hand in his for more than a moment ? But the sweet soul had taken it all so naturally ; her colour had never varied ; possibly her great deliverance had swallowed all lesser feelings for the time ; the man she loved had become her preserver, and this knowledge was so precious to her that it had lifted her out of her deep despondency.

But as he set forth to his work, he owned within himself that such things must not be—it were a stain on his integrity to suffer it ; from the first of Mildred's coming their intercourse had been free and unrestrained, but for the future he would time his visits when the other members of the family would be present, or, better still, he would keep Polly by his side, trusting that the presence of his young betrothed would give him the strength he needed.

Mildred did not seem to notice the change, it was effected so skilfully ; she was always better pleased when Olive or Polly was there—it diverted Dr. Heriot's attention from herself, and caused her less embarrassment ; her battered frame was in sore need of rest, but with her usual unselfishness, she resumed some of her old duties as soon as possible, that Olive might not feel overburdened.

' It seems as though I have been idle for such a long time,' she said, in answer to Dr. Heriot's deprecating glance at the mending beside her ; ' Olive has no time now, and these things are more troublesome to her than to most people. To-morrow I mean to take to housekeeping again, for Polly feels herself quite unable to manage Nan.'

Dr. Heriot shook his head, but he did not directly forbid the experiment. He knew that to a person of Mildred's active habits, anything approaching to indolence was a positive crime ;

it was better for them both that she should assert that she was well, and that he should be free to relax his vigilance; he could still watch over her, and interfere when it became necessary to do so.

Mildred had reason to be thankful that he did not oppose her exertions, for before long fresh work came to her.

The very morning after Dr. Heriot had withdrawn his silent protest, a letter in a strange handwriting was laid beside Mildred's breakfast-plate; the postmark was London, and she opened it in some little surprise; but Polly, who was watching her, noticed that she turned pale over the contents.

'Is it about Roy?' she whispered; and Mildred started.

'Yes, he has been ill,' and she looked at her brother doubtfully; but he stretched out his hand for the letter, and read it in silence.

Polly watched them anxiously.

'He is not very ill, Aunt Milly?'

'Not now; but I greatly fear he has been so. Mrs. Madison writes that it was a neglected cold, with a sharp attack of inflammation, but that the inflammation has subsided; he is terribly weak, and needs nursing, and the doctor insists that his friends should be informed.'

'But Dad Fabian is with him?'

'No, he is quite alone. The strangest part is that he would not suffer her to write to us. I suppose he dreaded our alarm.'

'It was wrong—very wrong,' groaned Mr. Lambert; 'his brother not with him, and he away from us all that distance; Mildred, my dear, you must go to him without delay.'

Mildred smiled faintly; she thought her strength was small for such a long journey, but she did not say so. Anxiety for his son had driven the remembrance of her accident from his mind; a slight attack of rheumatic gout, to which he had been subject of late years, prevented him from undertaking the journey as he wished.

'You will go, my dear, will you not?' he pleaded, anxiously.

'If Aunt Milly goes, I must go to take care of her,' broke in Polly.

Her face was pale, her eyes dilated with excitement. Olive looked on wistfully, but said nothing; it was never her way to thrust herself forward on any occasion, and however much she wished to help Mildred in nursing Roy, she did not drop a hint to the effect; but Mildred was not slow to interpret the wistfulness.

'It is Olive's place to nurse her brother,' she said, with a trace of reproof in her voice ; but though Polly grew crimson she still persisted.

I did not mean that—you know I did not, Aunt Milly !' a little indignantly. 'I only thought I could wait on you, and save you trouble, and then when he was better I could——' but her lip quivered, and when the others looked up, expecting her to finish her sentence, she suddenly and most unexpectedly burst into tears, and left the room.

Olive followed Mildred when she rose from the breakfast-table.

'Aunt Milly, do let her go. Poor Polly ! she looks so miserable.'

'It is not to be thought of for a moment,' returned Mildred, with unusual decision ; 'if no one but Polly can accompany me, I shall go alone.'

'But Polly is so fond of Roy,' pleaded Olive ; timid with regard to herself, she could persist with more boldness on another's behalf. 'Roy would not care for me half so much as he would for her ; when he had that feverish cold last year, no one seemed to please him but Polly. Do let her go, Aunt Milly,' continued the generous-hearted girl. 'I do not mind being left. If Roy is worse I could come to you,' and Olive spoke with the curious choke in her voice that showed strong emotion.

Mildred looked touched, but she remained firm. Little did Olive guess her reasons.

'I could not allow it for one moment, Olive. I think,' hesitating a little, as though sure of inflicting pain, 'that I ought to go alone, unless Roy is very ill. I do not see how your father is to be left ; he might have another attack, and Richard is not here.'

'I forgot papa,' in a conscience-stricken tone. 'I am always forgetting something.'

'Yes, and yourself in the bargain,' smiling at her earnest self-depreciation.

'No, please don't laugh, Aunt Milly, it was dreadfully careless of me—what should we all do without you to remind us of things? Of course papa must be my first thought, unless—unless dear Rex is very ill,' and a flush of pain passed over Olive's sallow face.

Mildred melted over this fresh instance of Olive's unselfish goodness ; she wrapped her arms fondly round the girl.

'Dear Olive, this is so good of you !'

'No, it is only my duty,' but the tears started to her eyes.

'If I did not think it were, I would not have proposed it,' she returned, reluctantly ; 'but you know how little care your father takes of himself, and then he will fret so about Roy when Richard is away. I never like to leave him.'

'Do not say any more, Aunt Milly ; nothing but real positive danger to Roy would induce me to leave him.'

'No, I knew I could trust you,' drawing a relieved breath ; 'but, indeed, I have no such fear for Rex. Mrs. Madison says it was only a slight attack of inflammation, and that it has quite subsided. He will be dreadfully weak, of course, and that is why the doctor has sent for us ; he will want weeks of nursing.'

'And you will not take Polly or Chriss. Remember how far from strong you are, and Rex is so exacting when he is ill.'

'Chriss would be no use to me, and Polly's place is here,' was Mildred's quiet answer as she went on with her preparations for the next day's journey ; but she little knew of the tenacity with which Polly clave to her purpose.

When Dr. Heriot came in that afternoon for his last professional chat with Mildred, he found her looking open-eyed and anxious in the midst of business, reading out a list for Olive, who was writing patiently from her dictation ; Polly was crouched up by the fire doing nothing ; she had not spoken to any one since the morning ; she hardly raised her head when he came in.

Mildred explained the reason of their unusual bustle in her clear, succinct way. Roy was ill, how ill she could not say. Mr. Lambert had had a touch of gout last night, and dared not run the risk of a journey just now. Olive must stop with her father, at least for the present ; and as Chriss was too young to be of the least possible use, she was going alone. Polly's name was not mentioned. Dr. Heriot looked blank at the tidings.

'Alone, and in your state of health ! why, where is Polly ? she is a capital nurse ; she is worth a score of others ; she will keep up your spirits, save you fatigue, and cheer up Roy in his convalescence.'

'You cannot spare her ; Polly's place is here,' replied Mildred, nervously ; but to her surprise Polly interrupted her.

'That is not the reason, Aunt Milly.'

'My dear Polly !' exclaimed Dr. Heriot, amazed at the contradiction.

'No, it is not, and she knows it,' returned the girl, excitedly ;

'ask her, Heriot ; look at her ; that is not the reason she will not suffer me to go to Roy.'

Mildred turned her burning face bravely on the two.

'Whatever reasons I have, Polly knows me well enough to respect them,' she said, with dignity ; 'it is far better for Roy that his aunt or his sister should be with him. Polly ought to know that her place is beside you.'

'Aunt Milly, how dare you speak so,' cried the girl, hotly, 'as though Roy were not my own—own brother. Have we not cared for each other ever since I came here a lonely stranger ; do you think he will get better if he is fretting, and knows why you have left me behind ; when he was ill in the summer, would he have any one to wait on him but me ?'

'Oh, Polly,' began Mildred, sorrowfully, for the girl's petulance and obstinacy were new to her ; but Dr. Heriot stopped her.

'Let the child speak,' he said, quietly ; 'she has never been perverse to you before ; she has something on her mind, or she would not talk so.'

The kind voice, the unexpected sympathy, touched Polly's sore heart ; and as he held out his hand to her, she crept out of her dark corner. He drew her gently to his side.

'Now, Polly, what is it ? there is something here that I do not understand—out with it like a brave lassie.'

But she hung her head.

'Not now, not here, before the others,' she whispered, and with that he rose from his seat, but he still kept hold of her hand.

'Polly is going to make a clean breast of it ; I am to hear her confession,' he said, with a cheerfulness that reassured Mildred. 'There is no time like the present. I mean to bring her back by and by, and then we will make our apologies together.'

Mildred sighed as the door closed after them ; she would fain have known what passed between them ; her heart grew heavy with foreboding as time elapsed and they did not make their appearance. When her business was finished, and Olive had left her, she sat for more than half an hour with her eyes fixed on the door, feeling as though she could bear the suspense no longer.

She started painfully when the valves unclosed.

'We have been longer than I expected,' began Dr. Heriot.

His face was grave, and Mildred fancied his eyes looked troubled. Polly had been crying.

'It was a rambling confession, and one difficult to understand,' he continued, keeping the girl near him, and Mildred noticed she leant her face caressingly against his coat-sleeve, as she stood there ; 'and it goes back to the day of our picnic at Hill-beck.'

Mildred moved uneasily ; there was something reproachful in his glance directed towards herself ; she averted her eyes, and he went on—

'It seems you were all agreed in keeping me in the dark ; you had your reasons, of course, but it appears to me as though I ought to have been the first to hear of Roy's visit,' and there was a marked emphasis in his words that made Mildred still more uncomfortable. 'I do not wish to blame you ; you acted for the best, of course, and I own the case a difficult one ; it is only a pity that my little girl should have considered it her duty to keep anything from me.'

'I told him it was Roy's secret, not mine,' murmured Polly, and he placed his hand kindly on her head.

'I do not see how she could have acted otherwise,' returned Mildred, rather indistinctly.

'No, I am more inclined to blame her advisers than herself,' was the somewhat cool response ; 'mysteries are bad things between engaged people. Polly kept a copy of her letter to show me, but she never found courage to do so until to-night, and yet she is quite aware what are Roy's feelings towards her.'

Mildred's voice had a sound of dismay in it—

'Oh, Polly ! then you have deceived me too.'

'You have no reason to say so,' returned the girl, proudly, but her heart swelled over her words ; 'it was that—that letter, and your silence, that told me, Aunt Milly ; but I could not— it was not possible to say it either to you or to Dr. Heriot.'

'You see it was hard for her, poor child,' was his indulgent comment ; 'but you might have helped her ; you might have told me yourself, Miss Lambert.'

But Mildred repelled the accusation firmly.

'It was no business of yours, Dr. Heriot, or Polly's either, that Roy loved her. Richard and I were right to guard it ; it was his own secret, his own trouble. Polly would never have known but for her own wilfulness.'

'Yes I should, Aunt Milly ; I should have found it out from his silence,' returned Polly, with downcast eyes. 'I could not forget his changed looks ; they troubled me more than you know. I puzzled myself over them till I was dizzy. I felt heartbroken when I found it out, but I could not have told Heriot.'

'It would have been better for us both if you had,' he replied, calmly ; but he uttered no further reproach, only there was a keen troubled look in his eyes, as he gazed at the girl's upturned face, as though he suddenly dreaded the loss of something dear to him.

'Heartsease, it would have been better for you and me.'

'Heriot, what do you mean?' she whispered, vehemently ; 'surely you did not misunderstand me ; you could not doubt the sincerity of my words, my love?'

'Neither the one nor the other,' was the quiet reply ; 'do I not know my Polly? could I not trust that guileless integrity as I would my own? You need not fear my misunderstanding you ; I know you but too well.'

'Are you sure that you do?' clinging to him more closely.

'Am I sure that I am alive? No, Polly, I do not doubt you ; when you tell me that you love Roy as though he were your own brother, that you are only sorry for him, and long to comfort him, I believe you. I am as sure that you speak the truth as you know it.'

'And you will trust me?' stroking the coat-sleeve as she spoke.

'Have I not told you so?' reproachfully ; 'am I a tyrant to keep you in durance vile, when your adopted brother lies dangerously ill, and you assure me of your power to minister to him? Miss Lambert, it is by my own wish that Polly goes with you to London ; she thinks Roy will not get well unless he sees her again.'

Mildred started. Polly had kept her thoughts so much to herself lately that she had not understood how much was passing in her mind ; did she really believe that her influence was so great over Roy, that her persuasion would recall him from the brink of the grave? Could Dr. Heriot credit such a supposition? was not the risk a daring one? He could not be so sure of himself and her ; but looking up, as these thoughts passed through her mind, she encountered such a singular glance from Dr. Heriot that her colour involuntarily rose ; it told her he understood her scruples, but that his motives were fixed, inscrutable ; it forbade questioning, and urged compliance with his wishes, and after that there was nothing more to be said.

But in the course of the evening Polly volunteered still further information—

'You know he is going with us himself,' she said, as she followed Mildred into her room to assist in the packing.

Mildred very nearly dropped the armful of things she was carrying, a pile of Roy's shirts she had been mending ; she faced round on Polly with unusual energy—

'Who is going with us ?   Not Dr. Heriot ?'

'Yes ; did he not tell you so ?   I heard him speaking to Mr. Lambert and saying that you were not fit to undertake such a long journey by yourself ; he did not count me, as he knew I should lose my head in the bustle ; very rude of him, was it not ? and then he told Mr. Lambert that he should see Roy and bring him back a report.   Oh, I am so glad he is coming,' speaking more to herself than Mildred ; 'how good, how good he is.'

Mildred did not answer ; but after supper that night, when Dr. Heriot had again joined them, she asked if he had really made up his mind to accompany them.

'You did not tell me of your intention,' she said, a little nettled at his reserve with her.

'No ; I was afraid of your raising objections and raising all sorts of useless arguments ; regret that I should take so much trouble, and so forth,' trying to turn it off with a jest.

'Are you going on Roy's account ?' abruptly.

'Well, not wholly.   Of course his medical man's report will be sufficient ; but all the same it will be a relief to his father's mind.'

'I suppose you are afraid to trust Polly with me then ? but indeed I will take care of her ; there is no need for you to undergo such a fatiguing journey,' went on Mildred, pretending to misunderstand him, but anxious if possible to turn him from his purpose.

But Dr. Heriot's cool amused survey baffled her.

'A man has a right to his own reasons, I suppose ?   Perhaps I think one of my patients is hardly able to look after herself just yet.'

'Oh, Dr. Heriot !' hardly able to believe it though from his own lips ; 'this is so like you—so like your usual thoughtfulness ; but indeed it is not necessary ; Polly will take care of me.'

'I daresay she will,' with a glint of humour in his eyes ; 'but all the same you must put up with my company.'

CHAPTER XXIX

THE COTTAGE AT FROGNAL

'Whose soft voice
Should be the sweetest music to his ear.'—BETHUNE.

THE journey was accomplished with less difficulty and fatigue than Mildred had dared to expect.

Dr. Heriot's attentions were undemonstrative but unceasing. For a greater part of the way Mildred lay back amongst her snug wrappings, talking little, but enjoying to the full the novelty of being the object of so much care and thought. 'He is kind to everybody, and now he has taken all this trouble for me,' she said to herself; 'it is so like him—so like his goodness.'

They were a very quiet party. Dr. Heriot was unusually silent, and Polly sat watching the scenery and flying milestones with half-dreamy absorption. When darkness came on, she nestled down by Mildred's side. From his corner of the carriage, Dr. Heriot secretly peered at the faces before him, under the guttering oil-lamp. Mildred's eyes had closed at last from weariness; her thin cheek was pressed on the dark cushion. In spite of the worn lines, the outline of the face struck him as strangely fair; a fine nature was written there in indelible characters; even in the abandonment of utter weariness, the mouth had not relaxed its firm sweet curve; a chastened will had gradually smoothed the furrows from the brow; it was as smooth and open as a sleeping child, and yet youth had no part there; its tints and roundness had long ago fled.

How had it been that Polly's piquant charms had blinded him? As he looked at her now, half-lovingly, half-sadly, he owned that she could not be otherwise than pretty in his eyes, and yet the illusion was dispelled; but even as the thought passed through his mind, Polly's dark eyes unclosed.

'Are we near London? oh, how tired I am!' she said, with a weary, petulant sigh. 'I cannot sleep like Aunt Milly; and the darkness and the swinging make me giddy.   One can only see great blanks of mist and rushing walls, and red eyes blinking everywhere.'

Dr. Heriot smiled over the girl's discontent.   'You will see the lights of the station in another ten minutes.   Poor little Heartsease.   You are tired and cold and anxious, and we have still a long drive before us.'

'It has not been so long after all,' observed Mildred, cheerfully.   She did not feel cold or particularly tired ; pleasant dreams had come to her ; some thoughtful hand had drawn the fur-lined rug round her as she slept.   As they jolted out of the light station and into the dark Euston Road beyond, she sat thoughtful and silent, reviewing the work that lay before her.

It was late in the evening when the travellers reached the little cottage at Frognal.   Roy had taken a fancy to the place, and had migrated thither the previous summer, in company with a young artist named Dugald.

It was a low, old-fashioned house, somewhat shabby-looking by daylight, but standing back from the road, with a pleasant strip of garden lying round it, and an invisible walk formed of stunted, prickly shrubs, which had led its owner to give it the name of 'The Hollies.'

Roy had fallen in love with the straggling lawn and mulberry trees, and beds of old-fashioned flowers.   He declared the peonies, hollyhocks, and lupins, and small violet-and-yellow pansies, reminded him of Castlesteads Vicarage ; for it was well known that Mr. Delaware clave with fondness to the flowers of his childhood, and was much given to cultivate all manner of herbs, to be used medicinally by the poor of the neighbourhood.

A certain long, low room, with an out-of-the-way window, was declared to have the north light, and to be just the thing for a studio, and was shared conjointly by the young artists, who also took their frugal meals together, and smoked their pipes in a dilapidated arbour overlooking the mulberry-tree.

Mildred knew that Herbert Dugald was at the present moment in Mentone, called thither by the alarming illness of his father, and that his room had been placed at Roy's disposal. The cottage was a large one, and she thought there would be little difficulty in accommodating Polly and herself ; and as Mrs. Madison had no other lodgers, they could count on a tolerable amount of quiet and comfort ; and in spite of the quaintness and homeliness of the arrangements, they found this to be the case.

Dr. Heriot had telegraphed their probable arrival, so they

werc not unexpected. Mrs. Madison, an artist's widow herself, welcomed them with unfeigned delight ; her pleasant, sensible Scotch face broadened with smiles as she came forward to meet them.

'Eh, he's better, poor lad, though I never thought to say it,' she said, answering Mildred's anxious look. 'He would not let me write, as I wished, for fear of alarming his father, he said ; but as soon as the letter was posted, he made me telegraph for his brother ; he arrived last evening.'

'Richard !' ejaculated Mildred, feeling things were worse than even she had expected ; but at that moment Richard appeared, gently closing the door behind him.

'Hush ! he knows you are here ;—you, I mean, Aunt Milly,' perceiving Polly now, with some surprise ; 'but we must be very careful. Last night I thought we should have lost him. Ah, Dr. John, how good of you to bring them ! Come in here ; we expected you, you see, Aunt Milly,' and he led them into poor Roy's sitting-room.

There was a blazing fire in the studio ; the white china tiles reflected a pleasant glow and heat ; the heavy draperies that veiled the cross-lights looked snug and dark ; tea was on the little round table ; a large old-fashioned couch stood, inviting, near. Richard took off Mildred's bonnet and hung it on an empty easel ; Polly's furs found a place on a wonderfully carved oak-chest.

There was all the usual lumber belonging to a studio. Richard, in an interval of leisure, had indeed cleared away a heterogeneous rubbish of pipes, boxing-gloves, and foils, but the upper part of the room was a perfect chaos of portfolios, books, and musical instruments, the little square piano literally groaned under the dusty records ; still there was a wide space of comfort round the tiled fire-place, where all manner of nursery tales leaped into existence under the kindling flame, with just enough confusion to be quaint and picturesque.

Neither Mildred nor Polly found fault with the suit of armour and the carved chair, that was good for everything but to sit upon ; the plaster busts and sham bronzes struck them as beautiful ; the old red velvet curtain had an imposing effect, as well as the shreds and scraps of colour introduced everywhere. Roy's velvet coat and gold-tasselled smoking-cap lay side by side with an old Venetian garment, stiff with embroidery and dirt. Polly touched it caressingly as she passed.

Mildred's eyes had noted all these surroundings while she

23

sat down on the couch where Roy had tossed for so many, many days, and let Richard wait on her; but her anxious looks still mutely questioned him.

'You shall go in and see him directly you are rested and have had some tea,' said Richard, busily occupying himself with the little black kettle. 'He heard your bell, and made a sign to me to come to you; he has been wishing for you all night, poor fellow; but it was his own fault, telegraphing to me instead.'

'You look fagged, Cardie; and no wonder—it must have been dreadful for you alone.'

'Mrs. Madison was with me. I would not have been without her; she is a capital nurse, whatever Rex may say. At one time I got alarmed; the pain in the side increased, and the distressed breathing was painful to hear, the pulse reaching to a great height. I fancied once or twice that he was a little light-headed.'

'Very probably,' returned Dr. Heriot, gravely, placing himself quietly between Mildred and the fire, as she shielded her face from the flame. 'I cannot understand how such a state of things should be. I always thought Roy's a tolerably sound constitution; nothing ever seemed to give him cold.'

'He has never been right since he was laid up with his foot,' replied Richard, with a slight hesitation in his manner. 'He did foolish things, Mrs. Madison told me: took long walks after painting-hours in the fog and rain, and on more than one occasion forgot to change his wet things. She noticed he had a cold and cough, and tried once or twice to dissuade him from venturing out in the damp, but he only laughed at her precautions. I am afraid he has been very reckless,' finished Richard, with a sigh, which Dr. Heriot echoed. Alas! he understood too well the cause of Roy's recklessness.

Polly had been shrinking into a corner all this time, her cheeks paling with every word; but now Dr. Heriot, without apparently noticing her agitation, placed her in a great arm-chair beside the table, and insisted that she should make tea for them all.

'We have reason to be thankful that the inflammation has subsided,' he said, gravely. 'From what Richard tells us he has certainly run a great risk, but I must see him and judge for myself.' And as Richard looked doubtfully at Mildred, he continued, decidedly, 'You need not fear that my presence will harass or excite him, if he be as ill as you describe. I will take the responsibility of the act on myself.'

'It will be a great relief to my mind, I confess,' replied Richard, in a low voice. 'I like Dr. Blenkinsop, but still a second opinion would be a great satisfaction to all of us; and then, you know him so well.'

'Are you sure it will not be a risk?' whispered Polly, as he stood beside her. She slid a hot little hand into his as she spoke, 'Heriot, are you sure it will be wise?'

'Trust me,' was his sole reply; but the look that accompanied it might well reassure her, it was so full of pity for her and Roy; it seemed to say that he so perfectly understood her, that as far as in him lay he would take care of them both.

Poor Polly! she spent a forlorn half-hour when the others had left; strange terrors oppressed her; a gnawing pain, for which she knew no words, fevered and kept her restless.

What if Roy should die? What if the dear companion of her thoughts, and hopes, should suddenly be snatched from them in the first fervour of youth? Would she ever cease to reproach herself that she had so misunderstood him? Would not the consequences of his unhappy recklessness (ah, they little knew how they stabbed her there) lie heavily on her head, however innocent she might own herself?

Perhaps in his boyish way he had wooed her, and she had failed to comprehend his wooing. How many times he had told her that she was dearer to him than Olive and Chriss, that she was the sunshine of his home, that he cared for nothing unless Polly shared it; and she had smiled happily over such evidence of his affection.

Had she ever understood him?

She remembered once that he had brought her some trinket that had pleased his fancy, and insisted on her always wearing it for his sake, and she had remonstrated with him on its costliness.

'You must not spend all your money on me, Rex. It is not right,' she had said to him more seriously than usual; 'you know how Aunt Milly objects to extravagance; and then it will make the others jealous, you know. I am not your sister—not your real sister, I mean.'

'If you were, I should not have bought you this,' he had answered, laughing, and clasping it with boyish force on her arm. 'Polly, what a child you are! when will you be grown up?' and there was an expression in his eyes that she had not understood.

A hundred such remembrances seemed crowding upon her,

Would other girls have been as blind in her place ? Would they not have more rightly interpreted the loving looks and words that of late he had lavished upon her ? Doubtless in his own way he had been wooing her, but no such thought had entered her mind, never till she had heard his bitter words, 'You are Heriot's now, Polly,' had she even vaguely comprehended his meaning.

And now she had gone near to break his heart and her own too, for if Roy should die, she verily believed that hers would be broken by the sheer weight of remorseful pity. Ah, if he would only live, and she might care for him as though he were her own brother, how happy they might be still, for Polly's heart was still loyal to her guardian. But this suspense was not to be borne, and, unable to control her restlessness any longer, Polly moved with cautious steps across the room, and peeped fearfully into the dark passage.

She knew exactly where Roy's room was. He had often described to her the plan of the cottage. Across the passage was a little odd-shaped room, full of cupboards, which was Mrs. Madison's sitting-room. The kitchen was behind, and to the left there was a small garden-room where the young men kept their boots, and all manner of miscellaneous rubbish, in company with Mrs. Madison's geraniums and cases of stuffed birds.

A few winding, crooked stairs led to Roy's room ; Mr. Dugald's was a few steps higher ; beyond, there was a perfect nest of rooms hidden down a dark passage ; there were old musty cupboards everywhere ; a clear scent of dry lavender pervaded the upper regions ; a swinging lamp burnt dimly in a sort of alcove leading to Roy's room. As Polly groped her way cautiously, a short, yapping sound was distinctly audible, and a little black-and-tan terrier came from somewhere.

Polly knelt down and coaxed the creature to approach : she knew it was Sue, Roy's dog, whom he had rescued from drowning ; but the animal only whined and shivered, and went back to her lair, outside her master's door.

'Sue is more faithful to him than I,' thought the girl, with a sigh. The studio seemed more cheerful than the dark, cold passage. Sue's repulse had saddened her still more. When Dr. Heriot returned some time afterwards, he found her curled up in the great arm-chair, with her face buried in her hands, not crying, as he feared, but with pale cheeks and wide distended eyes that he was troubled to see.

'My poor Polly,' smoothing her hair caressingly.

Polly sprang up.

'Oh, Heriot, how long you have been. I have been so frightened; is he—will he live?' the stammering lips not disguising the terrible anxiety.

'There is no doubt of it; but he has been very ill. No, my dear child, you need not fear I shall misunderstand you,' as Polly tried to hide her happy face, every feature quivering with the joyful relief. 'You cannot be too thankful, too glad, for he has had a narrow escape. Aunt Milly will have her hands full for some time.'

'I thought if he died that it would be my fault,' she faltered, 'and then I could not have borne it.'

'Yes—yes—I know,' he returned, soothingly; 'but now this fear is removed, you will be our Heartsease again, and cheer us all up. I cannot bear to see your bright face clouded. You will be yourself again, Polly, will you not?'

'I will try,' she returned, lifting up her face to be kissed like a child. She had never but once offered him the most timid caress, and this maidenly reserve and shyness had been sweet to him; but now he told himself it was different. Alas! he knew her better than she knew herself, and there was sadness in his looks, as he gently bade her good-night. She detained him with some surprise. 'Where are you going, Heriot? you know there is plenty of room; Richard said so.'

'I shall watch in Roy's room to-night,' he replied. 'Richard looks worn out, and Aunt Milly must recruit after her journey. I shall not leave till the middle of the day to-morrow, so we shall have plenty of time to talk. You must rest now.'

'Are you going away to-morrow?' repeated Polly, looking blank. 'I—I had hoped you would stay.'

'My child, that would be impossible; but Richard will remain for a few days longer. I will promise to come back as soon as I can.'

'But—but if you leave me—oh, you must not leave me, Heriot,' returned the girl, with sudden inexplicable emotion; 'what shall I do without you?'

'Have I grown so necessary to you all at once?' he returned, and there was an accent of reproach in his voice. 'Nay, Polly, this is not like your sensible little self; you know I must go back to my patients.'

'Yes, I know; but all the same I cannot bear to let you go;

promise me that you will come back soon—very soon—before
Roy gets much better.'

'I will not leave you longer than I can help,' he replied,
earnestly, distressed at her evident pain at losing him, but
steadfast in his purpose to leave her unfettered by his presence.
'Now, sweet one, you must not detain me any longer, as to-night
I am Roy's nurse,' and with that she let him leave her.

There was a bright fire in the room where Mildred and she
were to sleep. When Mrs. Madison had lighted the tall candle-
sticks on the mantelpiece, and left her to finish her unpacking,
Polly tried to amuse herself by imagining what Olive would
think of it all.

It was a long, low room, with a corner cut off. All the
rooms at The Hollies were low and oddly shaped, but the great
four-post bed, with the moreen hangings, half filled it.

As far as curiosities went, it might have resembled either
the upper half of a pawnbroker's window, or a mediæval corner
in some shop in Wardour Street—such a medley of odds and
ends were never found in one room. A great, black, carved
wardrobe, which Roy was much given to rave about in his
letters home, occupied one side ; two or three spindle-legged
and much dilapidated chairs, dating from Queen Anne's time,
with an oaken chest, filled up all available space ; but wardrobe,
mantelpiece, and even washstand, served as receptacles for the
more ornamental objects.

Peacocks' feathers and an Indian canoe were suspended over
the dim little oblong glass. Underneath, a Japanese idol smiled
fiendishly ; the five senses, and sundry china shepherdesses,
danced round him like wood-nymphs round a satyr ; a teapot,
a hunting-watch, and an emu's egg garnished the toilet-table ;
over which hung a sampler, worked by Mrs. Madison's grandmother ; two little girls in wide sashes, with a long-eared dog,
simpered in wool-work ; a portrait of some Madison deceased,
in a short-waisted tartan satin, and a velvet hat and feathers,
hung over them.

The face attracted Polly in spite of the grotesque dress
and ridiculous headgear—the feathers would have enriched a
hearse ; under the funeral plumes smiled a face still young and
pleasant—it gave one the impression of a fresh healthy nature ;
the ruddy cheeks and buxom arms, with plenty of soft muscle,
would have become a dairymaid.

'I wonder,' mused the girl, with a sort of sorrowful humour,
'who this Clarice was—Mrs. Madison's grandmother or great-

grandmother most likely, for of course she married—that broad, smiling face could not belong to an old maid; she was some squire or farmer's wife most likely, and he bought her that hat in London when they went up to see the Green Parks, and St. James's, and Greenwich Hospital, and Vauxhall,—she had a double chin, and got dreadfully stout, I know, before she was forty. And I wonder,' she continued, with unconscious pathos, 'if this Clarice liked the squire, or farmer, or whatever he may be, as I like Heriot. Or if, when she was young, she had an adopted brother who gave her pain ; she looks as though she never knew what it was to be unhappy or sorry about anything.'

Polly's fanciful musings were broken presently by Mildred's entrance ; she accosted the girl cheerfully, but there was no mistaking her pale, harassed looks.

'It is nearly twelve, you ought not to have waited for me, my dear ; there was so much to do—and then Richard kept me.'

'Where is Richard ?' asked Polly, abruptly.

'He has gone to bed ; he is to have Mr. Dugald's room. Dr. Heriot is sitting up with Roy.'

'Yes, I know. Oh, Aunt Milly, he says there is no doubt of his living ; the inflammation has subsided, and with care he has every hope of him.'

'Thank God ! He will tell his father so ; we none of us knew of his danger till it was past, and so we were saved Richard's terrible suspense ; he has been telling me about it. I never saw him more cut up about anything—it was a sharper attack than we believed.'

'Could he speak to you, Aunt Milly ?'

'Only a word or two, and those hardly audible ; the breathing is still so oppressed that we dare not let him try—but he made me a sign to kiss him, and once he took hold of my hand ; he likes to see us there.'

'He did not mind Dr. Heriot, then ?' and Polly turned to the fire to hide her sudden flush, but Mildred did not notice it.

'He seemed a little agitated, I thought, but Dr. Heriot soon succeeded in calming him ; he managed beautifully. I am sure Roy likes having him, though once or twice he looked pained— at least, I fancied so ; but you have no idea what Dr. Heriot is in a sickroom,' and Mildred paused in some emotion.

She felt it was impossible to describe to Polly the skilful tenderness with which he had tended Roy ; the pleasant cordiality which had evaded awkwardness, the exquisite sympathy that dealt only with present suffering ; no, it could only be stored sacredly in her memory, as a thing never to be forgotten.

The girl drooped her head as Mildred spoke.

' I am finding out more every day what he is, but one will never come to the bottom of his goodness,' she said, humbly. ' Aunt Milly, I feel more and more how unworthy I am of him,' and she rested her head against Mildred and wept.

There was a weary ring in Mildred's voice as she answered her.

' He would not like to hear you speak so despairingly of his choice ; you must make yourself worthy of him, dear Polly.'

' I will try—I do try, till I get heartsick over my failures. I know when he is disappointed, or thinks me silly ; he gives me one of his quiet looks that seem to read one through and through, and then all my courage goes. I do so long to tell him sometimes that he must be satisfied with me just as I am, that I shall never get wiser or better, that I shall always be Polly, and nothing more.'

' Only his precious little Heartsease ! '

' No,' she returned, sighing, ' I fear that has gone too. I feel so sore and unhappy about all this. Does he—does Roy know I am here ? '

' No, no, not yet ; he is hardly strong enough to bear any excitement. It will be very dull for you, my child, for you will not even have my company.'

' Oh, I shall not mind it—not much, I mean,' returned Polly, stoutly.

But, nevertheless, her heart sank at the prospect before her ; she would not see him perhaps for weeks, she would only see Mildred by snatches, she would be debarred from Dr. Heriot's society ; it was a dreary thought for the affectionate girl, but her resolution did not falter, things would look brighter by the morning light as Mildred told her, and she fell asleep, planning occupation for her solitary days.

Dr. Heriot's watch had been a satisfactory one, and he was able to report favourably of the invalid. Roy still suffered greatly from the accelerated and oppressed breathing and distressing cough, but the restlessness and fever had abated, and towards morning he had enjoyed some refreshing sleep, and he was able to leave him more comfortably to Mildred and Richard.

He took Polly for a long walk after breakfast, which greatly brightened the girl's spirits, after which Richard and he had a long talk while pacing the lawn under the mulberry trees ; both of them looked somewhat pale and excited when they came in, and Richard especially seemed deeply moved.

Polly moped somewhat after Dr. Heriot's departure, but Richard was very kind to her, and gave her all his leisure time ; but he was obliged to return to Oxford before many days were over.

Polly had need of all her courage then, but she bore her solitude bravely, and resorted to many ingenious experiments to fill up the hours that hung so heavily on her hands. She wrote daily letters to Olive and Dr. Heriot, kept the studio in dainty order, gathered little inviting bouquets for the sickroom, and helped Mrs. Madison to concoct invalid messes.

By and by, as she grew more skilful, all Roy's food was dressed by her hands. Polly would arrange the tray with fastidious taste, and carry it up herself to the alcove in defiance of all Mildred's warnings.

'I will step so lightly that he cannot possibly recognise my footsteps, and I always wear velvet slippers now,' she said, pleadingly ; and Mildred, not liking to damp the girl's innocent pleasure, withdrew the remonstrance in spite of her better judgment.

Dr. Heriot had strictly prohibited Polly's visits to the sickroom for the present, as he feared the consequences of any great excitement in Roy's weakened condition. Polly would stand listening to the low weak tones, speaking a word or two at intervals, and Mildred's cheerful voice answering him ; now and then the terrible cough seemed to shatter him, and there would be long deathlike silences ; when Polly could bear it no longer, she would put on her hat, coaxing Sue to follow her, and take long walks down the Finchley Road or over Hampstead Heath.

There was a little stile near The Hollies where she loved to linger ; below her lay the fields and the long, dusty road ; all manner of lights gleamed through the twilight, the dark lane lay behind her ; passers-by marvelled at the girl standing there in her soft furs with the dog lying at her feet ; the air was full of warm dampness, a misty moon hung over the leafless trees.

'I wonder what Heriot is doing,' she would say to herself ; 'his letters are beautiful—just what I expected ; they refresh me to read them ; how can he care for mine in return, as he says he does ! Roy liked them, but then——'

Here Polly broke off with a shiver, and Sue growled at a dark figure coming up the field-path.

'Come, Sue, your master will want his tea,' cried the girl, waking up from her vague musings, 'and no one but Polly shall get it for him. Aunt Milly says he always praises Mrs. Madison's cookery;' and she quickened her steps with a little laugh.

Polly was only just in time; before her preparations were completed the bell rang in the sickroom.

'There, it is ready; I will carry it up. Never mind me, Mrs. Madison, it is not very heavy,' cried the girl, bustling and heated, and she took up the tray with her strong young arms, but, in her hurry, the velvet slippers had been forgotten.

Mildred started with dismay at the sound of the little tapping heels. Would Roy recognise it? Yes, a flush had passed over his wan face; he tried to raise himself feebly, but the incautious movement brought on a fit of coughing.

Mildred passed a supporting arm under the pillows, and waited patiently till the paroxysm had passed.

'Dear Rex, you should not have tried to raise yourself—there, lean back, and be quiet a moment till you have recovered,' and she wiped the cold drops of exhaustion from his forehead.

But he still fought with the struggling breath.

'Was it she—was it Polly?' he gasped.

'Yes,' returned Mildred, alarmed at his excessive agitation and unable to withhold the truth; 'but you must not talk just now.'

'Just one word; when did she come?' he whispered, faintly.

'With me; she has been here all this time. It is her cookery, not Mrs. Madison's, that you have been praising so highly. No, you must not see her yet,' answering his wistful glance; 'you are so weak that Dr. Blenkinsop has forbidden it at present; but you will soon be better, dear,' and it was a proof of his weakness that Roy did not contest the point.

But the result of Polly's imprudence was less harmful than she had feared. Roy grew less restless. From that evening he would lie listening for hours to the light footsteps about the house, his eyes would brighten as they paused at his door.

The flowers that Polly now ventured to lay on his tray were always placed within his reach; he would lie and look at them contentedly. Once a scrap of white paper attracted his eyes. How eagerly his thin fingers clutched it. There were only a few words traced on it—'Good-night, my dear brother Roy; I am so glad you are better;' but when Mildred was not looking the paper was pressed to his lips and hidden under his pillow.

'You need not move about so quietly, I think he likes to hear you,' Mildred said to the girl when she had assured herself that no hurtful effect had been the result of Polly's carelessness, and Polly had thanked her with glistening eyes.

How light her heart grew; she burst into little quavers and trills of song as she flitted about Mrs. Madison's bright kitchen. Roy heard her singing one of his favourite airs, and made Mildred open the door.

'She has the sweetest voice I ever heard,' he said with a sigh when she had finished. 'Ask her to do that oftener; it is like David's harp to Saul,' cried the lad, with tears in his eyes; 'it refreshes me.'

Once they could hear her fondling the dog in the entry below.

'Dear old Sue, you are such a darling old dog, and I love you so, though you are too stupid to be taught any tricks,' she said, playfully.

When Sue next found admittance into her master's room Roy called the animal to him with feeble voice. 'Let her be, I like to have her here,' he said, when Mildred would have lifted her from the snow-white counterpane. 'Sue loves her master, and her master loves Sue,' and as the creature thrust its slender nose delightedly into his hand Roy dropped a furtive kiss on the smooth black head.

CHAPTER XXX

'I CANNOT SING THE OLD SONGS'

'Ask me no more : what answer should I give ?
　I love not hollow cheek or faded eye :
　Yet, O my friend, I will not have thee die !
Ask me no more, lest I should bid thee live ;
　　Ask me no more.

'Ask me no more ; thy fate and mine are seal'd :
　I strove against the stream and all in vain :
　Let the great river take me to the main :
No more, dear love, for at a touch I yield ;
　　Ask me no more.'

TENNYSON'S *Princess.*

RICHARD had promised to pay them another visit shortly, and
one Saturday evening while Polly and Sue were racing each
other among the gravel-pits and the furze-bushes of the people's
great common, and the lights twinkled merrily in the Vale of
Health, and the shifting mist shut out the blue distances of
Harrow and Pinner, Mildred was charmed as well as startled by
the sound of his voice in the hall.

'Well, Rex, you are getting on famously, I hear ; thanks to
Aunt Milly's nursing,' was his cheerful greeting.

Roy shook his head despondingly.

'I should do better if I could see something different from
these four walls,' he returned, with a discontented glance round
the room that Mildred had made so bright and pretty ; 'it is
absurd keeping me moped up here, but Aunt Milly is inexorable.'

Mildred smiled over her boy's peevishness.

'He does not know what is good for him,' she returned,
gently ; 'he always gets restless towards evening. Dr. Blenkinsop has been most strict in bidding me keep him from excitement and not to let him talk with any one. This is the first
day he has withdrawn his prohibition, and Roy has been in his
tantrums ever since.'

'He said I might go downstairs if only I were spared the trouble of walking,' grumbled Roy, who sometimes tyrannised over Aunt Milly—and dearly she loved such tyranny.

'He is more like a spoiled child than ever,' she said, laughing.

'If that be all, the difficulty is soon obviated. I can carry him easily,' returned Richard, looking down a little sadly at the long gaunt figure before him, looking strangely shrunken in the brilliant dressing-gown that was Roy's special glory ; ' but I must be careful, you look thin and brittle enough to break.'

'May he, Aunt Milly ? Oh, I do so long to see the old studio again, and the couch is so much more comfortable than this,' his eyes beginning to shine with excitement and his colour varying dangerously.

'Is it quite prudent, Richard ?' she asked, hesitatingly. 'Had we not better wait till to-morrow ?' but Roy's eagerness overbore her scruples.

Polly little knew what surprise was in store for her. Her race over, she walked along soberly, wondering how she should occupy herself that evening. She, too, knew that Dr. Blenkinsop's prohibition had been removed, and had chafed a little restlessly when Mildred had asked her to be patient till the next day. 'Aunt Milly is too careful ; she does not think how I long to see him,' she said, as she walked slowly home. A light streamed across the dark garden when she reached The Hollies ; a radiance of firelight and lamplight. 'I wonder if Richard has come,' thought Polly, as she stole into the little passage and gently opened the door.

Yes, Richard was there ; his square, thick-set figure blocking up the fireplace as he leant in his favourite attitude against the mantelpiece ; and there was Aunt Milly, smiling as though something pleased her. And yes, surely that was Roy's wraith wrapped in the gorgeous dressing-gown and supported by pillows.

The blood rushed to the girl's face as she stood for a moment as though spell-bound, but at the sound of her half-suppressed exclamation he turned his head feebly and looked at her.

'Polly' was all he said, but at his voice she had sprung across the room, and as he stretched out his thin hand to her with an attempt at his old smile, a low sob had risen to her lips, and, utterly overcome by the spectacle of his weakness, she buried her face in his pillows.

Roy's eyes grew moist with sympathy.

'Don't cry, Polly—don't ; I cannot bear it,' he whispered, faintly.

'Don't, Polly ; try to control yourself ; this agitation is very bad for him ;' and Richard raised her gently, for a deadly pallor had overspread Roy's features.

'I could not help it,' she returned, drying her eyes, 'to see him lying there looking so ill. Oh, Rex ! it breaks my heart,' and the two young creatures almost clung together in their agitation ; and, indeed, Roy's hollow blue eyes and thin, bloodless face had a spectral beauty that was absolutely startling.

'I never thought you would mind so much, Polly,' he said, tremulously ; and the poor lad looked at her with an eagerness that he could not disguise. 'I hardly dared to expect that you could waste so much time and thought on me.'

'Oh, Rex, how can you say such unkind things ; not care—— and I have been fretting all this time ?'

'That was hardly kind to Heriot, was it ?' he said, watching her, and a strange vivid light shone in his eyes. If she had not known before she must have felt then how he loved her ; a sudden blush rose to her cheek as he mentioned Dr. Heriot's name ; involuntarily she moved a little away from him, and Roy's head fell back on the pillow with a sigh.

Neither of them seemed much disposed for speech after that. Roy lay back with closed eyes and knitted brows, and Polly sat on a low chair watching the great spluttering log and showers of sparks, while Mildred and Richard talked in undertones.

Now and then Roy opened his eyes and looked at her—at the dainty little figure and sweet, thoughtful face ; the firelight shone on the shielding hand and half-hoop of diamonds He recognised the ribbon she wore ; he had bought it for her, as well as the little garnet ring he had afterwards voted as rubbish. The sight angered him. He would claim it again, he thought. She should wear no gifts of his ; the diamonds had overpowered his garnets, just as his poor little love had been crushed by Dr. Heriot's fascination. Adonis, with his sleepy blue eyes and fair moustache and velvet coat, had failed in the contest with the elder man. What was he, after all, but a beggarly artist ? No wonder she despised his scraps of ribbon, his paltry gewgaws, and odds and ends of rubbish. 'And yet if I had only had my chance,' he groaned within himself, 'if I had wooed her, if I had compelled her to understand my meaning.' And then his anger melted, as she raised her clear, honest eyes, and looked at him.

'Are you in pain, Rex ?—can I move your pillows ?' bending over him rather timidly. Poor children ! a veil of reserve had fallen between them since Dr. Heriot's name had been mentioned, and she no longer spoke to him with the old fearlessness.

'No, I am not in pain. Come here, Polly ; you have not begun to be afraid of me since—since I have been ill ?' rather moodily.

'No, Rex, of course not.' But she faltered a little over her words.

'Sit down beside me for a minute. What was it you called me in your letter, before I was ill ? Something—it looked strangely written by your hand, Polly.'

'Brother—my dear brother Rex,' almost inaudibly.

'Ah, I remember. It would have made me smile, only I was not in the humour for smiling. I did not write back to my sister Polly though. Richard calls you his little sister very often, does he not ? '

'Yes, and I love to hear him say it,' very earnestly.

'Should you love it if I called you that too ?' he returned, with an involuntary curl of the lip. 'Pshaw ! This is idle talk ; but sick people will have their fancies. I have one at present. I want you not to wear that rubbish any more,' touching her hand lightly.

'Oh, Rex—the ring you gave me ?' the tears starting to her eyes.

'I never threw a flower away the gift of one that cared for me,' he replied, with a weak laugh. ' " I never had a dear gazelle but it was sure to marry the market-gardener." Do you remember Dick Swiveller, Polly, and the many laughs we have had over him in the old garden at home ? Oh, those days ! ' checking himself abruptly, for fear the pent-up bitterness might find vent.

'Children, you are talking too much,' interposed Mildred's warning voice, not slow to interpret the rising excitement of Roy's manner.

'One minute more, Aunt Milly,' he returned, hastily ; then, dropping his voice, 'The gift must go back to the giver. I don't want you to wear that ugly little ring any longer, Polly.'

'But I prize it so,' she remonstrated. 'If I give it back to you, you will throw it in the fire, or trample on it.'

'On my honour, no ; but I can't stand seeing you wear such rubbish. I will keep it safely—I will indeed, Polly. Do please me in this.' And Polly, who had never refused him anything, drew off the shabby little ring from her finger and handed it to him with downcast eyes. Why should he ask from her such a sacrifice? Every ribbon and every flower he had given her she had hoarded up as though they were of priceless value, and now he had taken from her her most cherished treasure. And Polly's lip quivered so that she could hardly bid him good-night.

Richard, who saw the girl was fretting, tried by every means in his power to cheer her. He threw on another log, placed her little basket-work chair in the most inviting corner, showed her the different periodicals he had brought from Oxford for Roy's amusement, and gave her lively sketches of undergraduate life. Polly showed her interest very languidly; she was mourning the loss of her ring, and thinking how much her long-desired interview with Roy had disappointed her. Would he never be the same to her again? Would this sad misunderstanding always come between them?

How was it she was clinging to him with the old fondness till he had mentioned Dr. Heriot's name, and then their hands had fallen asunder simultaneously?

'Poor Roy, and poor, poor Polly!' she thought, with a self-pity as new as it was painful.

'You are not listening to me, Polly. You are tired, my dear,' Richard said at last, in his kind fraternal way.

'No, I am very rude. But I cannot help thinking of Rex; how ill he is, and how terribly wasted he looks!'

'I knew it would be a shock to you. I am thankful that my father's gout prevents him from travelling; he would fret dreadfully over Roy's altered appearance. But we must be thankful that he is as well as he is. I could not help thinking all that night—the night before you and Aunt Milly came—what I should do if we lost him.'

'Don't, Richard. I cannot bear to think of it.'

'It ought to make us so grateful,' he murmured. 'First Olive and then Roy brought back from the very brink of the grave. It is too much goodness; it makes one ashamed of one's discontent.' And he sighed involuntarily.

'But it is so sad to see him so helpless. You said he was as light as a child when you lifted him, Richard, and if he speaks a word or two he coughs. I am afraid Dr. Blenkinsop is right in saying he must go to Hastings for the winter.'

'We shall hear what Dr. John says when he comes up next. You expect him soon, Polly?' But Richard, as he asked the question, avoided meeting her eyes. He feared lest this long absence had excited suspicions which he might find difficult to answer.

But Polly's innocence was proof against any such surmises. 'I cannot think what keeps him,' she returned, disconsolately. 'Olive says he is not very busy, and that his new assistant relieves him of half his work.'

'And he gives you no reason?' touching the log to elicit another shower of sparks.

'No, he only says that he cannot come at present, and answers all my reproaches with jests—you know his way. I don't think he half knows how I want him. Richard, I do wish you would do something for me. Write to him to-morrow, and ask him to come; tell him I want him very badly, that I never wanted him half so much before.'

'Dear Polly, you cannot need him so much as that,' trying to turn off her earnestness with a laugh.

'You do not know—you none of you know—how much I want him,' with a strange vehemence in her tone. 'When he is near me I feel safe—almost happy. Ah!' cried the girl, with a sad wistfulness coming into her eyes, 'when I see him I do not need to remind myself of his goodness and love—I can feel it then. Oh, Richard dear! tell him he must come—that I am afraid to be without him any longer.'

Afraid of what? Did she know? Did Richard know?

'She seems very restless without you,' he wrote that Sunday afternoon. 'I fancy Roy's manner frets her. He is fitful in his moods—a little irritable even to her, and yet unable to bear her out of his sight. He would be brought down into the studio again to-day, though Aunt Milly begged him to spare himself. Polly has been trying all the afternoon to amuse him, but he will not be amused. She has just gone off to the piano, in the hope of singing him to sleep. Rex tyrannises over us all dreadfully.'

Dr. Heriot sighed over Richard's letter, but he made no attempt to facilitate his preparations for going to London; he was reading things by a clear light now; this failure of his was a sore subject to him; in spite of the prospect that was dawning slowly before him, he could not bear to think of the tangled web he had so unthinkingly woven—it would need careful unravelling, he thought; and so curious is the mingled warp and woof in the mind of a man like John Heriot, that while his heart yearned for Mildred with the strong passion of his nature, he felt for his young betrothed a tenderness for which there was no name, and the thought of freeing himself and her was painful in the extreme.

24

He longed to see her again and judge for himself, but he must be patient for a while, he knew ; so though Polly pleaded for his presence almost passionately, he still put her off on some pretext or other,—nor did he come till a strong letter of remonstrance from Mildred reached him, reproaching him for his apparent neglect, and begging him to recall the girl, as their present position was not good for her or Roy.

Mildred was constrained to take this step, urged by her pity for Polly's evident unhappiness.

That some struggle was passing in the girl's mind was now evident. Was she becoming shaken in her loyalty to Dr. Heriot ? Mildred grew alarmed ; she saw that while Roy's invalid fancies were obeyed with the old Polly-like docility and sweetness, that she shrank at times from him as though she were afraid to trust herself with him ; sometimes at a look or word she would rise from his side and go to the piano and sing softly to herself some airs that Dr. Heriot loved.

'You never sing my old favourites now, Polly,' Roy said once, rather fretfully, ' but only these old things over and over again !'

'I like to sing these best,' she said, hastily ; and then, as he still pressed the point, she pushed the music from her, and hurried out of the room.

But Mildred had another cause for uneasiness which she kept to herself. There was no denying that Roy was very slow in regaining strength. Dr. Blenkinsop shook his head, and looked more dissatisfied every day.

'I don't know what to make of him,' he owned to Mildred, one day, as they stood in the porch together.

It was a mild December afternoon ; a red wintry sun hung over the little garden ; a faint crescent moon rose behind the trees ; underneath the window a few chrysanthemums shed a soft blur of violet and dull crimson ; a slight wind stirred the hair from Mildred's temples, showing a streak of gray ; but worn and thin as she looked, Dr. Blenkinsop thought he had never seen a face that pleased him better.

'What a Sister of Mercy she would make,' he often thought ; 'if I know anything of human nature, this woman has known a great sorrow ; she has been taught patience in a rough school ; no matter how that boy tries her, she has always a cheerful answer ready for him.'

Dr. Blenkinsop was in rather a bad humour this afternoon, a fact that was often patent enough to his patients, whom he was given to treat on such occasions with some *brusquerie;* but with all his oddities and contradictions, they dearly loved him.

'I can't make him out at all,' he repeated, irritably, feeling his iron-gray whiskers, a trick of his when anything discomposed him ; 'there is no fault to find with his constitution ; he has had a sharp bout of illness, brought on, as far as I can make out, by his own imprudence, and just as he has turned the corner nicely, and seems doing us all credit, he declines to make any further progress !'

'But he is really better, Dr. Blenkinsop ; he coughs far less, and his sleep is less broken ; he has no appetite, certainly, but——' Mildred stopped. She thought herself that Roy had been losing ground lately.

Dr. Blenkinsop fairly growled,—he had little sharp white teeth that showed almost savagely when he was in one of his surly moods.

'These lymphatic natures are the worst to combat, they succumb so readily to weakness and depression ; he certainly seems more languid to-day, and there are feverish indications. He has got nothing on his mind, eh ?'—turning round so abruptly that Mildred was put out of countenance.

She hesitated.

'Humph !' was his next observation, 'I thought as much. Of course it is none of my concern, but when I see my patient losing ground without any visible cause, one begins to ask questions. That young lady who assists in the nursing—do you think her presence advisable, eh ?'—with another sharp glance at Mildred.

'She is his adopted sister—she is engaged,' stammered Mildred, not willing to betray the lad's secret. 'They are very fond of each other.'

'A questionable sort of fondness—rather too feverish on one side, I should say. Send her back to the north, and get that nice fellow Richard in her place ; that is my advice.'

And acting on this very broad hint, Mildred soon afterwards wrote to Dr. Heriot to recall Polly.

When Dr. Blenkinsop had left her, she did not at once return to the studio ; through the closed door she could hear Polly striking soft chords on the piano. Roy had seemed drowsy, and she trusted the girl's murmuring voice would lull him to sleep.

It was not often that she left them together ; but this afternoon her longing for a little fresh air tempted her to undertake some errands that were needed for the invalid ; and leaving a message with Mrs. Madison that she would be back to the early tea, she set off in the direction of the old town.

It was getting rapidly dusk as the little gate swung behind Mildred. When Roy roused from his fitful slumber, he could hardly see Polly as she sat at the shabby, square piano.

The girl was touching the notes with listless fingers, her head drooping over the keys ; but she suddenly started when she saw the tall gaunt figure beside her in the gorgeous dressing-gown.

'Oh, Rex, this is very wrong,' taking hold of one of his hot hands, and trying to lead him back to the sofa, 'when you know you cannot stand, and that the least movement makes you cough. Put your hand on my shoulder ; lean on me. Oh, I wish I were as strong and tall as Aunt Milly.'

'I like you best as you are,' he replied, but he did not refuse the support she offered him. 'I could not see you over there, only the outline of your dress. You never wear your pretty dresses now, Polly ?' reproachfully. 'I suppose because Heriot is not here.'

'Indeed—indeed—you must not stand any longer, Rex. You must lie down at once, or I shall tell Aunt Milly,' she returned, evasively.

He was always making these sort of speeches to her, and to-night she felt as though she could not bear them ; but Roy was not to be silenced. Never once had she mentioned Dr. Heriot's name to him, and with an odd tenacity he wanted to make her say it. What did she call him ? had she learnt to say his Christian name ? would she pronounce it with a blush, faltering over it as girls do ? or would she speak it glibly as with long usage ?

'I suppose you keep them all for him,' he continued, with a suspicion of bitterness in his tone ; 'that little nun-like gray dress is good enough for Aunt Milly and me. Too much colour would be bad for weak eyes, eh, Polly ?'

'I dress for him, of course,' trying to defend herself with dignity ; but the next moment she waxed humble again. 'I— I am sorry you do not like the dress, Rex,' she faltered. 'I should like to please you both if I could,' and her eyes filled with tears.

'I think you might sing sometimes to please me when he is not here,' he returned, obstinately ; 'just one song, Polly ; my favourite one, with that sad, sweet refrain.'

'Oh, not that one,' she repeated, beginning to tremble;
'choose something else, Rex—not that.'

'No, I will have that or none,' he replied, irritably. What
had become of Roy's sweet temper? 'You seem determined not
to please me in anything,' and he moved away.

Polly watched his tottering steps a moment, and then she
sprang after him.

'Oh, Rex, do not be so cross with me; do not refuse my
help,' she said, winding her arm round him, and compelling him
to lean on her. 'There, you have done yourself mischief,' as he
paused, overcome by a paroxysm of coughing. 'How can you—
how can you be so unkind to me, Rex?'

He did not answer; perhaps, absorbed in his own trouble,
he hardly knew how he tried her; but as he sank back feebly
on the cushions, he whispered—

'You will sing it, Polly, will you not?'

'Yes, yes; anything, if you will only not be angry with me,'
returned the poor girl, as she hurried away.

The air was a mournful one, just suited to the words :—

> 'Ask me no more: what answer should I give?
> I love not hollow cheek or faded eye:
> Yet, O my friend, I will not have thee die!
> Ask me no more, lest I should bid thee live;
>   Ask me no more.'

'Polly, come here! come to me, Polly!' for, overcome by a
sudden revulsion of feeling, Polly had broken down, and hidden
her face in her hands; and now a stifled sob reached Roy's ear.

'Polly, I dare not move, and I only want to ask you to
forgive me,' in a remorseful voice; and the girl obeyed him
reluctantly.

'What makes you so cruel to me?' she panted, looking at
him with sad eyes, that seemed to pierce his selfishness. 'It is
not my fault if you are so unhappy—if you will not get well.'

'Ask me no more; thy fate and mine are sealed.' The
plaintive rhythm still haunted her. Was she, after all, so much
to blame? Was she not suffering too? Why should he lay
this terrible burden on her? It was selfish of him to die and
leave her to her misery.

Roy fairly quailed beneath the girl's indignation and passionate sorrow.

'Have I been so hard to you, Polly?' he said, humbly.
'Are men ever hard to the women they love? There, the
murder is out. You must leave me, Polly; you must go back

to Heriot. I am too weak to hide the truth any longer. You must not stay and listen to me,' pushing her away with weak force.

It was his turn to be agitated now.

'Leave me!' he repeated, 'it is not loyal to Heriot to listen to a fool's maundering, which he has not the wit or the strength to hide. I should only frighten you with my vehemence, and do no good. Aunt Milly will be here directly. Leave me, I say.'

But she only clung to him, and called him brother. Alas! how could she leave him!

By and by he grew calmer.

'Forgive me, Polly; I am not myself; I ought not to have made you sing that song.'

'No, Rex,' in a voice scarcely audible.

'When you go back to Heriot you must tell him all. Ask him not to be hard on me. I never meant to injure him. The man you love is sacred in my eyes. It was only for a little while I hated him.'

'I will not tell him that.'

'Listen to me, dear! I ask his pardon, and yours too, for having betrayed myself. I have acted like a weak fool to-night. You were wiser than I, Polly.'

'There is nothing to forgive,' she returned, softly. 'Heriot will not be angry with you; he knows you are ill, and I—I will try to forget it. But you must get well, Rex; you will promise to get well for my sake.'

'Shall you grieve very much if I do not? Heriot would comfort you, if I did not, Polly.'

She made an involuntary movement towards him, and then checked herself.

'Cruel! cruel!' she said, in a voice that sounded dead and cold, and her arms fell to her side.

He melted at that.

'There, I have hurt you again. What a selfish wretch I am. I shall make a poor thing of life; but I will promise not to die if I can help it. You shall not call me cruel again, Polly.'

Then she smiled, and stretched out her hand to him.

'I would not requite your goodness so badly as that. You could always do as you liked with me in the old days, Polly—turn me round your little finger. If you tell me to get well I suppose I must try; but the best part of me is gone.'

She could not answer him. Every word went through her tender heart like a stab. What avail were her love and pity?

Never should she be able to comfort him again ; never would her sweet sisterly ministrations suffice for him. She must not linger by his side ; her eyes were open now.

'Good-bye, Roy,' she faltered. She hardly knew what she meant by that farewell. Was she going to leave him ? Was she only saying good-bye to the past, to girlhood, to all manner of fond foolish dreams ? She rose with dry eyes when she had uttered that little speech, while he lay watching her.

'Do you mean to leave me ?' he asked, sorrowfully, but not disputing her decision.

'Perhaps—yes—what does it matter ?' she answered, moving drearily away.

What did it matter indeed ? Her fate and his were sealed. Between them stretched a gulf, long as life, impassable as death ; and even her innocent love might not span it.

'I shall not go to him, and he will not return to me,' she said, paraphrasing the words of the royal mourner to harmonise with her measure of pain. ' Never while I live shall I have my brother Roy again.'

Poor little aching, childish heart, dealing for the first time with life's mysteries, comprehending now the relative distinction between love and gratitude, and standing with reluctant feet on the edge of an unalterable resolve. What sorrow in after years ever equalled this blank ?

When Mildred returned she found a very desolate scene awaiting her ; the fire had burnt low, a waste of dull red embers filled the grate, the moon shone through the one uncurtained window ; a mass of drapery stirred at her entrance, a yawning figure stretched itself under the oriental quilt.

'Roy, were you asleep ? The fire is nearly out. Where is Polly ?'

'I do not know. She left the room just now,' he returned, with a sleepy inflection ; but to Mildred's delicate perception it did not ring true. She said nothing, however, raked the embers together, threw on some wood, and lighted the lamps.

Had he really slept ? There was no need to ask the question ; his burning hand, the feverish light of his eyes, the compressed lips, the baffled and tortured lines of the brow, told her another story ; she leant over him, pressing them out with soft fingers.

'Rex, my poor boy !'

'Aunt Milly, she has bidden me good-bye,' broke out the lad suddenly ; 'she knows, and she is going back to Heriot ; and I —I am the most miserable wretch alive.'

CHAPTER XXXI

'She looked again, as one that half afraid
  Would fain be certain of a doubtful thing ;
  Or one beseeching, "Do not me upbraid !"
  And then she trembled like the fluttering
  Of timid little birds, and silent stood.'

                              JEAN INGELOW.

DR. HERIOT started for London the day after he had received
Mildred's letter ; as he intended, his appearance took them all
by surprise.

Mildred was the first to detect the well-known footsteps on
the gravelled path ; but she held her peace. Dr. Heriot's keen
glance, as he stood on the threshold, had time to scan the features
of the little fireside group before a word of greeting had crossed
his lips ; he noticed Polly's listless attitude as she sat apart in
the dark window-seat, and the moody restlessness of Roy's face as
he lay furtively watching her. Even Mildred's heightened colour,
as she bent industriously over her work, was not lost on him.

'Polly !' he said, crossing the room, and marvelling at her
unusual abstraction.

At the sound of the kind, well-known voice, the girl started
violently ; but as he stooped over her and kissed her, she turned
very white, and involuntarily shrank from him, but the next
moment she clung to him almost excitedly.

'Oh, Heriot, why did you not come before ? You knew I
wanted you—you must have known how I wanted you.'

'Yes, dear, I knew all about it,' he replied, quietly, putting
away the little cold hands that detained him, and turning to the
others.

A few kind inquiries after the invalid were met at first
very irritably, but even Roy's jealousy could not be proof
against such gentleness, and he forgot his wretchedness for a

time while listening to home messages, and all the budget of
Kirkby Stephen gossip which Dr. Heriot retailed over the cosy
meal that Mildred provided for the traveller.

For once Dr. Heriot proved himself an inexhaustible talker;
there was no limit to his stock of anecdotes. Roy's sulkiness
vanished; he grew interested, almost amused.

'You remember old Mrs. Parkinson and her ginger-cakes,'
Polly,' he said, with a weak ghost of a laugh; but then he
checked himself with a frown. How was it one could not hate
this fellow, who had defrauded him of Polly? he thought,
clenching his hand impatiently. Why was he to succumb to a
charm of manner that had worked him such woe?

Dr. Heriot's fine instinct perceived the lad's transition of mood.

'Yes, Polly has a faithful memory for an old friend,' he
said, answering for the girl, who sat near him with a strip of
embroidery from which she had not once raised her eyes. As
he looked at her, his face worked with some strong emotion;
his eyes softened, and then grew sad.

'Polly is faith itself,' speaking with peculiar intonation, and
laying his hand on the small shining head. 'You see I have a
new name for you to-night, Heartsease.'

'I think I will go to bed, Aunt Milly,' broke out poor Roy,
growing suddenly pale and haggard. 'I—I am tired, and it is
later to-night, I think.'

Dr. Heriot made no effort to combat his resolution. He
stood aside while Mildred offered her arm to the invalid. He
saw Polly hurriedly slip her hand in Roy's, who wrung it hard
with a sort of laugh.

'It is good-bye for good and all, I suppose to-night?' he
said. 'Heriot means to take you away, of course?'

But Polly did not answer; she only hid her red quivering hand
under her work, as though she feared Dr. Heriot would see it.

But the next moment the work was thrown lightly to the
ground, and Dr. Heriot's fingers were gently stroking the ill-
used hand.

'Poor little Polly; does he often treat you to such a rough
hand-shake?' he said, with a half-amused, tender smile.

'No, never,' she stammered; but then, as though gaining
courage from the kind face looking down at her, 'Oh, Heriot, I
am so glad he is gone. I—I want to speak to you.'

'Is that why you have been so silent?' drawing her nearer
to him as she stood beside him on the rug. 'Little Heartsease,
did you like my new name?'

'Don't, Heriot; I—I do not understand you; I have not been faithful at least.'

'Not in your sense of the word, perhaps, dear Polly, but in mine. What if your faithfulness should save us both from a great mistake?'

'I—I do not understand you,' she said again, looking at him with sad, bewildered eyes. 'You shall talk to me presently; but now I want to speak to you. Heriot, I was wrong to come here—wrong and self-willed. Aunt Milly was right; I have done no good. Oh, it has all been so miserable—a mistake from beginning to end; and then I thought you would never come.'

'Dear Polly, it could not be helped. Neither can I stay now.'

'You will not go and leave me again?' she said, faltering and becoming very pale. 'Heriot, you must take me with you; promise me that you will take me with you.'

'I cannot, my dear child. Indeed—indeed—I cannot.'

'Then I will go alone,' she said, throwing back her head proudly, but trembling as she spoke. 'I will not stay here without you—not for a day—not for a single day.'

'But Roy wants you. You cannot leave him until he is better,' he said, watching her; but though she coloured perceptibly, she stood her ground.

'I was wrong to come,' she returned, piteously. 'I cannot help it if Rex wants me. I know he does. You are saying this to punish me, and because I have failed in my duty.'

'Hush, my child; I at least have not reproached you.'

'No, you never reproach me; you are kindness itself. Heriot,' laying down her face on his arm, and now he knew she was weeping, 'I never knew until lately how badly I have treated you. You ought not to have chosen a child like me. I have tried your patience, and given you no return for your goodness; but I have resolved that all this shall be altered.'

'Is it in your power, Polly?' speaking now more gravely.

'It must—it shall be. Listen to me, dear. You asked me once to make no unnecessary delay, but to be your wife at once. Heriot, I am ready now.'

'No, my child, no.'

'Ah, but I am,' speaking with difficulty through her sobs. 'I never cared for you so much. I never wanted you so much. I am so full of gratitude—I long to make you so happy—to make somebody happy. You must take me away from here, where Roy will not make me miserable any more, and then I shall try to forget him—his unhappiness, I mean—and to think only of you.'

'Poor child,' speaking more to himself than to her ; 'and this is to what I have brought her.'

'You must not be angry with Roy,' continued the young girl, when her agitation had a little subsided. 'He could not help my seeing what he felt ; and then he told me to go back to you. He has tried his hardest, I know he has ; every night I prayed that you might come and take me away, and every morning I dreaded lest I should be disappointed. Heriot, it was cruel—cruel to leave me so long.'

'And you will come back with me now ? '

'Oh yes,' with a little sighing breath.

'And I am to make you my wife ? I am not to wait for your nineteenth birthday ? '

'No. Oh, Heriot, how self-willed and selfish I was.'

'Neither one nor the other. Listen to me, dear Polly. Nay, you are trembling so that you can hardly stand ; sit beside me on this couch ; it is my turn to talk now. I have a little story to tell you.'

'A story, Heriot ? '

'Yes ; shall we call it "The Guardian's Mistake" ? I am not much of a hand in story-telling, but I hope I shall make my meaning clear. What, afraid, my child ? nay, there is no sad ending to this story of mine ; it runs merrily to the tune of wedding bells.'

'I do not want to hear it,' she said, shrinking nervously ; but he, half-laughingly and half-seriously, persisted :—

'Once upon a time, shall we say that, Polly ? Little Hearts-ease, how pale you are growing. Once upon a time, a great many years ago, a man committed a great mistake that darkened his after life.

'He married a woman whom he loved, but whose heart he had not won. Not that he knew that. Heaven forbid that any one calling himself a man should do so base a thing as that ; but his wishes and his affection blinded him, and the result was misery for many a year to come.'

'But he grew comforted in time,' interrupted Polly, softly.

'Yes, time, and friendship, and other blessings, bestowed by the good God, healed the bitterness of the wound, but it still bled inwardly. He was a weary-hearted man, with a secret disgust of life, and full of sad loathing for the empty home that sheltered his loneliness, all the more,' as Polly pressed closer to him, 'that he was one who had ever craved for wife and children.

'It was at this time, just as memory was growing faint, that a certain young girl, the daughter of an old college friend of his, was left to his care. Think, Polly, how sacred a charge to this desolate man; a young orphan, alone in the world, and dependent on his care.'

'Heriot, I beseech you to stop; you are breaking my heart.'

'Nay, dearest, there is nothing sad in my story; there are only wheels within wheels, a complication heightening the interest of the plot. Well, was it a wonder that this man, this nameless hero of ours, a species of Don Quixote in his way, should weave a certain sweet fancy into his dreary life, that he should conceive the idea of protecting and loving this young girl in the best way he could by making her his wife, thinking that he would make himself and her happy, but always thinking most of her?'

'Oh, Heriot, no more; have pity on me.'

'What, stop in the middle of my story, and before my second hero makes his appearance? For shame, Heartsease; but this man, for all his wise plans and benevolent schemes, proved himself miserably blind.

'He knew that this girl had an adopted brother whom she loved dearly. Nay, do not hide your face, Polly; no angel's love could have been purer than this girl's for this friend of hers; but alas, what no one had foreseen had already happened; unknown to her guardian, and to herself, this young man had always loved, and desired to win her for his wife.'

'She never knew it,' in a stifled voice.

'No, she never knew it, any more than she knew her own heart. Why do you start, Heartsease? Ah, she was so sure of that, so certain of her love for her affianced husband, that when she knew her friend was ill, she pleaded to be allowed to nurse him. Yes, though she had found out then the reason of his unhappiness.'

'She hoped to do good,' clasping her hands before her face.

'True, she hoped to do good; she fancied, not knowing the world and her own heart, that she could win him back to his old place, and so keep them both, her guardian and her friend. And her guardian, heart-sick at the mistake he had made, and with a new and secret sorrow preying upon him, deliberately suffered her to be exposed to the ordeal that her own generous imprudence had planned.'

'Heriot, one moment; you have a secret sorrow?'

'Not an incurable one, my sweet; you shall know it by and by; if I do not mistake, it will yield us a harvest of joy; but I am drawing near the end of the story.'

'Yes, you have quite finished—there is nothing more to say; nothing, Heriot.'

'You shall tell me the rest, then,' he returned, gravely. Was she true to her guardian, this girl; true in every fibre and feeling? or did her faithful heart really cleave to the companion of her youth, calling her love by the right name, and acknowledging it without fear?

'Polly, this is no time for a half-truth; which shall it be? Is your heart really mine, or does it belong to Roy?'

She would have hidden her face in her hands, but he would not suffer it.

'Child, you must answer me; there must be no shadow between us,' he said, holding her before him. There was a touch of sternness in his voice; but as she raised her eyes appealingly to his, she read there nothing but pity and full understanding; for one moment she stood irresolute, with palpitating heart and white quivering lips, and then she threw herself into his arms.

'Oh, Heriot, what shall I do? What shall I do? I love you both, but I love Roy best.'

When Mildred re-entered the room, an hour later, somewhat weary of her banishment, she found the two still talking together. Polly was sitting in her little low chair, her cheek resting on her hand. Dr. Heriot seemed speaking earnestly, but as the door opened, he broke off hastily, and the girl started to her feet.

'I must go now,' she whispered; 'don't tell Aunt Milly to-night. Oh, Heriot, I am so happy; this seems like some wonderful dream; I don't half believe it.'

'We must guard each other's confidence. Remember, I have trusted you, Polly,' was his answer, in a low tone. 'Good-night, my dearest child; sleep well, and say a prayer for me.'

'I do—I do pray for you always,' she affirmed, looking at him with her soul in her eyes; but as he merely pressed her hand kindly, she suddenly raised herself on tiptoe and kissed his cheek. 'Dear—dear Heriot, I shall pray for you all my life long.'

'Are you going, Polly?' asked Mildred, in surprise.

'Yes, I am tired. I cannot talk any more to-night,' returned the girl, hastily.

Her face was pale, as though she had been weeping ; but her eyes smiled radiantly under the wet lashes.

Mildred turned to the fire, somewhat dissatisfied.

'I hope things are right between you and Polly,' she said, anxiously, when she and Dr. Heriot were left alone.

'They have never been more so,' he replied, with a mischievous smile ; 'for the first time we thoroughly understand ourselves and each other ; she is a dear good child, and deserves to be happy.' But as Mildred, somewhat bewildered at the ambiguous tone, would have questioned him still further, he gently but firmly changed the subject.

It was a strange evening to Mildred ; outside, the rain lashed the panes. Dr. Heriot had drawn his arm-chair nearer to the glowing fire ; he looked spent and weary—some conflicting feelings seemed to fetter him with sadness. Mildred, sitting at her little work-table, scarcely dared to break the silence. Her own voice sounded strange to her. Once when she looked up she saw his eyes were fixed upon her, but he withdrew them again, and relapsed into his old thoughtfulness.

By and by he began to talk, and then she laid down her work to listen. Some strange chord of the past seemed stirred in the man's heart to-night. All at once he mentioned his mother ; her name was Mildred, he said, looking into the embers as he spoke ; and a little sister whom they had lost in her childhood had been called Milly too. For their sakes the name had always been dear to him. She was a good woman, he said, but her one fault in his eyes had been that she had never loved Margaret ; a certain bitter scene between them had banished his widowed mother from his house. Margaret had not understood her, and they were better apart ; but it had been a matter of grief to him.

And then he began to talk of his wife—at first hesitatingly —and then, as Mildred's silent sympathy seemed to open the long-closed valves, the repressed sorrow of years began to find vent. Well might Mildred marvel at the secret strength that had sustained the generous heart in its long struggle, at 'the charity that suffered so long.' What could there have been about this woman, that even degradation and shame could not weaken his faithful love, that even in his misery he should still pity and cleave to her.

As though answering her thought, Dr. Heriot suddenly placed a miniature in her hand.

'That was taken when I first saw her,' he said, softly ; 'but it does not do her justice; and then, one cannot reproduce that magnificent voice. I have never heard a voice like it.'

Mildred bent over it for a moment without speaking; it was the face of a girl taken in the first flush of her youth; but there was nothing youthful in the face, which was full of a grave matured beauty.

The dark melancholy eyes seemed to rivet Mildred's; a wild sorrow lurked in their inscrutable depths; the brow spoke intellect and power; the mouth had a passionate, irresolute curve. As she looked at it she felt that it was a face that might well haunt a man to his sorrow.

'It is beautiful—beautiful—but it oppresses me,' she said, laying it down with a sigh. 'I cannot fancy it ever looking happy.'

'No,' he returned, with a stifled voice. 'Her one trouble embittered her life. I never remember seeing her look really happy till I placed our boy in her arms; he taught her to smile first, and then he died, and our happiness died with him.'

'You must try to forget all this now,' she said, alluding to his approaching marriage. 'It is not well to dwell upon so mournful a past.'

'You are right; I think I shall bury it from this night,' he returned, with a singular smile. 'I feel as though you have done me good, Mildred—Miss Lambert—but now I am selfishly keeping you up, after all your nursing too. Good-night.'

He held her hand for a moment in both his; his eyes questioned the pale worn face, anxiously, tenderly.

'When are you going to get stronger? You do me no credit,' he said, sadly.

And his look and tone haunted her, in spite of her efforts. He had called her Mildred too.

'How strange that he should have told me all this about his wife. I am glad he treats me as a friend,' she thought. 'A little while ago I could not have spoken to him as I have to-night, but his manner puts me at my ease. How can I help loving one of the noblest of God's creatures?'

'Can you trust Roy to me this morning, Miss Lambert?' asked Dr. Heriot, as they were sitting together after breakfast.

Polly, who was arranging a jar of chrysanthemums, dropped a handful of flowers on the floor, and stooped to pick them up.

'I think Roy will like his old nurse best,' she returned, doubtfully.

But Dr. Heriot looked obstinate.

'A new regime and a new prescription might be beneficial,' he replied, with a suspicion of a smile. 'Roy and I must have some conversation together, and there's no time like the present,' and with a grave, mischievous bow, he quietly quitted the room.

'Aunt Milly, I must go and match those wools, and get the books for Roy,' began Polly, hurriedly, as they were left alone. 'The rain does not matter a bit, and the air is quite soft and warm.'

Mildred shook her head.

'You had better wait an hour or two till it clears up,' she said, looking dubiously at the wet garden paths and soaking rain. 'I am going to my own room to write letters. I have one from Olive that I must answer. If you will wait until the afternoon, Dr. Heriot will go with you.'

But Polly was not to be dissuaded; she had nothing to do, she was restless, and wanted a walk; and Roy must have his third volume when he came down.

It was not often that Polly chose to be wilful, and this time she had her way. Now and then Mildred paused in the midst of her correspondence to wonder what had detained the girl so long. Once or twice she rose and went to the window to see if she could catch a glimpse of the dark blue cloak and black hat, but hours passed and she did not return.

By and by Dr. Heriot's quick eyes saw a swift shadow cross the studio window; and, as Polly stole noiselessly into the dark passage, she found herself captured.

'Naughty child, where have you been?' he said, removing her wet cloak, and judging for himself that she had sustained no further damage.

Polly's cheeks, rosy with exercise, paled a little, and she pleaded piteously to be set free.

'Just for a moment, Heriot. Please let me go for a moment. I will come presently.'

'You are not to be trusted,' he replied, not leaving hold of her. 'Do you think this excitement is good for Roy—that in his state he can bear it. He has been dressed and waiting for you for hours. You must think of him, Polly, not of yourself.' And Polly resisted no longer.

She followed Dr. Heriot, with downcast eyes, into the studio. Roy was not on his couch; he was standing on the rug, in his velvet coat; one thin hand grasped the mantelpiece nervously; the other was stretched out to Polly.

'You must not let him excite himself,' was Dr. Heriot's warning, as he left them together.

Poor Polly, she stood irresolute, not daring to advance, or look up, and wishing that the ground would swallow her.

'Polly—dear Polly—will you not come to me?' and Roy walked feebly to meet her. Before she could move or answer, his arms were round her. 'My Polly—my own now,' he cried, rapturously pressing her to him with weak force; 'Heriot has given you to me.'

Polly looked up at her young lover shyly. Roy's face was flushed, his eyes were shining with happiness, a half-proud, half-humble expression lingered round his mouth; the arm that supported her trembled with weakness.

'Oh, Rex, how wrong of me to let you stand,' she said, waking up from her bewilderment; 'you must lie down, and I will take my old place beside you.'

'Yes, he has given you the right to nurse me now,' whispered Roy, as she arranged the cushions under his head. 'I am more than your adopted brother now.' And Polly's happy blush was her only answer.

'You will never refuse to sing to me again?' he said presently, when their agitation had a little subsided.

'No, and you will let me have my old ring,' she returned, softly. 'Oh, Rex, I cried half the night, when you would not let me wear it. I never cared so much for my beautiful diamonds.'

A misty smile crossed Roy's face.

'No, Polly, I never mean to part with it again. Look here,' —and he showed her the garnets suspended to his watch-chain— 'we will exchange rings in the old German fashion, dear. I will keep the garnets, and I will buy you the pearl hoop you admired so much; you must remember, you have chosen only a poor artist.'

'Oh, Rex, how I shall glory in your pictures!' cried the girl, breathlessly. 'I have always loved them for your sake, but now it will be so different. They will be dearer than ever to me.'

'I never could have worked without you, Polly,' returned the young man, humbly. 'I tried, but it was a miserable failure; it was your childish praise that first made me seriously think of being an artist; and when you failed me, all the spirit seemed to die out of me, just as the sunshine fades out of a landscape, leaving nothing but a gray mist. Oh, Polly, even you scarcely know how wretched you made me.'

'Do not let us talk of it,' she whispered, pressing closer to him ; 'let us only try to deserve our happiness.'

'That is what he said,' replied Roy, in a low voice. 'He told me that we were very young to have such a responsibility laid upon us, and that we must help each other. Oh, what a good man he is,' he continued, with some emotion, 'and to think that at one time I almost hated him.'

'You could not help it,' she answered, shyly. To her there was no flaw in her young lover ; his impatience and jealousy, his hot and cold fits that had so sorely tried her, his singular outbursts of temper, had only been natural under the circumstances ; she would have forgiven him harder usage than that ; but Roy judged himself more truly.

'No, dear, you must not excuse me,' was the truthful answer. 'I bore my trouble badly, and made every one round me wretched ; and now all these coals of fire are heaped upon me. If he had been my brother, he could not have borne with me more gently. Oh,' cried the lad, earnestly, 'it is something to see into the depths of a good man's heart. I think I saw more than he meant me to do, but time will prove. One thing is certain, that he never loved you as I do, Polly.'

'No ; it was all a strange mistake,' she returned, blushing and smiling ; 'but hush ! here comes Aunt Milly.'

'Am I interrupting you ?' asked Mildred, a little surprised at Polly's anxious start.

She had moved a little away from Roy ; but now he stretched out his hand to detain her.

'No, don't go, Aunt Milly,' and a gleam of mischief shot from his blue eyes. 'Polly has only been telling me a new version of the old song—"It is well to be off with the old love before you are on with the new." After all, Polly has found out that she likes me best.'

'Children, what do you mean ?' returned Mildred, somewhat sternly.

Polly and even Roy were awed by the change in her manner ; a sort of spasm crossed her face, and then the features became almost rigid.

'Aunt Milly, don't be angry with us,' faltered Polly ; and her breast heaved a little. Did this dearest and gentlest creature, who had stood her in the stead of mother, think she was wrong ? 'Listen to me, dear ; I would have married Heriot, but he would not let me ; he showed me what was the truth—that my heart was more Roy's than his, and then he brought us together; it is all his doing, not Roy's.'

'Yes, it was all my doing,' repeated Dr. Heriot, who had followed Mildred in unperceived. 'Did I not tell you last night that Polly and I never understood each other so well;' and he put his arm round the girl with almost fatherly fondness, as he led her to Mildred. 'You must blame me, and not this poor child, for all that has happened.'

But the colour did not return to Mildred's face; she seemed utterly bewildered. Dr. Heriot wore his inscrutable expression; he looked grave, but not otherwise unhappy.

'I suppose it is all for the best,' she said, somewhat unsteadily. 'I had hoped that Polly would have been a comfort to you, but it seems you—you are never to have that.'

'It will come to me in time,' he returned, with a strange smile; 'at least, I hope so.'

'Come here, Aunt Milly,' interrupted Roy; and as Mildred stooped over her boy he looked up in her face with the old Rex-like smile.

'Dr. Heriot says I should never have lived if it had not been for you, Aunt Milly. You have given me back my life, and he has given me Polly, and,' cried the lad, and now his lips quivered, 'God bless you both.'

CHAPTER XXXII

A TALK IN FAIRLIGHT GLEN

O finer far ! What work so high as mine,
  Interpreter betwixt the world and man,
Nature's ungathered pearls to set and shrine,
  The mystery she wraps her in to scan ;
Her unsyllabic voices to combine,
  And serve her with such love as poets can ;
With mortal words, her chant of praise to bind,
Then die, and leave the poem to mankind !'
  JEAN INGELOW.

DR. HERIOT did not stay long in London ; as soon as his mission was accomplished he set his face resolutely homewards.

Christmas was fast approaching, and it was necessary to make arrangements for Roy's removal to Hastings, and after much discussion and a plentiful interchange of letters between the cottage and the vicarage, it was finally settled that Mildred and Richard should remain with the invalid until Olive and Mr. Lambert should take their place.

Mr. Lambert was craving for a sight of his boy, but he could not feel justified in devolving his duties on his curate until after the Epiphany, nor would Olive consent to leave him ; so Mildred bravely stifled her homesick longings, and kept watch over the young lovers, smiling to herself over Roy's boyishness and Polly's fruitless efforts after staidness.

From the low bow-window jutting on to the beach, in the quiet corner where Richard had found them lodgings, she would often sit following the young pair with softly amused eyes as they stood hand in hand with the waves lapping to their feet ; at the first streak of sunset they would come slowly up the shore. Roy still tall and gaunt, but with a faint tinge of returning health in his face ; Polly fresh and blooming as a rose, and trying hard to stay her dancing feet to fit his feeble paces.

'What have you done with Richard, children ?' Mildred would ask as usual.

'Dick ? ah, he decamped long ago, with the trite and novel observation that "two are company and three none." We saw him last in the midst of an admiring crowd of fishermen. Dick always knows when he is not wanted, eh, Polly ?'

'I am afraid we treat him very badly,' returned Polly, blushing. Roy threw himself down on the couch with a burst of laughter. His mirth had hardly died away when his brother entered.

'You have got back, Roy—that's right. I was just going in search of you. There is a treacherous wind this evening. You were standing still ever so long after I left you.'

'That comes of you leaving us, you see,' replied Roy, slyly. 'It took us just half an hour to discover the reason of your abrupt departure.' Richard's eyes twinkled with dry humour.

'One must confess to being bored at times. Keppel was far more entertaining company than you and Polly. When I am in despair for a little sensible conversation I must come to Aunt Milly.'

Aunt Milly was the universal sypathiser, as usual. Richard's patience would have been sorely put to proof, but for those grave-toned talks in the wintry twilights, with which the gray sea and sky seemed so strangely to harmonise. In spite of his unselfishness, the sight of his brother's happiness could not fail to elicit at times a disturbing sense of contrast. Who could tell what years rolled between him and the fruition of his hope ?

'In patience and confidence must be your strength, Richard,' Mildred once said, as they stood looking over the dim waste of waters, gray everywhere, save where the white lips touched the shore ; behind them was the dark Castle Hill ; windy flickers of light came from the esplanade ; far out to sea a little star trembled and wavered like the timid pioneer of unknown light ; a haze of uncertainty bordered earth and sky ; the soft wash of the insidious waves was tuneful and soothing as a lullaby. The neutral tints, the colourless conditions, neither light nor dark, even the faint wrapping mist that came like a cloud from the sea, harmonised with Mildred's feelings as she quoted the text softly. An irrepressible shiver ran through the young man's frame. Waiting, did he not know what was before him—years of uncertainty, of alternate hopes and fears.

'Yes, I know,' he replied, with an accent of impatience in his voice. 'You are right, of course ; one can only wait. As for patience, it is hardly an attribute of youth ; one learns it by degrees, but all the same, uncertainty and these low gray skies oppress one. Sea-fog does not enhance cheerfulness, Aunt Milly. Let us go in.'

Richard's moods of discontent were brief and rare. He was battling bravely with his disappointment. He had always been grave and staid beyond his years, but now faintly-drawn lines were plainly legible in the smooth forehead, and a steady concentrated light in the brown eyes bore witness to abiding and careful thought. At times his brother's unreasoning boyishness seemed almost to provoke him; want of earnestness was always a heinous sin in his judgment. Roy more than once winced under some unpalatable home-truth which Richard uttered in all good faith and with the best intentions in the world.

'Dick is the finest fellow breathing, but if he would only leave off sermonising until he is ordained,' broke out Roy, with a groan, when he and Mildred were alone; but Mildred was too well aware of their affection for each other to be made uneasy by any petulance on Roy's part. He would rail at his brother's advice, and then most likely digest and follow it; but she gave Richard a little hint once.

'Leave them alone; their happiness is still so new to them,' pleaded the soft-hearted woman. 'You can't expect Rex to look beyond the present yet, now Polly is with him—when he is stronger he will settle down to work.' And though Richard shook his head a little incredulously, he wisely held his peace.

But he would have bristled over with horror and amazement if he had known half of the extravagant daydreams and plans which Roy was for ever pouring into Aunt Milly's ear. Roy, who was as impetuous in his love-making as in other things, could not be made to understand that there was any necessity for waiting; that Polly should be due north while he was due south was clearly an absurdity to his mind, and he would argue the point until Mildred was fairly bewildered.

'Rex, my dear boy, do be reasonable,' she pleaded once; 'what would Richard say if he heard you? You must give up this daft scheme of yours; it is contrary to all common sense. Why, you have never earned fifty pounds by your painting yet.'

'Excuse me, Aunt Milly, but it is so difficult to make women see anything in a business point of view,' replied the invalid, somewhat loftily. 'Polly understands me, of course, but she is an exception to the general rule. I defy any one—even you, Aunt Milly—to beat Polly in common sense.'

'He means, of course, if his picture be sold,' returned Polly, sturdily, who feared nothing in the world but separation from

Roy. She was ready to eat bread and cheese cheerfully all her life, she thought. Both young people were in the hazy atmosphere of all youthful lovers, when a crust appears a picturesque and highly desirable food, and rent and taxes and all such contemptible items are delusions of the evil one, fostered in the brain of careful parents.

'Of course Rex only means if his picture sells at a good price. He will then be sure of work from the dealers.'

'There, I told you so,' repeated Roy, triumphantly, 'as though Polly did not know the ups and downs of an artist's life better than you, or even me, Aunt Milly. It is not as though we expected champagne and silk dresses, and all sorts of unnecessary luxuries.'

'Or velvet coats,' quietly added Mildred, and Roy looked a little crestfallen.

'Aunt Milly, how can you be so unkind, so disagreeable ?' cried Polly, with a little burst of indignation. 'I shall wear print dresses or cheap stuff. There was such a pretty one at sevenpence-halfpenny the yard, at Oliver's ; but of course Rex must have his velvet coat, it looks so well on an artist, and suits him so. I would not have Roy look shabby and out of elbows, like Dad Fabian, for the world.'

'You would look very pretty in a print dress, Polly, I don't doubt,' returned Roy, a little sadly ; 'but Aunt Milly is right, and it would not match my velvet coat. We must be consistent, as Richard says.'

'Cashmere is not so very dear, and it wears splendidly,' returned Polly, in the tone of one elated by a new discovery, 'and with a fresh ribbon now and then I shall look as well as I do now. You don't suppose I mean to be a slattern if we are ever so poor. But you shall have your velvet coat, if I have to pawn the watch Dr. Heriot gave me.' And Roy's answer was not meant for Mildred to hear.

Mildred felt as though she were turning the page of some story-book as she listened to their talk. How charmingly unreal it all sounded ; how splendidly coloured with youth and happiness. After all, they were not ambitious. The rooms at the little cottage at Frognal bounded all their desires. The studio with the cross light and faded drapery, the worn couch and little square piano, was to be their living room. Polly was to work and sing, while Roy painted. Dull ! how could they be dull when they had each other ? Polly would go to market, and prepare dainty little dishes out of nothing ; she would train flowers round the porch and under the windows, and keep chickens in the empty coop by the arbour. With plenty of eggs and fresh vegetables, their expenses would be trifling. Dugald had taught Rex to make potato soup and herring salad. Why, he and Dugald had spent he did not know how little a week, and of course his father would help him. Polly was penniless and an orphan, and it was his duty to work for her as well as for himself.

Mildred wondered what Dr. Heriot would think of the young people's proposition. As Polly was under age he had a voice in the matter, but she held her peace on this subject. After all, it was only a daydream—a very pleasant picture. She was conscious of a vague feeling of regret that things could not be as they planned. Roy was boyish and impulsive, but Polly might be trusted, she thought. Every now and then there was a little spirit of shrewdness and humour in the girl's words that bubbled to the surface.

'Roy will always be wanting to buy new books and new music, but I shall punish him by liking the old ones best,' she said, with a laugh. 'And no more boxes of cigarettes, or bottles of lavender-water ; and oh, Rex, you know your extravagance in gloves.'

'I shall only wear them on Sundays,' replied Roy, virtuously, 'and I shall smoke pipes—an honest meerschaum after all is more enjoyable, and in the evenings we will take long walks towards Hendon or Barnet. Polly is a famous walker, and on fine Sundays we will go to Westminister Abbey, or St. Paul's, or some of the grand old city churches ; one can hear fine music at the Foundling, and at St. Andrew's, Wells Street. Polly does not know half the delights of living in London.'

'She will know it in good time,' returned Mildred, softly. She would not take upon herself to damp their expectations ; in a little while they would learn to be reasonable. In the meanwhile she indulged in the petting that was with her as a second nature.

But it was a relief when her brother and Olive arrived ; she had no idea how much she had missed them, until she caught sight of her brother's bowed figure and gray head, and Olive's grave, sallow face beside it.

It was an exciting evening. Mr. Lambert was overjoyed at seeing his son again, though much shocked at the still visible evidences of past suffering. Polly was warmly welcomed with a fatherly blessing, and he was so much occupied with the young pair, that Mildred was at liberty to devote herself to Olive.

She followed her into her room ostensibly to assist in unpacking, but they soon fell into one of their old talks.

'Dear Olive,' she said, kissing her, 'you don't know how good it is to see you again. I never believed I could miss you so much.'

'You have not missed me half so much as I have you,' returned Olive, blushing with surprised pleasure. I always feel so lost without you, Aunt Milly. When I wanted you very badly—more than usual, I mean—I used to go into your room and think over all the comforting talks we have had together, and then try and fancy what you would tell me to do in such and such cases.'

'Dear child, that was drawing from a very shallow well. I remember I told you to fold up all your perplexities in your letters, and I would try and unravel them for you ; but I see you were afraid of troubling me.'

'That was one reason, certainly ; but I had another as well. I could not forget what you told me once about the bracing effects of self-decision in most circumstances, and how you once laughingly compared me to Mr. Ready-to-Halt, and advised me to throw away my crutches.'

'In other words, solving your own difficulties ; certainly I meant what I said. Grown-up persons are so fond of thinking for young people, instead of training them to think for themselves, and then they are surprised that the brain struggles so slowly from the swaddling-bands that they themselves have wrapped round them.'

'It was easier than I thought,' returned Olive, slowly ; 'at first I tormented myself in my old way, and was tempted to renew my arguments about conflicting duties, till I remembered there must be a right and wrong in everything, or at least by comparison a better way.'

'Why, you have grown quite a philosopher, Olive ; I shall be proud of my pupil,' and Mildred looked affectionately at her niece. What a noble-looking woman Olive would be, she thought. True, the face was colourless, and the features far too strongly marked for beauty ; but the mild, dark eyes and shadowy hair redeemed it from plainness, and the speaking, yet subdued, intelligence that lingered behind the hesitating speech produced a pleasing impression ; yet Mildred, who knew the face so well, fancied a shadow of past or present sadness tinged the even gravity that was its prevailing expression.

Olive's thoughts unfolded slowly like flowers—they always needed the sunshine of sympathy ; a keen breath, the light mockery of incredulity, killed them on the spot. Now of her own accord she began to speak of the young lovers.

'How happy dear Roy looks ; Polly is just suited for him. Do you know, Aunt Milly, I had a sort of presentiment of this, it always seemed to me that she and Dr. Heriot were making believe to like each other.'

'I think Dr. Heriot was tolerably in earnest, Olive.'

'Of course he meant to be ; but I always thought there was too much benevolence for the right thing ; and as for Polly— oh, it was easy to see that she only tried to be in love—it quite tired her out, the trying I mean, and made her cross and pettish with us sometimes.'

'I never gave you credit for so much observation.'

'I daresay not,' returned Olive, simply, 'only one wakes up sometimes to find things are turning out all wrong. Do you know they puzzled me to-night—Rex and Polly, I mean. I expected to find them so different, and they are just the same.'

'How do you mean ? I should think it would be difficult to find two happier creatures anywhere ; they behave as most young people do under the circumstances, are never willingly out of each other's sight, and talk plenty of nonsense.'

'That is just what I cannot make out ; it seems such a solemn and beautiful thing to me, that I cannot understand treating it in any other way. Why, they were making believe to quarrel just now, and Polly was actually pouting.'

Mildred with difficulty refrained from a smile.

'They do that just for the pleasure of making it up again. If you could see them this moment you would find them like a pair of cooing doves ; it will be "Poor Rex !" and "Dear Rex !" all the evening. There is no doubt of his affection for her, Olive ; it nearly cost his life.'

'That is only an additional reason for treating it seriously. If any one cared for me in that way,' went on Olive, blushing slightly over her words—'not that I could believe such a thing possible,' interrupting herself.

'Why not, you very wise woman ?' asked her aunt, amused by this voluntary confession. Never before had Olive touched on this threadbare and oft-maligned subject of love.

'Aunt Milly, as though you could speak of such a thing as probable !' returned Olive, with a slight rebuke in her voice. 'Putting aside plainness, and want of attraction, and that sort of thing, do you think any man would find me a help-meet ?'

'He must be the right sort of man, of course,'—'a direct opposite to you in everything,' she was about to add, but checked herself.

'But if the right sort is not to be found, Aunt Milly ?' with a touch of quaintness that at times tinged her gravity with humour. 'Didn't you know "Much-Afraid" was an old maid ?'

'We must get rid of all these old names, Olive ; they will not fit now.'

'All the same, of course I know these things are not possible with me. Imagine being a wet blanket to a man all his life ! But what I was going to say was, that if any one cared for me as Rex does for Polly, I should think it the next solemn thing to death—quite as beautiful and not so terrible. Fancy,' warming with the visionary subject, 'just fancy, Aunt Milly, being burdened with the whole happiness and well-being of another—never to think alone again !'

'Dear Olive, you cannot expect all lovers to indulge in these metaphysics ; commonplace minds remain commonplace—the Divinities are silent within them.'

'I think this is why I dislike the subject introduced into general conversation,' replied Olive, pondering heavily over her words ; 'people are for ever dragging it in. So-and-so is to be married next week, and then a long description of the bride's trousseau and the bridesmaids' dresses ; the idea is as paganish as the undertaker's plume of feathers and mutes at a funeral.'

'I agree with you there ; people almost always treat the subject coarsely, or in a matter-of-fact way. A wedding-show is a very pretty thing to outsiders, but, like you, Olive, I have often marvelled at the absence of all solemnity.'

'I suppose it jars upon me more than on others because I dislike talking on what interests me most. I think sacred things should be treated sacredly. But how I am wandering on, and there was so much I wanted to tell you !'

'Never mind, I will hear it all to-morrow. I must not let you fatigue yourself after such a journey. Now I will finish the unpacking while you sit and rest yourself.'

Olive was too docile and too really weary to resist. She sat silently watching Mildred's brisk movements, till the puzzled look in the dark eyes passed into drowsiness.

'The Eternal voice,' she murmured, as she laid her head on the pillow, and Mildred bade her good-night, 'it seems to lull one into rest, though a tired child would sleep without rocking listening to it ;' and so the slow, majestic washing of the waves bore her into dreamland.

Mildred did not find an opportunity of resuming the conversation until the following afternoon, when Richard had planned a walk to Fairlight Glen, in which Polly reluctantly joined ; but Mildred, who knew Roy and his father had much to say to each other, had insisted on not leaving her behind.

She was punished by having a very silent companion all the way, as Richard had carried off Olive ; but by and by Polly's conscience pricked her for ill-humour and selfishness, and when they reached the Glen, her hand stole into Mildred's muff with a penitent squeeze, and her spirits rising with the exhilaration of the long walk, she darted off in pursuit of Olive and brought her back, while she offered herself in her place to Richard.

'You have monopolised her all the way, and I know she is dying for a talk with Aunt Milly ; you must put up with me instead,' said the little lady, defiantly.

Mildred and Olive meanwhile seated themselves on one of the benches overlooking the Glen ; the spot was sheltered, and the air mild and soft for January ; there were patches of cloudy blue to be seen through the leafless trees, which looked like a procession of gray, hoary skeletons in the hazy light.

'Woods have a beauty of their own in winter,' observed Mildred, as she noticed Olive's satisfied glance round her. Visible beauty always rested her, Olive often said.

'Its attraction is the attraction of death,' returned her companion, thoughtfully. 'Look at these old giants waiting for their resurrection, to be "clothed upon," that is just the expression, Aunt Milly.'

'With their dead hopes at their feet ; you are teaching me to be poetical, Olive. Don't you love the feeling of those crisp yellow leaves crunching softly under one's feet ? I think a leaf-race in a high wind is one of the most delicious things in nature.'

'Ask Cardie what he thinks of that.'

'Cardie would say we are talking highflown nonsense. I can never make him share my admiration for that soft gray light one sees in winter. I remember we were walking over Hillsbottom one lovely February afternoon ; the shades of the landscape were utterly indescribable, half light, and yet so softly blended, the gray tone of the buildings was absolutely warm—that intense grayness—and all I could get him to say was, that Kirkby Stephen was a very ugly town.'

'Roy is more sympathetic about colours ; Cardie likes strong contrasts, decided sunsets, better than the glimmering of moon-light nights ; he can be enthusiastic enough over some things, I have heard him talk beautifully to Ethel.'

'By the bye, you have told me nothing of her. Is she still away ?'

'Yes, but they are expecting her back this week or next. It seems such a pity Kirkleatham is so often empty. Mrs. Dela-ware says it is quite a loss to the place.'

'It is certainly very unsatisfactory ; but now about your work, Olive ; how does it progress ?'

Olive hesitated. 'I will talk to you about that presently ; there is something else that may interest you to hear. Do you know Mr. Marsden is thinking of leaving us ?'

Mildred uttered an expression of surprise and disappoint-ment. 'Oh, I hope it is not true !' she reiterated, in a regret-ful tone.

'You say that because you do not know,' returned Olive, with her wonted soft seriousness ; 'he has told me everything. Only think, Aunt Milly, he asked my advice, and really seemed to think I could help him to a decision. Fancy my helping any one to decide a difficult question,' with a smile that seemed to cover deeper feelings.

'Why not ? it only means that he has recognised your earnestness and thorough honesty of purpose. There is nothing like honesty to inspire confidence, Olive. I am sure you would help him to a very wise decision.'

'I think he had already decided for himself before he came to me,' returned the girl, meditatively ; 'one can always tell when a man has made up his mind to do a thing. You see he has always felt an inclination for missionary work, and this really seems a direct call.'

'You forget you have not enlightened me on the subject,' hinted Mildred, gently.

'How stupid of me, but I will begin from the beginning. Mr. Marsden told me one morning that he had had letters from his uncle, Archdeacon Champneys, one of the most energetic workers in the Bloemfontein Mission. You have read all about it, Aunt Milly, in the quarterly papers. Don't you recollect how interested we all were about it ?'

'Yes, I remember. Richard seemed quite enthusiastic about it.'

'Well, the Archdeacon wrote that they were in pressing need

of clergy. Look, I have the letter with me. Mr. Marsden said I might show it to you. He has marked the passage that has so impressed him.'

'I am at my wits' end to know how to induce clergy to come out. Do you know of any priest who would come to our help? If you do, for God's sake use your influence to induce him to come.

'We want help for the Diamond Fields; Theological College Brotherhood at Middleport; Itinerating work; Settled Parochial work at Philippolis and elsewhere.

'We want men with strong hearts and active, healthy frames—men with the true missionary spirit—with fixedness of will and undaunted purpose, ready to battle against obstacles, and to endure peacefully the "many petty, prosaic, commonplace, and harassing trials" that beset a new work. If you know such an one, bid him Godspeed, and help him to find his way to us. I promise you we shall see his face as the "face of an angel."'

'A pressing appeal,' sighed Mildred; she experienced a vague regret she hardly understood.

'Mr. Marsden felt it to be such. Oh, I wish you had heard him talk. He said, as a boy he had always felt a drawing to this sort of work; that with his health and strength and superabundant energies he was fitter for the rough life of the colonies than for the secondary and supplementary life of an ordinary English curate. "Give me plenty of space and I could do the work of three men," and as he said it he stretched out his arms. You know his way, Aunt Milly, that makes one feel how big and powerful he is.'

'He may be right, but how we shall miss him,' returned Mildred, who had a thorough respect and liking for big, clumsy Hugh.

'Not more than he will miss us, he says. He will have it we have done him so much good; but there is one thing he feels, that Richard will soon be able to take his place. In any case he will not go until the autumn, not then if his mother be still alive.'

'Is he still so hopeless about her condition?'

'How can he be otherwise, Aunt Milly, when the doctor tells him it is only a question of time. Did you hear that he has resigned all share in the little legacy that has lately come to them? He says it will make them so comfortable that they will not need to keep their little school any longer; is it not good of him?' went on Olive, warming into enthusiasm.

'I think he has done the right thing, just what I should have expected him to do. And so you have strengthened him in his decision, Olive?'

'How could I help it?' she returned, simply. 'Can there be any life so noble, so self-denying? I told him once that I envied him, and he looked so pleased, and then the tears came into his eyes, and he seemed as though he wanted to say something, but checked himself. Do you know,' drooping her head and speaking in a deprecating tone, 'that hearing him talk like this made me feel dissatisfied with myself and—and my work?'

'Poor little nightingale! you would rather be a working bee,' observed Mildred, smiling. This was the meaning then of the shadowed brightness she had noticed last night.

'No, but somehow I could not help feeling his work was more real. The very self-sacrifice it involves sets it apart in a higher place, and then the direct blessing, Aunt Milly,' with an effort. 'What good does my poetry do to any one but myself?'

'St. Paul speaks of the diversities of gifts,' returned Mildred, soothingly. She saw that daily contact with perfect health and intense vitality and usefulness had deadened the timid and imaginative forces that worked beneath the surface in the girl's mind; a warped sense of duty or fear from the legions of her old enemies had beset her pleasure with sick loathing—for some reason or other Olive's creative work had lain idle.

'Do you recollect the talent laid up in the napkin, Olive?'

'But if it should not be a talent, rather a temptation,' whispered the girl, under her breath. 'No, I cannot believe it is that, after all, Aunt Milly, only I have got weary about it. Have I not chosen the work I liked best—the easiest, the most attractive?'

'Do you think a repulsive service would please our beneficent Creator best?'

Olive was silent. Were the old shadows creeping round her again?

'Your work just now seems very small by the side of Mr. Marsden's. His vocation and consecration to a new work in some way, and by comparison, overshadows yours; perhaps, unconsciously, his words have left an unfavourable impression; you know how sensitive you are, Olive.'

'He never imagined that they could influence me.'

'No, he is the kindest-hearted being in the world, and would not willingly damp any one, but all the same he might unconsciously vaunt his work before your eyes; but before we decide on the reality or unreality of your talent, I want to recall something to your mind that this same good Bishop of Bloem-fontein said in his paper on women's work. I remember how greatly I was struck with it. His exact words, as far as I can remember them, were—" that work—missionary work—demands fair health, unshattered nerves, and that general equableness of spirits which so largely depends upon the physical state. A morbid mind or conscience" (mark that, Olive) "is unfit for the work." '

'But, Aunt Milly,' blushing slightly, 'I never meant that I thought myself fit for mission work. You do not think that I would ever leave papa ?'

'No, but a certain largeness of view may help us to exorcise the uneasy demon that is harassing you. You may not have Bloemfontein in your thoughts, but you may be trying to work yourself into the belief that God may be better pleased if you immolate your favourite and peculiar talent and devote yourself to some repugnant ministry of good works where you would probably do more harm than good.'

'I confess some such thoughts as these have been troubling me.'

'I read them in your eyes. So genius is given for no purpose but to be thrown aside like a useless toy. What a de-gradation of a sacred thing ! How could you be such a traitor to your own order, Olive ? This vacillating mood of yours makes me ashamed.'

'I wish you would scold me out of it, Aunt Milly ; you are doing me good already. Any kind of doubt makes me positively unhappy, and I really did begin to believe that I had mistaken my vocation.'

'Olive will always be Olive as long as she lives,' returned Mildred, in a grieved tone ; but as the girl shrank back some-what pained, she hastened to say—'I think doubtfulness—the inward tremblings of the fibres of hope and fear—are your peculiar temptation. How would you repel any evil suggestion that came to you, Olive—any unmistakably bad thought, I mean ?'

'I would try and shut my mind to it, not look at it,' replied Olive, warmly.

'Repel it with disdain. Well, I think I should deal with your doubts in the same way ; if they will not yield after a good stand-up fight, entrench yourself in your citadel and shut the door on them. Every work of God is good, is it not ?'

'The Bible says so.'

'Then yours must be good, since He has given you the power and delight in putting together beautiful thoughts for the pleasure and, I trust, the benefit of His creatures, and especially as you have dedicated it to His service. What if after all you are right?' she continued, presently, 'and if it be not the very highest work, can you not be among "the little ones" that do His will? Will not this present duty and care for your father and the small daily charities that lie on your threshold suffice until a more direct call be given to you? It may come—I do not say it will not, Olive; but I am sure that the present work is your duty now.'

'You have lifted a burden off me,' returned Olive, gratefully, and there was something in the clear shining of her eyes that echoed the truth of her words; 'it was not that I loved my work less, but that I tried not to love it. I like what you said, Aunt Milly, about being one of "His little ones."'

CHAPTER XXXIII

'Some one came and rested there beside me,
  Speaking words I never thought would bless
Such a loveless life. I longed to hide me,
  Feasting lonely on my happiness.
    But the voice I heard
    Pleaded for a word,
Till I gave my whispered answer, "Yes !"'

'Yes, that little word, so calmly spoken,
  Changed all life for me—my own—my own !
All the cold gray spell I saw unbroken,
  All the twilight days seemed past and gone.
    And how warm and bright,
    In the ruddy light,
Pleasant June days of the future shone !'

HELEN MARION BURNSIDE.

It was with mingled feelings of pleasure and regret that Mildred saw the gray walls of the vicarage again. It was harder than she imagined to say good-bye to Roy, knowing that she would not see him again until the summer, but her position as nurse had long become a sinecure ; the place was now rightfully usurped by his young betrothed. The sea-breezes had already proved so beneficial to his health, that it was judged that he might safely be permitted at the end of another month to resume work in the old studio, by which time idleness and love-making might be expected to lose their novelty, and Mildred hoped that Polly would settle down happily with the others, when her good sense should be convinced that an early marriage would be prejudicial to Roy's interest.

It was very strange to find Chriss the only welcoming home presence—Chriss in office was a highly ludicrous idea. She had taken advantage of her three days' housekeeping to introduce striking reforms in the *ménage*, against which Nan had stormed and threatened in vain ; the housemaid looked harassed, and the parlour-maid on the eve of giving warning ; the little figure with the touzled curls and holland apron, and rattling keys, depending from the steel chatelaine, looked oddly picturesque in the house porch as the travellers drove up. When Mr. Marsden came in after even-song to inquire after their well-being, and Richard insisted on his remaining to tea, Chriss looked mightily haughty and put on her eyeglasses, and presided at the head of the table in a majestic way that tried her aunt's gravity. 'The big young man,' as she still phrased Hugh Marsden, was never likely to be a favourite with Chriss ; but she thawed presently under Mildred's genial influence ; no one knew so well how to bend the prickles, and draw out the wholesome sweetness that lay behind. By the end of the third cup, Chriss was able to remember perfectly that Mr. Marsden did not take sugar, and could pass his cup without a glacial stare or a tendency to imitate the swelling and ruffling out of a dignified robin.

At the end of the evening, Mildred, who had by that time grown a little weary and silent, heard the footstep in the lobby for which she had been unconsciously listening for the last two hours.

'Here comes Dr. John at last,' observed Richard, in strange echo of her thought. 'I expected he would have met us at the station, but I suppose he was called away as usual.'

Dr. Heriot gave no clue to his absence. He shook hands very quietly with Mildred, and hoped that she was not tired, and then turned to Richard for news of the invalid ; and when that topic was exhausted, seemed disposed to relapse into a brown study, from which Mildred curiously did not care to wake him.

She was quite content to see him sitting there in his old place, playing absently with her paper-knife, and dropping a word here and there, but oftener listening to the young men's conversation. Hugh was eagerly discussing the Bloemfontein question. He and Richard had been warmly debating the subject for the last hour. Richard was sympathetic, but he had a notion his friend was throwing himself away.

'We don't want to lose such men as you out of England, Marsden, that's the fact. I have always looked upon you as just the sort of hard worker for a parish at the East end of London. Look at our city Arabs ; it strikes me there is room for missionary work there—not but what South Africa has a demand on us too.'

'When a man feels he has a call, there is nothing more to be said,' replied Hugh, striking himself energetically on his broad chest, and speaking in his most powerful bass. 'One has something to give up, of course ; all colonial careers involve a degree of hardship and self-sacrifice ; not that I agree with your sister in thinking either the one or the other point to the right decision. Because we may consider it our duty to undertake a pilgrimage, it does not follow we need have pebbles or peas in our shoes, or that the stoniest road is the most direct.'

'Of course not.'

'We don't need these by-laws to guide us ; there's plenty of hardship everywhere, and I hope no amount would frighten me from any work I undertake conscientiously. It may be pleasanter to remain in England. I am rather of your opinion myself ; but, all the same, when a man feels he has a call——'

'I should be the last to dissuade him from it ; I only want you to look at the case in all its bearing. I believe after all you are right, and that I should do the same in your place.'

'One ought never to decide too hastily for fear of regretting it afterwards,' put in Dr. Heriot. Mildred gave him a half-veiled glance. Why was he so quiet and abstracted, she wondered ? Another time he would have entered with animation into the subject, but now some grave thought sealed his lips. Could it be that Polly's decision had had more effect on him than he had chosen to avow—that he felt lonely and out of spirits ? She watched timidly for some opportunity of testing her fears ; she was almost sure that he was dull or troubled about something.

'Some people are so afraid of deciding wrong that they seldom arrive at any decision at all,' returned Hugh, with one of his great laughs.

'All the same, over-haste brings early repentance,' returned Dr. Heriot, a little bitterly, as he rose.

'Are you going ?' asked Mildred, feeling disappointed by the shortness of his visit.

'I am poor company to-night,' he returned, hastily. 'I am in no mood for general talk. I daresay I shall see you some time to-morrow. By the bye, how is it Polly has never answered my last letter ?'

'She has sent a hundred apologies. I assure you, she is thoroughly ashamed of herself ; but Roy is such a tyrant, the child has not an hour to herself.'

A smile broke over his face. 'I suppose not ; it must be very amusing to watch them. Roy runs a chance of being completely spoiled ;' but this Mildred would not allow.

She went to bed feeling dissatisfied with herself for her dis-
satisfaction. After all, what did she expect? He had behaved
just as any other man would have behaved in his position; he
had been perfectly kind and friendly, had questioned her about
her health, and had spoken of the length of her journey with a
proper amount of sympathy. It must have been some fancy of
hers that he had evaded her eyes. After all, what right had
she to meddle with his moods, or to be uneasy because of his
uneasiness? Was not this the future she had planned? a fore-
taste of the long evenings, when the gray-haired friend should
quietly sit beside her, either speaking or silent, according to
his will.

Mildred scolded herself into quietness before she slept.
After all, there was comfort in the thought of seeing him the
next day; but this hope was doomed to be frustrated. Dr.
Heriot did not make his appearance; he sent an excuse by
Richard, whom he carried off with him to Nateby and Winton;
an old college friend was coming to dine with him, and Richard
and Hugh Marsden were invited to meet him. Mildred found
her *tête-à-tête* evening with Chriss somewhat harassing, and
would have gladly taken refuge in silence and a book; but
Chriss had begged so hard to read a portion of the translation
of a Greek play on which she was engaged that it was impossible to refuse, and a noisy hour of declamation and uncertain
utterance, owing to the illegibility of the manuscript and the
screeching remonstrances of Fritter-my-wig, whose rightful rest
was invaded, soon added the discomfort of a nervous headache
to Mildred's other pains and penalties; and when Chriss, flushed
and panting, had arrived at the last blotted page, she had
hardly fortitude enough to give the work all the praise it
merited. The quiet of her own room was blissful by comparison, though it brought with it a fresh impulse of tormenting
thoughts. Why was it that, with all her strength of will, she
had made so little progress; that the man was still so dangerously dear to her; that even without a single hope to feed her,
he should still be the sum and substance of her thoughts; that
all else should seem as nothing in comparison with his happiness and peace of mind?

That he was far from peace she knew; her first look at him
had assured her of that. And the knowledge that it was so
had wrought in her this strange restlessness. Would he ever
bring himself to speak to her of this fresh blank in his existence? If it should be so, she would bid him go away for a

little time ; in some way his life was too monotonous for him ; he must seek fresh interests for himself ; the vicarage must no longer inclose his only friends. He had often spoken to her of his love for travel, and had more than once hinted at a desire to revisit the Continent ; why should she not persuade him that a holiday lay within the margin of his duty ; she would willingly endure his absence, if he would only come back brighter and fresher for his work.

Fate had, however, decreed that Mildred's patience should be sorely tested, for though she looked eagerly for his coming all the next day, the opportunity for which she longed did not arrive. Dr. Heriot still held aloof, and the word in season could not be spoken. The following day was Sunday, but even then things were hardly more satisfactory ; a brief hand-shake in the porch after evening service, and an inquiry after Roy, was all that passed between them.

'He is beyond any poor comfort that I can give him,' thought Mildred, sorrowfully, as she groped her way through the dark churchyard paths. 'He looks worn and harassed, but he means to keep his trouble to himself. I will try to put it all out of my head ; it ought to be nothing to me what he feels or suffers,' and she lay awake all night trying to put this prudent resolve into execution.

The next afternoon she walked over to Nateby to look up some of her old Sunday scholars. It was a mild, wintry afternoon ; a gray haziness pervaded everything. As she passed the bridge she lingered for a moment to look down below on the spot which was now so sacred to her ; the sight of the rocks and foaming water made her cover her face with a mute thanksgiving. Imagination could not fail to reproduce the scene. Again she felt herself crashing amongst the cruel stones, and saw the black, sullen waters below her. 'Oh, why was I saved ? to what end—to what purpose ?' she gasped, and then added penitently, 'Surely not to be discontented, and indulge in impossible fancies, but to devote a rescued life to the good of others.'

Mildred was so occupied with these painful reflections that she did not hear carriage-wheels passing in the road below the bridge, and was unaware that Dr. Heriot had descended and thrown the reins to a passing lad, and was now making his way towards her.

His voice in her ear drove the blood to her heart with the sudden start of surprise and pleasure.

'We always seem fated to meet in this place,' he laughed, feigning not to notice her embarrassment, but embarrassed himself by it. 'Coop Kernan Hole must have a secret attraction for both of us. I find myself always driving slowly over the bridge, as though I were following a friend's possible funeral.'

'As you might have done,' she returned, with a grateful glance that completed her sentence.

'Shall we go down and look at it more closely?' he asked, after a moment's silence, during which he had revolved some thought in his mind. 'I have an odd notion that seeing it again may lay the ghost of an uneasy dream that always haunts me. After a harder day's work than usual, this scene is sure to recur to me at night; sometimes I have to leave you there, you have floated so far out of my reach,' with a meaning movement of his hand. Mildred shuddered.

'Shall we come—that is—if you do not much dislike the idea,' and as Mildred saw no reason for refusing, she overcame her feelings of reluctance, and followed him through the little gate, and down the steep steps beyond which lay the uneven masses of gray brockram. There he waited for her with outstretched hand.

'You need not think that I shall trust you to your own care again,' he said, with rather a whimsical smile, but as he felt the trembling that ran through hers, it vanished, and he became unusually grave. In another moment he checked her abruptly, and almost peremptorily. 'We will not go any farther; your hand is not steady enough, you are nervous.' Mildred in vain assured him to the contrary; he insisted that she should sit down for a few moments, and, in spite of her protestations, took off his great-coat and spread it on the rock. 'I am warm, far too warm,' he asserted, when he saw her looks of uneasiness. 'This spot is so sheltered;' and he stood by her and lifted his hat, as though the cool air refreshed him.

'Do you remember our conversation on the other side of the bridge?' he asked presently, turning to her. Mildred flushed with sudden pain—too well she remembered it, and the long night of struggle and well-nigh despair that had followed it.

'I wonder what you thought of me; you were very quiet, very sweet-voiced in your sympathy; but I fancied your eyes had a distrustful gleam in them; they seemed to doubt the wisdom of my choice. Mildred,' with a quick touch of passion in his voice such as she had never heard before, 'what a fool you must have thought me!'

'Dr. Heriot, how can you say such things?' but her heart beat faster; he had called her Mildred again.

'Because I must and will say them.   A man must call himself names when he has made such a pitiful thing of life.   Look at my marrying Margaret—a mistake from beginning to end; and yet I must needs compass a second piece of folly.'

'There, I think you are too hard on yourself.'

'What right had I at my age, or rather with my experience and knowledge of myself, to think I could make a young girl happy, knowing, as I ought to have known, that her endearing ways could not win her an entrance into the deepest part of my nature—that would have been closed for ever,' speaking in a suppressed voice.

'It was a mistake for which no one could blame you— Polly least of all,' she returned, eager to soothe this wounded susceptibility.

'Dear Polly, it was her little fingers that set me free—that set both of us free.   Coop Kernan Hole would have taught me its lesson too late but for her.'

'What do you mean?' asked Mildred, startled, and trying to get a glimpse of his face; but he had turned it from her; possibly the uncontrolled muscles and the flash of the eye might have warned her without a word.

'What has it taught you?' she repeated, feeling she must get to the bottom of this mystery, whatever it might cost her.

'That it was not Polly whom I loved,' he returned, in a suppressed voice, 'but another whom I might have lost—whom Coop Kernan Hole might have snatched from me.   Did you know this, Mildred?'

'No,' she faltered.   'I do not believe it now,' she might have added if breath had not failed her.   In her exceeding astonishment, to think such words had blessed her ear, it was impossible —oh, it was impossible—she must hear more.

'I am doubly thankful to it,' he repeated, stooping over her as she sat, that the fall might not drown his voice; 'its dark waters are henceforth glorified to me.   Never till that day did I know what you were to me; what a blank my life would be to me without you.   It has come to this—that I cannot live without you, Mildred—that you are to me what no other woman, not even Margaret, not even my poor wife, has been to me.'

She buried her face in her trembling hands.   Not even to him could she speak, until the pent-up feelings in her heart had resolved themselves into an inward cry, 'My God, for this—for these words—I thank thee !'

He watched her anxiously, as though in doubt of her emotion. Love was making him timid. After all, could he have misunderstood her words ? 'Do not speak to me yet. I do not ask it ; I do not expect it,' he said, touching her hand to make her look at him. 'You shall give me your answer when you like—to-morrow—a week hence—you shall have time to think of it. By and by I must know what you have for me in return, and whether my blindness and mistake have alienated you, but I will not ask it now.' He moved from her a few steps, and came hurriedly back ; but Mildred, still pale from uncontrollable feeling, would not raise her eyes. ' I may be wrong in thinking you cared for me a little. Do you remember what you said ? "John, save me !" Mildred, I do not deserve it; I have brought it all on myself, and I will try and be patient ; but when you can come to me and say, "John, I love you ; I will be your wife," you will remove a mountain-load of doubt and uncertainty. Ah, Mildred, Mildred, will you ever be able to say it ?' His emotion, his sensitive doubts, had overmastered him ; he was as deadly pale as the woman he wooed. Again he turned away, but this time she stopped him.

'Why need you wait ? you must know I——,' but here the soft voice wavered and broke down ; but he had heard enough.

'What must I know ?—that you love me ?'

' Yes,' was all her answer ; but she raised her eyes and looked at him, and he knew then that the great loneliness of his life was gone for ever.

And Mildred, what were her thoughts as she sat with her lover beside her, looking down at the sunless pool before them ? here, where she had grappled with death, the crowning glory of her life was given to her, the gray colourless hues had faded out of existence, the happiness for which she had not dared to ask, which the humble creature had not whispered even in her prayers, had come to her, steeping her soul with wondrous content and gratitude.

And out of her happiness came a great calm. For a little while neither of them spoke much, but the full understanding of that sacred silence lay like a pure veil between them. They were neither young, both had known the mystery of suffering— the man held in his heart a dreary past, and Mildred's early life had been passed in patient waiting ; but what exuberance of youthful joy could equal the quietude of their entire satisfaction ?

'Mildred, it seems to me that I must have loved you unconsciously through it all,' he said, presently, when their stillness had spent itself; 'somehow you always rested me. It had grown a necessity with me to come and tell you my troubles; the very sound of your voice soothed me.'

One of her beautiful smiles answered him. She knew he was right, and she had been more to him than he had guessed. Had not this consciousness added the bitterest ingredient to her misery, the knowledge that he was deceiving himself, that no one could give him what was in her power to give?

'But I never thought it possible until lately that you could care enough for me,' he continued; 'you seemed so calm, so beyond this sort of earthly passion. Ah, Mildred,' half-gravely, half-caressingly, 'how could you mislead me so? All my efforts to break down that quiet reserve seemed in vain.'

'I thought it right; how could I guess it would ever come to this?' she answered, blushing. 'I can hardly believe it now'; but the answer to this was so full and satisfactory that Mildred's last lingering doubt was dispelled for ever.

It was late in the afternoon when they parted at the vicarage gate; the dark figure in the wintry porch escaped their observation in the twilight, and so the last good-bye fell on Ethel Trelawny's astonished ear.

'It is not good-bye after all, Mildred; I shall see you again this evening,' in Dr. Heriot's voice; 'take care of yourself, my dearest, until then;' and the long hand-clasp that followed his words spoke volumes.

When Mildred entered the drawing-room she gave a little start at the sight of Ethel. The girl held out her hand to her with a strange smile.

'Mildred, I was there and heard it. What he called you, I mean. Darling—darling, I am so glad,' breaking off with a half-sob and suddenly closing her in her arms.

For a moment Mildred seemed embarrassed.

'Dear Ethel, what do you mean? what could you have heard?'

'That he called you by your name. I heard his voice; it was quite enough; it told me everything, and then I closed the door. Oh, Mildred! to think he has come to an end of his blindness and that he loves you at last.'

'Yes; does it not seem wonderful?' returned Mildred, simply. Her fair face was still a little flushed, her eyes were soft and radiant; in her happiness she looked almost lovely. Ethel knelt down beside her in a little effusion of girlish worship and sympathy.

'Did he tell you how beautiful you are, Mildred ? No, you shall let me talk what nonsense I like to-night. I do not know when I have felt so happy. Does Richard know ?'

'No one knows.'

'Am I the first to wish you joy then, Mildred ? I never was so glad about anything before. I could sing aloud in my gladness all the way from here to Kirkleatham.'

'Dear Ethel, this is so like you.'

'To think of the misery of mind you have both caused me, and now that it has come all right at last. Is he very penitent, Mildred ?'

'He is very happy,' she replied, smiling over the girl's enthusiasm.

'How sweetly calm you look. I should not feel so in your place. I should be pining for my lost liberty, I verily believe. How long have you understood each other ? Ever since Roy and Polly have come to their senses ?'

'No, indeed ; only this afternoon.'

'Only this afternoon ?' incredulously.

'Yes ; but it seems ages ago already. Ethel, you must not mind if I cannot talk much about this ; it is all so new, you see.'

'Ah, I understand.'

'I knew how pleased you would be, you always appreciated him so ; at one time I could have sooner believed you the object of his choice ; till you assured me otherwise,' smoothing the wavy ripples of hair over Ethel's white forehead.

'Women do not often marry their heroes ; Dr. Heriot was my hero,' laughed the girl. 'I chose you for him the first day I saw you, when you came to meet me, looking so graceful in your deep mourning ; your face and mild eyes haunted me, Mildred. I believe I fell in love with you then.'

'Hush, here comes Richard,' interrupted Mildred softly, and Ethel instantly became grave and rose to her feet.

But for once he hardly seemed to see her.

'Aunt Milly, my dear Aunt Milly,' he exclaimed, with unusual warmth, 'do you know what a little bird has told me ?' he whispered, stooping his handsome head to kiss her.

'Oh, Cardie ! do you know already ? Have you met him ?'

'Yes, and he will be here presently. Aunt Milly, I don't know what we are to do without you, but all the same Dr. John shall have you. He is the only man who is worthy of Aunt Milly.'

'There, that will do, you have not spoken to Ethel yet.'

Oh, how Mildred longed to be alone with her thoughts, and yet the sound of her lover's praises were very sweet to her; he was Richard's hero as well as Ethel's, she knew, but with Richard's entrance Ethel seemed to think she must be going.

'It is so late now, but I will come again to-morrow;' and then as Mildred bade her good-night she said another word or two of her exceeding gladness.

She would fain have declined Richard's escort, but he offered her no excuse. She found him waiting for her at the gate, and knew him too well to hope for her own way in this. She could only be on her guard and avoid any dangerous subject.

'You will all miss her dreadfully,' she said, as they crossed the market-place in full view of Dr. Heriot's house. 'I don't think any of you can estimate the blank her absence will leave at the vicarage.'

'I can for one,' he replied, gravely. 'Do you think I can easily forget what she has done for us since our mother died? But we shall not lose her—not entirely, I mean.'

'No, indeed.'

'Humanly speaking I think their chances of happiness are greater than that of any one. I know that they are so admirably suited to each other. Aunt Milly will give him just the rest he needs.'

'I should not be surprised if he will forget all his bitter past then. But, Richard, I want to speak to you; you have not seen my father lately?'

'Not for months,' he replied, startled at the change in her tone; all at once it took a thin, harassed note.

'He has decided to stand for the Kendal election, though more than one of his best friends have prophesied a certain defeat. Richard, I cannot help telling you that I dread the result.'

'You must try not to be uneasy,' he returned, with that unconscious softening in his voice that made it almost caressing. 'You must know by this time how useless it is to try to shake his purpose.'

'Yes, I know that,' she returned, dejectedly; 'but all the same I feel as though he were contemplating suicide. He is throwing away time and money on a mere chimera, for they say the Radical member will be returned to a certainty. If he should be defeated '—pausing in some emotion.

'Oh, he must take his chance of that.'

'You do not know ; it will break him down entirely. He has set his heart on this thing, and it will go badly with both of us if he be disappointed. Last night it was dreadful to hear him talk. More than once he said that failure would be social death to him. It breaks my heart to see him looking so ill and yet refusing any sympathy that one can offer him.'

'Yes, I understand ; if I could only help you,' he returned, in a suppressed voice.

'No one can do that—it has to be borne,' was the dreary answer ; and just then the lodge gates of Kirkleatham came in sight.

CHAPTER XXXIV

JOHN HERIOT'S WIFE

'Whose sweet voice
Should be the sweetest music to his ear,
Awaking all the chords of harmony ;
Whose eye should speak a language to his soul
More eloquent than all that Greece or Rome
Could boast of in its best and happiest days ;
Whose smile should be his rich reward for toil ;
Whose pure transparent cheek pressèd to his
Would calm the fever of his troubled thoughts,
And woo his spirits to those fields Elysian,
The Paradise which strong affection guards.'

BETHUNE.

AND so when her youth was passed Mildred Lambert found the great happiness of her life, and prepared herself to be a noble helpmeet to the man to whom unconsciously she had long given her heart.

This time there were no grave looks, no dissentient voice questioning the wisdom of Dr. Heriot's choice ; a sense of fitness seemed to satisfy the most fastidious taste ; neither youth nor beauty were imperative in such a case. Mildred's gentleness was the theme of every tongue. Her tender, old-fashioned ways were discovered now to be wonderfully attractive ; a hundred instances of her goodness and unselfishness reached her lover's ears.

'Every one seems to have fallen in love with you, Mildred,' he said to her one sweet spring evening when he had crossed the market-place for his accustomed evening visit. Mildred was alone as usual ; the voices of the young people sounded from the terrace ; Olive and Richard were talking together ; Polly was leaning against the wall reading a letter from Roy ; the evening sun streamed through the window on Mildred's soft brown hair and gray silk, on the great bowls of golden primroses, on the gay tints of the china ; a little green world lay beyond the bay window, undulating waves of grass, a clear sparkle of water, dim blue mists and lines of shadowy hills.

Mildred lifted her quiet eyes; their smiling depths seemed to hold a question and reproof.

'Every one thinks it their duty to praise you to me,' he continued, in the same amused tone; 'they are determined to enlighten me about the goodness of my future wife. They do not believe how well I know that already,' with a strange glistening in his eyes.

'Please do not talk so, John,' she whispered. 'I should not like you to think too well of me, for fear I should ever disappoint you.'

'Do you believe that would be possible ?' he asked, reproachfully.

Then she gave him one of her lovely smiles.

'No, I do not,' she returned, simply; 'because, though we love each other, we do not believe each other perfect. You have often called me self-willed, John, and I daresay you are right.'

He laughed a little at that; her quaint gentleness had often amused him; he knew he should always hear the truth from her. She would tell him of her faults over and over again, and he would listen to them gravely and pretend to believe them rather than wound her exquisite susceptibility; but to himself he declared that she had no flaw—that she was the dearest, the purest, a pearl among women. Mildred would have shrunk in positive pain and humility if she had known the extravagant standard to which he had raised her.

Sometimes he would crave to know her opinion of him in return. Like many men, he was morbidly sensitive on this point, and was inclined to take blame to himself where he did not deserve it, and she would point out his errors to him in the simplest way, and so that the most delicate self-consciousness could not have been hurt.

'What, all those faults, Mildred ?' he would say, with a pretence at a sigh. 'I thought love was blind.'

'I could never be blind about anything that concerns you, John,' she would return, in the sweetest voice possible; 'our faults will only bind us all the closer to each other. Is not that what helpmeet means ?' she went on, a soft gravity stealing over her words,—'that I should try to help you in everything, even against yourself ? I always see faults clearest in those I love best,' she finished, somewhat shyly.

'The last is the saving clause,' he replied, with a look that made her blush. 'In this case I shall have no objection to be told of my wrong-doings every day of my life. What a blessing it is that you have common sense enough for both. I am obliged to believe what you tell me about yourself of course, and mean to act up to my part of our contract, but at present I am unable to perceive the most distant glimmer of a fault.'

'John !'

'Seriously and really, Mildred, I believe you to be as near perfection as a living woman can be,' and when Dr. Heriot spoke in this tone Mildred always gave up the argument with a sigh.

But with all her self-accusations Mildred promised to be a most submissive wife. Already she proved herself docile to her lover's slightest wish. She did not even remonstrate when Dr. Heriot pleaded with her brother and herself that an early day should be fixed for the marriage ; for herself she could have wished a longer delay, but he was lonely and wanted her, and that was enough.

Perhaps the decision was a little difficult when she thought of Olive, but the time once fixed, there was no hesitation. She went about her preparations with a quiet precision that made Dr. Heriot smile to himself.

'One would think you are planning for somebody else's wedding, not your own,' he said once, when she came down to him with her face full of gentle bustle ; 'come and sit down a little ; at least I have the right to take care of you now, you precious woman.'

'Yes ; but, John, I am so busy ; I have to think for them all, you know ; and Olive, poor girl, is so scared at the thought of her responsiblities, and Richard is so occupied he cannot spare me time for anything,' for Richard, now in deacon's orders, was working up the parish under Hugh Marsden's supervision. Hugh had lost his mother, and had finally yielded his great heart and strength to the South African Mission.

'But there is Polly ?' observed Dr. Heriot.

'Yes, there is Polly until Roy comes,' she returned, with a smile. 'She is my right hand at present, until he monopolises her ; but one has to think for them all, and arrange things.'

'You shall have no one but yourself to consider by and by,' was his lover-like reply.

'Oh, John, I shall only have time then to think of you !' was her quiet answer.

And so one sweet June morning, when the swathes and lines of new-mown hay lay in the crofts round Kirkby Stephen, and while the little rush-bearers were weaving their crowns for St. Peter's Day, and the hedges were thick with the pink and pearly bloom of brier roses, Mildred Heriot stood leaning on her husband's arm in St. Stephen's porch.

Merrily the worn old bells were pealing out, the sunlight streamed across the market-place, the churchyard paths, and the paved lanes, and the windows of the houses abutting on the churchyard, were crowded with sympathising faces.

Not young nor beautiful, save to those who loved her; yet as she stood there in her soft-eyed graciousness, many owned that they had never seen a sweeter-faced bride.

'My wife, is this an emblem of our future life?' whispered Dr. Heriot, as he led her proudly down the path, almost hidden by the roses her little scholars' hands had strewn; but Mildred's lip quivered, and the pressure of her hand on his arm only answered him.

'How had she deserved such happiness?' the humble soul was asking herself even at this supreme moment. Under her feet lay the fast-fading roses, but above and around spread the pure arc of central blue—the everlasting arms of a Father's providence about her everywhere. Before them was the gray old vicarage, now no longer her home, the soft violet hills circling round it; above it a heavy snow-white cloud drooped heavily, like a guardian angel in mid-air; roses, and sunlight, and God's heavenly blue.

'Oh, it is all so beautiful!—how is one to deserve such happiness?' she thought; and then it came to her that this was a free gift, a loan, a talent that the Father had given to be used for the Master's service, and the slight trembling passed away, and the beautiful serene eyes raised themselves to her husband's face with the meek trustfulness of old.

Mildred was not too much engrossed even in her happiness to notice that Olive held somewhat aloof from her through the day. Now and then she caught a glimpse of a weary, abstracted face. Just as she had finished her preparations for departure, and the travelling carriage had driven into the courtyard, she sent Ethel and Polly down on some pretext, and went in search of her favourite.

She found her in the lobby, sitting on the low window-seat, looking absently at the scene below her. The courtyard of the vicarage looked gay enough; the horses were champing their bits, and stamping on the beck gravel; the narrow strip of daisy turf was crowded with moving figures; Polly, in her pretty bridesmaid's dress, was talking to Roy; Ethel stood near them, with Richard and Hugh Marsden; Dr. Heriot was in the porch in earnest conversation with Mr. Lambert. Beyond lay the quiet churchyard, shimmering in the sunlight; the white crosses gleamed here and there; the garlands of sweet-smelling flowers still strewed the paths.

'Dear Olive, are you waiting for me? I wanted just to say a last word or two;' and Mildred sat down beside her in her rich dress, and took the girl's listless hand in hers. 'Promise me, my child, that you will do the best for yourself and them.'

'It will be a poor best after you, Aunt Milly,' returned Olive, with a grateful glance at the dear face that had been her comfort so long. It touched her that even now she should be remembered; with an impulse that was rare with her she put her arms round Mildred, and laid her face on her shoulder. 'Aunt Milly, I never knew till to-day what you were to me— to all of us.'

'Am I not to be Aunt Milly always, then?' for there was something ineffably sad in the girl's voice.

'Yes, but we can no longer look to you for everything. We shall miss you out of our daily life. I do not mean to be selfish, Aunt Milly. I love to think of your happiness; but all the same I must feel as though something has passed out of my life.'

'I understand, dear. You know I never think you selfish, Olive. Now I want you to do something for me—a promise you must make me on my wedding-day.'

A flickering smile crossed Olive's pale face. 'It must not be a hard one, then.'

'It is one you can easily keep,—promise me to try to bear your failures hopefully. You will have many; perhaps daily ones. I am leaving you heavy responsibilities, my poor child; but who knows? They may be blessings in disguise.'

An incredulous sigh answered her.

'It will be your own fault if they do not prove so. When you fail, when things go wrong, think of your promise to me, and be patient with yourself. Say to yourself, "It is only one of Olive's mistakes, and she will try to do better next time." Do you understand me, my dear?'

'Yes, I will try, Aunt Milly.'

'I am leaving you, my darling, with a confidence that

nothing can shake. I do not fear your goodness to others, only to this weary self,' with a light caressing touch on the girl's bowed head and shoulders. 'Hitherto you have leaned on me; I have been your crutch, Olive. Now you will rely on yourself. You see I do not make myself miserable about leaving you. I think even this is ordered for the best.'

'Yes, I know. How dear of you to say all this! But I must not keep you. Hark, they are calling you!'

Mildred rose with a blush; she knew the light agile step on the stairs. In another moment Dr. Heriot's dark face appeared.

'They are waiting, Mildred; we have not a moment to lose. You must come, my dear wife!'

'One moment, John'; and as she folded the girl in a long embrace, she whispered, 'God bless my Olive!' and then suffered him to lead her away.

But when the last good-byes were said, and the carriage door was closed by Richard, Mildred looked up and waved her hand towards the lobby window. She could see the white dress and dusky halo of hair, the drooping figure and tightly locked hands; but as the sound of the wheels died away in the distance, Olive hid her face in her hands and prayed, with a burst of tears, that the promise she had made might be faithfully kept.

An hour later, Richard found her still sitting there, looking spent and weary, and took her out to walk with him.

'The rest have all started for Podgill. We will follow them more leisurely. The air will refresh us both, Olive;' stealing a glance at the reddened eyelids, that told their own tale. Olive so seldom shed tears, that the relief was almost a luxury to her. She felt less oppressed now.

'But Ethel—where is she, Cardie?' unwilling to let him sacrifice himself for her pleasure. She little knew that Richard was carrying out Mildred's last injunctions.

'I leave Olive in your care; be good to her, Richard,' she had said as he had closed the carriage door on her, and he had understood her and given her an affirmative look.

'Ethel has a headache, and has gone home,' he replied. 'She feels this as much as any of us; she did not like breaking up the party, but I saw how much she needed quiet, and persuaded her. She wants you to go up there to-morrow and talk to her.'

'But, Cardie,' stopping to look at him, 'I am sure you have a headache too.'

'So I have, and it is pretty bad, but I thought a walk would do us both good, and we might as well be miserable together,

to tell you the truth,' with an attempt at a laugh. 'I can't
stand the house without Aunt Milly, and I thought you were
feeling the same.'

'Dear Cardie, how good of you to think of me at all,'
returned Olive, gratefully.   Her brother's evident sympathy was
already healing in its effects.   Just now she had felt so lonely,
so forlorn, it made her better to feel that he was missing Aunt
Milly too.

She looked up at him in her mild affectionate way as he
walked beside her.   She thought, as she had often thought
before, how well the straitly-cut clerical garb became him—its
severe simplicity suiting so well the grave young face.   How
handsome, how noble he must look in Ethel's eyes !

'We are so used to have Aunt Milly thinking for us, that it
will be hard to think for ourselves,' she went on presently, when
they were walking down by the weir.   'You will have to put
up with a great deal from me, and to be very patient, though
you are always that now, Cardie.'

'Am I ?' he returned, touched by her earnestness.   Olive
had always been loyal to him, even when he had most neglected
her ; and he had neglected her somewhat of late, he thought.
'I will tell you what we must do, Livy ; we must try to help
each other, and to be more to each other than we have been.
You see Rex has Polly, but I have no one, not even Aunt Milly
now ; at least we cannot claim her so much now.'

'You have Ethel, Cardie.'

'Yes, but not in the way I want,' he returned, the sensitive
colour flitting over his face.   He could never hear or speak her
name unmoved ; she was far more to him now than she had
ever been, when he thought of her less as the youthful goddess
he had adored in his boyish days, than as the woman he desired
to have as his wife.   He no longer cast a glamour of his own
devising over her image—faulty as well as lovable he knew her
to be ; but all the same he craved her for his own.

'Not one man in a hundred, not one in a thousand, would
make her happy,' he said more than once to himself ; 'but it is
because I believe myself to be that man that I persevere.   If I
did not think this, I would take her at her word and go on my way.'

Now, as he answered Olive, a sadness crossed his face, and
she saw it.   Might it not be that she could help him even here ?
He had talked about his trouble to Aunt Milly, she knew.
Could she not win him to some confidence in herself ?   Here
was a beginning of the work Aunt Milly had left her.

'Dear Cardie, I should so like it if you would talk to me sometimes about Ethel,' she said, hesitating, as though fearing how he would like it. 'I know how often it makes you unhappy. I can always see just when it is troubling you, but I never could speak of it before.'

'Why not, Livy ?' not abruptly, but questioning.

'One is so afraid of saying the wrong things, and then you might not have liked it,' stammering in her old way.

'I must always like to talk of what is so dear to me,' he replied, gravely. 'I could as soon blot out my own individuality, as blot out the hope of seeing Ethel my future wife ; and in that case, it were strange indeed if I did not love to talk of her.'

'Yes, and I have always felt as though it must come right in the end,' interposed Olive, eagerly ; 'her manner gives me that impression.'

'What impression ?' he asked, startled by her earnestness.

'I can't help thinking she cares for you, though she does not know it ; at least she will not allow herself to know it. I have seen her draw herself so proudly sometimes when you have left her. I am sure she is hardening her heart against herself, Cardie.'

A faint smile rose to his lips. 'Livy, who would have thought you could have said such comforting things, just when I was losing heart too ?'

'You must never do that,' she returned, in an old-fashioned way that amused him, and yet reminded him somehow of Mildred. 'Any one like you, Cardie, ought never to lose courage.'

'Courage, Cœur-de-Lion !' he returned, mimicking her tone more gaily as his spirits insensibly rose under the sisterly flattery. 'God bless her ! she is worth waiting for ; there is no other woman in the world to me. Who would have thought we should have got on this subject to-day, of all days in the year ? but you have done me no end of good, Livy.'

'Then I have done myself good,' she returned, simply ; and indeed some sweet hopeful influence seemed to have crept on her during the last half-hour ; she thought how Mildred's loving sympathy would have been aroused if she could have told her how Richard and she had mutually comforted themselves in their dulness. But something still stranger to her experience happened that night before she slept.

She was lying awake later than usual, pondering over the

events of the day, when a stifled sound, strongly resembling a sob promptly swallowed by a simulated yawn, reached her ear.

'Chrissy, dear, is there anything the matter?' she inquired, anxiously, trying to grope her way to the huddled heap of bed-clothes.

'No, thank you,' returned Chriss, with dignity; 'what should be the matter? good-night. I believe I am getting sleepy,' with another artfully-constructed yawn which did not in the least deceive Olive.

Chrissy was crying, that was clear; and Olive's sympathy was wide-awake as usual; but how was she with her clumsy, well-meaning efforts to overcome the prickles?

Chriss was well known to have a soul above sympathy, which she generally resented as impertinent; nevertheless Olive's voice grew aggravatingly soft.

'I thought perhaps you might feel dull about Aunt Milly,' she began, hesitating; 'we do—and so——'

'I don't know, I am sure, whom you mean by your aggravating we's,' snapped Chriss; 'but it is very hard a person can't have their feelings without coming down on them like a policeman and taking them in charge.'

'Well, then, I won't say another word, Chriss,' returned her sister, good-humouredly.

But this did not mollify Chriss.

'Speaking won't hurt a person when they are sore all over,' she replied, with her usual contradiction. 'I hate prying, of course, and it is a pity one can't enjoy a comfortable little cry without being put through one's catechism. But I do want Aunt Milly. There!' finished Chriss, with another ominous shaking of the bed-clothes; 'and I want her more than you do with all your mysterious we's.'

'I meant Cardie,' replied Olive, mildly, too much used to Chriss's oddities to be repulsed by them. 'You have no idea how much he misses her and all her nice quiet ways.'

Chriss stopped her ears decidedly.

'I don't want to hear anything about Aunt Milly; you and Richard made her a sort of golden image. It is very unkind of you, Olive, to speak about her now, when you know how horrid and disagreeable and cross and altogether abominable I have always been to her,' and here honest tears choked Chriss's utterance.

A warm thrill pervaded Olive's frame; here was another

piece of work left for her to do. She must gain influence over the cross-grained warped little piece of human nature beside her; hitherto there had been small sympathy between the sisters. Olive's dreamy susceptibilities and Chriss's shrewdness had kept them apart. Chriss had always made it a point of honour to contradict Olive in everything, and never until now had she ever managed to insert the thinnest wedge between Chriss's bristling self-esteem and general pugnacity.

'Oh, Chriss,' she cried, almost tremblingly, in her eagerness to impart some consolation, 'there is not one of us who cannot blame ourselves in some way. I am sure I have not been as nice as I might have been to Aunt Milly.'

Chriss shook her shoulder pettishly.

'Dear me, that is so like you, Olive; you are the most funnily-constructed person I ever saw—all poetry and conscience. When you are not dreaming with your eyes open you are always reading yourself a homily.'

'I wish I were nice for all your sakes,' replied Olive, meekly, not in the least repudiating this personal attack.

'Oh, as to that, you are nice enough,' retorted Chiss, briskly. 'You won't come up to Aunt Milly, so it is no use trying, but all the same I mean to stick to you. I don't intend you to be quite drowned dead in your responsibilities. If you say a thing, however stupid it is, I shall think it my duty to back you up, so I warn you to be careful.'

'Dear Chriss, I am so much obliged to you,' replied Olive, with tears in her eyes.

She perfectly understood by this somewhat vague sentence that Chriss was entering into a solemn league and covenant with her, an alliance aggressive and defensive for all future occasions.

'There is not another tolerably comfortable person in the house,' grumbled Chriss; 'one might as well talk to a monk as to Richard; the corners of his mouth are beginning to turn down already with ultra-goodness, and now he has taken to the Noah's Ark style of dress one has no comfort in contradicting him.'

'Chrissy, how can you say such things? Cardie has never been so dear and good in his life.'

'And then there are Rex and Polly,' continued Chriss, ignoring this interruption; 'the way they talk in corners and the foolish things they say! I have made up my mind, Livy, never to be in love, not even if I marry my professor. I will be kind to him and sew on his buttons once in a way, and order him nice things for dinner; but if he sent me on errands as Rex does Polly I would just march out of the room and never see his face again. I am so glad that no one will think of marrying you, Olive,' she finished, sleepily, disposing herself to rest; 'every family ought to have an old maid, and a poetical one will be just the thing.'

Olive smiled; she always took these sort of speeches as a matter of course. It never entered her head that any other scheme of life were possible with her. She was far too humble-minded and aware of her shortcomings to imagine that she could find favour in any man's eyes. She lay with a lightened heart long after Chriss had fallen into a sweet sleep, thinking how she could do her best for the froward young creature beside her.

'I have begun work in earnest to-day,' she thought, 'first Cardie and now Chriss. Oh, how hard I will try not to disappoint them!'

Dr. Heriot had hoped to secure some five weeks of freedom from work, but before the month had fully elapsed he had an urgent recall home. Richard had telegraphed to him that they were all in great anxiety about Mr. Trelawny. There had been a paralytic seizure, and his daughter was in deep distress. They had sent for a physician from Kendal, but as the case required watching, Dr. Heriot knew how urgently his presence would be desired.

He went in search of his wife immediately, and found her sitting in a quiet nook in the Lowood Gardens overlooking Windermere.

The book they had been reading together lay unheeded in her lap. Mildred's eyes were fixed on the shining lake and the hills, with purple shadows stealing over them. Her husband's step on the turf failed to rouse her, so engrossing was her reverie, till his hand was laid on her shoulder.

'John, how you startled me!'

'I have been looking for you everywhere, Milly, darling,' he returned, sitting down beside her. 'I have been watching you for ever so long; I wanted to know what other people thought of my wife, and so for once I resolved to be a disinterested spectator.'

'Hush, your wife does not like you to talk nonsense;' but all the same Mildred blushed beautifully.

'Unfortunately she has to endure it,' he replied, coolly. 'After all I think people will be satisfied. You are a young-looking woman, Milly, especially since you have left off wearing gray.'

'As though I mind what people think,' she returned, smiling, well pleased with his praise.

Was it not sufficient for her that she was fair in his eyes? Dr. Heriot had a fastidious taste with regard to ladies' dress. In common with many men, he preferred rich dark materials with a certain depth and softness of colouring, and already, with the nicest tact, she contrived to satisfy him. Mildred was beginning to lose the old-fashioned staidness and precision that had once marked her style; others besides her husband thought the quiet, restful face had a certain beauty of its own.

And he. There were some words written by the wise king of old which often rose to his lips as he looked at her—'The heart of her husband does safely trust in her; she will do him good and not evil all the days of her life.' How had it ever come that he had won for himself this blessing? There were times when he almost felt abashed before the purity and goodness of this woman; the simplicity and truthfulness of her words, the meekness with which she ever obeyed him. 'If I can only be worthy of my Mildred's love, if I can be what she thinks me,' he often said to himself. As he sat beside her now a feeling of regret crossed him that this should be their last evening in this sweet place.

'Shall you be very much disappointed, my wife' (his favourite name for her), 'if we return home a few days earlier than we planned?'

She looked up quickly.

'Disappointed—to go home, and with you, John! But why? is there anything the matter?'

'Not at the vicarage, but Mr. Trelawny is very ill, and Richard has telegraphed for me. What do you say, Mildred?'

'That we must go at once. Poor Ethel. Of course she will want you, she always had such faith in you. Dr. Strong is no favourite at Kirkleatham.'

'Yes, I think we ought to go,' he returned, slowly; 'you will be a comfort to the poor girl, and of course I must be at my post. I am only so sorry our pleasant trip must end.'

'Yes, and it was doing you so much good,' she replied, looking fondly at the dark face, now no longer thin and wan. 'I should have liked you to have had another week's rest before you began work.'

'Never mind,' he returned, cheerfully, 'we will not waste

this lovely evening with regrets. Where are your wraps, Mildred ? I mean to fetch them and row you on the lake ; there will be a glorious moon this evening.'

The next night as Richard crossed the market-place on his way from Kirkleatham he saw lights in the window of the low gray house beside the Bank, and the next minute Dr. Heriot came out, swinging the gate behind him. Richard sprang to meet him.

'My telegram reached you then at Windermere ? I am so thankful you have come. Where is Aunt Milly ?'

'There,' motioning to the house ; 'do you think I should leave my wife behind me ? Let me hear a little about things, Richard. Are you going my way; to Kirkleatham, I mean ?'

'Yes, I will turn back with you. I have been up there most of the time. He seems to like me, and no one else can lift him. It seemed hard breaking into your holiday, Dr. Heriot, but what could I do ? We are sure he dislikes Dr. Strong, and then Ethel seemed so wretched.'

'Poor girl; the sudden seizure must have terrified her.'

'Oh, I must tell you about that; I promised her I would. You see he has taken this affair of the election too much to heart ; every one told him he would fail, and he did not believe them. In his obstinacy he has squandered large sums of money, and she believes this to be preying on his mind.'

'That and the disappointment.'

'As to that his state was pitiable. He came back from Kendal looking as ill as possible and full of bitterness against her. She has no want of courage, but she owned she was almost terrified when she looked at him. She does not say much, but one can tell what she has been through.'

Dr. Heriot nodded. Too well he understood the state of the case. Mr. Trelawny's paroxysms of temper had latterly become almost uncontrollable.

'He parted from her in anger, his last words being that she had ruined her father, and then he went up to his dressing-room. Shortly after a servant in an adjoining room heard a heavy fall, and alarmed the household. They found him lying speechless and unable to move. Ethel says when they had laid him on his bed and he had recovered consciousness a little, his eyes followed her with a frightened, questioning look that went to her heart, and which no soothing on her part could remove. The whole of the right side is affected, and though he has recovered speech, the articulation is very imperfect, impossible to understand at present, which makes it very distressing.'

'Poor Miss Trelawny, I fear she has sad work before her.'

'She looks wretchedly ill over it ; but what can one expect from such a shock ? She shows admirable self-command in the sickroom ; she only breaks down when she is away from him. I am so glad she will have Aunt Milly. Now I must go back, as Marsden is away, and I have to copy some papers for my father. I shall go back in a couple of hours to take the first share of the night's nursing.'

'You will find me there,' was Dr. Heriot's reply as they shook hands and parted.

CHAPTER XXXV

OLIVE'S DECISION

' Be good, sweet maid, and let who can be clever ;
  Do lovely things, not dream them, all day long ;
  And so make Life, Death, and that vast For Ever,
      One grand sweet song.'
                          CHARLES KINGSLEY.

ETHEL TRELAWNY had long felt as though some crisis in her life were impending.

To her it seemed impossible that the unnatural state of things between her father and herself could any longer continue ; something must occur to break the hideous monotony and constraint of those slowly revolving weeks and months. Latterly there had come to her that strange listening feeling to which some peculiar and sensitive temperaments are subject, when in the silence they can distinctly hear the muffled footfall of approaching sorrow.

Yet what sorrow could be more terrible than this estrangement, this death of a father's love, this chill cloud of distrust that had risen up between them !

And yet when the blow fell, filial instinct woke up in the girl's soul, all the stronger for its repression. There were times during those first forty-eight hours when she would gladly have laid down her own life if she could have restored power to those fettered limbs, and peace to that troubled brain.

Oh, if she could only have blotted out those last cruel words— if they would cease to ring in her ears !

She had met him almost timidly, knowing how heavily the bitterness of his failure would lie upon him.

' Papa, I fear things have not gone well with you,' she had said, and there had been a caressing, almost a pitying chord in her voice as she spoke.

' How should things go well with me when my own child

opposes my interest ?' he had answered, gloomily. ' I have wasted time and substance, I have fooled myself in the eyes of other men, and now I must hide my head in this obscurity which has grown so hateful to me, and it is all your fault, Ethel.'

'Papa, listen to me,' she pleaded. 'Ambition is not everything ; why have you set your heart on this thing ? It is embittering your life and mine. Other men have been disappointed, and it has not gone so very hard with them. Why will you not let yourself be comforted ? '

'There is no comfort for me,' he had replied, and his face had been very old and haggard as he spoke. It were far better that she had not spoken ; her words, few and gentle as they were, only added to the fuel of his discontent ; he had meant to shut himself up in his sullenness, and make no sign ; but she had intercepted his retreat, and brought down the vials on her devoted head.

Could she ever forget the angry storm that followed ? Surely he must have been beside himself to have spoken such words ! How was it that she had been accused of jilting Mr. Cathcart, of refusing his renewed overtures, merely from obstinacy, and the desire of opposition ; that she should hear herself branded as her father's worst enemy ?

'You and your pride have done for me !' he had said, lashing himself up to fresh fury with the remembrance of past mortification. 'You have taken from me all that would make life desirable. You have been a bad daughter to me, Ethel. You have spoiled the work of a lifetime.'

'Papa, papa, I have only acted rightly. How could I have done this evil thing, even for your sake ?' she had cried, but he had not listened to her.

'You have jilted the man you fancied out of pride, and now the mischief will lie on your own head,' he had answered, angrily, and then he had turned to leave the room.

Half an hour afterwards the heavy thud of a fall had been heard, and the man had come to her with a white face to summon her to her father's bedside.

She knew then what had come upon them. At the first sight of that motionless figure, speechless, inert, struck down with unerring force, in the very prime and strength of life, she knew how it would be with them both.

'Oh, my dear, my dear, forgive me,' she had cried, falling on her knees beside the bed, and raining tears over the rigid hands ; and yet what was there to forgive ? Was it not rather she who had been sinned against? What words were those the paralysed tongue refused to speak? What was the meaning of ¡those awful questioning eyes that rested on her day and night, when partial consciousness returned? Could it be that he would have entreated her forgiveness?

'Papa, papa, do not look so,' she would say in a voice that went to Richard's heart. 'Don't you know me? I am Ethel, your own, only child. I will love you and take care of you, papa. Do you hear me, dear? There is nothing to forgive—nothing—nothing.'

During the strain of those first terrible days Richard was everything to her; without him she would literally have sunk under her misery.

'Oh, Richard, have I killed my father? Am I his murderess?' she cried once almost hysterically when they were left alone together. 'Oh, poor papa—poor papa!'

'Dear Ethel, you have done no wrong,' he replied, taking her unresisting hand; 'it is no fault of yours, dearest; you have been the truest, the most patient of daughters. He has brought it on himself.'

'Ah, but it was through me that this happened,' she returned, shuddering through every nerve. 'If I had married Mr. Cathcart, he would not have lost his seat, and then he would not have fretted himself ill.'

'Ought we to do evil that good may come, Ethel?' replied Richard, gravely. 'Are children responsible for the wrong-doing of their parents? If there be sin, it lies at your father's door, not yours; it is you to forgive, not he.'

'Richard, how can you be so hard?' she demanded, with a flash of her old spirit through her sobs; but it died away miserably.

'I am not hard to him—God forbid! Am I likely to be hard to your father, Ethel, and now especially?' he said, somewhat reproachfully, but speaking with the quiet decision that soothed her even then. 'I cannot have you unfitting yourself for your duties by indulging these morbid ideas; no one blames you—you have done right; another time you will be ready to acknowledge it yourself; you have enough to suffer, without adding to your burden. I entreat you to banish these fancies, once and for ever. Ethel, promise me you will try to do so.'

'Yes, yes, I know you are right,' she returned, weeping bitterly; 'only it breaks my heart to see him like this.'

'You are spent and weary,' he replied, gently ; 'to-morrow you will look at these things in a different light. It has been such an awful shock to you, you see,' and then he brought her wine, and compelled her to drink it, and with much persuasion induced her to seek an hour or two's repose before returning to the sickroom.

What would she have done without him, she thought, as she closed her heavy eyes. Unconsciously they seemed to have resumed their old relations towards each other ; it was Richard and Ethel now. Richard's caressing manner had returned ; no brother could have watched over her more devotedly, more reverently ; and yet he had never loved her so well as when, all her imperiousness gone, and with her brave spirit well-nigh broken, she seemed all the more dependent on his sympathy and care.

But the first smile that crossed her face was for Mildred, when Dr. Heriot brought her up to Kirkleatham the first evening after their arrival. Mildred almost cried over her when she took her in her arms ; the contrast to her own happiness was so great.

'Oh, Ethel, Ethel,' was all she could say, 'my poor girl !'

'Yes, I am that and much more,' she returned, yielding to her friend's embrace ; 'utterly poor and wretched. Has he—has Dr. Heriot told you all he feared ?'

'That there can only be partial recovery ? Yes, I know he fears that ; but then one cannot tell in these cases ; you may have him still for years.'

'Ah, but if he should have another stroke ? I know what Dr. Heriot thinks—it is a bad case ; he has said so to Richard.'

'Poor child ! it is so hard not to be able to comfort you.'

'No one can do that so long as I have him before my eyes in this state. Mildred, you cannot conceive what a wreck he is ; no power of speech, only those inarticulate sounds.'

'I am glad Cardie is able to be so much with you.'

A sensitive colour overspread Ethel's worn face.

'I do not know what I should have done without him,' she returned, in a low voice. 'If he had been my own brother he could not have done more for me ; we fancy papa likes to have him, he is so strong and quiet, and always sees what is the right thing to be done.'

'I found out Cardie's value long ago ; he was my right hand during Olive's illness.'

'He is every one's right hand, I think,' was the quiet answer.

'He was the first to suggest telegraphing for Dr. Heriot. I could not bear breaking in upon your holiday, but it could not be helped.'

'Do you think we could have stayed away?'

'All the same it is a sad welcome to your new home; but you are a doctor's wife now. Mildred, if you knew what it was to me to see your dear face near me again.'

'I am so thankful John brought me.'

'Ah, but he will take you away again. I can hear his step now.'

'Poor girl! her work is cut out for her,' observed Dr. Heriot, thoughtfully, as they walked homewards through the crofts. 'It will be a sad, lingering case, and I fear that the brain is greatly affected from what they tell me. He must have had a slight stroke many years ago.'

'Poor, poor Ethel,' replied Mildred, sorrowfully. 'I must be with her as much as possible; but Richard seems her greatest comfort.'

'Perhaps good may come out of evil. You see, I can guess at your thought, Milly darling,' and then their talk flowed into a less sad channel.

But not all Mildred's sympathy, or Richard's goodness, could avail to make those long weeks and months of misery otherwise than dreary; and nobly as Ethel Trelawny performed her duty, there were times when her young heart sickened and grew heavy with pain in the oppressive atmosphere of that weary sickroom.

To her healthy vitality, the spectacle of her father's helplessness was simply terrible; the inertness of the fettered limbs, the indistinct utterance of the tied and faltering tongue, the confusion of the benumbed brain, oppressed her like a nightmare. There were times when her pity for him was so great, that she would have willingly laid down all her chances of happiness in this life if she could have restored to him the prospect of health.

It was now that the real womanhood of Ethel Trelawny rose to the surface. Richard's heart ached with its fulness of love when he saw her day after day so meekly and patiently tending her afflicted father; the worn, pale face and eyes heavy with trouble and want of sleep were far more beautiful to him now; but he hid his feelings with his usual self-control. She had learned to depend upon him and trust him, and this state of things was too precious to be disturbed.

Richard was his father's sole curate now. Towards the end of October, Hugh Marsden had finished his preparations, and had bidden good-bye to his friends at the vicarage.

Mildred, who saw him last, was struck with the change in the young man's manner ; his cheerful serenity had vanished —he looked subdued, almost agitated.

She was sitting at work in the little glass room ; a tame canary was skimming among the flowers, Dr. Heriot's voice was heard cheerfully whistling from an inner room, some late blooming roses lay beside Mildred, her husband's morning gift, the book from which he had been reading to her was still open on the table ; the little domestic picture smote the young man's heart with a dull pain.

'I am come to say good-bye, Mrs. Heriot,' he said, in a sadder voice than she had ever heard from him before ; 'and it has come to this, that I would sooner say any other word.'

'We shall miss you dreadfully, Mr. Marsden,' replied Mildred, looking regretfully up at the plain honest face. Hugh Marsden had always been a favourite with her, and she was loath to say good-bye to him.

'Others have been kind enough to tell me so,' he rejoined, twirling his shabby felt hat between his fingers. 'Miss Olive, Miss Lambert I mean, said so just now. Somehow, I had hoped—but no, she has decided rightly.'

Mildred looked up in surprise. Incoherence was new in Hugh Marsden ; but just now his clumsy eloquence seemed to have deserted him.

'What has Olive decided?' she asked, with a sudden spasm of curiosity ; and then she added kindly, 'Sit down, Mr. Marsden, you do not seem quite yourself ; all this leave-taking has tired you.'

But he shook his head.

'I have no time : you must not tempt me, Mrs. Heriot ; only you have always been so good to me, that I wanted to ask you to say this for me.'

'What am I to say?' asked Mildred, feeling a little bewildered.

He was still standing before her, twirling his hat in his big hands, his broad face flushed a little.

'Tell Miss Olive that I know she has acted rightly ; she always does, you know. It would be something to have such a woman as that beside one, strengthening one's hands ; but of

28

course it cannot be—she could not deviate from her duty by a hair's-breadth.'

'I do not know if I understand you,' began Mildred, slowly, and groping her way to the truth.

'I think you do. I think you have always understood me,' returned the young man, more quickly. 'And you will tell her this from me. Of course one must have regrets, but it cannot be helped ; good-bye, Mrs. Heriot. A thousand thanks for all you have done for me.' And before Mildred could answer, he had wrung her hand, and was half-way through the hall.

An hour later, Mildred stole softly down the vicarage lobby, and knocked at the door of the room she had once occupied, and Olive's voice bade her enter.

'Aunt Milly, I never thought it was you,' she exclaimed, rising hastily from the low chair by the window. 'Is Dr. Heriot with you ?'

'No ; I left John at home. I told him that I wanted to have a little talk with you, and like a model husband he asked no questions, and raised no obstacles. All the same I expect he will follow me.'

'You wanted to talk to me ?' returned Olive, in a questioning tone, but her sallow face flushed a little. 'How strange, when I was just wishing for you too.'

'There must be some electric sympathy between us,' replied her aunt, smiling. 'Nothing could have induced me to sleep until I had seen you. Mr. Marsden wished me to give you a message from him ; he was a little incoherent, but so far as I understand, he wished me to assure you that he considers yours a right decision.'

Olive's face brightened a little. Mildred had already detected unusual sadness on it, but her calmness was baffling.

'Did he tell you to say that ? How kind of him !'

'He did not stop to explain himself ; he was in too great a hurry ; but I thought he seemed troubled. What was the decision, Olive ? Has this helped you to make it ?' touching reverently the open page of a Bible that lay beside her.

The brown light in Olive's eyes grew steady and intense ; she looked like one who had found rest in a certainty.

'I have just been preaching to myself from that text : "He that putteth his hand to the plough and looketh backward," you know, Aunt Milly. Well, that seems to point as truly to me as it does to Mr. Marsden.'

'Yes, dearest,' replied Mildred, softly; 'and now what has he said to you?'

'I hardly know myself,' was the low-toned answer. 'I have been thinking it all over, and I cannot now understand how it was; it seems so wonderful that any one could care enough for me,' speaking to herself, with a soft, bewildered smile.

'Does Mr. Marsden care for you. I thought so from the first, Olive.'

'I suppose he does, or else he would not have said what he did; it was difficult to know his meaning at first, he was so embarrassed, and I was so slow; but we understood each other at last.'

'Tell me all he said, dear,' pleaded Mildred. Could it be her own love story that Olive was treating so simply? There was a chord of sadness in her voice, and a film gathered over the brightness of her eyes, but there was no agitation in her manner; the deep of her soul might be touched, but the surface was calm.

'There is not much to tell, Aunt Milly, but of course you may know all. We had said good-bye, and I had spoken a word or two about his work, and how I thought it the most beautiful work that a man could do, and then he asked me if I should ever be willing to share in it.'

'Well?'

'I did not understand him at first, as I told you, until he made his meaning more plain, and then I saw how it was, that he hoped that one day I might give myself heart and soul to the same work; that my talent, beautiful, as he owned it to be, might not hinder me from such a glorious reality—"the reality,"' and here for the first time she faltered and grew crimson, ' "of such work as must fall to a missionary's wife." '

'Olive, my dear child,' exclaimed Mildred, now really startled, 'did he say as much as that?'

'Yes, indeed, Aunt Milly; and he asked if I could care enough for him to make such a sacrifice.'

'My dear, how very sudden.'

'It did not seem so. I cannot make out why I was not more surprised. It came to me as though I had expected it all along. Of course I told him that I liked him better than any one else I had seen, but that I never thought that any one could care for me in that way; and then I told him that while my father lived nothing would induce me to leave him.'

'And what did he say to that?'

'That he was afraid this would be my answer, but that he knew I was deciding rightly, that he had never meant to say so much, only that the last minute he could not help it ; and then he begged that we might remain friends, and asked me not to forget him and his work in my prayers, and then he went away.'

'And for once in your life you decided without Aunt Milly.'

The girl looked up quickly. 'Was it wrong ? You could not have counselled me to give a different answer, and even if you had—' hesitating, 'Oh, I could not have said otherwise ; there was no conflicting duty there, Aunt Milly.'

'Dearest, from my heart I believe you are right. Your father could ill spare you.'

'I am thankful to hear you say so. Of course,' heaving a little sigh, 'it was very hard seeing him go away like that, but I never doubted which was my duty for a moment. As long as papa and Cardie want me, nothing could induce me to leave them.'

'I suppose you will tell them this, Olive ?'

'No, oh no,' she replied, shrinking back, 'that would spoil all. It would be to lose the fruit of the sacrifice ; it might grieve them too. No, no one must know this but you and I, Aunt Milly ; it must be sacred to us three. I told Mr. Marsden so.'

'Perhaps you are right,' returned her aunt, thoughtfully. 'Richard thinks so highly of him, he might give you no peace on the subject. When we have once made up our minds to a certain course of action, arguments are as wearying as they are fruitless, and overmuch pity is good for no one. But, dear Olive, I cannot refrain from telling you how much I honour you for this decision.'

'Honour me, Aunt Milly !' and Olive's pale face flushed with strong emotion.

'How can I help it ? There are so few who really act up to their principles in this world, who when the moment for self-sacrifice comes are able cheerfully to count the cost and renounce the desire of their heart. Ah !' she continued, 'when I think of your yearning after a missionary life, and that you are giving up a woman's brightest prospect for the sake of an ailing parent, I feel that you have done a very noble thing indeed.'

'Hush, I do not deserve all this praise. I am only doing my duty.'

'True; and after all we are only unprofitable servants. I wish I had your humility, Olive. I feel as though I should be too happy sometimes if it were not for the sorrows of others. They are shadows on the sunshine. Ethel is always in my thoughts, and now you will be there too.'

'I do not think—I do not mean to be unhappy,' faltered Olive. '"God loveth a cheerful giver," I must remember that, Aunt Milly. Perhaps,' she continued, more humbly, 'I am not fit for the work. Perhaps he might be disappointed in me, and I should only drag him down. Don't you recollect what papa once said in one of his sermons about obstacles standing like the angel with the drawn sword before Balaam, to turn us from the way ?'

Mildred sighed. How often she had envied the childish faith which lay at the bottom of Olive's character, though hidden by the troublesome scrupulousness of a too sensitive conscience. Was the healthy growth she had noticed latterly owing to Mr. Marsden's influence, or had she really, by God's grace, trodden on the necks of her enemies ?

'You must not be sorry about all this,' continued the girl, earnestly, noticing the sigh. 'You don't know how glad I am that Mr. Marsden cares for me.'

'I cannot help feeling that some day it will all come right,' returned Mildred.

'I must not think about that,' was the hurried answer. 'Aunt Milly, please never to say or hint such a thing again. It would be wrong ; it would make me restless and dissatisfied. I shall always think of him as a dear friend—but—but I mean to be Olive Lambert all my life.'

Mildred smiled and kissed her, and then consented very reluctantly to change the subject, but nevertheless she held to her opinion as firmly as Olive to hers.

Mildred might well say that the sorrows of others shadowed her brightness. During the autumn and winter that followed her marriage her affectionate heart was often oppressed by thoughts of that dreary sickroom. Her husband had predicted from the first that only partial recovery could be expected in Mr. Trelawny's case. A few months or years of helplessness was all that remained to the once lithe and active frame of the master of Kirkleatham.

It was a pitiable wreck that met Richard's eyes one fine June evening in the following year, when he went up to pay his almost daily visit. They had wheeled the invalid on to the sunny terrace that he might enjoy the beautiful view. Below them lay the old gray buildings and church of Kirkby Stephen. The pigeons were sitting in rows on the tower, preparatory to roosting in one of the unoccupied rooms; through the open door one had glimpses of the dark-painted window, with its fern-bordered ledge, and the gleaming javelins on the wall. A book lay on Ethel's lap, but she had long since left off turning the pages. The tale, simple as it was, was wearying to the invalid's oppressed brain. Her wan face brightened at the young curate's approach.

'How is he?' asked Richard in a low voice as he approached her, and dropping his voice.

Ethel shook her head. 'He is very weary and wandering to-night; worse than usual, I fancy. Papa, Richard has come to see us; he is waiting to shake hands with you.'

'Richard—ay, a good lad—a good lad,' returned the sick man, listlessly. His voice was still painfully thick and indistinct, and his eyes had a dull look of vacancy. 'You must excuse my left hand, Richard,' with an attempt at his old courtliness; 'the other is numb or gone to sleep; it is of no use to me at all. Ah, I always told Lambert he ought to be proud of his sons.'

'His thoughts are running on the boys to-night,' observed Ethel, in a low voice. 'He keeps asking after Rupert, and just now he fancied I was my poor mother.'

Richard gave her a grave pitying look, and turned to the invalid. 'I am glad to see you out this lovely evening,' he said, trying gently to rouse his attention, for the thin, dark face had a painful abstracted look.

'Ah, it is beautiful enough,' replied Mr. Trelawny, absently. 'I am waiting for the boys; have you seen them, Richard? Agatha sent them down to the river to bathe; she spoils them dreadfully. Rupert is a fine swimmer; he does everything well; he is his mother's favourite.'

'I think Ethel is looking pale, Mr. Trelawny. Aunt Milly has sent me to fetch her for an hour, if you can spare her?'

'I can always spare Ethel; she is not much use to me. Girls are generally in the way; they are poor things compared with boys. Where is the child, Agatha? Tell her to make haste; we must not keep Richard waiting.'

'Dear papa,' pleaded the girl, 'you are dreaming to-night. Your poor Ethel is beside you.'

'Ah, to be sure,' passing his hand wearily through his

whitening hair. 'I get confused ; you are so like your mother. Ask this gentleman to wheel me in, Ethel ; I am getting tired.'

'Is he often like this ?' asked Richard, when at last she was free to join him in the porch. The curfew bell was ringing as they walked through the dewy crofts among the tall, sleeping daisies ; the cool breeze fanned Ethel's hot temples.

'Yes, very often,' she returned, in a dejected tone. 'It is this that tries me so. If he would only talk to me a little as he used to do before things went wrong ; but he only seems to live in the past—his wife and his boys—but it is chiefly Rupert now.'

'And yet he seems restless without you.'

'That is the strangest part ; he seems to know me through it all. There are times when he is a little clearer ; when he seems to think there is something between us ; and then nothing satisfies him, unless I sit beside him and hold his hand. It is so hard to hear him begging my forgiveness over and over again for some imaginary wrong he fancies he has done me.'

'Poor Ethel ! Yet he was never dearer to you than he is now ?'

'Never,' she returned, drying her eyes. 'Night and day he engrosses my thoughts. I seem to have no room for anything else. Do you know, Richard, I can understand now the passionate pity mothers feel for a sick child, for whom they sacrifice rest and comfort. There is nothing I would not do for papa.'

'Aunt Milly says your devotion to him is beautiful.'

Ethel's face grew paler. 'You must not tell me that, Richard ; you do not consider that I have to retrieve the coldness of a lifetime. After all, poor papa is right. I have not been a good daughter to him ; I have been carping and disagreeable ; I have presumed to sit in judgment on my own father ; I have separated myself and my pursuits from his, and alienation was the result.'

'For which you were not wholly to blame,' he replied, gently, unable to hear those self-accusations unmoved. Why was she, the dearest and the truest, to go heavily all her days for sins that were not her own ?

'No, you must not blame him,' she continued, beseechingly. ' Is he not bearing his own punishment ? am I not bearing mine ? Oh, it is dreadful !' her voice suddenly choked with strong emotion. 'Bodily sufferings I could have witnessed with far less misery than I feel at the spectacle of this helplessness and mental decay ; to talk to dull ears, to arrest wandering thoughts, to listen hour after hour to confused rambling. Richard, this seems harder than anything.'

'If He—the Master I mean—fell under His cross, do we wonder that we at times sink under ours?' was the low, reverent answer. 'Ethel, I sometimes think how wonderful it will be to turn the page of suffering in another world, and, with eyes purified from earthly rheum, to spell out all the sacred meaning of the long trial that we considered so unbearable—nay, sometimes so unjust.'

Ethel did not trust herself to speak, but a grateful glance answered him. It was not the first time he had comforted her with words which had sunk deep into a subdued and softened heart. She was learning her lesson now, and the task was a hard one to poor passionate human flesh and blood. If what Richard said was true, she would not have a pang too many; the sorrowful moments would be numbered to her by the same Father, without whom not even a sparrow could fall to the ground. Could she not safely trust her father to Him?

'Richard, I am always praying to come down from my cross,' she said at last, looking up at the young clergyman with sweet humid eyes. 'And after all He has fastened us there with His own hands. I suppose it is faith and patience for which one should ask, and not only relief?'

'He will give that too in His own good time,' returned Richard, solemnly, and then, as was often the case, a short silence fell between them.

CHAPTER XXXVI

BERENGARIA

'I have led her home, my love, my only friend,
There is none like her, none.
And never yet so warmly ran my blood
And sweetly, on and on
Calming itself to the long-wished-for end,
Full to the banks, close on the promised good.

None like her, none.'—TENNYSON'S *Maud*.

Two years had elapsed since Olive Lambert had made her noble
decision, and during that time triple events had happened. Mr.
Trelawny's suffering life was over, Rex had married his faithful
Polly, and Dr. Heriot and Mildred had rejoiced over their first-
born son.

Mr. Trelawny did not long survive the evening when
Richard found him on the sunny terrace ; towards the end of
the autumn there was a brief rally, a strange flicker of restless
life ; his confused faculties seemed striving to clear themselves ;
at times there was a strained dilated look in the dark eyes that
was almost pitiful ; he seemed unwilling to have Ethel out of
his sight—even for a moment.

One night he called her to him. She was standing at the
window finishing some embroidery by the fading light, but at
the first sound of the weak, querulous tones, she turned her
cheerful face towards him, for however weary she felt, there
was always a smile for him.

'What is it, dear father ?' for in those sad last days the holy
name of father had come involuntarily to her lips. True, she had
tasted little of his fatherhood, but still he was hers—her father.

'Put down that tiresome work and come to me,' he went on,
fretfully ; 'you are always at work—always—as though you
had your bread to earn ; there is plenty to spare for you.
Rupert will take care of you ; you need not fear, Ethel.'

'No, dear, I am not afraid,' she returned coming to his side, and parting his hair with her soft fingers.

How often she had kissed those gray streaks, and the poor wrinkled forehead. He was an old man now, bowed and decrepit, sitting there with his lifeless arm folded to his side. But how she loved him—her poor, stricken father!

'No, you were always a good girl. Ethel, are the boys asleep?'

'Yes, both of them, father,' leaning her cheek against his.

'And your mother?'

'Yes, dear.'

'I had a fancy I should like to hear Rupert's voice again. You remember his laugh, Ethel, so clear and ringing? Hal's was not like it; he was quiet and tame compared to Rupert. Ethel,' wistfully, 'it is a long time since I saw my boys.'

'My poor dear, a long, long time!' and then she whispered, almost involuntarily, '"I shall go to them, but they shall not return to me."'

He caught the meaning partially.

'Yes, we will go to them—you and I,' he returned, vacantly, patting her cheek as she hung over him. 'Don't cry, Ethel, they are good boys, and shall have their rights; but I have not forgotten you. You have been a good daughter to me—better than I deserved. I shall tell your mother so when——'

But the sentence was never finished.

He had seemed drowsy after that, and she rang for the servant to wheel him into his own room. He was still heavy when she drew the curtains round him and wished him good-night; he looked placid and beautiful, she thought, as she leant over him for a last kiss; but he only smiled at her, and pressed her hand feebly.

That smile, how she treasured it! It was still on his lips when the servant who slept in his room, surprised at his master's long rest, undrew the curtains and found him lying as they left him last night—dead!'

'You have been a good daughter to me—better than I deserved. I shall tell your mother so when——'

'Oh, Ethel, he has told her now! be comforted, darling,' cried Mildred, when Ethel had thrown herself dry-eyed on her friend's bosom. 'God do so to me and mine, as you have dealt with him in his trouble.'

But for a long time the afflicted girl refused to be comforted. Richard was smitten with dismay when he saw her for the first time after her father's death. Her paleness, her assumed calmness, filled him with foreboding trouble. Mildred had told him she had scarcely slept or eaten since the shock of her bereavement had come upon her.

She had come to him at once, and stood before him in her black dress ; the touch of her hand was so cold, that he had started at its clamminess ; the uncomplaining sadness of her aspect brought the mist to his eyes.

'Dear Ethel, it has been sudden—awfully sudden,' he said, at last, almost fearing to graze the edge of that dreary pause.

'Ah ! that it has.'

'That afternoon we had both been sitting with him. Do you remember he had complained of weariness, and yet he would not suffer us to wheel him in ? Who would have thought his weariness would have been so soon at an end !'

She made no answer, only her bosom heaved a little. Yes, his weariness was over, but hers had begun ; her filial work was taken from her, and her heart was sick with the sudden void in life. For months he had been her first waking and her last sleeping thoughts ; his helplessness had brought out the latent devotion of her nature, and now she was alone !

'Will you let me see him ?' whispered Richard, not daring to break on this sacred reserve of grief, and yet longing to speak some word of comfort to her stricken heart ; and she had turned noiselessly and led him to the chamber of death.

There her fortitude had given way a little, and Richard was relieved to see her quiet tears coursing slowly down her cheeks, as they stood side by side looking on the still face with its changeless smile.

'Ethel, I am glad you have allowed me to see him,' he said, at last ; 'he looks so calm and peaceful, all marks of age and suffering gone. Who could have the heart to break that rest ?'

Then the pent-up pain found utterance.

'Oh, Richard, think, never to have bidden him good-bye !'

'Did you wish him good-night, dear ? I thought you told me you always went to his bedside the last thing before you slept ?'

'Yes—but I did not know,' the tears flowing still more freely.

'No—you only wished him good-night, and bade God bless him. Well, has He not blessed him ?'

A sob was her only reply.

'Has He not given him the "blessing of peace" ? Is not

His very seal of peace there stamped on that quiet brow?
Dear Ethel, those words, "He is not, for God took him," always
seem to me to apply so wonderfully to sudden death. You
know,' dropping his voice, and coming more closely, 'some
men, good men, even, have such a horror of death.'

'He had,' in a tone almost inaudible.

'So I always understood. Think of the mercy shown to
his weakness then, literally falling asleep; no slow approach of
the enemy he feared; no deadly combat with the struggling
flesh; only sleep, untroubled as a child; a waking, not here,
but in another world.'

Ethel still wept, but she felt less oppressed; no one could
comfort her like Richard, not even Mildred.

As the days went on, Richard felt almost embarrassed by
the trust she reposed in him. Ethel, who had always been
singularly unconventional in her ideas, and was still in worldly
matters as simple as a child, could see no reason why Richard
should not manage things wholly for her. Richard in his
perplexity was obliged to appeal to Dr. Heriot.

'She is ill, and shrinks from business; she wants me to see
the lawyer. Surely you can explain to her how impossible it
is for me to interfere with such matters? She treats the man
who aspires to be her husband exactly like her brother,' continued the young man, in a vexed, shamefaced way.

Dr. Heriot could hardly forbear a smile.

The master of Kirkleatham had been lying in his grave for
weeks, but his faithful daughter still refused to be comforted.
She moped piteously; all business fretted her; a quiet talk
with Mildred or Richard was all of which her harassed nerves
seemed capable.

'What can you expect?' he said, at last; 'her long nursing
has broken her down. She has a fine constitution, but the
wear and tear of these months have been enough to wear out
any woman. Leave her quiet for a little while to cry her
heart out for her father.'

'In the meantime, Mr. Grantham is waiting to have those
papers signed, and to know if those leases are to be renewed,'
returned Richard, impatiently.

With her his gentleness and sympathy had been unfailing,
but it was not to be denied that his present position fretted
him. To be treated as a brother, and to be no brother; to be
the rejected suitor of an heiress, and yet to be told he was
her right hand! No wonder Richard's heart was sore; he was

even aggrieved with Dr. Heriot for not perceiving more quickly
the difficulties of his situation.

'If my father were in better health, she would go to him ;
she has said so more than once,' he went on, more quietly.
'It is easy to see that she does not understand my hints ; and
under the present circumstances it is impossible to speak more
plainly. She wanted me to see Mr. Grantham, and when I
refused she looked almost hurt.'

'Yes, I see, she must be roused to do things herself. Don't
be vexed about it, Richard, it will all come right, and you cannot expect her to see things as we do. I will have a little
talk with her myself; if it comes to the worst I must consti-
tute myself her man of business for the present,' and Richard
withdrew more satisfied.

Things were at a low ebb just now with Richard. Ethel's
heiress-ship lay on him like a positive burden. The riches he
despised rose up like a golden wall between him and his love.
Oh, that she had been some poor orphaned girl, that in her
loneliness he might have taken her to his heart and his father's
home! What did either he or she want with these riches?
He knew her well enough to be sure how she would dread the
added responsibility they would bring. How often she had
said to him during the last few weeks, 'Oh, Richard, it is too
much! it oppresses me terribly. What am I to do with it all,
and with myself?' and he had not answered her a word.

Dr. Heriot found his task easier than he had expected. Ethel
was unhappy enough to be slightly unreasonable. She felt herself aggrieved with Richard, and had misunderstood him.

'I suppose he has sent you to tell me that I must rouse
myself,' she said, with languid displeasure, when he had unfolded
his errand. 'He need not have troubled either himself or you.
I have seen Mr. Grantham ; he went away by the 2.50 train.'

'I must say that I think you have done wisely,' returned
Dr. Heriot, much pleased. 'No one, not even Richard, has a
right to interfere in these matters. The will is left so that
your trustees will expect you to exert yourself. It seems a pity
that you cannot refer to them !'

'You know Mr. Molloy is dead.'

'Yes, and Sir William still in Canada. Yet, with an honest,
straightforward man like Grantham, I think you might settle
things without reference to any one. Richard is only sorry his
father is so ailing.'

'No, I could not trouble Mr. Lambert.'

'Richard has been so much about the house during your father's illness, that it seems natural to refer to him. Well, he has an older head than many of us ; but all the same you must understand his scruples.'

'They have seemed to me far-fetched.'

But, nevertheless, Ethel blushed a little as she spoke. A dim sense of Dr. Heriot's meaning had been dawning on her slowly, but she was unwilling to confess it. She changed the subject somewhat hastily, by asking after Mildred and the baby, and loading Dr. Heriot with loving messages. Nothing more was said about Richard until the close of the visit, when Dr. Heriot somewhat incautiously mentioned him again ; but, as he told Mildred afterwards, he spoke advisedly.

'You will not let Richard think he is misunderstood ?' he said, as he rose to take leave. 'You know he is the last one to spare himself trouble, but he feels in your position that he must do nothing to compromise you.'

'He will not have the opportunity,' she returned, with brief haughtiness, and turning suddenly very crimson ; but as she met Dr. Heriot's look of mild reproach, she melted.

'No—he is right, you are all of you quite right. I must exert myself, and try and care for the things that belonged to my darling father, only I shall be so lonely—so very lonely,' and she covered her face with her hands.

Ethel met Richard with more than her usual kindness when she saw him next ; her sweet deprecating glance gave the young man a sorrowful pang.

'You need not have sent him to see me, Richard,' she said, a little sadly. 'I have been thoughtless, and hurt you. I—I will trouble no one but myself now.'

'It was not the trouble, Ethel ; you must know that,' he returned, eagerly. 'I wish I had the right to help you, but——'

His voice broke, and he dropped her hands. Perhaps he felt the time had not come to speak ; perhaps an involuntary chill seized him as he thought of the little he had to offer her. His manner was very grave, almost reserved, during the rest of the visit ; both of them were glad when a chance caller enabled Richard, without awkwardness, to take his leave.

After this, the young curate's visits grew rarer, and at last almost entirely ceased, and they only met at intervals at the vicarage or the Gray House, as Dr. Heriot's house was commonly called. Ethel made no complaint when she found she had lost her friend, only Mildred noticed that she grew paler, and drooped visibly.

Mildred's tender heart bled for the lonely girl. Both she and her husband pleaded urgently that Ethel should leave her solitary home, and come to them for a little. But Ethel remained firm in her refusal.

'Your life is so perfect—so beautiful, Mildred,' she said, once, when the latter had pressed her almost with tears in her eyes, 'that I could not break in upon it with my sad face and moping ways. I should be more wretched than I am now.'

'But at least you might have some lady with you; such perfect loneliness is good for no one. I cannot bear to think of you living in a corner of that great house all by yourself,' returned Mildred, almost vexed with her obstinacy; and, indeed, the girl was very difficult to understand in those days.

'I have no friends but all of you dear people,' she answered, in the saddest voice possible, 'and I will not trouble you. I could not tolerate a stranger for a moment. Mildred, you must not be hurt with me; you do not know. I must have my way in this.'

And though Mildred shook her wise head, and Dr. Heriot entered more than one laughing protest against such determined self-will, they were obliged to yield.

It was a strange life for so young a woman, and would have tried the strongest nerves; but the only wisdom that Ethel Trelawny showed was in not allowing herself an idle moment. The old dreaming habits were broken for ever, the fastidious choice of duties altogether forgotten; her days were chiefly devoted to her steward and tenants.

Richard, returning from his parochial visits to some outlying village, often met her, mounted on her beautiful brown mare, Zoê. Sometimes she would stop and give him her slim hand, and let him pet the mare and talk to her leaning on Zoê's glossy neck; but oftener a wave of the hand and a passing smile were her only greeting. Richard would come in stern and weary from these encounters, but he never spoke of them.

It was in the following spring that Roy and Polly were married.

Roy had been successful and had sold another picture, and as Mr. Lambert was disposed to be liberal to his younger son, there was no fear of opposition from Polly's guardian, even if he could have resisted the pleadings of the young people.

But, after all, there was no actual imprudence. If Roy

failed to find a continuous market for his pictures, there was still no risk of positive starvation. Mr. Lambert had been quite willing to listen to Richard's representations, and to settle a moderate sum on Roy; for the present, at least, they would have enough and to spare, and the responsibility of a young wife would add a spur to Roy's genius.

Richard was not behind in his generosity. Already his frugality had amassed a few hundreds, half of which he placed in Roy's hands. Roy spent a whole day in Wardour Street after that. A wagon, laden with old carved furniture and wonderful *bric-à-brac*, drew up before The Hollies. New crimson velvet curtains and a handsome carpet found their way to the old studio. Polly hardly recognised it when she first set foot in the gorgeous apartment, and heaved a private sigh over the dear old shabby furniture. A little carved work-table and a davenport of Indian wood stood in a corner appropriated to her use; a sleep-wooing couch and a softly-cushioned easy-chair were beside them. Polly cried a little with joy when the young husband pointed out the various contrivances for her comfort. All the pretty dresses Dr. Heriot had given her, and even Aunt Milly's thoughtful present of house-linen, which now lay in the new press, with a sweet smell of lavender breathing through every fold, were as nothing compared to Roy's gifts. After all, it was an ideal wedding; there was youth, health, and good looks, with plenty of honest love and good humour.

'I have perfect faith in Polly's good sense,' Dr. Heriot had said to his wife, when the young people had driven away; 'she has just the qualities Rex wants. I should not wonder if they turn out the happiest couple in the world, with the exception of ourselves, Milly, darling.'

The wedding had taken place in June, and the time had now come round for the rush-bearing. The garden of Kirkleatham, the vicarage, and the Gray House had been visited by the young band of depredators. Dr. Heriot's glass-house had been rifled of its choicest blossoms; Mildred's bonnie boy, still in his nurse's arms, crowed and clapped his hands at the great white Annunciation lily that his mother had chosen for him to carry.

'You will not be late, John?' pleaded Mildred, as she followed him to the door, according to her invariable custom, on the morning of St. Peter's day; his wife's face was the last he saw when he quitted his home for his long day's work. At the well-known click of the gate she would lay down her work, at whatever hour it was, and come smiling to meet him.

'Where are you, Milly, darling?' were always his first words, if she lingered a moment on her way.

'You will not be later than you can help?' she continued, brushing off a spot of dust on his sleeve. 'You must see Arnold carry his lily, and Ethel will be there; and—and—' blushing and laughing, 'you know I never can enjoy anything unless you are with me.'

'Fie, Milly, darling, we ought to be more sensible after two years. We are old married folks now, but if it were not for making my wife vain,'—looking at the sweet, serene face so near his own,—'I might say the same. There, I must not linger if I am under orders. Good-bye, my two treasures,' placing the great blue-eyed fellow in Mildred's arms.

When Mildred arrived at the park, under Richard's guardianship,—he had undertaken to drive her and the child,—they found Ethel at the old trysting-place amongst a host of other ladies, looking sad and weary.

She moved towards them, tall and shadowy, in her black dress.

'I am glad you are here,' said Richard, in a low voice. 'I thought the Delawares would persuade you, and you will be quiet enough at the vicarage.'

'I thought I ought to do honour to my godson's first appearance in public,' returned Ethel, stretching out her arms to the smiling boy.

Mildred and Dr. Heriot had begged Olive to fill the position of sponsor to the younger Arnold; but Olive had refused almost with tears.

'I am not good enough. Do not ask me,' she had pleaded; and Mildred, knowing the girl's sad humours, had transferred the request to Ethel; her brother and Richard had stood with her.

Richard had no time to say more, for already the band had struck up that heralded the approach of the little rush-bearers, and he must take his place at the head of the procession with the other clergy.

She saw him again in church; he came down the chancel to receive the children's gay crowns. Ethel saw a broken lily lying amongst them on the altar afterwards. It struck her that his face looked somewhat sterner and paler than usual.

She was one of the invited guests at the vicarage; the

29

Lamberts were this year up at the Hall ; but later on in the afternoon they met in the Hall gardens : he came up at once and accosted her.

'All this is jarring on you terribly,' he said, with his old thoughtfulness, as he noticed her tired face.

'I should be glad to go home certainly, but I do not like to appear rude to the Delawares ; the music is so noisy, and all those flitting dancers between the trees confuse one's head.'

'Suppose we walk a little way from them,' he returned, quietly. No one but a keen observer could have read a determined purpose under that quietness of his ; Ethel's worn face, her changed manners, were driving him desperate ; the time had come that he would take his fate between his hands, like a man ; so he told himself, as they walked side by side.

They had sauntered into the tree-bordered walk, leading to the old summer-house in the meadows. As they reached it, Ethel turned to him with a new sort of timidity in her face and voice.

'I am not tired, Richard—not very tired, I mean. I would rather go back to the others.'

'We will go back presently. Ethel, I want to speak to you —I must speak to you ; this sort of thing cannot go on any longer.'

'What do you mean ?' she asked, turning very pale, but not looking at him.

'That we cannot go on any longer avoiding each other like this. You have avoided me very often lately—have you not, Ethel ?' speaking very gently.

'I do not know ; you are so changed—you are not like yourself, Richard,' she faltered.

'How can I be like myself ?' he answered, with a sudden passion in his voice that made her tremble ; 'how am I to forget that I am a poor curate, and you your father's heiress ; that I have fifties where you have thousands ? Oh, Ethel, if you were only poor,' his tone sinking into pathos.

'What have riches or poverty to do with it ?' she asked, still averting her face from him.

'Do you not see ? Can you not understand ?' he returned, eagerly. 'If you were poor, would it not make my wooing easier ? I have loved you how long, Ethel ? Is it ten or eleven years ? I was a boy of fourteen when I loved you first, and I have never swerved from my allegiance.'

'Never !' in a low voice.

'Never! When you called me Cœur-de-Lion, I swore then, lad as I was, that I would one day win my Berengaria. You have been the dearest thing in life to me, ever since I first saw you; and now that I should lose my courage over these pitiful riches! Oh, Ethel, it is hard—hard, just when a little hope was dawning on me that one day you might be able to return my affection. Was I wrong in that belief?' trying to obtain a glimpse of the face now shielded by her hands.

'Whatever I may feel, I know we are equals,' she returned evasively.

'In one sense we are not,' he answered, sadly; 'a woman ought not to come laden with riches to overwhelm her husband. I am a clergyman—a gentleman, and therefore I fear to ask you to be my wife.'

'Was Berengaria poor?' in a voice nearly inaudible; but he heard it, and his handsome face flushed with sudden emotion.

'Do you mean you are willing to be my Berengaria? Oh, Ethel, my own love, this is too much. Can you really care for me enough?'

'I have cared for you ever since you were so good to me in my trouble,' she said, turning her glowing countenance, that he might read the truth of her words; 'but you have made me very unhappy lately, Richard.'

'What could I do?' he answered, almost incoherent with joy. 'I thought you were treating me like a brother, and I feared to break in upon your grief. Oh, if you knew what I have suffered.'

'I understood, and that only made me love you all the more,' she replied, softly. 'You have been winning my heart slowly ever since that evening—you remember it?—in the kitchen garden.'

'When you almost broke my heart, was I likely to forget it, do you think?'

'You startled me. I had only a little love, but it has been growing ever since. Richard!' with her old archness, 'you will not refuse to see the lawyers now?'

He coloured slightly, and his bright look clouded; but this time Ethel did not misunderstand him.

'Dear Richard, you cannot hate the riches more than I do, but they must never be mentioned again between us; they must be sacred to us as my father's gift. I know you will help me to do what is right and good with them,' she continued, in her winning way; 'they are talents we must use, and not abuse.'

'You have rebuked me, my dearest,' returned Richard, tenderly; 'it is I who have been faithless and a coward. I will accept the charge you have given me; and thank God at the same time for your noble heart.'

So the long-desired gift had come into Richard Lambert's keeping, and the woman he had loved from boyhood had consented to be his wife.

The young master of Kirkleatham ruled well and wisely, and Ethel proved a noble helpmeet. When some years later his father died, and he became vicar of Kirkby Stephen, the parish had reason to bless the strong heart and head, and the munificent hands that were never weary of giving. And 'our vicar' rivalled even the good doctor's popularity.

And what of Olive and Hugh Marsden?

Mildred's words had come true.

There were long lonely years before Hugh Marsden—years of incessant toil and Herculean labour, which should stoop his broad shoulders and streak his dark hair with gray, when men should speak of the noble missionary, Hugh Marsden, and of the incredible work carried forward by him beyond the pale of civilisation.

There was no limit to his endurance, no lack of cheerfulness in his efforts, they said; no labour was too great, no scheme too impracticable, no possibility too remote, for the energies of that arduous soul.

Hugh Marsden only smiled at their praise; he was free and unfettered; he had no wife or child; danger would touch him alone. What should hinder him from undertaking any enterprise in his Master's service? But wherever he went in his lonely hours, or in his long sunshiny converse with others, he ever remained faithful to his memory of Olive; she was still to him the purest ideal of womanhood. At times her face, with its cloudy dark hair and fathomless eyes, would haunt him with strange persistence. Whole lines and passages of her poetry would return to his memory, stirring him with subtle sweetness and vague longings for home.

And Olive, how was it with her during those years of home duty, so patiently, so unselfishly performed? While she achieved her modest fame, and carried it so meekly, had she any remembrance of Hugh Marsden?

'I remember all the more that I try to forget,' she said

once when Mildred had put this question to her. 'Now I shall try no more, for I know I cannot forget him.' And again there had been that sadness in her voice. But she never spoke of him voluntarily even to Mildred, but hid in her quiet soul many a secret yearning. They were separated thousands of miles, yet his ·honest face and voice were often present with her, and never nearer than when she whispered prayers for the friend who had once loved her.

And neither of them knew that the years would bring them together again; that one day, Hugh Marsden, broken in health, and craving for a sight of his native land, should be sent home on an important mission, to find Olive free and unfettered, and waiting for him in her brother's home.

THE END

J. D. & Co.

Printed by R. & R. CLARK, *Edinburgh.*

BENTLEY'S FAVOURITE NOVELS

Each work can be had separately, price 6s., of all Booksellers in
Town or Country.

By JESSIE FOTHERGILL.

The 'First Violin.'
Borderland.
Healey.
Kith and Kin.
Probation.

By HELEN MATHERS.

Comin' thro' the Rye.

By MARCUS CLARKE.

For the Term of his Natural
Life.

By Mrs. ANNIE EDWARDES.

Ought We to Visit Her?
Leah : a Woman of Fashion.
A Ball-Room Repentance.
A Girton Girl.

By Mrs. RIDDELL.

George Geith of Fen Court.
Berna Boyle.

By Mrs. PARR.

Adam and Eve.
Dorothy Fox.

By E. WERNER.

Fickle Fortune.
No Surrender.
Success : and how he Won It.
Under a Charm.

By RHODA BROUGHTON.

Cometh up as a Flower.
Good-bye, Sweetheart!
Joan. | Nancy.
Not Wisely, but too Well.
Red as a Rose is She.
Second Thoughts.
Belinda.
'Dr. Cupid.'

By MARIE CORELLI.

A Romance of Two Worlds.
Thelma.
Ardath.
Vendetta.
Wormwood.

By HAWLEY SMART.

Breezie Langton.

By HECTOR MALOT.

No Relations.
(With illustrations.)

By Lady G. FULLERTON.

Ladybird.
Too Strange not to be True.

By HENRY ERROLL.

An Ugly Duckling.

ANONYMOUS.

The Last of the Cavaliers.
Sir Charles Danvers.

LONDON
RICHARD BENTLEY & SON, NEW BURLINGTON STREET
Publishers in Ordinary to Her Majesty the Queen

www.ingramcontent.com/pod-product-compliance
Lightning Source LLC
Chambersburg PA
CBHW022013110726
47901CB00006B/1503